The
Complete
Lion Mistress
Collection

Other books by R. A. Steffan

The Complete Horse Mistress Collection
The Complete Lion Mistress Collection
The Complete Dragon Mistress Collection
The Complete Master of Hounds Collection

Circle of Blood: Books 1-3
Circle of Blood: Books 4-6
(with Jaelynn Woolf)

The Last Vampire: Books 1-3
The Last Vampire: Books 4-6
(with Jaelynn Woolf)

Vampire Bound: Complete Series, Books 1-4

Forsaken Fae: The Complete Series, Books 1-3

Antidote: Love and War, Book 1
Antigen: Love and War, Book 2
Antibody: Love and War, Book 3
Anthelion: Love and War, Book 4
Antagonist: Love and War, Book 5

Diamond Bar Apha Ranch
Diamond Bar Alpha 2: Angel & Vic
(with Jaelynn Woolf)

The
Complete
Lion Mistress
Collection

R. A. Steffan

The Complete Lion Mistress Collection

ISBN: 978-1-955073-31-8 (paperback)

For information, contact the author at
http://www.rasteffan.com/contact/

Original cover art by Deranged Doctor Design

Second Edition: March 2022

Author's Note

The Lion Mistress is the story of four people who love each other. Be warned that unlike most books in the fantasy genre, it contains a fair amount of explicit sex — much of which is not remotely vanilla.

A special note for reverse harem lovers: I had never heard the term "reverse harem" when I wrote this series. It was always conceived as a poly romance story, just like *The Horse Mistress*. That said, it features one amazing woman who ends up with three adoring men at the end, and she is the glue that holds the four of them together.

The pace is medium burn, and the books contain strong LGBT content. If you dislike M/M, you'll dislike this series.

Table of Contents

The Lion Mistress: Book 1.. 1
The Lion Mistress: Book 2..259
The Lion Mistress: Book 3..537
Epilogue: Pride of Dreams...798

The Lion Mistress:
Book 1

ONE

It was strange that someone as quiet and timid as Vesh would leave such a noticeable hole in the world once he was gone.

Almost a week after the mob caught up to Vesh on the outskirts of Rhyth, Kathrael still occasionally found herself turning to speak to the space next to her where he was supposed to be. Each time, the person-shaped *emptiness* there jolted her back to that horrible evening spent hiding in the shadows, watching the fanatics jeering and laughing as they paraded the slender, battered corpse through the streets. Every such occurrence brought with it a tidal wave of fresh grief, along with renewed determination to succeed at her impossible, self-appointed quest.

Kathrael would have liked to place the blame for Vesh's carelessness—which ultimately turned out to be fatal— squarely at his own feet. It would have been easier to mourn him if she could work up a decent level of anger toward him at the same time.

But of course his death had been her fault, not his. Never his.

If she'd still been able to work, Vesh would never have started accepting riskier clients in order to earn enough money to feed them both. As a eunuch who had escaped the Priests' Guild, Vesh had been in high demand as a prostitute. However, he had also been a target of hatred.

With the foreign god Deimok gaining a foothold on the island of Eburos, the Priests' Guild no longer held the power they once did. The new faith—originally brought over from the continent by traders and visiting nobles—was a vicious and vengeful one. As the cult of Deimok grew larger and stronger in and around the city of Rhyth, practitioners of the traditional religion were increasingly singled out by groups of angry young men intent on venting their frustrations. These groups would harass anyone the cult leaders told them was responsible for Rhyth's current political and economic woes. Any poor soul unlucky enough to be accused of using witchcraft or having magical abilities was in immediate mortal danger — but eunuchs were also a popular target.

All of the priests of the Old Religion were eunuchs, but so far the rabble-rousers had not gained enough confidence to attack any of the temples directly. Vesh, though, had run away from his temple shortly after he'd been castrated. Without the protection of his Guild, he'd been easy prey. Lured to a secluded spot with the promise of generous payment for his services, Vesh had ignored Kathrael's pleas for caution. He'd been hungry. Desperate. They both had been.

So he'd gone off with a silver-tongued stranger, who doubtless had a gang of his friends waiting in secret. And now he was dead, leaving Kathrael alone in the world, without any means of income or support. No food, no home except whatever convenient doorstep or overhang she could find for shelter at night. Nothing, in truth, except for the clothes on her back.

But she couldn't afford to let that stand in her way. Because Kathrael had made a solemn vow to lead an uprising against the corrupt leaders and slave masters who held Rhyth in an iron grip, even as the city slowly rotted from within, descending into chaos and rioting.

First, though, there was one other thing she had to do. She was fucking well going to murder the cowardly bastard of a shape-shifter who'd been prophesied to lead them all to freedom, and hadn't.

The man who'd ruined her life.

✺

The morning dawned gray and stifling, matching Kathrael's dark mood precisely. Her stomach felt like an empty pit — a yawning chasm that ached for sustenance. She unwrapped her threadbare shawl from around her shoulders and contemplated the same question she had asked herself every day this week. What was it to be today? Begging, or stealing?

Of course the gods couldn't have been thoughtful enough to afflict her with some infirmity that people would find pitiable, but non-threatening. Lameness, or paralysis, maybe, or a missing limb or something. No, that would have been too bloody simple.

Instead, she sat at the crossroads with her shawl laid out in front of her in the dust to receive alms. Hours later, after countless passersby had glanced at her face, only to look quickly away and increase their pace until they were out of her immediate vicinity, she had only a single grubby coin to show for the morning spent abasing herself to complete strangers.

Once, she could have made ten times that much in the space of ten minutes, servicing some rich fop in a shadowed alley, fluttering dark eyelashes up at him as she pretended that his perfumed prick was the most delectable morsel that had ever passed her lips during the course of her short life. Now, she trudged to the nearest market, where an elderly, kind-hearted vendor would occasionally give her some of his damaged produce in exchange for such a meager sum.

Today, it was a pair of spoiled ground tubers, blackened on one side and reeking of mold. She accepted them silently, her face downturned, and scraped away the squishy parts with her fingers. Happily, someone had finally fixed the crank handle on the well at the edge of the square. The starchy white blobs were marginally more appealing after she'd rinsed them off, and it gave her something to drink with her pitiful meal as well.

With her stomach temporarily quieted, Kathrael found a shady spot to sit and think. Grief had dulled her wits. She'd allowed it to distract her from her goals. It was time to move, before she slipped into complacency and gradually starved to death, or was caught pilfering some insignificant item or bit of food.

She shuddered. Being thrown in the cells beneath the garrison would surely be a death sentence for someone like her... or, at the very least, a sentence that would make her long for death.

No. She had to find a new way. She had to move. If she didn't move now, she would never be able to. She wracked her mind, trying to think of fresh options. Her thoughts were cloudy, unfocused. Lack of sleep and decent nourishment was affecting her ability to think.

Think now. It will only get worse later, she reminded herself. A snippet of verse that her sister had used to croon, late at night when Kathrael couldn't sleep, wafted through her memory.

All who seek shelter shall find it.
All who grieve shall be comforted.
All the gods' children will receive solace.

Ask at the temple and gain the help you need.

Vesh would have laughed aloud at her. The temple had never meant solace for him, but rather, pain and suffering. It was, however, an avenue she had not tried before. The glimmer of a plan began to form, and she chewed absently at a thumbnail as she contemplated the possibilities.

She needed to act, while she still had the strength.

Vesh's old temple was further inside the central part of the city than she really liked to go these days. There was no getting around it, though. She arranged her shawl over her head and shoulders in such a way that it draped across the left side of her face, obscuring it in shadow. Her dress was in tatters, but there was nothing she could do about it. She would not be the only beggar girl inside the city walls, after all. Far from it.

Her bare feet were aching by the time she reached the city gate nearest the temple. The guard gave her a look of disdain and shoved her as she walked past, knocking her into a tall man wearing plain, well-mended clothing. He cursed, caught by surprise, but helped steady her as she staggered. It was on her tongue to thank him when she realized her shawl had slipped from her face in the confusion.

The man gasped sharply and jerked his hands away from her shoulders as if she had suddenly become red-hot. He stammered something and hurried away, wiping his hands on his tunic as if he feared she had contaminated him somehow.

Kathrael hurriedly covered herself again and made for the nearest alley where she could escape notice from others in the crowd who might have seen the man's reaction. The stab of hurt she had felt at his look of horror took her by surprise — she would have thought she was immune to such things by now. Perhaps it was because he had seemed as though he might be kind. Once upon a time, she might have used him somehow, playing on his sympathy for a poor, beautiful girl fallen on hard times.

Now, though, she was very much on her own. After regaining her bearings and making sure no one had taken any further notice of her, she rejoined the crowd trickling through the gate and headed in the direction of Vesh's temple, keeping her head down.

The sun was high in the sky when the impressive structure of wood and stone finally came into view. The new temples dedicated to Deimok were mostly shining white, built of polished marble and financed by the Emperor of Alyrios, sitting safe in his golden palace on the mainland across the channel. By contrast, the temples of the Old Gods still looked to be part of nature, made with local materials and designed to blend in with their surroundings.

Vesh's temple was dedicated to Naloth, god of rain and male fertility. Kathrael had always felt more of an affinity with Deresta—the goddess of the sun, fire, death, and warfare—but one did not go to Deresta's temple to beg for succor. Indeed, by rights, she should be visiting the temple of Utarr, Naloth's mate. For it was Utarr's Prayer of Solace that had risen earlier from the depths of Kathrael's memories, promising the chance of aid.

However, what she would be seeking was more than a simple meal or a handful of coppers to pay an irate landlord. To have any chance of success, she would need to find someone there who had cared for Vesh and might place value on their shared connection with him. Given that Vesh would have been stripped of all his titles and associations within the temple immediately upon running away, it was admittedly a gamble. That said, Vesh had been the kindest and best person Kathrael had ever known. She was confident that *someone* here would remember him in the same way she did.

The doors to the temple had been thrown open to let in fresh air. Kathrael was pleased to see that there were few people coming and going, and that the entryway was attended by a pair of acolytes who were barely more than boys. She approached them, eyes down, clutching her shawl over her scarred face so it would not slip free at an inopportune moment.

Addressing the younger, softer looking of the two, she said, "Please, brother, my situation is desperate and I have nowhere else to turn. I cast myself on your mercy. I beg you, can you take me to the kindest of the novices? I can barely bring myself to speak of the terrible thing which has befallen me."

From the corner of her eye, she watched the boy's expression transform from one of pleasure at being addressed as if he were in a position of power, to concern and sympathy as he took in her words and the way she hid part of her face as if ashamed. Without saying a single untrue word, she had conveyed to him that she had been assaulted, probably raped — perhaps impregnated. He would assume that the shawl over her face hid signs of a beating.

Most such victims chose to appeal to Naloth, as the arbiter of male behavior, so the situation would not be an unfamiliar one to either of the two acolytes. And, indeed, the youngster immediately moved to reassure her.

"Peace, sister," he said. "You have come to the right place. There are many here who can help you."

Kathrael hunched as if cowering, hiding her face further. "Only, I cannot — I cannot bear the thought of speaking to some gray-haired priest who would remind me of my f-father. Please, it must be someone young. Someone gentle, who will not judge me."

Those words, spoken in a voice quavering with suppressed emotion, perfectly described Vesh. She could only hope that like had called to like during his time here.

"Of course," said the acolyte, placating. "I know just the person. Come with me. I will take you to Novice Hameen. He is young, and he has always been kind to me."

"Thank you," she said, allowing relief to color her voice as she laid her free hand on his forearm and squeezed. "I didn't know where else to go. *Thank you.*"

"We are all here to serve, sister," the boy said, obviously pleased by the fawning. "Come. Follow me."

Kathrael allowed herself to be led into the relatively cool darkness of the temple. The acolyte guided her to a small, comfortable room with several seats and a low table holding food and wine. As soon as he left her to fetch Novice Hameen, she fell on the bread and fruit as if it might disappear at any moment, washing it down with wine straight from the jug.

How long had it been since she'd had access to as much fresh food as she could eat? She couldn't even remember. At the sound of approaching footsteps, she quickly rearranged everything that was left so that it looked a little less like the aftermath of an attack of gluttonous rats. When the novice entered, she was seated on the low wooden settle with her hands twisted in her lap, waiting quietly.

She glanced up at him, trying to gain an impression of his character — a skill she had cultivated during her days as a prostitute, and one that had stood her in good stead. Physically, Novice Hameen was Vesh's opposite in every way. Obese where Vesh had been skinny, even-featured while Vesh's features had exhibited a slightly asymmetrical character that served only to make him more interesting to look at. Hameen's eyes were also an unusual shade of pale gray, very different from Vesh's rich brown.

All of that was unimportant, however. Like Vesh, Novice Hameen projected an aura of compassion—a soul-deep kindness that could not be hidden or dimmed. He was also more or less the same age as Vesh had been. Kathrael let out a silent breath of relief, suddenly and irrationally certain that the two must have known each other.

"Welcome to the temple of Naloth," Hameen greeted in a clear, pleasant voice. "I am at your service, sister. What troubles you?"

Kathrael's heart pounded for a moment as she chose her words. "Brother Hameen, thank you for speaking with me. I believe we share a friend. Were you, by any chance, acquainted with a young novice who went by the name of Vesh?"

Hameen raised his eyebrows and regarded her in surprise. "Forgive me. That is not at all the subject I expected us to be discussing." He paused for a moment. "Surely you do not mean Novice Ta'vesh?"

It was Kathrael's turn to frown. "I knew him only as Vesh. A slender person, with a small gap between his front teeth, and his nose slightly bent as if it had once been broken?"

Hameen drew in a sharp breath and sat down rather abruptly in the chair across from her. "That describes Ta'vesh exactly, yes. His nose was broken when he was fourteen years old, by one of the other slave boys. I helped him set it, but it never healed quite right."

Kathrael swallowed hard, surprisingly affected by being here with someone else who had once called Vesh a friend. It had seemed since his death that without her to remember him, Vesh would disappear as if he had never existed. To know that others remembered—that others had been affected by him—was strangely comforting even as it made her grief rise once more.

"Do you know where he is?" Hameen asked eagerly, before bringing himself visibly under control. "I'm sorry. By rights, I should not even speak of him. He was formally cast out of the temple after he ran away."

"He is dead," Kathrael said. "Stoned to death by a mob last week, outside of the city."

Hameen's eyes closed in pain. "I had feared the worst, ever since he left. Yet even so, it's somehow worse to know that he survived so long, only to perish in the end." When he opened his strange, pale eyes again, they were wet. "Tell me, sister, how did you come to know him?"

"He befriended me when we were both living on the streets. We looked out for each other... or tried to." She lifted the shawl away from her face, meeting Hameen's gaze with her own. "He kept me alive and nursed me back to health after this happened."

The novice examined Kathrael's face without flinching, though his dark eyebrows drew together in sympathy. Although she avoided her own reflection like the plague, she knew perfectly well what he was seeing—scarred skin that had melted and run like wax, framing her useless, milky left eye. The burns extended down the left side of her neck and over the top of her breast, thankfully covered by the high neckline of her tatty, threadbare dress.

"What happened?" he asked kindly, and she suddenly realized that, aside from Vesh, he was the only person who had ever cared enough to ask.

She raised her chin. "I was a prostitute. We both were," she said, daring him to make an issue of it. "We were *good*, too. I could always tell if a man was safe to go with or not. This particular man was a good client. He always paid generously, and he never wanted anything too strange or distasteful in return."

Her attention turned inward, sliding back to that awful day the previous winter. "I didn't take his wife into account, unfortunately. She found out that he'd been spending the household savings to visit me. The man was a metalworker. One evening, his wife came to the inn where I always serviced him. She burst into the room and yanked me away from him by the hair. Before I could push past her and get to the door to run, she threw a vial of something at my face. I learned later that it was green vitriol. It's used to dissolve metal when making etchings."

Hameen winced.

"I didn't stop to think—I just ran. It wasn't so bad at first, but then it started to burn everywhere it had touched me. I couldn't get it off. Whenever I tried to wipe it away, it just spread the fire. I don't know how I managed to get back to where Vesh and I were staying, but somehow I did. One of the other women there wanted to soothe the burns with oil, but Vesh wouldn't let her. I remember that he dragged me out to the well and kept pouring buckets of water over me until I thought I would drown. At some point I must have passed out, because that's the last thing I remember from that night."

Novice Hameen had raised his hand to cover the lower part of his face in dismay as she spoke. When she finished, he took a deep breath as if centering himself, and returned it to his lap. "Ta'vesh's father was a metal smith. He would have known that oil would only make it worse. You are correct that he probably saved your life."

"Whereas I was unable to return the favor and save his."

"The friend I knew would no more have blamed you for such a thing than he would have blamed the sun for rising in the east," Hameen said.

Kathrael was silent for a moment. Vesh might not have blamed her, but she still blamed herself.

"He grew careless of his safety in his attempt to earn enough coin to keep both of us fed," she said eventually.

"If that is the case, then he must have thought you worth the risk." The young priest settled back in his chair and regarded her frankly. "Now, tell me what has brought you here. As appreciative as I am of knowing Ta'vesh's fate, I don't believe you sought me out solely to exchange memories of our beloved friend."

"No." Kathrael looked down, and then up again, preparing herself to lie to the first person who had shown her real kindness since Vesh's death. "I am utterly destitute, Brother Hameen. I have no means of making a livelihood. I cannot even beg—my face repels everyone who sees it. And yet, I am compelled to undertake a pilgrimage."

Hameen's brow crinkled again. "What sort of pilgrimage?"

"I must travel north to seek out the Wolf Patron, and try to convince him to aid us here in Rhyth," she said, forcing herself to meet Hameen's gaze squarely as she spoke.

There was a pause as the novice digested this.

"You speak of High Priest Senovo, the wolf-shifter of Draebard?" Hameen asked.

"He was Rhytheeri long before he fled over the mountains to live as a northerner," Kathrael said.

After the war five years ago, everyone in the south knew the story of the Wolf Patron, though numerous wild tales had grown up around the central truth. Senovo's parents sold him to the Priests' Guild as a young boy, when they could no longer afford to feed all of their children. He had grown up a slave, but he showed the intelligence and temperament required for eventual initiation into the priesthood.

Or so his owners had thought. When the High Priest ordered him to be dragged into the temple and forcibly castrated, Senovo changed into a wolf and tore his tormenters limb from limb. Only one survived to tell the tale, though he died of his injuries not long afterward. The wolf ran off and escaped into the wildlands, only to surface years later in human form as the powerful High Priest of the northern Draebardi tribe.

Along with the Draebardi Chieftain—rumored by some to be the Wolf Patron's lover—High Priest Senovo commanded an army of wolves that repelled an attempted invasion by the Alyrion Empire. Rhyth, situated on the southern coast of the island of Eburos, had maintained a lucrative trade partnership with the Empire in the years before the Emperor of Alyrios attempted to expand his reach by conquering northern Eburos. Since the unsuccessful incursion, however, the north had all but cut ties with Rhyth, turning instead to new, far-flung trading partners on the continent. Rhyth's supply of ore and gemstones from the productive northern mines had been strangled until it was a bare trickle.

Without valuable raw materials to trade, Rhyth was falling out of favor with the Empire, and now the city was struggling for its very survival.

"Perhaps the tales of the Wolf Patron's southern roots are true," Hameen allowed. "But what you propose is still an immense undertaking. Beyond the central fact that a young wolf-shifter did escape from the Temple of Deresta some years ago, the story is more legend than not."

"No," Kathrael said. "You're wrong. It is true. Being a prostitute puts a person in a position to hear a lot of talk. After a while, you gain a sense of what is truth and what is wishful thinking."

She didn't add that she had made it a lifelong mission to ferret out all the information she could about High Priest Senovo of Draebard. She also had one additional advantage that no one else knew about—she'd met the spineless son-of-a-bitch personally, on a sweltering summer day almost six years ago when her life had first begun sliding toward ruin… all thanks to *him*.

TWO

"Nevertheless," Hameen said, "you must be aware that the Priests' Guild does not give credence to the so-called prophesy of the Wolf Patron."

"Well, *of course* they don't," replied Kathrael. "The story doesn't exactly place them in a good light, does it?"

The priest shrugged. "Perhaps not. But, you must agree, the idea of an escaped slave returning as a figure of power to lead a slave rebellion sounds more like wishful thinking than reality. Such things happen only in stories."

Kathrael studied Hameen for a moment. "Tell me, Novice Hameen—were you a slave before you became a priest?"

"I was not," Hameen said after a short pause. "My parents purchased me a place as an acolyte when I first displayed unnatural urges for other boys as a youngster. Though I know, of course, that Ta'vesh was a slave before he was chosen for initiation."

"And I suppose your parents also paid for pain medicine and sleeping draughts for you during your novitiate? To ease your castration?" Kathrael asked pointedly.

"They did."

Her voice grew accusing. "Vesh had no such comfort or assistance."

Hameen looked pained. "I am aware. But slavery has been a reality in Rhyth for countless generations. It will take more than one shape-shifter to change it, however distasteful you or I might find the practice."

"So you won't help me?" Kathrael prodded.

The eunuch sighed. "I didn't say that. What, precisely, do you require of me?"

"Sandals," Kathrael said without hesitation. "A blanket. Traveling rations. Money, if possible."

"I cannot give you enough food and drink for such a long journey. Even if I could, you wouldn't be able to carry it all."

"But the rest?"

"I will find you a pair of sandals. And you may take my blanket—you have more need of it than I, whether you decide to attempt this journey or not. Stay here, and I will see if any coins have been deposited in the alms box that will not be missed." Hameen peered at her for a long moment. "I am doing this in Ta'vesh's memory, though he would probably not thank me for it. The pilgrimage you describe is fraught with danger, especially for a woman traveling alone."

"He's not here anymore to disapprove," Kathrael reminded him, "and you have my sincerest thanks."

Hameen stood. "I'll pray for you."

"I'm not certain anyone has ever done that for me before."

The novice shook his head. "No. Ta'vesh did, I feel sure. It wasn't the gods he was fleeing when he left the temple, it was the men."

Kathrael swallowed around the hard lump that rose in her throat, and nodded. "Perhaps so. Thank you again."

"Wait here. I'll return for you once I've gathered what I can." Hameen looked vaguely uncomfortable for a moment. "Afterward, I will take you to one of the back entrances to depart. You should not allow yourself to be seen if you can avoid it. The senior priests would not approve of what I am doing."

"I understand," she told him.

When he left, Kathrael ate the rest of the bread and stowed as many of the tart mayapples as she could fit into the pockets of her skirts. Before the sun had reached the top of the king's grand palace in the west, she was hurrying out of the temple through a small, little used door, laden with a sleeping roll and a bag of dried meat and cheese. A tiny ceremonial dagger nestled in the ragged sash tied around her waist—an unexpected addition.

Kathrael wondered if she would ever encounter Novice Hameen again. It seemed unlikely, as she fully expected to lose her life before she could successfully achieve her goals.

She hoped he would not be caught and punished for his unsanctioned generosity—her conscience was already heavy enough as it was.

There was no point in tarrying. Though it was already mid-afternoon, she might as well get underway. It wasn't as if she had anything holding her to the city, after all. And the sooner she was out of it, away from the crush of people, the safer she would be.

It was easier getting out than it had been getting in. She kept to the shadows and quiet side-roads, years of practice at remaining unnoticed holding her in good stead. She joined the crowd at the gate heading back to their homes outside of the walls after a day of commerce, and passed through unremarked. Not only were the guards more lenient about letting undesirables *out* of the city than letting them *in*, but also her bundle of possessions gave her an air of legitimacy despite her ragged clothing.

Once beyond the walls, she kept her head down and let the crowd carry her along until it started to thin. Her stomach was beginning to ache and gurgle unpleasantly, protesting the unexpected feast of fruit and bread after so long with almost nothing. Still, she was determined to get out into the rural areas north of the city. There, she could find a quiet patch of woods and hunker down for the night where no one would be likely to stumble across her while she slept.

The buildings and huts around her grew farther apart, separated by expanses of pasture and tilled land. These were the smallholdings, mostly owned by freefolk eking out an existence from the land. When Rhyth had been at the height of its power, there had been relatively few such holdings. Now, opportunity inside the city was drying up along with the trade across the sea, and anyone who could was moving back to the countryside.

Kathrael had grown up working the fields, but not here. She had been a slave on one of the large plantations further from the city, owned by some fat, wealthy noble who only deigned to ride out and survey his lands once or twice a year. Those places still existed, and from what she had heard, they were worse than ever as the overseers tried to extract even more labor from the slaves to meet the ever-increasing quotas demanded by the owners. With the raw materials and ore from the north cut off, the rich turned to agriculture to support their outrageous lifestyles… and the grain they sold was grown on the backs of slaves.

It was probably ironic that she had spent years as a prostitute extracting money from the same sort of men who had once owned her. They had been happy enough to pay her to dance and entertain their posh friends at the endless, decadent parties—*orgies*, more accurately—that seemed to serve as a sort of status symbol in the wealthy parts of the city, near the palace. Yet it never would have occurred to them to pay her for her years of backbreaking labor in the fields.

Fuck them all—every last one. Kathrael was going to tear down everything in this world that had tried to destroy her. She would see the slave owners thrown out into the streets, stripped of everything they'd stolen from her people, or she would die in the attempt.

The last few smallholdings were finally behind her, and the sun was dipping toward the horizon. Every muscle and joint in her body ached, unused to covering such distance in the space of a day. Her feet were on fire despite the too-large sandals Hameen had given her. She looked around. Her surroundings were uncultivated, a mixture of trees and grass. She left the road and made her way down a gentle embankment, to a flat area surrounded by shagbark trees.

The nuts were still green at this time of year, though she would have probably braved the resulting stomachache and eaten them anyway had she not managed to acquire food at the temple. As it was, she made a careful inventory of her supplies before the light faded, and measured out a small portion to eat.

Even though her gut was still churning from her earlier meal, she slowly chewed and swallowed the modest handful of dried goat meat strips and hard cheese. She did not know exactly how far away Draebard lay, but it was a long, long way. She knew it took people on foot a week to walk from Rhyth to the mountains. She would not only have to do that—she would have to *cross* the mountains and then travel on even farther, into the barbarian lands.

It would need all of her strength, and that meant eating as much and as often as she could.

It was dark when she finished her pitiful repast, washing everything down with weak, watered wine from the skin Hameen had given her. The wine would not last long in the summer heat, though she could stretch it by continuing to water it down further for a few days. After that... well... there were plenty of rivers running through the southern lands. The water in some of them was safe to drink, and the water from others wasn't. She would have to make do.

There was no need for a fire in the warm, humid weather, and lighting one would have drawn attention to her presence that she did not want. With nothing left to do, she unrolled Hameen's blanket and laid it on the ground. It smelled of sandalwood, and with no one here to see her do it, she buried her nose in the rough wool and breathed in.

It took time for her exhaustion to overcome the pain of her blistered feet and aching muscles, but eventually, she slipped into a heavy sleep, feeling a sense of freedom and purpose that she hadn't known in months... if not years.

Sunlight filtering through the leaves woke her the following morning. A light breeze from the north brought relief from the humidity. Kathrael's thin, starvation-weakened body protested movement with sharp aches and stiff, popping joints when she stretched. A moment later, her feet chimed in, reminding her of the blisters that had risen over the course of the day yesterday, as the straps of her unfamiliar footwear rubbed against the skin.

She flopped onto her back, and stared up at the ever-changing mosaic of leaves above her. It would be so easy to stay here. To rest for a few days and work her way through the bounty of food she'd received from the temple until it was gone.

It was nice here. No one would bother her. It would be so much easier.

You were never a quitter, Kath.

The half-heard whisper sounded exactly like Vesh. Kathrael bolted upright and whipped her head around, filled with irrational hope that the movement at the edge of her vision would coalesce into the slender, dark-haired form she knew so well. But it was only the wind rustling the grass. Her racing heart slowed, mired back into the dull listlessness of grief.

"Go away, Vesh," she told the empty glade. "You're dead."

The whisper of leaves moving in the breeze sounded like distant laughter.

Kathrael gritted her teeth and forced her body into motion. There was little that needed to be done before she could start moving again. She rolled up the blanket, ate a bit of cheese, and relieved herself in the tall grass. It was less painful to go barefoot, so she let the sandals dangle from her fingers as she climbed back up the slope leading to the little-used track she'd been following. With a brief glance at the sun to make sure she hadn't gotten turned around, she headed north.

By midday, she was struggling badly. The obvious thing would have been to stop and rest, but innate stubbornness, combined with confusion due to heat and exhaustion, had Kathrael convinced that if she stopped, she would never be able to start again.

The stretch of road she was on ran through a bit of forest, winding this way and that around trees that were too large and numerous to be easily cut down to clear the area for pasture or cropland. At least it was cooler in the shade. After taking a long drink of watered wine—now unpleasantly warm—from her wineskin, her thoughts began to clear. Ahead, she could just make out the sound of voices. There were two, both male, talking and laughing raucously. And they were coming her way.

She froze, caught in a moment of indecision. Should she hide, or keep walking? But then it was too late. The pair rounded the bend in front of her and paused. Caught, she fumbled with her shawl, drawing it quickly forward to obscure her scars.

"Well, well," said the one on the right. "What have we here?"

They were young—not boys, but barely men. The one who had spoken was tall and broad. The other was a few inches shorter, but wiry. Both were well, but not ostentatiously, dressed. Overseers' sons, perhaps, or members of a merchant family traveling from one village to another. The sixth sense that had kept Kathrael safe for most of her life immediately started tingling, raising the fine hair at the back of her neck.

"What're you doing out here all alone, love?" asked the one on the left, as the pair started walking toward her once more.

Kathrael turned her head to further obscure the left side of her face, but glared at them with her good eye. "I'm traveling. What does it look like?"

The broad one laughed, and the sound grated like a rusted axle. "It looks like that dress you're wearing is more holes than cloth — *that's* what it looks like. Where did a little beggar girl like you get that nice blanket and satchel? Did you steal it?"

"Maybe we should take a look in her bag. See what's in there. It might be money."

"It's moldy cheese and a bit of dried goat. Let me pass." Kathrael's free hand went to her sash, seeking the reassuring form of the dagger nestled there. Never mind that there were two of them, each towering over her, and she was on the verge of collapse from exhaustion.

"Nah, I don't think we will," said the wiry one. "Not until you let us have the bag."

She pulled the dagger free. It suddenly seemed very small and inadequate.

The broad one laughed. "What's that you've got there? A knitting needle? If you had another one, maybe you could mend that shawl."

Inspiration struck in a flash. She grabbed the shawl and pulled it back, revealing her face. Both of the men flinched, and the broad one took a step back. She bared her teeth. "Go ahead," she snarled. "Come a little closer. Touch me. Touch my satchel. I'd *love* to see what the two of you look like after you've caught the face-melting plague. Maybe you'd both like a kiss?"

The wiry one was still frozen in place like a statue, but his friend grabbed him by the arm and dragged him back. "*Fuck!*" he cursed. "You stay back, you crazy bitch!"

Kathrael took a step toward them, and spat at the wiry one's boots. He danced back as if he feared the gob of saliva might eat through the leather and contaminate him somehow.

"Naloth's balls!" Her target started hustling his friend around her on the road, giving her a wide berth. "Go find a hole to climb into and finish dying, you vicious cunt!"

Kathrael glared after them. "Thanks, but no thanks. I've got some people I need to take with me when I go."

"Leave her," said the other. "Come on, let's get *out of here.*"

Kathrael watched them hurry away, casting occasional glances over their shoulders at her as they kept to the side of the track, as if afraid to even walk on the same ground her bare feet had touched. She felt suddenly powerful, even as the familiar, crawling horror at what had happened to her face skittered through her stomach. Exhaustion momentarily banished, she turned her back on the rapidly disappearing figures and continued on.

By the time she collapsed onto Hameen's blanket, hours later, her exhaustion had returned tenfold. At least she'd managed to find a place to sleep near running water this time. After a night of restless sleep interrupted by bad dreams and throbbing pain, she spent a few minutes soaking her aching feet in the trickling brook. Some of the blisters had burst, and would no doubt infect. Her soles were bruised and scraped from walking miles barefoot the previous day.

She looked at her torn, threadbare underskirt for long moments before ripping strips from the bottom and using them to bind the worst of the damage. The sandals actually fit a bit better over the added bulk of the makeshift bandages, but even so, she could barely walk for the pain. Steeling herself to go on regardless, she shouldered her meager belongings and limped forward toward the line of mountains visible to the north, keeping her good eye focused on the distant goal.

By mid-morning, she was curled up by the side of the road, having broken her self-imposed vow not to stop, no matter what. Every step was agony. At some point she'd stumbled and, just as she had feared, once she'd gone down she couldn't find the strength to rise again. Now, the sun was beating down on her, making her head swim. Her wineskin was still more than half full after she'd filled it in the brook that morning, but she was afraid to drink it. Once it was gone, she had no way to get more if she couldn't even walk.

She thought that maybe she should want to cry, but all she could do was stare into the distance, blinking occasionally and feeling nothing.

She had no conception of time passing, but when her attention finally caught on distant movement in the direction from which she had come, the sun was high overhead. It was an emaciated donkey hauling a cart, with a figure walking alongside. Kathrael watched and waited, her shawl pulled up across her face, well aware that she couldn't get away even if she'd wanted to. A short time later, the cart pulled up next to her.

"Whoa, there!" said the drover. The donkey came to a stop and immediately cocked its hip to rest a hind foot, head drooping as if in sleep.

Looking up with her good eye, Kathrael tried to get a sense of the stranger. She was struck immediately by his face—his upper lip was split like a rabbit's. The strange gap in the flesh extended up to his nose, disappearing into one of his nostrils. She couldn't help staring; it was odd to see his gums and front teeth through the missing part of his lip, as if he was unfinished, somehow.

Upon seeing where her attention had landed, the man raised a hand, positioning loosely curled fingers in such a way that his disfigurement was hidden—obviously a habitual nervous gesture.

"Are you all right, miss?" he asked, the gap in his lip making some of the words come out oddly.

"No," Kathrael said honestly. "I need help. I have to get north, to the mountains, but I'm not used to traveling. My feet are blistered and bleeding, and I can't walk anymore."

"Oh," said the stranger, still hiding his lip and not meeting her gaze directly. His eyes flickered back to the cart, laden with melons. "Um, my employer would cane me if he found out I'd overloaded the donkey... but, well, you don't look like you weigh much. I could maybe take you to Penth, if you wanted? That's where I'm headed."

His nervous eyes skittered back to her, awaiting her answer. Instinct propelled her to shift her shawl back a bit, enough to give him a glimpse of her face. His breath caught.

"I'd like that very much," she said.

"What happened to your face?" he asked, completely guileless.

"I was burned," she said, rather than getting into the details. "What happened to your lip?"

"I was born this way. The midwife figured someone had put a curse on my mother."

Kathrael smiled up at him softly. "It must not have been a very good curse if she ended up with a son as kind as you."

Perhaps she should have felt guilt at manipulating such a simple soul, but she could find none as he smiled back, letting his hand fall away from his face. "You want to ride on the back?" he asked. "I can pile some of the melons higher to make space, but you'll have to make sure none of them fall out."

"I can do that," she said. "What's your name? I'm Kathrael."

"They call me Mouse, 'cause I look like a rodent," he replied, looking away again.

"What does your mother call you?" Kathrael asked.

"Livvy," he said. "My mother calls me Livvy."

"Well, Livvy, would you mind helping me up? I'm afraid I'm a proper invalid at the moment."

Her rescuer scrambled forward to help her to her feet, and gave her his arm to lean on as she hobbled to the cart. There was a rough board braced across the back of the thing, and Livvy rearranged the produce until he could take it off, giving her a place to sit with her feet dangling down off the edge. She eyed the rather precarious looking pile of melons and leaned back against it, using her arms to block the places where it seemed most in danger of collapsing once they set off. When she was situated, Livvy grinned at her and headed back to the front to get the donkey moving again.

Their progress was slow and bumpy, and Kathrael occasionally had to lunge after a stray melon attempting escape. Conversation was difficult in the rattling cart with Livvy out of her line of sight, walking beside the donkey. She gathered after a few shouted exchanges that he had been sent to Penth by his employer, who was also his uncle, when the man had heard that vendors in the village were paying high prices for produce after blight had destroyed the local crops.

It was a two-day trip, but Livvy's uncle still expected to turn a tidy profit even after giving his nephew enough coin to stay overnight at a town along the way.

"You could… uh… stay with me," he called over his shoulder, stumbling a bit over the words. "If—if you need a place to sleep tonight, I mean."

"In fact, I do. That's very generous of you, Livvy." Kathrael felt herself returning to firmer ground. She recognized that stammering male hopefulness of old. And she knew now that even with her disfigurement, she had the means to pay her debt to her unexpected benefactor using a form of coin that she had long assumed to be completely devalued.

⚜

Hours later, the cart rattled and juddered its way into a collection of ramshackle buildings clustered near the convergence of two rivers. To call the place a *town* was being somewhat generous, but this was apparently to be their destination for the night.

"We're here!" Livvy called back to her, as he guided the donkey to a falling-down barn near what Kathrael assumed was the way-house. A boy emerged from the sagging structure, all elbows and knees and sharp, jutting cheekbones. He and Livvy conversed in low voices as Kathrael set about the painful process of getting down from the back of the cart.

While it had been a relief not to have to walk, the jouncing, jarring ride had done little more than add a new set of aches to her existing ones. Her head pounded from the combination of exhaustion and the hot sun. Her back and shoulders were knotted with strain, and her feet still felt like they were on fire.

Nevertheless, she was determined to walk into the way-house under her own power, so she gritted her teeth and forced rebellious muscles into use. Her gait was hitching and stilted as she gimped along. Livvy noticed immediately, and hurried to offer her a supporting arm.

"Easy, there," he said. "You look like a stiff wind would fell you."

"I'll be all right," Kathrael said, trying not to lean on him too much. "It's just cramps from sitting in the wagon so long."

Her companion frowned, dubious. "Well, if you say so. I paid the boy to care for the donkey and watch over Uncle's produce tonight. Let me get us a room and you can rest while I see about dinner."

"And here I thought we'd be dining on melons," she joked weakly.

Livvy laughed, his free hand coming up to cover his harelip—a nervous tic. "Gods, no," he said. "At this time of year, even the thought of eating melon makes me ill."

The proprietor of the way-house was a sour-faced old man who eyed them with suspicion as they entered. Kathrael twitched her shawl forward a bit more over the side of her face and straightened away from Livvy's supporting arm as much as possible.

She let the men's voices wash over her and tried not to draw attention to herself as they haggled. How different things had once been, when drawing men's attention was her livelihood. And yet, she had drawn Livvy's attention easily enough today. She let him help her up a short flight of stairs that squeaked and flexed alarmingly under their weight, down an uneven hallway to a crooked doorway standing invitingly open.

The room could have been moldy and infested with fleas, and it still would have been the nicest place she'd slept in for weeks. Surprisingly, though, it was fairly well kept. The straw mattress sat on an actual bed frame rather than the floor—which had been swept recently. The small table nearby held two candles and a flint striker.

Livvy deposited her on the edge of the bed, and she had to stifle a moan of pleasure at the idea of sleeping on something softer than the ground.

"Why don't you lie down for a bit while I bring up some food?" he asked.

She smiled and nodded silently, though she had no intention of lying down. The gods knew when she'd be able to get up again, once she did.

Dinner was thick gruel and weak ale that smelled like horse piss. Kathrael wolfed it down without tasting it, manners forgotten in the face of hot, nourishing food. When the bowl was scraped clean and the flagon, emptied to the last dregs, she came back to herself enough to notice Livvy watching her while trying not to be obvious about it. A faint flush of embarrassment traveled up the unscarred side of her neck to color her face.

She willed it down. After tomorrow—assuming Livvy was still willing to take her all the way to Penth—she would never see him again. Let him stare his fill. At least he had helped her.

"You, um, you must be tired," he said when they had both finished the humble meal. "I can... take a couple of blankets and sleep on the floor, I guess."

She stilled. It was time to pay for her passage, aching body or no.

THREE

Kathrael loosened the frayed laces holding the front of her bodice together, and looked up at Livvy with her good eye. "Don't be silly," she said. "You should sleep on the bed with me."

Livvy caught his breath, and Kathrael could see his gaze darken in the candlelight. He started to speak, but the words caught in his throat. He had to swallow hard before he could reply. "I've never slept with a girl before. You know... because of my lip. Father always says no girl is likely to want me, and I should just get used to it."

"But that's not true. I want you, Livvy," Kathrael lied. She glanced down, a calculated move. "Unless you find my scars repulsive..."

It was a surprise how much the beat of silence affected her, as if her heart had suddenly decided that this awkward young man's opinion of her mattered, without bothering to consult her head. She looked up again to find him staring at her open-mouthed.

"No!" he said quickly. "No, I'm just surprised is all. I never expected—"

"Come here then, and sit next to me," Kathrael told him. He did, carefully not touching her. Nervous excitement rolled off of him in waves. She continued, "So, you've never even gone to the temple, then? Dallied with the novices?"

He shook his head and looked down. "Father said there wasn't any point. It would just make me want what I couldn't have."

Kathrael angled her body toward him, one hand coming to rest on his tense thigh as the old, familiar dance came back to her. "Well, that's simply not true. I'm sure you're not the only person in Rhyth with a harelip, Livvy. Perhaps you'll find a nice girl who looks like you do, and you'll fall in love with each other."

Several expressions chased each other across Livvy's open face as she watched, and slid her hand a little higher. "Or... maybe a girl with scars?" he asked, utterly artless.

The smile Kathrael pasted on felt like it would crack her damaged face. "Perhaps so," she managed. To forestall any further conversation, she cupped his cock through his loose trousers, drawing a groan from him.

He was large and hard, and when she knelt between his legs on sore, creaking knees to unlace his clothing and free him from his smallclothes, he grasped the edge of the mattress tightly with both hands. His prick reeked of stale sweat, and she had to battle nausea as she sucked him off. He was the first man she had serviced since her face was ruined, and the scars around the left side of her mouth pulled painfully as her lips stretched around him. Thankfully, his lack of experience had him coming down her throat in great spurts after mere moments.

Later, she lay back on the bed, making encouraging noises as he rutted into her. There was no oil-filled lamp in the room, nor was there any grease, or anything else she could use to ease the way into her dry passage. Despite the gob of spit that she'd managed to surreptitiously smear over him, the familiar push-pull between her legs went beyond the usual vague discomfort, spilling over into full-fledged pain as flesh that had lain untouched for months stretched to accommodate Livvy's large cock.

She had learned years ago to retreat inside her mind at such times, but something about letting another person this close to her scars and hurts brought a terrible sense of vulnerability to the fore. By the time Livvy finally cried out and shuddered through his second release, Kathrael's skin was crawling in a way it hadn't for years.

Afterward, she lay very still and quiet in his sweaty grip. When his loud snores filled the room, she wriggled free and pulled on her ruined dress with jerky, uncoordinated movements, covering herself. Then, she curled up on the rough wooden boards of the floor and fell into an exhausted sleep.

⋙ ☙ ⋘

A hand on her shoulder woke her the following morning, and she was unable to suppress her flinch. Sleeping with someone nearby who wasn't Vesh was a terrifying prospect. She never would have let herself drift off had she not already been on the verge of collapse.

"Hey," Livvy said. "S-sorry. I didn't mean to startle you. Why are you on the floor?"

Kathrael's tongue felt thick and dry as she unstuck it from the roof of her mouth to reply.

"I was... too hot," she said eventually, after casting around for a reasonable sounding excuse. "I didn't want to wake you with my tossing and turning."

Livvy frowned, looking unhappy, but he only said, "Oh. I see."

"Is it time to leave?" Kathrael asked, hoping to distract him.

"Yeah," he said. "Did, uh, did you still want to come with me the rest of the way to Penth?"

What Kathrael *wanted* was to flee the room and never see him again, but that wouldn't get her any closer to Draebard. "If you're willing to take me, yes."

Livvy nodded. "All right. Well. You'll have to get out of the cart before we reach the edge of the village. If any of Uncle's contacts tell him I've been taking on passengers, I'll be in big trouble."

"That's fine," Kathrael said. "I appreciate you helping me, Livvy. You're a good person."

In fact, Livvy's plan sounded better than fine. If he dropped her off on the road somewhere, he wouldn't expect a repeat of last night before they parted. Which suited Kathrael right down to the ground.

Livvy blushed, embarrassed by the compliment. "It's nothing, really. I just like to help where I can, you know?" He cleared his throat. "If you, uh, want to wash, there's a ewer of water and a bowl in the hallway. I'll see if I can talk the innkeeper out of some bread or something, and then we should go."

"Of course." Kathrael forced another smile and hobbled into the hall to rinse off her face.

Livvy disappeared down the rickety stairs, and she looked around the now-deserted space to make sure she was truly alone. The other doors were closed and no sounds emerged from within, so she hiked up her torn skirts and ran the damp cloth between her legs. There was no blood, thankfully, though her flesh was raw and aching. The cool cloth went some way toward soothing it, but she was nearly as sore from last night's coupling as she had been after her first few painful times at the tender age of thirteen.

She sighed. It would get better in a couple of days, and it seemed unlikely that she would be called upon to repeat the performance anytime soon.

When Livvy returned with a couple of hunks of two-day-old brown bread, she was as ready to face the day as she could be, under the circumstances. She knew she would barely have made it half a league today if forced to walk on her own, but the food and drink combined with a few hours of sleep had at least revived her enough that she could manage sitting on the back of the melon wagon for a few more hours.

It was cooler than the previous day, and cloudy. At first, Livvy kept up an intermittent stream of banal small talk, shouted awkwardly back and forth between his place in front with the donkey and her perch on the back of the wagon. By late morning, it began to rain—a steady drizzle—and the talk dried up even as the parched dirt turned to mud. Kathrael let the chilly water drip down her hair and the back of her neck, shivering a bit as her wet clothing clung to her skin.

She was so thin these days that she had no defense against changes in temperature, and she dreaded the coming winter. Perhaps, she thought as another round of trembling took her, she would be dead by then. Perhaps that would be preferable—particularly if she was able to gain her revenge first.

Late in the afternoon, the cart rolled to a stop on the uneven road. The rain had finally ceased, and the returning sun steamed the moisture back out of the ground, making the air thick and humid. Livvy appeared at the rear of the wagon.

"Time for me to get off?" Kathrael asked, and the young man nodded reluctantly.

"Penth is in the valley, just over the crest of this hill," he said. "It's not far. I, uh, wish I could keep you with me..."

Livvy was a sweet, decent young man, for all that he was awkward and uncouth. Even so, something about the wording made Kathrael's stomach churn and a shiver travel up the length of her spine.

Keep you with me...

Like a possession. Like an object—something to be *owned*.

The pasted-on smile seemed harder to conjure each time she summoned it. "I have to keep heading north, Livvy. And you have to get back to your uncle. Remember what I said, though. I'm sure there's someone out there for you. You just have to find her."

Livvy's face twisted through a complicated mixture of hope and disappointment, before he darted forward and kissed her undamaged cheek. She forced herself not jerk away from the contact.

"You'll be all right, though?" he asked.

"Of course I will," she said airily, as if such a question was ridiculous. "Go on. Off with you, now. Thank you again for helping me."

Livvy caught his lower lip in his teeth and chewed on it before nodding and turning away. A moment later, the cart rattled forward, leaving Kathrael standing on the side of the road with her waterskin and satchel, sandals clasped in her hand. She looked past the slow-moving cart and the young man shooting occasional glances over his shoulder at her as he crested the hill leading down to Penth.

The mountains had been at her back as she traveled in the wagon, but they were noticeably closer now than they had been yesterday. A genuine smile flickered over her features for an instant as she looked at the rugged peaks. Her satchel still contained food and a few precious coins. The waterskin was heavy at her shoulder. Her feet ached, but not with the unbearable stabbing pain that had brought her to her knees the morning before. The blisters were already starting to scab over, protected by the bindings torn from her skirts.

She could keep going.

Kathrael started limping slowly toward the village of Penth.

The blight had obviously hit Penth hard. The fields outside the village were mostly wilted and yellow, with immature, wrinkled vegetables withering on the vine. The air smelled of rot. In the town itself, people in the street gave her wary glances, their eyes flicking up only briefly before returning to the ground in front of them. Gaunt cheeks and sunken eyes were everywhere. The scent of desperation clung to them.

Kathrael kept her head down and tried to blend in, aided in doing so by her own jutting, starvation-sharpened bones. Penth was a good-sized settlement, somewhat larger than she had assumed it would be. As she wandered the streets toward the center of town, she began to realize that she was once again trapped by circumstance.

She'd had vague thoughts of using her meager collection of coins to purchase supplies for the next leg of her journey — the mountain crossing. The sad collection of food she now carried might conceivably suffice to get her *to* the mountains, but it would come nowhere close to getting her *over* them.

Livvy's generosity had gained her two meals she hadn't needed to acquire for herself, but it had also landed her in a place where food was scarce and unbelievably costly. There was a crowd in the marketplace; its mood restless as townsfolk vied for meat and produce that simply wasn't there.

After only a few minutes of walking stall-to-stall, Kathrael learned that her handful of coppers would buy her precisely nothing of use in Penth. The ugly atmosphere soon drove her onto a side street, the fine hair at the back of her neck prickling with unease.

From ahead came the sound of another crowd, this one punctuated by cries of excitement and occasional laughter rather than angry muttering. Curious, Kathrael followed the noise until the narrow street opened out into a second open square, paved with flagstones and surrounded by two-story, whitewashed buildings.

At one corner of the square, a collection of wagons and people dominated the crowd's attention. She could see a large number of children clustered near the front, laughing and hopping up and down in an attempt to see over the shoulders of those in front of them. As was her habit, Kathrael kept to the shadows and skirted the edge of the crowd until she reached a set of steps leading up to a sheltered doorway. There, she was able to get a decent view of what was going on without attracting attention.

It was a band of traveling entertainers, as she had half-suspected. A well-fed man in flamboyant dress stood atop a small wooden platform, waving his hands and sweet-talking the crowd. With few other options open to her at the moment, she settled in to watch for a bit.

The troupe was a small one, but included some very strange — even shocking — individuals. An exceptionally tall, skeletally thin man danced with a tiny, misshapen women who would barely have come up to Kathrael's waist. At the end of the dance, the woman clambered up the spokes of the wagon wheel so the man could take her in his arms like a child. They kissed to the sound of raucous jeers from the children, and titters from the adults.

A lad with no arms sat at a wooden table near the raised platform, playing a game of dice using his toes. Occasionally, he would pause to grasp a flagon between the soles of his feet, contorting himself to lift it to his lips and take a drink.

Another man—normal looking, though his expansive stomach set him immediately apart from the skinny townsfolk—made his way through the crowd, a young boy with large, sad eyes balanced on his hip. A girl the same age trailed behind him, one small hand gripping the bottom edge of the man's intricately embroidered tunic. In his free hand, he carried an upturned hat.

Kathrael was not close enough to hear the conversation as he moved from person to person in the crowd, but after a few soft words from the unhappy boy-child, many of the audience members who had been singled out gasped in surprise and nodded, sometimes taking a step back in shock. More often than not, they or the people around them would flip coins into the hat immediately afterward. She wondered what caused the reaction, but did not dare get closer to find out.

One thing was certain, however. The performers were making money. Quite a bit of it, in fact.

Half-formed ideas and plans circled Kathrael's mind as she continued to watch the spectacle. She was in a strange town, where the people were already desperate and unlikely to have much sympathy for a beggar, especially a hideously scarred one. Before her stood men who had money—enough money that the upturned hat was already sagging under the weight of coins after only a few minutes. If she followed them to wherever they stayed for the night…

Well. They would need to go to sleep sometime.

She'd have to make it to a town beyond the reach of the blight, but the money in the hat would be enough to buy food, and sturdy boots, and new clothes for her journey. Movement from one of the wagons caught her attention, breaking her free of her thoughts. The back of the cart was enclosed by bars, like a cage or a cell. Within, a tawny, four-legged shape rose and stretched, jaws cracking in a wide yawn to reveal sharp fangs.

It was a lion—thin and covered in scars, but still one of the most beautiful things Kathrael had ever seen. She caught her breath, unable to look away. The animal swept its ears back, and green-flecked eyes locked on hers without warning, pinning her in place in the sheltered doorway. Her heart jolted and began to beat double-time.

She tore her gaze away with considerable difficulty when the man on the platform raised his voice again, addressing the crowd.

"Ladies and gentlemen! I give you the main attraction. The king of predators, tamed and reduced to the gentleness of a kitten by the indomitable power of my will!" He turned to his partner, still carrying the boy while the girl clung to him. "Laronzo, *release the lion!*"

There were several shouts of fear around the square as the second man stepped up to the wagon and unlatched the barred door. Mothers hurried forward to drag their children away from the front rows. The lion shook itself and jumped down from the back of the cart before padding over to the raised platform and leaping nimbly onto it to stand next to the leader of the company.

"Now, now," said the man. "There's no cause for alarm, I assure you. Your young ones are as safe as they would be with a baby lamb. Watch!"

His partner joined him on the dais with the two children, and plopped the boy in his arms unceremoniously onto the lion's back. The child immediately grabbed the animal's scruffy mane, completely without fear. A moment later, the little girl wrapped her arms around the lion's neck, and Kathrael was hit with a flash of memory so strong it nearly sent her to her knees.

The wolf growled, its hackles rising as it crouched in front of her, keeping the overseer with the whip at bay. Kathrael gaped up at the legend made flesh standing less than an arm's length away, hope surging in her young breast.

She righted herself from where she lay sprawled on the ground and crept forward, wrapping her arms around the wolf's bristling shoulders fearlessly.

"Lupi?" she asked, tears running unchecked down her cheeks. "The gods have finally sent you for us, after so long?"

Kathrael thrust a hand out to steady herself against the doorframe behind her, caught between the past and the present even as the audience looked on in amazement.

"As you see," the man continued, "this beast is completely under my control. Only the strongest of wills can overpower the spirit of a lion, and I am pleased to count myself among that number."

The lion wrapped a large paw around the little girl and swiped its broad tongue across her hip, drawing a giggle from her. The audience gasped, but she only clung harder and buried her face in its mane. Kathrael stared as if entranced as the man on the platform motioned for his partner to drag the children away, and then guided the animal through a series of tricks as one might do with a pampered lapdog.

He seemed totally unconcerned for his safety, supremely confident of his control over the beast. Kathrael wondered if she was imagining the sense that the lion was humoring its jailer, biding its time until… *what*?

At the end of the show, however, the beast leapt lightly back up into its cage. It flopped down next to the bars and yawned again, its eyes returning unerringly to Kathrael in her shadowed hiding place. She couldn't help the shiver of reaction that skittered up her spine.

⌇⌇⌇

That night, she sat huddled in a small hollow behind two scrubby bushes on the outskirts of Penth, waiting for the moon to rise. Exhaustion circled like a carrion bird, threatening to swoop in and carry her off to unintended sleep at any moment. She knew, though, that this might be her only chance to get the money she needed to continue her journey. There was every possibility that the traveling entertainers would be heading off for greener pastures in the morning.

The group had chosen a campsite a little way outside of the town. Kathrael had been hard-pressed to keep up with them on her aching feet, even with the relatively slow pace of the heavily laden wagons.

Something rustled in the darkness and she blinked her eyes open with a jerk, unaware of having closed them. To her relief, she found the camp illuminated only by a faint silver glow of moonlight. The two men she took to be the owners had finally retired to their enclosed caravans, and the fire had burned down to embers.

Earlier, before night had fallen, she'd watched as the pair herded the others into various caravans with bars on the windows, and locked them inside. It made something inside her itch and prickle, but she told herself firmly that it wasn't why she was here. These people were not her responsibility.

And yet, a voice in her head taunted, *you vowed to Elarra that you would free all the slaves in the south. Does that not make them your responsibility?*

At least the little voice didn't sound like Vesh this time. Yes, she had vowed to her sister when they were children that she would lead an uprising against the slavers. But first, she *would* have her revenge. She deserved that much out of life, surely. And *revenge* meant getting across the mountains.

In the moonlight, the camp was completely quiet. Kathrael slipped on silent feet from her hiding place and into the circle of wagons. Someone had left a crust of bread and the dregs of a cup of wine next to the remains of the fire. Kathrael ate and drank without thought, finishing every drop, every crumb.

She was just looking around, trying to decide the best way to find where the money was stashed without waking anyone, when a soft noise pierced the silence.

"Psst!"

Her heart thudded in her ribcage and she froze, *caught*, but no cry of alarm followed that first quiet sound. She cast around in the near darkness, silently cursing her blind, useless left eye. Eventually, her gaze came to rest on the lion's cage. The animal was nowhere to be seen. Instead, a naked man crouched inside facing her, his arms resting casually through the bars as he watched her.

FOUR

Favian of Draebard took a deep breath and knocked on the door to the High Priest's private quarters in the back of the temple. He'd always known it would be a challenge to convince his mentor that he was truly ready to undergo his novitiate into the priesthood, but the situation was starting to become ridiculous. It was time to speak plainly, and finally hash out the argument once and for all.

There were low voices coming from within, though the conversation paused at the sound of his knocking. As it was fairly late in the evening, it came as no surprise to Favian that the High Priest was not alone in his rooms. And indeed, it was not Senovo, but Carivel—Draebard's Horse Mistress— who opened the door for him.

"Oh! Hello, Favian. Come on in," she said with a sheepish smile, rubbing a hand over the back of her neck as she stood back to let him pass. She was barefoot, dressed casually in a man's tunic and breeches—clearly not intending to leave anytime soon. "We were just discussing some village business. Have you eaten? There's a bit of roast left."

"Hi, Carivel. Thanks, but I ate earlier with the other acolytes. I just need to speak with Senovo, if he has time. You and Andoc as well, I guess, since you're here."

Carivel mouthed a silent "*ahh*" of understanding, and waved him into the room.

Chief Andoc looked up as he entered, a smile brightening his ruggedly handsome face. "Join us, Favian. What can we do for you tonight?"

Next to him, Senovo leaned back in his chair and lowered the goblet he'd been holding to the table before him. His black hair hung loose over his shoulders, freed from the tightly plaited queue favored by members of the priesthood. He raised a dark, finely sculpted eyebrow at his protégé, a question in his gold-green eyes.

Andoc and Carivel had been Favian's formal guardians since he lost his father several years ago. His mother had died giving birth to his sister, Frella, when he was still quite young. After his father was killed in an accident while traveling, Senovo had immediately taken both Favian and Frella under his wing, welcoming them into the temple and ensuring that their day-to-day needs were met. Soon afterward, Andoc and Carivel had used their positions of authority within the village to make a more permanent arrangement for the siblings. None of the three had ever attempted to replace his dead parents, but nonetheless, he and Frella had quickly come to rely on them as family.

Favian was more grateful to the eccentric trio seated before him than he could express. Now, though, he needed to make Senovo, in particular, understand that it was time for him to move on to the next stage in his life. He swallowed, and licked his dry lips to wet them.

"High Priest Senovo," he said, "I formally request that you either agree to let me undergo my novitiate and elevate me to the priesthood, or throw me out of the temple altogether."

Understanding flooded Senovo's features. "Favian—" he began, looking pained.

Favian didn't give him a chance to continue. "I have completed all of the requirements to join the priesthood, and expressed my desire to dedicate myself to the gods' service. *Several times*, in fact," he added dryly. "I can only assume that your continued resistance to my request means you do not consider me worthy of becoming a novice priest."

Senovo closed his eyes for a moment and sighed. "Of course it doesn't, Favian," he said, "as you know perfectly well. I merely wish to ensure that you truly understand what you will be undertaking, Little Brother. Once done, it can never be undone."

Favian relaxed his stiff stance enough to lean his hands on the table, meeting Senovo's gaze evenly across the expanse of wood. "I know you're only trying to protect me, Elder Brother," he replied, echoing the less formal term of address used between members of the temple, "but in the end, it's my life. *My* choice."

Andoc, along with Carivel, had been watching the confrontation silently. Now, the village chief looked at Senovo and rolled his eyes. "It's not as if you haven't tried every trick you could think of to talk him out of it already, *amadi*," he pointed out, one hand resting on the back of Senovo's chair with casual familiarity. "He wants to be a priest, and he wants to be a eunuch. It's a completely different situation than the one you suffered as a young man."

Carivel ran a hand through her close-cropped hair, ruffling it. "There's nothing that says you have to do it personally, is there? The castration, I mean," she asked Senovo with a frown.

The High Priest pinched the bridge of his nose between his forefinger and thumb. He was silent for a long moment before speaking again. "No. No, there is not." He looked back up at Favian, pinning him with an intense gaze. "Very well, Favian. Give me your word that you are truly running *toward* the priesthood—not running *away* from your physical desires or inclinations… and I will agree to your request."

Favian forced himself to hold that too-knowing gaze and reply in an even voice, "You have my word."

It was the truth, now that Ithric was gone, seemingly for good—sneaking away from Draebard months ago in the middle of the night, without so much as an explanation or a goodbye.

Well… it was *mostly* the truth, at any rate, and Favian refused to feel guilty about the small deceit.

Senovo's eyes burned into his for another beat before he blinked and said, "In that case, I will speak to Healer Sagdea. She is the most qualified person in Draebard to perform the procedure, in any case. Brother Eiridan can assist her in my stead."

"Congratulations, Favian," Carivel said quietly. "I've always said you were going to be a terrific priest someday."

"We're all very proud of you, you know," Andoc put in. "It took courage to beard our stubborn High Priest in his den and state your case. Carivel's right—you'll make a great priest."

"Thank you," Favian said, the words meant for all three of them, but his attention still focused on Senovo.

Senovo huffed out a breath. "Don't thank me yet, Favian. You may assume that my reluctance to see you castrated stems merely from my own unfortunate initiation into the Priest's Guild, but there is also another matter to address."

Favian felt a moment's confusion before he realized what Senovo meant.

"Ah," he said. "Right. I'd almost forgotten about the dream."

Andoc's expression sharpened immediately, and Carivel drew in an audible breath.

"*The dream?*" Andoc echoed. "What dream are we discussing, here, and why is this the first I've heard about it?"

Favian opened his mouth to speak, but Senovo beat him to it. "Favian has many dreams, Andoc. He shared this one with me not long after the battle at Llanmeer, but it didn't seem relevant until his novitiate approached. It did, however, have many of the hallmarks of a true vision. Favian?"

Favian cleared his throat. "Yes, it felt like a seer's dream at the time. You have to understand, it's been years ago, now, so it's pretty hazy, I'm afraid. But I was definitely lying in my room, recovering from the novitiation ceremony. I think it was a few days afterward. And there was this girl…"

⚜

Later, after his guardians had extracted every detail from him that he could remember, Favian left them to their discussion and went to find Limdya. She had offered earlier to keep his sister Frella company while he spoke to Senovo, and she'd made him promise to tell her everything once he returned.

Limdya and her two sisters had been orphaned in the Alyrion attack on Draebard, only a few months before Favian's own father had died. She'd been a huge help to both him and Frella as they dealt with their grief and fear for the future. In return, Favian had assisted her wherever he could with her job at the horse pens—she had been the first girl ever accepted as an apprentice there. Well, the first girl if you didn't count Carivel, who had originally gained her position at the pens because everyone thought she was a boy.

At any rate, Limdya had never been allowed near the horses when she was growing up, so she was at a considerable disadvantage compared to the other apprentices. Since Favian had worked at the pens before becoming a temple acolyte, he was happy to tutor her in horsemanship whenever he was able. Though he was confident his decision to leave the pens and join the temple had been the right one, he still missed the horses, and it was good to get out with them when his other duties allowed.

In the beginning of their friendship, it quickly became obvious that Limdya had something of a crush on him.

Which was, well… *awkward*. Though Favian had always craved close relationships and emotional intimacy with females and males alike, he had only ever been sexually attracted to men. Unfortunately, such liaisons were strictly taboo in Eburosi society—to be caught with another man could result in exile at the very least.

Not that Favian thought Andoc would actually throw him out of the village, of course. Rumor had it that their fearless chieftain had entertained his share of male lovers in his own misspent youth. And there was also the fact that Andoc and Carivel were handfasted to a eunuch High Priest—though the controversial three-way relationship had brought its own measure of scandal when it first became public knowledge.

Still, a eunuch being with a man was *different*. Not encouraged, exactly. But… tolerated.

A few months after they had become close, Favian haltingly told Limdya all of this, terrified that she would pull away in disgust once she knew of his unnatural leanings. She sat very still and quiet for several long moments after his flood of words had finally dried up, before leaning forward and pulling him into a tight hug.

"It's not fair," she'd said, her voice full of sadness on his behalf. "It's no more fair than saying that women can't tend the animals or men can't be healers. It's just so… *stupid*—all of it!" She pulled back, wiping away tears. "Sorry, I'm being an idiot." She gave a wet laugh, obviously directed at herself. "Apparently, I have a type, when it comes to men. The *unavailable* type."

"You'll find someone, Limdya," he'd told her with complete certainty. He placed a kiss on her forehead, even as relief poured through him that she hadn't reacted with anger or hurt. "If it weren't for the sex thing, we could go get handfasted tomorrow as far as I'm concerned. I *do* love you. I just don't… *desire* you."

Her smile was watery. "That's a tempting offer," she said. "I want children, though. Lots of them. And I *do* want to be desired, Favian." Her eyes grew far away. "Maybe someday…" When she looked at him again, her usual playful good humor had returned. "I'm afraid you'll just have to put up with me as a friend."

He'd smiled back at her and made some light quip, but inside, he'd longed for someone in his life who was more than *just a friend*.

As it turned out, Limdya hadn't needed to wait long before love found her—in the form of Dalon, Carivel's assistant at the horse pens. He was a few years older than her, and their relative positions in the village made it awkward at first, but Favian was convinced that their feelings for each other were genuine. They had been together for almost two years, and were now discussing entering into a more permanent arrangement in the fall.

Still, Limdya had made good on her promise of continued friendship, and she was the one he went to whenever he needed support or a sympathetic ear from someone close to his own age. Now, she was waiting for him with Frella in the room he and his sister shared in the temple.

Frella must have heard his footsteps approaching, because she yanked open the door, eyes wide, and asked, "*Well?*"

"He said yes," Favian confirmed, and caught Frella when she squealed with excitement and threw herself into his arms.

Limdya appeared in the doorway, a smile making her round, soft features glow. "Congratulations, Favian. When is the ceremony?"

"Two days from now," he told her, flooded with a strange combination of relief and nervousness.

She nodded her understanding before turning sober. "What about the dream, though? You remember the one I mean? Did you tell them about the girl with the knife?"

"Yes, I did." Favian disentangled himself from his sister and crossed to sit down on his bed. "Senovo knew already, but I recounted everything I could remember about it to all three of them, which unfortunately wasn't as much as I'd have liked."

"It might not even happen, you know," said Limdya, though she sounded doubtful. "Not all of your dreams come true."

"Thank goodness," Frella put in, her face screwing up in disgust. "Remember that one you told us about where no one in the village could find any clothes, and everyone had to go around naked? *That* would have been a real nightmare."

Limdya laughed, clear and light. "It all depends on the person in question, sweetheart. Am I right, Favian?"

Favian blushed to the roots of his hair, remembering with perfect clarity how Ithric's body had looked in the odd dream—lean and perfect and covered with old scars. "No comment," he said.

"Eww," groaned Frella. "Why do you two have to say things like that?"

Limdya only laughed harder. "It'll all make sense someday, sweetheart—you'll see. And may the gods help the male population of Draebard when that day finally comes."

At the age of ten, Frella had already perfected the art of the offended flounce. She employed it now. "Ugh," she said over her shoulder in a tone of disgust. "You're *awful*, Limdya! I don't have to listen to this. I'm going to go and tell the others the news!"

"Don't mention the dream," Favian called after her. "I don't want it to turn into some great big deal!"

Ever since he had begun to exhibit signs of the second sight at the age of fourteen, Favian's gift had been a mixed blessing, at best. At first, he had only dreamed of catastrophic events—terrible things that left him wracked with guilt when they came to pass in reality. Later, he started to foresee stupid, meaningless things. People slipping and falling in the mud after a rainstorm, or spilling their drinks. Piglets escaping from the hog pens—that sort of thing.

Eventually, his dreams seemed to settle along a sort of middle ground, of things that were important, but not world ending. Possibly this was only because Draebard had been relatively quiet in recent years, since the war. Whatever the case, Favian wasn't about to complain. He didn't think he could have maintained his sanity with death and destruction playing out behind his closed eyelids at night.

"Here," said Limdya, drawing him back to his surroundings. "I brought some ale from the cookhouse. We'll celebrate with a toast."

"Thanks," Favian said, accepting a cup from her. Limdya's older sisters still ran their late mother's cookhouse, and even though Limdya no longer worked there, she always seemed able to get the best food and drink for any occasion.

"To Novice Favian," Limdya toasted with a smile, raising her own clay cup.

Favian could not contain his pleased grin as he touched his cup to hers. "It does have kind of a nice ring to it, doesn't it?"

"It does indeed, my friend," Limdya agreed. "So, are you going to have a last fling before the ceremony? See your balls off in style, so to speak?"

Favian choked on his mouthful of ale. "Limdya!" he said after he managed to clear his throat. "Be serious! Who exactly in Draebard am I going to fuck?"

Limdya sobered. "I *was* being serious. You could have a night with one of the novices, couldn't you? Or maybe even another acolyte. Even if people found out, I don't think they'd hold it against you. You're *almost* a eunuch now, after all."

He laughed, but it was a weak sound. "Oh, gods, no. I couldn't. It would be like bedding a family member." He shook his head and gave a little shudder, dismissing the frankly disturbing image. "Besides," he added, "I don't really go for eunuchs."

Limdya let out an unladylike snort of amusement, as Favian had intended. It seemed she wasn't ready to let it pass so easily, though. "I just think it's sad that you'll never get a chance to really experience it. As a man, I mean. I know eunuchs still *do* have sex, of course—some of them, at least. But it must be really different for them, right?" She paused, frowning. "Don't you want to at least know what it's like?"

Favian looked down, studying his ale. "I do know what it's like," he said quietly.

Limdya was silent for a long moment, before blurting, "Oh, my gods. You don't mean… you and Ithric—?"

"Once," Favian confirmed, and added in a voice laced heavily with irony, "right before he left, in fact."

"But I thought you two could barely stand each other!" Limdya said.

"That's because Ithric is an infuriating ass," Favian muttered.

Limdya made a dismissive noise. "*Dalon* is an infuriating ass, but that doesn't mean I'm not in love with him." Favian could practically see her rearranging things inside her head to accommodate this new information. "Merciful Utarr. Everything makes *so* much more sense now. He broke your heart, didn't he?"

Favian scoffed to hide the way his chest ached. "Don't be ridiculous. I'm fine. It could never have worked between us anyway. What would a novice priest want with a scruffy, itinerant shape-shifter?"

What, indeed?

Limdya opened her mouth to say something else that Favian was fairly sure he didn't want to hear. Fortunately, approaching footsteps and a ragged cheer from the hallway interrupted her. Moments later, several of Favian's fellow acolytes and novices poured into the too-small room, armed with flagons of wine liberated from the refectory.

Reston grabbed Favian in a one-armed hug and ruffled his hair. "Congratulations, Little Brother. Frella just told us the good news. Think the gods will forgive us in the morning if we get you thoroughly plastered tonight to celebrate?"

Favian took a deep breath and gave his melancholy thoughts a firm shove to one side. "I think there's only one way to find out. Pour me a cup?"

FIVE

Kathrael approached the lion cage without realizing she was doing it, getting close enough to confirm that the animal really wasn't inside.

"You were at the performance this evening," said the young man, his voice pitched low. "What are you doing here?"

His features were angular—pleasing to the eye in the faint illumination, though with a heavy northern cast to the brow and chin. His nose had been broken at some point. Whoever set it had done a better job than Hameen had done with Vesh's nose, but there was still a decided lump about a third of the way down its length. His tangled mane of wavy hair was dark in the moonlight, but not black. Brown, perhaps. His lean, sinewy body was covered in a patchwork of scars, visible as thin silver lines against his darker skin.

His eyes were piercing and strangely intense.

"Where is the lion?" Kathrael blurted.

"It's around," the stranger said, still seeming strangely relaxed for someone crouched naked in a dangerous animal's cage and talking to an intruder in the middle of the night.

With a sudden flash of mortification, Kathrael realized that her shawl had fallen to her shoulders, leaving her face uncovered. The man hadn't even reacted.

"Why are you here?" he asked again, still watching her with those strange, faintly glowing eyes.

Once again, words came out of Kathrael's mouth before she consciously decided to speak them. "I'm going to steal money from the men who own you."

The young man's eyes widened, his expression caught between amusement and offense. "They don't *own* me!"

"You're naked and locked in a cage," Kathrael pointed out, though it seemed highly unlikely he could have missed those two facts.

The stranger's smile was sharp, dangerous, and short-lived. "Locking me in a cage helps them sleep better at night.

Anyway, I can't leave this place quite yet." His gaze turned assessing. "You could do something for me, though."

Kathrael's own expression turned wary. "You're not going to raise the alarm?"

"Not now, certainly. Maybe in a bit."

By rights, Kathrael should have run at that point. Instead, she glared at him through her good eye.

He ignored her sour look and continued, "You won't be able to get anywhere near Turvick's money stash, you know. He keeps it under his mattress… and he's a light sleeper."

"Then I'll knock him out first," Kathrael said.

"You could try that, I guess," the man agreed. "Of course, then you'd still have to deal with Laronzo. They sleep in the same caravan."

A bush rustled nearby. Kathrael jumped, but it was only some small night creature, probably looking for scraps. Her heart began to sink as she cast around for ways to get a bag of money away from two men twice her size within the enclosed space of a caravan… and came up empty.

"So, will you help me?" the stranger asked.

"You want me to let you out? Why should I help you?"

He looked at her oddly. "No, I told you, I can't leave just yet. And, well, to be more accurate, it wouldn't actually be *me* you'd be helping. You'd be helping the twins. They need to get away from here—the sooner, the better."

Kathrael had no idea why she was still standing around talking. And yet… "What twins?"

"You saw them earlier. The two children. This place isn't good for them."

She remembered the very young boy and girl who had clung fearlessly to the lion. Remembered their huge, sad eyes. "What can I do for a couple of children barely off the breast?" she asked sharply. "I can't even keep *myself* fed and clothed!"

The man didn't react to her sudden anger. "The boy reads minds," he said in a quiet voice. "Thoughts, emotions, intentions. Turvick and Laronzo are cold-hearted thugs, driven by greed. The others here are frightened. Trapped. Humiliated at being forced to display their differences for people's entertainment, day in and day out; locked up like animals at night."

Instinctive, superstitious wonder flooded Kathrael, followed closely by nausea at the idea of someone so young constantly having such ugliness forced into his mind.

The stranger continued. "Laronzo drags the boy through the crowd during performances, telling the rubes what they're thinking. It hurts Dex to be surrounded by strangers like that, but if he resists, they separate him from his sister." His eyes grew hard and dangerous. "I don't know the nature of her gift. I don't know if anyone does. She never speaks — not that I've heard, at least. But if she and her brother are forcibly parted by more than a few dozen paces, they scream in agony as though they're both being burned by flames."

Kathrael choked on a gasp, and swallowed it down harshly. "What are you asking of me? I told you, I'm barely keeping my own body and spirit together."

"I'm asking you to rescue them and take them back to their family. Turvick stole them from the village of Darveen a little over a week ago. It's east of here — only two days' walk from Penth."

She was silent for a long moment, listening to the tiny night noises around the camp. "I don't have enough food left for a two-day journey with children," she said eventually.

The stranger raised a sardonic eyebrow, his expression turning wry. "The money stash is well-guarded, but the provision wagon — not so much." He jerked his chin toward a cart off to their left. "It's right over there. It's not locked. Help yourself, just leave enough for the rest of us for a day or two. Food's scarce around Penth."

Kathrael's eyes widened and she hurried over to the wagon. As promised, it was laden with wooden boxes — none of them secured. Her stomach growled, and she immediately set about stuffing as much food as she could carry into her leather satchel. When it was full, she slung a second wineskin over her shoulder, and rearranged everything as best she could in the boxes to hide the pilferage.

"The twins are in the caravan behind you," came the quiet voice from the lion's cage.

She stilled. There was nothing to stop her leaving with the food and never looking back. It was madness to try to take children with her through the wilderness to Darveen. The twins were, what? Three, perhaps four years of age?

She thought of frantic toddlers screaming as they were ripped away from mothers, from siblings — families torn from each other and dragged onto the auction block. Sold and shipped across the land like cattle. Her heart thudded painfully in her chest and she had to stand still for a long moment and just breathe.

It was madness, yes. But Kathrael had been mad for some time now. She opened her eyes and went to examine the twins' caravan. It was not nearly as sturdy-looking as most of the other wagons, or the lion cage. There were bars on the small windows and a lock on the door, true, but the wood around the lock was cracked with age and riddled with woodworm. She supposed that it didn't take much to keep a couple of small, frightened children from escaping during the night.

After exploring the warded locking mechanism with her fingers, she returned to the lion cage and its mysterious occupant. "I'll have to break the lock," she said. "It will make noise."

The sharp smile returned. "You'll need a distraction, in that case. I've got just the thing." He sobered. "Do you know how to get to Darveen?"

"Go east?" she offered dryly.

"The main road from Penth splits beyond the bridge over the river. You'll need to take the south fork, and then turn east again at the crossroads beyond the forest."

"All right," she said. "But what about you?"

"Turvick is heading north to the towns along the west coast, on the other side of the mountains. He thinks it will be safer to exhibit his show there, and he's probably right," said the man. "I need to head north anyway—might as well get free food and transportation for the journey. He's supposedly got a ship booked for our passage in a few days."

With the hysteria in Rhyth and the surrounding lands over people who showed evidence of magic, Turvick was smart to run. Sooner or later, someone would start the wrong kind of talk about his human exhibits, and a mob would show up, baying for blood. In fact, that probably explained why they were camped away from town.

"I'm heading north as well," Kathrael said, apropos of nothing. She couldn't explain her odd fascination with the strange young man. He seemed a little bent in the head, to be perfectly honest, and yet she couldn't stop herself from drawing out the conversation. Perhaps it was merely a case of like calling to like, she thought wryly.

He smiled again, and there was less of a manic edge to it this time. "Perhaps I'll see you there, in that case. Now, though, you'd better get a move on. Try to break the lock. If Turvick or Laronzo wake up, I'll make sure their focus stays on me while you get the twins away."

"How?" she asked, still not liking the element of risk involved in such a half-baked plan.

"Easy," he said, the sharp grin returning. "Safe journey, Little Cat."

With that, he stretched and shook himself, and suddenly there was a skinny lion with a scruffy mane lounging against the bars of the cage where a lean, crazy-eyed man had crouched a moment before.

Kathrael staggered back in shock, nearly falling to the ground as she tripped over her own feet. A moment later, though, she was creeping back up to the bars as if drawn by an invisible cord.

Of course.

Even though she was dizzy with reaction, she could barely hold back the harsh laughter that wanted to rise up. *How many people could say they'd met not one shape-shifter, but two?* She only hoped this meeting would not herald the same kind of turmoil that had turned her life upside down six years ago.

The lion blinked glowing eyes at her. She lifted a hand, reaching through the bars to cradle the animal's jaw. It rubbed its head against her palm like an overgrown mouser in the granary, its eyes never leaving hers.

"Well, lion-boy," she said. "Aren't you just full of surprises?"

The beast shoved her hand playfully with its blocky head, a low rumble that might have been amusement—or encouragement for her to get a move-on—rising from its chest.

"Yes, yes—fine," she groused. "I'm going. You should know, though, that the last person I met who was like you ruined my life. If your crazy plan ends up with me locked in a caravan and being exhibited to gawping crowds as the *Wax-faced Girl* or some such, I'm going to take it *very personally.*"

At least you'd have food, said the voice that sounded like Vesh. *And you could learn more about the lion-boy.*

And I'd be a slave again, in all but name, she thought, before shaking herself free of the argument.

"Right," she said decisively. After a final scratch of the lion's soft cheek, she pivoted and moved toward the burned-out remains of the campfire with steady deliberation. One of the stones from the fire ring would do nicely to break the half-rotted wood around the lock. She selected a rounded stone that fit easily in her hand. It was still warm from the earlier fire, and the deep heat against her palm was soothing.

The lion tracked her movement as she crept over to the twins' caravan. "Dex?" she called in a quiet voice, hoping it would be enough to wake the children. "Dex, wake up. You don't know me, but I've come to take you and your sister back to Darveen. To your home. I'm going to break the lock on your door, and then we have to sneak away very quietly. Do you understand?"

There was only silence from within. Kathrael sighed.

"Well, stay back from the door if you can hear me." With a final glance back at the lion, who was still watching with interest, she hauled off and slammed the heavy stone into the soft wood around the lock. There was a loud cracking noise as it hit, and she held her breath. There was no time to worry, though, so she hit the lock a second time, and a third, her sore joints and aching muscles already protesting the effort.

Eventually, the aged wood gave way, and the splintered door creaked open on abused hinges. By this time, there was a commotion coming from the largest and finest of the caravans, as the owners awoke and scrambled out to see what was causing the noise. Desperate not to be seen, Kathrael clambered into the twins' wagon and pulled the ruined door shut behind her as best she could.

It was dark inside except for a square of moonlight coming through the bars of the small, east-facing window. However, she could sense two small bodies nearby, huddled together in a corner.

"Shh," she whispered. "It's all right. I won't hurt you. We need to hide for a minute. The lion-boy said he would cause a distraction. Then we can run."

The nature of the distraction became clear an instant later, when a deafening roar came from the direction of the lion's cage, followed by the rattle of wood and metal as a heavy body slammed against the bars repeatedly. Kathrael risked a glance through the window. Across the camp, the owners were hurrying toward the animal's cage, half-dressed in sleeping robes and carrying wooden staves, shouting to each other in confusion.

"What's wrong with him?"

"He's gone crazy—he'll break out! Stop him!"

She caught her breath in a gasp as the men started flailing their staves at the lion through the bars, trying to beat it off before it damaged the sturdy cage with its apparent escape attempt. The lion only fought harder, ignoring the blows.

A small hand closed around Kathrael's forearm, startling her, and then she was looking into Dex's large sad eyes, his face pale in the square of moonlight.

"They won't kill him," said the child. "They need him. For the show."

She swallowed, unwilling to acknowledge the depth of her worry for the crazy lion-boy she'd only just met. "We should go," she said instead. "Will you come with me back to Darveen?"

Dex's sister crawled forward to join her brother. The tiny girl stared at Kathrael's face for a long moment. Then, she and her brother shared a quick look, and she nodded.

"We can go home?" Dex asked.

"I'll do my best to get you there," Kathrael replied, unwilling to promise what she wasn't at all sure she could deliver. "Quick—get anything you need. We have to leave now."

"We only have our clothes," Dex said. "Well, our clothes, and Fish."

The little girl nodded, and clutched a lump of stuffed burlap to her chest that might, at a stretch, be described as fish-shaped.

"Come along, then. Quiet as you can." She eased the battered door open just enough to help the two children down from the wagon and follow them out before shutting it as best she could with the doorframe bent. With one of their hands in each of hers, she guided them back so that the bulk of the caravan was between them and the lion's cage. She was unable to control her flinch at the sound of wood hitting flesh, followed by a yowl of pain.

"Hurry," she hissed urgently, and led the twins away from the camp and into the brush where she had been hiding earlier. They struggled to keep up on their short legs.

With luck, the pair would not be missed until morning. *Luck* had not been a friend to Kathrael over the years, however, so she kept the children moving. When they began to flag, she carried them, ignoring the protests of her own abused body. She had toiled under sacks of grain as a girl working in the fields, so the weight—and the pain of an aching back as she bore it—was no stranger to her.

Now, though, she was barely recovered from her collapse on the road north of Rhyth. When she could go no further, she found the first sheltered spot among the trees and bushes that seemed to offer a temporary haven, and sank to the ground gratefully.

She had been following the rising moon, but with the moon now overhead, it would be too easy to lose her sense of direction. Better to lie low until sunrise started to paint the east. It was hard to see details in the shadow of the rustling leaves above them, but the two siblings both seemed very quiet and pale.

"Are you hungry?" she asked, rummaging in her pack for something to give them.

The girl nodded, and reached for the unleavened bread Kathrael handed her.

"I'm thirsty," said the boy.

"Here." She handed him the heavy waterskin and helped him hold it so he could drink his fill. "Better?"

He nodded.

"So," she said, addressing the girl. "I know your brother is called Dex. What's your name? I'm Kathrael."

The girl only shook her head and looked away. Kathrael wondered if she truly could not speak, or if she merely chose not to as the result of some trauma or fear.

"She pretends she doesn't have a name," said Dex. "But she does. She just doesn't like it."

Kathrael gave her an assessing look. "Well, then… what would you *like* to be called?"

"She wants to be called Petra," Dex said, leaving the mystery of Petra's speaking ability—or lack thereof—unsolved.

"Is that right, Petra?" Kathrael asked. The girl nodded, still silent.

"All right, you two," she continued. "We're staying here tonight. I have a blanket if you're cold. Do you think you can sleep while I keep watch?"

"I don't know," said Dex.

"Try," Kathrael said in a dry voice. "Tomorrow will be a very long day."

Petra took the blanket when she offered it. Kathrael felt around until she found a hollow at the base of a tree where she could lean back to listen to the night sounds around them. She was fairly confident that the twins would fall asleep within moments of lying down, even in such unfamiliar surroundings. They had to be exhausted—she certainly was.

An edge of surprise cut through the gray fog of weariness shrouding her mind when Petra crawled half into her lap and curled up to sleep there, rather than lying down nearby. Dex snuggled up against them a moment later, and as she had suspected, their breathing evened out into sleep within minutes.

She sat still as a statue, unwilling to risk waking them. The little girl's warm, trusting weight in her arms was a stark *might-have-been* that made her heart ache.

⤞ ⚜ ⤝

When Kathrael jerked awake some time later, it was light. She had not intended to sleep, although that had probably been unrealistic. Their hiding place hadn't been discovered— not that there was truly much risk of it without a fire or anything else to mark their presence.

Petra was watching her with large, liquid eyes.

Kathrael stared back, realizing with a sudden jolt that she had not given her scars a single thought since last night when she'd been talking to the lion-boy. Neither he nor the twins had reacted to her disfigurement in any way. She would have put it down to the nighttime darkness and the stressful situation, but even now in the dappled morning sunlight, Petra was watching her without a hint of fear or repulsion.

"They don't matter," Dex said from where he was sitting nearby, tousle-haired, and with a smudge of dirt on his cheek.

He reads thoughts, she reminded herself, feeling a wash of superstitious unease.

"'M sorry," he muttered. "I can't help it. It's all right, though. You're a good person. It doesn't hurt."

"I'm really not, you know," Kathrael said, the words slipping out without conscious thought.

"Petra needs to pee," Dex said, in the disconnected way that young children often seemed to converse. Petra nodded agreement, still staring at Kathrael's face from inches away.

Kathrael blinked, and forced her mind back to the practical. "Right. I imagine we all do. Then we'll eat something and be on our way. The sooner we start, the sooner you two can get home."

And the sooner I can get moving in the right direction again.

The three of them prepared for the day as best they could with their limited resources. Kathrael had to fight the urge to gorge on the food she had stolen from the provisions cart, knowing that not only would they need it for the rest of the trip, but also that it would probably make her sick. She ate a reasonable portion and tried her best to ignore the way her hands itched to grab more and stuff it into her face like some kind of savage.

After making sure that the children's needs were seen to as far as was possible, Kathrael readied them to set off.

"I need one of you to walk while I carry the other one," she said. "When you get tired, let me know and we'll switch."

"I can walk," said Dex.

"Very well. Tell me if I'm going too fast, though."

Dex nodded, and followed her as she hitched Petra against her hip and settled the satchel, skins, and blanket over her shoulders.

The day seemed to creep by, and Kathrael had the constant feeling that they were barely making progress. It didn't help that she was keeping them away from the road as much as possible, unwilling to risk being seen while they were still so close to Penth. When the river appeared through gaps between the trees with the fork in the road visible beyond, it was a relief. At least they were following the correct route, if nothing else.

Kathrael took a chance and quickly crossed the bridge before returning to the cover of the trees and brush. It was too dangerous to risk ruining the food if the river turned out to be deeper than expected, and she probably would have had to take the twins across one at a time.

She cursed silently when a farmer saw them from a distance, but the odds of the brief sighting coming to anything were negligible. No doubt the farmer had more important things to attend to than immediately running to

Penth and gossiping about a woman in a tattered dress with two small children. He was almost certainly too far away to see her scars.

As the day wore on, they had to stop more and more frequently to rest. Even carrying one of the youngsters, such travel was too much to ask of children so young. She tried carrying both of them again for a while, but her own strength was simply not up to the task. When Kathrael finally admitted defeat for the day, they still had not reached the crossroads.

That night, she tried once more to keep watch, and once more fell asleep. A nightmare woke her, accompanied by the sound of stifled sobs from the blanket next to her. It took a few moments to get her bearings and remember where she was, but then she was leaning over to check Petra, who was still crying.

"You dreamed," Dex said, making the simple words sound like an accusation. His own voice was a little quivery around the edges.

"Oh, gods," Kathrael said softly. They could see into her mind. Feel what she felt. They were so *young*. " —I'm sorry."

"You can't stop dreams," the boy said.

She ground her teeth together. "Oh, yes, I can. Go back to sleep. It won't happen again tonight, I promise."

Dex gave her a skeptical look, but went back to soothing his sister. Before too long had passed, they were both asleep once more. Kathrael leaned her back against a rough patch of bark, determined not to sleep any more before morning.

At first, she thought about the lion-boy. She hoped he was all right after being beaten by his captors. She still couldn't explain her fascination with him. By rights, she should be wary of shifters, to say the least. They certainly seemed to have a knack for thrusting her into dangerous circumstances with little thought for the consequences to her life.

As the dawn slowly lightened the east to reveal a sky heavy with slate-gray clouds, her thoughts naturally turned to the Wolf Patron, and what she had planned for him. Sometimes it seemed that her desire for revenge was all that kept her from collapsing in a heap by the side of the road somewhere and never getting up again. The idea of a slave rebellion was too big—too *distant*—to truly seem real. For all that she had vowed to make such a rebellion happen, there were so many obstacles to overcome, she fully expected to be dead before it ever came to be.

There was only one obstacle between her and Senovo of Draebard, though — the mountains. And people crossed the mountains all the time. The sharp little ceremonial dagger still nestled in Kathrael's sash, and all it would take was a single thrust.

What would it feel like to kill a man?

Would the blade slide in easily, or would she have to force it with all her strength? Where would be the best place to strike? He would probably be facing her. The heart? Would his ribs get in the way, though? Maybe the stomach? Or a slashing cut to the throat? She pictured the way the blood would spray out, coating her as he clutched at his neck and collapsed to the ground.

Though she had kept her promise not to sleep and dream, her eyes had still fallen shut as she sat thinking. So it came as a shock when a small, soft hand cradled her unscarred cheek. She opened her eyes with a gasp to find Petra looking at her from barely a hands' width away.

"Don't," said the little girl, very distinctly. She sounded unutterably sad.

Kathrael quashed the small stab of guilt that threatened to pierce her righteous indignation over the Wolf Patron's actions all those long years ago.

"So you *do* speak, then," she said instead.

Petra just looked at her with brown eyes that seemed far too old for her young face.

Their final day of travel grew terribly hot and humid as the morning wore on. They came upon the crossroads fairly early on. Dex perked up as they looked out from a copse of trees nearby. He pointed one chubby finger toward a monument stone sitting like a sentinel at the corner where the two tracks met.

"I've been here before!" he said with some excitement.

"Home is that way," Kathrael told them, indicating the road that disappeared into the woods in the direction of the mid-morning sun.

Dex tugged at her hand, the familiar landmark lending him new energy. "Let's go!"

Kathrael hitched Petra higher onto her hip and surveyed their surroundings. There was a cart pulled by oxen approaching from the west, and a man carrying a large sheaf of grain on his back to the south, though he was moving away from them. Neither had much reason to pay attention to them, and they were quite some distance from Penth by now.

Judging it was worth the risk, she let go of Dex's hand long enough to pull her shawl over the scarred side of her face. When she was certain that she was well covered, she led the way onto the road and headed east. They were able to make good progress for perhaps half an hour before the road grew busier and she took them back into the trees.

Shortly after midday, the skies opened. There was no shelter even in the woods, and all she could do was take the blanket from her back and tell the twins to hold it over their heads as they walked. The ground grew muddy and treacherous, so she took them back onto the road, confident that few other people would be out and about in the storm.

The rain continued into the afternoon, until all three of them were soaked to the bone. Though unpleasant, it was at least still fairly warm. Only when the skies cleared did a brisk breeze from the north begin to cool things off and make her shiver.

They walked on, and Kathrael was starting to worry that she would deliver the children to Darveen only for them to succumb to the coughing sickness, when the village appeared in the distance.

"Home!" Dex cried, and shoved at her until she let him down from her arms. He grabbed Petra's hand and they ran forward, their weariness and discomfort forgotten.

"It's still quite a distance," Kathrael called to them, but their childish excitement was too great for such practicalities to move them. Instead, she let them wear themselves out, and caught up when they had covered perhaps a third of the remaining distance.

The sun was slanting toward evening and their clothing was finally beginning to dry on their bodies when the bedraggled trio got close enough to the modest village to attract attention.

"Dex? Lalla?" said a middle-aged woman standing in front of a hut at the edge of the settlement. "Gods above! Is that really you?" The basket she was carrying sagged in her grip as her attention turned to Kathrael. "Who are you, girl? What are you doing with these children? And why are you hiding your face?" Without giving Kathrael a chance to answer, she turned back toward the hut and yelled, "Boys! Come here! I've caught the girl who kidnapped Shayla's twins! *Hurry!*"

SIX

Ithric stayed in the form of the lion for nearly two days after the twins' escape. In many ways, it was easier to bear the pain of his newly acquired bruises and aches that way. The lion lived only in the moment, nursing its hurts with slow swipes of its tongue, but with no concerns about what was happening outside of the confines of the camp and its immediate surroundings. No worries about the twins, or the girl who had helped them.

The troupe was still traveling toward the coast, and Ithric could smell the distant tang of salt in the air. They were far away from Penth now, traveling in the opposite direction from where he'd sent the twins and their unlikely rescuer. After a few fruitless hours spent riding around on two of the draft horses, searching for the children the morning after Ithric's distraction, Turvick and Laronzo had apparently given up on recapturing them.

It was time to put the second part of his admittedly hare-brained scheme into play.

He waited until his two captors were puttering around the fire, getting things in the camp ready for evening, before shifting back to human form with a piteous groan.

"*Ahh,*" he cried, rolling over onto his side in the dirty straw and clutching his ribs. "It hurts! Turvick, is that you? Laronzo? Why did you beat me?"

Both men had looked up at his words, and Turvick approached the cage with cautious steps. "Finally decided to shift back, boy?" he asked. "You're lucky I didn't cut my losses in Penth and put a spear through your heart. What the hell possessed you? Did you help the twins escape somehow?"

Ithric glared at him through the bars, still cradling his bruised torso. "How could I have helped *anyone* do *anything* when I'm stuck in this cage? I was trying to warn you, you morons!"

"Mind your tongue, boy!" Turvick snapped.

"If you wanted to warn us of something, why didn't you just change back to human and tell us?" Laronzo asked, still hanging back a few paces as if he expected Ithric to shift back to animal form and attack at any moment.

"Because of the witch, of course!" Ithric said, as if it was obvious.

"Because of the *what*?" Laronzo said, taken aback.

Ithric stared at him as if he was an idiot—no great feat of acting.

"The *crone*. The old woman who snuck into camp and spirited the children away! I asked her what she was doing and she put a curse on me. I shifted into animal form and couldn't shift back—I've been stuck as the lion for nearly two days now! She must have been a witch. The gods only know what she wanted with those poor children." He shuddered theatrically and touched his fingers to his forehead and heart in a superstitious gesture. "I tried to get your attention so you could stop her, but then you started hitting me for no reason!"

Laronzo looked at Turvick. "I guess that sort of makes sense, doesn't it?" he said in an uncertain tone. "He seems all right now, at any rate..."

"Shut up, Laronzo," said the other man, before turning his attention back to Ithric. "What did this supposed *witch* look like, boy? How did she break the lock?"

Ithric met Turvick's gaze with wide, innocent eyes. "She was tall and stooped, with long hair that was nearly white. I'm not sure I've ever seen anyone that old before. She pointed at the lock and muttered something, and it just kind of exploded. That was when I started making noise, trying to wake you."

Turvick glared at him for long moments, as if hoping to make him look away. When Ithric did not flinch or look down, he eventually growled, "Fine. There's nothing to be done about it now—not if we want to reach the ship on time for our passage north."

Ithric shrugged his agreement.

"The witch stole a bunch of our food, though," Laronzo said. "We've barely got enough now to make it to the coast."

"I know," said Ithric. "I saw. It's not like I could do anything to stop her, though, was it?"

Turvick regarded him with a sneer. "Maybe not, but I'm still inclined to take it out of your rations, not ours. Lions don't need to eat all that often anyway, right?"

As he had not been given any food since the night of the twins' escape, this came as no great surprise—even though the mere talk of food was making his stomach rumble and growl audibly.

"Fuck you, Turvick," he said in a tired voice. "You're a real bastard sometimes, you know that? Isn't he a real bastard sometimes, Laronzo?"

Laronzo looked startled, like he hadn't expected to be drawn into the conversation in such a way. His mouth opened, but no words came out. Ithric hid a smirk at the sight, taking his amusement wherever he could find it these days.

"Think you're funny, boy?" Turvick asked, unperturbed. "Just you remember—if the lion takes a step wrong, it won't be your flea-bitten hide I take it out on, it'll be the others. And if you shift into human form where the rubes can see you, your fellow freaks will be the ones to suffer for it. Clear?"

"Very," Ithric said. "Unlike some people here, I'm not mentally deficient."

Turvick stared at him like one might stare at a smear of manure on one's boot sole. "You think? Makes you wonder why you're the one in the cage, then, doesn't it?"

"Not really," Ithric replied, and gave his captors the too-wide smile that Favian had once told him people found deeply disconcerting.

Turvick only made a noise of disgust and stalked away, gesturing sharply for Laronzo to follow him.

When they were gone, Ithric slumped back against the bars and gave in to the ache of an empty belly, the throb of slow-healing bruises, and the carefully hidden pang of worry for his fellow captives... for the escaped twins... for the angry, desperate girl who had risked herself to rescue them on the strength of a complete stranger's request.

Despite his bravado, he was finally beginning to realize just how far in over his head he'd ended up. Ithric sighed. He'd always hated swimming.

SEVEN

"Wait, no—" Kathrael said, taken by surprise as the woman shouted for help. Stupidly, she had not thought much beyond the act of physically getting the children back to Darveen. *Of course* her ragged clothing and disfigured face would make her appear some sort of miscreant and raise the villagers' suspicions.

She thought about running, but knew it was hopeless. She had been traveling on aching, blistered feet, carrying a child and a heavy pack for two days. Her skirts were still heavy with rainwater, and she wouldn't get fifty steps before she was caught. Besides, running would only make her seem guilty of something.

Three young men ranging from adolescence to perhaps twenty-five were jogging toward them—the woman's sons, she suspected.

"Put that little girl down and back away!" barked the oldest, his voice like a whip-crack.

Petra clung to Kathrael, seeming frozen in place, while Dex grabbed a fistful of her skirt and held tightly. *They can feel the fear and anger around them*, she remembered, and made a conscious effort to stay calm.

"You're scaring them," she said as evenly as she could, "I'm just trying to get them back to their family."

One of the men grabbed her by the arm, and the woman darted in to pull Petra from her grasp.

"Tell it to the village council," said her captor, only to flinch back a moment later as he peered under her shawl. "What the—! What's wrong with your *face*?"

"They're just burn scars," she said through gritted teeth, unable to quell the unwelcome pitch and roll of her stomach at his tone of disgust.

He relaxed a bit, renewing his grip on her arm as he blew out a noisy breath. "Utarr's tits, I'm surprised you could get within five paces of a child, looking like that."

Dex had pulled away from Kathrael to follow his sister as the woman carried her a safe distance away, but he spoke up at that. "She helped us!"

"Come away, child," said the woman. "Let the adults deal with this. Poor things—you're soaked! We must get you back to your parents so you can dry off and warm up..."

Kathrael's spirits sank as the twins were led away, throwing worried glances over their shoulders as they headed into the village.

"Come on, you," said the oldest of the three brothers, as he grasped her other arm and tugged her forward. "Perron, go find someone from the council and tell them what happened. We'll take the girl to the square in front of the meeting hall."

Kathrael let them tug her forward, and wondered if she was about to be strung up or burned at the stake, courtesy of another shape-shifter. *Serves me right*, she thought, anger at the injustice of it all flooding her and banishing her exhaustion from the demanding journey.

They arrived in front of the modest building a short time later, just as the youngest brother came hurrying back with a white-haired elder in tow.

"What's this?" demanded the old man, peering at Kathrael through rheumy eyes as he approached. "Good grief! What's the matter with this girl? Does she have some kind of disease?"

"She says they're just burns," said one of the pair holding her.

"I have a tongue!" Kathrael flared. "I can speak for myself!" She jerked against her captors' hold, but the movement was weak and ineffectual—her lack of strength only made her angrier.

The old man raised an eyebrow. "Then perhaps you'd care to explain what you were doing with Shayla's children, girl. Darveen has no mercy for kidnappers."

She glared through her good eye, a lifetime of anger threatening to rise up and swallow her whole. "Am I an idiot? Why would I bring kidnapped children back to the place where they would be recognized after—what? A week? Two? Does the village council of Darveen intend to execute me for rescuing them and returning them home?"

Two more elders joined them from inside the meeting hall, drawn by the ruckus and shouting.

"Calm yourself, girl," said the taller one, a great hulking man with an iron gray beard and a bald, shiny head. "We are not barbarians. You will be given a chance to state your case, and if the council deems you guilty, you will be branded on the cheek as a criminal and expelled from the village."

Branded. On the cheek. Kathrael had to fight completely inappropriate, hysterical laughter. Of course. Of *course* they would want to burn her face.

"*Stop!*" cried a man from across the village square. Kathrael twisted in her captor's grip and saw a plain-faced man running toward them, holding Petra securely against his hip. A pale woman hurried along a few steps behind, holding Dex as she tried to keep up. Kathrael nearly sagged in relief.

The newcomer slid to a stop, panting for breath. "Stop," he said again, quieter this time. "Let her go."

The man on Kathrael's left looked to the little knot of elders for guidance, and the bald man nodded cautiously. She snatched her arms back the instant her guards' grips loosened, and rubbed resentfully at the bruises they'd left.

"You have something to say, Melko? Shayla?" the first elder asked, squinting at the couple with his weak eyes.

"Yes, I have something to say!" said the twins' father. "This woman is innocent. My son says he and his sister were kidnapped by the two men who came through the village a couple of weeks ago with the traveling show. She rescued them and brought them home."

Melko and Shayla approached her. Both looked startled when they got a good look at her face, but Dex laid a hand on his mother's cheek and said, "Don't be scared, Mama. Look deeper."

Shayla blinked and stepped forward to stand face to face with Kathrael. "Forgive me for staring. Rudeness is a poor way to greet the woman who saved my family. You've returned my heart and soul to me, stranger. *Thank you.*"

To Kathrael's surprise, the woman reached out and drew her into a one-armed embrace. Unless you counted Livvy's sweaty, post-coital clutch, no one had embraced her since before Vesh died. Her breath caught, instincts torn between the need for human contact and the desire to flee and hold herself safe from the dangers presented by such vulnerability.

Shayla must have felt her stiffen, because she pulled away with a final light squeeze of Kathrael's shoulder. Her husband turned to address the small knot of elders.

"I accept this woman into my home and consider her under my family's protection," he said. "Does the council take issue with this?"

Kathrael turned to see what the response would be. The bald man shook his head. "Of course not, Melko. If you are satisfied with the girl's innocence then the council has no reason to intervene." His attention turned to Kathrael, though he looked uncomfortable as he took in the ruin of her face. "You'll have to forgive us, young woman. The village of Darveen is very protective of its children, and the twins are… special."

"The village of Darveen wasn't protective *enough*, apparently," Kathrael said in a bitter tone. "Since you let them be taken from under your noses."

"Believe me," Shayla said quietly. "I've been blaming myself since the moment I came back from hanging the washing and found them gone."

"The important thing is that they're back now," said Melko, holding Petra a little tighter. The little girl smiled in utter contentment and burrowed her face into her father's neck. "Thanks to you," he continued. "Please, allow us to make you welcome in our home, and accept our deepest apologies for the misunderstanding. We can never repay you, but we can at least provide you with food and a clean bed."

All at once, reaction to the journey and the ugly confrontation washed over her, leaving her dizzy and weak. She nodded, lost for both words, and the strength to speak them.

"She doesn't feel well," Dex said from his perch against his mother's hip.

Shayla put the boy down and he immediately reached up to take Kathrael's hand. A moment later, Shayla put a gentle arm around her shoulders, steadying her. "Come, please. It's not far. Let me help you."

Kathrael nodded and let herself be led, the buzzing in her ears drowning out the sound of conversation behind her as Melko exchanged some final words with the elders. She was dimly aware of entering a modest house and being guided to a neat, comfortable looking bed. Gentle hands helped her pull off the tattered remains of her wet dress, and replace it with a soft linen shift. Her head hit a down-filled pillow that felt like resting on a summer cloud, and the world went black.

She awoke later to the sound of cheerful humming and the scent of cooking meat. She lay very still for several moments, disoriented, with absolutely no idea where she was. A warm weight against her side drew her attention to where Petra lay curled in the space between her arm and body, watching her, and everything came flooding back. She craned around to look on her other side and found Dex laid out on his stomach like a starfish in the generous bed, his hair sticking out in every direction as he blinked into wakefulness.

"Mama, she's awake," he slurred, still sounding mostly asleep himself.

Light footsteps approached and Kathrael tensed, but it was only Shayla. "Hello, there," she said, wiping her hands on her apron. "I was starting to think you'd sleep straight through the day and into the night."

"How long—?" Kathrael rasped, her throat feeling like sand.

"It's late afternoon," said Shayla, reaching out a hand to help her extricate herself from the little girl and sit up. "You arrived early yesterday evening."

"Oh," she said, her mind still mired in sleep. She looked down at herself, noticing the borrowed shift properly for the first time. A jolt of fear hit her squarely in the chest—*where was the satchel with her food? Where was her blanket? Her dagger?*

"They won't steal your things," Dex said, answering the unspoken thought. "It's all right by the bed."

"Yes," Shayla said, evidently well practiced at following Dex's one-sided conversations. "It's all right there. Well, except your dress. I had thought to mend it for you while you rested, but I'm afraid it's a bit beyond my ability."

"A bit beyond help, you mean," Kathrael said, relaxing as she realized that she was safe here.

Shayla smiled. "I imagine that old dress has some stories to tell. Have you traveled up from Rhyth, then? I thought I recognized the style. It must have been beautiful when it was new."

Kathrael hadn't owned it when it was new, of course, but there was no point in saying so. "Yes," she said instead.

"I'm traveling north, over the mountains. I was in Penth when one of the other people stuck in that awful traveling show asked me to help Dex and Petra."

Shayla looked surprised for a moment. "She told you her name was Petra?"

Kathrael shook her head. "Not exactly. Dex said she preferred it. She only spoke to me once, and only a single word."

Shayla looked at her daughter, eyebrows furrowed. "You really are set on that name, aren't you, sweet one?"

"Yes," Petra said, meeting her mother's eyes with her wide, brown ones.

"Perhaps we'll speak with the elders about a name changing ceremony."

Petra's face lit up, and Dex muttered, "About time," under his breath. When Kathrael looked at him, he shrugged. "She goes on about it *constantly*," he explained. Kathrael shook her head in wonder and amusement, trying to imagine what it must be like for the two siblings to be connected in such a way.

"Why *Petra*, though?" she asked, curious.

It was Shayla who answered. "That was my grandmother's name. She had the same gift as the twins. Sometimes looking into their eyes is like seeing her alive again."

Kathrael digested that for a moment. "I'd never even heard of such a gift before."

Shayla's expression turned pensive. "It's a dangerous time to be gifted. I worry for the future, but I suppose it's in the gods' hands."

Though she maintained a healthy skepticism when it came to putting things in the gods' hands, Kathrael was loathe to say so aloud in the presence of the small family. She was saved from having to come up with anything else to say by the sound of the door.

"I'm back," called a male voice—Melko. "Is she awake yet?"

"She is!" Shayla called back. She patted Kathrael's shoulder. "There's clothing of mine for you to wear folded over the back of the chair. I'll keep Melko out of your hair while you get dressed, and then we'd love you to join us for dinner."

"Thank you," Kathrael said, momentarily overwhelmed by the sudden free availability of food, clothing, and shelter.

"Come on, you two." Shayla herded the children off of the bed and out of the room. "Let's leave your friend in peace for a few minutes."

The door closed, leaving Kathrael in silence that seemed to echo after the friendly presence of Shayla and the twins. She looked around. The house was a pleasant, well-furnished space that confirmed her muddled impression from last night of a family that was comfortably well off. The smart thing to do would be to grab everything of value that she could carry and disappear through the window as soon as darkness fell.

And yet... what kind of person would that make her?

She picked up the dress hanging over the chair and held it against her body. It was a plain piece of clothing — the dress of a tradesman's wife, cut from sturdy material and without ornamentation. It would hang on her bony frame. It would also be the nicest clothing she'd worn in months. She shrugged out of the shift and pulled it on, cinching up the belt to hold it in at the waist so the bodice didn't gape too badly. When she was decent, she padded out into the main room on bare feet.

Melko greeted her with a broad grin. "There's our hero!" he said, and she felt a flush of surprise. As far as she knew, Kathrael had never been anyone's hero before. It was a very odd feeling, to say the least. "Are you feeling better after some rest, I hope?" Melko continued.

"Yes, thank you," Kathrael said hesitantly, still wrong-footed at being treated like a normal person deserving of care and attention.

"Well, I hope you're hungry," he said. "It looks like Shayla has made us enough stew to feed the entire village."

Kathrael's stomach cramped with hunger at the words.

"She's *starving*, Papa," Dex said solemnly from his perch on a stool near the table. His tone made it clear he was using the word in its literal meaning, and Melko's smile faltered and fell away.

"Not anymore. Not while you're under my roof," he told her, his voice going quiet. "Come. Sit. Please. Can I get you wine?"

Kathrael blushed and nodded, still unprepared for the depth of Melko and Shayla's gratitude, and the hospitality they offered her so freely. "Yes. Wine would be… very nice. Thank you."

When they had all seated themselves and partaken of the hearty stew, Melko sat back in his chair and regarded her. Kathrael was still working her way slowly through a third bowl, sopping up the rich broth with chunks of freshly baked flatbread, but she looked up when she became aware of the others' eyes on her.

"Shayla said you were planning on crossing the mountains," he said. "I've been thinking about what you'll need for the journey."

Kathrael blinked at him, uncomprehending.

"It gets cold up there, even in the summer," he continued, "and the terrain is rugged and rocky. You'll need decent boots, and a tent hide to use for shelter. Clothes for traveling. Dried rations, so you can carry enough food with you to get across."

"I'll manage," she said cautiously, wondering why he seemed so intent on pointing out all the things she lacked.

"I have no doubt that you'd find a way," he agreed, "but I think we can help you with those things."

"It's the least we can do," added Shayla.

She stared at them.

"I don't understand," she said.

"Our oldest son died last year," Shayla said, adding to Kathrael's confusion with the apparent *non sequitur*. "He was about your size, I think. His things… I couldn't…" She trailed off.

"We still have his boots and clothing," Melko explained.

"And I could take in one of my dresses to fit you. Our neighbors borrowed our traveling tent last year and never gave it back. We don't ever use it. But they still have it, and we'd like to give it to you, along with some of our food stores. We don't need as much now with Persy gone, and it was a good harvest last year."

Kathrael continued to stare, her spoon dipping slowly in her hand, forgotten, until it slipped out of her fingers and clattered in the bowl. "I don't know what to say."

"Say *thank you*," Dex advised.

"Thank you," she said in a weak voice.

The world ran on commerce, she knew — at least it did when neither party was strong enough to take what they wanted by force. Kathrael's whole life had been commerce.

She'd been born as a commodity, to be sold or traded. After escaping slavery — or, at least, trading one form of slavery for another — she had bartered her body for what she had needed.

When that had no longer been an option, Vesh had made a foolish trade, wasting resources to keep her alive when she could no longer keep up her end of the bargain. There were intangible resources involved in commerce sometimes, she knew. Vesh had acted on sentiment, not self-interest.

There were few sentiments as strong as those between family members — parent and child, brother and sister. Kathrael had returned Melko and Shayla's children to them. Perhaps it was not so surprising after all that they would wish to pay her somehow for her actions. Food and clothing were commodities they could afford, and so they would give these things to her in return for Dex and Petra's safe recovery.

"If there's anything else we can do?" Shayla offered.

"No," Kathrael replied, feeling more certain of the situation now. "Clothing and supplies would be immensely helpful, thank you."

At the couple's insistence, Kathrael stayed two more days with them, resting and regaining her strength. True to their word, Melko and Shayla assembled a practical traveling outfit for her, composed of Persy's thick-soled boots and breeches, with a modified split skirt to wear over them and a fitted bodice that could be worn with or without a linen shift underneath.

Her worn blanket from Novice Hameen was joined by a light tent hide. The tent could be draped over a branch or propped over a short central pole that doubled as a walking stick for rough terrain. Not only was her belly full from three days of Shayla's excellent cooking, but her leather satchel was filled to bursting with dried meat, fruit, and rendered tallow for the journey. She also carried a single wineskin. Melko had advised her to ration it until she got into the mountains, where there were numerous small springs and brooks with clean, safe water to drink.

Finally, on the morning of the fourth day, she readied herself to depart. Shayla met her at the door with a swath of lightweight woven fabric in her hands, dyed a striking shade of purple.

"I have one more thing for you," she said. "I noticed that your shawl was in a similar state to your old dress. I'd like you to take this to use instead, assuming you want it. It was my mother's. I never wear it, and it's too fine a shawl to sit unused, waiting for the moths to destroy it."

Kathrael reached out a hand to take the delicately woven cloth, feeling the silky strands slide across her fingers. "It's beautiful," she said. "Are you sure—?"

"I'm sure," replied Shayla without hesitation. "Here. Put it on."

Kathrael set down the satchel and tent roll so she could remove her old, worn shawl and slip the new one over her head and shoulders. It seemed to weigh nothing and settled easily in place, a fold falling across the left side of her face to hide her scars.

"It suits you," Shayla said.

They were joined by Melko, holding each of the twins' hands in his. "Go with the gods, Kathrael of Rhyth. Should you ever pass this way again, you will always have friends in Darveen."

"Thank you, Melko. Shayla. You've both been very kind," she said, before crouching down to the twins' level. "And you two—be good, and stay away from strange men, all right?"

Dex nodded. "We will. Remember, you're a good person," he told her solemnly.

Petra darted forward to hug her. "Bye," she said.

"Goodbye," she replied, trying not to give into sentiment as she straightened away.

Shayla and Melko had been immeasurably kind to her, but their debt to her was surely repaid by now. As tempting as it might be to stay in this welcoming, generous place, that generosity would not extend indefinitely. It would be far too painful to watch their gratitude fade into resentment as she became more and more of a burden to them. Better to leave while they still felt they owed her. She had what she needed from them. That should be enough, shouldn't it?

With that thought firmly in mind, she set off from the comfortable little house and did not look back. Ahead lay the mountains, and beyond—Draebard.

EIGHT

The morning of Favian's novitiate dawned muggy and overcast. He had been up for hours already, ever since Senovo's light grip on his shoulder woke him from a strange dream full of half-remembered voices and a feeling of vague regret.

The High Priest's eyes shone in the flickering light of the single candle he'd brought with him. "Come, Favian. It's time to purify yourself before the ceremony. I won't insult you by asking if you're still certain you wish to proceed."

In fact, nervousness had slammed into Favian's stomach with all the subtlety of a runaway wagon the moment he'd realized that *it was today, it was time, this was really going to happen now.* Nervousness was different than uncertainty, however, so he mustered a wan smile for the man who had cared for him and his little sister these last several years.

"Thank you for that, Elder Brother," he said, managing to project dry humor rather than stark terror, fortunately. "Are you sure Frella will be all right?"

One of the strictures surrounding the novitiation was the ban on contact with anyone outside of the Priests' Guild or the Healers until after the ceremony was complete. Limdya had shared a meal with Favian yesterday, while Andoc and Carivel had wished him well last night and taken Frella to stay with them for the duration.

"Your sister will be fine," Senovo reassured. "She is worried for you, but that's only natural. She is happy for you as well, and she has many friends to keep her company until she can see you again."

Favian nodded and tried to compose himself, aware that he was only worrying about Frella as a distraction from worrying about himself.

"Up with you, now, Little Brother," Senovo said. "We will bathe in the river before you perform your devotions to the gods. The Healer will arrive soon after sunup."

The entire temple had woken early in a show of solidarity, priests and acolytes emerging into the darkness of predawn, shedding robes and wading into the slow-moving waters of the river at the sheltered bend behind the sprawling structure of stone and wood. They were largely silent as befitted their peaceful, deserted surroundings.

Priest Eiridan—a pleasant-faced man with intelligent eyes and a noticeable pot belly who had come to Draebard's temple from the village of Meren a number of years before—guided Favian to a calm pool near the edge of the river and helped him lather himself from head to foot with herb-scented lye soap. When he was satisfied, Eiridan took him back out into the current and urged him down to rinse. Favian held his breath, feeling the water tug at him as it flowed past the negligible obstruction caused by his submerged body.

How easy to let oneself float away under the onslaught, he thought as the rushing river filled his senses. *How much more difficult to stand against the torrent and move upstream.*

Eiridan guided him up to the surface with a gentle touch under his chin. Favian emerged into the cool morning air, his eyes and nose stinging as he shook the water from his face. He staggered a bit as his balance shifted in the current, but a firm grip on his shoulder steadied him. He looked to his right to find that Senovo had joined them, his own black hair hanging in a wet mass between his shoulder blades.

"There is one final thing to address," his mentor said, "if you would allow me the honor."

Favian nodded, wide-eyed, and let Senovo lead him up the pebbled beach and into the bathing room at the back of the temple. A sturdy chair had been placed next to a table holding a ewer of water, a basin, and several candles; an oil lamp hung nearby. Favian sat, tipping his head back at Senovo's direction. The High Priest picked up the wickedly sharp blade that lay next to the basin, glinting in the yellow lamplight.

Favian closed his eyes trustingly, his heart beating a complicated rhythm as the razor slid over the front half of his scalp, shaving the hair away as was customary for a proper priest's queue.

Gods above. I'm going to be a priest, he thought with something like awe. *I'm finally going to be what I was born to be.*

Senovo shaved the blond hair away with the greatest of care, leaving the back half of his skull untouched. Perhaps it was the emotion of the day making Favian maudlin, but the love in that careful touch made tears prickle at the back of his eyes. How difficult must it be for Senovo to see *any* of his acolytes undergo castration after what had been done to him as a young man? Much less *Favian*, who was as close to a son to him as any eunuch could ever have.

When Senovo was finished, he carefully brushed the stray hairs from Favian's forehead and straightened. Favian reached out a hand and closed it around Senovo's wrist before he could step away. The High Priest froze, the wicked blade still held in his sure grip.

"Thank you," Favian said, craning around to meet his mentor's green-flecked eyes with his blue ones.

The mask of *High Priest* slipped for a moment, revealing the vulnerable man beneath. "You are most welcome, Little Brother. The look of the priesthood suits you."

Favian smiled up at him, helplessly fond, feeling his earlier nervousness slip away. "I had an excellent role model," he said, serenity settling in place across his shoulders like a comfortable cloak.

"I'll be sure to tell Brother Eiridan you said so," Senovo replied with a flash of his customary self-deprecating humor, a small smile quirking one side of his own lips in response. "Now, though, you should visit the altar and prepare yourself for the ceremony. The sun is almost up."

"Yes, Elder Brother," he said. "And... don't worry. Everything will be fine."

"I believe that's supposed to be my line," said Senovo, raising an eyebrow. "Go, Favian. I will see you after the ceremony." His voice turned wry. "Though you may not be in any condition to remember it. Nevertheless, we will watch over you."

The altar room was almost completely dark, illuminated by a single candle on the large stone slab dedicated to Naloth and his goddess, Utarr. Favian knelt in the small circle of light, hands folded and resting on the warm stone, head bowed.

I know that we humans don't truly understand all that you have attempted to tell us, he thought. *I'm trying to do the right thing. I swear that I will dedicate myself to your service. I will help all of your children who have need of me, to the best of my ability. Only... I cannot give up on the idea that there's someone out there, waiting for me. Surely you wouldn't have given Carivel and Andoc to High Priest Senovo if it were truly wrong for a priest to desire such a thing?*

I don't know why you made me the way I am. These urges for men — they're so strong. So overpowering. I hate the loss of control that they make me feel. It will be a relief to finally be free of them. Perhaps that's what the gods intended all along. Perhaps I was given these... inclinations... so that I would be drawn to the priesthood to escape them.

I hope that's the case, anyway. I just want to do what's right. But... I also hope... that I won't always have to do it alone. Perhaps you'll show me a dream to point the way. Perhaps —

Eiridan's low voice interrupted his prayer. "Brother Favian. The Healer is here. It is time." Favian looked up, and the priest handed him a cup of brown liquid, earthy-smelling and laced with the sharp hint of herbs. "Drink now, and I will help you back to your room."

Favian took a deep breath and let it out. While he'd knelt in front of the altar, the gray light of a cloudy morning had crept in around the edges of his awareness. He closed his eyes and tipped the cup back, letting the contents slide over his tongue. The liquid was rich and complex, with a hint of bitterness. He swallowed until nothing was left but a few dregs, and handed it back to Eiridan.

The older priest helped him to his feet and kept a hand cupped under his elbow as they made their way through the quiet hallways, to the familiar room that Senovo had set up for him and Frella after their father's death. He swayed a bit as they rounded the final corner, the sleeping draught beginning to hit him at the same moment he saw the other temple denizens arrayed along the final stretch of hall like an honor guard.

Reston and Crenelo, who had survived the temple massacre during the Alyrion attack all those years ago... Brother Feldes, who prepared their food every night, channeling his nurturing tendencies into providing the temple with nourishment... slender Mithral, the youngest acolyte, his hazel eyes seeming huge in his thin face... all of the others, meeting his eyes one by one, standing silent and proud as he walked past.

Again, Favian felt tears rise. Perhaps his inability to hold them back this time was a side effect of the sleeping draught. Eiridan guided him through the door of the room, where Healer Sagdea waited for them with her long white hair bound up in braids. A clean apron covered her simple gray robes.

"Help him lie down," she said, her voice softened somewhat from its usual brusque tone. "I can see that the draught is already taking effect."

Hands helped Favian down to lie on the bed, and his vision swam at the change in elevation.

"'S all right," he slurred. "'M all right. Tell S'novo not to worry…"

"We'll tell him, lad," Sagdea said, as if humoring him. "Now, just close your eyes for a few minutes, and everything will be fine."

Favian snickered, suddenly overcome with amusement at the way everyone seemed to feel the need to reassure everyone else about his castration. He opened his mouth to explain the joke, but before he could make the words come out, colors exploded behind his closed eyelids and his awareness floated away through the rafters above him, disappearing into the darkness like mist.

The mountains were nothing like Kathrael had pictured them. She'd thought they must be stately. Peaceful. An oasis of nature, largely free from the touch of men. Instead, they were a terrible, haunted place. Wind whistled through the rocks and trees, leaching the moisture from her skin and making her lips crack and bleed.

It was cold at night, as Melko had warned — unnaturally so, for summertime. In the daytime, the sun baked her, reddening any exposed skin until it peeled. Something about the air near the top had a strange effect on her body and mind. Her heart labored, beating hard and fast even when she stopped to rest. She was light-headed. Dizzy. Her muscles ached constantly from the steady climb, keeping her awake at night.

One might have assumed that things would get better once she crested the top of the trail and started down the northern slope. However, almost six years after what had become known as the Massacre at the Western Pass, the northern slope was still a strange wasteland of rocks, scrub, and the creaking skeletons of burned trees.

And, of course, where was she going, madwoman that she was? She was heading to Draebard to confront one of the men who had turned the mountain forest into a raging inferno, trapping and burning to death hundreds of Alyrion soldiers as they marched toward the northern villages.

With no leaves or branches overhead to dampen it, the wind was even worse on this side of the range. It keened and shrieked at night, threatening to blow her sad little tent down around her. Worse, as her journey wore on, it started to sound like voices. Or rather, it started to sound like one very specific voice.

"*Help me, Kath,*" Vesh whispered in her ear as she lay in pitch darkness, exhausted and trying to sleep. "*Help me, please!*"

Kathrael pressed her palms to her ears as hard as she could and screwed her eyes shut. "You're dead, Vesh. I may be losing my mind, but you're *still dead*, damn you! I *can't* help you!"

"*Don't leave me,*" Vesh said in the same strange, attenuated voice. "*don't leave me alone…*"

Tears squeezed between the tightly closed lids of her good eye, cold on her cheek as the wind whipped around her through gaps in the tent. "Fine!" she nearly screamed. "Fine! You can stay, only *please* shut *up!*"

Vesh didn't shut up. On the contrary, his voice was joined by others as the hours passed. Her mother. Her sister. The baby that had perished in her womb, years ago. Kathrael curled up in a tight ball and hid her head in her arms, trying to hold on until morning.

⁊‧᯾‧ᡷ

When she finally emerged from the foothills days later, everything inside her had been scoured away except for the overwhelming need to reach Draebard and find the Wolf Patron… to *end* things, one way or another. Unseen presences still hovered around her, harrying her forward toward her goal. In moments of clarity, she knew with utter certainty that without the supplies that Shayla and Melko had given her, her body would have perished somewhere on the mountain pass, along with her wits.

As it was, the sole of one of her boots was coming loose, and her food was almost gone — which would have been more alarming if she hadn't become too disoriented to remember to eat and drink most of the time. All that mattered now was putting one foot in front of the other. So she walked, and she walked, and she walked.

Even with her face covered, other travelers gave her a wide berth, something in her bearing proclaiming the dangerous madness that threatened to swallow her whole. Whenever she reached a crossroads, she would wait for the next person to pass and waylay them, hissing, *"Which way to Draebard?"* Inevitably, they would blanch and stammer directions, at which point Kathrael headed whichever way they were pointing until she became lost again and had to accost the next unlucky person.

When she rounded a bend in the logging road she was following and came upon a large village in the valley below, surprise momentarily snapped her out of her fugue. This had to be it. This had to be the place. The last people who had directed her made it sound close by. Kathrael's heart sped up. There, in front of her in the distance, was the temple—the sprawling single-story building unmistakable with its enclosed courtyard and beaten metal icons adorning the walls.

He was there. The Wolf Patron had to be *right there.*

She looked around at her surrounding. Her vision swam in and out of focus. Voices still whispered in her mind, making it hard to think, and she clutched at her temples angrily, releasing a cry of frustration.

A plan. She needed a plan. She would hide until nightfall and sneak inside. If she couldn't find the Wolf Patron, she would use her knife to capture the first wide-eyed acolyte she found and demand to be taken to him. And then... and then... she would run forward and sink her dagger into him again and again until he stopped haunting her dreams.

And it would all be over. Either they would catch her and execute her for killing their High Priest, or else she would escape and make her way back to Rhyth to help the slaves.

"You know better, Kath," Vesh whispered, his breath tickling her ear. *"It will never be over. Not ever."*

Kathrael let out a ragged sob and stumbled into the forest, hunching up at the base of a tree to wait for evening.

Favian tossed and turned, his head moving restlessly from side to side. His mind spun in lazy, drugged circles that were only partially effective as a distraction from the deep ache between his legs where his balls had previously hung.

Healer Sagdea had done the deed neatly and efficiently with the assistance of Priest Eiridan, while Favian snored and drooled under the influence of the powerful sleeping draught. Or so Reston and Crenelo had informed him afterward in cheerful tones, during one of the woozy stretches when he could actually stay awake and aware enough to understand speech.

Gods, his sac *really hurt*. He stared up at the rafters, trying to focus on the way the heavy beams moved in slow, surreal waves when he was fairly sure they were supposed to stay still and support the thatched roof. Why had he woken up in the first place? Things had been fine when he was asleep. Maybe it was Frella who had disturbed him? But that couldn't be right. His guardians had taken his little sister away to stay in their quarters while Favian recovered. So if it hadn't been Frella, then what had awakened him?

Oh, yes.

The girl. That was it. He looked back to the doorway to see if he'd imagined her. Which, apparently, he hadn't. Or at least, if so, he hadn't *stopped* imagining her yet, because she was definitely still there.

He didn't think she was supposed to be in his room, hovering inside the door like a ghost while he lay naked under the light woven blanket, drugged out of his mind and barely able to string together a coherent sentence.

"Wha—?" he asked, his tongue feeling thick and dry.

He stared at her profile as she peered into the hallway— dark-haired, golden-skinned, fine-boned. Pretty, if one happened to be interested in such things. Which Favian wasn't, particularly. At the sound of his voice, she whirled to look at him, and a tendril of shock wormed its way past the fluffy layer of wool stuffed inside his head.

The other half of her face was horribly scarred, the flesh looking nearly melted in places. Her eye on that side was wide open and milky.

"Shh!" she said sharply.

The world went gray at the edges for a moment. When it came back, she was standing next to the bed, and there was a wicked little blade pressed under Favian's chin. He snapped his jaw shut reflexively.

It had been sheer luck finding a sick, defenseless novice alone in his room in the quiet hallway of the temple barracks. Candles illuminated the modest space, which contained cots for two people. The young man lay on his back, looking up at her with hazy blue eyes. He was strikingly attractive in that exotic northern way, she noted distantly, with fine features and a chiseled jaw. His hair was a shade of pale gold that she had never seen before, and his eyes were the color of the sky just after dawn. The combination lent him an almost unearthly air of beauty.

She pressed the blade a little more firmly into the skin of his neck.

"This is Draebard, yes?" she asked, just to be sure. He started to nod, only to stop short as the knife jabbed into the flesh of his neck. She took the aborted gesture for assent, and her racing heart beat even faster. "Good. Now, priest-boy, unless you want me to open up your guts like a fish, take me to the shape-shifter called Senovo. I have unfinished business with him."

The novice stared at her blearily as if trying to make sense of her words. She was just gathering herself to try to drag him to his feet by force when they were interrupted by a voice from the doorway.

"That will not be necessary. I am here."

"Step away from the bed," said a second voice, deep and commanding. "*Now.*"

Kathrael whirled in shock, the sudden movement making her dizzy. *No, wait, he couldn't be here yet. She wasn't ready to face him now—*

But there he was, standing just inside the doorway. Clad in the white robes of a High Priest, with his tightly plaited black hair and dark southern complexion, it could be no one else. He was flanked on one side by a powerful man with a withered leg who leaned on a stout walking stick, and on the other, by a slender, androgynous boy with close-cropped hair and a soft, beardless chin, who sighted down the shaft of a small bow and arrow pointed at her.

"You heard him," said the boy, drawing the bowstring back another fraction. "Step *away.*"

This wasn't how it was supposed to happen. She'd meant to take him by surprise, but now there were three of them, and she couldn't—

Kathrael raised the dagger in front of her defensively—an instinctive movement. Before she could even blink, the lame man's walking stick flashed out and her hand exploded in pain, the little knife flying from her grip to skitter along the flagstones and come to rest next to the wall. She cried out and lunged after it, only to be intercepted by a gray shape that slammed into her, rolling her onto her back and knocking the breath from her lungs.

The large wolf pinned her beneath its body, its rank breath puffing in her face. A snarl curled its lips, revealing sharp canines as Kathrael stared at the beast, transfixed.

How appropriate that you should be the one to finally take my life, she thought. *How terribly, pathetically apt.*

She had failed. She had failed at *everything*. Kathrael looked up, meeting gold eyes ringed with green, trying to draw breath into her lungs and failing. The buzzing in her ears grew until it threatened to drown out everything else. Suddenly, the wolf stiffened above her, its snarl subsiding as it leaned down to snuffle at her face and neck. A moment later, the body pinning her in place twisted impossibly, and a slender eunuch with piercing green-gold eyes gripped her shoulders, staring down at her in shock.

"*You?*" he said, as if the word had been punched from him. "I *remember* you. Merciful gods. You're... *alive?*"

Kathrael tried desperately to suck air into lungs that did not want to work properly, and couldn't manage more than a wheeze. Gray fog flowed in from the edges of her vision and smothered her until she finally slipped down into darkness.

NINE

*"*There's only one punishment for thieving, you little bitch!*"* In her dreams, Kathrael would always be a skinny thirteen-year-old girl, powerless against the forces that controlled her life. Vesh's spirit had been right—she would never escape this. *Never.* Perhaps this was to be her punishment in death, to relive the dream again and again for all eternity.

The overseer's whip whistled down and laid a line of fire across her back as she cowered, holding in the screams that wanted to escape. Once... twice... and, then—

"Stop right there!" shouted a female voice with a heavy, unfamiliar accent. Kathrael gaped up in amazement as a barbarian woman galloped up from nowhere and reined her horse to a halt. The woman was dressed in leather and fur, with feathers braided in her hair—wild and beautiful. She nocked an arrow into her bow and steadied her mount with her knees as she trained the weapon on Kathrael's tormenter.

More barbarians followed. A powerful man swung down from his saddle and handed his horse off to a boy who was still mounted. The man's sword scraped ominously as he drew it from his belt and stalked toward the overseer, careful to keep out of the female warrior's line of fire.

"Back away from the girl," he ordered, and, oh, wait, she knew *that voice now. It was the same voice that had ordered her to back away from the sick novice's bed.*

In her dream, the overseer lowered his whip and took a single step back. Another of the newcomers dismounted—a slender eunuch in white robes.

"What is the meaning of this?" the overseer demanded. "What business of yours is this? A barbarian, a woman, a priest, and a beardless boy?"

"I might be a barbarian," said the powerful man, "but if you think I'm going to let you whip a little girl bloody, you're even stupider than you look."

Kathrael cringed. Everyone knew that angering an overseer just made things worse. And indeed, the man's face grew red with outrage as he puffed himself up.

"How dare you! These slaves are the property of Master Iaden of the Five Lakes! Set yourself against me, and you set yourself against him."

The woman drew the arrow back another fraction and sighted down it. "Wow. That would probably sound really impressive if we had any idea whatsoever who this Master Iaden was," she said in a dry voice, her aim never faltering.

Kathrael tried to crawl away from the confrontation, toward the other slaves, desperate to put more distance between herself and the whip. With a cry of rage, the overseer lifted the weapon to strike her again. Before it could fall, however, an angry wolf appeared between them as if from thin air, ears flat back against its head and lips curled in a dangerous snarl.

Confusion erupted around Kathrael, as the slaves began to point and cry, "Lupiandas! Lupiandas!"

Kathrael fell backwards onto the ground in surprise, her mouth open as she stared at the large animal standing protectively in front of her. Could it be? Could the prophecy have finally come to pass? She righted herself and crawled forward, wrapping her arms around the wolf's bristling shoulders, fearless.

"Lupi?" she asked, hope flooding her breast even as her back throbbed with fire. "The gods have finally sent you for us, after so long?" Tears spilled over and trailed down her cheeks, unchecked.

The wolf allowed the embrace, continuing to hold the overseer at bay with bared teeth and a sinister growl. In the distance, hoof beats thundered, heralding the approach of more riders. Elarra darted forward and snatched Kathrael away from wolf. Taken by surprise, she gasped and tried to break free — to return to the Wolf Patron's side — but her older sister's grip was strong and sure.

"Hurry!" Elarra cried, and ran after several of the other slaves as they darted toward the tall grain and the woods beyond.

Kathrael found herself dragged along with them, even as she cried, "No, no — wait!" and tried to look back over her shoulder to where the powerful barbarian man was holding the wolf back, keeping it from tearing out the overseer's throat by virtue of a hand on the back of its neck. "What are you **doing**, *Elarra?" she wailed. "The Wolf Patron is* **here**! *He has come for us — he will lead us to freedom!"*

"He did lead us to freedom, little sister," Elarra said between gasping breaths as they ran. "We are free! Now, **run**!"

Kathrael clamped her jaw shut and ran.

He will come for us, she thought, as they hid in a sheltered hollow that night, hungry and sore.

He will return and lead us to a better life, she thought, as they stole food from a farmhouse, then used a sharp piece of flint to try to saw through the stiff leather collars sewn onto their necks.

He will help us rise up against the Masters and free all the slaves, she thought, as Elarra kissed her forehead and headed off into the city with two of the other women, to try to procure food and money for them by selling their bodies.

Oh, gods. He's not coming back. He's left us all to die, she thought, when Elarra failed to return. I'm alone. I'm all alone now, and I don't know what to do. What do I do?

Kathrael gasped, jerking awake. Her hand throbbed, and her chest ached, and her spirit was empty, filled with dust and cobwebs. Someone had laid her on a straw mattress somewhere, maybe still in Draebard's temple. Not that it mattered. She was alone.

No, that was wrong. There was someone seated by the closed door. The chair was tipped back on two legs, its occupant resting one booted foot casually on the footboard of the simple bed. It was the boy with the bow and arrow from earlier. He sat slouched in the precariously balanced chair, arms folded across his chest. His face seemed too old to be so young, with fine creases around his eyes and lips despite the lack of stubble on his soft chin.

Upon noticing that she had awoken, he let the chair settle back on to four legs and leaned forward to look at her. "You're the slave girl from the field outside of Rhyth." His voice was a low contralto. "The one we saved from being whipped."

Kathrael sneered and turned on her side to put her back to him.

"When you ran," the boy continued, "Senovo was certain you would be recaptured and killed. He wept for you, you know."

And what good did his tears do me, or anyone else, she wanted to ask, but even those simple words seemed like too much effort. She huddled in on herself, relieved when her captor didn't try to talk to her anymore. Eventually, sleep overcame the hunger pangs in her belly and the pain in her hand, and she slid back down into dreams.

✙

The next time she woke, it was a slow emergence into the realms of consciousness rather than an abrupt transition. Two voices were speaking in low tones nearby. The sense of their words emerged in fits and starts.

"… have to figure out what we're going to do with her sooner or later, *amadi*…"

"… while she's unconscious…"

"Perhaps not, but…"

Her sudden realization that the voices belonged to the Wolf Patron and the man with the withered leg, and that they were talking about her, caught at her awareness and dragged her more fully awake. She kept her eyes closed and her breathing even, not wishing to give herself away.

"She had a dagger pressed to Favian's neck, Senovo." There was controlled anger in the powerful man's tone. "I won't let her stay here in Draebard. She'll have to be expelled from the village, at the very least."

"No. I forbid it."

"It was you she was coming after. I'd think you of all people would understand the danger she represents."

"I have extended her the amnesty of the temple, as is my right as High Priest. Do not oppose me on this, Andoc. She is under my protection, as she should have been under my protection years ago."

The powerful man—*Andoc*—blew out a frustrated breath. "And you think Chief Volya would have let us drag a little girl along with us to the meetings in Rhyth, just because we felt bad for her? Should we have freed all of the slaves we came across on the journey and brought them with us as well?"

There was a stretch of silence. "Perhaps we should have. Whatever the case, it's immaterial. She is here now, and I will not see her harmed further."

"I'm more concerned about whether she would see you harmed further, given the chance."

"She is unarmed, half-starved, and has barely regained consciousness in the last day and a half. Save your concern for whether she will recover from whatever has befallen her in the years since we last saw her."

Another stretch of silence. "Yes. All right, *amadi*, your point is taken. Those scars…"

"Indeed."

"Just be careful. And if you can't manage that on your own behalf, do it for Favian. He's the one who was in danger of having his throat slit."

"Of course."

"How is he today, anyway?"

"The Healer is letting him spend more time awake without pain draughts. She says that the incision is closing well and he should be up and about for short periods within the next couple of days."

"That's good to hear. Does he remember — ?"

"He does, and I've already had to bar him from coming here to sit with her. I doubt I'll be able to stop him once Sagdea clears him to leave his bed."

A sigh. "You've been a terrible influence on that boy. Or possibly a wonderful one. I haven't decided yet."

"I've been no more of an influence on him than you and Carivel."

The Chief snorted. "Right. Sure you haven't. Keep telling yourself that, *amadi*." There was the sound of rustling clothing — someone standing up. "Come on. We both need to meet with the elders about the ore production from the eastern mines. And, of course, about the… other matter."

"I'll be there momentarily."

The door opened and closed, the sound of a wooden walking stick tapping rhythmically against flagstones announcing the Chief's departure. Some sixth sense told Kathrael that the Wolf Patron had remained behind, watching her silently. The knowledge should have elicited some sort of reaction within her — anger, fear, her long-banked desire for revenge — but Kathrael couldn't muster anything. Only the desire to sleep again, and hopefully never wake up.

There was nothing left for her in this world. If the gods were just, she would have died on the mountain, or under the fangs of a slavering wolf. But when had the gods ever been just?

Eventually, the door opened and closed a second time, as the Wolf Patron exited on silent feet. Some time later, darkness claimed her again.

"Wake up," said an unfamiliar voice. "You've slept enough. I've brought a Healer to see you. You need to eat and drink something, and no one here wants to have to force it down your throat."

Kathrael blinked gritty eyes open almost against her will. It was daytime, and she was still in the same plain room, lying on the same straw mattress. The sick novice with the golden hair and blue eyes was gazing down at her, looking just about as awful as Kathrael felt. He was terribly pale, with dark circles under his eyes and lines of pain bracketing his full lips.

"Sit *down*, Favian," said a cranky female voice from nearby. "Preferably before you fall down."

"Well, I would—only it hurts to sit, Healer," said her would-be hostage. "Probably on account of you cutting my balls off last week."

"Don't be cheeky," said the Healer. "Remember who brought you into this world. I'll remind you that you were the one who insisted on coming here with me. For that matter, you were the one who insisted on becoming a priest. It's a little late to start complaining about it now."

"Who's complaining?" the golden-haired boy asked rhetorically. Kathrael watched with a dull expression as his attention returned to her, his blue gaze taking in the ruin of her face. "Now, come on, you—sit up a bit. You can lean against the headboard."

Kathrael opened her mouth to tell him where he could take his brisk demeanor and sympathetic glances, but a dry croak emerged instead. She descended into helpless coughing.

The novice held out a metal goblet and waggled it back and forth invitingly. "It'll be easier to tell me to go fuck myself if you have a drink first."

Kathrael gritted her teeth and struggled into a sitting position, using muscles that felt as weak as a newborn kitten's. She grabbed the goblet with an angry movement, sloshing watered wine over the rim. Once she had drained it, she shoved it back at the novice's chest.

"Go fuck yourself," she rasped.

He fumbled the cup for a moment before steadying it, and grinned. "Can't," he said cheerfully, and indicated his lower body with a brief sweep of his free hand. "Eunuch."

Kathrael continued to glare at him. "Get creative. You can use a rusty javelin point for all I care."

His expression morphed into one of mock hurt, and he placed his hand over his heart as if struck. "That's not a terribly nice thing to say to the person who brought you food and wine, now is it? And I thought we were getting along so well."

Completely against her will, Kathrael's stomach rumbled audibly at the mention of food. Again, she cursed her traitorous body that seemed so intent on *surviving* when there was nothing left to survive *for*.

The cranky, white-haired Healer stepped back into Kathrael's line of sight.

"Let's have a look at you," she said, and reached out toward Kathrael's face with one gnarled hand.

She shrank back instinctively, drawing in a sharp breath.

"*Wait*," said the novice. "Healer, this woman is a former slave."

Kathrael held her breath, looking back and forth between the two of them mistrustfully—unsure what the novice was getting at.

The Healer eyed the novice with irritation. "And? Don't be ridiculous, Favian. It's not as though I'm going to hurt her."

The young man—Favian—nodded. "I know that, Healer. Only—" He met Kathrael's gaze with a searching one of his own. "Being examined can be a bit unpleasant. A bit intrusive. But if you want Healer Sagdea to stop doing something, you can tell her and she will. It's your body. I just... thought you should know that." The words trailed off, sounding a bit sheepish.

Kathrael stared at him as if he'd grown a second head, complicated feelings warring in her chest, filling the space that had been empty since she'd woken on the plain bed in this small room.

The Healer huffed as if she found the whole thing terribly tiresome. "Well, of course it's your body, young woman. And if you'd like it to recover, I would strongly suggest that you let me examine you. Preferably before I perish of old age."

Kathrael clenched her jaw against the unwelcome tangle of emotion and tried to return to the empty place where she didn't have to feel anything. "Do what you will. I won't stop you." *Or help you,* she added silently.

"How very accommodating of you," the old woman said in a dry voice.

"Do you want me to stay, or go?" asked the novice.

Kathrael mustered enough energy to glare at him. "I want you to go find that rusty javelin."

He shrugged. "Sorry to disappoint you, but the warriors in Draebard aren't big on javelins. I think they're more of a southern thing, actually. I'll just be outside in the hallway."

The Healer pointed an imperious finger at him. "Take that chair with you and *sit down.*" Her voice dropped to a mutter. "I should have kept you confined to your room for another day, stubborn boy." When the door closed behind the novice, her attention returned to Kathrael, who merely continued to glare. "Right, then. Let me take a look at you."

The examination was as unpleasant and personal as the novice had warned it would be. Kathrael submitted to being poked and prodded, disappearing inside herself as she had been prone to do whenever someone else was touching her body. She answered all of the Healer's questions and mumbled commentary with stony silence. Only when the woman explored her scarred cheek with gentle fingers did she suck in a surprised breath and jerk away.

"Don't—" she gasped, the word torn from her against her will.

The Healer only raised an eyebrow. "Does it pain you?"

Kathrael pressed her lips together and looked away, determined not to let herself be engaged in further pointless conversation.

"Fine," said the old woman. "If you don't want to talk, I will. You are chronically undernourished, and you have a heavy infestation of intestinal parasites. I'll wager that your joints ache, and you suffer from frequent muscle cramps. Your stools are irregular and your stomach pains you frequently. Your scars are about six months old. They are well healed given the obvious severity of the burns that caused them. Not from a fire, I don't think. The pattern is wrong. Boiling water or hot oil, maybe. It matters little at this point. The conjunctiva around your blind eye are inflamed. I suspect the capacity to produce tears in that eye was damaged. You might consider wearing a patch to protect it from debris and further injury."

Every word was true, but Kathrael remained stubbornly silent regardless.

"Let me call Favian back in," the old woman said with a sigh. "No doubt he'll insist on helping with your treatment. You're lucky you picked such a kind-hearted young idiot to threaten with a knife, my dear. Most would be clamoring to the village elders for your punishment and expulsion after such a thing."

"More fool him," Kathrael growled, despite herself.

The Healer only shook her head and went to retrieve Favian, who was looking, if anything, even more ghastly than before.

She retrieved the chair as well, and plunked it down next to the bed, shoving the novice into it without ceremony.

"*Ow*," he complained, shooting her a sullen look that sat poorly on his finely drawn features. "I did mention the part about how it hurts to sit, yes?"

"My heart bleeds for you," retorted the Healer. "Now, there are two problems with our young guest that need to be addressed most urgently. First, I'm prescribing a mixture of honey, raw garlic, and roasted winter squash seeds four times a day for the next week, to get the intestinal worms under control."

Kathrael closed her eyes, convinced that she could feel worms wriggling in her belly now that the Healer had described the problem.

"She should take the mixture on an empty stomach, between meals," the old woman continued. "The parasites will make it difficult for her to gain weight even with sufficient food, but start her out with frequent small meals anyway. Moisten everything with rich broth and cook it well so that it's easy to chew and digest. Avoid bread and sweet fruit for now; they will feed the parasites more than they feed her."

Now hunger was warring with the roiling nausea.

"The second issue is more your area than mine, Favian," said the Healer. "I am concerned that this young woman is suffering from a derangement of the mind as well as the body. Not surprising, perhaps, given what she must have experienced."

Kathrael's eyes flew open, a sudden rage burning through her and sweeping away her earlier determination not to be drawn into any discussion.

"Derangement of the mind?" she mimicked. "You speak of madness? Yes, I am mad! I have been *mad* for some time now! So, what will you do with this dangerous madwoman in your midst? Perhaps you'd like to brand what's left of my face, like they threatened to do in the last village where I stopped! Or lock me away in a cage, like the boy I met outside of Penth!"

Favian leaned forward, looking at her intently, but without either fear or pity. "Neither of those things are going to happen," he said matter-of-factly. He wove his fingers together and rested his chin on his joined hands. "Most mad people don't have the drive and focus to plan and execute a difficult journey with almost no resources at their disposal. So tell me what makes you think you're mad."

The rage was replaced in an instant by fear and exhaustion so strong that she shook with it, shivering like a child lost in a blizzard. Out of nowhere, tears pressed at the back of her good eye, burning like vitriol.

"I am haunted by spirits," she said in a tiny, lost voice, the words jerked free from her chest on by one. She hated that voice instantly. *Hated* the weak, helpless person that she had become. That she had always been? And yet, the words continued to come, pulled from her even as she tried to stem the flood. "Ghosts. So many ghosts. They torment me constantly. I don't know how to make them stop!"

Her hands were shaking, clenched in the blanket covering her. The novice stretched forward and covered the nearest with one of his own, steadying it. "Tell me about these spirits," he said, sounding genuinely interested.

Kathrael swallowed convulsively, and began to talk.

She told Favian and the Healer about Vesh—about who he'd been in life and who he was in death. She told them about her sister, who'd dragged her to freedom and then disappeared without a trace, leaving Kathrael alone in a world that cared nothing for her. About her mother, whose spirit had died long before she'd borne two daughters for the masters who owned her, body and soul.

Whenever her voice grew hoarse, Favian stopped her and urged her to drink more watered wine and eat a bit of the stew he'd brought earlier. By the time she finally trailed off, unable to speak of the way her dead, unborn infant daughter cried inconsolably in the depths of night, the bowl was empty and the cup had been refilled twice.

She blinked, looking blankly around the small room, overcome by a wave of surrealism. *This is all just another dream*, she thought. *It cannot possibly be anything else.* Dizziness assailed her, but a gnarled hand steadied her shoulder and guided her back down to lie prone on the bed.

"That was a lot to get out," said the Healer. "Now that you've eaten and had something to drink, you should sleep some more, young woman."

"Someone will be nearby when you wake," said the novice. "And for what it's worth, I don't know if your spirits live inside your head or outside of it. But whatever the case, I think it's clear that they care about you a great deal, to hover so near."

Kathrael's face twisted in pain at the words. She hid it in the bedding, curling away from the young man and the old woman. "Go away," she croaked. "Go away and leave me alone, *please*."

"Of course, if that's what you wish," Favian said kindly. "But remember—you are in the temple now, where you will gain the help you need."

She gripped the bedding tighter, and steeled herself not to respond.

TEN

The belly of the lumbering cargo ship was dark, damp, and fetid. The lion hated it, and would have hated it even if Turvick hadn't insisted on shackling him with an iron collar chained to the wall.

The smell of briny water was thick in the air. Timbers creaked as the waves buffeted them. It made him nervous. Lions *could* swim, if there was a good reason to do so, but they would also avoid it if there were any other option. And here, shackled to a wall in this strange den of floating logs, the lion's instincts were screaming that if the water started coming in, it would mean certain death.

He paced restlessly, irritated by the way the damp, filthy straw stuck to his footpads, but not wishing to lie down on it, either. It was night. Faint slivers of starlight crept in through gaps in the boards above, and a larger chink came down through the open hatch leading to the outside world above. It was more than sufficient for him to see his surroundings, though it would have seemed like near-complete darkness in his human form.

The others were all asleep in their moldering cloth hammocks. No. Wait. There was movement from the corner. The short, stunted female was climbing carefully out of her sleeping place and tiptoeing across the distance separating them. The lion ceased its pacing and focused its attention on the other humans, who slept on, oblivious.

"Ithric?" she whispered, when she was close enough to reach out and touch him. There were damp trails running down her cheeks, and her voice sounded wet. Congested. "Can I talk to you?"

There was a mental shift as his human alter ego stirred. The lion allowed the change to happen, settling into the background as his flesh rippled and twisted. Ithric blinked and steadied himself against the dirty floor for a moment, briefly disoriented in the darkness after spending several days in animal form. The heavy metal collar settled uncomfortably around his bare throat and he raised a hand to ease it.

After a moment of holding his breath and listening, it seemed clear that they had not awoken the others. "What is it, Rona?" he asked, the low whisper made hoarse by thirst. "Has something happened? You're crying…"

Rona's voice trembled when she replied, "I'm scared, Ithric. I don't know what to do. I-" She swallowed hard. "I think I'm pregnant. I've missed my moon bleeding twice now."

Ithric blinked in surprise and took a moment to digest that. "And you think the father is—"

"It's Nimbral's. It has to be. There hasn't been anyone else."

Ithric blew out a silent breath. Nimbral was the skinny giant that Turvick and Laronzo had paired with Rona as a bizarre couple for the purposes of the traveling show. He'd known they cared for each other, but he hadn't realized they'd actually, well, *coupled*. He stared for a beat, trying to wrap his brain around the logistics involved before shaking his head and deliberately letting it go.

"I never thought I might get pregnant. But… but I did, and now I'm afraid this baby is going to kill me. Nimbral is so big, Ithric, and I'm so small. What if—"

"We need to get you out of here, Rona. We need to get you to a Healer," Ithric interrupted, unease growing in the pit of his stomach. For weeks now, he'd been contenting himself with the vague hint of a plan. Get north, where he had friends who would help, assuming he could get word to them somehow. Take any chance that presented itself to get the others away from Turvick. It had worked with the twins—at least, he hoped it had. But how often would such circumstances arise, in reality? Rona needed help *now*. Or at least, *soon*.

"Turvick won't let me go. Even if he would, I'm not leaving without Nimbral!" Rona's voice was shaking again, growing louder as she grew more emotional.

"Well," said a voice from across the hold, "isn't that touching."

Turvick. Ithric tensed, a sense of deep foreboding sweeping over him. Sparks flew in the corner where Turvick lay, as he struck a flint. A candle flared into life.

"Pouring your heart out to the beast-man, love?" Turvick asked, the candle illuminating his sneer as he rose and moved closer to them. Rona scurried backward, trying to keep distance between them.

"We were just talking," Ithric said, in an attempt to draw the man's attention onto himself.

Turvick stopped a couple of paces beyond the length of chain attaching Ithric to the wall. "Yes. You were *talking*. I heard. And I seem to recall warning you what would happen if you stepped out of line. Do you remember, I wonder?"

Ithric paled. "You said I wasn't to change form in front of the rubes. You never said anything about talking to Rona and the others!"

"I said *if you take a step wrong*, boy." Turvick's face in the candlelight was twisted in anger. Around them, the others were waking at the commotion. "Laronzo! Get my whip."

"What's going on?" Laronzo asked, barely awake.

"Nothing that concerns you," Turvick snapped. "Now stop asking stupid questions and do as I say!"

Ithric leaned forward until the collar bit into his neck, anger rising from the pit of his stomach. "You wouldn't dare whip a defenseless woman," he said in a low, dangerous voice.

"You have no idea what I would or wouldn't dare," Turvick said. "But as it happens, I have no intention of whipping your little friend. Watch and learn, boy. And think twice the next time you want to have a nice little chat with one of your fellow freaks."

Laronzo handed him the whip and took the candle when Turvick thrust it into his hand. Their captor stalked over to the hammock where Nimbral was cowering and grabbed the huge man by the shoulder, toppling him out onto the floor.

"No!" Rona screamed. She scrambled over and grabbed Turvick's leg, only to go flying when he kicked her carelessly away.

Nimbral was still sprawled on the floor, trying to get his feet under himself. He was immensely tall, but Ithric knew he was not very strong. In fact, his joints pained him terribly most of the time, and he tended toward clumsiness. Now, Turvick easily shoved him onto his hands and knees, ignoring his startled cry. The whip rose and fell, and the cries became screams.

Nausea flooded Ithric's gut and his heart pounded against the cage of his ribs like a drum. The lion rose up without his conscious realization and took over, lunging against the metal collar and subsiding back in frustration when the heavy chain did not give way. A deafening roar of anger echoed around the hold, joining the shrieks of pain and fear.

Kathrael tossed and turned. It was the dream again. The same fucking dream. For days now, she had submitted meekly to Favian and the Healers' care. She let them feed her. She swallowed the rank mixture that made the worms die and pass out of her body — a process so foul and nauseating that she heartily wished for death on more than one occasion.

Otherwise, she was blank and distant.

Silent.

Broken.

After the surge of anguish buried inside her had briefly spilled over into words, she found her spirit once again empty but for the whisper of haunting voices... and, of course, dreams.

She was thirteen again, skinny and knock-kneed. Elarra had left days ago to try to sell her body in the city. In the dream, she was caught endlessly in that moment of horror when the realization that her sister wasn't coming back finally penetrated her mind and stuck fast. No one was coming for her. When Elarra and the other women failed to return on the morning after they'd left, the other slaves who had run away with them had gone off to try to find work or something to steal.

One of the boys urged her to come with them, but she had refused — foolishly believing that Elarra would return soon with a bag full of money and an entertaining story about why she was so late. Perhaps she would even have the Wolf Patron in tow, ready to lead them in a glorious uprising against the Masters.

But of course, Elarra didn't return. And neither did he.

She was alone on the outskirts of an unfamiliar city — an abandoned child with no food, no water, no money, and no friends. She was going to starve. She was going to die, alone and afraid. She was —

Something cold and wet nudged her arm, jerking her free of the old, familiar wash of panic. She bolted upright with a startled cry, awareness of her surroundings filtering in as her heartbeat began to slow from its staccato rhythm. She was in Draebard, in the temple. In the room where she had been ever since she failed in her quest for revenge. The soft light from a single oil lamp illuminated her surroundings.

The wolf was looking up at her.

It was seated on the floor next to the bed, resting its head flat on the edge of the straw mattress and watching her with a quizzical expression—as unthreatening as a wolf could possibly be. When her breathing evened out from its panicked tempo, the animal placed a paw on the mattress and half-crept, half-wriggled onto it until it could nuzzle at her face and neck, as if in reassurance.

Kathrael froze, every muscle strung tight. Air caught fast in her throat and stuck there painfully, only to erupt without warning into an ugly sob. Every terrible thing she had experienced seemed to rise up at once from her chest, trying to choke her on its way out, escaping as painful, wracking tears. She crumpled forward, catching herself against the slender wolf's unexpected strength—grabbing handfuls of thick fur and hanging on for dear life. The animal took her weight without complaint and continued to lick at whatever part of her it could reach.

Merciful gods.

The Wolf Patron had finally come to rescue her from the nightmare of her life... six years too late. She closed her eyes tightly, and cried harder.

⤙ ⚜ ⤚

Favian woke from a restless doze to the muffled sound of weeping. He looked across at Frella, still sound asleep in her bed on the other side of the room. The noise was further away, coming from down the hall somewhere. Realization struck, and he rolled upright, getting silently to his feet with teeth gritted against the slowly fading ache between his legs.

The room and the hallways beyond were as familiar to him as his own hand, even in the dark. As he had suspected, the sound of sobbing grew louder as he approached the room where the nameless girl who had threatened him with a knife was recuperating. The door was open a few inches, light from the lamp he'd left burning for her escaping into the hallway to form an irregular wedge of weak illumination.

He knew he should go and alert one of the more experienced priests to come help her—as a brand new novice, he was hardly qualified to offer counsel to someone in as much pain as their reluctant guest obviously was. But for some reason, the thought of leaving her like this for even that short time was unbearable—he had to at least let her know that she wasn't alone, that people here would help her. That *he* would help her.

When he pushed the door open another few inches and looked inside, Favian was more than a little shocked to find the wolf with her. Senovo had been avoiding her to a noticeable degree, ostensibly because he thought his presence would only upset her more, but also, Favian knew, because he blamed himself for not somehow saving her as a young girl when they had briefly met outside of Rhyth, years earlier.

Now, though, she was clinging to him with the desperation of a drowning woman, weeping as if she would die. The sight pierced his chest like an arrow, even though he knew, intellectually, that weeping was a definite step forward from the frightening apathy she'd exhibited for the last few days.

"Hey," he said softly from the doorway, alerting the pair to his presence. She tensed, but did not release her death grip on the wolf's fur. "It's all right. You're all right. You're not alone any more. I'm just going to go get Senovo a robe for when he changes back, and I'll come sit with you. You're fine—you're safe here."

He hurried back to his room and grabbed a spare set of dun robes from the chest. When he returned, Senovo had shifted into human form and was holding the girl against his chest. Her lank hair hung in a dark curtain across her face, obscuring it. Something about the sight made Favian want to weep himself—perhaps it was the stricken look on his mentor's face, or the girl's air of utter vulnerability now that her stony anger had finally dissolved into grief.

"Here," he said in a quiet voice, and draped the simple garment over Senovo's shoulders. Senovo thanked him with a look. Favian sat down on the other side of the bed and waited to see what their guest needed.

She cried for a long time—the exhausted weeping of a child who had lost everything. Favian was more familiar with that kind of weeping than he cared to dwell on, though even after his father died, he had never been nearly as alone as the broken girl in front of him. He'd had Frella, who loved him and needed him to be strong for her. He'd had Senovo and

Carivel. Andoc. A village full of people who'd known him his entire life.

But even then, he'd wanted to curl up and die. He couldn't imagine what the young woman shuddering in Senovo's arms was going through. Something about her called to him, for all that their first real meeting had taken place with a dagger pressed to his throat. Maybe it was the fact that he'd dreamed her, years ago. Or maybe it was the courage she'd shown, crossing the mountains alone—borne along on the crest of her anger despite a failing, half-starved body.

Now, she sucked in a wet, noisy breath and shoved at Senovo with all of her remaining strength. He let her go immediately and vacated the bed, donning the robe Favian had brought him properly and doing up the fastenings.

"I wanted you dead," she grated, her voice roughened by tears and mucus. She still kept her face down, hiding behind the curtain of dirty hair.

Senovo folded himself into the chair near the bed. "I'm not surprised."

"Maybe I still do," she added.

Senovo only nodded, though she could not see the movement. "Though it will admittedly sound self-serving, I can tell you with some certainty that bloody revenge against those who have wronged you does not, in the end, make things better."

He was talking, Favian knew, about the priests that the wolf had killed during his escape from the southern temple. Even now—against all reason—he still blamed himself for their deaths. However, an injured wolf's moment of madness was a far different thing than traveling half the length of Eburos for the sole purpose of killing a man, though Favian kept that opinion to himself under the circumstances.

The girl ignored his words and continued. "The idea of revenge has been all that kept me from curling up by the side of the road to die, these past weeks. I would wake in the morning, and think *today I will get closer to Draebard. I will take my revenge on the Wolf Patron, and then*—" She cut herself off, still not looking at either of them. "But now I have failed. What am I without that anger to keep me going? An escaped slave with a disfigured face, alone in a strange land? There is nothing left for me. What do I *do* now?"

Senovo closed his eyes. "What you can. We all do what we can. It is, in the end, the only choice we have."

"*You left us.* You came in and upended our world, and then you disappeared without a trace." She finally looked up, glaring at Senovo with her good eye. "*Why didn't you come back?*"

Senovo's shoulders fell for a bare instant before he squared them and met her accusing gaze. "I was a terrified boy who ran away from my masters, and didn't stop running until Rhyth was just a strange, distant place that people spoke of as if it was a completely different world. When our traveling party came across you, on the way to the talks at the southern palace six years ago, I'd never even heard of the prophecy of the Wolf Patron. I am not who you think me to be—and for that, I am sorry."

The girl continued to glare. "You are still the Wolf Patron, whether you want to be or not."

"Perhaps so," Senovo allowed, sounding suddenly very tired. "But I cannot be the savior you want me to be."

"And so the southern slaves will continue to suffer under the Masters' yoke while you hide here in your temple, wearing your white High Priest's robes."

Favian could see the barb strike home, but Senovo merely said, "I wish it could be different. Perhaps salvation will still come for those suffering in the south, just from a different source."

The girl scoffed. "There is no one else. Now, leave me. Both of you. Get out of my sight. It makes me sick to look at you."

Senovo nodded, and rose to go without comment. Favian followed his lead, but paused by the bed.

"We're going now," he said. "But I'll be back in the morning."

⤖ ⚜ ⤕

Kathrael didn't think she'd ever cried as much in her life as she did over the course of that dark, endless night. She also couldn't remember ever feeling worse physically than she did when the sun finally hoisted itself over the horizon by slow degrees, spilling gray light through the room's small window. As bad, perhaps—but not worse.

Her head pounded, and her throat burned, and her stomach ached, and her eyes felt like someone had tried to set fire to them — even the one that could no longer make proper tears. Not for the first time in recent days, she lay there looking at the blurry rafters above her and fervently wished to die.

What she got instead was Favian, poking his head through the door a scant few moments after warning her of his approach with a maddeningly cheerful flurry of knocks. She stared at him with swollen eyes in a puffy red face and silently dared him to offer some comforting remark about it.

"I made you some willow bark tea," he said. "Drink it and come with me. You look awful, and frankly, you smell worse. I've drawn a warm bath for you, which I hope you appreciate, since hauling heavy buckets around with a half-healed scrotum is not the most fun I've ever had in my life."

"Then you shouldn't have bothered," Kathrael rasped, not moving.

"I did mention the part about you stinking like ten-day-old fish, yes?"

"Maybe I'm actually dead and just haven't realized it yet."

Favian pinched her upper arm without warning and she yelped, jerking upright in surprise. "Nope," he said. "Still alive, notwithstanding the smell. Now drink your tea before it gets cold. It'll help with your headache. That was always my least favorite part about crying my eyes out, personally."

He more or less shoved the tea into her hands, and she took it as a self-defensive measure to keep it from spilling over her lap. The curls of steam rising from the clay cup were undeniably soothing. At this point, she was desperate enough for the pain in her head to stop that she drank the bitter brew. When she was done, she shoved the empty cup back at him with as little care as he had shown. The small flash of satisfaction when he fumbled it and barely rescued it from shattering on the floor took her by surprise.

He shot her a look and set the cup aside. "Come on. Up. Bath. You'll feel much better afterward, I assure you."

"No."

He raised an eyebrow. "Come with me and I'll answer one question on any subject completely truthfully. No second thoughts, no backing down."

Despite herself, she eyed him with a speculative expression, a wisp of curiosity curling through the fog of misery that shrouded her. "Fine," she said, and tried to get up—only for her knees to buckle.

Favian grabbed her arm without comment and steadied her as she rose on shaky feet. Shockingly, the same legs that had carried her over the mountains had seemingly forgotten how to work at all, after days spent bedridden. To her surprise, though, the novice's touch did not repel her. Quite the opposite—something about it reminded her sharply of nights spent curled up with Vesh, safe in arms that demanded nothing of her but quiet affection. Tears threatened to rise again, though she would have sworn she'd cried herself dry last night. She swallowed them back, angry at the weakness.

Favian was looking down at her oddly. When she frowned at him, he seemed to shake himself free of his reverie. "Sorry," he said. "It's just—I thought you'd be taller."

She ignored the strange observation. "Are we going to stand here all day? I thought you were the one who was offended by my stench."

A smile pulled at his full lips before he hid it. "Just so. Let's go, then."

Their progress through the halls of the village temple was depressingly slow. They passed a handful of acolytes going about their business, all of whom nodded to Favian and kept their eyes carefully averted from her disfigured face. The bathing room was at the back of the structure. Kathrael could hear a river flowing nearby through the open doors and windows in the large room. The place was humid and smelled faintly of mildew.

She thought back to the spectacular bathhouses in the wealthy quarter of Rhyth, with their intricate mosaics and tiled pools fed by hot springs. When she had been younger and beautiful, in demand by wealthy fools with too much money, she had been part of the entertainment at such places on numerous occasions. There, the air had smelled of sulfur and cedar smoke. She had adored the bathhouses.

The simple bathing room in the temple of Draebard was a poor substitute, but it had a deep copper tub filled with steaming water, and a cloth hanging next to a container of soft lye soap. Now that she was here, Kathrael couldn't deny the appeal of finally being clean. Aside from a rag and a bowl of water in the village where Livvy had stopped on the way to Penth, and, later, at the twins' home in Darveen, she had not washed properly in weeks.

"You're still pretty shaky," Favian observed as he helped her to the bath and let her lean against the rim to balance. "Would you like me to stay and help you?"

She unlaced the neck opening of the shift they'd dressed her in and let it fall free of her shoulders to puddle on the ground. Her gaze met his, challenging.

"Stay if you want, priest-boy. I was a whore for *years*, you know. A good one, too. You're freshly cut, you say?" She looked down the length of his body and back up at his face, hit by the sudden desire to do something that would shock him and finally put the disgust she expected to see into his expression. "Probably wondering if your prick still works, right? I'll get it up for you if you'd like."

Favian didn't reply, but helped her step out of the circle of linen around her ankles and into the tub, where she sank down into the blood-warm water with an undeniable sigh of pleasure. When she was settled, he pulled a chair up to the head of the tub and sat down.

"Well?" she insisted, looking up at him.

"It still works," he said quietly, lathering up the rag and handing it to her. "To an extent, at least. I gather it takes a few weeks for all of the changes to happen."

"So whip it out. I'll make you feel good — pay you back for nursing me like a sick babe this last week." She raised an eyebrow, still looking him square in the eye and daring him to back down. "I've never sucked off a fresh-cut eunuch before."

A faint blush did rise to his cheeks, but his expression remained open and unguarded. "I'm afraid you're not really my type, in that regard."

Understanding dawned. "Oh. Queer?" she asked.

"Sort of," he said, still blushing. "I could only ever get hard for men, though I had my share of romantic crushes on girls and boys both, growing up. I guess you could say that makes me queer. Thankfully, before long, I won't be that way anymore — instead, I'll be nothing at all."

She stared at him, surprised by his candor. "And you *wanted* that?"

His brow furrowed. "Draebard isn't Rhyth. No one here is forced into the Priests' Guild." His voice had gone hard on the last sentence but it softened again, growing reflective. "To answer your question, yes, I wanted it. Sex and lust have brought me nothing but heartache. I'm happy to be done with them."

The memory of tearing agony as a fat old man forced his way into her thirteen-year-old body for first time flickered across her mind's eye, followed by the flash of a glass vial filled with vitriol. She sank back in the bath, abandoning her attempt to goad him. "I know the feeling," she said on a breath. "You're right. You're better off without it, and so am I."

He shrugged. "Well. Don't get me wrong. There can be a beauty to it sometimes. I'm coming to appreciate that, now that it's no longer something I have to worry about personally. Brother Eiridan has started letting me sit in on some of the intimate counseling now that I'm a castrate, and I can understand the appeal from a purely aesthetic perspective."

Kathrael scoffed and ran the soapy rag over her body, scrubbing at the travel grime. "Pah! Don't be fooled," she said, not even trying to hold back the bitterness. "Sex is a transaction, nothing more. It's what women give men so they'll stay in a handfasting, and what prostitutes give men for money."

Favian looked troubled, but he said nothing.

Kathrael dunked her head back to wet her greasy hair. She worked soap into the tangles, enjoying the feel of the lather against her scalp. "So," she said. "You promised me the answer to a question."

That got his attention again. "You've already asked several very personal questions, you do realize."

She waved his words away. "Those didn't count."

Amusement flitted across his features. "If you say so. What's your question?"

She looked at him, her good eye burning into his. "Who is the Wolf Patron to you?"

Favian answered without hesitation. "He's my High Priest. My mentor."

"No. Not good enough." A little rivulet of soapy water dribbled down her cheek, but she ignored it.

"I—" The young priest blinked, taken aback. "Well... he's the man who accepted me into the priesthood with open arms when I thought that I would never find a place in life where I could fit in. He's the one who ignored the rules and brought my sister to live at the temple when we were orphaned less than a year later. He was like a parent to her… to both of us, really. I love him deeply."

"In the south," Kathrael said, "he is known as a powerful mage who was prophesied to save us all from the overseers' yoke… and didn't."

"Prophesied by whom?" Favian asked. "He's a shape-shifter, yes. But believe me when I tell you, shifters are only people—no better or worse than anyone else." He shook his head before continuing. "How was he even supposed to be aware of this *prophecy*? There was a war coming in the north, and we all knew it. A terrible, unwinnable war. Is it such a surprise that he would focus his efforts on helping the land that had taken him in and given him a life, rather than running back to the place that had enslaved and mutilated him?"

"The war was years ago," she said stubbornly. "And I've heard the stories about the Battle of Llanmeer, where he led an army of wolves to defeat the Alyrions. He *is* powerful. He could have come."

Favian was silent for a moment. "I'm… not sure an army of wolves would help the slaves in Rhyth," he said. "Who would they attack? Slavery is not a battle in a war."

She scowled. "You know nothing about it."

Favian lowered his gaze. "No. I suppose you're right about that." He looked up at her again. "But you still can't expect one man to walk in—on four legs or two—and magically fix things, just because someone said it was going to happen. Prophesy is a tricky business, and I say that with more authority on the subject than most."

She shrugged, dismissing his words angrily. "Tell it to the child who has just been pulled from his mother's breast and sold to the highest bidder."

He chewed his lip for a moment before speaking. "I'm sorry," he said with every indication of sincerity. "I wish I had a better answer."

Kathrael made a noise of disgust and went back to washing, suddenly aware that she'd been arguing passionately with him, her spirit filled with the familiar fire that had deserted her after her failed attempt at revenge. In addition, the steaming bath and the willow bark tea had cleared her aching head. She was clean and fed, her belly free of parasites. For the first time since before Vesh was murdered, she felt like a human being again… and she had no idea what to do with the realization.

Favian helped her rinse and oil her hair. He was silent as he steadied her while she dried off, and he hovered nearby as she walked back to her room unaided. Someone had aired the bed and put fresh blankets on it while they'd been gone, but she found, unexpectedly, that the idea of lying down in it did not appeal.

"I'm sick of the sight of this bed," she said.

Favian looked surprised, but pleased. "Then come to the refectory and have a meal. You can meet some of the others."

A faint sense of trepidation washed over her as she began to think about what her actions must have looked like to these people whose High Priest she had tried to attack. A dangerous madwoman with a scarred face, intent on murder and wielding a knife. It was an uncomfortable realization.

Sometimes madness isn't permanent, whispered a familiar voice, tickling her ear.

She must have gone still and silent for too long, because Favian was watching her carefully. "What is it? Are you all right?"

She shook her head. "It was only Vesh, talking to me. I'm all right now."

He nodded, accepting the words with an ease that made something inside her chest relax and unknot after weeks of tension.

"You know," he said, "it seems strange that I know the names of the spirits that surround you, but not yours."

She was quiet for a long moment, remembering what it was like to be somewhere that people cared enough to want to know what you were called. "Kathrael," she said. "My name is Kathrael."

ELEVEN

Kathrael did, in fact, accompany Favian to eat in the temple's communal dining area, where several of the priests and acolytes were gathered for a meal after their morning devotions. Some of the younger boys at the heavy trestle table had difficulty looking at her directly, and she caught one brown-haired lad staring fixedly at her scars with an expression of sick fascination on his face.

She suddenly wished for the fine woven shawl that Shayla had gifted her — she had been so ill and distraught that it had only now occurred to her to wonder where her meager belongings were.

The High Priest was notably absent, though the others appeared to defer to an oddly matched pair of senior priests. One — an immensely fat eunuch with heavy jowls and sandy brown hair — was ladling bowls of fragrant cooked cereals from a large cauldron. Despite the ready access to food she'd enjoyed over the last few days, Kathrael's stomach rumbled at the smell. The second priest was seated at the table, but rose as she and Favian entered. He was younger and thinner, though still with the noticeable pot belly that many eunuchs seemed to acquire as they aged. His eyes drew her attention — they were the kind of eyes that saw deeply, and kept secrets.

"Greetings," he said, in an accent notably different than Favian's. "It's good to see you up and about, honored guest. I am Brother Eiridan, and this is Brother Feldes." He indicated the fat priest, who dipped his head in a small bow. "Please, join us for breakfast. The High Priest has instructed that we serve you as best we are able during your stay here. Would you care for a bowl of spiced barley meal?"

Kathrael stood frozen inside the doorway, looking at the nervous acolytes fiddling with their spoons and trying to remember how to be around people. Priest Eiridan's intelligent eyes followed her gaze, and he cleared his throat softly.

"You'll have to forgive some of our number for their discomfort regarding your facial scars," he said, his tone unconcerned and forthright. "It is a natural human reaction to empathize with the pain that must have been involved, and then immediately think about what it would be like to have such a thing happen to oneself. They do not intend disrespect, and the reaction will fade as they have a chance to interact with you for a few minutes."

His blunt speech was refreshing, and she decided that she liked him. "I'm used to it... or should be, at least," she said hesitantly. "Thank you. I would like a bowl of barley; it smells delicious."

The fat priest—Feldes—smiled and puffed up as if she'd complimented him personally. "Of course, my dear," he said in the same strange accent. "Have as much as you like. It's one of my favorite recipes. My grandmother used to make it for breakfast on festival days when I was a child, back in Meren."

"Thank you," she said again, and took the bowl he handed her. Favian gestured her to a seat at the end of the table. He sat next to her on the hard wooden bench—somewhat gingerly, she noted—and she wondered if he was purposely using his presence at her side to insulate her from the group of strangers further down the table.

She focused on her bowl and the delicious contents. Chunks of fruit had been stewed in with the barley, and autumn spices had been added with a liberal hand. Around her, the conversation turned back to other things, and she relaxed a bit.

Apparently there was, in fact, a festival planned for that evening. Eiridan and Feldes were explaining to the younger acolytes what would be required of them as the townsfolk celebrated. In Rhyth, the festivals devoted to the Old Gods had long ago devolved into excuses for the wealthy to flaunt their wealth, the drunkards to drink more wine than usual, and the corrupt to revel in their corruption. That said, it was also a good opportunity to make money as a prostitute, particularly if one also had a talent for dancing or playing a musical instrument.

In Draebard, festivals sounded like much simpler affairs. Plentiful, rich food, games, storytelling, mind-altering substances, and lots of people having sex in public. Though perhaps, she thought wryly, they were not so different from the celebrations in Rhyth after all.

"You're welcome to attend, of course, if you'd like to get out of the temple for a night," Favian said quietly, startling her.

She looked at him, her brows drawing together in a frown. "I'm not likely to get stoned or branded as a criminal if I set foot outside, then?"

He looked at her in consternation. "No. I would hardly have suggested it if that were the case. Aside from you and me, the only people who know the details about the night of your arrival are Senovo, Andoc, and Carivel. Well... and Healer Sagdea, I suppose. But it's not like any of them are going to go spreading rumors around."

"They're not rumors when they're true," Kathrael muttered.

"Even so..." Favian shrugged. "The High Priest of Draebard has offered you sanctuary, and everyone in the village will respect that. You are free to go, wherever and whenever you choose." His voice lowered further, for her ears alone. "I've been on the wrong end of your knife, Kathrael and I don't think you really would have pressed the point into my throat. Am I wrong?"

A bubble of dizziness made her head spin for a moment, as she pictured scarlet blooming from Favian's neck, trickling down to soak the linen of his robes.

"No," she whispered, the stewed cereal she'd eaten suddenly settling in her belly like lead. "You're not wrong." She pushed the bowl away and swallowed hard.

The corner of Favian's lip quirked up in a brief, sad smile. "Yeah—I didn't think so."

"... Favian?" She and Favian both looked up somewhat guiltily as Brother Feldes called Favian's name, obviously not for the first time.

"I'm sorry, Elder Brother," Favian said. "Could you repeat that?"

"I asked if you were recovered enough to assist at the festival tonight, Favian," said the priest with a faint huff.

The novice flushed. "Oh... yes. Of course. Though I might need to sit down and rest occasionally."

"Certainly, Little Brother," said Eiridan. "Do only what you are able. Now, if everyone is finished, there is much to prepare."

"I do believe that was a hint," Favian said in a whispered aside. "Are you all right on your own now?"

"Yes," she said, her mind still whirling. "Go and do priest things, priest-boy. I'll be fine."

In fact, she was completely exhausted after the small amount she had done this morning. She supposed it would take time to recover her strength, such as it was. And there was also the fact that she had been awake for most of the night weeping like a babe. Even now, her face felt puffy and hot. She wished again for her shawl, and shot a hand out to stop Favian as he was leaving.

"Where are my things?" she asked. "My clothes and satchel?"

"They're in the chest at the foot of the bed," he said. "Everything except your dagger, that is. I'll see if I can get that back for you later today."

She frowned. "You would give me back my knife, after what I did to you?"

"As long as you're not still intending to use it on Senovo, or anyone else in Draebard — why wouldn't I?"

Kathrael looked at him closely, trying to understand him. "I can't make sense of you," she said eventually.

He shrugged. "For what it's worth, I can't make sense of a lot of things in life," he replied. "Sometimes you just have to accept what's around you and move on. Try to get some more rest, all right? I'll see you later."

Kathrael shook her head lightly and let him go. She was still a bit shaky as she made her way back to the room where she'd spent the last week, but walking was growing easier the more she did it. The comfortable bed seemed to call to her, the clean blankets warm and sweet smelling. Within moments of her head hitting the pillow, she was fast asleep, deep in blessedly dreamless slumber.

Hours later, a knock at the door woke her. She expected Favian to appear, but instead it was the deep-eyed priest with the forthright manner, Eiridan.

"Forgive me for waking you," he said, hovering just inside the doorway. "Favian said you were thinking about attending the festival, and it will be getting underway shortly."

She glanced at the window, surprised to find that darkness was rapidly falling and she had slept the day away. "Oh," she said. "Thank you. I didn't realize it was getting so late."

Eiridan smiled, then sobered. "I daresay you still need the rest. If I may, I'd like to ask you something while I'm here. Young Favian has been quite worried about you these last days. I have been tasked with assisting his education in the arts of counseling those in need, and he shared with me that you are beset by spirits who speak and interact with you."

Kathrael drew the blanket up around her, suddenly defensive. "What of it?"

"The spirit world is a particular interest of mine, as it happens. I was merely wondering if you would be willing to speak with me about the matter in more detail at some future time."

She relaxed marginally. "Oh. I... suppose that would be all right. You know about such things, then?"

"I've studied it as much as I'm able to, but it's not a well-understood phenomenon. That's why I'd be fascinated to hear about your experiences. Also, if you're not averse, I'd like to have Favian sit in on the discussion. He still has much to learn about the world beyond the visible."

Strangely, the idea of having her self-appointed nursemaid present was a rather comforting one. Perhaps this priest with the disconcerting eyes could help her quiet the voices somehow—especially her inconsolable baby.

"Very well. I'll talk to you both," she said, "as long as you promise not to have me caged up as a madwoman after you hear what I have to say."

"You don't seem mad to me," Eiridan said, "for what it's worth."

"Maybe not now," she said, the words coming out without her intending them, "but I think I might have been, before."

Eiridan tipped his head, considering her words. "It's possible, certainly. Sometimes madness is only temporary."

She couldn't help her startled huff of laughter. Eiridan looked at her questioningly.

"Sorry, it's nothing. Only... one of the spirits said very nearly the same thing to me earlier today."

His features lit with understanding, then amusement. "So, a *wise* spirit, no less. Fascinating. I look forward to hearing more. Now, though, I'll leave you to ready yourself for the evening. Is there anything you need?"

"No, I'm fine," she said.

"Enjoy Draebard's hospitality, in that case. May the gods' blessings be upon you."

Eiridan tipped his head respectfully and withdrew, leaving her to ponder the turn her fortunes had taken. She rose on stiff legs and dressed, carefully arranging the shawl over her face to cover her scars. Outside, night had fallen, and the town was illuminated by torchlight. Bonfires dotted the village green, the smell of roasting meat permeating the air.

Feeling suddenly uncertain, Kathrael kept to the shadows and did not join in the revelry. Around her, people were drinking and laughing, helping themselves to the plentiful food as they talked and joked. The aroma of burning herbs wafted to her hiding place, heady and complex. Drums beat a primal rhythm in the open area at the center of the village, and several men and women were dancing, eyes closed, lost in their own worlds.

Once, she would have prowled through the crowd like a tigress, drawing the eyes of every man who saw her. Now, she was a wraith, haunting the edges of the feast—a timid woodland creature hoping for scraps, but terrified of discovery.

Perhaps she should have stayed in the temple. But she was here now, and it made sense to familiarize herself more with the village and its people. To that end, she continued her slow circuit, moving from shadowed building to shadowed building without drawing attention to herself.

At one point, she saw Favian wandering through the crowd with a wineskin slung over his shoulder, stopping to greet passersby and refill their cups or goblets. She watched him, momentarily torn between gaining his attention and staying hidden. He moved to speak with a young couple who smiled and called a friendly greeting at his approach. The rosy-cheeked woman got up from her perch on the man's lap to kiss Favian on the cheek and embrace him. When she released him, she took his hand and tugged him over to sit with them. Favian followed willingly, a smile lighting his attractive features.

Kathrael left him to it and moved on, not acknowledging a small pang at seeing him so comfortable among his close friends.

Away from the central green, things were quieter. Trees grew at the edge of the village, a series of trails and small clearings also lit by the ubiquitous torches. Here, Kathrael wandered at the edges of the circles of light, enjoying the peaceful, pleasant night. As the evening wore on, couples began to filter into the forest — giggling women and the low voices of men intent on bedding them.

Such things held no interest for her, and she wandered deeper into the woods, following the string of flickering torches through the winding maze of trails. At the farthest extent of the illuminated area, more voices filtered through the leaves — *familiar* voices.

The Draebardi chieftain, Andoc. The smooth-faced boy who had been guarding her room when she first woke up after her thwarted attack.

The Wolf Patron.

The High Priest's low voice cut off with a gasp, followed by a soft moan. She crept closer, as if drawn by an invisible cord.

The three of them were in the last clearing lit by torchlight, with only darkness beyond. They were naked, and Kathrael was surprised to see that the slender boy had breasts — not a boy at all, then, but rather a coltish, angular woman with narrow hips and the sort of rangy muscles that were only gained through hard use.

A leather harness buckled snugly around her pelvis. Kathrael recognized the type from her days around Rhyth's brothels — rich men at orgies would sometimes pay to watch one woman fucking another with such a device, which held a fake cock of wood or leather in place over a girl's cunt.

Somewhat to her shock, the boyish woman was using it to fuck Senovo with slow, rolling thrusts of her hips as he lay sprawled back against Andoc's broad chest. Andoc had settled himself against a convenient tree trunk and was cupping Senovo's face in his hands, kissing his lips like one drinking from a chalice.

She watched, unable to look away, as the woman changed her angle of attack and thrust in deeper. Senovo bucked under her and cried out into the kiss. She remembered that Vesh used to claim he could still get some pleasure from being fucked under certain circumstances. Kathrael had been skeptical at the time, but despite being a eunuch, Senovo's small prick bobbed out, stiff and ready, and he writhed on the fake cock with every indication of enjoyment.

The odd, androgynous woman reached down and wrapped a fist around his modest shaft, pumping in time with her thrusts. Before long, he trembled through a release as strong as any Kathrael had seen from an uncut man—his moans swallowed by the Draebardi chief's demanding kiss.

After he went limp and pliant between them, the pair manhandled the spent eunuch onto his front. The woman pressed his leg out of her way and thrust into him again, his body yielding to the assault with a new shudder. His head was resting on Andoc's thigh now, and he rubbed his cheek against the man's hard cock like a cat. Andoc hissed out a breath, and Senovo braced himself on shaky arms so he could wrap his lips around the hard length. He bobbed up and down in slow movements, matching his tempo to the woman's thrusts.

Andoc's hand came up to rest on the back of his head, fingers tangling in the long black plait of hair. "So good, *amadi*," he breathed, his voice impossibly tender. "Love you both so much..."

The words twisted something inside Kathrael's chest painfully. She clenched her jaw. *Men will say all sorts of things during sex*, she reminded herself. *It doesn't mean anything.* In the clearing, Senovo moaned around the cock he was sucking, and let the hand on his head press him smoothly down to take it to the root.

"I will never, ever get enough of this," said the woman in a low, shaky voice, her hand sliding up the relaxed curve of Senovo's spine. "I love you two so much it hurts."

Kathrael had absolutely no idea what the strange, boyish woman was getting out of her playacting. Still, she was smart to play the man's role as long as the others allowed it. Better to be the taker than the taken.

A rustle behind her hiding place in the shadows made Kathrael jump. But it was only Favian, approaching quietly along the illuminated trail. He must have seen her movement, because he came over to her immediately, greeting her with a smile.

"There you are," he said quietly, in deference to the various lovers scattered around the woods. "I thought I saw you head back here earlier. Everything all right? What are you doing hiding back here all alone?"

She saw the moment his attention moved past her, to the clearing beyond. His face twisted into an expression of amused horror—with the emphasis on the horror.

"Aaand there's a mental image I really could have done without, thanks *so* much," he muttered under his breath. "Could we, er, go someplace else? *Now?*"

She allowed him to lead her back the way they'd both come, unable to let his obvious discomfiture pass unremarked. "Problem, priest-boy? I thought it was a pretty passable performance, myself. Your mentor's cock-sucking technique seems quite... *practiced...*"

"Right. Just stop talking. Seriously."

Amusement bubbled up inside her and she laughed at him; she couldn't help it. How long had it been since she *laughed*?

"It's *not funny*," Favian said, the words belied by twist in his lips as he tried to keep his expression suitably severe. His face was still beet red.

"It is a *bit* funny," she retorted. "You're going to make a sorry excuse for a priest if seeing people having sex makes you blush like a virgin. I can picture you now at your first handfasting, stammering over the vows with your cheeks glowing like a pair of hot coals."

"Don't insult the person who drew you a hot bath this morning." Favian glared at her, not terribly convincingly. "It's not the sex, it's the *people who raised* me having sex. Which they do. All. The. Fucking. Time. It's almost a running joke at this point." He gave up his attempt at severity and ran a hand over his face, a snort of appalled laughter escaping from behind it. "They probably thought they were safe, way back here in the woods."

"Who's the woman?" Kathrael asked, finally having pity on him. "I thought she was a man."

"Oh, that's Carivel. Draebard's Horse Mistress. We all thought she was a boy for years, after she first moved here. Turns out she's sort of... both. The way she explains it, she was born with a male spirit in a female body." He shrugged. "She's just Carivel, really. You sort of have to take her as she is."

"Actually, from where I was standing, it looked like she was the one doing the taking."

Favian emitted a sort of choked noise.

Kathrael laughed again, but then she sobered. She had known of a young male prostitute in Rhyth who had dressed and acted like a woman. She'd only spoken to him briefly on a couple of occasions, but he'd been one of the first to be targeted by the cult members. He hadn't survived long.

"Who is she to the Wolf Patron, and your Chief?" she asked, bringing herself back to the present. "They say in the south that Senovo and Andoc are lovers. I guess that part was true, at least."

"They're bondmates."

She frowned. "Andoc and Carivel, you mean?"

"No, all three of them. They were handfasted six years ago, before the Alyrion invasion."

"Three people can't enter into a handfasting together," Kathrael said. "And Senovo is a eunuch."

"Well, obviously they *can* enter into a handfasting, since they did exactly that," Favian replied. "To be fair, though, I think it's the first time it's happened. The High Priest in Meren has second sight. He foresaw their union in a vision, and performed the ceremony himself."

"Oh, so it was a *prophecy*?" she goaded, feeling her good mood begin to sour. "How interesting."

"It was a vision," Favian reiterated, "and it was something that all three of them desired to do. So they did, at which point it turned out to be a *true* vision. Second sight can be a tricky business."

"Words, priest boy. Just words."

Favian shrugged. "It's the truth. Prophecies are meaningless unless they come to pass. I can say that the sun is destined to disappear from the sky and leave the world in darkness, but unless it happens, I'm just flapping my lips."

"The sun disappeared from the sky a couple of hours ago," Kathrael pointed out in a dry tone. "And it's dark right now."

He shot her a look. "You know what I mean."

She blew out a sharp breath of irritation through her nose and let the argument lie.

"Have you eaten?" Favian asked, changing the subject as they emerged from the woods and headed back into the village.

"No," she said, not adding that she'd been afraid to come forward and interact with anyone long enough to get food. Now, though, the smell of succulent pork and beef was making her stomach rumble.

"Well, come with me, in that case. I'll introduce you to some people. There are definite benefits to being friends with a member of the family who run the village cookhouse."

Kathrael screwed up her courage and gestured ahead of them. "All right—if you're sure. Lead on, then."

⚜

When the festival had finally run its course, with the last drunken holdouts stumbling back to their own huts or someone else's, the temple denizens made their way back to collapse into their own beds for a few hours. Several of the older acolytes—and some of the younger priests who still took pleasure in such things—were looking decidedly well fucked, if Favian was any judge. He marveled for the thousandth time how anyone could use sex in such a casual way, taking fleeting pleasure and then just moving on as if nothing of import had happened.

Once again, he felt a quiet surge of relief that he would soon be beyond such things.

Now, though, he was bone-tired. Everything had gone smoothly in the village—no brawls had marred the celebration of the gods' bounty, and it appeared that everyone had enjoyed themselves. Even Kathrael had relaxed a bit after he'd introduced her to Limdya and Dalon, unbending enough to wish him a good night as she left for her own room.

The elders who no longer had much interest in attending such festivals had taken the village children out to the summer horse pastures to camp under the stars. This meant, of course, that their parents would have the evening to relax without worrying. Frella was out with them, so Favian had their room to himself tonight. With a sigh of relief, he fell into bed, and was soon fast asleep.

Some time later, he dreamed.

The lion growled low in its throat, stalking toward the man in the gaudy tunic and breeches with dangerous intent. Around Favian, the crowd was muttering nervously, milling around. The big cat roared in anger, and someone at the front screamed. A moment later, people were running... scrambling to get out of the village square... blocking his view.

He cast around for somewhere higher, where he could climb up and try to get the beast's attention. Terrified people shoved past him, threatening to send him to the ground. Favian was yelling something, trying to move against the tide — his words lost in the noise and meaningless to his own ears. Soon, he was left at the edge of the ever-expanding clear space left behind as the crowd fled. The lion surged forward, tackling its victim to the ground even as he turned to run.

Without warning, the beast's head jerked up, its attention drawn from its prey to Favian. A moment later, there was a twisting change, *and Ithric crouched over the downed man, looking frantically at Favian with wide, shocked eyes. The man on the ground scrabbled for something at his belt, and a shiny knife appeared in his hand.*

Favian cried out a warning. The knife jabbed up, towards Ithric's unprotected side —

"No!" The strangled cry echoed around the empty room. Favian clawed his way upright among the tangled blankets, dizzy and nauseous. He lunged for the edge of the bed, barely making it before the contents of his stomach burned their way up his throat and splattered onto the flagstone floor below as he heaved.

⚜

Kathrael lay in bed, staring up into the darkness. Her thoughts circled endlessly, keeping her from slumber — her own fault for sleeping the day away, she knew. A noise drew her attention, and she sat up. If she hadn't already been wide awake, she would never have heard the strange, choked cry, muffled nearly to nothing by the walls separating her from whoever had called out.

She froze for a moment, unsure what — if anything — to do.

Go, Vesh whispered. *You want to go and help, so go and help.*

No one should be all alone in the dark of night, Elarra added.

"You left me alone in the night," she reminded both of them.

Yes, but they *didn't,* said Vesh.

It was true. The Wolf Patron — damn his hide — had come to her and roused her from her nightmares. Minutes later,

Favian had followed the sound of her weeping to sit with her while she grieved. She sighed and rolled to her feet, glad that the world no longer tilted and swayed when she did so. Perhaps she was finally regaining her health under the priests' care.

She lit a candle, then padded over to the door and opened it, listening. Faint sounds of distress were coming from her right, and as she got closer they resolved into the unmistakable sound of vomiting.

It could have been as innocuous as an acolyte who had overindulged during the festival earlier… but members of the temple were discouraged from such things when they had public duties to perform. And there had been a cry a few moments ago—

Another noise of pain emerged from behind the closed door, and Kathrael reached up to knock. When there was no answer, she opened the door with a tentative push, unsure what she was likely to find. The flickering light from the candle she was carrying illuminated Favian, clutching the bedpost with one hand and his stomach with the other as he heaved another thin stream of bile onto the floor.

"Favian!" she exclaimed, hurrying forward and setting the candlestick on the table by the bed.

Favian gasped in a breath as if drowning and clutched at her arm. "Kathrael," he croaked, "I have—I have to—"

"Do you need to throw up again?" she asked, more than a little frightened by his demeanor. "Should I get someone? The Healer?"

He shook his head, still clinging to her arm. "I have to see Senovo. Please! *Please* help me get to him."

"I'm not sure you should try to get up," she said dubiously, but she braced herself as he used his grip on her arm to pull himself upright, barely keeping his feet clear of the mess on the floor.

"Wait," she said, and picked up the candle again. She slung his arm across her shoulders, but he was reeling. The candle guttered dangerously as they wavered, threatening to plunge them into darkness. "Favian, you're scaring me!"

"I'm sorry," he said. "I can't—" He managed to get his feet under him a bit more squarely. "I *have* to talk to Senovo *right now. Please*, Kathrael!"

If nothing else, perhaps Senovo would know what to do to help him, she thought. Assuming they could get there without Favian collapsing in a heap first.

"All right, I'll take you," she said finally. "You'll have to direct me, though. I don't know where we're going."

He gave a tight nod and stumbled toward the door, leaning on her heavily. They staggered through the hallways into a part of the temple where she hadn't been before, away from the public spaces. Eventually, they fetched up against an unassuming wooden door. Favian knocked frantically and burst into the room beyond without waiting for an answer.

Inside, the space was illuminated by an oil lamp. It was spacious and well furnished, with an open doorway leading to a second room beyond.

"Who's there?" called a startled voice, and a rumpled, half-dressed figure entered the circle of light. It was the woman Kathrael had taken for a man — Carivel. Her eyes widened in alarm. "Favian?" she said, and hurried forward, giving Kathrael a wary glance as she took Favian's arm and steadied him. "What is it? What's wrong?"

"I had a dream," Favian said, sounding very young and frightened. "Carivel, I have to tell Senovo, I have to—"

"Right," Carivel said, sounding inexplicably grim. "Just breathe for a minute, Favian—you look like you're about to pass out." She twisted to call over her shoulder. "Senovo!"

"I'm here." The Wolf Patron emerged from the other room, his eyes sliding over Kathrael and cataloguing her presence at Favian's side for an instant before his attention settled firmly on his protégé. He took the arm that Carivel had been holding and urged Favian to a chair. "Sit, Little Brother. Andoc is awake and will be here momentarily. Do you want to wait for him?"

Favian shook his head. "Ithric is in danger," he said, all in a rush.

Kathrael had remained stubbornly at Favian's side, for all that she was bewildered by his strange behavior. Why would a grown man — albeit a young one — go running to his guardians after a nightmare? And why would those guardians seem so worried about a mere bad dream? Without understanding exactly why, she moved to stand behind Favian's chair and put a protective hand on his shoulder. Again, the Wolf Patron's sharp, amber-green eyes took note of the gesture, and she stared at him, daring him to make something of it.

He was more concerned about Favian, though, and crouched down in front of him at eye level. "You had a dream about Ithric?"

Favian nodded, tension cording the muscles under Kathrael's hand. At that moment, Andoc limped in from the other room where the three had apparently been sharing a bed, bare-chested, bleary-eyed, and bracing his bad leg with the same walking stick he'd used to disarm Kathrael on the night of her arrival, when she'd threatened Favian with her dagger.

Andoc pulled up a second chair and sat in it. "Favian? You had a vision? Tell us."

Kathrael blinked. A *vision*? Did he mean—

Favian took a deep breath as if steeling himself. "I was in a strange village. I didn't recognize it. Ithric was threatening a man—an oddly dressed man. His clothes were very bright and elaborate. There was a crowd, but they were frightened. They started screaming and running away." He broke off in a hoarse cough, and swallowed hard. Carivel moved to the table and poured him a cup of wine, which he sipped before continuing.

"I couldn't see past the people trying to get away. I was pushing against the crowd, yelling something to Ithric, and trying to get closer. He—"

Favian cut himself off and curled forward as if he would be sick again. Senovo took him by the arms and steadied him, even as Kathrael tightened her grip on his shoulder.

"He… saw me. He looked right at me, and changed. But the man had a knife. He… lifted it to plunge it into Ithric's side, and—" Favian breathed deeply for a moment. "I woke up."

Andoc sat back heavily in his chair, lifting a hand to rub over the lower half of his face. He appeared suddenly pale in the lamplight… almost as pale as Favian. Senovo glanced over his shoulder, and the two exchanged a look.

"He's alive, then," Andoc said.

"So it would appear," Senovo replied softly.

Favian looked between them, confusion twisting his features. "What do you mean, *he's alive*? Someone's going to kill him! We have to find him somehow!"

There was an awkward silence, as Andoc seemed poised to speak, but didn't.

"Tell him," Carivel said, sounding angry. "He deserves to know. Andoc, you should never have agreed to keep it a secret from him. And Senovo and I should never have gone along with it."

TWELVE

"What secret, what are you talking about?" Favian was shaking now, under Kathrael's grip.

Andoc closed his eyes for a brief moment, then met Favian's gaze squarely. "A few months ago, Ithric came to me and asked to be one of my spies in the south. I warned him that it was dangerous, but he said he was tired of wintering in the north, and that there was nothing holding him here. He was going south anyway, and I might as well make use of him—his words, not mine, Favian."

Favian's trembling turned to full-blown shuddering. "And you *agreed* to this?" The words were very nearly a shout.

Andoc was still pale, but he didn't back down from Favian's anger. "I figured that at least if I was paying him to spy for me, he'd be in regular contact. And he'd also have money to live on. Things were fine for a while. We were getting regular updates via the messengers that run back and forth through the port at Llanmeer."

The Chief paused again. "But... a few weeks ago, I stopped getting any news from him at all. The last report had been normal, and then, just... nothing. I was honestly afraid that he was dead, but... well, it seemed needlessly cruel to tell you, when I didn't have any solid information to offer."

Favian shook off her hand and surged to his feet. "You sent a *shape-shifter* to be a spy in *Rhyth*? They *burn* shape-shifters in Rhyth!"

Kathrael froze, her breath catching in her throat.

Andoc got to his feet as well, as did Senovo. "I didn't send him anywhere, Favian. He was going, and he asked, and I agreed. I'm sorry—I know you two had been... whatever you were to each other. But I also know you were barely on speaking terms when he left. He specifically asked me not to tell you where he was headed."

Favian drew breath to say something, but Kathrael beat him to it.

"This *Ithric*—you say he is a shape-shifter?"

Suddenly, she was the center of attention. She felt a flush rise up her neck, and swallowed. "Does he, by chance, take the form of a lion?"

Favian whirled on her. "How do you know that?"

Her heart was pounding in her ribcage at the sudden revelation. "I met a boy who could change into a lion outside of Penth. He was part of a traveling show. They were keeping him in a cage."

"They were *what*?" Favian breathed.

"The two owners were exhibiting him as a tame lion. They also had several other people in the show who were... different, I suppose you'd say. A very short woman and a very tall man. A boy with no arms. They were all virtual prisoners of the two men named Turvick and Laronzo. Your friend, Ithric—he talked me into rescuing a pair of young children who could read minds, and returning them to the village where they'd been kidnapped."

Favian collapsed back into the chair from which he'd risen only moments before. "Ow," he said blankly, presumably when the impact jarred the half-healed scars from his recent castration.

"Well, *shit*," Carivel said. "There can't be that many lion-shifters running around in the south, can there? Did he tell you his name?"

"No," Kathrael said. "He looked like a northerner, though. Shaggy hair, skinny, lots of scars. A bit bent in the head."

"Definitely Ithric, then," Favian said in a heavy tone. He looked back at Andoc. "We have to go rescue him. You *can't* leave him stuck in a cage somewhere in the south, especially now that you know his life is in danger."

"He's not in the south any more," Kathrael interrupted, remembering something else the lion-boy had said.

"He's not?" Favian asked. "How could you know?"

She shook her head. "The men who ran the traveling show were planning on going north by sea, to one of the western ports. They thought it would be safer than staying in the south, and they were probably right."

"Perhaps there is method to Ithric's madness," Senovo murmured.

Andoc looked at him sharply. "You think he's trying to get back to Draebard?"

"He did say that he needed to get north. He wouldn't let me help him escape when I freed the children," said Kathrael.

"We have to find him. Rescue him," Favian said, addressing Andoc again. "We know where he is. The place I saw in my dream—it, well, it might have been a western port village. We could ask around. People would remember a traveling show like that!"

"Favian," Andoc said, his voice regretful. "I can't send an armed party into unaffiliated villages and start demanding things. The tribes in the west want nothing to do with Draebard and its allies these days. If we go rattling our swords within their territories, they're likely to start uniting against us, and that's the last thing the north needs right now."

"Then don't send an armed party! Send—I don't know—send a group from the temple!" Favian was leaning forward now, his voice growing increasingly desperate.

Senovo crossed his arms. "And would you count yourself among such a group, Favian? You do realize, if your dream is a true vision, then Ithric isn't in danger *until you see him*. Your own presence is part of the very sequence of events you wish to thwart."

Favian sank back, covering his face with one hand as he tried to regain his composure. "It will be different this time. This time, I know exactly what's coming. I know exactly what to *avoid*."

Kathrael could keep silent no longer. "Wait. You're a *seer*, Favian? You… dream the future?"

Favian let out a noise that could almost have been laughter, were it not so laced with bitterness. "I dreamed *you*, the night you snuck into my room with a knife and demanded to see Senovo. I dreamed you *years* ago."

Kathrael could barely take in this new disclosure, so close on the heels of the revelation about the lion-boy she'd met near Penth.

Favian shrugged. "I did tell you that I spoke with more authority than most people on the subject of prophesy," he said, the same bitterness still heavy in his words.

"I suppose you did, at that," she said faintly.

Andoc shifted, drawing their attention. "Favian, we'll have to speak with the elders about your dream, and what, if anything, is to be done about it. Senovo's right, though. The fact the he was whole and safe when you saw him in the dream means that we have time to decide what to do."

"You don't know that," Favian shot back. "We have no idea what's happening to him!"

"Nevertheless, I won't act rashly on this," Andoc said, and it was clear from his tone that he considered the matter closed. "Not even for Ithric, Favian. Give me a day or two. Now, are you all right? You looked ready to collapse when you came in here earlier."

"I'm fine now," Favian said in a tight voice. "It's not me you should be worrying about."

With that, he rose to his feet again, shaking off Kathrael's hand when she moved to help him.

"Favian—" Carivel said, but he was already opening the door and stalking out.

With nothing else to do, Kathrael followed him, throwing a nervous glance over her shoulder at his three guardians. Carivel was frowning. Andoc was scrubbing his hand over his face. But the Wolf Patron met her look with one of his own, and Kathrael knew he was urging her to stay with Favian and keep an eye on him.

She turned and hurried from the room.

Unfortunately, she had been paying more attention to keeping Favian upright than memorizing their route on the wavering journey from his room to his mentor's. It took a couple of wrong turnings before she was able to successfully retrace their steps. When she caught up with Favian back at his room, it was to find him scrubbing away at the puddle of sick next to his bed. He dipped a rag in a bucket of water and rubbed it back and forth over the flagstones with short, angry movements, not looking up at her arrival.

"Is the Chief wrong about your friend being safe?" she asked, leaning a shoulder against the heavy wood of the doorframe and crossing her arms over her chest.

"He's not my friend," Favian said, biting off each word like it had personally offended him.

Kathrael raised a skeptical eyebrow, but he couldn't see it from where he was crouched, cleaning up his mess. "That doesn't really answer my question."

Favian threw the rag in the bucket with a sharp flick of his wrist. "I don't *know*, all right? Just because he was alive and not obviously injured in the dream doesn't mean that they aren't starving him, or torturing him, or—"

With a pang, she remembered the sound of wood hitting flesh as the lion distracted its captors so Kathrael and the twins could get away unnoticed. There was no point in relating that to Favian, though—not now. "They weren't doing any of those things when I spoke with him," she said, which was technically true.

Favian flopped down on a clean part of the floor, leaning his head back against the edge of the bed and staring up at the rafters.

"If he's not your friend, who is Ithric to you?" she asked.

"No one. He's no one to me." Favian was still burning holes in the ceiling with his gaze. "He's an infuriating prat without an ounce of good sense or self-preservation."

"Then I imagine he'll still be an infuriating prat in a day or two, when your Chief Andoc has had a chance to speak to the village elders. Can you get back to sleep?"

Favian shrugged and rolled his head upright. "No point," he said with a sigh. "It's almost dawn. I should finish cleaning up this mess, and then maybe I'll go start chopping up vegetables for Brother Feldes. I imagine everyone else will be dragging this morning after the festival last night."

"All right," she said, and gestured imperiously for a clean rag. "I'll help you, in that case."

⚜

The following day had a vaguely dreamlike quality. At mid-morning, the children and their chaperones trooped back into the village. Other than that, Draebard was quiet, with everyone who could do so sleeping off their hangovers. Kathrael was tired, but she was also determined not to sleep another day away and end up lying awake at night.

She helped Favian for a while, and met his sister Frella when she returned. The young girl was bold and intelligent for her age. She stared at Kathrael fearlessly for a moment, and it seemed she was on the cusp of asking about her scarred face. Instead, though, her searching gaze turned to her brother.

"Something happened to you," she said. "Did you dream?"

"Yes," Favian said.

"Bad?" Frella asked.

"Bad for Ithric," her brother replied.

Her face twisted into a frown. "Oh. You're going to try to stop it, aren't you?"

"Maybe."

Frella looked at him for a long time, and nodded as if resigned.

After witnessing the odd, abbreviated conversation between the siblings, Kathrael went out to wash her clothes in the river. Favian, meanwhile, was called away to attend to the morning devotions. At midday, he reappeared and took her to the horse pens, of all places. Kathrael had never so much as touched a horse before. She was a bit shocked to find that the northerners let girls as well as boys care for the animals.

"Carivel's doing, mostly," Favian explained. "She'd already inherited the position of Horse Master while everyone still thought she was a man. When her secret came out, she just sort of... stayed there. Though there are other tribes where women do men's jobs. The Mereni even have a female Chief and a female First Warrior. Meren is only a couple of days east of here, and our tribes are close allies."

"Your tribe is strange, priest-boy," she said, looking around at the powerful animals with equal amounts of admiration and trepidation. "But... I think I like it."

Favian smiled, though he was still pale and distracted. "Here. Let me introduce you to the last colt I ever trained before I left the horse pens to become an acolyte in the temple. I still like to come out here and visit him when I need to clear my mind."

Unlike the rest of the village, the horse pens were bustling with people. "The animals need to be fed and cared for, whether there was a festival or not," Favian explained.

A girl who had been shoveling manure in one of the corrals looked up as they passed and waved; Kathrael recognized Limdya, and gave a tentative wave in return. Ahead, a smaller pen held a handful of horses kept for use during the day, while the others were turned out to graze on the rolling pastures north and west of the village. Her attention was caught by two creamy white animals standing nose to tail in one corner, contentedly swishing flies from each other's faces.

Favian whistled, soft and low. The shorter of the two horses immediately pricked his ears toward the sound and gave a low nicker.

"That's Ozias and Audris," Favian said. "They're brothers. The shorter one was born the morning after Alyrion soldiers attacked the village during the night and massacred the priests in the temple. One bright spot in a terribly dark day, I suppose you could say."

The horse had wandered over to meet them at the fence as Favian spoke. He nudged the young priest with his nose before turning to sniff at Kathrael, who took a nervous step back.

"He's so big," she said.

"He's far from the largest horse in the herd," Favian told her. "Don't yield your personal space to him like that. Horses are prey animals. It's easy enough to get them to move away." He made a small waving motion with his hand to demonstrate, and the white horse moved back obligingly. "Come here and stretch out your hand, palm down. Let him sniff it and greet you like he would another horse."

Kathrael stepped back up to the fence and reached over it. The horse arched his neck and snuffled at the backs of her fingers. Its breath tickled warm and damp over her skin as she watched in fascination.

"He's beautiful," she breathed. The other white horse joined them to see what its brother found so interesting. "They both are."

"Cream-colored horses are rare. These belonged to the old chief, Volya, but they passed to Andoc after he died. They're trained for battle as a chariot team, though you can also ride them, obviously."

"Maybe *you* can ride them," Kathrael said as the second horse took its turn sniffing her hand. "The closest I've ever come to riding is sitting on the back of a melon cart pulled by an ancient donkey."

Favian smiled. "I'll teach you someday, if you like. Or Carivel will. She's far better than I am, in any case."

Before she could protest that Carivel probably had no interest in teaching her anything after she'd threatened both Favian and Senovo with a knife, a small disturbance in the herd drew her attention. A short black and white horse with a barrel-shaped body and a ridiculously extravagant mane came trotting toward the white horses, shaking its head and pinning its ears flat against its blocky skull.

The creamy animals whirled and fled the scene as if their tails were on fire, retreating to the far side of the pen.

The conqueror tossed his head up and down once in victory and stretched it over the top rail of the fence, only to let out a terrific sneeze that sent a fine mist of snot over both Favian and Kathrael.

Favian sighed. "Hello to you, too, troublemaker. Kathrael, meet Kekenu — Carivel's horse."

Kathrael looked from the little horse, to Favian's long-suffering expression, and back again, before bursting out into peals of laughter.

That evening, Favian was called away to the village meeting house, where Kathrael expected he was being questioned by the elders about the details of his dream. The deep-eyed priest, Eiridan, had invited her earlier to dine with him and continue their discussion from the previous evening. Favian had originally intended to join them, but she decided there was no reason not to go on her own, since he was needed elsewhere.

Brother Eiridan met her in the large hall housing the altar to Utarr and Naloth. He ushered her into a cozy room just off the annex, where bowls of soup and plates of flatbread awaited them. Kathrael wasn't sure she would ever get used to the ready supply of hearty, delicious food. Despite the fact that she had eaten three meals already today, her stomach gurgled and growled in anticipation. She had to force herself not to fall on the food like a scavenger attacking a fresh carcass.

Eiridan merely poured her a goblet of wine, and offered a simple blessing before devoting himself to his own meal. Kathrael waited until he had taken the first mouthful and followed suit, trying not to slurp her soup.

Perhaps in deference to her obvious single-mindedness around food, the priest did not attempt to keep up a conversation as they ate. She was surprised to find that the silence was surprisingly comfortable. When she was finished, her stomach full to bursting and a feeling of warm drowsiness sliding over her like a warm blanket, Eiridan sat back in his chair and laced his fingers together over his round belly.

"Well, I believe Brother Feldes has outdone himself tonight. That was a truly excellent meal," he said in his mild, oddly accented voice.

Kathrael gave him a hesitant smile. "Yes. I still have to pinch myself whenever someone just offers me food like that. I've never eaten as well as I have since I arrived here."

Eiridan nodded. "I gather food was difficult to come by when you were in Rhyth, and on your journey over the mountains."

The smile twisted bitterly, and Kathrael looked down. "I used to make money by selling my body, but I'm afraid there wasn't much demand for a prostitute with a ruined face. Times were hard. My friend Vesh did what he could to feed both of us, but in the end, desperation made him careless and he lost his life for it."

"That is a true tragedy," the priest said sadly. "Your friend Vesh is one of the spirits who speaks to you, I take it?"

"Yes. He was the first, though he is not the loudest." A faint cry, as if from a restless babe, pricked at the edge of Kathrael's hearing.

She looked up again to find Eiridan still regarding her solemnly. "Please feel free to ignore any of my questions that you find too painful or intrusive," he said, "but I confess, I find your situation very interesting. The gods teach us that the human spirit returns to the sky from whence it came on the smoke of the funeral pyre, even as the body returns to the earth as ashes. Can I assume... that your noble friend did not receive a proper funeral after his death?"

The piercing stab in her chest took Kathrael by surprise, and she had to pause for a moment to breathe. "No," she said, once the pain had subsided to the more familiar dull ache. "He was stoned to death by a mob from the cult of Deimok. They... paraded his corpse through the streets. I don't know what they did to him... to *it*... afterward. I was too afraid to follow them back into the heart of the city."

"Understandably so," Eiridan said, his tone grave, but devoid of either pity or censure. "One wonders if his spirit fled to you for safe haven after it parted from his body. He must have great trust in you to give you that most vital part of himself, if that is the case."

The ache grew deeper. "If so, it was misplaced trust. It was looking after me that got him killed in the first place."

"I can't help disagreeing with your assessment," said Eiridan, leaning forward now to regard her. "Have you not safeguarded his spirit in the weeks since his death? Did you not undertake a journey of great difficulty to come to a place where we might be able to help him find peace?"

"I didn't come here because of Vesh," she said, only to catch her breath as the rest of Eiridan's words settled in her awareness. "Wait. You think you can free my spirits and help them find peace? Really?"

"I don't know. I'm afraid such a situation has never arisen before within my experience. However, the members of the temple of Draebard will try to help you in any way we can. And if we fail, there are other more experienced priests in neighboring villages with whom we can speak. Now, tell me, do the other spirits share the same circumstances? Violent death? Lack of a funeral?"

Kathrael steeled herself to think about the others. "Some do," she said in a faint tone. "Some I'm not sure about. My mother. My sister—she disappeared. I don't know what happened to either of them. But... the worst is—" Her voice cracked, and she broke off, not having intended to speak of it in the first place.

Eiridan frowned. "Go on, please—if you can. I wish only to understand, and to help."

"My baby," she whispered after a long moment of indecision.

The priest breathed out slowly. "The spirits of lost children always haunt their parents, Kathrael. *Always.*"

Tears rose up without warning and burned their way down her unscarred cheek. She curled into herself, chest hitching silently in time with the plaintive cries of an infant that only she could hear. Soft fingers pressed a clean cloth into her hand, and Eiridan perched himself on the edge of the table nearby. Not touching. Just sitting with her quietly as she cried.

Eventually, she regained enough control of herself to speak. "I'm not a parent. I was thirteen when I first sold my body to a man. Barely fourteen when I fell pregnant. I was small. Thin, even then. My belly was just beginning to swell when I woke up one morning with blood soaking my thighs. One of the other women had some experience as a midwife. I think she felt sorry for me—she cared for me and kept me alive, but my..." She swallowed hard. "... my baby girl was dead. The miscarriage damaged me inside, the woman told me afterward, and I guess she was right. I never became pregnant again."

"Fourteen is very young to fall pregnant. You were still a child yourself."

She made a dismissive noise, and wiped at her face with the cloth in disgust. "I hadn't been a child for years."

"Perhaps not in spirit," Eiridan allowed. "But in body, you were."

She shrugged a shoulder angrily, and he let the silence stretch.

"She cries at night sometimes," Kathrael whispered after the pause grew too heavy. "Inconsolably."

"And nothing is more painful to a mother than her child's cries," Eiridan offered in a quiet voice.

Tears threatened again, but she swallowed them back. "I told you, I'm not a mother!"

"I think, in your heart, that you are." Eiridan stood and returned to his chair on the other side of the low table, giving her space. "I wonder, Kathrael… does your unborn child cling to you, or do you cling to her?"

She glared at him. "Why would I cling to this pain?"

"Why, indeed?" he replied unhelpfully.

"You said you'd help me," she reminded him. "You said you'd help my spirits find peace."

"Yes," Eiridan replied. "And to that end, I would like to consult with the other priests on the matter, but I will need your permission to do so."

Her heart froze for a moment. "Not the Wolf Patron."

A furrow appeared between Eiridan's brows, but then his expression smoothed and he nodded. "The others, though?"

She hesitated, and nodded her assent.

Eiridan dipped his chin in acknowledgement. "Thank you. For now, I will offer a thought of my own. From what I have been able to learn about cases like yours, physical weakness and illness lower the veil between this world and the spirit realm. As the body grows closer to death, it becomes easier to communicate with the other side. It is very possible that as you regain your strength and health, that veil will rise again on its own. Tell me, have the voices changed at all or grown less frequent since you've started to recover physically?"

Kathrael thought back carefully over the last few days. "Except for my baby, they aren't as angry or frightened as they were when I was traveling. In the mountains, it was as if my desperation was feeding theirs, and vice versa. But since I started feeling stronger, I suppose it's true that I don't hear them as often, and that they are calmer."

"That is encouraging," said Eiridan. "I'll speak to the others and see if they have any further ideas to offer. In the mean time, don't hesitate to come to either Favian or myself if you need anything."

She nodded, but didn't rise. He took his leave and closed the door behind him to give her privacy. She sat there for a very long time, staring at the beaten metal sculpture hanging on the far wall, and thinking.

Favian left the meeting that night as frustrated as when he'd arrived. The elders listened carefully to his recounting of the dream, asked several pertinent questions about it, and then dismissed him without another word. He knew they'd be up until the small hours, debating things seemingly for the sole purpose of listening to the sound of their own voices. He *knew* they'd *hem* and *haw* and end up doing absolutely nothing, because the gods forbid they should ever just *act* without first dissecting every single aspect of the situation until they managed to convince themselves that action was unnecessary.

Unsure what else to do to distract himself, Favian poked his head into his room just long enough to confirm that Frella was there, and peacefully asleep. Then, he went further down the hall to check on Kathrael.

The door was open, and a candle burned inside. Unlike his sister, Kathrael was awake, seated on the bed with her knees curled up to her chest and her arms wrapped around them. She had been staring at the candle flame as if attempting to find meaning within it, but she looked up as Favian lifted a hand to rest against the rough wood of the doorframe.

"How did your meeting go?" she asked.

"About like I expected it would," Favian said, knowing his voice sounded tired and bitter. "How did *your* meeting go?"

She lifted her shoulders in a shrug and let them drop, her gaze turning back to the candle.

Favian sighed. "Did Brother Eiridan do that thing where he assures you he just wants to discuss something with you because he finds it such an interesting subject, and then twenty minutes later you realize that you're telling him about your deepest, darkest secrets while blubbering like an infant? Because I've always hated that trick."

Kathrael's expression twisted in pain, and a sob jerked its way free of her chest as she hid her face against her knees.

Favian's brows drew together in sympathy. "I guess that's a *yes*, then."

Something about her demeanor had changed in the last day or two. Favian couldn't have put his finger on it, exactly, but he knew what to do now, nonetheless. Without a word, he climbed onto the bed, crossing to sit on the side closest to the wall with his back leaning against the headboard, so she could move away from him easily if she needed to.

She was still crying. He put an arm around her shoulders and eased her out of her tightly curled ball to rest next to him. She flinched in surprise at his touch, and froze for a moment. Just as he once would have done with a frightened horse, Favian stayed still and unthreatening, letting her decide what to do. He wasn't surprised, however, when she gave in with a shudder of trembling muscles and let him settle her against his side.

In many ways, Favian knew he had been lucky. Though his life had included more than its fair share of tragedy, he had never lacked for people to love and comfort him when he was in need. He could barely imagine facing such things with no one there to help.

"I'm here," he said. "You're not alone with your spirits anymore, Kathrael."

She shuddered again and dragged her breathing under control, still not looking at him. "We talked about my baby," she said in a voice so low it was barely audible.

"You had a child?" Favian asked.

"No. No, I didn't. I *almost* had a child. But I didn't, and now I can never have children again."

He nodded his understanding. "My mother died giving birth to Frella. I never understood why the gods seem bent on making what should be a happy occurrence into a tragedy so often."

"I wouldn't have been able to support her even if she'd lived," Kathrael said in a tone of defeat. "She just would have died a bit later, is all."

A terrible thought hit him. "Is she one of the voices that haunt you?"

Kathrael nodded against his shoulder. "She... cries sometimes. At night. She's always hungry, or scared, and I can't do anything to fix it, because she's dead."

Favian made a small noise of pain and tightened his arm. "Oh, Kathrael."

"I think I could live with the others," she continued. "But when she wakes me in the middle of the night, sometimes I just want to die."

Favian swallowed the lump of emotion that tried to clog his throat. He reached up with his free hand to tip Kathrael's chin toward him—to make her meet his eyes—and was a bit surprised when she let him.

"When that happens, you come and get someone, you understand?" he said, willing her to accept the words. "You wake me, or Eiridan, or anyone else in the temple for that matter. Kathrael—promise me. Don't face that pain alone. Not here. Not now, when there are people to help."

"Help how?" she asked. "What can you or anyone else do to quiet my dead baby?"

"I don't know. Maybe there's something, or maybe there's nothing. But we can at least be there, with you."

She was silent, digesting this.

"Do you promise?" he asked again.

She paused and spoke slowly, as if feeling the words out. "If... I think your presence will help, I will come and wake you, Favian."

It wasn't exactly a heartfelt vow, and he noticed she didn't say anything about seeking help from the others. That might become a problem in the next few days, but he suspected it was about the best he could hope for from her right now.

He nodded his understanding. "Good."

They sat silently for a long time, lost in their own thoughts. Favian couldn't help wondering about the feeling of rightness as he held her against his side. She fit in a way he would never have expected—filled a gap he hadn't realized was there. How had a woman who greeted him with a knife against his jugular and a threat against the man he loved like a father become so important to him in the space of two short weeks?

He was still pondering the question when exhaustion from the dream last night and the emotion of the day dragged him down into sleep.

⁓ ♔ ⁓

Kathrael jerked awake to the sound of a small throat being cleared. It was light outside—after a fashion, at least. The sort of murky gray light that heralded a cloudy dawn in the offing. Her neck ached—the result, apparently, of having slept sitting up for the entire night. Of having slept—the entire night—while leaning against Favian's side.

Favian's sister was regarding her steadily from beside the bed. Kathrael flushed without knowing exactly why, and nudged Favian's ribs with her elbow. He snorted awake and groaned, his hand flying to his own neck.

"Ugh," he said. "What… what time is it?"

"A little bit before Feldes or one of the others comes looking for you, I imagine," Frella said, and Kathrael couldn't help being impressed by her ready command of irony at such a young age.

"Oh," Favian said, and wiped a hand over his face. Kathrael sheepishly sat up and let him have his arm back. He shook it out to get the blood flowing and gave her a wan smile in return.

Frella was still watching the two of them with her arms crossed in front of her—a tiny princess with rumpled bed-hair. "What did the elders say last night, Favian? Are you going to go and rescue Ithric?"

"They didn't say anything," he replied, sounding tired. "And… maybe."

"Can I come with you, if you do?"

"*No*," Favian said immediately.

She frowned. "You're *not* going alone." It wasn't a question.

"No one's going anywhere, alone or otherwise, until the elders make their decision," said Favian.

Frella's piercing gaze flicked back to Kathrael. "*You*. You'll help make sure he doesn't do anything stupid, yes?"

"*Frella*." Favian said reproachfully, before Kathrael could fashion a response with her groggy wits. "Stop being rude. I'll be along in a minute, all right?"

The girl looked rebellious, but she did leave to give them a moment of privacy.

"Sorry about that," Favian said.

Kathrael stretched, feeling her spine crack and pop. "Don't be. She's your sister. She's just worried about you. About the lion-boy, too, it sounds like."

For some reason, that last part brought a faint flush to Favian's cheeks. "Yes, well," he said, not sounding thrilled. "She always did like him. Kindred spirits, I suppose."

A moment later, the quiet rustling of robes heralded a second visitor. Kathrael looked up to find the Wolf Patron darkening her door, though his attention seemed to be for Favian alone.

"Favian," he said. "Andoc wishes to speak with you."

Kathrael felt Favian tense beside her.

"Of course," he said, and clambered somewhat awkwardly off the bed. Before he left, he gave her a searching look. "Will you be all right?"

She nodded. "Go on, priest-boy. Don't leave your Chief waiting. I hope you receive the news you seek."

"Thanks," he said. "Don't stay cooped up in here by yourself today, Kathrael. I'll see you when I can."

"*Go*," she prodded. "Don't worry about me, I'll be fine." With a faint jolt, she realized that she actually meant the words. Favian was already leaving, but when she looked to the doorway, the Wolf Patron was once again regarding her with that odd, speaking look. He held her gaze for a moment before turning to follow Favian. As before, the silent exchange left her off-balance and restless in her own skin.

He sees *you*, Vesh whispered unhelpfully. *They all do, here.*

She shook off the strange feeling and swung her feet off the bed. There was nothing stopping her from curling up to sleep some more, but the prospect was not as appealing as she might have expected. She was, in fact, surprisingly rested after the night spent leaning on Favian's shoulder. No dreams or voices had disturbed her — it had been as if she'd closed her eyes, and opened them a mere moment later, but the whole night had passed peacefully.

After a bit of thought, she rose and washed with the bowl of water on the bedside table. Perhaps Priest Feldes would appreciate an additional pair of hands in the kitchens again this morning.

The fat, fussy priest welcomed Kathrael with enthusiasm and set her to stirring batter for the brown, fruit-filled cakes he was planning on serving that morning.

"Brother Eiridan spoke with me about your unseen voices," he said casually, once the preparations for breakfast were in hand.

Her expression must have soured on hearing Eiridan's name, because Feldes immediately looked sympathetic. "Ah. I can see you have been a victim of our esteemed brother's belief that wounds of the spirit must be lanced in a similar manner to wounds of the body, in order to prevent festering. He did mention that you'd become rather upset during your discussion."

"He shouldn't have tricked me into talking to him," she muttered, anger warring with embarrassment.

"I fear you do him a disservice, my dear. That's the thing, you see—he truly is interested. Fascinated, in fact. You should have heard him going on about the metaphysical implications of lost spirits clinging to a loved one. I could barely shut him up long enough to get a word in edgewise."

She glanced up, curious despite herself. "And did you come up with a way to quiet them?" she asked.

"I'm afraid not, child. That said, Brother Eiridan is planning a journey back to our old village to speak with the High Priest there. I gather you do not wish to include our own High Priest in your confidence, which is certainly your right. While Senovo is undeniably a powerful man, at the end of the day, he is also a young one. High Priest Jyrrel is more experienced, and has seen much in his life. He may well have fresh wisdom to offer us."

Her irritation with Priest Eiridan faded considerably upon hearing how much trouble he was putting himself to on her behalf. "I'm… not used to people going to such effort for me," she said. "Or any effort at all, to be perfectly honest."

Feldes only smiled. "I told you—he's interested. He can also become a bit, shall we say, *single-minded* about things on occasion. Ask him sometime about his studies into the written symbols the Alyrions and Rhytheeri use to communicate information without a messenger. Or don't, unless you want to be treated to an hour's lecture on the subject."

"I've seen those symbols," she said in mild surprise. "I only learned a handful of them, though."

"Good gracious. In that case, I'd definitely advise you to steer clear of the subject unless you have a spare week or two to devote to answering Eiridan's questions."

Suddenly and without warning, the emptiness that was her life now nearly overwhelmed her. She no longer had any goals to achieve. No mountains to cross, no fantasies of bloody revenge to give her strength when her body threatened to fail. Who *was* she now? And... who had she been before?

Some of this must have showed on her face, because Feldes frowned. "Are you all right, my dear?"

"Yes," she said on a faint quaver. "Sorry. It just occurred to me that should Priest Eiridan wish to question me for two weeks about Rhytheeri symbols, I... really have nothing more pressing to do with my time."

Feldes nodded his understanding. "I see. Well, for what it's worth, you are free now to make whatever new goals and plans you choose. And I would suggest doing so promptly, if only so you *will* have a good excuse to avoid his questions on the subject. Right now, however, you can help me divide up this batter and get it in the ovens."

It was evening before Kathrael saw Favian again. She'd spent the day finding odds and ends to keep herself busy, even screwing up her courage to take the leftover fruit cakes out to the apprentices at the horse pens. Limdya greeted her cheerfully and helped her distribute them, and Dalon gave her a friendly nod from across the yard where he was instructing a young boy about something involving a mass of tangled leather harness straps.

To her surprise, the boyish Horse Mistress herself stopped Kathrael as she was preparing to leave and return to the temple. She tensed, well aware that Carivel was still less than pleased with Kathrael's grief-fueled plan to get revenge on High Priest Senovo—not to mention her willingness to go through Favian to do so.

As it turned out, it was the latter person that Carivel was interested in.

"Have you seen Favian?" she asked, and up close, Kathrael could see that the crease in her brow stemmed not from anger, but from worry.

"Not since this morning," Kathrael said warily. "Why?"

"I need to talk to him, and he's been avoiding me. He is — unfortunately — quite skilled in avoidance when he wants to be." The worried frown grew deeper.

"Did the Chief have bad news for him this morning, then?" Kathrael asked.

Carivel seemed unsurprised that she knew of Favian's meeting with Andoc. Perhaps the Wolf Patron had told her of finding Favian in Kathrael's room. "He had news that Favian didn't want to hear, certainly."

She felt a twinge of anger on Favian's behalf warm her belly. "The elders will not act to help his friend?"

"They aren't friends. But, no, the elders won't sanction anything that might ruffle feathers in the west." Carivel took a deep breath and let it out. "They plan to wait and see if Ithric can get free on his own, or if this traveling show you described will come within the territory of Draebard and its allies."

"Favian didn't take it well," Kathrael guessed.

"To put it mildly, yeah." She ran a hand through her close-cropped hair. "So if you see him, tell him I need to speak with him, all right?"

"I'll tell him."

"Thanks," Carivel said, her lips twisting into something that tried to be a smile, and failed.

But Favian was conspicuously absent that afternoon, and when she finally did see him, it was because he found her, not the other way around. She was taking a bucket of scraps from the evening meal outside to the feed the chickens when Favian appeared from the shadows.

"I need you to relay a message to Frella for me," he said without preamble.

"What kind of message?" she asked.

"Tell her I had to leave, and that I'll be back as soon as I can. But don't tell her until tomorrow."

"You're going after him." She didn't bother to phrase it as a question.

"I don't have a *choice*. No one else will do anything!" Favian pressed his hands under his armpits, visibly reining in his need to *act*. "Will you give Frella the message?"

Something clicked inside of Kathrael's mind, settling into place with a heavy sense of utter rightness. "Sorry, priest-boy. I'm afraid I can't."

He looked surprised. Hurt, even. "Why not?"

"Because," Kathrael said, "I'm going with you."

THIRTEEN

Favian's expression of betrayal morphed back into one of surprise. "It... might be dangerous," he said after a momentary pause. "I probably shouldn't let you come. And for that matter... why would you even offer? You don't owe me anything."

She raised an eyebrow and drew herself up to her admittedly not-very-impressive height. "First, priest-boy, let's get something straight. You don't *let* me come along. I choose to come with you, and then I do it. End of story. Second, you helped me when you had every reason not to. And the lion-boy helped children he barely knew get to freedom, when he could have asked for his own freedom instead. Why should I *not* try to help you both in return?"

"It will be a difficult journey," said Favian, still obviously off-balance. The look she gave him took only a few seconds to penetrate, and he blushed. "Right. Sorry. That was a bit stupid, wasn't it."

"A bit," she allowed dryly, thinking of hunger and thirst and blisters bleeding on her feet. "You're forgiven, though. Now, tell me you at least have a plan?"

He nodded. "I have most of what we'll need gathered together and hidden in the woods behind the temple. You should see about getting some more food from the kitchens, though—I only packed for one. I'll, um, I'll see if my friend Lundis will relay the message to Frella in the morning, so she knows what's happening."

"She would figure it out, regardless, you know. She's smart, your sister."

"Yes, well. I'd feel better leaving her the message anyway." Favian took a deep breath and let it out. A faint puff of steam formed in front of his face and dissipated almost immediately—the first hint of autumn had cooled the evening air to a slight nip. "Beyond that," he continued, "we just need to wait until she's asleep and sneak out to the horse pens. There's usually a guard posted at night, but they all know me. I'll tell them neither of us could sleep and we wanted to come out and calm our minds for a few minutes."

"You want me to ride a horse?" Kathrael asked, a feeling of trepidation creeping over her for the first time.

"Well... I'd planned to take two horses, so Ithric could ride back," Favian said. "That's probably still the best plan—you can ride double with me since you don't have any experience. The horses can handle it—you barely weigh anything."

Kathrael was still nervous about this aspect of the scheme, but she could hardly back out now. Besides, there *was* something rather appealing about the idea of sitting on top of one of the great beasts' backs. Especially if someone else was controlling it.

"All right," she allowed. "I suppose I can manage that." A new thought came to her. "What about your—" she gestured toward his crotch. "You know. Won't riding be painful?"

"Probably," Favian said with a grimace. "Walking will take too long, though, and a wagon would be just as uncomfortable—assuming I could even sneak a wagon out of town successfully, which is doubtful."

She shrugged. "If you say so. You'll come and get me when it's time, then?"

"If you're still certain you want to do this, yes."

"I'm certain." She suddenly remembered her visit to the horse pens earlier in the day. "Oh! I almost forgot. The Horse Mistress was looking for you. She wanted to talk to you."

Favian's expression snapped closed. "Yeah. Not happening."

"Your decision, priest-boy," she said. "I'm just relaying the message."

"If she wanted to say something, it would have been more useful for her to say it during the meeting with the elders," he said tightly, before visibly forcing himself to relax. "Frella can pass on my message to the others—including Carivel—in the morning."

"Fine," Kathrael said. "I'll get us some more food and wait for you in my room. Don't worry, we'll find your lost shape-shifter, Favian."

He tried for a smile, though it didn't reach his eyes. "Thank you, Kathrael. I'll see you later tonight. Be ready."

It was very late when Favian finally crept into Kathrael's room. She was propped up in bed, half-dozing while she waited for him. Nevertheless, the instant she heard the swish of his robes, she was completely alert. The prospect of having a *purpose* again was intoxicating—surprisingly so.

The whispers of half-heard voices that had floated around the dark recesses of the room as she napped dissipated like mist in the sunlight, and she swung her feet down to rest on the floor. She was dressed in the traveling clothes Shayla had found for her. Someone at the temple had repaired the sole of her left boot. Her satchel was full of food; her dagger nestled at her waist.

She was ready.

"Sorry to be so long," Favian said in a low voice. "Frella got it into her head to stay up and *make sure I didn't do anything foolish*, as she put it. It took forever for her to finally drift off."

"She's going to be furious with you," Kathrael observed.

"Yes," Favian agreed. "She is. Fortunately, she's my sister, so she's pretty much obligated to forgive me. Especially when we bring Ithric back with us."

Kathrael was unavoidably reminded of her own sister heading off to the city with promises of bringing food and money back when she returned.

Do you forgive me, little sister? Elarra whispered from the shadows.

I don't know, she thought. Aloud, she held her peace.

They snuck out through a back entrance, thereby avoiding the sleepy acolyte posted at the main door to help anyone who had need of the priests during the night. The air was crisp and chill, a prelude of things to come. The waning moon played hide and seek in the clouds, intermittently illuminating their surroundings with pale silver light. Even so, Kathrael kept a hand on Favian's arm to help guide her steps. Having a blind eye had reduced her night vision considerably, whereas Favian was so familiar with the village that he moved with as much confidence as if it had been daylight.

The sound and smell of many large animals gathered in one place heralded their arrival at the horse pens.

Favian paused, looking around. "There's no guard tonight. That's strange."

Kathrael felt a prickle of unease, but shrugged it off. "Maybe he just went off for a piss or something."

"Maybe," Favian said, sounding unconvinced. "Well, I guess we'd better take advantage of it, whatever the case. Come on. We'll need saddles and bridles from the tack shed."

He led her to a large structure with a simple shed-roof, situated not far from the corrals where the horses milled about restlessly in the dark. The door creaked on iron hinges as he pulled it open, and they both froze when a familiar voice from inside said, "It's about bloody time. I expected you hours ago, you know."

Sparks flew as the unseen speaker struck a flint, and a moment later, a hanging lamp flared to life, revealing Carivel. She and Favian stared at each other for a long moment.

"Well, shit," Favian said, breaking the awkward silence.

"Does Senovo know you still curse like that, *Novice Favian*?" Carivel asked in a dry tone, before her attention caught and held on Kathrael.

"Probably." Favian sounded tired. "He knows most things, in my experience."

"Are you here to stop us, Horse Mistress?" Kathrael asked, tilting her chin up to level a glare at Carivel. "Everyone has gone to great lengths to assure me that I'm not a prisoner here. I assume the same can be said of Favian."

The twitch of Carivel's lips suggested an emotion somewhere between irritation and amusement. Her attention turned to Favian, and it was to him that she directed her reply. "If I were here to stop you, I probably wouldn't have sent away the guard. I also wouldn't have gone to the trouble of saddling Kekenu, Audris, and Ozias while I waited."

"You... what?" Favian asked, looking lost.

Carivel huffed in annoyance. "I was planning on coming with you, you clod. It's not as if we were going to let you go off alone."

"*We?*" Favian echoed, still very obviously lagging several steps behind in the conversation.

Carivel rolled her eyes and made a low noise of disgust. "Yes, *we*. You think the others didn't know to expect this?" Her gaze flicked back to Kathrael, who was watching her warily. "I'll admit, however, that we didn't take *you* into account. Why are you here, Kathrael?"

In general, Kathrael appreciated the northerners' frankness, but for some reason the question still rankled. "I'm going with him, of course. The lion-boy deserves better than your village elders' abandonment."

Carivel's expression softened incrementally. "Yes. Yes, he does. That said, no one wants to see this thing turn into a diplomatic incident that spawns some messy intertribal conflict."

"Which is why you shouldn't go, Carivel," Favian said, having evidently caught up with the two of them once more. "You're known. I'm not."

"I am actually capable of pretending to be someone else for a week or two, Favian," Carivel pointed out.

"After riding in on a loudly colored black and white pinto, with Andoc's two white stallions in tow?" Favian shot back. He frowned suddenly. "Why did you choose them, anyway? I was going to borrow a couple of nondescript bays or chestnuts."

"Because they would make it much easier for Andoc and Senovo to find us if something went wrong," Carivel said.

"Favian's right about one thing, though," Kathrael interrupted. "If you are known to these other tribes, and you're so worried about provoking a *diplomatic incident*, then you shouldn't come. He isn't going alone. I'll be with him. Nobody in the north knows me. I'm not anyone special."

Carivel's eyes burned into her for a long, uncomfortable moment.

"You came all the way here from Rhyth on foot, is that right? By yourself?" she asked eventually.

"I rode for one day and part of another on the back of a donkey cart. Other than that, yes."

"And you managed to complete that kind of a journey without proper supplies?"

"When I started out, I didn't even have shoes."

The Horse Mistress's gaze drilled into her for another few heartbeats. "And why should I trust you alone with Favian after what you tried to do to him?"

Kathrael willed down the flush that was threatening to rise to her face. "Because *he* does. And you trust *him*."

"Let the two of us go, Carivel," Favian said earnestly. "We'll find Ithric and bring him back."

Carivel let out a slow breath through her teeth. "Favian... I understand why you have to go. I know you *have* to see the contents of your dream in the waking world, or else you couldn't have *Seen* it in the first place. But... after what you saw in your vision, how can you be so confident of bringing Ithric back safely?"

Kathrael had wondered that as well, though she could hardly claim to be an expert in such things. Her experience with *prophecy* to date had been a singularly painful and unfulfilling one.

"This is different," Favian replied earnestly. "Before, there was never any good way for me to influence what I saw. But I know what to do this time."

She saw the moment Carivel made her decision—saw it in the dip of her chin and the faint slump of her shoulders. "All right, Favian. Though I hope to the gods I'm not making a mistake."

"If so," he said, "it's not your mistake to make, Carivel. It's mine."

She shook her head, a tiny movement. "At least tell me you've gathered supplies for yourselves."

"They're hidden at the edge of town," he told her.

She frowned, and rummaged under her jerkin. "Well, then. Here. You'd better have this," she said, pulling out a cloth purse tied with a drawstring. She tossed it to Favian, who fumbled it one-handed before rescuing it from falling. It looked heavy; the contents clinked and jingled.

"That... is a lot of money," Favian said, sounding distinctly taken aback.

For her part, Kathrael couldn't help the way her eyes widened in awe. It was... quite possibly the most money she'd ever seen gathered together in one place. Carivel only shrugged.

"Andoc's contribution. You might need it," she said. "You being a priest now will probably help, but even so— mind that you keep a lookout for bandits."

"We will," said Favian, and moved forward to embrace her. "Thank you."

Carivel closed her eyes and squeezed back. "You can thank me by coming back safe. Preferably with Ithric in tow." She stepped back and turned to regard Kathrael. "That goes for you, too. Don't do anything to make me lose faith in Favian's judgment, all right?"

Kathrael did flush that time, but Carivel only stuck out a hand. After a moment, Kathrael gripped it forearm to forearm, an unspoken pact.

Carivel led them out into the darkness, where she had left the three horses tied to the fence. They were laden with saddles, bridles, saddlebags, loops of extra rope and various other sundries for traveling. She efficiently transferred some of the supplies from the splotchy black and white horse to the two white ones. The animals' coats reflected the moonlight, making them appear almost luminous in the murky night.

When everything was arranged to her satisfaction, she clapped Favian on the shoulder. "Off with you, then. Ithric is waiting. May the gods smile on your endeavors and return you safe and whole."

"Goodbye, Carivel," Favian said. "Tell the others we promise to be careful. We'll see you again soon."

With that, he took up the horses' reins. "Come on, Kathrael. We'll have to circle around and pick up the supplies at the western edge of the village. I want to get a bit of distance behind us tonight before we stop to rest."

"Lead on," she said, and followed along next to the shorter horse's shoulder when Favian headed off toward his hiding place.

☙ ⚜ ❧

An hour later, they were cantering along the western road at a steady pace. Favian had padded the seat of the saddle with a thick fur folded into a square and tied into place with twine, but he still found it more comfortable to balance his weight in the stirrups, gripping with his knees and letting his seat hover an inch or two above the saddle.

It would have been unpleasantly chilly with the wind in his face on the unexpectedly brisk night, but Kathrael was a warm weight pressed along his back. At first, her arms had clamped around his stomach almost hard enough to squeeze the breath out of him, and he could feel her pounding heartbeat even through their clothes. It hadn't taken long for her to get the feel of the horse's motion, though, and now she balanced more easily behind him while keeping a light grip around his waist.

They were riding Ozias, the colt who had been born the day after the Alyrion attack. He was the shorter of the two horses by about half a hand, and his gait was smoother than his brother's. Audris cantered next to them, his head even with his sibling's shoulder. Favian held the second stallion's lead rope looped once around the pommel and gathered in his right hand along with Ozias' reins.

"Doing all right?" he called back to Kathrael. He felt her nod in response, her cheek pressed against his left shoulder blade.

"It's not like I expected it to be," she replied, raising her voice over the wind. "I thought it would be bouncier!"

"That's because we're not trotting," Favian said in a wry tone. "And we won't be, if I can possibly help it."

Truth be told, it was probably foolish to undertake such a journey by horseback so soon after being castrated. He was no longer used to spending hours in the saddle every day, as he had been when he was Carivel's apprentice at the horse pens. For now, it was true that he could ride comfortably enough in the half-seat people used for crossing rugged terrain and jumping obstacles, but his thigh muscles would surely pay the price tomorrow, and all the days that followed.

"Do we have a plan, beyond showing up in a village and interrogating people about a traveling show that may or may not have passed through?" Kathrael asked, distracting Favian from his fretting.

"I thought we could claim that Ithric is your brother and your sole means of support, and that I'm helping you look for him after he was kidnapped," Favian said.

"My sole means of support? Because of my face, you mean," Kathrael said.

Though she maintained her grip around Favian's middle, he could feel something in her closing off. Favian had been so focused on cobbling together a plan that might help them find Ithric, he'd only realized at that very moment how it might sound to Kathrael.

"Would that... be all right?" he asked. "Sorry—it was more than a little presumptuous of me."

"No," she said. "It makes sense. He should be my bondmate, though, not my brother. He looks too northern, and I look too southern. No one would believe we're related."

"In that case," Favian said, trying for levity but unable to keep the bitterness from creeping into his voice, "my condolences on your unfortunate handfasting match."

There was silence behind him, though Favian felt Kathrael relax again after her earlier tension.

"I don't understand you, priest-boy," she said eventually. "One would almost think you hated this person you're going to such lengths to save."

It was Favian's turn to lapse into silence, as the horses' hooves ate up the road beneath them.

"I don't hate him," he said, several minutes later. "Things would actually be quite a bit simpler if I did."

Kathrael digested that as they rode on, her arms tightening around him.

⤙ ⚜ ⤚

They stopped a few hours later, when Favian could no longer keep his eyes from drifting shut every few minutes. It was still dark, but he thought he could detect a faint tinge of lighter sky behind them, in the east.

"We should get some rest," he said, and stifled the yawn that tried to come out with the words. "If we head back into the trees a bit, I don't think anyone will bother us."

Kathrael had progressively sagged against him as the night wore on, but she roused herself at his words. "Did you know I once scared off a pair of men who wanted to rob me on the road north of Rhyth?"

"No," Favian replied, "but I can't say I'm all that shocked, really. What did you do?"

"I uncovered my scars and threatened to give them the *face-melting plague*. They couldn't get away fast enough."

Favian was caught between amusement at the mental image, admiration at her utter fearlessness, respect for her formidable resourcefulness, and a surprisingly strong surge of protectiveness at the idea of thieves threatening her.

"We'll keep that particular defense in reserve for emergencies, I think," he said, not sure what else would be appropriate to say.

She snorted, sleepy and self-deprecating. "I believe that may be the only time I've ever been grateful for having this ruin of a face. There was something strangely satisfying about watching them scamper off in terror."

"I guess there would be, at that," he agreed, and linked elbows with her to help her slide down from Ozias' back. Her knees wobbled, and he kept a grip on her forearm until she steadied herself. "It takes a minute to get your land legs back sometimes," he told her. "Especially the first few times."

"So I see," she agreed wryly, taking a few tentative steps to get the muscles working again.

Favian could already feel the burn in his own legs from riding in a half-seat for so long. He dismounted cautiously, not wanting to make a fool of himself by folding into a crumpled heap on the ground, but fortunately his legs held his weight with only a moderate protest.

"There was a creek running alongside the road earlier—I could hear it," he said. "Let's see if we can find it, and maybe a clearing with enough grass so the horses can graze while we sleep."

He couldn't make out her expression in the dark, but the frown was audible in her voice. "Won't they run off?"

"We'll hobble them so they don't wander far," he explained. "I'll show you how it's done in the morning, when there's light to see."

They cautiously followed a wide, well-traveled animal track deeper into the trees. The horses heard the trickle of water before they did, and perked up, pressing forward with new energy. Before long, the woods opened up into a pleasant glade, with a babbling creek running along one edge.

"Perfect," said Kathrael. "Look, there's a big tree that fell down over here. There's space under the trunk where we can shelter out of the wind."

While it was not dangerously cold by any means, it was bordering on uncomfortable even without the added breeze caused by the horses' speed as they had traveled. And Favian hadn't missed the way Kathrael's chilly hands had burrowed into the folds at the front of his robes as they rode. She was not quite the same skeletal figure who had snuck into his sickroom that first night, but she still had barely an ounce of fat on her body. She was also a southern girl, born and bred.

"Are you cold?" he asked. "I can make a fire."

"As long as it won't draw the wrong sort of attention," she said cautiously.

"No reason why it should. We're back quite a way from the road, and the only other sign of people we've seen were campfires back near the crossroads we passed an hour ago." Favian tied up the horses as he spoke and began to unpack bedrolls and saddlebags. "Are you hungry?"

"I'm always hungry these days, it seems. Here, give me the tent hide."

They worked with an easy rapport, getting things set up for a few hours' rest and settling the horses to drink and graze. Kathrael gathered wood, and Favian started the fire with a pinch of the highly flammable powder that the priests used for effect during ceremonies. They heated bowls of water from the stream to boiling and used it to rehydrate some of the dried meat and root vegetables they carried with them.

Despite his earlier exhaustion, once he'd bedded down, Favian couldn't seem to quiet his mind enough to fall asleep. He tried to keep his tossing and turning to a minimum, painfully aware of Kathrael curled up in her blanket next to him. Some time later, it became apparent that his efforts to be still had been for nothing.

"Can't sleep?" Kathrael asked.

"No," he answered with a sigh. "Sorry. Am I keeping you awake?"

She scooted up to sit, leaning against the heavy bole that they were using as the main support for the tent. "No. The spirits are restless tonight. Maybe they're remembering the last time we traveled."

She shivered a bit, whether from cold or disquiet, he didn't know. Following an instinct, he wrapped an arm around her back and drew her against him, blanket and all.

"Your baby?" he asked, and she shrugged a shoulder under his grip.

"All of them," she said.

He frowned. "Is there anything I can do?"

"I don't need your sympathy, Favian," she said. "Distraction would be good, though. What is it that keeps *your* mind from rest after such a long day?"

He blew out a breath. "Just worry. Worry about the journey, worry about finding Ithric, worry about what happens if we *do* find him. Stupid, really... worry won't help with any of it. It'll just make me exhausted tomorrow."

"You're as tense as a rabbit staring down a pack of hunting dogs," she observed. "Here. Budge up a bit."

She ducked out from under his arm and shoved him around until she could sit behind him, her legs on either side of his and her skirts bunched up at the small of his back.

"What are you—" He broke off with a grunt as strong fingers dug into the muscles of his shoulders. "Agh! Wait—I don't think—"

"Shut up, priest-boy," Kathrael said, her words tickling his ear. "If I were trying to seduce you, you'd know it. Trust me."

"*Nngh*," he said, as agony where her vicious fingers were stabbing into him melted into pleasure. "Kathrael... you don't have to—"

"Didn't I tell you to shut up? I remember that part distinctly."

Another terribly undignified, choked-off moan of pleasure-pain slipped past Favian's control, after which he clamped his lips together and did as he was told. It was not unlike being trampled by a herd of very small horses... if the horses knew exactly how to trample him in such a way that their hooves hit *every. Single. Knot. In. His. Back.*

When she was finally satisfied with her efforts at torture, he would have been shaking like a newborn calf, had doing so not seemed like far too much work when his body was this relaxed.

Somehow, he'd ended up flat on his stomach during the process, with his right cheek mashed into the blanket. "Ow," he said into the rough wool. "I think."

"Can you sleep now?" Kathrael asked.

Favian thought about it for a moment, his mind moving like thick treacle.

"... maybe?" he hazarded. She was still leaning against his left hip, and he felt her shiver. "You're still cold," he said, and rolled onto his side with some considerable effort. "Come here. It'll be warmer together."

She came without protest, somewhat to his surprise. He arranged her in front of him, so she was between the fire and his body. When the blankets were wrapped around them and the warmth from both sides had begun to penetrate her chill, he felt her relax into his embrace with a silent sigh of relief.

Again, Favian was struck by how *right* it felt to have her there. Some considerable time must have passed as he lay there soaking up the feeling and trying to quantify it, because she stirred in his arms and asked, "Still awake?" in a sleepy voice.

"Sorry," he apologized again, vowing to stay camped here in the morning until she, at least, had gotten some decent rest.

"Don't apologize," she said, still in that soft-edged, middle-of-the-night voice. "I'm the queen of restless nights. No room to say a word, me."

Perhaps it was the late hour, darkness poised to give way to dawn. Or perhaps it was his own unusually relaxed state, coupled with lack of sleep and distraction over Ithric. Whatever the case, his thoughts moved straight to his mouth and out past his lips without any pause for censure.

"Do you ever think that it would be nice to have this kind of closeness without the complication of sex getting in the way?"

She shrugged in his arms, and yawned. "There's no *would be*. It *is* nice." She snuggled back against him. "I haven't had anything like this since Vesh died. I missed it. You remind me of him sometimes, you know."

Favian's heart ached for her—a sharp pang. "I take that as a very high compliment," he said.

"You do realize," she said around another yawn, "that if this was all you wanted out of life, you didn't need to get your balls cut off. Women would have lined up to get their claws into you."

"It's not *all* I wanted. I do have other reasons for choosing to become a priest," he clarified. "Though I must say, in my experience, women aren't usually terribly interested in a man who can't get it up for them."

She made a dismissive noise. "The only thing women get out of sex is children, and the illusion of security." She paused before adding, "Or, if they're smart, money."

Favian frowned at the tart tone of her reply, and tamped down his knee-jerk inclination to dispute it. This was not the time to have an in-depth discussion about a subject that obviously cut Kathrael close to the bone, but he filed it away to pursue later. Was it merely the bitterness of a woman who had been forced into a life of prostitution, or had Kathrael truly never found any pleasure in the gifts of the body?

For all that Favian was happy to see the back of his own lustful desires, it certainly wasn't because he'd found them un-pleasurable. In fact, it was a bit too much the opposite problem. Lust had led him into what was perhaps the worst decision he'd ever made in his life. And, because the gods' sense of humor was often more than a little sick... here he was, months later, riding pell-mell toward that very same bad decision.

Time passed, and Kathrael made a soft snuffling noise, sliding into sleep within the circle of his arms. A few minutes later, the warm, slumbering weight of her paired with the quiet rasp of her breathing pulled Favian down into darkness as well.

The sun was well up in the sky when the two of them woke, hours later. The fire had burned to ashes, but late summer was already wresting control back from autumn, driving the temperature and humidity up to something more seasonable.

Favian was still nursing that trampled-by-tiny-but-vicious-horses feeling, though to be fair, the tension that had gripped his neck and shoulders for days was all but gone. His legs, on the other hand, were every bit as stiff and sore as he'd expected they would be, and he knew he was going to have to grit his teeth and sit his ass down in the saddle for much of the day today, painful as it would certainly be.

Kathrael wasn't moving much better after her first experience riding double.

"I thought this was supposed to be easier than walking?" she observed as she gingerly climbed back up behind Favian, the two of them riding Audris this time.

"Faster, anyway," Favian replied as he fussed around with the fur pad on the seat of his saddle, trying to keep as much pressure as possible off of his newly healed scar. If he rounded his lower back and rocked back on his seat bones, it was just about tolerable. Though that probably wouldn't be the case a few hours from now. "Maybe we'll start off at a walk for a bit, to warm up our muscles."

"My muscles are on fire already, thanks," came the sarcastic reply.

They headed off, rejoining the road and continuing their westward trek.

"Where exactly are we going?" Kathrael asked. "Do you know the villages in the west?"

"To an extent," Favian said. "My father was born in Teth, so I figured we'd start there since I have blood ties with them. I thought about starting at the southernmost port town, but I'm sure they would have been there already and moved on. We'd end up chasing them. I think it'll be more efficient to start further north. If they've been to Teth already, we'll still need to head north to catch up, but we'll be much closer to them. And if they haven't been there, we'll know to head south until we come across them. Or at least, until we come across word of them."

"That makes sense, I suppose."

"It's a big area to search," Favian admitted. "But the good news is, there are only a handful of large villages and towns scattered through the region."

"People will be talking about a show like that for weeks, I'm sure," Kathrael said. "It should be easy enough to gain word of it."

"That's what I'm counting on. I just hope the Chief of whatever village we end up in will be sympathetic to us, and not to the men running the show. He should be, I think, after we tell them Ithric's a shape-shifter."

Kathrael was silent for a moment. "In the south, you definitely wouldn't want to tell them that."

Favian frowned. "This isn't the south, thank the gods. People still revere shape-shifters here. Though the fact that Ithric isn't in the priesthood is going to raise some eyebrows."

"I take it the lion-boy is a bit more attached to his balls than you were to yours?"

"To put it mildly." Favian shook his head, thinking of the blazing rows they'd had on the subject over the years. "He has rather strong feelings on the matter, in fact."

"Well, maybe he's a special case, since he has to take care of his poor, disfigured bondmate." Kathrael's voice oozed honey.

Favian snorted. "Believe me, the highlight of this entire thing is going to be seeing his face when he finds out that he's *married*. He's… er… not really the type to settle down."

"That's all right," said Kathrael philosophically. "Neither am I."

FOURTEEN

Over the following hours of travel, Favian assured Kathrael that they were making good progress toward Teth, though riding became increasingly miserable as the day wore on. Kathrael could feel Favian alternately lifting himself to hover over the saddle, and settling down in an uncomfortable looking slouch. Neither seemed to give him much relief.

For her part, the muscles of her back and legs were burning with overuse, every rhythmic, rocking stride making them ache a little more. They slowed often to let the horses blow, and stopped at the occasional stream to water them. By mutual agreement, however, they did not dismount to eat or drink themselves. It would be far too hard to get back on and keep going afterward. Instead, they slowed to a walk and ate dried fruit and cheese straight from the saddlebags, washing it down with watered wine from one of the wineskins.

It was only the memory of her journey over the mountains and the hardship she had endured that kept Kathrael from begging Favian to stop early so they could rest. Her back might be aching, and her thighs might be starting to chafe—but things could be so much worse. They had food and drink. They had shelter and adequate clothing. They even had fast transportation—and, in fact, Favian assured her that they would reach Teth sometime the following day.

She could bear her discomfort for the space of a day, as Favian was bearing his.

Even so, it was a relief when the sun touched the western horizon, throwing long shadows behind them.

"No need to ride through the night tonight," Favian said. "I think we can both use a full night's rest."

"You'll get no argument from me," she replied.

The pair found another suitable spot for camping and dismounted with matching groans of discomfort. The terrain had changed over the course of the day, patchy forests giving way to open grasslands. They had seen a few fellow travelers as they rode, and Kathrael kept her face carefully covered with her shawl. While a couple of people had stared in interest at the unusual white horses, none had shown any further interest in them beyond an occasional muttered, "Good day, Brother," to Favian in his dun-colored priest's robes.

The two of them repeated the same steps they'd gone through the previous night to set up camp, the process made considerably easier this time by the slowly fading light of dusk. Favian showed Kathrael how to help unsaddle the horses and rub them down. She was still a little nervous around the animals when she was on the ground, but at the same time there was something both thrilling and delightfully *forbidden* about working with them.

She—a slave girl, a prostitute, the lowest of the low— was caring for a tribal chieftain's prized white horses. And they were as docile under her touch as they would be for any seasoned Horse Master. All her life, she had been taught that a woman's spirit was too weak to control the spirits of animals.

Who's the weak one now? she thought as Ozias nuzzled a tidbit of dried mayapple from her palm.

Never you, Kath, Vesh whispered, the noise fading into the rustle of tall grass around her.

When the horses were settled and the campfire was merrily crackling away in the warm twilight, they cooked a simple meal. Kathrael ate with ravenous single-mindedness, though she noticed Favian only picked at his food.

"You should eat," she said around a mouthful of bread and cheese. "Keep your strength up."

Favian's smile was wan; his face, pale. "Maybe after I stop aching quite so much. It's making me a bit queasy right now."

She swallowed and looked more closely at him. "You need to figure out something different for riding tomorrow. It can't be good for you when you're still not completely healed. Maybe we could alternate riding and walking?"

"The wound is closed and scarred over," he assured her quickly. "I guess it's just the inside that still needs more time. Whatever the case, I'd rather not walk. As it is, we'll make Teth late tomorrow afternoon if we don't run into any delays. But if we walk part of the way, we might have to camp for a third night."

"Well, it's your choice," she said. "I'd offer to work on it for you like I did last night with your back..."

He blushed and laughed, as she had intended. "Kind of you to offer, but I *really* don't think that would help the situation, unfortunately."

"Just trying to be helpful, priest-boy," she said, all innocence.

He snorted. "Of course you are. Nothing at all to do with the fact that you think it's funny when you can make me blush." He sobered. "How about you let me return the favor, instead? You were moving earlier like your back hurt."

Kathrael paused with the half-eaten slab of bread held poised, halfway to her mouth. She was strangely taken aback. It was one thing to offer some of the skills she'd picked up as a whore—she'd truly enjoyed massaging the tension from Favian's muscles until he melted into relaxation beneath her touch. But to have someone offer the same to her?

She had remained frozen for too long. Favian was looking at her carefully.

"Did I say something wrong, Kathrael?" he asked.

She blinked, breaking free of her paralysis. "No," she said slowly. "You didn't say anything wrong. I just... didn't expect you to offer, is all."

Favian settled further against the saddle he was using as a backrest and regarded her with his pale blue eyes. "Oh? Why wouldn't I, though? It only seems fair."

She did him the courtesy of thinking about the question for a few moments before answering.

"It's just that... women do things for men, to make them feel better and give them pleasure. Not the other way around. Men... *take*."

For some reason, that made him look sad.

"Haven't you ever been with a man who wasn't paying for your services? A man *you* chose to be with?" he asked.

Her temper flared. "I *chose* to be with all of them!"

He didn't rise to her anger. Nor did he back down. "But only for money, is that right? Never because you wanted it for yourself?"

"Please! Am I a fool, to give my body away for free?" She was still angry. Defensive. "It was bad enough when I was getting paid for it."

Favian let out a breath through his teeth. "It's true then, what you hinted at last night. You've never felt physical pleasure from any of your liaisons?"

She made a derisive noise. "Women don't get pleasure from being fucked. Some of them pretend to, but it's just a lie."

He was still looking at her in a way that made her want to squirm. "I assure you," he said, with evident sincerity, "it's not a lie. Have you never even touched yourself for pleasure? Sex with a man can produce those same feelings, and more."

"Why would I want to touch myself?" she asked, genuinely confused. Occasionally, men would ask a whore to touch herself while they watched, and the more experienced women had advised Kathrael to writhe around and moan while she was doing it because it made the man more excited.

But her cunt had always been swollen and uncomfortable when she was working regularly, and rubbing it mostly just chafed unless she could sneak some oil onto her fingers first. She'd never once found it pleasant.

Favian continued to stare at her as if he suspected her of having him on, but when she only looked back in confusion, he eventually said, "Many woman—*most* women, I would have thought—touch themselves to feel good and provoke a sexual release. Just as most men do."

She stared at him. "I think these women have been telling you fairy stories, Favian. Like I said, some women pretend to enjoy it because men like that sort of thing. Some men do, anyway—in my experience, most don't actually care one way or the other."

Her companion seemed lost for words, confirmed a moment later when he said, "I'm not sure how to even begin to respond to that."

"Why are you so surprised?" she asked. "I thought you didn't like sex anyway?"

"No, I *loved* sex," Favian replied. "I thought about it all the time, or at least it felt like I did. Sex with men, that is to say. It was almost obsessive… and *that* was the part I didn't like."

"So you went and got your balls cut off?" She was deflecting, she knew—trying to move him away from the uncomfortable topic by pissing him off, but she couldn't seem to stop herself.

He still wasn't rising to the bait, though, leaning back against his saddle in such a relaxed and thoroughly unthreatening manner that it made her want to shake him until his teeth rattled.

"I got castrated because I wanted to be a priest, for a variety of reasons that we can discuss in more detail if you're interested. But a happy side effect has been that, yes, I'm no longer obsessed by the idea of sex. I don't hate the idea. I don't love the idea. It's just a thing that people do with each other to feel good. When it's used to give mutual pleasure and express love, it's quite beautiful, really. When it's used as a weapon to hurt someone, it's very, very ugly. When it's used as a cold transaction with no meaning behind it—" Favian paused, searching for the words he wanted. "— it's... rather sad, I suppose."

"Spoken like a man," she managed to spit, not liking the way his words prodded at something deep inside her chest.

He shrugged. "Like a eunuch, at any rate. Now, since we're apparently going to have to agree to disagree on that subject for the moment, *would* you like me to work on your back? I assure you, I'm only interested in repaying the favor from last night, and making it a little easier for you to ride tomorrow." He paused. "Well. There might also be the aspect of distracting myself from the ache between my legs for a bit, too. But don't tell anyone."

The air escaped Kathrael's lungs in a slow sigh that took most of her defensive anger with it. Favian was a eunuch, and a hopelessly naive one, at that. He was offering. She would be a fool to pass up that offer when her back was tied up in painful knots.

"Fine," she said, trying to say it a sharp enough tone to convey that she still thought him a fool. She wasn't at all sure it worked.

She finished her bowl of reconstituted meat and parched grains, wiping up the last traces with a chunk of coarse bread. Favian still hadn't managed more than a few mouthfuls of his own food, so he poured the remains into a covered container by the fire for the morning meal.

After everything was cleaned up and packed away for a quick start the next day, Favian went off to check the horses one last time while she laid out the bedrolls. Since the night was fair and there were no convenient trees around, she decided to forego the tent.

"The horses seem happy," Favian observed upon his return. "Though why wouldn't they be? They're surrounded by a sea of grass."

"Simple pleasures," she said, accepting the peace offering implicit in the change of subject. "I can appreciate the appeal of a full belly and a warm, dry night."

"I'm sure you can, more than most people," Favian replied. "Now, let's see if we can give you the chance to appreciate a back that isn't tied up in knots." He indicated the buckskin leather bodice that Kathrael was wearing over her linen under-blouse. "Do you want to take that off first?"

It was odd to have a man—or a eunuch, rather—ask her to disrobe for some reason other than sex. She shrugged, and loosened the laces on the bodice enough that she could shimmy out of it. In the muggy, late summer warmth and the privacy of their campsite, she untied the heavy split skirts she wore over her breeches, and stepped out of those as well. Finally, she toed off the worn pair of boots Shayla had given her, and settled herself on the ground cloth she'd put down at the edge of the firelight, where they would sleep tonight.

Favian knelt behind her, his knees bracketing her hips. "Where does it hurt?"

"All over," she said tartly.

"Hmm, you're *ever* so helpful, you know," Favian teased, and his large hands closed over her shoulders, warm and heavy.

It was a bizarre feeling. Vesh would occasionally sling an arm around her shoulders as they sat together, or pat her on the back, or hold her when she was upset—but he had never pressed strong fingers into her muscles and kneaded away the tension there.

Kathrael knew she had been a little bit cruel with Favian last night, digging into his rigid back without mercy to get at the knots as quickly and efficiently as possible. By contrast, Favian started with slow, firm movements to warm and relax her muscles. She was admittedly tense in the unfamiliar situation, for all that she'd trusted Favian enough to sleep peacefully in his arms on two separate occasions now.

This seemed... different somehow, perhaps because it was completely new territory for her.

"All right?" Favian asked, gathering her heavy length of dark hair and draping it over her shoulder so he could get at the back of her neck.

She grunted in reply as his thumbs dragged along taut tendons.

"This wasn't exactly the best introduction to horseback riding," he apologized. "Though I suppose it's something of a trial by fire. You'll probably develop a decent seat by the time we get back to Draebard, purely out of self defense."

A small noise slipped past her control as his palms slid down the strained muscles framing her spine, fresh blood flow tingling in their wake.

"Tell me more about this plan you have for rescuing our lion-shifter," she said, mostly as a way to distract herself from the dark magic Favian's hands were working on her abused back. "You said that this time would be *different* from your other visions—that you knew what to do. What did you mean by that?"

Favian's fingers stilled for a moment before continuing their delicious torture. Kathrael squirmed and hissed out a sharp breath as the heel of one hand pressed into a knot, rocking back and forth until the tension melted away.

"In the past, either I wasn't closely enough involved in the events I was seeing to have much of a direct impact on them, or else the event in question was already happening when I saw it, so nothing I did would make a difference. Assuming I *wanted* to make a difference in the first place, which wasn't always the case."

Kathrael frowned, thinking about it. "But if you saw Ithric get stabbed..."

"I saw the knife flash up toward his body," Favian clarified, "as I was standing at the edge of the crowd, yelling something to get his attention."

"Same thing, surely?" Kathrael asked, the pitch of her voice rising abruptly on the last word as Favian's fingers hit another knot. She cleared her throat. "I still don't understand what you think you can do to stop it."

"Simple," Favian said. "I know he could hear me—he looked straight at me. So I'm going to yell, 'Watch out, he has a knife,' as loud as I possibly can."

Kathrael blinked. "Well, as plans go, that's... direct, I suppose."

She felt Favian shrug behind her, and draw in a slow breath. "I've been over it a hundred times in my mind, and it's what I can do. I have to believe that by not showing me the moment when the knife struck home, the gods are telling me I can save him."

There was a heartbreaking air of vulnerability behind the words. Favian's hands had worked back up the length of her back as he spoke, and now rested on her shoulders again. She reached up to cover one of them with her own. "I hope you're right."

"Me, too," he whispered.

Without thinking, she twisted around until she was half-facing him, and brushed her lips against his in a chaste kiss. "You're a good friend, Favian of Draebard," she said. "Or perhaps a good enemy. I still don't claim to understand what you and the lion-boy are to each other."

"Then you're in excellent company," Favian said into the small gap between them.

Suddenly remembering herself, she sat back, giving him space. "Sorry," she said. "I know women aren't your type, but I really wasn't trying to make you blush that time."

Favian smiled, the faintest quirk of his lips. "I told you before, Kathrael—I've had feelings for both men and women... but I could only ever get it up for men." His amusement grew more visible. "However, since it's unlikely I'll be able to get it up for anyone in the future, I suppose that's rather leveled the field." The smile faded into thoughtfulness. "Though I'm surprised, I'll admit. You haven't had a single good thing to say about physical affection between men and women."

Kathrael looked down and to the side. "I never kissed them," she muttered.

When Favian frowned in confusion and ducked his head to regain eye contact, she swallowed and continued in a more normal tone. "Kissing isn't sex. I never used to kiss the men I was servicing." She glanced away again, honesty compelling her to add, "Not... voluntarily, anyway."

Favian breathed out softly, and she clenched her jaw. Those forced kisses had always been far worse than any other perverse degradation she'd participated in for money. Sweaty hands wrapped in her hair or gripping the back of her neck... foul breath suffocating her as a slimy tongue forced its way into her mouth. It always sent her awareness scurrying into the hidden places in her mind within seconds. Sometimes she lost entire hours that way, only a blank space in her memory and a sense of rage left behind when she came back to herself.

Favian's forehead came to rest gently against her own. "Oh, Kath..." he said, as if she'd just told him the saddest story he'd ever heard. The tips of his fingers came up to brush against the left side of her face, trailing over the twists of scar tissue with a pressure so light she could barely feel it through the damaged flesh, for all that the gesture brought the burn of tears to her good eye.

He tipped up her chin with the barest suggestion of a touch, and she followed, stretching forward until her lips brushed his a second time. He met her with a sweetness that threatened to shatter her heart into a thousand diamond-edged shards. His lips were dry, a bit chapped... his hand came up to cup her scarred cheek as if it were precious rather than ugly. Her chest did hitch then, but she had cried enough tears to last a lifetime these past days. Instead, she poured the feelings into the press of their lips.

Whereas another man might have tried to take control of the kiss and deepen it, Favian seemed utterly content to continue with light, butterfly touches, undemanding of more. Eventually, when she was warm and heavy with the slowly settling weight of pent-up emotion, he stroked his thumb over her cheek and eased away. Her eyes had closed at some point; she blinked them open until he came into focus, pale-skinned and golden-haired in the flickering firelight. His blue eyes were as bottomless as the ocean.

"I won't see anyone else take from you what you do not freely give," he said, and a hint of his earlier sadness still lingered behind the words. "Never again, Kath. *Not ever.*"

"Are you going to be my protector, Favian?" she asked, knowing that such ideas were the province of youthful foolishness and naivety. Wishing, in this moment, that they were not.

"I think," Favian said after a beat, "that you are perfectly capable of being your own protector. But I fully intend to be the person who proves to you that you are deserving of protection."

She stared at him in silence, trying to wrap her mind around his words and failing. After a while, he had pity on her and kissed her forehead, breaking the moment.

"Come on," he said, urging her to turn around again. "You must be tired. I know I am. Lie on your stomach, and

I'll try to get those last few knots in your back. Then we'll sleep."

Relieved by the offer of distraction, she did as she was instructed and stretched out on the blankets, pillowing her head on her arms. Her thoughts still circled restlessly, but the long day combined with the slow kneading of Favian's fingers along the length of her spine soon had her drowsing. She was only vaguely aware when he finished with a final slow stroke down her back, and lay down next to her. He pulled a blanket over them both, and she rolled over without conscious thought to fit herself against his side. She fell asleep soon after, to the sounds of night insects chirping in the grass.

The nightmare jerked her awake hours later. She sat up with a pounding heart, clammy sweat beading on her face and chest.

Help me, daughter, her mother begged. *Why did you abandon me?* Kathrael could vividly see her lifeless eyes, staring in blank hopelessness as her sister Elarra pulled Kathrael away and ran from the overseer. Ran from the Wolf Patron. She and Elarra had abandoned the old woman when they left. Had *abandoned their mother.*

The squalling cry of a hungry baby echoed strangely at the edge of Kathrael's hearing, and she moaned in denial, clapping her hands over her ears. It did nothing to muffle the noise, and she moved to pull at her hair instead, trying to distract herself with pain.

"No…" she whispered, as the cries grew in pitch and volume. "I can't help you — you're dead. You're all *dead —*"

She gasped and flinched in surprise when a hand touched her arm.

"Kathrael?" a voice asked, dragging her into a slightly greater awareness of her surroundings.

Favian. It was Favian, and what a fool she'd been to hope that just because she'd spent two peaceful nights in his arms, somehow that meant he could magically keep the ghosts away while she slept.

"Kath?" he asked again. "Talk to me, please. Did you have a nightmare?"

She nodded, not sure if the movement was visible in the faint glow of burning embers from the fire, but unable to offer more as the baby's cries grew still louder, nearly drowning out his concerned voice.

"Is it the spirits?" he asked, his firm grip on her shoulder grounding her as she shook. He paused, and continued, "Is it your baby?"

She made a noise of pain and clutched at her head again. "Yes," she said, barely recognizing her own voice. "She's starving. She's *scared*. I—I can't..."

Favian clasped her other shoulder as well, squeezing until she looked at him with a wild expression.

"Kathrael," he said in a firmer voice, "she's not starving. She's in the spirit world. She didn't starve. She just... died. Quietly, inside you. I don't know why she cries at night, but I have a feeling that when you get upset it only makes it worse. Can you take a few deep breaths for me? Try to focus on me, and on your surroundings."

Kathrael stared at him and tried to breathe. Gradually, her heart rate slowed, though the cries continued to tug painfully at her heart. For the first time in many days, the old, familiar feeling of wanting to die washed over her, leaving her shaky and nauseous.

"I can't do this..." she said. "I can't keep *doing* this! *Why won't they leave me alone?*"

Favian looked nearly as upset as she was, and there was pain in his voice when he said, "I'm so sorry, Kath. I wish I knew what to do."

"I don't need your pity!" she flared. "It doesn't help! It only makes me feel worse!"

He swallowed and forced his expression into something more neutral. "What, then? What did you do before, when you were alone?"

She thought back, to *before*. It was surprisingly difficult to do so. "I... moved. I got up and started walking again. I... don't honestly know if I would have made it over the mountains at all, if not for the spirits harrying me along." She paused, and swallowed. "Can we just go? Right now?"

Favian looked taken aback for only a moment, before he nodded. "Of course. I doubt either of us would be able to sleep any more tonight, anyway. Let me stir up the fire so we can see what we're doing to pack up the camp. You roll up the blankets, and I'll get the horses ready."

Her relief was a palpable thing. "Thank you," she breathed, and rose on unsteady feet to start putting their belongings to rights.

Favian built up the fire and retrieved the horses, saddling them with the efficiency of long practice. Kathrael helped him fasten the saddlebags and bedrolls in place, trying to focus on her task rather than the plaintive cries of distress whispering through the windblown grass.

When they were ready, Favian said, "I want to try something different today. I've thought of a way I might be able to ride more comfortably, but you won't be able to ride behind me safely while I'm doing it. I'd like you to ride Audris by yourself, while I ride Ozias."

That caught her attention, dragging it forcibly back to her companion. "What? I don't know how to control him. All I know how to do is hang on and not fall off!"

"I'll still be leading you by a rope attached to his halter," Favian replied quickly. "You won't have to steer him. The only difference is that you'll have to hang onto the saddle for balance instead of hanging onto me."

She thought about this for a moment and decided it would actually provide a useful distraction. "All right. I can do that, I think. Can we go now?"

"Yes, we're going." Favian brought Audris over and showed her how to step up onto his bent knee and into the saddle. He fussed with the stirrups until they were the right length and arranged her feet in them. Once he'd demonstrated how to hold the reins, he stepped back and gave her a critical once-over.

"If something happens and he gets loose, sit up straight in the saddle, plant your seat, pull back on both reins smoothly, and say *whoa*. If I catch you pulling on the reins otherwise, I'll channel my inner Carivel and give you a verbal reaming you won't forget. Those reins are attached to a hunk of metal in your horse's mouth and several people—myself included—put a lot of effort into training him to trust his rider not to hurt him with the bit."

"Yes, *sir*," Kathrael said, laying the irony on thick, even though his distraction really *was* helping. "Such an authoritative streak you've been hiding all these weeks, priest-boy. I had no idea."

His mouth quirked as if he was hiding a smile. "Well," he pointed out, "I *was* raised by a village chieftain, a High

Priest, and a Horse Mistress. You'd expect some of it to have rubbed off on me at some point."

Still holding both horses' ropes, he gave a final look around the fire-lit campsite to make sure they hadn't forgotten anything. Apparently satisfied, he kicked dirt over the campfire until it was thoroughly smothered, plunging them into darkness. The white horse Kathrael was riding snorted at the sudden change and the smell of smoke, but barely shifted beneath her. She gathered the reins in one hand as Favian had shown her, and hooked her fingers under the pommel of the saddle so she wouldn't accidentally tug on them.

There was the sound of movement in the darkness next to her as Favian mounted and got himself settled. It was after moonset, and only a handful of stars peeking between patchy clouds lent any sort of illumination. She could make out the white blur beneath her and another one to the side, but that was all.

"Let's see if this will work," Favian muttered, to the accompaniment of more shifting and rustling. "Huh. That's not so bad. A little precarious, maybe. Let's just hope we don't run into any unexpected excitement along the way. Ready?"

"Yes, please," she said, impatient to be going.

"All right, then—off we go. Hold onto the saddle, and try not to grip with your legs—that's the cue to make him go faster."

Favian clucked softly to the horses, which moved off at an easy walk. They headed back toward the road and started the trek westward toward Teth. She held on and tried to sway with the horse's movements, as the sound of a crying babe rose and fell around her.

Kathrael gritted her teeth and focused on staying atop Audris as he ambled along next to his sibling. She was only vaguely aware of time passing, of the sky gradually growing lighter at their backs. As if it was some sort of signal, at the first rays of light from the rising sun, the ghostly cries of distress faded into silence.

She sagged in relief, her free hand coming to rest on the firm shoulder of the animal beneath her.

The movement caught Favian's attention. "Better now?" he asked, peering at her closely in the uncertain morning light.

"I can't hear her any more," Kathrael said, "or any of the others."

"Good," he replied. "You were so quiet—I was worried."

There was nothing to say to that, so she only shrugged, already exhausted though the day had scarcely started.

"If you're ready, we can let the horses lope for a while," he continued. "Do you think you're steady enough up there?"

"I think so," she assured him, aware that any additional speed they could manage would get them to Teth more quickly.

She looked at Favian properly for the first time since they'd left their camp, and realized that he was riding half-sideways, with his right leg hooked over the pommel of his saddle and his weight resting cockeyed on his right hip.

"Is that safe?" she asked.

He only grinned. "Oh, yes—as long as absolutely nothing unexpected happens."

"I'm not sure that's particularly reassuring," she said. He *was*, after all, the one controlling her horse, as well as his own.

"That's why I rode Ozias and gave you Audris, even though Audris is a bit harder to sit." Favian reached down to rub his horse's withers. "Ozias will look after me. He's known me his whole life."

"So it's helping with your… problem, then? Because, and I'm sorry to be the one to say this, but you do look a bit ridiculous."

He rolled his eyes at her. "Yes, it's much more comfortable, thank you. I can even switch sides if my muscles start to get cramped. But perhaps I'll swing my leg back over before we ride in to my father's old village. I wouldn't want to embarrass you."

"Ha," she said, though she was painfully aware that it was more likely that his own reputation would suffer among his clansmen for being associated with someone as disfigured as she was. Still, his plan to use her scars to their advantage was a clever one. And, somewhat oddly, it did make her feel a bit better about what they were likely to encounter in their search for the traveling show.

"Sit up straight and hold on," Favian warned her. "We're going to speed up now."

Kathrael sat back and renewed her grip on the saddle as Audris surged into a rolling canter, his hooves skimming over the road in a steady, three-beat rhythm.

FIFTEEN

Teth was a bustling little village surrounded by lush pastureland and inhabited, it seemed, by far more cattle than people.

"Draebard has its horses," Favian said when he saw her staring at the large herds of black and red cattle. "Teth has its cattle. Definitely try the cheese while we're here. It's excellent."

As he had promised, Favian slung his leg back over the saddle to ride normally as they approached the edge of town. Kathrael nervously tugged her shawl forward, struck anew by how odd it had been not to have to worry much about the reaction to her face while she was staying in the temple in Draebard.

"Hullo!" Favian called as they rode up to the cluster of buildings and huts. "It's Favian—Renthro's son. Is Sula around? Or Vineet?"

Several people looked up from what they'd been doing, and a man with light brown hair called back, "Favian? Well now, it's *Novice* Favian, I see! Welcome back. Your aunt and uncle are probably out with the cattle." He paused upon noticing Kathrael. "Uh, hello, miss. Welcome to Teth."

Kathrael only nodded, keeping her face hidden.

"Thank you," Favian said, drawing the man's attention back to him. "It's Kesin, isn't it?"

The man grinned. "You remember! I wasn't sure you would—you were just a boy when we last met. I must say, I'm surprised to see you in those robes. Thought you were horse-crazy. Apprenticed to Draebard's Horse Master, weren't you?"

"It's a very long story, I'm afraid," Favian said.

Kesin nodded. "I bet it is. Well, I won't keep you from your kin. You remember where their grazing lots are?"

"I think so," Favian said. "It was a pleasure to see you again, Kesin. May the gods' blessings be on you and yours."

"Thank you, Brother," Kesin said with another smile. "It's good to see you doing so well. Goodbye, miss."

"Goodbye," Kathrael said softly, averting her face from the man's curious gaze.

Favian led them further into the village, greeting people who recognized him and others who merely recognized his position as a visiting priest. Eventually, they came to a smallholding at the northern edge of the settlement. Favian rode past the house with its thatched roof and window boxes of fragrant herbs. Behind the humble structure was a larger one, apparently for livestock. Cattle were penned nearby, mooing occasionally.

"Aunt Sula?" Favian called. "Uncle Vineet?"

A moment later, the door to the barn flew open and a middle-aged woman with hair the same pale gold as Favian's rushed out.

"Favian?" she said in disbelief. "Favian! Merciful Utarr, it really is you!"

Favian dismounted in time to meet his aunt as she threw her arms around him and hugged tight. He hugged back, and Kathrael could see the crooked smile that curled his lips at the bittersweet reunion with his dead father's kin.

"It's really me," he confirmed.

"What's all this ruckus?" a new voice asked. A powerful man with bushy eyebrows and hair just beginning to turn gray approached from the direction of the pens.

"Vineet!" Sula said. "Favian has come for a visit!"

"Is that so?" Vineet said, striding up to Favian with a grin. "Let's have a look at you, then!" He gave Favian a critical once-over before pulling him into a back-slapping embrace. "The temple life suits you, boy. Still living in Draebard with that Wolf Priest?"

"I am," Favian replied once they parted. "It's good to see you, Uncle. Good to see both of you."

"And who's this?" Sula asked politely, smiling up at Kathrael where she still sat on Audris' back, her shawl hiding her face.

"Ah—forgive my poor manners," Favian said, returning to the horses so he could help her down. "This is Kathrael. She's actually the reason for my visit. We're looking for her bondmate, who was recently abducted. Kathrael, this is Sula, my father's sister, and her husband, Vineet."

"Hello," Kathrael said, still not looking at them directly.

"Oh, my goodness!" Sula said in sympathy. "You poor dear—abducted, you say?"

Vineet was peering curiously at her, trying to see under her shawl.

"Are you unwell, young woman?" he asked, a note of caution seeping into his voice.

"Kathrael was burned rather badly some months ago," Favian said smoothly. "She suffered scarring that made it impossible for her to continue in her chosen trade. Since then, she's been completely reliant on her bondmate for their livelihood. We have reason to believe that his abductors are heading north, following the towns near the coastline. When she appealed at the temple for assistance, I offered to help her search for him."

Kathrael reluctantly lifted her head, giving them a glimpse of what lay behind the shadow of her shawl. Sula gasped, and Vineet took an involuntary step back. Kathrael told herself firmly that she didn't care, and met Vineet's look of horror with a challenging one of her own.

"Gods above," Vineet said. "Yes… I suppose you couldn't manage much for yourself, looking like that."

"*Vineet*," Sula hissed.

Kathrael glanced at Favian, and saw a tendon tighten in his jaw. "You'd be surprised," he said, even though it contradicted the story he himself had concocted for them. He gave himself a slight shake, and continued, "At any rate, you can understand how important it is that we find Ithric and return him home safely."

"Of course," Sula said. "But how can we help?"

"Not sure how you expect to find this man with so little to go on," Vineet added gruffly. "He could be anywhere, assuming he's even still alive."

Apparently, tact was not a trait that Favian's uncle possessed in excess, but Favian merely replied, "He's alive. He's being held prisoner by the owners of a traveling show that exhibits people and animals as curiosities.'

"The show with the freaks, you mean?" Vineet blurted. "I saw that one! Gods above, her husband isn't the one with no arms, is he?"

Kathrael's heart pounded, half in excitement and half in outrage at the man's callousness. Beside her, Favian sucked in a sharp breath.

"They were here in Teth?" he asked, straining forward like one of the overseer's hounds scenting prey. "*When?*"

"Yes. About a week ago," Vineet said. "Something like that, anyway."

"No," Sula put in. "It was nine days ago that they left. I remember because Janna's baby boy was sick that day."

"How long were they here?" Favian asked sharply. "Did they say where they were going next?"

"Calm down, lad," Vineet said. "Goodness—anyone would think it was your own bondmate you were tracking. Let me see, now... I think they were only here for three days or so—"

"Yes, that's right," Sula confirmed.

"No idea where they were headed, though," Favian's uncle added.

"Did they socialize with anyone when they were staying here?" Kathrael asked.

Vineet avoided looking at her as he answered. "Well, the freaks pretty much kept to themselves—"

Of course they did, you fool, Kathrael thought. *They're prisoners.*

"—but the two who seemed to be in charge spent a fair amount of coin in the tavern, of an evening," he finished, still directing his words to his nephew rather than to her. "You might go and have a word with old Clarry, Favian."

"Thank you, I will," Favian said, throwing her a brief, apologetic look. "I don't suppose we could prevail on you to provide beds for the night? We'll have to head out first thing in the morning."

"Of course—" Sula began, but Vineet cut her off and spoke over her.

"I dunno, lad," he said, "we're a bit hard up for space. And your cousin is feeling poorly right now. I, uh, wouldn't want to give her a shock with, well, you know..."

He gestured a bit awkwardly toward Kathrael, who continued to stare at him with a level gaze. Beside her, Favian stiffened.

"Vineet!" Sula chided again. "He's family!"

"Hush, Sula," he said, a bit harshly. "Look, Favian, I just think it would be best if your friend stayed elsewhere. You know what they say about bringing bad luck into a house. This family has already had more than its share of ill fortune."

Kathrael had never before seen Favian go as cold as he did at Vineet's words.

"Of course, Uncle," he said, all traces of his earlier affection vanished. "We wouldn't dream of imposing. Thank you for your help—we'll stay at the temple instead. Give my love to Cousin Trina and tell her I hope she feels better soon."

"Favian—" Sula said, sounding terribly sad.

Favian dredged a smile for her and gave her another embrace. "It's all right, Aunt Sula. Being a priest has its advantages. We won't lack for hospitality tonight."

"Tell Frella hello for me," Sula said. "I've still never gotten to meet her."

"We'll have to remedy that one day," said Favian, giving her a final squeeze and releasing her. "Goodbye. It was good to see you."

"Goodbye, Favian," she replied. "Be careful, please. I couldn't bear to lose another family member senselessly."

"Father's death wasn't senseless," Favian said without hesitation. "He died doing what he could to protect Eburos from invasion by the Empire. Mother's wasn't either. She died bringing Frella into the world. But nevertheless, we'll be careful—don't worry."

"Goodbye, lad," Vineet said stiffly. "Take care of yourself, eh?"

"Of course," Favian said evenly. "You do the same, Uncle."

With that, he helped Kathrael climb up onto her horse's back and followed a moment later, taking the reins and leading her away. Except for the occasional greeting to passersby, Favian was silent during the journey to the temple, and Kathrael let him stew until they approached the large building.

"You could have sent me to stay at the temple while you spent more time with your kin," she said finally.

Favian shook his head. "Just because someone is family doesn't automatically make their actions acceptable. I feel bad that Sula was caught in the middle, but for me to argue with her husband would have put an unnecessary strain on their relationship, while sending you away would have made me as bad as Vineet."

"You're very calculating sometimes," Kathrael observed. "That always surprises me about you."

Favian looked at her. "All priests are calculating, to some degree. Part of the training for the priesthood is to place ourselves outside of a situation rather than becoming embroiled in it. I've always struggled with that, but I guess the lesson finally stuck in the end."

Kathrael thought of Favian stumbling frantically to his mentor's rooms in the aftermath of his prophetic dream about Ithric. She thought of his obsessive quest to change the future against all odds.

"Of course it did," she murmured.

After securing a couple of rooms in the temple and enjoying a meal of cold meats and onion soup, Favian left Kathrael to rest while he went to speak with the tavern owner. He ignored the small stir caused by a priest in a drinking establishment and strode up to the filthy wooden counter, trying his best not to limp on legs that still felt sore and shaky from far too much time perched awkwardly in the saddle over the past few days.

Old Clarry was a grizzled, stoop-shouldered man with one ear missing. "Evening, Brother," he said, somewhat warily. "Not used to seeing your type in here. Not local, are you? Can't say as I rightly recognize you.'

"I'm Renthro's son, as it happens," Favian said, already grown tired of repeating it. "Just visiting relatives on my way to find the owners of a traveling show that came through recently."

Clarry made a considering noise. "Heard he passed away a few years back, is that right? Renthro, I mean."

"That's right," Favian said in a flat tone. "He was traveling in winter and his horse fell into a crevasse."

"Huh," said the tavern keeper. "Pity, that."

Favian silently recited a short stanza from the religious histories about the importance of tolerance, feeling his temper fraying at the continual reminders of the tragedy that had torn his and Frella's lives apart when they were younger.

"Yes," he said in an even tone. "It was a terrible loss. Now, about that traveling show…"

"Y'mean the freaks?" Clarry asked, pausing to swipe out a dirty tankard with an equally dirty rag.

Favian mentally repeated the words of the stanza a second time and took a deep breath. "That's the one. I gather the owners drank here when they were in town? I don't suppose they mentioned where they were headed next? It's vital that I speak with them."

Clarry frowned. "Vital, eh? What would a priest need to talk about with the likes of them? Queer bunch, if you ask me."

Favian gritted his teeth, giving up on the stanza and trying to channel Senovo's endless patience, instead. "We have... a mutual acquaintance."

Clarry shrugged. "Huh. If you say so. It's true the big one liked to flap his lips when he came in. Tarvick, his name was—or something like that. Said they was heading up to Gebrall, and then on to Woodhaerst. Planning to go right along the length of the coast, they were, and spend the winter up north somewhere. Crazy, if you ask me. Shoulda headed east to the big towns like Venzor and Llanmeer, instead."

"Hmm," Favian said, noncommittal, trying to ignore the fast tripping of his pulse. "Well, thank you—that's exactly what I needed. I'll stop disconcerting your customers now, and get out of your way."

"Aye. That's prob'ly for the best," Clarry agreed with a philosophical tilt of the head, and went back to transferring dirt from one goblet to another with the grungy old rag.

⤛ ♕ ⤜

Kathrael looked up as Favian burst into the tiny sleeping cell she had been allocated in Teth's temple. He was bristling with energy, pacing back and forth in the cramped, inadequate space.

"They're in Woodhaerst," Favian said, his arms crossed tightly in front of his chest. "Or they will be in the next day or two. If we're fast enough, we can catch them before they leave."

"You got the information you needed, then? That's wonderful, Favian."

He nodded, a jerky movement, his eyes far away in the light of the flickering candle. She reached out and grabbed his arm, pulling him to sit on the edge of the bed, where he fidgeted.

"What's wrong?" she asked. "You're pulled tighter than a bowstring."

He took a deep breath and let it out. "Nothing. Everything. Sorry—it's strange, being here. I want to get going, now that we have what we need."

"In the morning," she said firmly. "You're exhausted. We both are."

"I know. I know. Not that I could sleep right now." His knee was jiggling up and down, a nervous movement that put her teeth on edge.

"Can you get a sleeping draught from one of the priests here?" she asked.

He groaned. "Ugh. I guess so, but I practically lived on those things for more than a week after my novitiate. I think they've started to lose effectiveness."

"Then maybe you should go… pray, or something?" She stared at him critically, and he had the good grace to look abashed.

"Yes, sorry. Maybe I should. Don't mind me — try to get some rest. We haven't had all that much the past two nights."

To Kathrael's surprise, he leaned forward and kissed her forehead — a warm, lingering press of lips — before leaving her to her rest. She was not terribly surprised, however, when hours later, a familiar body slid into the narrow bed behind her and slung an arm over her waist, spooning around her back. Only half awake, she snuggled into the welcoming warmth and drifted off again.

Eighteen leagues north of Teth, a lion paced restlessly in its cage, eyes glowing in the darkness. Ithric's ribs and hipbones stood out starkly against his scruffy late-summer pelt. It suited Turvick to starve him these days. The man saw it as a way to weaken his captive, physically and mentally. He seemed not to realize how this new cruelty was affecting Ithric's animal mind — the lion was ready to lose control at the slightest additional provocation.

Ithric's human sensibilities had grown increasingly confused over the weeks since Rona had confessed her pregnancy to him in the darkness of the ship's hold. After brutally whipping Nimbral — the baby's unlikely father — as punishment, Turvick had threatened the same for Rona if Ithric dared to shift into human form again.

At the time, Ithric had vowed to get Rona away to safety and find a healer to help her with the dangerous pregnancy, but as the days and weeks passed without an opportunity to make good on his promise, his grip on control in animal form was slipping, His mind increasingly descended into thoughts of tooth and claw and bloody revenge.

Not that Turvick was taking any chances with him. In addition to feeding him just enough to keep him alive and able to perform at the shows, Turvick had started making Laronzo hold a knife to Rona's stomach whenever Ithric was out of his cage. The human part of him was terrified that his control would snap, and the lion would savage one or both of the bastards — getting Rona and her unborn child killed in the process.

Ever since the embarrassing fiasco with Favian months ago in Draebard, Ithric had told himself over and over that he didn't need anyone. Being a spy in Rhyth had been challenging, while also providing the occasional excitement he craved. The whole place was a tinderbox waiting for the right spark, and the darker part of him had reveled in the atmosphere of imminent havoc — the prospect of seeing everything torn down and burned. It was a part of himself of which he wasn't particularly proud, and one he could now admit came to the fore when he was left on his own for too long.

Ithric's decision to reveal himself as a shape-shifter to Turvick and Laronzo had been spur-of-the-moment. Favian would doubtless describe it as another example of his willful self-destructiveness, but he'd be wrong. When he'd seen the way the others were being maltreated and kept prisoner by Turvick and his partner, he'd decided on the spot to do something about it.

Since people as strange and unique as Rona, Nimbral, and Arnav would be in as much — if not more — danger on their own in the south, he'd done the only thing he could think of at the time. He'd offered to join Turvick's show, claiming that he was terrified of being discovered and burned at the stake for his shape-shifting ability. Turvick had been easy enough to convince. His eyes had immediately grown wide, shining with avarice at the thought of possessing a tame lion that would follow his every command.

Laronzo, on the other hand, had rightly been wary — worried that if Ithric was discovered, they'd be dragged down with him by the followers of Deimok. Ithric saw the potential in this immediately, and casually planted the idea of going north in Turvick's mind. It was safer there, he'd mentioned, making sure his voice sounded suitably wistful.

At first, he'd been rather proud of the plan. Get north, get everyone free from Turvick's clutches, and take them somewhere he knew people... Venzor, for preference, or perhaps Meren. Even Draebard, in a pinch, though he tamped down the stab of pain and longing which came hard on the heels of that particular thought.

But Turvick hadn't been satisfied with his existing troupe of human oddities. When he'd kidnapped the young twins in Darveen, Ithric blamed himself. If not for his plan to get north, they would never have been anywhere near Darveen. For the first time, he realized that he'd been pulled in deeper than expected. Only the lucky and completely unforeseen appearance of the beautiful, bitter girl with the scarred face had allowed him—hopefully—to undo the mistake that had nearly cost the twins their family and their freedom.

Even now, he had no way to confirm that his angry visitor had kept her word and returned the children safely... but something about her made him feel confident that she had.

Now, it was Rona in danger. Every week that passed increased the risk that the dangerous pregnancy would damage her tiny body, perhaps fatally. And Ithric had no idea what to do. His original plan to subtly guide Turvick east, toward the places where people might know him, had relied too heavily on Turvick's continued trust. That was a complete joke now. Turvick didn't trust him a finger's width after the twins' disappearance and the scene with Rona on the ship.

He was stuck, and while it frightened him—the *human* part of him—it only made the lion angrier. Without the chance to take human form occasionally, he was slowly losing his will to the animal's. Once again, just as he had when he was spying in Rhyth, Ithric was overwhelmed by a sense of tumbling faster and faster toward calamity. This time, however, it was a far more personal sort of calamity. He might have started this journey with the intention of saving the others, but now it seemed far more likely that he would bring them all to blood and ruin.

Tomorrow they would arrive in Woodhaerst and start performing again. Turvick would attempt to control Ithric by threatening Rona, and Ithric would attempt to control his inner animal and not rip Turvick's throat out regardless. Everything was spiraling out of control, and he had no idea how to stop it.

The lion growled low in its chest and continued pacing obsessively, back and forth along the short length of the filthy cage.

>⚜<

Kathrael would never have imagined being able to cover such a long distance in such a short span of time. Now that Favian had a firm goal in mind, he was relentless, pushing Kathrael, their two horses, and himself to the limit.

She continued to ride on the second horse as a means of spreading the load more evenly between them, with Favian still controlling both animals. Her seat and legs felt like they were one big, aching bruise from the days of riding, but she said nothing—well aware that Favian had his own issues stemming from long hours in the saddle. Besides, as they closed in on their quarry, Kathrael found his single-mindedness catching. What had begun as *Favian's quest to save Ithric* had somehow become *their quest to save Ithric.*

She only hoped that the lion-boy would have the good grace not to get himself killed after all the trouble they'd gone to in trying to rescue him.

They rode late into the night and snatched a few hours' sleep, only to rise before the sun and begin again. As they cantered along the rutted and pockmarked road that paralleled the coastline, Favian gave her little pointers and let her practice controlling the stallion she rode while he kept slack in the rope connecting them. Even during these lessons, though, she could tell that Favian's spirit was straining toward Woodhaerst, his mind only partly on the here and now.

Her own spirits were restless—especially Vesh, who whispered doubts and misgivings in her ear.

If your golden-haired priest fails in this endeavor, it will surely break him.

What if the lion-boy's death is only the first?

There was a panicked mob in his vision… what if they turn on him, like they turned on me? What if they turn on you?

"Shut up, Vesh," she muttered through gritted teeth. "You're not helping."

Favian glanced at her. "What was that? Sorry, I couldn't hear."

"Nothing," she said more loudly.

The town of Gebrall came and went; they didn't stop. They barely slowed, in fact. She wondered what the townsfolk made of the priest and the woman with the veiled face riding through the village green on a pair of white horses, shouting questions about which day the traveling show had left their town. Favian seemed satisfied with the answers provided by the confused residents, and the two of them immediately traveled on.

Kathrael was desperately tired, and she knew Favian was, too. When she found herself nodding off in the saddle, her body slipping sideways for a heart-stopping instant before she grabbed her horse's thick mane and righted herself, she turned to her companion in the dim light of the crescent moon.

"Favian, we have to stop! The horses are exhausted. I'm exhausted. You're exhausted. One of us is going to get hurt, and then where will we be?"

Even though she couldn't see the muscle ticking at the corner of Favian's jaw, she could imagine it easily enough in the stubborn silence that followed.

"We're almost there," he said after a lengthy pause.

"Then we'll still be almost there in a few hours," she said, and carefully gathered up the reins to slow her mount to a walk as he had showed her. Favian was forced to follow suit or risk being jerked from his precarious sideways position by the rope he was holding. She continued, "Look, I know you're in a hurry to get there, but I fell asleep and nearly slid right out of the saddle just now. We're stopping."

The horses were eager for the rest, too, their low snorts echoing rhythmically as they huffed and blew.

Favian seemed to come back to himself. "I'm sorry, Kath. Of course we'll stop."

"It smells like rain, as well. We should put up the tent," she pointed out.

He groaned, but veered them off the road in search of a suitable site to camp. "Rain is all we need."

Kathrael shrugged, though he probably couldn't see it. "The weather is the weather. There's nothing to be done about it. Besides, rain will slow heavy caravans more than it slows us."

"Yes... I suppose you're right," Favian said in resignation.

They reached a small copse of trees, and he dismounted. She followed, hitting the ground on shaky legs. It was difficult to stay awake as she helped him unsaddle the horses and set up the tent in the near dark, but the alternative was to get soaked when the rain moved in. To save time, they didn't bother with a campfire. As it was, heavy clouds swallowed the sliver of moon just as they were moving the bedrolls inside the makeshift shelter.

Kathrael fell asleep shortly thereafter to the sound of raindrops hitting the thick hide stretched above them.

Gray light was peeking through the tent flap when she woke. Favian was already outside, heedless of the steady drizzle as he packed the saddlebags.

"Did you sleep?" she called, worrying that he'd stayed up fretting all night.

"Some," he replied. "You were out like a snuffed candle, though. Sorry I pushed so hard yesterday."

"It's all right. I want to get to him, too. Is there food?"

Favian gestured to a pair of saddlebags next to the tent. "Nothing hot, I'm afraid. A fire seemed like too much of a challenge in this weather."

She nodded and rummaged for some bread and dried meat, washing down the simple repast with watered wine. They finished packing the tent and saddled the horses, who seemed cranky and unenthusiastic about the prospect of being rained on all day. Donning cloaks, they clambered onto the animals' backs with stiff movements and made their way up to the road, which was already growing slick and muddy.

"Almost there," Favian said under his breath, as if reminding himself. "Not much longer now."

SIXTEEN

It was the morning of the troupe's final day in Woodhaerst, and the lion flicked its ears back in displeasure as a gust of wind blew another spattering of cold raindrops through the bars of the cage. Laronzo had thrown Ithric a joint of rotten meat the night before, after days of nothing but stale water. He'd fallen on the stinking haunch without a second thought, but now his belly churned and gurgled, adding to the day's general misery.

Perhaps the rain would prevent Turvick from putting on the show that afternoon, and Ithric wouldn't be forced to fight the primal and increasingly overpowering urge to sink his teeth into the man's neck and taste human blood spurting over his muzzle.

We mustn't do it. We mustn't do it. We can't. Remember Rona. Remember the baby, he thought like a chant. The lion's lip curled, its rasping tongue swiping out as if to savor the imagined gore.

The sun was almost directly overhead when the rain finally stopped and the clouds parted. Kathrael threw back the hood of her wet cloak, aware of Favian doing the same thing beside her.

"Look," he said, pointing into the valley ahead of them as they crested a small hill. "There it is."

Kathrael couldn't hold back a sigh of relief. Even though they only had Favian's vague calculations of travel times for a group of slow-moving caravans to go on, she could *feel* that they were close to their target.

"He's here," she said. "I know he is."

Favian nodded, and she thought he felt it, too. They were close. "Come on," he said. "Let's go get him."

They cantered down the gentle slope leading to the outskirts of town. The place was a tiny speck compared to Rhyth, but it was still much larger than Teth and most of the other villages she'd seen in the north, Draebard included. It would not be as simple as riding in and finding the village green; they would have to search for their quarry.

"Were they in the central square when you saw them before, in Penth?" Favian asked, lifting his voice over the wind so he could be heard.

Kathrael thought back to the blighted southern town, surprised at how distant the memories seemed. Even though it had been mere weeks, nearly every single aspect of her life had changed since then.

"No," she said, "they were set up in another plaza a few blocks away. Penth was a bit bigger than this, though. Does Woodhaerst even have more than one square?"

Favian shook his head in frustration. "I've never been here before, so I have no idea. We'll have to ask." He chewed his lower lip for a moment. "The temple should be easy to find. Someone there will almost certainly know, and we can tell them the owners are imprisoning a shape-shifter. That way we'll have some support if things get ugly."

Kathrael didn't bother to point out that Favian's vision pretty well guaranteed things *would* get ugly. Instead, she merely nodded agreement. "Good idea. Do all of the temples in the north wield as much political power as the Wolf Patron's? Can the priests here force Woodhaerst's chief and elders to free the other people that the owners are keeping prisoner?"

"I don't know," Favian said. "My understanding is that the temples in the west don't hold as much sway as they do in places like Draebard and Meren, but they'll still be more likely to take us seriously than the council would—assuming the council would even agree to see us in the first place."

"The temple it is, then."

They were at the edge of the town now, and as they rode further in, the roads grew narrow and twisting. The ground was still muddy from the morning's rain, and the familiar stench of many people living in a small area—food and waste and piss and sweat—assailed Kathrael's nose, making her realize that she had barely noticed the smell in the smaller villages like Draebard and Teth. The twisted tangle of homesickness and dread the scents evoked took her by surprise.

It didn't take long to get directions to the temple from a merchant selling ceramic cups at the side of the road. The large building was adorned with the now-familiar northern style of artwork in stone, wood, and beaten metal. It seemed to be dedicated to the goddess of war and flame, Deresta. Kathrael, who had always identified strongly with She-Who-Burns, felt herself relax a bit at the idea that the goddess was somehow standing behind them at the culmination of their quest.

They tied the horses nearby and approached the main doors, where a pudgy acolyte with reddish hair greeted them. He bowed to Favian and looked quickly away from Kathrael after catching a glimpse of her face.

"Welcome to the temple, Honored Guests," he said, recovering smoothly. "How may I assist you?"

Favian stood straight, his hands clasped inside the sleeves of his dun robes. "I am Favian of Draebard, novice to Senovo, the Wolf Priest. I must speak to your High Priest on a matter of great urgency."

Kathrael was a bit taken aback to hear Favian name his famous mentor so casually, especially after Chief Andoc had made it clear that he would not countenance any action among the western tribes that might be seen as interference by Draebard. Nonetheless, the strategy was effective—the acolyte's eyes widened, and he stammered, "Of… of course, Elder Brother. I will go immediately and see if he is available. Come with me, please, and I will take you to a room where you may wait and refresh yourselves."

They were brought to a small room off the main annex, where wine and fruit awaited them on a low table. Kathrael ate and drank while Favian paced. Eventually, she glared up at him and said, "Sit *down*, Favian. Do you want to greet the High Priest looking like a madman?"

Favian growled, but compromised by standing still against the far wall. He faced the door, staring at it with an intensity that made his blue eyes burn and his already chiseled features harden into marble. Kathrael couldn't help staring in turn, struck oddly and unexpectedly by his beauty. Something inside her flared into warmth at the sight, but she was distracted from regarding him when Woodhaerst's High Priest swept in.

"Greetings, my children," he said in a raspy voice, and the salutation might have been insulting were it not for the man's obviously advanced age. "What brings you to my temple after such a long journey?"

Favian bowed deeply. "Greetings, Respected Elder. I am Novice Favian of Draebard, and my companion's name is Kathrael. We have reason to believe that a shape-shifter is being held captive within the town of Woodhaerst." The old man had been looking curiously at Kathrael's face, but now his eyes shot back to Favian as he continued, "Tell me, please—is there a traveling show in town right now, exhibiting people as oddities?"

"There is," the High Priest replied cautiously. "In fact, there has been much talk of it the past two days. I understand that this rather distasteful show has another unusual exhibit as well—"

"A tame lion?" Favian suggested, his voice grim.

The priest let out a slow breath between his lips. "Indeed. You claim this beast is actually a shape-shifter's animal form? That is a very serious allegation, Novice Favian."

"I don't claim it. I know it," Favian said evenly.

"Not only that," Kathrael added. "The owners are keeping all of their exhibits as prisoners."

Favian drew the old man's attention again before he could ask how Kathrael could know such a thing.

"The shifter in question is Kathrael's bondmate. He was abducted several weeks ago. She sought assistance at the temple, and we have been chasing them ever since," he explained.

"Your bondmate?" the High Priest asked in surprise. "This shape-shifter is not a member of the priesthood?"

"They were already handfasted when his ability first manifested itself," Favian said, a bit too quickly.

Kathrael drew her shawl back, exposing herself to the priest's gaze. "Ever since I was burned, Ithric has been my sole means of support," she said, throwing herself into the role. "I cannot earn a living now. Without him, I would be destitute. He refused to cut the handfasting thongs and abandon me for a life in the temple."

The old man regarded her with a mixture of pity and thoughtfulness. "It is an unusual situation, certainly. Though it is highly irregular for a shape-shifter to remain outside the purview of the temple, I suppose this young man's motives were noble enough. What precisely are you asking of me, Novice Favian? Are you here on the Wolf Priest's behalf?"

"I am here on Kathrael's behalf, to see her husband freed, along with the other people being held captive by these men for their own profit. Nothing more, nothing less." Favian's voice had gone as hard as his features, and Kathrael held her breath, waiting to see how the High Priest would respond.

He frowned, contemplating Favian's words for long moments before nodding thoughtfully. "I will speak to Chief Ezrol about the situation and see if he is willing to take action. You must understand that I hold very little sway with the council, but the fact that this young man is a shape-shifter brings the situation within the scope of the temple to some degree."

"Thank you, Elder Brother," Favian said, still looking tense. "Time is of the essence. Based on what we've learned of these men, it is likely that this will be their last day in Woodhaerst before they move north again. Do you know where this show is being held?"

The priest shook his head. "I fear I have no taste for such things. A moment, please. Young Peltres may know the answer."

He stuck his head out the door and called for Peltres. The red-haired acolyte who had greeted them hurried in a moment later. "Yes, Elder Brother?" he asked in a nervous voice, his eyes still skating away from Kathrael's scars.

"Do you know where the men exhibiting the lion are going to be this afternoon?" the High Priest asked.

"I believe they are set up in the square behind the meeting hall, High Priest," the boy said. "Though, of course, I would not attend such a thing myself."

"Of course not, Little Brother. Don't worry, you are not in trouble," The old man assured. "In fact, go to the meeting hall right now, and ask the Chief if he would consent to meet with me on a matter of some urgency. I will follow behind in a few minutes."

"Yes, Elder Brother," said the boy, and hurried off after a final wide-eyed look at Favian and Kathrael.

"Is the meeting hall within walking distance, then?" Favian asked.

"It is," the High Priest confirmed.

"In that case, we will follow your acolyte and find the men we're looking for." The hard look had returned to Favian's eyes.

The High Priest frowned. "It would be better if you waited until I can speak with the town's leaders."

"No," Favian retorted. "It really wouldn't. Good day to you, Elder Brother, and thank you for your assistance."

He gestured Kathrael to precede him out of the room, and they left the High Priest frowning in confusion behind them.

"Are you sure we shouldn't wait for help?" she asked, as they hurried toward the entrance to catch up to the red-haired acolyte.

"I'm sure. I've already seen what will happen. There were no guardsmen or other priests around, which isn't a surprise since I know how long it can take to get a council of elders to take action on *anything*." Favian cupped her elbow and pointed ahead to where Peltres was speaking to another boy in the entryway. "Come on."

Kathrael hid her face as they followed the acolyte along the twisting roads and alleys. She was honestly grateful for the excuse to stretch her legs after so much time riding. The town of Woodhaerst seemed to be a relatively prosperous settlement, if a somewhat chaotic one. Just the sort of place that would appeal to men with a controversial traveling show, actually. She wondered how much money they'd made here, on the backs of the people they were mistreating.

"This is the meeting hall, Novice Favian," Peltres said nervously, indicating the long building they were approaching. "The square is behind it, one street over."

Favian was already looking in that direction as if he could see straight through the walls separating him from their destination. "Thank you. We'll be fine from here."

"Yes, thank you," Kathrael echoed, even though the boy still seemed terribly awkward around her. "Go and deliver your message. We'll need some help before things are done and dusted, I suspect."

The acolyte nodded and hurried toward the entrance of the hall. Favian was fairly vibrating with nervous energy, and she took his hand when he extended it. The two of them headed with single-minded purpose toward the next street, and whatever awaited them there.

As they approached, Kathrael could hear the same kind of crowd noise that had drawn her to the show in Penth—people laughing, talking, the occasional shout of excitement. Her heart beat faster, and Favian's hand tightened around hers. They emerged, moments later, into the southern edge of the square, which was absolutely packed with people — *hundreds* of them.

"They must be at the other end," Kathrael said, over the noise of rowdy spectators. "I can't see a thing!"

Favian was craning his head, trying to see over the wall of people. Kathrael was much shorter, and all she could make out was the row of shoulders in front of her. A ragged cheer of excitement filtered back to them from the front of the crowd, adding to their frustration at not being able to see what was happening.

"This is no good," Kathrael shouted in Favian's ear, standing on tiptoe to do so. "You try to get closer. I'm going to skirt around and see if I can find a vantage point off to the side."

He nodded, his attention focused on what he could not see. They were still at the very back of the crowd, so Kathrael slipped away, retracing their steps and hurrying down the road until she came to an alley which presumably backed along one of the sides of the square. She could still hear the crowd clearly, even with a row of close-set buildings separating her from the mass of people.

When she judged she was behind the area where the caravans were set up, she started looking for a way to get back to the plaza. Eventually, she was forced to climb over a rickety section of wooden fence between two narrow houses, but once she'd managed it, she was rewarded with a relatively clear view of the show from behind.

The lion cage was on the far side of one of the other wagons, half hidden from her line of sight, but she could see tawny haunches and a tail lashing back and forth angrily. A jolt of mingled excitement and worry hit her upon seeing Ithric, alive and in the flesh. Though the gods had never done much for her up to this point, she couldn't help sending up a quick prayer that the lion-boy would survive whatever was to come next.

With difficulty, she tore her gaze away from that lashing tail and took in the rest of the scene. It was very much as before, only without the presence of the twins. She couldn't help the surge of satisfaction she felt over her role in that. The boy with no arms was seated at his table, feeding himself with a spoon held in his toes. Nearby, the tall man danced with the short woman.

This time, she was close enough to take in their haggard countenances as they capered and performed for the crowd. She wondered what these people had endured since she saw them last, and vowed that whatever else happened today, she *would* see them safe at the end of things... even if they were unable to save Ithric from his prophesied fate.

Kathrael looked around herself, seeking a path that would get her closer and perhaps give her a better view of the cage. The strange couple's dance ended to a round of whoops and bawdy catcalls. As it did, the man in charge— Turvick, she recalled—stepped up on his platform to gain the crowd's attention and begin his spiel about the tame lion.

Her attention was caught, however, when the shorter, fatter man—Turvick's partner, who had dragged the twins around the crowd during the show in Penth—moved quietly to grab the tiny woman's arm. She *cringed* at his touch, and tried half-heartedly to struggle away as he dragged her behind the shelter of the caravans. Kathrael's jaw clenched, her hand gripping the edge of the fence she was standing next to until the knuckles turned white.

Something was deeply wrong with the scene, and every instinct she possessed screamed at her to act. But act how?

She looked around again. The unnaturally tall man who had been dancing with the small woman stood empty-armed now, his face pale as milk. Turvick's partner had positioned himself in such a way that he and his tiny captive were not obvious to the crowd, but could still be seen by anyone standing to the side or behind them, as Kathrael currently was. A moment later, the man drew a wicked looking knife and pressed the tip to the woman's belly. Kathrael caught her breath, her own stomach clenching in empathy.

Just then, the woman's captor turned his head and looked straight toward the lion's cage. Kathrael followed his gaze and found the lion, fully visible now, staring fixedly back at him with glowing eyes. Suddenly, everything fell into place. They were using the small woman as a hostage against Ithric's good behavior while he was in the form of a lion.

Indeed, Turvick was stepping up at that very moment to open the lion's cage, his face twisted in a sneer now that he was facing away from the crowd. There was a familiar litany of fearful cries from the crowd as the animal jumped down from its enclosure, and Turvick immediately started giving his reassurances about the animal's docility.

To Kathrael's eye, Ithric looked anything but docile at that moment. His lithe body was fairly vibrating with anger. Halfway to the raised platform, the lion froze. As it had in Penth, its head turned slowly until it was looking straight at her. This time, instead of being afraid, Kathrael let her features twist into a sharp, predatory smile. The lion's lip curled, and a low, rumbling snarl rolled across the space separating them. The crowd muttered nervously in the background.

Suddenly, glaringly cognizant of what she needed to do, Kathrael straightened from her hiding place and stalked directly toward the man holding the knife.

Favian shoved his way through the claustrophobic press of people, trying to get to the front. Already, the sick feeling that always overcame him when reality started to synchronize with one of his visions was washing over him, made worse by the stench of unwashed bodies and rotting garbage around him.

He elbowed his way between two burly men. One of them growled and grasped his sleeve, only to let it drop an instant later when his partially shaven head and priest's robes penetrated the man's awareness.

"Let me pass," Favian said, barely recognizing his own voice. Some combination of his tone and the man's innate respect for the priesthood caused him to squeeze back against his companion for an instant so Favian could slip through.

Ahead of him, gasps and cries of fear erupted from the crowd. His heart pounded triple time as he pressed forward against the wall of people once more, this time catching a sharp—though probably accidental—elbow to the sternum for his troubles. He staggered a bit as the crowd heaved, pushing back from whatever had alarmed the people at the front.

As if I can't guess, he thought, somewhat desperately, trying to stand his ground and not be swept backward by the people jostling around him.

Favian gritted his teeth and jammed a shoulder between the next two people in front of him, attempting to widen the space enough to force his way through.

The man holding the knife to the tiny woman's belly must have seen Kathrael move toward him from the corner of his eye, because his head whipped around from where he'd been craning to watch Turvick force the lion to perform for the crowd.

"Who are you?" he demanded angrily. "You can't be back here!"

Kathrael, still flooded with righteous anger, ignored him and addressed his terrified captive instead. "Don't be scared," she said. "When he drops the knife, run."

The woman stared at her with wide, frightened eyes, even as the man frowned and said, "What—?"

Kathrael pulled her shawl down and twisted her face into a snarl, cutting off his indignant question. The man's face paled and he took an unconscious step backward, the knife slipping from his limp grip to clatter on the flagstones lining the plaza. The short woman stamped on his toes with one tiny boot and darted away, running for the tall man she'd been dancing with earlier. He crouched and met her with open arms, holding her close.

With a final sneer at Turvick's dumbstruck partner, Kathrael turned her attention to the lion. The animal looked from the mismatched couple embracing each other tightly, to the shocked man in front of Kathrael—unarmed now as he backed slowly away from her. Its glowing gold-flecked eyes tracked slowly back to Turvick, whose body jolted as if he'd been struck. Suddenly, all of the sneering bravado he'd displayed earlier around the dangerous animal drained away in a moment, and he stumbled back a step. The lion prowled forward on silent paws, pacing him with clear intent.

⤙ ♔ ⤚

Favian shoved his way between two women, finally close enough to the action to see over the shoulders of those still remaining in front of him. His heart seized as his eyes caught and held on Ithric, his imposing animal form now bony and scarred from whatever had been done to him over the months since he'd left Draebard. As Favian watched in horror, the lion faced off with a portly man in a gaudy tunic and breeches, who backed away in obvious fear... just as he had foreseen.

The beast growled low in its throat, stalking its victim with dangerous intent. Around Favian, the crowd was muttering nervously, milling around. The big cat roared in anger, and someone in the front row screamed. A moment later, people were running... scrambling to get out of the packed village square... buffeting him as they pushed past... blocking his view.

He cast around for any kind of high ground—a wagon, or a barrel, or *anything* where he could climb up and try to get the beast's attention, but there was nothing. Terrified people continued to shove at him, threatening to send him to the ground.

Favian yelled at the top of his lungs, trying to get the lion's attention. "Ithric! *Ithric!*"

A moment later he was standing—battered and bruised—at the edge of the ever-expanding clear space left behind as the crowd fled. The lion surged forward, tackling its prey to the ground even as the gaudily dressed man turned to run.

"Ithric!" Favian cried again. "Be careful, you idiot! *He's got a knife!*"

Without warning, the beast's head jerked up, its attention drawn from its prey to Favian. A moment later, there was a twisting *change*, and Ithric crouched over the downed man in human form, looking frantically at Favian with wide, shocked eyes. The man on the ground scrabbled at his belt, and a shiny dagger appeared in his hand.

Favian shouted in dismay. The knife jabbed up even as Ithric tried to twist away, and blood sprayed from Ithric's unprotected side as it hit home.

SEVENTEEN

Ithric cried out as his side erupted in agony, cutting through the remnants of the bloodlust that had turned his feline vision red and made his mouth water with the need to tear into Turvick's flesh. The dual shocks of the knife wound, along with the unexpected change of form, threatened to send him reeling—but his earlier anger gave him the strength to knock the knife from his tormentor's hand.

The pair rolled over, grappling, and the pain in Ithric's side spiked as Turvick's weight settled on top of him. Ithric roared in the man's face, his voice barely human, and kneed him as hard as he could between the legs. Turvick grunted and tried to curl up, giving Ithric the chance he needed to roll them over again. Wheezing, he straddled the fucking bastard who had terrorized his fellow captives for so long, and smashed his fist into the man's ugly face, over and over until he stopped moving.

The world was narrowing down to a tunnel, his vision going gray and the noises around him sounding oddly attenuated. For this reason, he didn't see the owners of the hands that closed around his upper arms and pulled him away from the unconscious man lying underneath him.

"I'll kill him," he gasped, struggling weakly to get back to the body on the ground. "Lemme—"

"Let's leave something for the others, yes?" said a low, musical female voice. "Guards should be here before long to sort things out, and hopefully someone from the council, or at least from the temple."

Ithric craned to look at the woman's scarred face, blinking as his fuzzy mind made the connection. "Little Cat? I was right, then—thought it was you. Told you we'd meet again..."

"Now who's predicting the future?" said a second painfully familiar voice, sounding grim.

Ithric rolled his head to the other side, confirming that, first, he hadn't been hallucinating Favian's presence earlier and, second, that he was really growing *very* dizzy now.

"Oh. It's you," he said. "What in the gods' names are *you* doing here?"

Even with his wavering vision, Ithric could see the tendons working at the corners of Favian's jaw.

"Good to see you, too, you cock-sucking son of a bitch," Favian said, his tone deceptively mild. "Now shut up, and I swear by all that's holy that if you die on me after all this, Ithric, I will fucking kill you."

"Language," Ithric chided in an annoying singsong voice, and promptly passed out in their arms.

Favian swallowed hard, holding panic at bay by a mere thread as Ithric went limp against them. His eyes sought Kathrael's face. She was pulling Ithric's left arm out of the way so she could get a clear view of the bloody gash in his side.

"Is he—?" Favian asked, the words pulled from him almost against his will.

"He's still breathing," Kathrael said, hitching herself around so she could tear a strip of cloth from the hem of her skirts. "I think he just fainted."

Favian placed a hand flat over Ithric's naked chest, feeling the slow rise and fall for himself, along with the thrum of a still-beating heart. He took a deep breath and dragged his eyes away to scan the nearly deserted square.

"We need a healer," he said.

"We *need* you to keep your head on straight in case that crowd we just panicked turns into a mob and comes back for us," Kathrael retorted, wadding up the strip of cloth and pressing it hard to the gory knife wound. "Favian, you're the only person here with any kind of authority whatsoever. The rest of us are freaks in their eyes. We might as well have targets painted on our backs if those frightened people decide to come after us with torches and pitchforks."

Favian looked around again, truly taking in the scene. Turvick's other three captives had closed in around his now weaponless partner, trapping the man against the side of one of the caravans. Despite the fact that one of the three people surrounding him only came up to his stomach and another had no arms, he looked utterly terrified—the expression of someone who knew exactly what he deserved for his crimes, and was staring his comeuppance in the eye.

A short distance away, Turvick himself lay in a heap on the muddy cobbles, still out cold, his breath coming in wet wheezes. Favian looked down again, at Ithric's pale, slack face, and made himself move. He eased Ithric down to lie with his head in Kathrael's lap. She steadied his limp body and continued to press the wad of cloth hard to his wound, looking up long enough to give Favian a reassuring nod.

He glanced down at himself. There was mud and blood staining his robes, but he straightened them into a semblance of order and dragged his tattered composure together.

"Wait. Don't harm him," he called to the three strange people arrayed in a hostile half-circle around Turvick's partner. "Guards will be coming any minute, and they mustn't find you doing anything threatening."

The tiny woman looked up at him uncertainly as he came closer. "Who are you? What business of yours is this?"

"Kathrael and I are friends of Ithric," he said, which was much simpler than explaining that he'd been in love with the shape-shifter and gotten his heart trampled into the mud for his troubles. For good measure, he added, "Kathrael is also the one who rescued the twins and took them back to their family."

The armless boy looked at him sharply with dark, flashing eyes. "The children are safe? She took them back to Darveen?"

"She did. They were reunited with their mother and father, safe and sound."

"Is Ithric dead?" the woman asked, her face still gray with fear and anger.

"No!" Favian said, too loudly. He forced himself to modulate his voice to something approaching normality. "No. He's wounded, though. I don't know how badly. He needs a healer. Guards will be here soon. I'll call for one then."

"Rona needs a healer, too," said the unnaturally tall man. Of the three, he looked the most likely to lose control and tear the cowering man in front of him limb from limb.

Favian looked at the small woman again. "Are you hurt?"

She shook her head, two spots of color rising in her pale cheeks. "Pregnant." Her eyes moved of their own volition to the tall man, and Favian blinked, putting the pieces together with some surprise.

She continued, "I'm afraid the child will kill me if it's too big. Ithric promised to get me away to a healer, but Turvick overheard us talking. That's when things started to get really bad." She wrapped her arms around herself. "He whipped Nimbral. Started withholding food from Ithric, and forbade him to change into human form. He made Laronzo threaten me with a knife whenever the lion was out of his cage, because he was afraid Ithric would kill him otherwise." Her gaze swept over to the man Ithric had beaten unconscious. "Did he?"

"No," Favian said. "Just punched him in the face a few times before we pulled him away."

"Pity," Rona said with a dark look.

A noise drew their attention. Guards were jogging across the square toward them, weapons drawn.

"Please. Stay where you are, all three of you." Favian told them. "Don't make any threatening moves. I'll talk to them."

"Why should we trust you?" the tall man asked, still sounding combative.

Favian gestured around. "Because you have no one else to trust."

He turned away and walked forward with raised hands to meet the guards before they could get too close. The man in front came to a halt a few steps away from him and scanned the plaza, gesturing for his compatriots to stop as well.

"I am Priest Favian of Draebard," Favian said, the title still not coming naturally to him. "Thank you for coming— there are people injured and we are in urgent need of assistance."

The guards' leader regarded him with wary eyes. His sword was still drawn, but he held it lowered at his side. "Brother Favian," he acknowledged cautiously. "There were reports of an escaped lion attacking people; part of this traveling show that's been camped in town for the last few days."

"No lions here now, as you can see," Favian said, gesturing around the largely deserted space. "Just two cruel and greedy men preying on those weaker than themselves for their own gain."

He was playing for time, more than anything—hoping that the High Priest had spoken with the chief and the elders, and that help would arrive from that quarter.

"There *was* a lion in the show," the guard said, still looking as though he was as likely to detain them all as to send for a healer to attend the injured. "The cage is empty now."

"That wasn't a lion," Favian said, playing his only available card. "It was a shape-shifter held captive, beaten and starved into submission. He's right over there, and he's wounded. He *needs* a *healer*."

The man appeared surprised, and followed Favian's pointing finger to where Ithric lay limp in Kathrael's hold. Kathrael had already replaced her shawl, covering her face, so she looked like any passerby might, who had stopped to help.

"Miss?" the guard asked. "Did you see any of this?"

Kathrael nodded, still not lifting her head. "I did. I was right up front." She pointed at Turvick's partner, careful to keep her face angled away. "That man was in the back, threatening the small woman with a knife. He didn't think anyone in the crowd could see him, but I was off to the side. The lion changed into this boy and tried to help her, but the owner over there grabbed him and tried to stop him.

"They fought, and the owner stabbed him before the shape-shifter knocked him unconscious. The others got the small woman away from the man who was threatening her. This priest saw what was happening and came to help."

It was a masterful performance, and Favian dove in to play his part. "That's right. I've been chasing these men for some time. There were reports that they had kidnapped a shape-shifter, and were holding other people against their will as well. Apparently it was all true."

From behind him, Turvick's partner finally managed to find his tongue. "No! Don't listen to them—they're lying! These freaks turned on us for no reason! Look what they did to Turvick!" He pointed at his crumpled partner with a shaking finger.

The guards looked somewhat bewildered by the deluge of conflicting information, and their leader appeared to be fighting the beginnings of a headache.

"Look," he said. "I've got a frightened mob outside the square, multiple reports of a dangerous wild animal attacking people, and a collection of freaks who look intent on murder. What are you suggesting I do? Pat everyone on the head and send them on their way?"

Favian's temper surged, making his fists clench inside the sleeves of his robes. "I'm *suggesting* you send someone for a healer before the injured shape-shifter currently bleeding all over the cobblestones ends up a *dead* shape-shifter!"

"Do as the priest says," came a new voice, and Favian's head whipped around to see a powerful man with close-cropped brown hair approach. The elderly High Priest flanked him, following a step behind.

The guard's demeanor immediately changed. He stepped back and gave a short half-bow. "Of course, sir. Right away," he said, and gestured one of his men to go in search of help.

The new arrival surveyed the motley group of injured and uninjured with an impatient sigh. "Had a bad feeling about this lot when they pulled into town three days ago," he muttered. "Should've paid more attention to my gut, obviously." He jerked his chin toward Ithric's naked form. "This your shape-shifter?"

Not mine. Never mine, Favian thought bitterly, but aloud, he only said, "Yes, that's him." He had to fight the urge to step in front of Ithric and Kathrael protectively as the newcomer walked over and reached down, lifting Kathrael's shawl enough to peer underneath. She said nothing in response to the man's presumption, but Favian could sense her covering a flinch. His fists clenched harder.

"Huh," the man said. "That's a real mess, all right. Guess you weren't exaggerating about her, Oslud."

The High Priest nodded. "Their story had the ring of truth to it, Chief Ezrol. The fact that the young man in question is not a member of the temple *is* rather irregular, but nonetheless, holding a shape-shifter against his will is a serious offense against the gods."

"We weren't holding him against his will!" Turvick's partner cried, evidently sensing the tide turning against him. "He joined us voluntarily—practically begged us to let him in!"

"Lies!" Kathrael replied indignantly, changing course effortlessly to play the part of Ithric's wife. "Did he beg you to starve him, or put these scars on his body? He's skin and bones! You kidnapped him from our home village!"

The Chief shook his head impatiently. "Maybe he was kidnapped, or maybe he was looking for an easy way out of an unhappy handfasting to a disfigured woman. Whatever the case, it's clear that he's been mistreated, and I won't have folks saying that I allowed such treatment of a shape-shifter in my town. Guards, take that man and his partner away and lock them up while the council decides what to do with 'em. As for the rest of these... people..."

He looked uncertainly at Rona, her tall, thin mate, and the boy with no arms.

Favian stepped in quickly. "Perhaps they could stay at the temple until more permanent plans can be made. They are welcome to come back to Draebard with us when we leave. High Priest?"

The old man jerked as if startled. "What? Oh, yes... that would probably be for the best."

One of the guards had grabbed a bucket of water from the well at the corner of the plaza while they were talking. He dumped it unceremoniously over Turvick's head, making the man splutter and gasp as he was dragged roughly back to consciousness. More guards pulled him to unsteady feet, while others edged warily past the three still holding his partner at bay.

When the pair were escorted away with their hands tied behind them — Turvick staggering drunkenly between two of the large men — Favian felt a modicum of his tension ease. When a dark-haired, middle-aged healer arrived, clutching a satchel of herbs and bandages, it eased a bit more.

After a brief double take at the collection of strange individuals standing around, she fussed over Ithric's wound and peeled his eyelids back to check his pupils. "I'll need a stretcher, and someplace clean and quiet to work," she snapped.

The High Priest finally seemed to shake himself free of his stupor, and gestured toward the southern edge of the square. "Come. Everyone, back to the temple. It would be best for you to keep out of the public eye after the panic earlier."

The healer's sharp gaze flicked over the others, landing for a moment on Favian's bloodstained robes. "Is anyone else hurt, aside from the one who was dragged out of here a few minutes ago?"

The tall man, Nimbral, stepped forward. "Rona needs help," he said, and gestured at the tiny woman.

The healer looked at her pale countenance. "Are you ill, then?"

The short woman shook her head. "I'm pregnant. It's his."

Rona nodded up at Nimbral. The healer blinked in surprise, echoing Favian's earlier response, and blew out a large breath. "Right. Well. First things first. Let's get your friend seen to, and then we'll talk." She glanced around at the remaining guards. "Now, where's that stretcher?"

⚜

"Will he live?" Favian asked some time later, his arms wrapped tightly around himself.

Kathrael was relieved to be back in the quiet solitude of the temple after the tense scene in the plaza, but she, too, looked to the sharp-featured healer in concern. The blood pouring from Ithric's wound had slowed to a trickle after the stretch of time she'd spent keeping pressure on it, but he showed no signs of waking even after all the jostling and prodding.

"Hmm," said the woman in a non-committal tone, sounding eerily like Favian's friend in Draebard, Healer Sagdea. Perhaps all healers in the north were crotchety by nature.

"The knife left a ragged tear, but it didn't look as deep as it could have been," Kathrael offered to fill the silence. It was true—she'd seen more knife wounds than she cared to admit among her fellow prostitutes over the years. This one—while messy—was not as bad as some she'd seen.

"I've had worse…" came a slurred voice from the bed.

"Ah, that's what I was waiting for," said the healer, even as Favian hurried forward to hover at her shoulder. "How do you feel, young man?"

Ithric pried sticky eyelids open and tried to wet his mouth with his tongue. "Like I've been starved, kept in a cage for weeks, and then knifed," he said eventually. "Why? How do I look?"

Kathrael raised an eyebrow. "Like you've been starved, kept in a cage for weeks, and then knifed," she confirmed, and turned away to pour him a cup of the medicinal tea the healer had prepared earlier.

Ithric frowned suddenly. "The others? Are they —"

"Your friends are safe. They're here in the temple," the healer told him.

Ithric relaxed back, and let Kathrael support his head so he could sip at the warm liquid. When he had swallowed a few sips, he coughed and winced as the movement pulled at the wound. "Rona needs a healer. She's pregnant," he rasped.

"I am aware," said the woman. "Though I'd've thought you'd be more worried about your own condition."

Ithric only lifted a shoulder and let it drop. His eyes skated around Favian and came to rest on neutral territory, staring at the rafters above. "Just another scar," he mumbled. "'S worth it if it means the others are safe."

Favian had stepped back from the bed after it became obvious that Ithric was awake and more-or-less aware. Now, he inhaled sharply as if about to say something, but no words followed. Kathrael looked between the two of them with interest, trying to decipher them.

The healer made a noise of disapproval. "You're very lucky, as it happens. The blade slid along one of your lower ribs rather than piercing deeper, into your organs. As long as the wound does not putrefy, it should heal well enough."

"Not to worry, in that case," Ithric said, sounding weary. "I have the constitution of a lion."

The woman regarded him with interest. "It's true, then? You are a shape-shifter?"

"It's true," Ithric said, still in the same flat tone. "Why? Do you want a demonstration?"

The healer chewed her lip as if strongly considering it, before her professional ethics stopped her. "No, no," she said. "You shouldn't tax yourself. I've just never met one before, that's all. Well… I should go speak to the dwarf, I suppose. Get some rest, now, and have your friends bring you some light broth to drink in a few hours. Keep the bandages clean, and I'll look in on you later this evening."

Ithric nodded carelessly and let his eyes slip closed. Favian was standing against the wall now, his arms still tightly crossed, face pale even though Kathrael would have expected him to be relieved that Ithric was awake and seemed to have his wits about him.

Since it seemed no one else was going to respond, she said, "Thank you, Healer. Your help is much appreciated."

The woman merely nodded and waved a hand in acknowledgement, before gathering her things together and bustling out of the room. Favian was still staring silently at Ithric's sleeping form from his place against the wall. There was a chair next to the bed, so Kathrael sat. She brushed back a lock of Ithric's tousled auburn mane of hair and hooked it behind his ear before looking up.

"You did it, Favian," she said in a quiet voice. "You saved him. Aren't you happy?"

"Yes," he whispered, his face pale and his expression closed off. A moment later, he turned abruptly and strode from the room, not looking back.

Kathrael stared after him for the span of several breaths before returning her attention to the injured shape-shifter on the bed. "What's your story, lion-boy?" she asked. "How did you hurt each other so badly, without managing to cut the cord that draws you together?"

Ithric slept on, oblivious.

When Favian had still not returned hours later, Kathrael made a brief, unsuccessful search for him. Unwilling to leave Ithric too long on his own, and confident—or at least, *mostly* confident—that Favian would not actually take the horses and leave, she returned to the borrowed sick room.

When she entered, it was to find her charge awake again, regarding her with clear hazel eyes.

"What happened to the twins?" he said.

She smiled, remembering the task with which he'd challenged her, and the little family's joy when they had been reunited. Looking back, she thought that his request might have been the only thing that kept her spirit from sliding into complete ruin during those dark and hopeless days. Somehow, he had seen good in her. The *children* had seen good in her, as well—and *they* had the power to see straight into her thoughts.

What might she have become, if not for that small reminder of love and light?

"They're safe at home with their mother and father," she said, a hint of pride slipping into her tone. "Why? Did you doubt me?"

"Never for a minute," Ithric said.

Kathrael suddenly remembered their cover story. "Oh, I almost forgot. You should know that we've been telling everyone you and I are handfasted. You didn't join the priesthood because you've had to provide for me ever since my face was ruined. Apparently, I'd be lost without you."

Ithric looked at her oddly. "And people buy that story after meeting you?"

She couldn't hold in the unladylike snort. "Please. Why wouldn't they?" She drew her shawl forward and ducked her head bashfully, falling into the persona of the helpless damsel. "I'm *ever* so demure, you know. And I've been so *terribly* worried about you since you were kidnapped from our village..."

Ithric smirked despite his weakness, clearly amused. "Oh, dear. You poor little thing—my heart bleeds, just thinking about it." He shook his head slowly and looked her up and down. "So. We're handfasted, eh? In that case, you'd probably better tell me your name. Might raise a few eyebrows otherwise."

"It's Kathrael," she said, and offered him a drink of the pale broth sitting in a cup next to the bed.

He made a noise of surprise around the mouthful of liquid and swallowed it. "So I was right! You really are a Little *Kat*."

She mock-glared at him. "Who are you calling *little*, lion-boy?"

He laughed, only to pull up short, one hand flying to the rusty stain seeping through his bandages. "*Ow*. All right. No laughing, apparently. Why don't you tell me how you met our Most Holy and Exalted Brother Favian, instead? That should sober me right up."

"She held a knife to my throat and tried to use me as a hostage to get to Senovo," said Favian from the doorway. "We've been great friends ever since."

Kathrael blushed a bit, but Ithric apparently had other things on his mind as he stared at Favian with a complicated expression, taking in his appearance with a slow, head-to-toe sweep of his eyes.

"Huh," he said. "Looks like I missed a few things since I left. Nice new robes you've got there. Love the hair. So, how are the balls?"

Favian's blue eyes were as cold as a glacier in the mountains. "Absent," he said with sharp, precise elocution.

"*Finally.* What about you? You've managed not to get burned at the stake yet, I gather?"

Ithric grinned, showing teeth. It was not a nice expression. "Not yet. Sorry to disappoint you."

Kathrael looked from Ithric to Favian and back again. "The healer said you were to drink that broth, lion-boy," she said. "Perhaps you two can wait to eviscerate each other until after it's finished?"

"Happily," Ithric said. His stomach rumbled a moment later. Kathrael handed him the cup, pleased to see that his hands were steady as he lifted it.

"Yes, by all means," Favian added. "I'm well acquainted with how much Ithric appreciates the hospitality of the temple."

"One cage is much the same as another," Ithric said pleasantly, and slurped the broth.

Favian's face clouded in anger, and he stalked out of the room without another word. Kathrael watched him go, and turned back to regard Ithric. "You shouldn't wield your claws so thoughtlessly, you know. He's been a wreck ever since he had a vision of you being stabbed. Perhaps you both ought to go a little easier on each other, whatever happened between you in the past."

Ithric looked surprised for a moment, the cup held frozen an inch from his lips. Then he finished the movement and took another thoughtful mouthful. "A vision? I suppose that answers the question of what he's even doing here," he said after he'd swallowed. "If he had a dream about it I guess he'd have to come. Otherwise he couldn't have seen it in the first place."

Kathrael attempted to wrap her mind around that, and failed. "Prophecy gives me a headache," she decided. "It's ridiculous."

"As ridiculous as a person turning into a lion?" Ithric said lightly, and Kathrael got the impression he was relieved to have a distraction from his earlier thoughts about Favian.

"As ridiculous as children who can see other people's thoughts," she agreed. "Seriously, though—I'm swearing off prophecy from now on. It's exhausting."

Ithric let out a breath of laughter and flinched again as pain from the wound flared. "You might need to rethink the company you're keeping, in that case." He set the empty cup aside. "Now—I hate to be an ingrate, but I don't suppose there's anything more substantial than broth to be had? I would *murder* for some roast mutton right now."

EIGHTEEN

For the next several days, Favian was a ghost. On those rare occasions Kathrael saw him, he was always deeply involved in conversation with Ithric's fellow captives. Once, she stayed for a bit to see what they were discussing. Apparently, Favian was attempting to talk them into coming back to Draebard, with mixed success.

Rona and Nimbral were at least somewhat open to the idea, mainly because the healer here in Woodhaerst had given Rona an answer she did not want to hear.

"She said I should kill the baby," the small woman said, and stroked a hand over her belly. "She even offered to make the tea for me that would do it. I don't *want* to kill it. It's *ours.*"

There was a stubborn lilt to her voice, and the giant next to her put a large hand around her shoulder.

"Sagdea is one of the most respected healers in the north," Favian said. "Maybe she will know of some other way."

"I just want to go home," said Arnav, the armless boy. "I don't want to live in the north."

"Will your family take you back?" Kathrael asked bluntly.

"Why wouldn't they?" he shot back, sounding angry. "It's not my fault I was born like this!"

"Where are you from, Arnav?" Favian asked.

"Rhyth," he muttered, sullen.

"Rhyth is tearing itself apart," Kathrael pointed out. "No one is safe there—certainly no one... *different.* I should know."

"It's still where I belong," said the boy, glaring daggers at her.

Kathrael felt a surprising flush of homesickness, and wondered at it. It would be madness to leave the safe haven she'd found in Draebard and return to a place that wanted her dead. So why did thoughts of the humid nights and the chaos of city life make her heart ache? She could only shake her head, suddenly unable to answer Arnav with words.

Since Favian seemed more likely to do Ithric further bodily injury than to nurse him, Kathrael spent most of her time in the shape-shifter's sick room. It was no hardship. The fascination she'd had for him ever since their first brief meeting showed no signs of waning. Quite the opposite. Ithric was quick-witted and self-deprecating, full of humorous quips and completely unselfconscious in her company.

He looked at her as no one else had since before her injury. Even Vesh had gazed at her with regret afterward, as though he felt he should have protected her somehow. As though her scars were his personal failing. Livvy, of the harelip and the guileless mind, had looked at her as one looks at a mirror—fascinated by her *because* of her scars, rather than *despite* them. Favian and the twins looked past the ugly injury, to what lay underneath.

But Ithric... Ithric simply did not appear to see the scars. He looked at her as any man might look at a beautiful woman. Drinking her in. Appreciating her. It touched something inside of her that she had not realized was broken—a place that longed to be *wanted*, for exactly what she was.

It was ridiculous.

Why would anyone want damaged goods, when the world was full of buxom beauties with soft, unblemished skin and clear, twinkling eyes? Shape-shifters were still revered in the north—that was obvious enough. Though Ithric's refusal to join the priesthood made him something of an oddity, Kathrael had no doubt that women would still fight each other for a single moment of his time, hoping to gain status from the association. Hoping that the gods' gift of animal transformation would somehow rub off on them and bring luck to their own lives.

And yet, Ithric still watched her with eyes that seemed to caress her.

Ridiculous.

Dusk was leeching the last of the day's light from the windows when she nudged the door open with her foot and backed into his room, holding a heavy tray and a pitcher. It was the fifth evening since their arrival, and Ithric's subsequent injury. He was already up and around, though he could not go far and he still tired easily.

"It took the better part of a week, but I finally came through with the mutton," Kathrael said without looking at the bed. "I hope you're suitably appreciative."

She pushed the door closed with her hip and turned around, only to find a lion sprawled among the blankets, regarding her with lazy eyes. Kathrael froze, staring at the animal in fascination. The beast had a puckered, half-healed gash along its ribcage, and a pile of damp, chewed-up bandages trailed over the edge of the straw-stuffed mattress and onto the floor below.

Before she could do more than stand there, gaping in wonder, the figure twisted unnaturally. Her gaze slid away from the odd wrinkle in reality as if unable to gain purchase on it. When she focused again, Ithric lay naked in the bed, looking sheepish.

"Sorry about that," he said, and threw a corner of the blanket carelessly over his lap. "When Turvick wouldn't let me change into human form, I thought I'd go mad with it... yet here I am, only a few days later, and already the lion is growing restless. Hope I didn't scare you."

Kathrael broke free from her paralysis and walked toward him to place the tray on the small table next to the bed. "You didn't scare me. Just gawping, for which I apologize. It's an impressive form."

"D'you think so?" he asked, looking oddly shy. "I've always felt a bit scrawny and flea-bitten. Still, I suppose I should count myself lucky that I don't transform into a field mouse or something." He chuckled. "I met some bears up north who told stories about a man who changed into a turtle. No idea if they were being serious or not."

Kathrael poured some wine for them and handed him a cup. "There are other shape-shifters in the north, then?" she asked, intrigued.

Ithric took a deep swallow and nodded. "Oh, yes. There are the bears—almost a dozen of them, though they mostly keep to themselves. And Senovo, of course. Also, there's an old woman down south who lives as a vixen—if she's still alive, that is. I haven't seen her since before the invasion." He frowned. "I imagine there would be more if the priests didn't try to castrate or sequester anyone who shows the ability. That's why the bears stay way up in the wastelands, away from people."

It had the sound of old resentment. Kathrael gained a sudden flash of insight into at least part of the conflict between Ithric—the shape-shifter who refused to be castrated—and Favian, the seer who'd *wanted* to be castrated.

"How did you avoid being drawn into the Priests' Guild, anyway?" she asked, curious.

Ithric gave a little self-deprecating snort. "Simple. I ran away and hid. Spent most of my time in animal form, because it was warmer, but I also nearly starved to death before Senovo found me and took me under his patronage. I was an adolescent lion with no pride to support me, and no experience hunting. I ate a lot of stringy rabbits and carrion that winter, let me tell you."

Kathrael smirked, and handed him a plate. "Well, I guess you'd better enjoy the mutton while you have the chance, in that case."

Ithric grinned in return, but there was a glint in his eye as he said, "Oh, I've gotten considerably more skilled since then, believe me."

"Not much help when you're locked in a cage, though," Kathrael pointed out, gesturing toward his body, which didn't have a trace of fat on it.

Ithric sobered. "Yeah. That was admittedly not my finest hour. Thought I could help the others by playing along with Turvick and his crony. But I just ended up making things worse."

His sullen tone surprised her. "Oh, come now. It all worked out in the end, didn't it?" she said.

With a sour expression, Ithric replied, "*Sure* it did. Because what I really need more than anything else is to be indebted to someone who holds me in utter contempt. The perfect ending to a complete fiasco."

"What? You mean *Favian*?" she asked in surprise, wondering how two otherwise intelligent people could possibly have gotten so twisted up. "Did the healer give you some funny herbs when I wasn't looking?" She shook her head and went back to sopping up gravy with a hunk of bread. "I really can't figure you two out."

Ithric mirrored her, returning his attention to his food. "There's nothing to figure out. He wasn't who I thought he was, and I wasn't who he thought *I* was. End of story."

And you're both mad as a box of frogs, Kathrael thought, but didn't say. It was increasingly apparent that someone needed to bang their fool heads together, and she was coming to the uncomfortable realization that she was the only candidate for the job.

She had once witnessed a fire at a storage building in Rhyth's dockyards. The place had been full of barrels of creosote. She had a nasty feeling that this confrontation would be just as explosive.

Her opportunity for head banging came sooner than expected. The following evening, Favian overcame his reluctance to enter Ithric's presence and knocked on the door as she and Ithric were eating a meal of fish and mixed greens.

Ithric looked up warily, but Kathrael said, "Favian! Come join us. I've barely seen you in the past two days."

Favian entered, his leery expression matching Ithric's perfectly. "I've already eaten, thanks. Sorry I disappeared on you, though. The council has been hearing the complaint against Turvick and Laronzo. I've been wrapped up in that." He stood just inside the doorway, looking uncomfortable. Someone had finally gotten the bloodstains out of his robes, and the front of his skull was freshly shaved, making him look every inch the respectable young priest.

"Nice of you to let me know about the hearing ahead of time," Ithric said in a deceptively conversational tone.

Favian's eyes narrowed. "I offered at the beginning to bring you in to give testimony, but the elders declined. I think they're a bit in awe of you. The gods alone know why."

"Probably worried that he'll bring a curse down on the town if they offend him somehow," Kathrael said, and Ithric made a noise of disgust.

"Anyway, your presence—or lack thereof—was a moot point, as it turned out," Favian continued. "Turvick and Laronzo will be branded as kidnappers and taken back to Gebrall , where they'll be put on the first boat heading back to one of the southern ports."

"Good," said Ithric. "Anything else?"

"Yes," Favian said stiffly. "We need to either send a message back to Draebard, or head back there ourselves. Otherwise, we're likely to have people out searching for us before long, which is exactly the kind of thing Andoc and the elders wanted to avoid."

"So leave for Draebard, in that case," Ithric said easily. "What's stopping you?"

Kathrael looked back and forth between them, and decided that it was a good time to start poking the hornets' nest with a pointy stick. "He wants to know if you're well enough to leave *with* us, lion-boy. Don't be dense."

As casually as she could, she set her half-eaten plate aside and rose, wandering over to stand next to Favian. If that action *happened* to place her in front of the room's only exit, and if she *happened* to lean back against the closed door so that that the only way to leave would be to go through her bodily... well. Running away wasn't the answer for these two. It had obviously done them no favors in the past.

"And why would I want to come with you?" Ithric asked in a tired, flat voice.

"Don't you need to report back to your spymaster?" Favian said pointedly, and Ithric couldn't hide a brief flash of surprise. Kathrael settled back, prepared for the tinderbox to burst into flame.

"I have no idea what you're talking about," Ithric said after a beat, displaying impressive sincerity given that he was blatantly lying through his teeth.

"You might as well save your storytelling ability for something else, you ass. Andoc spilled everything," Favian shot back. "Including the part where you specifically asked him not to tell me where you'd gone."

Ithric huffed in disgust and crossed his arms defensively. "I guess it's a good thing I'm the spy, and not him. So much for honor among thieves."

"Says the man who snuck away from Draebard in the middle of the night."

"What? Can you think of a *better* time for sneaking?" Ithric retorted.

A stony silence descended as the two of them glared at each other across the width of the room. Kathrael pursed her lips, waiting for the tension to break and wondering if she could come up with any additional fuel to throw on the smoldering embers.

"Gods," Ithric spat eventually, running his hand through his hair with an angry movement. He rose and paced, still keeping most of the room between himself and Favian. "I need to get out of this place. It's driving me mad."

Kathrael frowned. "Out of Woodhaerst?"

"Out of the temple," he clarified, letting his eyes pin Favian for a bare instant before returning to Kathrael. "It makes the lion restless. As I said before, one cage is very like another."

"So what's stopping you?" Favian said, echoing Ithric's earlier snide remark. "I'm sure you could find a bed to warm elsewhere in town."

The mocking bitterness of his tone hid hurt beneath. Kathrael frowned, an idea forming—one that could either get right to the heart of the matter, or backfire quite spectacularly on her.

"If you're looking to relieve your restlessness, lion-boy, I'd be happy to help you out. I was a prostitute in Rhyth for years, you know," she said in an arch tone. "For you, it'd be on the house. I like you—and we *are* supposed to be bondmates, you know."

Favian turned to her, agape—his face a picture of shock and… betrayal? Ithric just looked surprised.

She steeled herself to ignore the pang she felt at hurting Favian, and pressed on. "You've been locked away for weeks with no company, after all. You must be about ready to burst by now. So, how about it? Favian has already turned me down—no accounting for taste." She paused, as if considering. "Though, to be fair to him, he is a *bloody* good kisser. Maybe he'd like to stay and watch us."

Ithric was definitely on the back foot, staring at her like she'd grown a second head. He blinked once, slowly, and regarded her like some sort of unfamiliar puzzle.

"Tempting offer, Little Cat," he said a moment later, recovering himself, "but I make a point of only taking lovers who are in heat for me. And, though you might like me well enough, you are decidedly *not* in heat right now."

"Oh… so, you mean lovers like Favian, then?" she asked in an innocent tone, and felt Favian freeze beside her. She didn't think he was even breathing.

Ithric's face grew hard, and he let out an unpleasant bark of laughter. "Favian chose to mutilate himself rather than feel desire. You shouldn't take his rejection personally,

Kathrael. He won't be in heat for you, me, or anyone else... not ever again."

Kathrael gave them both pitying looks. "For a lion, Ithric, you sure don't see what's right in front of you very clearly. And for someone with the second sight, Favian, you are surprisingly blind."

Favian and Ithric stared at her for a handful of heartbeats before turning back to each other in perfect unison. Favian's fists clenched, and he leaned forward as if bracing for a physical attack.

"What is there to see? He *left*," he accused, his armor finally shattering to reveal the depth of hurt underneath. He glared at Ithric with anguished eyes. "You took everything I had to give, and talked about a future together, and then you *left* me without a single fucking word!"

Kathrael leaned against the door again, and hoped that things wouldn't actually descend into fisticuffs.

Ithric's fingers were digging into the back of the wooden chair so hard the knuckles turned white as the pair stared each other down. It was like watching a hungry lion square off with an angry bull aurochs, Kathrael thought. Or at least, it would have been... if the aurochs secretly *wanted* to be devoured.

"I talked about a future," Ithric said, his voice grating like stone on stone. "And you threw it back in my face."

"What?" Favian said, confusion touching his features. "I didn't—"

He straightened, and Ithric shoved the chair aside and took three steps forward, raising a hand to point in Favian's face. "You made it absolutely clear that you found the idea of having your balls cut off more appealing than the idea of *being with me*! Of *course* I left! What the hell else was I supposed to do?" He grimaced and clutched at his side, the growing force and volume of his words paining his half-healed wound.

Favian reeled back a step as if struck. He was breathing hard, his face flushed with righteous anger. "But... that *was* our future, Ithric! Once I became a priest, we could have been together without censure. No one could have stopped us, or made us outcasts! When you got angry and tried to talk me out of it, I didn't know what to think. I've wanted to be a priest since I was thirteen and realized that the world wasn't going to magically change and welcome my kind. The temple was the only place I had ever found acceptance. I was looking forward to sharing that future with you, until you pulled out a knife and hacked that dream to pieces."

His voice went quiet at the end, sounding terribly sad, and Kathrael held her breath.

Ithric made an inarticulate noise of pain and stumbled forward, grabbing Favian's shoulders and shoving him against the wall with a thump, Favian's hands came up to grip Ithric's arms as if he would try to throw off his hold—or perhaps drag him closer.

"You shouldn't have to mutilate yourself to be with another person," Ithric said. His voice was pained; pleading, though anger still colored his tone as well.

They clutched at each other almost desperately for a few moments, before Ithric pulled back just enough to cup Favian's face and draw him into a rough kiss, lips and teeth clashing. When they parted for breath, Ithric pressed their foreheads together. "Why would you *do* that?" he asked. "I never asked for that! I didn't *want* that sacrifice!"

Favian closed his eyes. "It's my body, Ithric. It's my choice. I *want* to be a priest. I want to help people, and serve the gods. And I want to be with you, but only if you accept my right to be who I was destined to be."

"I don't understand why you won't fight to change things," Ithric said. "It's *wrong!*"

Favian eased him back at arms' length to look at him, but it was Kathrael who answered.

"There's no honor in fighting a battle you can't possibly win," she said, thinking of the slaves she'd left behind in the south. The ones she'd vowed to save. "It's just another way to commit suicide."

Silence settled over the room for a long moment.

"Six years ago," Favian said slowly, "a eunuch couldn't enter into a handfasting, you know. Certainly, no one would have credited three people becoming bondmates, like my guardians did. And before Leader Magoldis of the Mereni rose to power, the idea of a female becoming the chieftain of a tribe would have been ludicrous."

He looked at Ithric as if willing him to understand. "It isn't time yet for this to change. When the time comes, it will happen."

Ithric looked at him, his anger drained away, leaving only sadness behind. "But, Favian, how will that time ever come if we don't stand up and say *no*?"

Favian could only shake his head, looking lost. "I don't know, Ithric. But... can we disagree about it, and still agree that... maybe... we were both wrong all those months ago in Draebard? I'm really not keen on getting my heart broken a second time — not when I've only just now gotten you back."

There was a pause as they looked at each other, finally seeing one another clearly, it seemed. Ithric appeared to deflate, all the fight draining from him, leaving behind only the weak, injured young man Kathrael had spent the last few days nursing back to health.

"Tell you what," he countered. "How about we start by agreeing that we're all knackered, and there's a very comfortable bed in this room that would be even more comfortable with company. We can fight again in the morning."

"I should probably leave you two alone," Kathrael said, surprised by the sharp ache that the words brought.

Ithric frowned. "Why?" he said, even as Favian looked at her with rueful eyes and said, "Er... no. You probably *shouldn't*. We don't have a good record when left to our own devices."

A thread of surprise wove through her pall of worry and loneliness. She glanced between the two of them, feeling something like hope trying to take hold in her breast.

"Stay, Little Cat," said Ithric. "Please. I've been without a pride for far too long. In fact, if you'll both forgive the presumption..."

He unfastened the borrowed robe he was wearing and turned around to let it drop. A moment later, the lion dropped onto all fours and slunk around to face them, snuffling the air curiously with a deep *whuff... whuff... whuff* noise.

Favian sagged, all of the tension flowing from his spine, leaving him propped against the wall, utterly limp. "Bastard," he whispered, his voice empty now of the bitterness that would have underpinned the word as little as an hour ago.

The lion butted up against him with its head, and Favian dropped to his knees, throwing his arms around the heavy shoulders and burying his face in the scruffy mane. He was trembling visibly.

The animal gazed up at Kathrael, serene, and she succumbed to her own need for reassurance. When she knelt next to Favian and put a hand on his shoulder, he released his grip on Ithric with one arm and used it to pull her properly into the embrace. She came willingly, leaning against him, and against the lion's easy strength. The beast rubbed its head companionably against her body, a low rumble rolling through its chest.

"I'm sorry I dragged you into the middle of our mess, Kath," Favian said against her hair. "It wasn't my intention—truly."

"You didn't drag me, priest-boy," Kathrael pointed out, settling more fully against them. "I stuck my nose in because I wanted to. I make my own choices, remember?"

He choked on a huff of laughter. "Right. I know you do. You will stay with us, though?" There was a tentative note to the question, and she lifted her head enough to see his face.

"Are you sure you want me to? You've got him back now, Favian." She took a deep breath, the next words surprisingly difficult to get out. "You're not obligated to me, you know, just because we shared a blanket or a bed a few times."

Favian stared at her for a moment, his brow furrowed. "Kathrael. Do you really believe I can only care for one person at a time? If so, you've obviously forgotten who raised me. And you heard Ithric—he craves a pride of his own in the same way Senovo needs his pack around him. I... wasn't lying when I said that Ithric and I don't do well on our own."

She couldn't help the relief that bubbled up and flowed through her like an underground spring. She pressed the undamaged side of her face against Favian's chest to feel his heart beating, and whispered, "I'll stay, then."

The lion butted her again and slipped free of Favian's hold. It padded over to the low bed and jumped onto it with a lithe movement, settling among the mass of blankets. Bandages still circled its torso. The animal craned to sniff at them and chew at a loose edge.

"*Ah!* Don't, Ithric," Favian chided, pushing to his feet and offering Kathrael a hand up to follow him. "Leave them. Those bandages are there for a reason."

The lion curled a lip and shook its head in disgust. Kathrael couldn't stop the helpless smile that stretched her face. Favian saw the expression, and a shy, fond look slid over his own features.

"Gods," he said after a moment, rubbing a hand over his face, "I could sleep for a week. Maybe I *will* use some of the money Carivel gave us to send a messenger back to Draebard. I think we'd all benefit from a bit more time to recover before we try to travel."

"Not all of us—Rona doesn't have forever," Kathrael reminded him. "She needs to make a decision about the pregnancy soon."

Favian nodded. "Yes, you're right, of course. A day or two, then. That won't make much difference in the pregnancy, but it will give us a little more of a chance to rest, and for Ithric to heal."

"You think he'll come with us?" she asked.

"I hope so," Favian said, barely more than a breath, and turned to strip down to his linen shift and smallclothes. "Come on, Kathrael. Sleep. You need it, too."

It was true. Alone in her borrowed room, sleep had been slow to come and quick to leave as voices rustled around her, half-heard. She removed her outer layers and pinched the candles out before feeling her way to the bed. She wasn't sure what it said about her that she was more at ease with the idea of sharing a bed with a lion than she would have been at sharing it with Ithric in human form.

The lion-boy no more a danger to you than the priest is, came Vesh's ghostly voice from the shadowed, unseen corners of the room. *You're safer in their bed than you would be sleeping alone in yours.*

It was a startling realization. It was also something that Ithric must have understood inherently from the depths of his animal instincts. The pride. Safety in numbers. *Family.*

"Kath?" Favian asked, and she became aware that she must have frozen in place, staying quiet too long in the dark.

"Sorry," she said, shaking herself free. "Vesh just said something insightful, that's all."

"Oh, yes?" Favian replied. "What did he say?"

Kathrael worried her bottom lip for a moment. "I'll… tell you in a bit. I need to think about it for a minute, first."

She felt her way to the edge of the mattress. The lion was sprawled along the far side of the bed. Favian had arranged himself in the middle, and after a moment of fumbling, Kathrael pressed herself along the length of his back. She snuck an arm around him from behind, and he covered it with one of his own, holding her in place against him. She lay there for some time, the quiet of the room broken only by the raspy sound of the large cat's breathing.

"I've lost everyone I ever dared to get close to," she said slowly, feeling the truth of the words settle in her belly even as she said them. "I'd come to believe that I was fated to always be alone. But... even if there's always a chance of suffering more loss... I can still choose not to be alone. Even though it's hard. Even when it places my heart at risk. *We* can choose... not to be alone."

Favian was quiet for a long moment before he quoted softly, "*All who seek shelter shall find it. All the gods' children will receive solace.*"

Kathrael let the words soak into her, remembering a sweltering market square in Rhyth where she'd stared at a pair of rotten ground tubers and first decided to seek help at the temple. Those words had marked the beginning of a journey that she had expected — perhaps even hoped — would lead to bloody revenge followed by a quick death.

Instead they had led... *here.*

Where would they lead next?

Kathrael's dreams that night were strange, but not frightening. Wolves and lions lounged around on low divans in a sumptuously appointed Rhythian house, attending a feast while she and Vesh danced for them. Slaves cheered and slapped their thighs in appreciation from the corner, where they guarded the wealthy host and his family — bound and gagged, kneeling on the floor.

The music in the background faded away like mist as she groaned into wakefulness. She stretched, her muscles tingling pleasantly. Her eyes blinked open, to be greeted by early morning light slanting in through the small eastern window, painting everything gold.

Next to her, Favian slumbered on despite the jostling. It was, she suspected, the first full night of sleep he'd managed since they left Draebard, if not before. No wonder he was dead to the world. With a little jolt of surprise, she realized that Ithric, by contrast, was awake and in human form on

Favian's other side, propped up on an elbow and looking down at him with a thoughtful, intent expression.

When he noticed her awake, his attention shifted to her and he gave a rueful smile. "Good morning, Little Cat. Sleep well?"

A hint of amusement lifted the corner of her mouth as she watched Favian drooling onto the bedclothes between them. "Perhaps not *quite* as well as Favian seems to be doing, but I can't complain. You?"

"I always sleep well," Ithric replied in a dismissive tone. "Lions are *champion* sleepers."

She let out a breath of laughter and rolled up on an elbow opposite him.

Ithric regarded her with interest for a long moment. "So," he said eventually. "I have to ask. You and Favian..."

She looked down for an instant before making herself meet his eyes again. "Bit of a long story. He wasn't lying—I really did put a knife to his throat and try to use him as a hostage to get to High Priest Senovo."

Ithric continued to stare at her as if trying to figure her out. "That probably wasn't the wisest choice of hostage on your part, you do realize."

"Well," Kathrael said, "in my defense... it sort of worked. The Wolf Patron *did* come."

"Yeah, I'll just bet he did," said Ithric. "With claws and fangs, no doubt. I'm surprised you're still in one piece."

She looked away again. "My own well-being wasn't high on my list of priorities at the time. Even if I'd known who Favian was, which of course I didn't."

"Hmm... I guess I've been in that place one or two times, myself," Ithric said, in a tone that made her think he probably had. His tone lightened deliberately. "So, afterward... let me guess. Favian immediately went all *mother hen* on you and wouldn't leave you alone?"

She looked at Favian's sleeping form and let the back of a finger stroke down the length of his upper arm. "Something like that, I suppose. To be fair, I was in pretty dire need of a mother hen. Or at least, of a friend. I still am, really."

"A friend who's a good kisser?" Ithric prodded, still eyeing her like she was a delicate wooden puzzle box and he wanted the key. "Or was that part just for the shock value?"

She couldn't help the faint blush that traveled up her neck. "Well... yes. It *was* for the shock value... but it's also true. I think we both needed someone for support. Not to worry, though, lion-boy. I know his heart lies with you. I've no intention of getting between you."

Ithric made a dismissive noise. "Don't be ridiculous, Little Cat. I've never understood the idea of ownership when it comes to love." He smirked. "In fact, if you ever *do* have the urge to get between us, I, for one, would be more than happy to oblige."

She snorted, though his words inspired a strange curl of sensation in her belly that was surprisingly pleasant. "I wasn't lying about being a prostitute either, lion-boy," she shot back. "So let's just say that if I *were* to take you up on that offer, it wouldn't be the oddest place I've ever been. Far from it."

Ithric raised an eyebrow. "Well, *well*. How intriguing," he teased. "Right now, though, I'd be interested in hearing more details about Favian's kissing skills. I'm a bit surprised that he was inclined, now that he's... you know."

"I'm a eunuch, Ithric. That doesn't mean I'm made of wood," came a sleep-roughened voice from below them.

Ithric looked down in surprise, but recovered quickly. "Well, certainly your prick isn't, I'm guessing. How long have you been awake?"

"Since somewhere in the vicinity of the *mother hen* jab," Favian said, peeling opening one bloodshot eye to glare up at him.

"Right. *No fighting*, you two," Kathrael insisted, pinning each of them with a meaningful look. "Not yet, anyway. It's far too early."

"Seconded," Favian agreed, and closed his eyes again.

Ithric rolled his eyes and said, "Fine. We'll fight later. Now, however, I have to test a theory. I assume it's not too early for this?"

With no further warning, he leaned down and caught Favian's lips in a sweet kiss that was completely at odds with their violent clash of teeth and lips the previous evening.

NINETEEN

Favian made a muffled noise of surprise that tailed off into a soft whine. The earlier curl of warmth in Kathrael's belly intensified, making her breathe in sharply. One of Favian's hands closed around her forearm as if to ground himself, while his other wrapped around the back of Ithric's head to hold him in place.

The kiss went on and on, as if all the words the pair could not say aloud were contained in it. Kathrael watched in fascination as a tear slipped free from the corner of Favian's closed eyes and trickled down his smooth temple.

When they finally parted and Favian spoke, his voice was unsteady. "No… never too early for that."

"Definitely better than fighting," Ithric agreed, his own voice hoarse.

Kathrael gently freed her arm from Favian's grip and thumbed away the little trail of salt water on the side of his face. "For the gods' sakes, you two, be *happy*, will you? You have a second chance now. Don't waste it."

On impulse, she leaned down and kissed Favian's warm, slick lips. He met her with a languid slide of mouth on mouth that turned the strange warmth in Kathrael's belly heavy and liquid.

When she pulled away with a final stroke of his cheek, he said, "I *am* happy." His gaze turned back to Ithric. "This is all I ever wanted, Ithric. Just this… just to be with you. I wondered for so many years if I would ever be able to have this kind of closeness with anyone."

There was still wariness behind Ithric's eyes. "As I recall, you used to want other things from me, as well—before you had that part of yourself cut out and thrown away like garbage." His voice grew rough on the final words.

Favian sighed out a slow breath and dragged himself into a sitting position. He took Ithric by the shoulders and met his challenging, almost *angry* gaze with sad blue eyes. "Ithric. What do I have to do to make you understand that I didn't join the priesthood as a way to spite you? *It wasn't about you.*" He shook his head as if to draw back some of the sharpness of his words, and started again. "I was already an acolyte in the temple when I first met you, you know. I knew even then that my life was destined for the gods' service. My urges for men — for *you* — terrified me."

"There's nothing *terrifying* about sex. Or lust," Ithric shot back. "Aren't you priests always on about it being one of the gods' greatest gifts to their children?"

A furrow formed between Favian's eyebrows. "Not everyone experiences desire the same way you do, Ithric. I was already having prophetic visions I couldn't escape — often showing terrible, tragic things that I was powerless to prevent. The last thing I needed was something else in my life that I couldn't control — my *own body* rebelling against me at the most inappropriate times."

"It was only a problem because you were constantly fighting yourself," Ithric insisted. "Denying yourself. *Don't* try to tell me you didn't like what we did when you finally stopped avoiding things and more or less jumped me."

A very faint worried tone had entered his voice. Despite her self-professed lack of interest in such things now that she no longer relied on sex to survive, Kathrael couldn't help wondering what, exactly, had passed between the two of them back in Draebard.

Favian was still frowning. "Ithric… we nearly tore each other apart. Before you left, we *did* tear each other apart. I don't want a lifetime of that."

Kathrael couldn't help adding, "I've seen how lust hurts other people. I've profited from offering my body as an outlet for lust, but I could never understand the way men seem oblivious to the harm it does."

Ithric shot her a hurt look that clearly said, *not you, too?* He straightened away from Favian's grip. "You're both wrong. Sex should be a source of joy and pleasure for everyone involved, whether it's tender or tempestuous. I never wanted to hurt you, Favian. I just wanted to be with you. But every time we got close, our rough edges grated together. And the closer we got, the deeper the wounds became. But I simply can't understand your desire to destroy that part of yourself rather than try to heal it."

Favian sighed and hooked a hand around the back of Ithric's neck. "It *is* healed now. This is what I wanted, Ithric. I am… finally… as I was meant to be."

There was a considerable pause. "But you no longer desire me," Ithric said, as if the words were being pulled from him one at a time, and Kathrael got the feeling that they were finally getting to the heart of the complicated tangle between them.

Favian made a pained noise of negation and pulled Ithric forward to press another kiss to his lips. This time, Ithric was the one who looked to be on the verge of tears.

"Ithric," Kathrael said, when Favian released him and rested their foreheads together. "That's not true. If you'd seen him after he dreamed the vision about you... if you'd seen how frantic he was about getting to you... saving you... you wouldn't ever say such a thing. It was as if nothing else in the world existed for him, except the danger to *you*."

The shape-shifter looked at Favian with something akin to hope.

"I don't lust after you now, it's true," Favian said into the space between them. "But I still want to be close to you. In all ways, Ithric. In whatever way you want. Please don't run away from me again. *Please*."

Ithric's breath escaped in a rough hitch, as if he'd been punched. "Then don't make it sound like my desire for you is some sort of disease. Like it's hurting you."

Favian's hand gripped tighter. "Those were Kathrael's words, not mine. She and I have... something of a disagreement about matters of sex and desire. It's true that it hurt when I was younger, not to be able to feel desire for anyone society told me I was *supposed* to desire. I don't know. Maybe I wasn't as strong as you, or maybe it was easier for you since you desire men and women both.

"Whatever the case, I bought into the idea that I was broken, somehow, because I only felt lust for men. Maybe I shouldn't have bought into it. But, Ithric, don't you see? I'm a eunuch now. Nobody in Draebard cares if we're together. They might roll their eyes behind our backs and shake their heads in virtuous despair over us, but not a *single person* would object aloud."

Ithric's eyes were still closed. "I never asked you to make that sacrifice. I never *wanted* you to."

Favian reached up and kissed the pained crease between Ithric's brows. "No," he said. "You didn't. I chose to do it on my own. Now it's done, and I don't regret it, Ithric. I *don't*."

Silence stretched as Ithric digested this.

"Well," Kathrael said into the heavy atmosphere of the room. "That's not *completely* accurate, is it? He regretted it just a bit on the three-day horseback ride from Draebard to Teth."

The tension broke, and Ithric choked on a pained bark of laughter. "Yeah. I'll just bet he did." He ran a hand through his messy hair, leaving it in further disarray. "Gods, *look* at us. The shifter, the eunuch, and the girl who hates sex, all curled up together in bed."

Favian snorted through his nose and flopped, boneless, against the headboard. "When you put it like that..." He scrubbed a hand over his face, rubbing the sleep from his eyes. "I guess we probably deserve each other."

"No, Favian, you're wrong," Kathrael said, sobering. "I don't deserve any of this."

Ithric blinked at her. "Why ever not?"

Favian snaked an arm around her shoulders and pulled her down to rest against his side. "Yes, you do, Kath. You deserve life, and health, and happiness as much as any other person."

"I'm not sure I know how to be happy," she said slowly. "It seems... I don't know. *Selfish*, I guess, when there is so much wrong with the world."

Ithric reached across to hook a lock of her dark, sleep-tangled hair over her ear, and she felt a moment of surprise that the light touch did not make her flinch.

"Can't you find happiness in taking action to right those wrongs?" he asked. "Like when you rescued the twins, or helped free all of us from Turvick and Laronzo's clutches? There's nothing selfish about that."

She thought about his words, mulling them over for long moments. "I suppose... when I first met you and you convinced me to help Dex and Petra, I was too wrapped up in my own grief and desire for vengeance to feel much of anything. And when Turvick and his partner were taken away for punishment, I mostly just felt relief." She paused again. "But, it does make me happy to think of the two of you being reunited... maybe having the life together that you almost threw away."

"And kissing Favian?" Ithric asked in a sly tone. "Because that certainly makes *me* happy."

Favian blushed pink. "Doing it, you mean? Or watching *her* do it?"

"Both," Ithric said, as if the answer should be obvious.

Blood warmed Kathrael's face as well, and she wondered at it. Wondered that she should blush like a virgin over the idea of kissing when she had known such depths of depravity and humiliation throughout her short life.

"Yes. That did make me happy as well. You're right," she admitted quietly. "And… I think this would, too."

She sat up in Favian's embrace and leaned across his body, stretching out a hand to the lion-boy. Ithric's eyes lit with interest, and he followed her touch on his cheek willingly. She held her breath as their lips touched, a flash of worry piercing her chest that he would grab her and try to *take*, now that she had offered.

Instead, though, he kept the kiss as light and chaste as Favian had on that first night beside the campfire. Gradually, she relaxed, chiding herself as she realized that Favian would never have let Ithric press her too hard, assuming he had been inclined to do so in the first place. Even now, Favian's hand rested protectively between her shoulder blades, his thumb stroking back and forth as he watched her kissing his old lover.

After a few moments, Ithric pulled back a fraction in favor of rubbing his stubbled cheek along her scarred one. His lips brushed her ear, and he buried his nose in her hair for a moment before straightening away.

She caught her breath and looked at him — suddenly, painfully aware of the picture she made. Scarred face. Blind, milky eye. Unkempt hair in desperate need of a wash. Yet Ithric still looked at her with an appreciative gaze, not flinching away from the ugliness that she knew was there.

"My scars don't repulse you," she said with renewed wonder. "They didn't, even on that first night outside of Penth."

Ithric's brow furrowed. "Well, no. Why would they?"

"They repulse most people," she said, thinking of every person who had ever gasped and looked away, stepping back as if bad fortune and disfigurement might somehow be contagious.

"Yes," Ithric replied, "but you have to understand — most people are fools, in my experience." He reached out to brush fingertips over the patch of damaged flesh, sliding from her cheek, to her jaw, to her neck — following the trail where the vitriol had dripped down. "The lioness with scars on her face is always the most sought after. She's the strongest—she fought, and survived."

Kathrael caught her breath against the unexpected sob that tried to rise up. "I didn't fight," she said in a hoarse whisper. "I just ran. I've been running for half of my life."

"Kath. No. You *survived*," Favian reiterated, turning her head with a touch to her chin so she was forced to meet his gaze.

It was too much. She squeezed her eyes shut. "I take it back—I was wrong earlier. I'm sorry. Could you both go back to fighting now, please?"

Ithric huffed a breath of laughter through his nose. "Nope—not just now, I'm afraid. Maybe later. You were right—it's too early. In fact, if we're done with the soul baring for a bit, I'm going back to sleep. Might as well take advantage of being the invalid while I have the chance." He stretched carefully, several joints in his spine popping. "Someone wake me when there's food?"

"Shameless hedonist," Favian accused, affection underlying the insult.

"Yep, that's me," Ithric said, shuffling around to make himself as comfortable as he could with his wound still half-healed. He curled up on his side against Favian's hip and closed his eyes, humming in appreciation when Favian's fingers stroked through his hair.

They were quiet for some time, leaning against each other while Ithric dozed.

"I should see about hiring a fast rider this morning to take a message to Draebard for us," Favian said eventually. "They'll only be a few days ahead of us, but I'd like to avoid having search parties out for us if I can."

"Mmm," Kathrael agreed, half-asleep herself. A thought assailed her. "Do you think the priests would be willing to draw a bath and lend me some soap and hair oil? I'm tired of being grimy."

Favian shrugged, a look of interest lighting his pleasant features. "I don't see why not, especially if we haul our own buckets. I'll join you. It would be nice to be clean, you're right." He poked Ithric, who groaned. "Ithric. Bath? You definitely need one."

Ithric batted his hand away. "Lemme sleep. Not s'posed to get the bandages wet, anyway. Bring me a bucket to wash in afterward or something."

"Do lions hate water as much as cats?" Kathrael wondered aloud.

"Eh. *Hate* is a strong word," Favian said, extricating himself from the tangle of blankets and limbs so the could rise. "*Dislike*, maybe. Though how it's any less savory than cleaning oneself with one's own tongue is something of an open question…"

"I'm not listening to this," Ithric mumbled.

"Of course you aren't," Favian agreed, and leaned over to run his fingers over Ithric's cheek in a brief caress. "Go to sleep. We'll be back later with food. And a bucket."

"*Mmph*," Ithric said, and fell asleep again.

She and Favian dressed quietly and left. Outside the door, Favian paused and let the wall take his weight, the night's events catching up with him. "He's still weak," he said. "That was a nasty wound."

"It's healing fast," Kathrael replied, and stepped close to wrap her arms around him. His chest rose and fell once within her grasp.

"Even so," he said, clearly thinking about how close Ithric had come to death. "A few inches lower, and…"

Around them, the temple was waking for the day. Kathrael pulled away and nudged Favian to move. "Hey. *Enough*," she said. "Come on. Bath first. You can fret later."

⚜

The novice priest who showed them where to find buckets, soap, and rags for washing was somewhat harried, and rushed off as soon as Favian thanked him.

"There's to be a public handfasting later today," Favian explained. "The couple are high in status, and I gather the priests are under pressure to make the ceremony a suitable spectacle for the crowd. In fact, I've been co-opted into distributing wine to the guests. The couple's families have a history of conflict, and apparently the High Priest believes that keeping everyone well-lubricated will reduce the chance of friction."

Kathrael snorted, placing a pair of water buckets onto metal hooks over the large hearth to heat them. "Right. Unless they get *too* drunk, and then all bets are off. Have fun straddling *that* fence."

Favian grinned, a sight Kathrael had sorely missed. "At least if the ceremony devolves into a brawl, I can just go back to Draebard afterward. That goes a long way toward taking the pressure off."

"True enough," she agreed. "Where's the hair oil? There must be some here…"

After a quick rummage, they located a vial of oil and a wooden comb on a small shelf opposite the bronze tub. Kathrael attacked the tangles matting her long hair to pass the time while the water warmed.

"There was a time not so long ago when I would have been appalled at the idea of my hair being dirty and unkempt," she said, the thought sitting oddly.

"I imagine it's different when you rely on your appearance for your livelihood," Favian offered. "But it's also hard to keep up with things like that when you're being dragged around from village to village by a half-crazed priest."

He moved to pick up a couple of buckets of cold water and dump them in the bronze washtub in an attempt to cover his obvious discomfort.

She raised an eyebrow. "I've told you, Favian. I make my own choices. Besides, it was far better than sitting around Draebard with no purpose beyond chopping vegetables for Brother Feldes and feeding the chickens."

He shot her a glance that was oddly shy. "Yes. Well. Thank you, anyway." He put the buckets aside and watched her fighting with a stubborn mat of hair. "Here. Let me? I think you'd better rub some oil into the snarls first or you're going to have chunks missing by the time you're done."

Again, Kathrael was taken aback by the unexpected offer—though perhaps she shouldn't have been. Maybe this was something else that was different in the north. Maybe men, or eunuchs, at least, really didn't see anything odd about cosseting a woman just for the sake of it. She slowly handed over the comb.

Favian took it and set it aside so he could work oil into the worst tangles. When he started methodically combing out her hair, starting near the bottom, the gentle tugging against her scalp sent strange tingles down Kathrael's spine. She closed her eyes, letting her guard down in a way she rarely had before, enjoying the pleasant, shivery sensation rather than questioning it.

It only took minutes for Favian to work out the final snags. The water in the buckets over the fire was not terribly hot, but they dumped it into the tub anyway rather than stand around waiting any longer. Favian filled another bucket to hang over the hearth while they washed — for Ithric, Kathrael presumed.

"You first," Favian said, a cheeky look crossing his face as he added, "You need it more."

Kathrael mock-glared at him. "I'd be offended if you weren't so obviously right about that." She checked the temperature, which was at least lukewarm rather than chilly, and removed her clothing to reveal flesh that was finally starting to fill out again after having been starved down to skin and bones for months.

To her surprise, rather than blushing and turning away, Favian was watching her. "You're looking much better than the first time you shed your clothing in front of me, Kath. I hope you're feeling better as well?"

Indeed, it was she who had to fight a blush. She stepped lightly into the tub and lowered herself into the water as she thought back to those horrible months of starvation.

"It's strange even trying to think back to those days," she said, after a thoughtful pause. "Hunger was an ache that never left. My guts cramped from all the worms in them, and my joints flared with pain at every movement. Even before the vitriol attack, I never really had enough to eat. Or else it was just parched grains, no meat or vegetables, and I would be hungry again in no time even if I ate until my stomach was full. This is the first time in my life that I've had all the nourishing food I could eat for months at a time."

Favian nodded. "Healer Sagdea says that without enough of the right kind of food, nothing in the body works the way it's supposed to." He paused to smile in amusement. "And Priest Feldes says that one cannot nourish the spirit without first nourishing the body."

Kathrael smiled as well. "Brother Feldes has a very fine spirit indeed." She began to wash herself, and hummed in appreciation when Favian brought over a rag to scrub at her back, along with a pitcher to pour water over her hair so she could soap it up and rub the soft strands together between her palms until they were squeaking.

"You know," she said idly, "Rhyth has some very fine bath houses. I only ever got to make use of them when I was working, but I do miss them sometimes. They were much grander than a metal tub sitting in a back room."

Favian made a noise of interest. "Oh yes? When we stayed in the palace at Rhyth, there was a huge tub in every guest room. We were all rather amazed by that, as I recall… though less so, once we realized that the buckets to fill them were hauled by child slaves." His voice grew sad at that, but he shook it off. "We didn't see much of the city outside the palace walls. It was beyond anything I've ever imagined, though. The scale of it was breathtaking."

"There are hot springs under parts of the city," Kathrael said, remembering. "Where they bubble up, the rich families built huge stone buildings full of mosaics and marble-lined pools big enough to swim in—at least some of them. There are steam rooms, with cold pools for dipping afterwards, and the whole place smells of cedar and fragrant herbs."

Favian watched her silently for a long moment before speaking. "You miss Rhyth, don't you. Even with everything that happened there."

She looked up at him, feeling vulnerable. "Your life has not been without pain either. Do you consider Draebard any less your home because bad things happened there?"

"No," he replied without hesitation. "I don't."

She nodded, and went back to rinsing herself off. Favian directed her head back with a light touch and poured water over her hair, setting off a new round of shivery tingles. After running a bit more oil through the dark strands and rinsing a final time, she sighed and gestured for a length of burlap toweling hanging nearby.

"Your turn," she said, and stepped out to dry herself.

Again, to her surprise, Favian merely nodded and stripped off his priest's robes and linen underthings, baring himself to her interested gaze with no apparent hesitation. His body was trapped somewhere between that of a muscular young man and that of a soft eunuch—not enough time had passed yet for his waist to thicken and his body hair to completely disappear.

Her gaze was caught by a twisted mass of scar tissue under his left collarbone, at the juncture of torso and shoulder. He glanced over, saw her looking, and smiled ruefully.

"I wasn't always a temple acolyte," he explained. "I probably had no business on a battlefield at that age, but I ended up on one just the same. Driving a chariot, to be precise. I failed to duck at the appropriate moment, and took an arrow through the shoulder. I'm afraid that's the only battle scar I have worth showing off, but at least it's a fairly impressive one."

Somehow, the imperfection made him seem more relatable, even though it had occurred under circumstances with which Kathrael had absolutely no experience. She shook herself free of her strange fascination, and pointed out, "You do have at least one other scar of interest now, you know."

At that, he huffed out a breath of laughter. "I'm not sure it's the sort of scar one shows off. And frankly, it's not much to look at as far as I can make out. It's surprisingly small."

"But surprisingly painful."

Favian shrugged, and stepped into the tub. "I think the arrow was worse, actually, though it didn't stay as bad for as long. Both of them were important steps toward the priesthood; I made the decision to leave the horse pens and join the temple not long after my shoulder injury."

Well," Kathrael said, feeling suddenly shy, "I for one, am glad you did. Even if Ithric isn't."

Favian grimaced and took up a soapy rag. "That's a very old argument, as I'm sure you gathered. I don't expect to break any new ground with it at this late date."

Kathrael gave herself a final scrub with the burlap and hung it back on its peg. Still naked, she padded over and dragged a chair to the head of the tub, so she could sit and return the favor of washing Favian's back.

"He's just scared that it means you don't want him any more, Favian," she said.

He frowned. "I told him I did. Twice."

"You told him, but I don't think he heard you. Not properly."

Favian didn't object when she freed his plait of blond hair and began unraveling it to wash.

"I thought I was completely clear," he said, the furrow between his eyebrows deepening.

Kathrael stopped running her fingers through his fine hair and leaned around to consider him. "Far be it from me to interfere, but I suspect actions will speak louder than words in this case."

He looked thoughtful for a moment. "Maybe you're right. The last time—the *only* time—we were together, it wasn't exactly what you'd call... subtle. Not that horny adolescents are generally known for their subtlety in such things."

"Not really, no," Kathrael agreed.

To her surprise, Favian reached up and drew her into a brief kiss. "Thank you. I wasn't exaggerating when I told you that the two of us are utter shite on our own. It really does help to have someone outside the quagmire available to throw us a rope. And it hasn't escaped me that we're only here in the first place because you engineered the whole thing."

"Least I could do," she said. "*I'm* only here because you two saved me."

He smiled and brushed wet fingers across her cheek. "I'm not at all sure that's true. But if it is, I consider the debt more than repaid."

She gave into the urge to press into his palm, soaking up the touch with closed eyes. "Everything will work out, Favian," she said. "You'll see."

A little while later, they returned to Ithric's sick room with supplies in tow.

"Food," Kathrael announced, setting the large bowl of stew on the table next to the low bed. She poked Ithric's shoulder when he only mumbled in response, and he pried open bleary eyes.

"Bucket," Favian added, setting down the heavy wooden pail full of steaming water. He had a couple of clean rags and a length of toweling slung over his shoulder. A small pot of soft lye soap nestled in his free hand, along with the stoppered vial of hair oil.

Ithric stretched, still somewhat gingerly. "Well, now," he said around a yawn. "I suppose I could get used to this."

"Best not," Favian shot back, "unless you're planning on getting skewered on a regular basis."

"Spoilsport," Ithric said, voice light.

"Come and eat, both of you," Kathrael commanded as she dragged the room's single chair over next to the small table. "I'm hungry, and if you don't want me to eat your shares as well, you'd better do something about it now."

That brought Ithric shuffling over to the edge of the bed immediately, and he took the wooden spoon she handed him with a smile. Favian followed a moment later. They huddled around the hot food, sharing the bowl with only a minimum of jousting and parrying for the choicest bits.

Favian lost interest before she and Ithric did, putting aside his spoon and leaving them to scrape up the rest of the thick stew. He wandered back to the bucket and untied the fastenings of his robes, removing both robes and shift until he was clad only in linen smallclothes, slung low on his hips.

Kathrael watched in something like amusement as Ithric, drawn to the movement in the corner of his eye, turned and did a rather comical double take.

His eyes narrowed warily. "What are you *doing*, Favian?"

Favian took up one of the rags and dipped it in the bucket. "What does it look like I'm doing? If I'm going to help you wash, I'd rather not splash water all over my robes."

With a look of consternation, Ithric rose slowly from his perch at the edge of the bed and stalked toward him. He was still naked except for the swathe of bandages after his transformation during the night—completely unselfconscious. Kathrael was treated to a fine view of the play of wiry muscles in his back and buttocks as he crossed the room. He stopped half a step too close to Favian, pressing into his space and looking down into Favian's blue eyes from his slight advantage in height.

"Oh?" he asked, his voice low and a little dangerous. "You're going to *help me wash*, are you?"

Favian did not back down. Kathrael knew that in his place, she would have been sorely tempted to do so under the force of that intense gaze. Instead, he merely widened his eyes into a clear *you're an idiot* expression and lifted the wet rag. "Well, *yeah*," he said. "I thought you were the one who wanted to play the invalid? Now turn around so I can start on your back."

They were a study in opposites, and Kathrael found she could not look away as she lounged back in the sturdy wooden chair. Ithric was lean and hungry, his wiry physique hinting at a surprising turn of strength and speed, given his lack of bulk. His mane of messy hair was dark, with ruddy highlights. Favian, by contrast, was sleek and well fed, the changes in his body already beginning to soften the angular lines of male muscle. His hair glinted gold in the sunlight streaming from the room's high window. His eyes were pale and deep like clear water as he and Ithric stared each other down.

Eventually, reluctantly, Ithric turned his back to Favian, revealing a haunted, hopeful expression to Kathrael's fascinated gaze. She let the corner of her lips curve up—a smile of reassurance that did nothing to ease Ithric's tension. At the first touch of the soapy rag, his eyes flickered closed. His brows were still drawn into an expression of the most exquisitely agonized desire.

Kathrael could not have explained what it was that caused her heart to beat faster in anticipation as she watched Favian wash the sweat and grime from Ithric's body with slow, deliberate strokes of the rag. He took infinite care around the bandages, and continued lower. When he reached around to slide the cloth along the crease of Ithric's hip, a hand shot out with catlike speed and grabbed his wrist in an uncompromising grip.

Ithric spun them around so Favian was facing him and growled, "If you're intending to stop any time soon, now would be a *very* good time to do so."

Still un-cowed, Favian met his eyes squarely. "I have *no intention* of stopping, you ass. Now either quit moping and take what you really want, or let me get back to what I was doing."

A low rumble rolled through Ithric's chest. A heartbeat later, the rag fell to the floor with a wet slap as Favian was summarily pinned on his back on the bed—the aurochs finally ready to be devoured. Kathrael held her breath, hypnotized by the sight.

"You should be careful what you ask for, Favian," Ithric said in a hoarse voice.

TWENTY

Favian arched up against him, testing the hold and falling back when it did not falter. "I've decided that *careful* isn't really my thing any more. Sorry to disappoint."

Ithric made another low noise and fell on Favian's throat, kissing and biting his way down the pale column of flesh. He loosed his grip on Favian's wrists, and Favian brought a hand up to the back of his neck to hold him in place. Ithric licked and nuzzled his way over Favian's chest and stomach, his hands scrabbling at the ties of the smallclothes that were now the only thing separating them. He rubbed his cheek against Favian's groin through the cloth and breathed in. Something jolted unexpectedly in Kathrael's belly, flaring into life at the sight.

"You smell different," Ithric accused, mouthing at Favian through the damp linen.

Favian's voice was a bit breathless. "They scent their soap differently here, I think."

The stubborn laces finally gave way to Ithric's fumbling and he tugged the underclothes down impatiently so he could get at Favian's skin directly. "No," he insisted. "*You* smell different."

"Really?" Favian asked, sounding curious but not alarmed. "Huh."

Ithric wrestled the smallclothes the rest of the way down and off. He resumed his place and shoved Favian's leg to the side, exposing him further. "Let me see you. I have to see what you did to yourself—"

"Ithric," Favian soothed, reaching down to run a hand through Ithric's hair. "There's not much to see. It's just a little scar, and an empty flap of skin…"

Ithric ran gentle fingers over Favian's cock. Favian closed his eyes in pleasure and let his head fall back, baring his neck. "You're not even *hard*," Ithric said, sounding as if the fact caused him physical pain.

Kathrael watched in silence, caught up in a way she never would have foreseen, mentally urging them to work it out—to come to an understanding after so many months of aching for each other.

Favian ran his hand down to Ithric's chin and made him look up, meeting his eyes. "I don't *need* to be hard. It's better this way, really. I want to feel *you*, Ithric... not my own desperation for release."

When Ithric didn't answer, Favian pulled him up the length of his body and sealed their lips together. Ithric made a noise somewhere between a whine and a sob into the kiss, before pressing him further down into the mattress.

When they finally parted for air, Favian met Ithric's eyes again. "I *do* still want you," he said, sounding as breathless as Kathrael felt. "*Please.* You *have* to believe me. Take me now, Ithric. Let me feel how much you want me in return."

Ithric looked so overwhelmed that it finally broke Kathrael free of her trance. She roused herself enough to get up from the chair and move to the discarded bathing supplies, where she picked up the vial of oil.

"You'll want this," she said, knowing well enough what was coming next after her long friendship with Vesh. "Take it slow. Don't... hurt him." Her voice went quiet on the final words, a note of pleading entering without her realizing it.

Ithric's hazel eyes flew to hers, but it was Favian who spoke. "Kath. He's not going to hurt me."

He lifted a hand to cup her cheek, making her look at him and see his expression of confident serenity. She felt another little shiver of reaction.

"No." Ithric had recovered enough for speech. "Little Cat... it's not going to be like that. I'd hurt myself long before I ever hurt him."

"Stay with us," Favian continued, still cupping her face. "Stay and watch. You'll see."

She hesitated for a long moment before nodding, still feeling shivery, her skin running hot and cold. She told herself it was only so she could be sure that Ithric wasn't too rough... that Favian hadn't taken on more than he expected. "All right," she said, and forced herself to quip, "Probably best to have a professional present, I suppose."

Ithric peered down at Favian with a strange expression. "So, how come you were never this uninhibited when you still had balls?" he asked.

Favian blushed, but actually appeared to give the question serious consideration. "I... suppose I didn't want to disappoint the people I respected, before. Now that I'm a eunuch, there's no one to disappoint. No one to shock."

"I think you shocked *him*," Kathrael pointed out, indicating Ithric with a flick of her eyes.

Favian smiled, and gave a little roll of his hips where they were pressed against Ithric's. "Well... maybe a bit. He'll get over it, though."

Ithric growled and thrust into the crease of Favian's hip. "I'm over it." He lifted his body away from Favian's so he could urge him to move.

Favian rolled over onto his stomach and hitched one leg up and to the side. His eyes sought out Kathrael, who was still more-or-less frozen next to the bed. "You're all right, though, Kath? Aren't you?"

She pulled her cynicism around her like a cloak and raised a supercilious eyebrow, despite the faint, tripping beat of her heart against her ribs. "Don't be daft. I doubt either of you could come up with anything that I haven't see dozens of times, priest-boy, if not hundreds. The rich men of Rhyth do *so* love their orgies."

With that, she returned to her perch on the chair near the bed, haughty as any queen. Of course, her sudden desire to sit down had *nothing* to do with the way her knees were turning to jelly. Ithric's eyes tracked her with interest for the span of a few breaths before he returned his attention to the bed.

"You know, Favian, I did actually manage to invite myself to a handful of those, and our Little Cat is not exaggerating." He poured a thin stream of oil over his fingers and trailed them along Favian's spine. "They have all sorts of interesting ideas about sex in the great houses." His fingers disappeared between Favian's buttocks and his forearm flexed. "Sometimes, though, the simplest things are still the best."

Favian hissed between his teeth, his eyes falling shut. His spine curved, and he scrabbled a bit against the tangled furs and blankets underneath him. Ithric poured more oil directly onto Favian's exposed flesh and set the vial aside. His free hand stroked up Favian's back and closed around his nape, steadying him.

Kathrael had tensed a bit in her chair at Favian's reaction to being breached, remembering well the unpleasant burn of being taken in that particular way. When Favian's eyes flew open, though, they were dark and pleasure-drugged, the pupils blown wide. The next sound torn from his throat was undeniably one of encouragement—a low groan.

Ithric looked every inch the hungry predator, yet despite his insistently throbbing prick leaving little smears of seed against Favian's hip, he merely continued to tease and work Favian open with unhurried movements. Kathrael made the mistake of looking at the shape-shifter's face, and the expression of desperate love there hit her like a blow.

The curl of shivery warmth in her belly burst into flame without warning, only to turn hot and liquid a moment later. It flowed down to the place between her legs and settled there, making her sex swell. On the bed, Favian gasped and keened as Ithric pressed deeper, pushing back now against the fingers breaching him as if trying to get *more*. Kathrael *knew* Favian, and she knew that he was utterly incapable of putting on that kind of an act—his pleasure truly was real.

Kathrael's cunt pulsed at the realization, and some of the liquid heat squeezed out from between her swollen labia. She caught her breath audibly in surprise, wondering in a daze if she had somehow forgotten her moon time and started to bleed. This felt... *different*, though—slick, and wet, and oh-so-good against her suddenly sensitive inner lips.

Her small gasp of shock had attracted the others' attention. They stilled, and Favian dragged his wits back together to look at her with eyes that barely focused. "Kath?" he asked.

She didn't answer, unable to do more than stare at him with parted lips as her nipples hardened and rubbed deliciously against the linen of her shift.

Favian's eyes grew more intent, and Ithric was looking at her in worry now as well. She blushed scarlet.

"*Kath.*" Favian's voice was sharper now. "Say something. Have we upset you? Brought back bad memories, or—"

Suddenly, Ithric's nostrils flared. He breathed in slowly, as if scenting the air. His eyes lit with pleasant surprise. "No..." he said, drawing out the word. "It's all right, Favian. It looks like I spoke too soon earlier. I do believe our Little Cat is in heat for us after all."

Favian blinked, lifting his upper body to get a better view of her. The movement brought his back against Ithric's chest. Ithric looped a possessive arm around Favian's torso and grinned at her over his shoulder. The sight made a new pulse of wetness dampen the material of her underskirts.

"Kathrael?" Favian prompted yet again. "Is that true?"

She could only gape at them helplessly, swept away by her body's unexpected response. "I—" she managed eventually. "I don't know. I feel strange all of the sudden..."

"Good strange?" Ithric asked, as if he already knew the answer.

She nodded.

"Do you want us to stop what we're doing?" Favian said.

"No!" she said immediately. "No. Don't stop—"

Ithric's eyes went lazy and wicked. He reached down to close his teeth over the line of muscle running from Favian's neck to his shoulder, biting down. Kathrael's gaze fell on the small patch of skin with sudden, single-minded focus, and the sound Favian made went straight to her sex.

"Ithric!" he gasped, and batted the shape-shifter away.

Ithric backed off with a smug look and went back to regarding her. "Touch yourself, Little Cat. If you don't want to join in with us, you can watch and play with yourself while I take him."

Kathrael's heart was pounding now, but—

"I don't... I've never..." She trailed off, unable to manage a full sentence.

Ithric's brow furrowed. "You've never touched yourself?"

"I've never enjoyed it."

Favian's expression settled into a kind of gentle affection that did nothing whatsoever to quiet the whirlwind of emotions in her mind. "Try, if you want to," he said. "You might find that it feels different this time."

Ithric kissed the mark he'd made on Favian's skin and urged him back down on the bed, their attention returning to each other—much to Kathrael's relief. Could Favian have been right? Was this the pleasure he insisted so ardently that women could feel, as well as men?

"What about you, Favian? Can you still come?" Ithric asked, returning his fingers to Favian's slick opening.

Favian stretched like a cat. "I'm not sure," he said in a dreamy voice. "The other novices say that some eunuchs can, and some can't. As long as you keep doing *that*, I don't really care, to be honest."

"What, *this*, you mean?" Ithric asked, his wrist twisting.

Favian grunted and tried to press back against his fingers again. Kathrael's sex grew so full and heavy that it was almost uncomfortable. When she shifted against the hard seat of the chair to ease it, a new wave of pleasure skittered up her spine. She rocked her hips back and forth in tiny, instinctive movements, riding the little surges of liquid pleasure.

Ithric continued to stretch and tease Favian with his fingers, stopping at intervals to dribble more oil over the place he was breaching. Favian's mouth was open in an expressive *oh* of pleasure, the rest of his body gradually relaxing, growing heavy under the slow, merciless ministrations.

The tips of Kathrael's pebbled nipples ached terribly as they brushed against her chemise with every breath. With a groan, she pulled the laces free and tugged the loose material open, letting it fall over one shoulder until the breast on that side was exposed to the cooling air. She palmed the smooth globe with a soothing motion, trying to quell the fire, and breathed in sharply as a new jolt of pleasure rushed from the taut bud of flesh straight to her throbbing cunt.

Favian was moaning, now — his limp body wracked with tremors every few moments. "Please," he mumbled, "please… *Ithric*. Need you… I need you *right now*. Let me feel you. *Please…*"

Ithric looked nearly as undone as Favian did. He leaned down until his front pressed against Favian's back, and his lips were next to Favian's ear. "You'll have me," he said. His forearm flexed again, and Favian *keened*, arching off the bed.

The ache in Kathrael's sex was too great to ignore any longer. Feeling inexplicably wanton, she squeezed and pinched her exposed breast with one hand while hitching up her skirts an inch at a time with the other. On the bed, Ithric had pulled free of Favian's body and was oiling up his cock, which was hard and leaking. His gaze locked with Kathrael's for an instant, their faces wearing mirrored expressions of need.

Favian turned over to lie on his back, and Ithric's gaze was drawn back to him as if pulled there by an inescapable force.

"I have to see you," Favian explained, still sounding half-gone.

Ithric crawled into the cradle of his spread legs. "I'm right here," he said. "I'm not going anywhere, Favian, I promise. Never again."

Favian surged up to kiss him, and Ithric groaned into his mouth. Kathrael pulled up the front of her skirts the final few inches until she could worm a hand underneath, and lifted her left leg to rest her foot on the edge of the bed. She cupped her swollen sex at the same moment Ithric curled his hips and pressed into the depths of Favian's body.

The thatch of hair between Kathrael's legs was soaked with the moisture her sex had produced. It was slick and warm, and a faint smell reminiscent of seaweed and musk floated to her nostrils. *This must be what Ithric smelled earlier,* she thought, and shivered. *He knew...*

Now, he and Favian were rocking together with lazy movements, never breaking the kiss as their bodies entwined, pressing ever closer. Ithric reached down to hook a hand under Favian's knee and pull his leg up. He thrust in again, and Favian gasped into the kiss.

Kathrael slid a fingertip between her outer lips, exploring the folds inside. Each movement sent shocks of pleasure through her body, growing sharper and more insistent when she touched the nub of flesh at the top that had always been painfully oversensitive before. Now, sliding a fingertip around it in slow circles felt like flying... felt like gliding up the side of a mountain, rising ever higher in hopes of seeing what lay on the other side.

"Missed you," Ithric was saying against Favian's lips. "Missed you so much, Favian. And *you*, Little Cat," he continued, and Kathrael made a needy noise upon hearing the endearment, "what you did... thank you... feels so good to have you both here..."

The warm desire in Kathrael's belly surged higher, a feeling like nothing she had ever experienced. Favian wrapped his arms around Ithric and pressed him close, skin to skin.

"Come for me," he whispered, and both Ithric and Kathrael cried out.

If Kathrael had been gliding before, now she was falling free, plunging into the warm depths of a welcoming sea as her sex throbbed and clenched, flooding her body with an ecstasy she had never even dreamed existed. She washed up on the shore long moments later, still sprawled in the chair, feeling dizzy and drugged with pleasure.

Favian still held Ithric as he twitched and shuddered in the aftermath of his own release, his face buried in the juncture of Favian's neck and shoulder.

"So beautiful," Favian said, "the pair of you."

Kathrael slowly drew her fingers away from her slick sex, jerking in surprise as the movement pulled another shivering aftershock from her spent body.

"Favian," she said after a long pause, her voice as raspy as if she'd been shouting, "I never *knew...*"

Ithric moved his head so that he could look at her while still resting his cheek against Favian's collarbone. His brows drew together. "Was that really your first time, Little Cat?"

Kathrael could only nod, a flush rising up her neck.

Ithric looked surprised for a moment, but then his face cleared and he smiled. "It's good, isn't it?" The smile transformed into a mischievous smirk. "Hey... maybe Favian's not so bad at this priest stuff after all."

Favian poked Ithric hard in the side—his *uninjured* side—and Ithric flinched. "Ow," he complained, lifting his upper body enough to glare down at his tormentor.

"He's right, though," Kathrael managed. "You're not bad at the priest stuff at all." She paused, taking stock of her body. "Only... am I supposed to feel like I'm a helpless puddle of warm mush afterward?"

"Oh, *definitely*," Ithric replied. "That's how you know you're doing it right."

"I guess that's good, then," she managed, sliding down a bit further in the chair.

Favian was still watching her, warm satisfaction on his face. "It's even better with someone else's arms around you afterward," he suggested.

She considered the offer, eyeing the warm bed piled with furs and blankets, along with the two sated men curled up in it. Both of them were awaiting her response with interest, but no indication of impatience. She realized that she was free to decline, and they would treat her no differently than if she accepted. She could *choose*, without fear of losing them.

A soft voice whispered in her ear. *You're not their whore, Kath. You're no one's whore. You're their beautiful, scarred lioness, who fought and survived.*

A lump rose in her throat, and she swallowed around it. Without a word, she rose on shaky legs and untied her skirts. They fell to the floor by the bed, leaving her clad only in her chemise, which still gaped obscenely, half unlaced. Favian nudged Ithric to move over and shuffled toward the center of the mattress, leaving an inviting space next to him.

When she curled up in it, Favian eased an arm under her shoulders, supporting her head on his chest. Ithric threw an arm and a leg over him from the other side.

He was right. This was even better. She was still mired in drowsy lassitude, but the slow brush of fingers along the swell of her shoulder sparked a pleasant tingle across her sensitized skin. She let her own fingers trail across Favian's chest, and felt gooseflesh rise in their wake.

"What about you, Favian?" Ithric mumbled into Favian's neck. "Did you come?"

Favian was quiet for a moment, framing his response. "Not exactly. It's kind of hard to explain. It feels quite a bit different now. Still very pleasurable, but it doesn't build in the same way it used to. While I'm not sure I'd go out of my way to seek it out on my own, I definitely want this with you as often as you'd like. It makes me feel very close to you both. Very open."

Ithric's eyes were closed, though his expression appeared thoughtful. "Hmm... there's a joke in there somewhere about you being *opened*, but I'll restrain myself."

"How kind of you," Favian said, sounding deeply unimpressed. Kathrael snorted in amusement.

"I'm not sure how I feel about sharing a bed with a lover and not making them come," Ithric continued, still sounding half asleep. "Makes me feel selfish."

"Well, don't," Favian said, with a bit of asperity. "Because I'm enjoying getting something out of it beyond a few seconds of release and a mess of spend coating my belly. If you really need a project related to giving people orgasms, maybe you and Kath should talk."

Ithric smiled, his eyes still closed. "Maybe we should. Later, though. Sleep now."

"You've slept half the day already," Kathrael couldn't help pointing out, even though she was on the verge of dozing, herself.

"Invalid, remember?" Ithric muttered.

"You should both sleep," Favian said. "If I'm gone when you wake up, it's because I had to go help with the handfasting. I'll be back sometime this evening, though. If I'm feeling particularly charitable, I might even bring some leftover food and wine back with me."

Ithric yawned, arching his spine before settling back against Favian's side. "Mmm. Bring pork, if they have it. Or goat. Goat's good, too..."

Kathrael fell asleep to the rumble of Favian's soft chuckle under her cheek.

The sound of a crying infant woke her some considerable time later, the noise persisting even as the dregs of the dream that had spawned it slipped away. She gasped and sat upright, disoriented. The last light of evening barely illuminated the room. There was a man next to her in the unfamiliar bed, sleeping with his back turned. He was naked, and the smell of sex permeated the air.

Without stopping to think, Kathrael scrambled back, half falling to the floor and crawling away until she fetched up against a wall, her daughter's anguished cries ringing in her ears. She slapped her hands against the sides of her head and squeezed hard, to no avail.

How could she have been so foolish as to fall asleep? Even now, the man was rolling over, her clumsy movements having awoken him. Had he paid her yet? Where was the money? Maybe she could get it and get away before he tried to fuck her again. The baby's cries grew into high-pitched screams, and she whimpered, unable to think clearly.

"Little Cat?" The question was tentative; the tone, worried. "Little Cat, what's wrong? Did you have a nightmare?"

The man rolled into a sitting position. A swathe of linen bandages crisscrossed his torso, and the sight penetrated her confused mind.

Ithric.

She let out a gasp of relief, still hazy on where she was and what was happening, but knowing deep in her bones that she was not in physical danger, at least.

"Kathrael," Ithric said, "Hey. You're scaring me now. Tell me what's wrong."

She shook her head, pressing fingers into her temples, unable to focus properly on both him and her baby. "I—I can't..."

Ithric was moving—rising from the bed and giving her a wide berth as he rummaged for smallclothes and a set of robes. "Right. I don't know what's happening, but I'm going to get Favian. Just stay here, Little Cat. Don't move. Don't do anything. Promise me."

She could only shake her head again, wishing with all her might that she could reach into her skull physically and rip those agonized cries out by force. She was only distantly aware of the door opening and closing as Ithric left.

The events from earlier in the day started to filter past the hazy veil of sleep and nightmare as she sat next to the wall, rocking back and forth. How could she have let herself feel such happiness while her baby's spirit was hungry and frightened? What kind of a person did that make her? She was surrounded by the dead—by people she had failed in *every conceivable way*. What *right* did she have to pleasure?

Time was meaningless, marked only by the jerky movements of her body as she continued to rock. Eventually, the door opened again, barely penetrating her awareness.

"She panicked out of the blue," Ithric was saying. "Stumbled out of bed and crawled over to the wall. She hasn't said a word, she just sort of whimpers. I didn't know what to do—"

"I'm not sure there *is* anything to do." Favian's voice that time, sounding grim. She tried to latch onto it, her eyes searching the deepening gloom for him.

Light flared as Ithric lit the lamp. Favian crossed to her and dropped to his knees. His soft hands covered her own and pulled them gently from her temples. "Kath," he asked, "is it your baby again?"

She nodded, still unable to speak, and leaned forward until her throbbing head rested against his sternum.

"Baby?" Ithric asked, from somewhere nearby. "Favian, what are you talking about? What's going on?"

Favian's chest expanded and fell in a deep breath. "For some reason, Kathrael attracts the spirits of the dead—people she's lost. They speak to her. Sometimes, they torment her. No one is quite sure why."

Kathrael choked on a sob, and one of Favian's arms came around her, holding her to him. She was dimly aware of movement as Ithric crouched at her side—close, but not touching.

"A baby, though?" Ithric asked, sounding appalled.

"M-my daughter," Kathrael managed in a quavering voice. "She d-died in my womb when I was—" She gulped, choking, and had to pause before she could go on. "When I was fourteen."

Ithric let his breath out.

Favian rubbed her back, and she shook with the need to somehow flee the painful reminder of her failure as a mother. As a woman.

"Kathrael says the baby's spirit is always hungry. Frightened," Favian said, still grim. "We've talked with the other priests, but so far no one has been able to come up with a way to help someone who's already dead."

Kathrael shuddered, and pressed back against Favian's light hold. "I-I need to *move*. I can't just sit here, I'll go mad!"

Favian's arms slipped away, but Ithric's hand fell on her shoulder. "Wait," he said. "Please, Little Cat—just for a minute. Help me understand. There's something that doesn't make sense to me. Why would a spirit feel hunger? You said your daughter died before she was born. How would she even know what hunger *is*?"

Kathrael hugged herself, torn between the desire to flee and the desire to collapse into their arms and shatter. "I don't *know*!" she said.

"What are you getting at, Ithric?" Favian asked. "Surely Kathrael is in a better position than either of us to judge?"

"It just doesn't make sense, Favian," Ithric repeated. "Think about it. *Frightened...* now *that* makes sense. Has anyone actually tried to help the poor kid?"

"*Help, how*?" Kathrael forced out, nearly at the end of her tether. "*She's dead!*"

"Ithric—" Favian began in a quelling tone.

"No. Just let me think out loud," Ithric interrupted. "She might be dead, but her spirit is *here*. I mean, how do you soothe any frightened baby? Has anyone *attempted* to offer her comfort?"

"How *can* I?" Kathrael nearly shouted, hating the hysterical undertone of her voice.

"We don't understand what you're suggesting, Ithric," Favian said, his calm at odds with her upset.

Ithric rose and urged Kathrael to shaky feet. "Just let me try something, you two. Please… give me your trust for a handful of minutes. Honestly, it doesn't look like anything we try could make the situation much worse than it already is, does it?"

Kathrael could only shake her head, trying not to latch onto false hope. Even so, it was easier to stop fighting and let herself be led, so desperate was she for *anyone* to proffer some sort of salvation from her private hell of self-loathing and despair.

"I think we're both open to any ideas you or anyone else might have," Favian said, echoing her thoughts. "But you'll still have to explain what you intend."

Ithric urged her toward the bed, and Favian added an arm to support her from the other side as well. "It's exactly what I said," Ithric offered. "What do you do when a baby cries, if it's not because of hunger? You soothe them."

Kathrael shuddered again. "I can't even touch her…"

Ithric guided her to the center of the bed and put a hastily folded blanket against the headboard for her to lean against. "No," he said, his voice sad. "But you can try to let go of your own pain over her loss, and be the comfort she needs. Babies always take their cues from their mothers."

That stopped her. Shock suffused her as the harsh truth of what he was saying cut through her haze of pain and self-hatred. No one in their right mind would hand a squalling baby to a person who was curled up rocking in the corner with their hands over their ears to block out the sound of the cries.

"Favian," Ithric urged, as Kathrael sat frozen on the bed in the wake of her epiphany. He gestured Favian to join her. Favian climbed in and sat next to her, shoulder to shoulder, his mouth twisting into a frown as she looked to him for guidance.

"As much as it pains me to say so," he said, "Ithric might just be onto something. Will you let him try to help?"

She nodded, still struck dumb. Her eyes slipped to Ithric as he crawled in to bracket her on the other side, only to squeeze shut a moment later when the wails echoing in her ears grew even more desperate.

"I'm so sorry, Kathrael," Ithric said. "I know it must hurt you. But she's just a baby. All she wants is to feel safe. To know that she's protected by people who care about her."

Tears rose up and spilled from Kathrael's good eye. "I couldn't protect her," she whispered.

Favian wrapped an arm around her and drew her close against him. "You're protecting her spirit. You're protecting her memory. You came to a place where other people could try to help. And, gods help me, I think you may have just stumbled on the person with the answer."

Unable to take any more, she buried her face against him and wept. All of the tightly held anguish she'd been caging in her chest escaped in a river of salt water that ran down her undamaged cheek. Ithric scooted up to rest against her back, one hand sliding up and down her arm in a soothing motion.

She cried for a long time. *I'm sorry, my precious daughter,* she thought. *I'm so sorry I tried to shut you out. To push you away. I didn't understand — I didn't know what else to do. I still don't, really. I love you, though. So much. I will always love you...*

Gradually, the sound of soft humming penetrated her awareness. She came back to her surroundings enough to realize that the low, soothing noise came from Ithric. He was still at her back, rocking her back and forth with tiny movements. Her chest settled, the rhythm of her congested breathing broken only by an occasional hitch as he started to sing in a surprisingly fine, clear tenor.

"I left my baby lying there,
lying there, lying there;
I left my baby lying there
To go and gather wineberries."

It was a lullaby; one she had not heard before. A new sob choked her, and she buried her face in Favian's linen robes.

"Ho-van, ho-van gorry o go,
Gorry o go, gorry o go;
I've lost my dearest baby-o..."

Favian stroked her head as she listened, the words of the song competing with the baby's cries. Cries that were slowly growing weaker.

"I saw the little yellow fawn,
yellow fawn, yellow fawn;

But never saw my baby.

"I found the otter on the lake,
on the lake, on the lake;
But could not find my baby."

Her daughter's cries subsided into soft whimpers, and Kathrael's heart skipped a beat, stealing her breath away for a moment.

"Ho-van, ho-van gorry o go,
Gorry o go, gorry o go;
I never found my baby-o.

"The faeries took my baby home,
baby home, baby home;
I'll see her when I'm dreaming."

The words trailed off, and Ithric returned to humming. Favian's light voice joined him, and a moment later, the voices of other unseen presences joined the harmony. Vesh. Her sister. Her mother. Even after Ithric and Favian's voices went silent, the lullabies continued—songs from the southern slave camps, songs from the temple.

Kathrael lifted her tear-stained face, looking around the room in wonder. Her daughter's spirit cooed and burbled quietly, the tiny, anguished wraith finally at peace.

"Kath?" Favian asked, his thumb coming up to brush away the tear track from her unscarred cheek.

Oh, my daughter, she thought. *My dearest baby. I think… I think… maybe… we don't have to be afraid any more.*

"Thank you," she whispered aloud. "Thank you both so much.

TWENTY-ONE

The three of them sat curled together in the flickering glow of the single lamp for a long time after the lullaby ended. The ghostly voices faded slowly into silence, the transition so gradual that Kathrael could not have said when they finally slipped back behind the unseen veil.

Favian insisted on leaving long enough to get them food, and watched carefully to ensure that Kathrael ate her share.

Afterward, they talked for *hours*. Kathrael learned that Ithric had turned into a lion for the first time seven years earlier, when bandits attacked his family on the road and killed his parents. He savaged one while in animal form, and the other three fled, leaving Ithric and his older sister alive.

"Alyndra tried to drag me to the temple as soon as we got back home to Venzor. She and the High Priest were both ignoring me, even though I was standing right there, talking about me becoming an acolyte like it was a foregone conclusion. So I waited until dark and ran away." He ran a hand through his ragged mane of hair, mussing it. "Alyndra was furious with me for leaving her alone before our parents could even have a proper funeral, and I was furious with her for trying to make me a prisoner of the Priests' Guild."

"It wouldn't have been like that," Favian interjected.

Ithric raised an eyebrow. "Wouldn't it?" he shot back in a deeply skeptical tone. "Not everyone in the northern temples shares Senovo's views on such matters, Favian. If he hadn't found me and taken me back to Draebard with him, I have no doubt that I would have been hounded into the temple if I'd ever dared show my face around people again."

Favian shook his head and breathed out sharply through his nose. Although he was practically radiating disagreement, Kathrael could see him rein himself in to avoid an argument.

"Anyway," Ithric continued, "things still aren't good between Alyndra and me. I heard she got handfasted a couple of years ago, but we haven't spoken since the summer after I ran away."

"Maybe it's time to try mending things," Favian offered. "I can't imagine being at odds with Frella for years on end. Life's too short. All three of us have learned that lesson far too well, I think."

"Maybe so," Ithric said.

In return for Ithric's story, Kathrael haltingly told him about her own life. When she spoke of her first disastrous meeting with the Wolf Patron, his eyes widened.

"Wait," he said. "*You're* the little slave girl from south of Rhyth?" His eyes flew to Favian, who nodded.

"Kath and I disagree to a considerable degree on the concept of prophecy," he said, "but I can't help thinking that our meeting—and everything that came after—was fated."

"Apparently I'm shorter in person than I was in his Seer's dream," Kathrael quipped, still uncomfortable with the idea that her actions had somehow been preordained.

"It's probably just because I was lying down in the dream," Favian replied, his lips quirking with rueful humor.

Ithric flopped back against the headboard of the bed, boneless, and shook his head. "Crazy—all of it. Completely demented, from start to finish." He reached over to grasp a cup of the rich wine Favian had brought them, and lifted it. "Ah, well— here's to fate."

Favian saluted him with his own cup, and Kathrael followed suit. "To fate," Favian said wryly.

"So," Ithric continued, "We're taking Rona, Nimbral, and Arnav to Draebard with us. Then what?"

Favian frowned, confused. "What do you mean, *then what*?"

"Well," Ithric said slowly, "I mean… I should probably have a word with Andoc about the state of things in the south, and I did promise Frella I'd teach her knife throwing. I expect there will be a fair amount of thoroughly enjoyable buggery in our future, Favian, and I'm definitely open to exploring new and exciting ways to make Kathrael come, if she's amenable."

Kathrael flushed. "I'm amenable," she mumbled.

Ithric made a *there you have it gesture*. "So, aside from all that, and singing the occasional lullaby as required… what's next? Little Cat? What are your plans now that you've successfully rescued everyone who was under old Turvick's thumb?"

Surprised, Kathrael flashed back to her so-called *plans* from when she started this unlikely journey. She couldn't stifle the snort of harsh, derogatory laughter that escaped.

"Oh... nothing much," she said in a voice laced with heavy sarcasm. "Once I'd traveled across the mountains and taken my bloody revenge on the Wolf Patron for abandoning the southern slaves, I was going to trek *back* across the mountains and lead a rebellion against the Masters in Rhyth without his damned help. Obviously."

Ithric's eyes lit with interest. "Oh? Were you now?" he asked, as if her ironic tone had bypassed him completely. "Hmm. All right—I'm in. Let's do that, then."

She blinked. "Ithric... I was out of my head at the time. Mad as a bag of weasels. One escaped slave girl can't lead a revolution—it's ridiculous."

Ithric only smiled at her, all innocence. "Oh... so you're saying you need a *shape-shifter* to help?" The smile sharpened—grew dangerous.

Kathrael's mouth opened, but no words came out.

Fortunately, Favian did not suffer from the same problem. "Ithric! Are you *soft in the head*? They *burn* shape-shifters in the south!"

"I know," Ithric said slowly, as if to an imbecile. "I was there. Don't you consider that a good reason to try and change things?"

"They also stone eunuchs who dare to step out from under the temple's protection," Kathrael said quietly.

"Yes. They do," Ithric agreed, sobering. "Favian, I don't think you understand how bad things are in Rhyth. The city is ready to tear itself apart. And if it falls, I don't think I have to tell you who's going to step in and take over."

"The Alyrions," Favian breathed.

"They're halfway there already," Ithric confirmed.

"More than that, I'd say," Kathrael said. "The cult of Deimok is growing in power all the time. The priests of the Old Religion are weak in the south. They will not stand against it for much longer."

"You're right, then—you *do* need to talk to Andoc," Favian said, sounding grim. "You both do. But, Ithric, he's not going to countenance starting a revolution."

Ithric raised an eyebrow. "I think you might be surprised."

"And how will starting a slave revolt even *help*, if the Alyrions are waiting for exactly that?" Favian asked.

Kathrael put her cup aside and laced her fingers together, looking down at them. "Almost half of the population is silenced right now, Favian. The slaves don't want to worship a foreign god. They don't want to bow down to an Emperor. They want the same thing you want in the north. Freedom. Dignity. A say in their own futures."

Favian flopped back into his chair as if he'd been pushed there by an unseen hand.

"Nothing more than all the gods' children deserve, surely. Would you disagree, Favian?" Ithric prodded.

There was a pause. "No," Favian said, very quietly. "Of course I don't disagree. Of *course* they deserve it. But where would three people even begin with such a thing?"

Kathrael's chest tightened at his words. *Three people*, he'd said. Was this really to be her life, now? Could it actually be true?

"I… don't have the faintest idea," she admitted. "I wasn't joking when I told you I was mad at the time."

Ithric smiled again. "Well, I suppose the *obvious* thing would be to talk to the leaders of the escaped slaves in the underground movement and see what they think. I know several of them — I suspect they'd have a few thoughts on the subject."

Both Favian and Kathrael stared at him with open mouths, and he shrugged.

"Hello? Spy, remember? What did you *think* I've been doing all these months?" He rose and stretched before leaning down to kiss first Kathrael, and then Favian. "First things first, though."

"Yes. Right," Favian said, once he'd managed to stop gaping. He shook his head, appearing to come back to himself with some difficulty. "Draebard. *Home.* Rona still needs help, Frella is almost certainly ready to strangle me for running off without her, and you two *definitely* need to speak with Andoc — *at length.*"

Ithric nodded, his expression agreeable. Kathrael felt suddenly light, unburdened, as if she might float away and soar into the sky at any moment.

"Yes. Draebard first," she echoed, nearly giddy with thoughts of the future. "And I want to do that orgasm thing again, too. *Lots.* That was really nice."

A grin split Ithric's face, and his eyes moved from one to the other of them with lazy affection. "Oh, *absolutely*," he said. "As often as you like, Little Cat. Also, the buggery. Can't forget the buggery, can we?"

End of Book 1

THE LION MISTRESS:
BOOK 2

ONE

Kathrael hummed a soft lullaby as the wagon jounced and juddered over the rutted road. She and her fellow travelers were somewhere between Woodhaerst and Venzor, where they planned on stopping for the night. She shifted position, trying not to disturb Ithric as he lay dozing, his head pillowed on her lap. Still humming, she resumed stroking her fingers through his messy mane of hair, and he sighed in contentment.

"I think we're getting close now," Favian called from the driver's seat. "Everyone doing all right back there?"

Ithric mumbled something under his breath and immediately went back to sleep. Kathrael looked up at her fellow passengers, Rona, Nimbral, and Arnav, who were sprawled in varying degrees of comfort against the other side of the wagon bed. Nimbral nodded and adjusted his grip around his tiny partner, curled up in the space next to his unnaturally tall form. Arnav shrugged a bony shoulder, looking bored. The movement was made strangely disconcerting by his lack of arms.

"We're fine, Favian," Kathrael said. "Do you want me to wake Ithric so he can direct you once we get there?"

Venzor was nearly a day and a half out of their way on the journey back to Draebard. But they had decided to make the detour so Ithric could visit his estranged sister, who had been recently handfasted and whom he had not seen in years.

"No, let him sleep," Favian said, looking over his shoulder. "I figured I'd head for Andoc's mother's home and get directions from there. Trust me—Iseboa would do me serious bodily injury if she found out I'd stopped in Venzor without visiting her."

Kathrael nodded, and went back to her quiet lullaby. Ithric settled deeper in her lap, while across from her, Rona stroked a hand absently over her belly—unconsciously soothing the unborn child that lay within. At the edges of Kath's hearing, the spirit of her own lost baby fussed for a few moments, only to subside when Vesh's ghostly voice joined hers in the simple melody.

I never pictured you as a nursemaid, Vesh, she thought, a feeling of mild amusement lifting one corner of her lips.

I did have four younger brothers and sisters, you know, Vesh shot back. *And it's good to feel her at peace, finally.*

Kathrael's throat tightened. *Yes,* she agreed. For so long, the tiny wraith had wailed and cried inconsolably during the night, driving Kathrael to the brink of madness with guilt and grief over her inability to help her dead, unborn daughter. It had taken Ithric to finally make her see that the ghostly infant did not need her guilt; she needed Kathrael's strength and comfort.

Three nights ago, he and Favian had held Kathrael between them as she wept, her pain finally spilling over as she grieved the miscarriage she had suffered years ago when her half-starved fourteen-year-old body had been unable to sustain the pregnancy. Ithric had sung a soft lullaby, soothing her lost child's fear until the cries finally subsided, replaced by peace and contentment.

Kath already had many reasons to care for Favian, but that gesture had instantly cemented her love for Ithric as well. She was more than content to extend their difficult journey back to Draebard if it meant that the injured lion-shifter would have a chance to reconcile with his only living relative after such a long estrangement.

The wagon hit a particularly deep pothole and lurched, causing Ithric to grunt in pain as his wound was jarred. Kathrael thought she heard a low curse from Favian as well. Not surprising, really. Favian's recent castration during his initiation into the priesthood had not been helped by days of riding, as he and Kathrael raced to find and free Ithric from the clutches of the men who had held him prisoner, along with the motley group of misfits huddled now on the other side of the wagon.

Once it was decided that Rona, Nimbral, and Arnav would travel with the three of them to Draebard, Favian had used most of their remaining money to purchase a wagon, harness, and additional supplies for traveling.

They had originally brought two horses from Draebard, planning to let Favian and Ithric ride, with Kathrael riding double behind one of them. The addition of three more people—all of them with physical challenges that made travel difficult—prompted Favian to change his plans. Now, the two cream-colored horses were hitched side by side, pulling a decidedly aged and battered wagon behind them. Six passengers crowded into the inadequate space, resting on bundles of their supplies.

Ithric had eyed the ancient conveyance with misgivings when Favian first pulled up to the temple and reined the horses to a halt.

"Just so we don't break a wheel or snap an axle the first time we hit a rut," he said skeptically.

Favian had glared at him. "Don't even say it, Ithric. Don't even *think* it, all right?"

"Well," Kathrael put in optimistically, "it's certainly nicer than the melon wagon I rode on to get to Penth."

"*Thank you*," said Favian. "At least *someone* is suitably appreciative."

To his credit, the old rattletrap was holding together well enough so far. And it really was better than the alternative. Nimbral was a fantastically tall man, but his joints pained him. Rona was pregnant, and would have had difficulty keeping up with her short stature and bowed legs. Arnav could walk, but without arms he would have been unable to carry supplies. Also, Ithric was still recovering from a knife wound, though he would doubtless have protested that he was fine if someone had brought it up.

The wagon might not have been *comfortable*, precisely, but it was efficient. And now, it was bringing them to the place where Ithric—not to mention the Draebardi chief, Andoc—had grown up. Kathrael could not deny that she was curious as the settlement came into view in the valley below.

Venzor was a good-sized village, larger than both Draebard and Woodhaerst. Their party had made good time—it was only mid-afternoon, and people still bustled along the streets running through the town. Several of the townsfolk paused to stare at the unusually colored horses, pointing and muttering amongst themselves. Kathrael ducked her head and subtly twitched her shawl forward to more completely cover the scars marring the left side of her face.

She wondered if the white horses were already known in their owner's former village. It was clear that Favian had been here before, perhaps with his guardians, because he chose a route through the town without hesitation, heading for a quiet side road lined with large, neatly kept cottages.

"Ithric," Favian called. "Wake up. We're at Iseboa's place."

Ithric blinked open hazel eyes shot with flecks of green and stretched cautiously. He smiled up at Kathrael. When she gave his head a final stroke, he pressed into the contact, catlike.

"At least we're fairly well assured of a warm welcome on that front," he replied in a dry tone. "Though you'll forgive me if I let you take care of the introductions, and explain why we're landing on her with a small army."

"I'm sure the truth will suffice," Favian shot back in the same tone. He pulled up in front of a cheerful cottage with ivy growing on the walls and boxes of herbs in the windows. "We're about to find out, at any rate."

Ithric levered himself upright, gritting his teeth as his half-healed wound made itself known. He clambered into the driver's seat, taking the reins so Favian could climb down— the young priest's movement made a bit awkward by his dun-colored novice's robes. At the same moment, a plump woman with dark hair shot through with iron gray came around the side of the house, carrying a basket of linens against her hip.

She froze upon seeing the two white horses standing in front of her home. The basket dropped to the ground, unheeded. The woman's eyes flew to Favian and lit up with surprised joy. Kathrael gathered that this must be Iseboa, Andoc's mother.

An instant later, the woman hurried forward. Favian met her halfway.

"Favian!" she exclaimed, and threw her arms around him tightly. "Oh my goodness, it's so wonderful to see you!"

"Hello, Iseboa," Favian said warmly, returning the embrace with obvious affection. "Sorry to show up with no warning and company in tow. You're looking well. How have you been?"

"All the better for seeing you, sweetheart. Look at you! *Novice* Favian, now. I'm so proud of you," she replied with a smile. She pulled back enough so she could see the others. Her eyes widened at the odd assortment of individuals, but she covered the reaction of surprise immediately. Her smile returned an instant later as she recognized Ithric, who waved back sheepishly.

"Hi, Iseboa," he said, and Kathrael was more intrigued than ever to meet the woman who could apparently turn the self-assured, irreverent shape-shifter into a contrite adolescent with a single look.

"Ithric!" Iseboa said. "By all the gods and goddesses. Come over here, right this instant."

Favian grinned and moved to stand at the horses' heads so Ithric could climb meekly down for inspection. "Don't hug him too tightly, please," Favian warned. "He was wounded in the side recently and we've only just got him patched back together."

"Hug him? I should box his ears for staying away so long!" Iseboa immediately belied the words by wrapping her arms carefully around Ithric's shoulders and giving a gentle squeeze. He had to lean down a bit to get to her level.

"Sorry," Ithric mumbled, and Kathrael thought she could detect a blush coloring his features. "It just seemed like things would be better if I stayed away. How is Alyndra?"

His tone was hesitant—simultaneously worried and hopeful—and Iseboa stretched up to press a kiss to his forehead before releasing him.

"She's well, Ithric. You have a nephew now, you know—she gave birth to a healthy boy a couple of months ago." Ithric breathed in sharply, but Iseboa only shook her head. "First things first. Please, everyone come inside, and you can introduce me to your friends. Favian—there's a bucket of clean water by the back door if you'd like to give the horses a drink before you tie them up. I'll see about sorting out some refreshments for us."

"Thank you, Iseboa," Favian said, his voice full of affection. "Kath? Would you mind helping me with the horses? We'll join the rest of you in a few minutes."

"Of course," Kathrael replied, somewhat relieved to have a job to focus on, truth be told.

She helped Arnav down from the back of the wagon, while Nimbral helped Rona. Leaping lightly to the ground after them, she went around to the front to hold the horses so Favian could unhitch them and get the water bucket. Audris nudged her in the shoulder with his muzzle, and she scratched his forehead absently while she waited.

Within minutes, Favian had stripped the animals of their harness and offered them a drink, his years as an apprentice in Draebard's horse pens lending an effortless efficiency to his actions. He and Kathrael tied the two horses up to a hitching post in the shade by the side of the house.

"Will our supplies be safe in the wagon?" Kathrael asked as Favian gave Ozias a final pat and led the way toward the front door.

He snorted. "Anyone stupid enough to steal from a wagon parked in front of Iseboa's house deserves exactly what they'd get. It will be fine."

Kathrael's lips twitched. "She does seem rather… forceful. In a decidedly motherly sort of way."

"Oh… you have *no idea*," Favian replied. "Now, come on. Even I'm not cruel enough to leave Ithric to her tender mercies for more than a few minutes with no support."

He entered without knocking, and Kathrael eased her way in behind him. The cottage was good-sized, but seemed crowded with seven people in the main room. The space was homey and inviting, littered with the tools of a weaver's trade — distaffs and spindles of brightly colored yarn, frames holding partially completed blankets, and piles of folded, finished cloth stacked hastily out of the way.

In their brief absence, Iseboa had distributed drinks in mismatched cups to everyone in the room. She appeared a moment later with two more, giving one to Favian and the second to Kathrael. She smiled tentatively as she handed over Kathrael's cup. Kathrael ducked her head instinctively to put the damaged side of her face in shadow, but tried to return the smile.

"I met everyone else while you and Favian were outside," Iseboa said, breaking the small moment of awkwardness. "I'm Iseboa, Favian's grandmother." She gave a gentle laugh. "Or perhaps, more accurately, his grand-guardian. Though *grandmother* rolls off the tongue so much more easily, wouldn't you agree?"

"I'm Kathrael," she answered, feeling oddly shy.

"Well, it's lovely to meet you, Kathrael," Iseboa said with evident sincerity. "Please make yourself comfortable and try to forgive the clutter. So, tell me — how did you, Favian, and Ithric come to be acquainted? Were you also part of that horrible traveling show that Ithric has been telling me about?"

Kathrael opened her mouth, but there was really no way to make "I took your grandson hostage at knifepoint and tried to use him as a hostage to get to your son's bondmate" sound anything other than awful. Before she had to try, Favian rescued her.

"Kathrael and I met in Draebard. She had traveled all the way over the mountains, searching for Senovo," he said, tactfully remaining silent about the details. "By pure chance, she'd already met Ithric along the way, and helped rescue two children who were being held prisoner by the men running the show."

It still made Kath want to cringe whenever Favian or someone else from Draebard softened the truth of her arrival there, downplaying her grief-fueled scheme to enact vengeance on the Wolf Patron.

You should be grateful, Vesh whispered.

I suppose I should be, she thought, *but mostly it just makes me queasy.*

Iseboa was looking at her with new interest. "You walked all the way from Rhyth? Good heavens, Kathrael. You must have been very determined to find Senovo, indeed."

Something about Iseboa made her want to tell the truth. She swallowed, and took a deep breath before speaking.

"You could say that, yes. The Wolf Patron and I met briefly when I was only a child. I was a field slave in the agricultural area north of Rhyth. He and the others from Draebard turned my life upside down that day, and then disappeared without a trace." She paused, thinking back to those dark times. "Over the years, I came to hold him responsible for every bad thing that happened in my life. When I left Rhyth to journey north, I'd just seen the only person I'd ever called a friend stoned to death by a mob. I was, in fact, very determined to find Senovo — so I could take vengeance on him."

Iseboa looked deeply troubled. She was silent for a moment, as were the others. Kathrael realized that aside from Favian and Ithric, no one present knew the details of her background. No doubt she had shocked them as well, but she would not hide from her actions — not in front of a woman who clearly cared for both Favian and Senovo as family. Iseboa deserved to know to whom she was offering the hospitality of her home and hearth.

"Since you are here, now, with Favian and Ithric," Iseboa began slowly, "I am confident that vengeance is no longer your goal. I… grieve for all that you have endured in your life, Kathrael… but you must know that my son's bondmate—the person you call the Wolf Patron—is a good man."

Around them, the others remained quiet, letting the unexpected scene play out. Kathrael chose her words carefully.

"In the south, he is more legend than man. He is the powerful mage who was supposed to return to lead us to freedom. Instead, he appeared in our lives just long enough to hold an overseer at bay while a handful of us escaped. Then he vanished immediately afterward, leaving us to either scratch out a bare existence through petty theft and prostitution, or starve to death."

Iseboa reached behind her for a chair and sat down heavily. Kathrael pressed on, needing to finish.

"That was all I ever knew of him until I crossed the mountains, Iseboa. I expected to find a cold, uncaring statue when I snuck into the temple in Draebard in search of him. Some sort of detached, haughty demigod. Instead I found a man, like any other. Better than many. He spared me when he could have condemned me; extended his protection and ensured that I was nursed back to health when he could have turned his back on me."

Andoc's mother still held Kathrael's gaze. "*That* is the man *I* know," she said quietly.

Kathrael nodded, not disputing it. "When I look at him, my heart still sees the Wolf Patron. But my mind knows now that he is a person, not a legend—and that, while his presence was undeniably a catalyst in my own life, he is not responsible for all the world's ills."

Favian cleared his throat, drawing Iseboa's attention. "Kathrael is too hard on herself, Iseboa."

Kathrael looked at him frankly. "On the contrary. You are too soft on me, Favian."

"You were stricken by grief, and that grief drew you toward a place where you could find help," he argued. "I, for one, am glad it did."

To her utter surprise, Ithric came up behind her and wrapped an arm around her stomach, resting his chin on top of her head. "That makes two of us," he said. She could feel his words rumble through his chest where he pressed against her back.

Iseboa looked between the three of them speculatively. "I think perhaps all three of you found something different than you expected to find. If so, I am pleased for you, and pleased that what could easily have been a tragedy seems to have become a redemption, of sorts." She blinked, drawing herself visibly away from the topic. "Now, though—Ithric. *Are* you here to visit Alyndra? She and the miller's son have a place of their own now. It's in a different part of town from your parent's old hut."

Kathrael felt Ithric's ribcage rise and fall as he blew out a breath. He let his arm fall away from her and moved to stand next to her. Kathrael tried not to miss the contact.

"I am," he said. "Though I don't hold out much hope that things will go any differently than last time."

The last time, Kathrael knew, had been several years ago, and had resulted in nothing more than a bitter argument followed by an unhappy parting. Iseboa obviously knew this, too, because her mouth turned down unhappily.

"It's worth a try, Ithric," she said gently. "Many things have changed since then, and family is important."

Kathrael thought of her family of birth—all lost now. She thought of the family she had gained, the tentative new bonds still tender and delicate. Untried.

"I know it's important, Iseboa," Ithric was saying. "That's why I'm here."

"You've grown up," Iseboa observed fondly.

"Matter of opinion, that," Favian muttered under his breath. Ithric shot him a dark look, but didn't rise to the bait. Iseboa glanced at him as well, and she seemed to see more than expected. With a sudden flash of insight, Kathrael wondered if she was remembering her own son and his eunuch lover in their younger days.

Whatever the case, she merely quirked a brief, secret smile and turned back to Ithric. "Would you like me to take you to her? Or will you stop for a meal first?"

Ithric appeared unsure, and again, Kathrael was struck by how off balance he seemed here in his home village. "I'd prefer to go now," he said after a short pause. "I'm afraid I don't really have much of an appetite at the moment."

"Do you want us to come with you?" Favian asked, both his voice and expression soft now, despite his earlier teasing.

Ithric sighed audibly, looking from Favian to Kathrael and back again. "No. Not really. Though I do appreciate the offer. This is on me, and if it goes badly I'd rather not have an audience, if it's all the same."

Kathrael nodded, understanding very well what he meant. A moment later, Rona's soft voice piped up from the corner, where she was seated in a comfortable chair next to Nimbral.

"If she's not pleased to see you, Ithric, she's a fool." Rona blushed a bit when their attention turned to her, but didn't back down. "You came all the way here to see her. If she won't reconcile with you, it's her loss." Her tone grew emphatic on the final words, even as her cheeks flushed bright pink.

"Thanks, Rona," Ithric replied, with a sad smile that faded almost immediately. He seemed to steel himself, and turned back to Iseboa.

She gave a small nod and addressed the rest of them. "Favian, I hope I don't have to tell you to make yourself at home. In fact, if you wouldn't mind rummaging around in the kitchen, you can put together something for the others to eat while I'm gone. Just use whatever looks good." Favian nodded. "As for the rest of you, my place is yours. Please make yourself comfortable and let Favian know if you need anything. I'll be back before long."

"Thank you," Arnav said from his perch on a stool by the table. The others echoed him as Iseboa gave them a last smile and went to throw a light cloak over her dress.

Kathrael looked up at Ithric's face, still lined with uncertainty. On instinct, she stretched up on tiptoe to brush a light kiss over his stubbled cheek. He let out a breath, a bit of the tension draining from his rigid stance. A moment later, Favian pushed away from where he'd been leaning hipshot against the end of the table and crossed to stand in front of him.

"Just say what you need to say, Ithric. You can't control whether she's ready to hear it or not." He cradled Ithric's face and guided his head down so he could press a kiss to his forehead before letting him go.

Ithric nodded, eyes closed, and straightened away. "Yeah. That doesn't make it any easier, though."

"Most things worth doing are difficult, lion-boy," Kathrael offered.

He smiled again, though it didn't reach his eyes. "Wise words, Little Cat." Iseboa had returned as they spoke, and he turned to her. "Ready?"

She nodded. "I am. We'll see you all later. Make sure Favian feeds you properly in the mean time."

"I'll take care of it," Favian assured. "Good luck, Ithric. May the gods smile on your endeavors."

"Ever the priest," Ithric said lightly, and followed Iseboa out the front door.

Alyndra's new home was in the northern arm of the village, close to the gristmill. Ithric was relieved that Iseboa seemed content to let him stew in silence as they walked, rather than offering platitudes or trying to engage him in small talk.

It was decidedly odd, being with her like this. The last time he had been in Venzor was many years ago—before the war, and only a few months after he had shifted form for the first time during the bandits' attack on the road outside of town. On that occasion, too, Iseboa had offered to accompany him to try to make peace with his sister.

Time seemed to waver back and forth between the present and the past, even though he was no longer a frightened boy, alone and in hiding. Maybe he *should* have let Favian and Kathrael come along... but no. This was something that he and Alyndra needed to work out between them, if it even could be worked out.

"Here it is," Iseboa said, indicating a modest hut that was decidedly crook-cornered in places, but neatly kept and covered in a fresh coat of whitewash. "Do you want me to stay? I could wait outside and walk back with you afterward if you'd like."

As a youngster, Ithric had barely known Iseboa—only by name, as a customer of his father's who would come in to buy combed wool every few weeks. He had really only spent time in close contact with her twice—when, as a boy, he'd come back to Venzor to speak with Alyndra... and now.

Even so, there was something about her that drew people; he was no exception. Without hesitation, he turned and wrapped her in a brief embrace, which she returned—being careful of his wounded side.

"No," he said. "It's fine. Go back and take care of the others. I know where we are—I can find my way back to your place afterward with no problems. Thanks for bringing me, Iseboa... *again.*"

She smiled, a wry expression. "We do seem to be making a habit of this, don't we? Good luck, Ithric."

He tried to smile in return, and she turned with a wave to head back to her home and her houseguests. Ithric looked back toward the little hut, then took a deep breath to steady himself before marching up and knocking on the door.

The afternoon light was slanting into evening, now. It was Alyndra's bondmate who answered the door—already home after finishing his day's work at the gristmill.

Yando was a powerful young man, whom Ithric remembered only vaguely from his childhood. Even then, their parents had intended Alyndra to join with him, but he and Ithric had not interacted much. For this reason, it wasn't really a surprise when Yando showed no recognition upon seeing his face.

"Yes?" he asked, faintly wary. "Can I help you?"

Ithric suddenly became aware of the picture he must present. He'd had nothing when Favian and Kathrael freed him from the traveling show, where Turvick had been forcing him to stay permanently in the form of the lion. No possessions, no money, not so much as a stitch of clothing to call his own. Now he was wearing a threadbare set of acolyte's robes from the temple in Woodhaerst, over Favian's extra pair of breeches and worn sandals. Hardly the model of respectability.

He'd been silent too long. A light voice came from the back room of the small hut, as familiar as his own despite the changes adulthood had wrought.

"Who's there, Yando?" Alyndra asked, entering the front room with a small bundle held close to her chest.

Ithric swallowed, his breath catching in his chest. "Lyndie?"

Alyndra froze just inside the connecting doorway with a high-pitched gasp, her face going white as milk. "Ithric?" she asked in a tiny voice.

Yando looked from his pale wife to Ithric. "You're Ithric?" he asked, in a tone that could not remotely be described as friendly. His gaze returned to Alyndra. "Lyn? Do you want me to let him in, or throw him out on the street?"

TWO

Ithric had to restrain the growl that wanted to rumble through his throat. *Try it*, he thought, as the inherent threat from another male who would keep him from his sister made his hackles rise. He reminded himself forcibly that he was the outsider here, and he hadn't exactly expected a warm welcome. The lion stirred briefly in discontent, but subsided.

"Let him in," Alyndra said in a hesitant voice, after a pause long enough to stab at his heart. "Ithric, what are you *doing* here?"

Ithric slipped past Yando's wary bulk, fine hairs on his arms and neck still prickling at the territorial protectiveness rolling off of the other man in waves.

"I came to see you, Alyndra," he said, stopping several steps away. "Why else?"

His eyes were drawn to the bundle in her arms. She gripped the baby closer in an unconscious gesture. "It's been *years*, though! The last I heard, you'd left Draebard and no one had heard from you or knew where you'd gone. I... worried that you might be dead."

"I'm not dead," he pointed out helpfully. "And it seems that you've been busy since I've been gone." Again, he looked at the bundle, longing to see the tiny form nestled inside the soft swaddling.

Alyndra's eyes grew wet. "I've moved on, Ithric. I'm living my life."

The breath left his lungs in a slow, silent exhale. "Of course you are, Lyndie. So am I. I just thought... maybe we could make our peace, so those lives didn't have to be completely separate anymore."

Yando was standing across the room, his arms folded over his chest. "She's not the one who built that wall, Ithric. You are."

"*Yando*," Alyndra said softly, before Ithric could respond. "Don't. It's all right."

Yando shrugged, looking unhappy, but subsided to lean against the wall by the door.

Ithric peered around the tiny hut, a question he'd been wondering about since he'd first seen the unprepossessing place slipping past his lips. "Why did you move out of Father and Mother's hut, Lyndie? Especially with a baby on the way. There would have been a lot more space if the two of you had stayed there."

Alyndra's face closed off. "I had to sell it to pay the dowry. There was no other way to get the money, with them dead and you gone."

"You sold Ma and Da's hut?" he blurted in shock, before the rest of the words penetrated properly.

Now anger flooded her features. "What else was I supposed to do, for Deresta's sake? Sit around waiting for my ne'er-do-well brother to reappear and hand me bags of money? I would have been waiting a long time, as it turns out!"

"And I would have had a hell of a time earning money for you when I was stuck in the temple as an acolyte!" he shot back, his own anger rising to match hers.

The baby squalled, and Yando stepped forward from his position out of the way, once more looking ready to throw him bodily from the house. Ithric subsided, immediately appalled with himself.

"Oh, gods, Alyndra," he said, voice full of contrition, "I'm sorry. I was afraid this would happen—it's a big part of why I stayed away. Look... you have every reason to be angry with me. And *of course* you had to sell the hut. You were absolutely right to do so."

Some of the anger drained from her face, but her voice was still wary. "I'm sorry, too, Ithric. I... know now that I should have talked to you all those years ago when our parents died, before I dragged you to the temple. I didn't know what else to do after you shifted and killed that bandit on the road. I was scared, and grieving, and I was just a *child*. But... I can't bear having you in and out of my life like this, disappearing for years at a time without so much as a word."

He started to protest that it would be different now— only to catch himself before the words emerged. He was leaving for Draebard, and from there, for Rhyth. For how long? How long did it take to foment a slave rebellion? And would he even be alive at the end of it?

He swallowed hard. "I understand," he said instead. "And, Alyndra—I *am* sorry for the pain I've caused you."

Alyndra looked at him, her face twisting as a choked noise of stifled tears escaped her control. Ithric's heart ached.

"I think it would be best if you left now," Yando said.

Ithric took a deep breath and nodded. "I will. Only, could I see my nephew first? This... might be the only chance I'll get."

Alyndra paused for a moment before she nodded, still obviously holding back tears. She crossed the few steps between them and tilted her upper body to reveal the face of the perfect little baby boy resting in her arms. A lump rose in Ithric's throat, and he reached out one callused finger to stroke the smooth forehead with its little curl of dark hair—the barest of touches.

"Oh, Lyndie," he breathed. "He's beautiful."

The baby snuffled, making little suckling motions with his lips, and Ithric fell immediately and profoundly in love. He looked up into Alyndra's large brown eyes. "What's his name?"

"Uthric," she whispered, her voice suspiciously hoarse.

Ithric felt the burn of tears at the back of his eyes for the first time in years, and closed them, breathing slowly to regain control. He opened them again and stretched over to kiss Alyndra's temple.

"I'll leave now," he said around the lump in his throat. "I love you, Lyndie. I swear I never meant to hurt you."

She was crying openly now, tears trickling down her cheeks. "I know, Ithric. I never meant to hurt you, either. Goodbye."

⁂

Walking away from the cramped little hut was one of the hardest things Ithric had done in recent memory. Evening had stolen the light while Ithric spoke with Alyndra, and that suited him just fine. For all that Venzor had been his home growing up, he found he had absolutely no desire to be recognized by anyone who had known him back then.

So he kept to the deepening shadows, face down, shoulders slouched, and made his way back to Iseboa's cottage, where the only people he really wanted to see right now awaited him.

He opened the door without knocking, making free with Iseboa's hospitality as he knew she preferred. Kathrael looked up immediately when he entered, and the others followed suit.

"How did things go?" she asked, her low, musical voice washing over him, soothing.

"We fought. Just like we've always fought ever since we were children," he said carelessly, as if it didn't matter. "Cute baby, though. Takes after me in that respect, I'll wager. Maybe he'll grow up to be a shifter, too... the poor little sod."

Kathrael frowned at his words, and Favian was looking at him with a too-knowing expression that he *really* didn't like. Ithric wasn't accustomed to being *understood*. Not like this. No wonder he and Favian had expended so much energy keeping each other at a distance for so long. Having someone *know* him like this was honestly rather terrifying.

To make things even worse, Rona spoke up hesitantly from her seat in the corner. "I'm sorry things didn't go well, Ithric. You've still got us, though."

Ithric's chest ached, but he pasted on his customary disconcerting grin, aware that doing so would make him look like a complete asshole. "No cause for being sorry, Rona. It's nothing more or less than I expected. Not a big deal."

"Family's important, Ithric," said Arnav, surprising him a bit. Normally, Arnav could be counted on to stay aloof from these kinds of personal discussions. Not sure what else to do, Ithric just shrugged.

"So, do we have a plan for tomorrow?" he asked, changing the subject with a distinct lack of subtlety.

Favian was still looking at him with something far too close to pity for Ithric's taste, but it was Iseboa who rescued him.

"You're all welcome to stay here tonight, if you don't mind the cramped conditions," she said. "I borrowed some blankets from the neighbors on my way back, and I think we can make it work." She hesitated. "I assume you'll want to head out for Draebard in the morning? Not that I'm trying to kick you out, mind. I'd love for you to visit longer."

From the corner of his eye, Ithric saw Rona run a hand subconsciously over her belly, even as Favian said, "Thank you, Iseboa. As much as I'd like a longer visit, we really need to get home. I sent a message ahead to Draebard letting them know roughly when to expect us, and I don't want to worry them by being late."

"You'll have to take messages to everyone for me," Iseboa said. Her eyes twinkled. "I have a particularly scathing one for my son regarding how long he's left it between visits."

Favian chuckled. "I'll be happy to deliver it, though I draw the line at boxing his ears for you."

Iseboa laughed, effortlessly dispelling the tension that had thickened the atmosphere after Ithric's return. "Fair enough, I suppose." She looked around the room. "Well, you must all be exhausted. Can I get you anything else, or would you like to retire for the night?"

"You've been too kind already," said Arnav. "We're fine. You'll have to show us where you want us to bed down."

Nimbral levered himself to his feet, hunching a bit to keep his head clear of the bottoms of the rafters. "I'll help you carry bedding," he said, and Ithric felt a small twinge of amusement penetrate his black mood at how quickly the pair had fallen under Iseboa's spell.

"Actually," Favian said, "I need to take the horses to the pens to be cared for, before everyone there leaves for the night. Ithric, would you mind coming along to show me the way?"

Ithric swallowed a sigh, knowing perfectly well when he'd been outmaneuvered. "Yes, fine," he said.

He was not surprised in the least when Kathrael added, "I'll come along, too. I'd love a chance to see more of your village, Ithric."

He didn't bother to point out that it was dark outside. "Come on then, both of you. It's getting late."

Andoc's cream-colored horses were ghostly silver forms in the near darkness. Ithric took the taller one, Audris, and Favian took Ozias. Once they were underway, Kathrael hooked a hand through the crook of Ithric's free arm and walked with him. He couldn't deny that the small point of contact eased some of the tension in his neck and shoulders.

To his surprise, the two of them seemed content to walk with him in silence, letting him lead the way to the large collection of horse pens where Venzor's herd was kept. Favian took the lead upon their arrival, speaking to the rather harried looking lad who was in charge of the pens that evening. The boy was eager enough to make a good impression on the visiting priest with the fine white horses, however, and before long, the two stallions were installed in a clean, dry pen with hay and water, munching contentedly.

Of course, the walk back to Iseboa's house was a different story from the walk out to the pens. The horse facilities were located away from the village proper, to keep the flies and the smell from being a nuisance. While they were still in the quiet area beyond the outskirts of the town, Favian put a hand on Ithric's elbow and pulled him to a stop.

Ithric let Favian step around so they were facing each other, and immediately felt his defensive armor snap into place without any conscious decision on his part.

"You know," Favian said, "you don't have to hide from us by acting like an obnoxious asshole."

"Language," Ithric chided, more out of habit than anything.

Favian looked at him, unimpressed. "You're allowed to be upset, Ithric. Neither of us buys into this act that your fight with Alyndra hasn't affected you at all."

Ithric gazed down at Favian's handsome features, pale in the evening darkness, and felt another sigh lift and lower his ribcage. "Oh?" he said. "So… if I'm allowed to be upset, does that also mean I'm *allowed* to deal with being upset in my own way?"

Kathrael moved closer until she was standing at his side. "Of course it does, lion-boy. Favian's just being a priest. Try not to blame him — I don't think he can really help it." She stretched up until she could catch his mouth in a tender kiss, and Ithric closed his eyes, leaning into the soft press of lips almost in spite of himself.

They parted after a few moments, and she continued, "He does have a point, though. You don't *have* to hide from us. Gods know you've already seen me at my most pathetic. Turnabout is fair play, after all."

Something settled in Ithric's chest, and on impulse, he pulled Favian in for a matching kiss. He came willingly.

"Look, you two," he said once Favian had pulled back to breathe. "I'm not going to have a big discussion about my feelings. I spoke with Alyndra. We started fighting and then stopped ourselves before things got too nasty. She doesn't want me in and out of her life with no rhyme or reason, and I guess I can see her point about that, even if I don't agree with it. She let me meet my nephew, and afterward we said goodbye. I suppose it was closure of a sort. End of story."

"That's better," Favian said. "I'm not asking you to collapse into weeping—"

"Of course he isn't. Weeping all over people is my job," Kathrael interjected wryly.

"—but you don't have to shut us out completely. That's all," Favian finished.

To be fair, the discussion hadn't ended up being as painful as Ithric had expected it to be. He shrugged. "I'm not really the share-and-care type, Favian... but I'll try to keep a lid on the *acting like an obnoxious asshole* part, anyway. Though I'm sure you'll be happy to remind me if I slip up."

"Hey, what do you know—progress!" Favian said with fake enthusiasm, and pulled Ithric in for another brief kiss. "Come on. Let's get back and get some sleep. Tomorrow's going to be another long day."

Kathrael took Ithric's hand, her fingers feeling small and delicate as they entwined with his. Favian walked on his other side, bumping shoulders companionably now and then. All in all, the occasional moments of irritation paled before the sense of rightness he felt at having them both here. In fact, if he were being brutally honest about things, he *did* feel a bit better for having told them the details of his conversation with his sister.

He shook his head at himself, snorting softly in dismay.

⚜

When they got back, Iseboa was waiting up for them, curled in a padded chair with a colorful woven blanket thrown over her legs. The others had bedded down, though the occasional rustling and restless movement showed that they had not yet fallen asleep.

"You three are welcome to the bedroom," she said in a low voice. "You know where it is, Favian. I put out fresh bedding for you." A yawn cracked her face, and she covered it with one hand.

Favian shook his head fondly and crossed to give her a hand up from the chair. "Nonsense," he said, already herding her toward the doorway leading to the back of the cottage. "We are *not* turning you out of your bed after the six of us descended on you unannounced."

"It's no problem..." Iseboa began, only for Favian to cut her off.

"Nope. Not happening. This is purely selfish, I assure you, Iseboa. If you think I'm going back and tell Andoc I made you sleep in a chair so I could have your bed, you are sorely mistaken."

That startled a low laugh from her, and she put her hands up in surrender. "All right, Favian. You win. There are more blankets stacked in the corner. Make yourselves as comfortable as you can and I'll see you all in the morning."

"That's more like it," Favian said.

"Goodnight," Ithric added, and Kathrael echoed him right afterward.

"Sleep well," Iseboa said fondly, and disappeared into her room.

Favian fussed around making a nest of blankets for them, and they stripped off their outer layers before curling up together. Though he was tired and his side was sore after a day of hard travel and emotional upheaval, Ithric could not seem to settle. His restless mind turned his conversation with Lyndie over and over, picking at the details in a way that was unusual for him.

Though he was trying not to move too much, it became apparent that he was keeping Favian and Kathrael awake regardless. At least the rhythmic snores and quiet breathing from the other side of the room proclaimed the fact that Rona, Nimbral and Arnav were not having the same difficulties.

Eventually, Kathrael rolled onto her side and looked at him, her good eye shining in the low orange glow of the hearth fire's embers. "Can't sleep?" she whispered, and hooked a lock of his unruly hair behind his ear.

He shook his head, and felt Favian lifting himself up on an elbow on his other side. They were silent for a very long time as Ithric turned things over in his mind.

"She named her baby Uthric," he said quietly, the words slipping free before he'd consciously decided to speak them.

Rather than answer with words, Favian and Kathrael wrapped him up in their arms. No one had ever really… *done* that for Ithric before. Not since he was a very small boy, anyway. His breath hitched once and evened out, warmth spreading through his body that had nothing to do with the nearby hearth.

His mind finally let go of the endlessly circling thoughts that had been plaguing him, and his eyelids grew heavy. He fell asleep to the flutter of Favian's breath against his neck and the brush of Kathrael's hair against his shoulder.

They left in the morning, saying their goodbyes and vowing to deliver Iseboa's messages to her son, his bondmates, and Favian's sister Frella. The rest of the trip to Draebard passed uneventfully, though they were all tired and cranky by the end from long hours spent in the jouncing, jarring wagon. Nevertheless, the old rattletrap made it all the way back without losing any major components or leaving them stranded by the side of the road, so Ithric counted them lucky enough.

It didn't take long for a cry to go up as their approach to Draebard was noticed. Ithric gazed at the bustling place he'd never really expected to see again. His occasional home, of sorts—though one he'd been happy enough to see the back of after his disastrous liaison with Favian that spring. Now, however, he was returning—with both Favian and Kathrael at his side—to the people who had accepted him and his shape-shifting ability to a far greater degree than his own village ever had.

In moments, Andoc himself came hobbling out of the village hall with his walking stick, meeting them as Favian pulled the horses to a halt at the edge of the village green.

"Favian! *Ithric*," he said with feeling. "Oh, thank the gods. When you dropped out of contact, Ithric, you had me half convinced that you'd died, you know."

Ithric eased himself down from the driver's seat where he'd been keeping Favian company during the last leg of the journey.

"There seems to be a lot of that going around," he said, thinking once more of Alyndra. "I'm sorry I worried you, though. Not to mention, I'm sorry to have retired so unexpectedly as your spy." He accepted Andoc's hand, gripping it forearm to forearm. "That said, I do have some rather interesting things to report, now that I'm here to do it in person." He paused. "Well... I say interesting..."

"But what he means is *alarming*," Favian cut in.

By this time, Kathrael had disembarked and joined them, her shawl pulled forward to cover the scarred side of her face. Ithric took note of the fact and frowned, struck by her sudden self-consciousness now that she was back among the people who'd taken her in. He shook the thought off a moment later, but resolved to ponder her reaction in more detail when he had a free moment.

Now, though, the news of their arrival had apparently reached the temple, because a slender form with messy chestnut hair was flying toward them at great speed, her legs pumping in her skirts as she ran.

"Ithric!" Frella cried, and nearly tackled him to the ground with the strength of her hug when she flung herself into his arms. "Oh, Favian, you did it!"

She was so obviously happy to see him that he swallowed the pain of his jarred wound and lifted her off the ground to swing her around. "Hey, kitten," he murmured, and set her down again. "Staying out of trouble?"

"More than *you* are," she accused. "Why did you leave without saying goodbye?"

"Frella!" Favian said in a quelling voice. "He's been hurt—try not to squeeze the stuffing out of him, will you?"

Immediately, she let Ithric go and backed off a step. "Oh... sorry," she said sheepishly.

Instead, she rounded on her brother. "I'm furious with you, by the way. But I guess you're forgiven for sneaking off since you brought Ithric back safely."

"Well, that's a relief," Favian teased, before his attention was caught by Senovo's approach.

The High Priest looked very grateful indeed to see them all safe and sound. He placed a hand on Favian's shoulder and squeezed it. "You were successful, then, Little Brother. I'm glad. Welcome back, Ithric. Kathrael."

Kathrael only gave a wary nod in reply, so Ithric answered for both of them. "Thanks, Senovo. It's good to be back. We, uh, didn't come alone, though."

The others had remained in the back of the wagon—trying, Ithric thought, not to draw attention to themselves. A small crowd of gawkers was already gathering around the little reunion. Several people followed his gaze, only to gasp as they noticed the odd assortment of individuals huddled in the back of the rickety conveyance.

Andoc did a surprised double take himself, but recovered quickly. Senovo blinked, but immediately moved to greet the three refugees from Turvick's show.

"Welcome," he said in a formal tone. "I am High Priest Senovo of Draebard. Please allow me to offer the hospitality of the temple for as long as you have need of it."

"Senovo," Ithric said, taking over the introductions, "Andoc—these are my friends, Arnav, Rona, and Nimbral. They were also being held captive by two men running the traveling show where I've been stuck for the last several weeks."

"Pleased to meet you all," Andoc said, limping over to join them. "Any friend of Ithric's is welcome in Draebard for as long as you care to stay."

"Thank you," Rona squeaked, clearly somewhat overawed at meeting the two men who had such a fearsome reputation in the south.

"Rona has need of a consultation with Healer Sagdea at her earliest convenience," Ithric put in quickly, well aware that the delay in getting Rona the care she needed was largely his fault.

"I can go fetch her now, unless you need me for something here," Kathrael said, speaking up for the first time.

"By all means," Andoc said. "And it's good to have you back safely as well, Kathrael."

Kathrael looked vaguely uncomfortable at his words, and ducked away without comment to find the healer.

"I'll go take the horses and wagon to the pens and let Carivel know we're back," Favian offered. "You should let Sagdea take a look at you, too, Ithric."

"I'm just fine, mother hen," he groused, though his heart wasn't in it. "I'll help Senovo get everyone settled, and go see what state Carivel's old hut is in these days."

"Musty and cluttered, at a guess," Andoc offered wryly. "Take a bit of time to rest and recuperate, Ithric, and then we'll talk. Now, though, I'd better get back to the elders and let them know what's going on." He clapped a hand on Ithric's shoulder. "It really is a relief to see you in one piece, by the way."

"Nonsense," Ithric said in a light tone. "You should know that it takes more than a little prick with a knife to stop me. In fact, if Favian hadn't distracted me at a critical moment, the lion would have eaten the little prick in question for breakfast."

"I heard that!" Favian called back over his shoulder as he headed for the horse pens.

"You were meant to!" Ithric called back in the same tone.

Shortly thereafter, they all went their separate ways, leaving the village gossips chattering behind them.

Senovo helped Ithric get Nimbral, Rona and Arnav settled in the temple, and went to see about acquiring food for them. When the healer arrived, with Kathrael tagging along behind, she raked her eyes over Ithric in a way that he found deeply discomfiting. He knew that look, which was almost certainly the prelude to much poking and prodding in his near future.

"What's this about a knife wound, young man?" the healer asked caustically.

"It's nearly healed," he muttered, and her answering harrumph had a decided *we'll see about that* flavor to it. To deflect her attention from him and hopefully put off the inevitable, he added, "Rona needs your help right now, far more than I do."

Sagdea's gaze lit with interest as she took in the others. "Oh?"

Rona stood, lifting her chin. "I'm with child. A healer in Woodhaerst said it could kill me if I didn't end the pregnancy soon. But I don't *want* to kill our baby."

Her eyes slid to Nimbral, and Ithric saw Sadgea follow her gaze. The old healer's mouth turned down in a frown.

"I see," she said. "Well, come with me and let's have a look at you. Then we can talk." Nimbral made as if to rise, but the healer stopped him with an imperious finger. "No. You stay here. I will speak with Rona first. You can join us to discuss things afterward. Ithric, get one of the priests to join us for that part, if you would."

"Yes, Healer," Ithric said. The two women left to go to one of the private rooms, and Nimbral immediately got up to pace. "If anyone will know what to do, it's Sagdea," he continued.

"It's true," Kathrael offered. "She is very knowledgeable."

"There is *nothing* to do, except what the other healer already told us," Nimbral said in a tight voice. "It's my fault she's in danger. I just want her safe."

Ithric could only sigh. "I know you do, Nimbral."

With nothing else to contribute, he and Kathrael waited with Arnav and Nimbral, the time crawling by. Favian returned from the pens, smelling faintly of horse, and Ithric looked up as he entered.

"Sagdea is with Rona now," Kathrael informed him.

Favian nodded his understanding.

Nimbral cleared his throat. "The healer said she wanted to talk to us both afterward, and that a priest should be there." He hesitated. "Would you...?"

"Of course I will, Nimbral, as long as Rona is comfortable with me being there."

Ithric felt the same faint tinge of surprise that he always did when Favian did something priest-like, and tried to shake it off. It was just so... odd... being with someone who embodied all the things Ithric had tried to fight against for almost half of his life.

And yet, neither Favian nor Senovo had ever tried to force him into the temple. None of the priests in Draebard had. They only seemed concerned with performing their duties to the townsfolk—helping where they were needed and offering succor to the lost, just as he had been lost when Senovo first found him. Just as Kathrael had been lost when she snuck into the temple, mad with grief and starvation, and tried to take Favian hostage.

It was difficult to reconcile these people with the idea he had of the temple, growing up—a cage guarded by rigid, self-important old eunuchs who cared only for tradition and appearances. Perhaps, if he had grown up in Draebard, he would not have felt the need to flee when his abilities first manifested. Perhaps he would have stayed with Alyndra, gotten support as they grieved their dead parents, received help as he struggled to deal with his strange, unexpected gift.

His thoughts were interrupted when Rona reentered, Sagdea following a step behind. Tears flowed freely down the small woman's face.

THREE

"Come, Nimbral," Sagdea said. "It's time for me to speak with both of you. Favian, will you be joining us?"

Favian looked to Rona. "Would that be all right, Rona?"

Rona nodded, standing in the doorway with her arms wrapped tightly around herself. Nimbral quickly crossed to join her, his large hand covering her small shoulder.

"Come, then," Favian said kindly. "There's a private room down the hall where we can all sit and talk about this. Follow me."

Once the four had left, Ithric stirred, restless and wrong-footed after the obviously bad news. "I should go see about making Carivel's hut habitable," he said, needing something to do.

Kathrael looked up at him, frowning in evident confusion.

"She never uses it since she's been handfasted to Andoc and Senovo," he explained. "She gave me use of it years ago and I normally stay there whenever I'm in Draebard."

"Oh, I see," she said, her face clearing. "Do you want any help?"

He shook his head. "Nah. Why don't you stay here and let Favian know where I am. The two of you can join me later—" He paused, a hint of uncertainty entering his mind unbidden. "—if you want to."

Kathrael looked at him with something uncomfortably close to pity. "Ithric," she said. "I don't think there's any question that Favian wants to be wherever you are, assuming his duties permit it. And I want to be with both of you, whether it's in a room at the temple, or a borrowed hut, or a tent in the middle of nowhere. We'll be along as soon as we can."

Her words made something swell in Ithric's chest, squeezing out the misgivings that had tried to take up residence. He cleared his throat. "In that case, I'll try to have it cleaned up by then. You might want to bring food with you—I don't have any money and I'm not sure where the remains of our traveling rations will have ended up after the wagon was unloaded."

"I'll wheedle something from Brother Feldes in the kitchens, don't worry," she assured him.

Ithric turned to Arnav. "Do you need anything before I head out? Will you be all right here?"

"Of course I will—we're fine here. Stop fussing and go get your place cleaned up for your lovers, Ithric."

Ithric couldn't stop the faint flush of pleasure that suffused him at Arnav's words, despite the pall cast by Rona and Nimbral's sad news from the healer.

"All right, then, I will." He gave Kathrael a quick wink. "I'll see you later, Little Cat. Oh—and a word to the wise." His eyes slid back to Arnav, and he smirked. "*Don't* let him talk you into playing dice for money."

"Spoilsport," Arnav said, his voice sour.

Kathrael shot Arnav a speculative look. "Hmm... well now you've piqued my curiosity. How about we play for something else, in that case? I've still got that stash of honey candy Favian bought in Woodhaerst."

Arnav's eyes lit up.

"Deal," he said immediately.

Ithric shook his head and left them to it.

It was fairly late in the evening before Kathrael and Favian were able to make their way from the temple to Carivel's hut at the edge of town. Kathrael carried a skin of ale over one shoulder, and Favian had a bag of clean clothing and bedding in one hand and a jar of fish stew in the other.

Kathrael hadn't been quite sure what to expect, when it came to the hut. As Horse Mistress, Carivel was high in status and might well have had a large home. Ithric had made the place sound rather modest, though, and indeed, when they arrived at the hut Favian indicated, it was tiny and in obvious need of repairs.

Probably why Carivel stays in the High Priest's grand rooms at the temple, or the Chief's home, she thought.

Still, humble though it was, it might as well have been a palace to someone like her who had lived on the streets for so long, sheltering in doorways and scurrying from place to place like a rat.

Home is wherever your family happens to be, Vesh whispered.

So it is, at that, she agreed, and followed Favian up to the oddly off-center door.

Ithric had hung a lit lamp from the doorpost, casting an inviting half-circle of light around the entrance. More light shone from inside, through the single small window, and Kathrael gathered that he had been busy in their absence.

Favian, who had been quiet and melancholy after his discussion with Rona and Nimbral, stepped up to the door and awkwardly transferred the bag he was carrying to his other arm. He hesitated before knocking.

"What is it?" Kathrael asked.

Favian huffed out a breath and shook himself free of his brief reverie. "Nothing. I just realized that the last time I knocked on this door was when I stumbled here drunk as a loon and more or less threw myself at Ithric."

Understanding flooded her. "A lot has changed since then," she pointed out.

The door opened, revealing Ithric, shirtless, yesterday's bandages wrapped around his middle. "So it has," he agreed. "I smell food — stop lurking and come inside, both of you."

"Hello to you, too," Favian said, before shaking his head and brushing past Ithric through the door.

Ithric ushered Kathrael through as well and took the skin from her. "Make yourselves comfortable, but avoid the chair in the corner. I think one of the legs is about to fall off."

"You bring us to the nicest places, you know," Favian teased, and set the stew down on a rickety table.

Kath looked around, taking in the layer of dust and cobwebs that still clung to some of the corners. It was a single room, perhaps three times as large as the acolytes' sleeping cells in the temple. One of the rafters had split and was sagging under the weight of the thatched roof in a somewhat alarming fashion. Ithric had cleaned up the area around the hearth and a straw palliasse, moving the sparse collection of furniture to the central area. A small fire burned merrily, providing illumination and keeping back the faint chill of the evening.

The place was cozy, safe, and filled with the two people she cared about most. Kathrael decided there and then that she liked it.

"I half expected you to bring Frella along," Ithric observed. "You know she's always welcome, Favian."

Favian quirked a smile and flopped down on the mattress lying on the floor. Somewhat to Kathrael's surprise, no cloud of dust erupted—Ithric must have aired it and filled it with fresh straw earlier.

"We spent some time together before I left the temple. She informed me in no uncertain terms that she'd gotten accustomed to having our room to herself while I was gone," Favian said. "I also told her about the three of us, by the way—not that it would have taken her long to figure it out on her own."

"Good," Ithric said.

Kathrael frowned and asked, "So... she's not upset by that?"

Favian's brow furrowed. "Why would she be? Remember who raised us. Besides, she adores Ithric, for some reason that completely escapes me—"

"It's called *good taste*," Ithric interrupted.

"—and she likes you as well, Kath," Favian finished.

"She does?" Kathrael asked, oddly taken aback.

Favian stared at her. "Well... yes?"

Ithric was looking at her closely as well, and she felt a flush of self-consciousness rise up her neck. "You're doing that thing again," he said.

"Doing what thing?" she countered, feeling suddenly defensive.

"Acting all self-conscious, Little Cat," Ithric said. "I noticed it as soon as we arrived here in Draebard."

"I don't know what you mean," she muttered, not meeting his eyes.

You care about their opinion of you, here, her dead sister murmured in her ear.

"Shut up, Elarra," she said under her breath.

"Kath?" Favian asked.

She took a deep breath and pulled herself free of the uncomfortable muddle of emotions that had risen. "Sorry. Just spirits *being irritating*." She glanced up at them. "I guess I didn't even realize I was doing it." She deliberately reached up and pushed her shawl back to fall around her shoulders. "Let's just eat, all right?"

Ithric shrugged, letting it go easily—for which Kathrael was really quite grateful.

"Suits me," he said, reaching for the stoppered jar of stew and wincing a bit when his wound pulled. "I'm hungry."

Favian went to the dusty shelves at the side of the room and pulled down three cups. "You're always hungry," he said, giving the clay vessels a dubious look and wiping them out on the hem of his robes before bringing them over. He poured ale and shared it out while Ithric rummaged for spoons.

As they had in Woodhearst, they huddled around the little table and ate the stew straight from the container. Kathrael felt her earlier tension drain away by degrees, as she focused on the hot food and the warm companionship of sharing a meal.

"What did Rona decide, Favian?" Ithric asked around a mouthful, his tone growing somber.

Favian looked at him with an earnest expression. "I have to be careful about answering questions regarding situations like this, where I'm acting as a priest, Ithric. In this case, though, I can tell you that there has been no decision yet. Beyond that, you'll need to ask Rona or Nimbral directly."

Ithric looked at Favian with an expression Kathrael couldn't quite categorize. "You know," he said in a conversational tone, "I was thinking earlier today that if I'd grown up in Draebard rather than Venzor, I might have had a somewhat different view of the temple, and priests in general."

"If I'd grown up in Draebard rather than Rhyth, I *definitely* would have," Kathrael added. The northern temples she'd seen — and Senovo's in particular — could have been an entirely different world than that of the sanctimonious southern Priests' Guild with its slaves and its cloying aura of hypocrisy.

Rather than appearing pleased at the compliment, Favian seemed to deflate, his expression growing sad. "I'm sorry that's the case. It... bothers me that there are so many places on Eburos where the temple is not the haven for the people that it's supposed to be."

Her appetite for food sated, Kathrael put her spoon aside and gave in to the impulse to put her arms around Favian and rest her head on his shoulder. "All you can do is be the kind of priest that those others aren't, Favian," she said. "And you're already doing exactly that."

"Maybe," Favian said, unconvinced, even as Ithric looked at them with an expression of almost painful fondness.

"Please tell me that you two are done with everything for tonight, so I can take you to bed now," he said, and Kathrael felt the strange little jolt of warmth grow in her belly, that only these two seemed able to conjure.

"Yes," she said.

"Yes," Favian echoed, "but don't think I didn't notice you wincing in pain earlier. Did you try to do too much today and reopen the wound?"

"No," Ithric sighed, "I did not try to do too much today and reopen the wound, Favian. It just takes time for these things to heal." He looked down at his side and started unwrapping the bandages, which had grown grungy over the last couple of days traveling. "Here. See for yourself—I should let it get some air anyway. Please don't fuss. If I wanted that, I'd have let Healer Sagdea run me to ground this afternoon."

Favian breathed out sharply through his nose.

"He's just worried about you, lion-boy," Kathrael said. "You can hardly blame him. People aren't supposed to have holes in them like that."

Ithric rolled his eyes, and immediately waggled his eyebrows at them. "Maybe not holes like *that*..."

Favian picked up Kathrael's spoon and threw it at his shoulder. Ithric yelped in surprise.

"Observe, the master of seduction at work," Favian said in a dry tone. "It's a good thing you're pretty to look at, Ithric."

Ithric grinned, and stalked around the table to them. He leaned down, his lips a hairsbreadth from Favian's. "You love me, really," he said into their shared air. Kathrael hummed in appreciation as he closed the space between them and kissed Favian deeply. Arousal curled in her belly—all the day's cares forgotten in an instant.

Favian groaned into the kiss as Kathrael stretched up and nuzzled at the hinge of his jaw. "Yes," he said on a breath as he and Ithric parted for air. "I do. Both of you."

A wicked idea prickled at the edges of Kathrael's mind, and she smiled, giving Favian's jaw a final nip. "Tell me, Favian," she asked, her tone purposely innocent, "have you ever sucked a cock before?"

Ithric's eyes darkened, and he answered her smile with a predatory one of his own. "He's *had* his cock sucked, certainly. I can personally attest to that."

A flush rose on Favian's neck and cheeks, though it might have been embarrassment or a reaction to the memory. "And sadly, I must confess that the encounter you're referring to—plus the one in Woodhaerst, of course—is the sum total of my sexual experience with men."

Ithric's eyes lit with interest. "Your experience with *men?*" he echoed. "Favian, you *dog*, is there something you'd care to share with us?"

Favian groaned and squeezed his eyes shut. "Fine. Yes. I tried to have sex with a girl when I was sixteen. Needless to say, the experiment didn't get very far. And before you ask, *no*, I will not tell you who it was... beyond saying that it wasn't Limdya."

Ithric made a little waving motion with one hand as he settled a hip on the edge of the table. It creaked alarmingly. "*Details*, Favian. *Details*. You don't get to drop something like that into the conversation without expanding on it."

Kathrael sat back in her own chair, surprised by the depth of her own curiosity. "Under the circumstances, I can't help agreeing," she said, intrigued to see Favian's blush deepen.

He looked at the cobwebbed rafters and muttered, "I can't believe you two want to hear about something this embarrassing." But he cleared his throat gamely. "Right. So you both know that I've always had romantic feelings for both men and women, but only ever had sexual urges for men."

They nodded. "Well, as I got older and talked more with the other acolytes, I thought maybe I'd just never given sex with women a proper chance. So I... let Reston set me up with someone..."

"You realize you're just making us *more* curious about who it was," Ithric said.

"*Too. Bad*," Favian reiterated.

"You're making *him* more curious, he means," Kathrael corrected. "I don't actually care who it was."

Favian gave her a side-eyed look. "Look. Do the two of you want to hear this story or not?"

"Sorry," Ithric said—not, in point of fact, sounding particularly sorry. "Do please continue."

"Yes, go on, priest-boy," Kathrael added. "I'm intrigued."

With a put-upon sigh, Favian resumed the story. "So, apparently Reston's friend had, well, a *thing* for temple acolytes. I thought it would be a good way to start out, because she didn't want to do anything that might get her pregnant. We met in the woods after dark, and she barely said a word to me — just started kissing and touching me."

"Ugh," Ithric interrupted. "I hate that. I mean, if we're going to fool around, can we at least have a conversation first?"

Kathrael looked between them, once again beset by the idea that they were somehow having her on. "You two are both very strange. You realize that, yes?"

"We are?" Ithric asked, frowning.

Her tone was wry as she answered. "When I was a whore, I didn't run into many men who desired an extended conversation before being serviced."

Ithric looked thoughtful for a moment. "Huh. I suppose I've usually been the one doing the servicing, personally — although there was never any money involved. Not that the sex wasn't mutual — that isn't what I mean. Most of the people I've been with were quick enough to reciprocate, and we were both happy at the end of things. But... a lot of them only wanted the novelty of sleeping with a shape-shifter. So it was always refreshing to be with someone who at least wanted to talk for a bit first."

Kathrael shook her head, trying to conceive of a woman asking a man to service her, and the man agreeing.

Ithric continued, "It sounds like you were in about the same situation, Favian. You were with someone who was more interested in *what* you were than *who* you were."

With a shrug, Favian replied, "I suppose so. Whatever the case, it was just... awkward. I enjoyed the kissing well enough, but — no surprise — I couldn't get hard for her. I ended up just touching her until she came, though I could tell she was still disappointed. Like it was a personal insult to her that she couldn't arouse me."

"Did you dislike touching her?" Kathrael asked, curious.

"The whole situation was tangled up with my sense of failure and not having lived up to her expectations, so I don't tend to recall it fondly." Favian looked at her directly, his blue eyes deep in the light from the hearth. "Honestly, though, it wasn't that I was repulsed or anything. She was beautiful, and it was interesting seeing what made her respond. I liked watching her come. I... think I might enjoy that sort of thing with someone I care about."

His brows drew together as if he were choosing his words carefully. "As long as that person understood what I could and couldn't offer them, that is. Particularly now that I'm a eunuch."

Love for the kind-hearted young priest surged in Kathrael's breast unexpectedly. It swirled together with the arousal that had surfaced earlier, forming a heady mix more potent than strong wine. She stretched forward and kissed him, framing his face in her hands.

"Favian," she said when they parted, "you still have no idea how many women would have jumped at the chance to have you, if you'd offered such a thing." Her voice went low and hoarse. "But I'm selfishly glad you never did."

"So am I," Ithric added, and there was a decided rasp to his voice as well.

"I just don't want to promise you more than I can give, Kath," Favian said. "I don't ever want to see that look of disappointment on your face."

She was still cradling his head in her hands. "*Stop*, priest-boy. What use do I, of all people, have for your lust? You know me. You *know* that's not what I need from you." She kissed him again. "You've already given me what I need, in a thousand small ways. Tonight, let me teach you a new way to please Ithric. And after the two of us make him lose control, we'll decide what we want to do together."

A small noise escaped Ithric's throat, claiming their attention. "Little Cat," he said, "if you don't want to be exposed to a man's lust, you need to stop talking like that."

She only smiled. "I've already seen *your* lust, lion-boy. And — trust me — I know just what to do with it." It was true. Maybe she wasn't ready yet to submit to it directly, but Ithric's desire neither frightened her nor dampened her own recently discovered ardor. She would show Favian another way to make the man he loved so desperately feel good, and she would gain pleasure from watching him do it.

"Yeah... that's definitely not helping," Ithric said.

"Well, get undressed, then," she said, her tone matter-of-fact. Because she knew he would not take offense, she asked,

"Have you washed today? I'm not fond of the smell of stale sweat on a prick."

Indeed, rather than get angry, he laughed. "Not to worry, Little Cat. I had a scrub at the edge of the river before the sun went down. I promise not to knock you both unconscious with my stench."

Her lips twitched as she tried to contain her own amusement. "Good," she said. "Now, clothes off and lie on the mattress."

"Pushy," he observed, clearly delighted despite his teasing remark. He rose from his perch on the edge of the table and walked a few steps toward the straw palliasse before turning back to them and starting work on the laces of his trousers. "What about you? Can we see you naked this time, Little Cat? I must admit, that particular image has been on my mind rather frequently of late."

Favian roused himself from where he'd been sitting next to her, quiet and thoughtful after their earlier exchange. He turned in his chair to watch Ithric disrobe with obvious appreciation. A devilish gleam lit his eyes.

"What do you mean, *we*? I've already seen Kath naked… on more than one occasion, in fact." He leaned back, arms crossed casually. "And she's just as beautiful as you've probably imagined."

Warmth suffused Kathrael's body, as ridiculous as the reaction was. She had known, growing up as a teenage prostitute in Rhyth, that she was attractive. After her disfigurement, though, she had only ever thought of herself as ugly. Until these two, no one had tried to disabuse her of the notion—but where others flinched from her appearance, *they* only ever looked at her with love.

Ithric's cock twitched visibly in his smallclothes. "You keep dropping these things into the conversation unexpectedly, Favian. If I didn't know better, I'd accuse you of doing it on purpose."

"We were just bathing together, lion-boy," Kathrael explained. She flushed a bit, and added, "Though on the first occasion, I'm afraid I *did* offer to suck him off." She pretended to pout. "That was when he spurned me, you know. My poor vanity may never recover."

Favian snorted at her. "You were only offering because you thought it would shock me. Which, to be fair, it kind of did."

"Yes—guilty, I'm sorry to say," she admitted.

"Well, it's up to you what you want to do tonight, Little Cat, of course," Ithric said, looking at the two of them with transparent affection. "I do realize you're not interested in more right now, so just be aware that I'll keep my hands to myself, either way."

She smiled at him, full to bursting with the feeling of security and belonging she felt in the presence of this oddly matched pair. Rather than answer in words, she rose from her chair and met his eyes directly, her hands going to the laces holding her buckskin bodice closed.

His own fingers stilled in their task of undressing as his attention centered completely on her. She breathed in sharply in surprise as Favian's voice whispered, "May I?" from close behind her, and his hands settled over hers.

Her tense muscles relaxed immediately, and she let him take over, removing her clothing piece by piece. Heat pooled in her belly, heavy and liquid. Ithric watched from a few steps away, utterly entranced. Favian's fingers did not so much as brush her skin accidentally as he worked, and after a few moments she covered one of his hands with hers.

"You needn't be quite so careful, Favian," she told him, craning to catch a glimpse of his face. "Your touch has never made me feel anything but safe."

He exhaled, his warm breath tickling her. "I'm glad," he said.

When he skimmed his hands up her bare sides, lifting her chemise over her head and dropping it onto the pile of clothing at their feet, Kathrael was struck by a strange sort of split experience. Part of her was remembering the countless times she had bared herself to a man with only bitter, cold ashes filling her heart. The rest was rooted firmly in the present, marveling at the way Ithric's eyes felt like a physical touch as they roamed over her naked skin.

How two things could be so superficially similar while affecting her in such a profoundly different way was utterly beyond her understanding.

"Kathrael," Ithric breathed. "You are a work of art. Thank you for giving us this." His eyes tore away long enough to meet Favian's over her shoulder. "Favian... please let me see you, too. Let me see you together."

Favian's smile was audible in his voice. "Only if you finish what you started with those trousers and smallclothes at the same time. I'd hate to distract you any more than Kath already has."

"Deal," Ithric said, and finished shucking off his clothing and boots as Favian disrobed behind her.

By the time Ithric straightened from toeing off his boots and stepping out of his loose trousers and underthings, Favian was naked, standing behind Kathrael with a bare inch of space between them — close enough that she could feel the heat of his body.

Without even thinking about it, she leaned back, closing the distance between them until skin met skin. His arm came to rest loosely around her ribcage. The difference in their heights meant that when she tilted her head back, it fit perfectly into the hollow over his collarbone.

They stared at Ithric — the hard, lean lines of his body now uncovered and illuminated by the flickering glow from the hearth — and he stared at them in return, naked hunger in his gaze.

"I must have done something recently to please the gods," he said in an unexpectedly conversational tone of voice, "though for the life of me, I can't think what it might have been."

"Concocting a plan to get the twins to safety? Beating that bastard Turvick to a pulp?" Kathrael suggested. She paused, giving the next words special weight. "Comforting my baby when no one else could?"

"Ah... but I already got my reward for that, Little Cat," Ithric said, his tone softening.

Favian's arm tightened around her even as a lump rose in her throat. "Lie down for us, Ithric," he said. "Not everything has to be earned, you know. Sometimes good things can happen simply because we wish them to."

Kathrael twisted in Favian's gentle hold until she could press a kiss to his jaw, wanting desperately to believe that such a thing could be true. Ithric smiled — a hesitant quirk of the lips that was completely different from his usual disconcerting, predatory grin. "Well, now. Who am I to argue with two beautiful people who want to suck my cock?" he asked, and sank down gracefully onto the straw mattress in the corner.

He stuffed a couple of lumpy old pillows behind him to support his upper body against the wattle-and-daub wall, and settled into a comfortable slouch. Finally, he arched up a bit so he could place his forearms behind the small of his back, wrists crossed, with his weight pinning them in place when he relaxed back.

"There you go," he said, still smiling that tiny smile up at them. "I'm all yours. Do as much or as little as you like, both of you — I'll just lie back and enjoy whatever you come up with."

Kathrael could practically feel the approval radiating from Favian, who still stood behind her, watching Ithric over her shoulder. Part of her was struck by how ridiculous it was to think that she, who had been a whore for years, needed such consideration for something as simple as sucking a man's prick.

A larger part of her, though, was more grateful for the gesture than she could possibly express. She and Favian could take their time, try different things, stop to talk about it if they needed to, and no hand would tangle unexpectedly in her hair, forcing her head down in impatience until she choked.

She was... *safe*. Completely and utterly safe, here in Ithric and Favian's bed.

"Hmm. We'll do our best to make it memorable, in that case," Favian teased, giving her a final light squeeze with his arm before leading the way toward the bed.

She followed and brushed past him to settle herself in the space between Ithric's hips and the wall, leaving Favian on the side of the bed that faced the rest of the room. There, he would have more room to maneuver his larger frame. He sat down, his attention immediately focusing on Ithric's prick, which was hard already even though they had not yet touched him.

"You're starting at the wrong end, Favian," she chided, letting fond amusement color the words.

Confusion furrowed Favian's brow. "Am I?" he asked.

She rolled her eyes at him. "*Men*," she said. "You all have minds like a straight, narrow track through the forest."

Ithric snickered, and she mock-glared at him.

"*Hush*, lion-boy. Now, watch and learn, Favian," she said, and indulged herself by stretching up until she could catch Ithric's lips in a kiss.

FOUR

Ithric's noise of amusement transformed instantly into one of appreciation. After a leisurely slide of lips, she moved down to his neck... his collarbone... the hollow of his shoulder. She was aware that Favian was following her lead, demanding a kiss of his own and then mirroring her down the length of Ithric's lean body. She had never been quite so... *present*... while exploring a man's body before—letting her lips feel the warmth of salty flesh, trying to taste the difference between unblemished skin and the scars that littered his torso.

The knife wound was on Favian's side—still angry red and puckered, the deepest part not quite closed over yet. She heard Favian exhale sharply as he reached it, obviously still affected by the memory of that terrible moment when the knife flashed up and sprayed crimson.

"Favian," Ithric said. "*Hey*. It's all right. I'm all right. I'm starting to think that blasted dagger hurt you more than it hurt me."

"Sorry," Favian whispered against the skin of Ithric's side.

"Don't be sorry," said Ithric. "Just... keep doing what you're doing, all right? It's a lot more enjoyable than talking about a stab wound."

It was Kathrael's turn to snort in unladylike amusement. "High praise, indeed," she observed. "I'm not sure anyone has ever compared my seduction technique to a festering wound before."

That was enough to break Favian free of his unhealthy fixation, and surprise an appalled laugh out of him.

"What can I say?" Ithric offered, smirking down at her. "I'm not like those *other* men you've known—"

His voice wavered on the last word, as she drew her tongue down the crease of his hip.

"Mmm-hmm," she hummed against the tender, ticklish skin. "Of course you aren't. Now *that's* more like it."

Favian followed her lead on the other side, and Ithric said, "So—I'll just shut up now, shall I?" There was a decidedly breathless quality to the words, and Kathrael smiled in satisfaction.

She reached across Ithric's body to guide Favian toward her with a touch on the cheek. They kissed, cheeks brushing against their victim's stiff, twitching shaft with tantalizing, barely-there touches. Ithric groaned, tailing off into a gasp when Kathrael broke off the kiss to flick the tip of her tongue up the side of his prick. Again, Favian mirrored her, and she played with him, their tongues tangling as they kissed and teased around Ithric's cock.

Ithric was breathing hard, little noises escaping his control every now and again when one of them curled a tongue around his shaft or licked over the head.

"Maybe I spoke too soon," he managed. "This might actually be *worse* torture than—" He swallowed audibly. "—than a knife wound."

Kathrael pulled back enough to ask, "Are you complaining, lion-boy?"

He laughed. "*Definitely* not."

She smiled in satisfaction, and decided it was time to have pity on him. "Take him in your mouth, Favian—just the head. Swirl your tongue. See if you can taste the salt of his seed in the slit." Her smile turned wicked as she looked up the length of Ithric's body from where she rested against his hip. "Watch his face while you do it."

Ithric let out a sort of choked noise. His pupils were blown wide, black nearly swallowing the ring of hazel around them as Favian gamely shifted to get a better angle and licked over the blunt head of his cock. Favian looked up at Ithric's slack face as Kathrael had instructed, and let his lips slide down, stretching around the hard flesh.

Kathrael smiled as Ithric shuddered, trying to hold himself still. She stroked Favian's cheek, and trailed her fingers down to tickle Ithric's sac.

Ithric's balls drew up tight at the ghost of a touch, and he gasped, "Shit—*ah!* Favian, I—"

With no more warning than that, his stomach muscles clenched and he was coming. Favian jerked back in surprise, unprepared, and a rope of sticky white hit the side of his face. Ithric grunted, the rough noise dragged from his throat as he jerked and spilled.

There was a rather protracted moment of silence afterward as Favian sat up and wiped a gob of Ithric's spend from his chin, broken only by the culprit's ragged breathing as he sagged back on the bed.

"Well, Kath," Favian said, examining the mess coating his fingertips, "apparently we are *just that good*, despite my relative lack of experience. Who knew?"

"Oh... my... *gods*," said Ithric, finally regaining the power of speech. "I—cannot believe that just happened. I am never going to live this down for as long as I draw breath, am I?"

Kathrael's lips twitched as she tried not to react visibly. "Not to worry, lion-boy," she said, aware that her amusement was coming through in her voice, but unable to resist teasing him, just a little. "Once upon a time, you'd have been my favorite kind of client."

That was too much for Ithric, who descended into choked laughter. When he got control of himself, he looked sheepishly at Favian. "Seriously, though—I am *really* sorry about that." His eyes flicked to Kathrael. "Little Cat? Kiss him for me, please, while I lie here for a few moments, stewing in my own humiliation."

"Hmm," she said slowly, as if considering, "Well... I suppose I can manage that. If you *insist*."

Smiling, she took Favian's hand and sucked his fingers clean. "Hey," he said with a frown, "Kath. You don't have to—"

She pulled off with a pop and smirked at him. "I'm not doing this for your benefit, Favian."

Her eyes flicked to Ithric, and Favian followed her gaze in time to see their companion watching with his mouth hanging open.

"Ah," Favian said. "Right. Point taken."

She leaned forward to lick up the smear of spend left on his cheek and chin, and whispered in his ear. "*This* part is for your benefit, though," she said, and brushed her lips against his.

Favian hummed approval and relaxed into the kiss, one hand coming up to cradle her head as they explored each other over Ithric's spent body. Somewhat to her surprise, Kathrael's arousal had never waned—not even during Ithric's unexpectedly premature release. Now, it flowed through her body unhindered, sinking slowly to settle in her sex, where slick warmth squeezed out to coat her inner folds.

She moaned in pleasure, and Favian swallowed the noise.

"I can smell your desire, Little Cat," Ithric said in a low, hoarse voice. "Will you let us watch you again while you come?"

The words ignited new fire in her veins, and she tore free of the kiss with a gasp. "Yes," she said, thinking of the sense of security she'd felt when Favian had stood behind her earlier with his arm looped around her waist. "Favian, will you... hold me, this time?"

Hesitant, she met his deep blue gaze with her good eye, and his face softened. "Happily, Kath. Anytime you desire it, and for as long as you want."

She darted in to kiss him again, and the three of them shifted around on the bed by unspoken agreement. Ithric ceded the pile of pillows to the two of them and lay on his side next to the wall, propped up on an elbow to watch. Favian leaned back, taking Ithric's previous spot and guiding Kathrael to recline against his chest, cradled in the space between his legs.

"Comfortable?" he asked.

She lay back, basking in the feeling of being held. Cherished. Her sex ached and throbbed under Favian's solicitous care and Ithric's hot gaze. "Almost," she said, and threw a leg over one of his, exposing herself to the cooling air. "There. Much better."

"You know," Ithric said appreciatively, "if I'd realized that afternoon we spent together in Woodhaerst was your first time, I'd have paid closer attention."

"You were a bit distracted, as I recall," she pointed out, and was rewarded by Favian's chest rising and falling behind her as he chuckled silently.

"Just a bit," Favian said.

"Well... maybe so," Ithric agreed. "But I'm not distracted now."

The low rumble of his words ratcheted Kathrael's desire higher, and her reply was breathless. "No. I can see that."

Unwilling to hold back a moment longer, she ran her hands over her breasts. The nipples pebbled beneath her palms. The resulting jolt of pleasure was just as sharp as she remembered from the last time, and her eyes slipped closed as she savored it. She needed another pair of hands, she thought, so she could do this and rub her sex at the same time.

The faint sound of laughter tickled the edges of her hearing.

You're an idiot, Kath. But I love you anyway. Vesh's ghostly whisper in her ear startled her, but realization dawned an instant later.

"Oh!" She twisted, trying to see Favian's face. "Favian? Would you... touch me? Only if you want to, though—"

"Tell me where," he said without hesitation. "And you'll have to let me know if you don't like something. All right?"

She nodded, and let her head fall back against the hollow of his shoulder. "All right." Her voice was breathy. "My breasts... please. Touch my breasts?"

Favian had one arm wrapped loosely around her already. He slid his hand up until it was cupping her left breast, exploring the weight and texture of it. Her eyes slipped shut.

"Beautiful," Ithric breathed from his place next to them, where he was watching, but not touching them.

Kathrael moaned softly and let her hands drift down, over her stomach, leaving Favian to play with her breasts. She slid fingertips over her slick folds, marveling anew at this strange bliss that she had never even known her body could experience.

The rapture was building, if anything, even more quickly than it had in Woodhaerst—fed by her delving fingers and heightened further by an unexpected shock of pleasure as Favian plucked her taut nipples between his fingers.

"I love that we can make you feel this way, Kath," he whispered.

"*I* love that we get to watch while you experience these things for the first time," Ithric added. "It's the most precious gift you could give us."

She made a needy noise, twisting restlessly in Favian's arms.

"Let me kiss you while you come," Ithric said impulsively. "Would you like that?"

She caught her breath at the image, which only served to throw more fuel on the fire of her arousal. "Yes," she said. "Kiss us both, lion-boy. I—I do want that."

Ithric sat up, a bit awkwardly as he favored his hurt side. He braced a hand on Favian's shoulder and brushed his lips across Kathrael's scarred cheek before his attention moved to Favian. The two of them kissed, tender and sweet, so close to Kathrael that she could feel Ithric's stubble brush her temple when she rolled her head toward them.

Ithric's heat radiated above her, and Favian's soaked into her from behind. She was surrounded by them. Cocooned. Protected. When Ithric moved back to take her mouth in a slow kiss, she thought her heart might pound its way right out of her ribcage.

The first time Ithric had kissed her, it had been almost chaste. Now, he turned the slide of lips and tangle of tongues so filthy that Kathrael grew dizzy with need, her fingers moving faster over her sensitive flesh. Sometime, she thought in a daze, she would spend hours with them like this, floating on an undulating wave of sensation with the outside world only a distant memory.

Now, though, it was too much. Favian turned his head to kiss and nuzzle at the shell of her ear, and just like that, her release swelled and crashed over her. A raw, animal scream of ecstasy tore free from her throat, and Ithric swallowed it—drinking her cries like hot mulled wine, licking deep into her mouth to chase the dregs. Stealing her breath away.

She slumped against Favian's body, lightheaded, pleasure buzzing under her skin as Ithric let her up for air with a final light nip to her lower lip. Favian's hands had gentled, cupping her breasts and sending little aftershocks singing along her nerves.

"Oh," she breathed, "I *do* love that."

Ithric brushed a thumb over her lower lip, swollen and slick from kissing. "So," he said, "do I."

"Would this be a good time to say *I told you so*?" Favian asked, all innocence. He slid his hands down to rest across her belly, holding her close to him.

"*No*," she said, only to reconsider a moment later. "Well, *yes*, probably—since I'm too wrecked to manage a decent rebuttal. You know what? Go ahead and be smug about it, if it makes you happy. It's worth it."

Favian snorted, and Ithric laughed outright.

"I just don't understand, though," Kathrael continued, still floating on her happy little cloud. "I mean... seriously.

How many men have I *been* with? Why has it never felt like this before now?"

Ithric laced his hand with Favian's across her stomach, his thumb rubbing back and forth over Favian's knuckles. "Maybe our smug bastard of a priest was right earlier, and we really are *just that good*."

Favian kicked him lightly in the shin. "As gratifying as it would be to take full credit, I think it's more likely related to what Healer Sagdea said. Remember? You told me that even before you were injured, there was never enough to eat. And she always says that without enough of the right kind of food, nothing in the body works the way it's supposed to."

"Huh," Ithric said. "That does make a fair amount of sense, to be honest."

Kathrael pondered Favian's words, at least as much as she was able while her mind was so deliciously sated and sleepy. "Maybe," she allowed. "I think it's you two as well, though. Because I certainly don't have the least bit of interest in running back to any of my old clients' beds and trying this."

"*Good*," Ithric said, his voice a low rumble that made her shiver.

"Good," Favian echoed in a lighter tone. "Because not a single one of them deserves you."

She smiled, and turned so she could nuzzle her cheek against his chest. "You're a hopeless romantic, priest-boy."

"*Shh*. Don't spread it around," Favian said. He stretched beneath her. "Come on, you two. Sleep. It's getting late."

Ithric stretched as well, still being careful of his injured side. "You sure?" he asked. "Feels like we've kind of been neglecting you tonight. You want anything more first?"

"I've got *exactly* what I want, right here," Favian shot back. "Or I will have, once we're all settled under the covers together."

"Put him in the middle, Ithric," Kathrael said around a huge yawn. "He'd like that."

Without waiting for the object of their discussion to weigh in with an opinion on the matter, Ithric sat up to give them each a final kiss, and clambered over them to get on Favian's other side. After they'd wriggled around to find comfortable positions under the blanket with Favian wrapped up between them, Ithric let out a great sigh of relaxation.

"We need to talk to Andoc in the morning," he said. "Then I want to go out for a bit to see if I can bring back some game for the cookhouse, and get a few coins in my purse. Though... I suppose I'll have to buy a purse before I can implement the second part of that plan, since I don't actually own one anymore."

"You hunt, Ithric? Really?" Kathrael asked, already more than half-asleep.

Amusement laced Ithric's reply. "I'm a lion, Little Cat. Of course I hunt."

The following morning dawned clear and warm. It was growing late in the season, but after a short stint of brisk nights and cooler days, summer seemed to have wrested back control of the weather for the time being.

It was still a decidedly odd experience for Kathrael to wake up feeling healthy and rested, in safe surroundings and with warm bodies lying next to her that she actually *wanted* there.

"Good morning," Favian greeted softly.

"Mmm," she agreed, rubbing sleep from her eyes. On Favian's other side, Ithric slept on, his face pressed into Favian's shoulder.

Still speaking quietly, Favian continued, "I need to go see to my duties at the temple. Did you want to come along, or stay here and get a bit more sleep?"

"Sleep," she said immediately. Despite the shabby surroundings of Carivel's abandoned hut, the idea of lounging in bed this morning felt positively luxurious.

"Enjoy yourself, in that case," Favian said, and stretched forward to kiss her. "I'll see you later, when we all meet with Andoc. Rest well."

"Until then," she said around a yawn, and let him disentangle himself so he could rise and dress. She rolled over into the warm spot he had vacated. Ithric mumbled something and pressed against her side as he had been pressing against Favian's a few moments earlier.

When she next woke, the slant of sunlight through the window proclaimed it to be mid-morning. She stretched, her body sliding against the lithe form of the shape-shifter lying next to her. Kathrael's flank rubbed against something hard, and Ithric made a sleepy noise, his hips flexing into the contact.

She froze, caught and held for a moment between her old life and her new one—her body unsure how to react. Ithric blinked awake, looking around with bleary eyes as he took in their surroundings. A wide yawn cracked his jaw, and he shuffled back to give her some space.

"Morning, Little Cat. Sorry to rut on you like that—thought you were Favian for a minute there." His brow furrowed. "Speaking of which, where *is* Favian?"

The easy way in which Ithric apologized for his sleep-muddled actions and moved on to other things settled her instincts. Her body subsided into warm relaxation once more. "Well... unlike some of us, he actually has responsibilities," she said. "He's off being priestly, and said he'd see us when we meet with Andoc. Which... I suppose we'd better start thinking about, considering how late it's getting."

Ithric groaned and threw off the blanket, unconcerned with his nakedness. "Yes, you're right. Not," he added with a sly smile, "that Andoc is known for being much of an early riser himself. Come on... there's a bucket in the corner if you want a quick wash first. I'm afraid I didn't think to lay in anything for breakfast, though."

⚜

Kathrael overrode Ithric's mild grumbling and dragged him to the temple to eat. Afterward, they met Favian, who looked decidedly grim. Ithric took one look at him and his expression fell.

"Rona," he said. "Did she—?"

"She's recovering," Favian said, and Kathrael's own heart sank at the knowledge that the small woman must have followed the healer's advice to end her pregnancy.

"I should talk to her," Ithric muttered, sounding terribly sad.

Favian put a hand on his shoulder and shook his head. "Not now. Give her some time first, Ithric. She's not alone—Nimbral is with her, and Sagdea is checking on her frequently."

Ithric nodded, looking unhappy.

Kathrael could well imagine how Rona would be feeling, and, indeed, her sudden disquiet seemed to rouse the tiny spirit of her own lost baby, who fussed with restless cries at the edge of her awareness. She took a centering breath, closed her eyes, and focused inward, humming a low tune under her breath.

Ithric's keen ears caught the nearly inaudible sound, and he glanced at her quickly. "Sorry, Kath. I wasn't thinking. Not a good subject. Did we upset her?"

Kathrael forced a smile, brief though it was. "It's all right Ithric. Don't worry about it. Rona is your friend. Of course you're worried."

Somewhat to her surprise, Ithric eased her into a light embrace, tucking her head under his chin. "Even so," he said.

The little wraith was already quieting, though—returning to sleep. Nonetheless, Kathrael stayed where she was for a few moments, soaking up the contact as Ithric held her and Favian rested a hand on the back of her hair, stroking over the smooth strands.

"It's fine," she reiterated. "Really. She's fine now." Reluctantly, she straightened, and they let her go easily. "Is Andoc ready to meet with us, Favian?"

"I'm sure he'll make time," Favian said. "Senovo let me know that Andoc would be at the meeting house until midday, so we can catch him there if we leave now."

Favian took a deep breath as they exited the temple. The day was gray and the air heavy with the promise of rain, matching Favian's mood precisely. It seemed deeply unfair that so many women suffered and died bringing children into the world, and that so many children never even survived long enough to see that world.

Rona had been utterly distraught, obviously torn apart by the decision she had made. Only the healer's insistence that the child would not survive its birth any more than Rona would had convinced her to take the tea that would save her life. She had done so early this morning under Sagdea and Favian's watchful gaze, and now both her body and spirit were suffering the effects.

Favian had been secretly relieved when the elderly medicine woman chased him out of the room to give her patient privacy after the cramps and sickness started—though part of him felt guilty over that relief.

Now, he led Ithric and Kathrael toward the meetinghouse, where a whole new set of problems awaited.

Despite Ithric's opinion on the matter, Favian did not expect that Andoc would look favorably on the shape-shifter's rather hare-brained plan to help Kath rally the slaves in Rhyth to revolt.

You're part of that plan, too, a little voice in his head reminded him, but he set it aside firmly. It was a moot point, surely. The whole thing was ridiculous. It could never work—it would just get them all killed if they tried. Andoc would no doubt decide the same. Which was good, since Favian could barely comprehend the idea of losing either Ithric or Kathrael now that the three of them had found each other.

Couldn't they just forge a life here in Draebard, where it was safe?

He stifled a sigh. They had reached the meeting hall, where Zolis and another young warrior that Favian didn't know well flanked the entrance.

"Well, now!" Zolis said. "I heard you were back, Ithric, but I could hardly credit it. Come to the barracks sometime and we'll have a few drinks."

Ithric smiled, and Favian wondered if other people could see the strain behind it. "Sure," he said. "Give me a few days to get settled and you're on."

Zolis waved them into the structure and called after them. "Don't forget you still owe me three pieces of silver from that game of dice last spring!"

Ithric lifted a hand in acknowledgement, and Kathrael raised an eyebrow at him even as Favian sent him a faintly disapproving look.

"Gambling, lion-boy?" she asked. "I'm *shocked.* And after your little lecture to me yesterday, as well."

Ithric huffed. "Maybe I should introduce Zolis to Arnav."

Favian was spared responding as they reached the main hall. Low voices could be heard from within. Andoc was seated with four men and two women from the council of elders around one end of the large table that dominated the room. He looked up as Favian entered the open doorway.

Favian had not spent much time in the meetinghouse in his lifetime, but those few occasions when he had entered this room had been memorable. He was momentarily overcome with the recollection of running here as fast as his legs could carry him after hearing that his father had been lost while traveling. Favian had crashed to a halt against the sturdy timbers of this very doorframe, yelling abuse at Andoc and the elders for sending his father on such a dangerous journey during winter to negotiate a treaty with his old village of Teth.

He blinked rapidly, forcing the past away.

"Good morning. Come in, all of you," Andoc called, gesturing them to seat themselves at the table, across from the council. "I've just been explaining the situation to the others. Ithric, you said you have news that we need to hear?"

Ithric cleared his throat, folding his hands in front of him on the table. "I do. I assume Andoc told you all that I was spying for him in Rhyth before I was captured and taken away from the city by men exhibiting unusual people as oddities."

One of the women leaned backed in her chair. It was Lanessa, the widow of old Elder Tolmac. She'd taken his place on the council when he died two years previously. "So he did, young man, though one wonders what possessed you to volunteer for such a thing. The south is not safe for those with the Old Magic."

"The south is not safe for spies, whether they have the Old Magic or not, Elder," Ithric retorted. "Spying is not, by its nature, a safe pursuit."

"These days," Kathrael added quietly, "the south is not safe for *anyone*. Rhyth is tearing itself apart."

"Is this true?" one of the others asked, directing the question to Ithric. Favian felt a flash of annoyance that even now, so many on the council would discount the words of a woman, even though that woman had lived in the south all her life.

"Kathrael has more insight than I regarding the long-term changes in and around Rhyth," Ithric said, echoing Favian's thoughts. "She is, after all, a native."

"What, exactly, is happening there?" Asked the other woman at the table, her iron gray hair falling over her shoulders as she leaned forward. "What makes you think things are coming to a head?"

"The Alyrions are scaling back their support of the puppet regime in Rhyth. Unrest is growing. The north cut trade with the south to a trickle after the war six years ago," Ithric said, "and now Alyrios is cutting trade in response, since they can no longer get the raw materials they want."

"The rich families in Rhyth are trying to replace that trade with grain exports," Kathrael put in, her voice sure even though she hid her face in shadow. "But even the southern river deltas can only grow so much food—and most of it is grown by slaves. The people are growing ever more hungry, impoverished, and desperate."

Ithric laced his fingers together, looking grim. "The cult of Deimok is growing stronger all the time, feeding on people's fears and desire for violence. Mobs roam the streets, stoning people. Drowning them. Burning them. The entire city is a tinder pile, waiting for the right spark to set it aflame."

Favian couldn't help the faint shiver that traveled up his spine.

There was a long moment of silence before Elder Dantrell, a white-haired old man with a long beard and a bald patch on top of his head, spoke. "As sad as all this is for the people who live there, surely if Rhyth falls, that is a *good* thing for the north?"

Favian could *feel* Kathrael bristle next to him. "With the cult of Deimok gaining power with the common people, and the government composed of weak Alyrion pawns, who do you think is going to move in and take over if everything falls to pieces?" she snapped.

Ithric was calmer, but his words were no less forceful. "The Alyrion withdrawal of support has ulterior motives. They are seeking actively to destabilize the region."

There was a low murmur as several of the elders leaned over to confer with their neighbors. Favian's own pulse sped up as he thought about their words, even though he had heard the information already.

Andoc raised his hand to get everyone's attention, and the others quieted. "This is as serious as you led me to believe, you three. However, it also sounds like the events you describe are almost inevitable at this point. I think our focus now must be on sharing this news with our allies and devising a strategy for defense should the worst occur, and the Empire gain a solid foothold south of the mountains."

Ithric took a breath. "There is another power in the south that no one is taking into account. At least, not yet."

Andoc frowned. "What power is that?"

"The slaves," Kathrael said quietly, and Andoc breathed in sharply.

"While everyone else is focused on the unrest in the streets, the slaves have been quietly organizing," said Ithric. "They lack resources and support, but I have met secretly with several members of the underground resistance working to free slaves and mobilize them against the rich families and the overseers."

Favian held his breath.

"Are you suggesting," Andoc said slowly, "that the northern tribes support this resistance group openly?"

The elders started murmuring to each other again. Ithric smiled his unnerving smile for a bare instant before it was gone.

"I'm not suggesting anything, just telling you what I saw, Chief. There's only one group in Rhyth that could tip the balance in an unexpected direction right now. But they'll need help."

"*Unexpected* does not necessarily equate with *good*, young man," said Elder Dantrell.

"Nor does it necessarily equate with *bad*," Favian said, surprising himself by speaking up.

Andoc flicked an eyebrow at him, as if Favian had surprised *him*, as well. Favian looked away, still not quite ready to forgive his guardian for letting Ithric become his spy in the first place, thus allowing him to run headlong into danger. Not for the first time in his life, he wished he'd never heard of Rhyth, or Alyrios.

Rhyth is Kath's home, though. The thought came unbidden.

"We'll need to discuss this new information, obviously," Andoc was saying. He paused, and Favian's eyes snapped back to him. "But I think it's clear that we will have more need than ever for reliable spies in the coming months."

Ithric leaned back in his chair and crossed his arms. A faint chill passed through Favian's chest at what Andoc was clearly implying.

"Well," said Ithric, "I realize that I fell a bit short of the mark last time. That said, I have the advantage of a native guide now." His gaze moved deliberately to Kathrael.

Kathrael lifted her chin, no longer hiding in the shadow of her shawl. "Yes, he does," she agreed, and the cold feeling in Favian's chest intensified, as the reality of what they were proposing—and what it would mean to Favian's life—truly began to set in for the first time.

FIVE

"I think that went fairly well," Ithric said, as the three of them left the meetinghouse and headed across the green. He was feeling rather flush with the accomplishment of having brought the council such valuable information, and he could sense Kathrael radiating a sort of quiet determination next to him.

Favian had seemed awfully subdued since they exited the building, but Ithric figured he was still stewing over Andoc having sent Ithric to spy in Rhyth and then keeping it a secret from him. He was distracted from pursuing that line of thought when a familiar voice hailed them.

"Hey, Favian!"

All three of them turned, and Ithric recognized the small, dark-haired form of Keenan approaching, a wide grin splitting her face. The Mereni archer had been a frequent visitor to Draebard ever since Ithric had been here. She and Carivel had become friends before the war, when they first hatched the plan of training archers to fight from horseback rather than on foot or from chariots. Years later, she was still a fairly common sight in the village, traveling here from Meren two or three times a year, often with her bondmate Ciero in tow.

Now, though, Ithric's eyes were drawn to the noticeable bulge in her normally flat stomach.

"Keenan!" Favian greeted. "How are you?"

"Never better," she said, smoothing a hand over her belly and confirming Ithric's suspicions about the bump there. "Hello, Ithric! Good to see you again." Her attention settled on Kathrael, and she blinked, but recovered quickly. She stuck out a hand. "I don't think we've met. I'm Keenan. Friend of Carivel's—but don't hold that against me."

Taken aback, it took Kathrael a moment to return the gesture, gripping Keenan's wrist briefly before letting go. "Kathrael," she said. "I'm a… friend of Favian and Ithric's."

"Pleasure to meet you," Keenan said easily, before returning her attention to all three of them. "Ciero and I arrived a couple of days ago. I have a new style of bow that I wanted to show Carivel. We figured we'd better come now, since travel will only get harder over the next few months."

"Do I take it that congratulations are in order?" Favian said.

Keenan laughed. "*Finally*, yes. And to think, it only took six-and-a-half years!"

Ithric spared half a glance at Kath to see how she was reacting, but she only looked a bit wistful. "Well, congratulations," he said, meaning it. "Good things come to those who wait... or so I've been told. Not really my forte, waiting—though this would seem to lend some credence to the idea."

Keenan chuckled. "Maybe so. Well, I won't keep you. Ciero and I are staying at the way-house. We should all have a meal together or something while I'm here. Just... not first thing in the morning, please, unless you want to watch it come right back up."

Favian frowned. "Sagdea might have something for that, you know."

The tiny archer only smiled. "If it gets too bad I'll talk to her. Mostly, though, it just comes with the territory. I can live with it, if a baby is the end result. Good to see you... and nice to meet you, Kathrael."

With a cheery wave, Keenan resumed her trek toward the horse pens, and Favian seemed to slide right back into his dark thoughts. As it happened, though, Keenan's sudden appearance had given Ithric an idea. Unfortunately, he needed to talk to them about something else first.

"I've had a thought, you two," he began. "One I didn't share with Andoc and the council. Favian, you in particular are going to hate this."

The opening he'd offered Favian was about a league wide, so Ithric was surprised when he didn't walk through it, but only replied, "Great," in a dark tone.

"What is it, lion-boy?" Kathrael asked.

"If we're going to travel south together as a group, we'll need some sort of cover story," he said. "Some reason why we're traveling, and an excuse to get cozy with all different types of people."

"Yes?" Kathrael asked cautiously. "And you've come up with such a reason, have you?"

He grinned, quick and sharp. "I have. I thought we could travel as a troupe of entertainers, heading south from village to village until we get to Rhyth. Tell me, Little Cat, do you have any relevant skills?"

That got Favian's attention. "You want us to pretend to be a *traveling show*?" His expression was horrified.

"What do you mean, *pretend*?" Ithric asked. "You either *are* a traveling show, or you're not. Though we'd have to find a role for you beyond blessing the onlookers and standing around looking pretty, I suppose. Kathrael, what about it?"

Kathrael's reply was very quiet. "I can play the *sithaa*. And… I used to dance."

"Perfect," Ithric said. "I learned fire-eating from a tribe up north when I was younger, though I'm pretty rusty. Also, I do love to tell a good story."

Meanwhile, Favian's face had gone red, then paled. "You are *not* exhibiting yourself as a lion," he said.

Ithric's lips twitched, though the smile did not reach his eyes, and his voice was sober when he replied. "No. Best not. Too much chance of talk since I'd need to shift back and forth all the time."

"I don't like this, Ithric." Favian's haunted expression from earlier returned. "You're running into this thing headlong, without any respect for how incredibly dangerous it is."

Ithric looked at him in surprise. "You think I don't know being in the middle of a city on the edge of revolt is dangerous, Favian? Really?"

Favian rounded on him. "It's not just *you* now, Ithric. It's the people you love. And the people *they* love, who will be left behind if we leave and don't come back." His jaw worked as he visibly restrained himself. "Look. I need to go and… check on Rona. We can talk about this later, all right?"

Without waiting for a reply, Favian turned sharply and headed for the temple.

"Ithric." Kathrael's tone was solemn, and he tore his attention away from the retreating figure to look down at her. "You must realize—while I may have been a performer—of sorts—at one time, I can't *be* that person any more. Unless you want to display me as an object of repulsion, no one is going to pay money to watch a disfigured woman dance and play a musical instrument."

The old, immature part of Ithric wanted to bristle at their lack of faith in him. But the new part—the part that aspired to be good enough to lead and protect his pride—was stronger. *Fortunately.* He put his hands on her shoulders and urged her to meet his eyes.

"Kath," he said. "I know you believe that. But you're wrong. Come with me, please. There's someone I want you to meet."

Kathrael followed Ithric through a tangle of side roads, trying not to let her misgivings show. It had been one thing talking about a grand plan to unify the slaves against the corrupt government of Rhyth when they were safely tucked together in bed at the temple in Woodhaerst, flush with success at having bested Turvick and his crony.

It was, as she was discovering, quite another to contemplate the actions they would need to take for such a thing to *actually happen.* She had not been oblivious to Favian's realization earlier of just what, exactly, he had agreed to do. She and Ithric were outcasts. Refugees. But Favian had a home… a family… a *sister.* He had a vocation he loved. He had just become a novice priest mere *weeks before,* for the gods' sakes—after putting in years of work to attain that very position.

And now, they were asking him to pull up the roots he had grown over the course of a lifetime, all so he could follow them on an insane quest to a place where he would be a target of hatred—in constant danger of sudden, violent death.

Vesh's kind face flashed before her eyes, with his dark eyes and crooked nose, and his beloved, much-missed smile. Could Kathrael bear to see Favian's battered body dragged through the streets by a jeering mob? Could she survive having his ghostly voice haunt her in the depths of night? A deep shiver ran through her that had nothing to do with the temperature.

They arrived at the way-house, a sprawling jumble of a structure that had obviously been added onto many times over the years. Ithric's earlier manic enthusiasm had subsided into something more centered, and she wondered why he had brought her here.

"Keenan's husband Ciero was a warrior when he was younger," Ithric said, "but he lost his hand in a battle. Now he's an artist. I want you to meet him, so I can talk to you both about an idea I had after realizing he was here."

"All right," she agreed, still subdued after the turn her thoughts had taken since leaving the quiet protection of Carivel's hut this morning.

Ciero, it turned out, was seated at a bench in the small courtyard behind the way-house. He rose to greet them when Ithric hailed him, a smile on his broad, pleasant features.

"Ithric, isn't it?" he said, before his gaze moved to her and stuttered to a stop at her scarred face, as many people's did. "Oh," he continued, tearing his eyes away. A slight blush rose on his light skin. "I'm so terribly sorry. You'll have to forgive my rudeness. You'd think I of all people would know better." He sheepishly raised the stump of his right arm, which ended in an ugly pucker of flesh below the elbow.

Kathrael felt blood rise to her face, but swallowed her momentary surge of embarrassment. "I'm… quite used to it," she said. In her eyes, the northerners' tendency to actually acknowledge their rudeness and apologize for it was infinitely preferable to the alternative of being an invisible outcast—unremarked and untouchable. "I'm Kathrael. We met your wife earlier today."

Ithric smoothly took up the conversation. "I hope you'll forgive the presumption, Ciero—I know we're not properly acquainted. But your reputation precedes you, as they say."

Ciero laughed. "Well, I don't know about that," he said. "But flattery is always appreciated, regardless. What can I do for you?"

"I was wondering if it would be possible to commission some sort of half-mask for Kathrael, to cover her scars," he said, and Kathrael gave him a sudden, sharp look. "Something as beautiful as she is, though that may be asking rather a lot, I realize."

Ciero raised an eyebrow, and returned his attention to her face. This time, though, the look was interested, assessing, as if he was measuring her damaged features.

"Hmm," he said. "I don't see why not. It might take a mixture of different materials…"

"Ithric," Kathrael began, not sure what words she intended to follow his name.

He looked at her, a faint furrow between his brows. "Have you never even thought of it before, Kathrael?"

"No," she said, after a moment of silence. "I honestly hadn't."

His eyes softened. "I've watched you, Little Cat. It's not the scars on your face, you know. When you think people are judging you for your appearance, you... hide. You turn inward, and show the scars you carry *inside*. Those are the ones I hate to see."

Her breath caught on the inhale, and she had to swallow to clear her throat. No one had ever put it in quite that way before, and the truth of it entered her heart like a sharp metal spear point.

She thought of armor, the leather and metal that warriors donned to protect the soft parts underneath. She thought of the shield of beauty she had used for years as a prostitute, to protect the wounded child inside. She thought of Ithric and Favian at her side, ready to step in front of her and protect her against anything that might harm her, from without or within.

"If... you think such a thing can be made," she said, addressing Ciero slowly, and with a faint quaver in her voice, "I... believe I would like that very much."

Ciero's expression had softened at Ithric's words to her, and he nodded. "I can't guarantee how it will come out, but it would certainly be my honor to attempt it. Would you be willing to let me take a clay impression of that side of your face? It would make it easier for me to work on the mask without having to constantly pester you for measurements and fittings. I'm supposed to meet some friends for a meal shortly, but I could do it late this afternoon if you're free."

Free. The word, used so casually, made something swoop in her chest. A smile curled her lips. "Yes," she said, "I'm free."

⚜

A short while later, she and Ithric walked back along the winding tangle of roads, both quiet and lost in thought. When she took his upper arm and used it to pull him to a stop so she could stretch up and press a kiss to his lips, he seemed surprised.

"What was that for?" he asked. "Not that I'm complaining, mind you."

She looked up at him. "If you have to ask, lion-boy, you wouldn't understand."

The smile he gave her in return crinkled the corners of his eyes, and she thought perhaps he understood more than she was giving him credit for. He pressed a kiss of his own to her scarred temple, and they started walking again.

"Do you want to come out to the hunting grounds with me?" he asked. "I still intend to make a bit of money today if I can, and I think the shagbark nuts are finally ready for gathering if you've a mind to make a few coins yourself. Charyal and her sisters always pay a fair price for supplies for the cookhouse."

Even with the gray clouds gathered overhead, the idea of going out into the wilderness to keep Ithric company and gather nuts for a few hours sounded infinitely preferable to moping around the temple or Carivel's hut with nothing to do.

"Deal," she said. "I should get a bag or something to hold them. Do you need to go get weapons for hunting?"

He laughed, a low rumble that unexpectedly ignited a spark of arousal in Kathrael's belly. "Oh… *Little Cat*," he said. "I won't be using weapons."

They walked the rest of the way to Carivel's hut in companionable silence. Once there, Ithric pulled a moth-eaten cloth bag with a drawstring out of the dusty storage chest in one corner of the room. Then, he began to strip efficiently, throwing her a lopsided grin when she made a teasing, appreciative noise.

He tied a loincloth around his hips a moment later, then took down a small knife and old, cracked leather sheath from where they hung on a peg on the wall. He fastened it to the thong holding up the loincloth, and straightened. "Simpler to shape-shift this way," he explained. "Ready?"

She nodded, and let him lead the way out. He was barefoot, but seemed completely unbothered by it as he took them to the eastern edge of the town and beyond, into the woods. This, she remembered, was the area that had been lit with torches during the summer festival that took place shortly before she and Favian had left Draebard to look for Ithric, weeks ago. Pairs and trios of lovers had used the maze of trails and grottos for semi-public trysts, their gasps and murmurs filling the night air.

"Why, *Ithric*," she teased. "I recognize this place. Surely you haven't brought me out here for nefarious purposes?"

He snorted. "Not without Favian here to join us, no. This really *is* the way to the hunting grounds." His gold-shot eyes caught hers, returning the teasing. "Though I do believe you've been having wicked thoughts about me, Little Cat... which I *thoroughly* encourage."

She couldn't really deny it, so she didn't try. "Well, if you insist on going around in nothing but a breechclout..."

Ithric only smirked. "Here. I'll do you one better that that." He untied the simple knot in the thong holding the loincloth in place and pulled it free — unconcerned by his nakedness as he flipped the thong, the attached knife sheath, and the length of soft buckskin over a low-hanging branch. "There are shagbark trees scattered all through this area, but I seem to recall a larger concentration a little way further down that trail." He pointed to Kathrael's right.

"And where will you be?" she asked.

"There are some open fields further east that usually have deer and boar in late summer and autumn," he said. "I'm complete shite at hunting in forests, so that's why I'm heading for open ground. Don't feel like you have to wait for me — I can meet you back at Carivel's hut if you get bored. Not sure how long I'll be... that's kind of up to the prey."

Kathrael was still utterly intrigued by the lion, but she only said, "All right. Let's meet at the temple, though. I want to see Favian. He seemed off today."

Ithric's tone turned wry. "Well, if you insist. I guess I'm going to have to give up and get used to the temple, under the circumstances."

It was Kathrael's turn to snort. "You've just taken a priest as a lover, so I should think so, yes." She waved him off. "Go on, then. Go catch dinner."

He gave her a last, devilish look. "You know, by rights I should make you do this. It's usually the lioness that hunts, in a pride."

"Then I hope you like mice and bugs," she shot back, "because that's about all you'd be likely to get. And even then, only the slow ones."

He laughed aloud. "Not so you'd notice, no. I suppose I'll just have to muddle through on my own, in that case."

With a quick wink in her direction, he dropped to all fours and shifted. Kathrael caught her breath; entranced anew by the powerful beast that crouched where a naked man had stood mere moments before.

The lion shook himself and stretched, jaw cracking open in a wide yawn. He stalked forward on silent paws and rubbed his cheek against her hip. Her chest swelled with emotion as she reached a hand down to trail over the tawny hide covering hard muscles. Ithric twined around her, the movement smooth as water, and her fingers trailed along his spine as he left her to head for the hunting grounds. A final flick of his tail caressed her leg, and he was gone, prowling into the shadows and disappearing from view.

Kathrael watched the place where he had been for a long moment. She breathed in deeply, feeling the humid air and the scents of forest life fill her lungs. Around her, the leaves rustled softly as a light breeze stirred the heavy air. A strange sense of peace overcame her in this place of complete solitude, and she looked around, searching for the distinctive ragged trunks of the trees she needed. One caught her eye just off the trail Ithric had indicated, and she headed for it, bag in hand.

🦐 ♔ 🦐

When the old cloth bag was somewhat more than half full, she pulled the drawstring closed and set it at the base of a huge tree. If she filled it any fuller, it would be difficult to carry back to the cookhouse. Not to mention the fact that the ancient burlap already looked strained to bursting in places, in danger of giving way at any moment.

Restless, she looked around the small glade where she'd found herself after following Ithric's directions to the collection of shagbark trees and the distinctive four-lobed nuts littering the ground beneath them. The wind had picked up, the sounds of the forest growing almost musical as it played through the branches overhead.

Her mind kept veering back to Ithric's words at the way-house, turning them over and over.

When you think people are judging you for your appearance, you... hide, he'd said. *You turn inward, and show the scars you carry* inside. *Those are the ones I hate to see.*

Once, her body had been a comfortable home—the only home she'd had, at times. She hadn't flinched to have people look at it, to have them watch her, naked or clothed, as she displayed herself while dancing... while making music... while prowling through a crowd, looking for her next mark.

All that had changed in the span of time it took firelight to flash against the edge of a glass vial of vitriol.

One could only watch so many people cringe, blood draining from their faces as they beheld one's scars, before one began to flinch away from oneself, she supposed. And yet... did her disfigured face make her body any less graceful? Would it make her music any less lyrical?

If her scars were hidden behind a mask—something beautiful and eye-catching—would she be any different to an onlooker than what she had been before? A strange urge rose from the depths of her being, pulling her arms out to her sides, fingers trailing gracefully like the flight feathers on a bird's wings. The loose sleeves of her chemise caught the wind, as if she might, in fact, be able to fly away, borne aloft on the strong currents.

She closed her eyes, the first smattering of raindrops pelting her face, the soft noise joining the music of nature around her. She could barely breathe as the sense of something settling back into place within her skin overcame her, nerves alight as surely and brightly as they had been during her throes of ecstasy in Favian and Ithric's bed.

The feeling bubbled over into movement. Unable to stay still, she spun in place. Her feet carried her with dancing steps into the center of the glade. Raindrops pattered against her skin and hair, cool in the humid early afternoon. She swayed and stretched in time to the beat only she could hear, feeling her muscles strain with the unaccustomed movement.

Kathrael leapt and twirled, only to wobble and crash to the ground in a heap as her knees failed to support her on the landing. She flopped back in the grass, unhurt, but wondering how she had ever allowed herself to draw so tightly inward, hiding away from the world and growing weak.

No more.

Fat raindrops splattered her face and neck as she lay there, blood pumping through her body, lending strength to muscles long unused in such a way. Kathrael decided there and then that she would dance again, scarred face or no. She rolled to a seated position and began to methodically stretch her joints and muscles, as she used to do before performing in front of a crowd of rich Rhytheeri orgy-goers.

With time and effort, she knew, that which had grown weak could become strong again.

The hours passed without Kathrael's conscious realization, until the rain subsided and a shaft of weak sunlight slanted through a gap in the clouds. The angle of the light startled her—it was already mid-afternoon, and her muscles were trembling with exertion, warm and shaky after extended use.

Aware that she needed to get back in time to meet with Ciero, she returned to the bole of the old tree and picked up her threadbare bag of nuts. It seemed even heavier than before after her exertion, but for some reason, rather than disheartening her, the thought made her smile.

She headed carefully back down the trail, the bag slung over her right shoulder. Ithric's breechclout and knife still hung over the branch where he'd left them earlier, a sure sign that he had not yet returned from his hunt. Just when she had decided to leave him to it and head back into the village, she heard the low *whuff... whuff... whuff* of heavy, animal breathing coming from a short distance away.

Hoping that there was nothing *else* as large as a lion roaming the forest so close to Draebard, Kathrael stood her ground. She was rewarded a few moments later when the lion reappeared from the dappled shadows under the trees, padding slowly toward her with the neck of a dead stag clamped in its powerful jaws. The deer's limp form dragged along the ground under the lion's body, as it stepped carefully around its burden.

"You did it!" she greeted, looking the stag over with something like admiration. "That's certainly an impressive kill."

Ithric set the unfortunate hart down at her feet and shifted form, steadying himself for a moment before rising smoothly to his feet and wiping at a smear of red on his jaw.

"Not bad," he agreed, and craned around to look at a blossoming bruise on his side, a few inches below the nearly healed knife wound. "He got a good kick in at the end, though I don't hold it against him. Fair's fair, I suppose, given that I was trying to kill him at the time."

Kathrael winced at the ugly purple and blue mark blooming on his torso. The skin at the center was scraped from the drag of a sharp hoof, but Ithric didn't seem terribly bothered by the small injury, so she didn't make a fuss.

"Do you need some help carrying it back?" she asked. "We could probably find a branch to tie its feet to, and carry it on our shoulders."

"Nah," he said, tying on his loincloth and immediately crouching with the knife to gut and field-dress the animal. "I can get it, and it looks like you've got a good load of nuts there already. Thanks, though."

She shrugged agreement. After only a few minutes, Ithric had the stag's innards cleaned out and was tossing everything except the heart, liver, and kidneys into the brush for the scavengers to clean up. The light rain, which had temporarily stopped, began to fall again.

Kathrael watched it patter against Ithric's bare skin, making shiny trails as the droplets ran down. It was a bit of a shock to realize that she was thinking about licking the rivulets dry with her tongue. She blinked. What on earth had Ithric and Favian awakened in her? It was as if a whole new aspect of her spirit had suddenly sprung to life, fully formed and ravenous for nourishment.

She looked back to Ithric's face, only to find him watching her in turn, the corner of his lips turned up and a sly sparkle in his eye.

"I don't know what you're thinking, exactly, but I'm reasonably sure I approve," he said. "For now, though, I should get this meat back before the liver starts to spoil. Ready?"

"Yes, ready," she confirmed, though her mouth was slightly dry.

Ithric slung the stag's carcass over his shoulders, while she hefted the drawstring bag of shagbark nuts, and they headed for Charyal's cookhouse to surrender their bounty.

SIX

Favian felt like he was wandering around in a daze. He'd returned to the temple to sit with Rona and Nimbral after parting from Kathrael and Ithric at midday. Rona was miserable, wracked by pain as her body rejected and expelled the contents of her womb. Nimbral was pale and worried, alternately pacing the room and folding himself into a too-small chair to clasp one of Rona's hands between both of his.

It took more effort than it should have for Favian to stay focused on his role as their priest, a state of affairs which wove a thin thread of anger through the gray fog that hung over him. Anger at himself for his distraction. Anger at Ithric and Kathrael for not being content with what the three of them could have together, here in Draebard. More anger at himself for having gone along with their scheme in the beginning, rather than somehow talking them out of it before the ridiculous idea took hold.

This was *madness*.

Yet here he was, still distracted from the important responsibility he had to Rona. He took a slow, silent breath and let it out. He was rescued a moment later by Healer Sagdea's return.

"Good evening, Favian," Sagdea greeted—not that Favian was finding much good about it.

"Healer," he acknowledged. "Is it time for another examination?"

Rona gave a low moan from the bed.

"I'm afraid so," said the healer. "Go get dinner and some rest, Favian. I'll watch over her tonight. If I'm able to recover the remains for a funeral ceremony, I'll let you know."

Favian nodded. The pair had expressed the desire for such a ceremony earlier. After having become acquainted with Kathrael—and, more to the point, with Kathrael's ghosts—Favian thought that was probably a wise idea. "I'll inform the High Priest so he can prepare."

Rona's voice was weak. "The—the Wolf Patron will bless my baby's spirit himself?"

Favian felt his heart lurch once more for Rona's loss, and crossed to the bed to take up her free hand. "Of course he will, Rona."

She burst into tears, and he let her hand slip free as Nimbral curled forward in the chair across from him to enfold her tiny body with his. Feeling horrible about the whole situation—the crushing unfairness of it all—he excused himself and left Rona to the elderly healer's care for a few hours.

He was surprised to find Ithric and Kathrael waiting for him in the refectory. Given Ithric's distaste for everything related to the priesthood, coupled with the amount of time he'd been forced to spend in temples lately, Favian had assumed he'd have to trek out to Carivel's hut to find them. But here they were, seated at one of the trestle tables, a bowl of something fragrant and steaming in front of each of them and a third sitting untouched nearby, evidently set out for him.

Ithric sensed his approach first, but it was Kathrael who spoke. "The healer said she was on her way to kick you out for the night. Join us and eat something?"

Favian collapsed onto the bench, the press of his thoughts a nearly physical weight.

"How's Rona?" Ithric asked.

"About like you'd expect," Favian said tightly. "What she's going through isn't a pleasant or easy process."

Again to his surprise, Ithric didn't push. He only nodded and said, "You'll let me know when she's up to visitors?"

"Of course," Favian murmured, staring into his bowl.

"Eat, Favian," Kathrael said again.

Favian picked up the spoon and ate with listless movements, barely tasting the bowl's contents.

As Kathrael went back to her own meal, something caught the corner of Favian's eye and he looked at her more closely. "Kath? Is that... *potter's clay*? Why do you have potter's clay on your face?"

Kathrael's hand lifted to the scarred side of her face as if she would be able to find the smears of reddish brown by feel. "Oh! I thought I got it all earlier."

"We went to see Ciero today," Ithric said, as if that was an explanation.

Favian blinked. "Is Ciero teaching you to throw pottery? I... didn't know he even worked with clay."

Oddly, a flush traveled up Kathrael's neck. "No," she said. "Nothing like that. He wanted a mold of the side of my face so he... could... make me a mask." The final words came out in a rush.

With a frown, Favian regarded her closely for a moment. "Kath, you don't need to hide your face here. If people react badly, that's on them, not you. No one who matters in Draebard is going to judge you for your scars."

She met his gaze squarely. "Perhaps I don't *need* to, Favian. And I certainly don't intend to wear it all of the time. But there may be circumstances where I *wish* to. And I will not always be in Draebard."

Just like that, the feeling of gray suffocation settled over Favian again. He looked back down at his tasteless meal. "Oh. Well. Yes. Of course not."

Ithric sighed. "If you've got something to say, Favian, just say it."

Suddenly, Favian could not summon the energy to even begin to talk about what truly needed to be discussed. "It's nothing," he said. "Just, you know... Rona. Look, I should stay here tonight in case I'm needed. You two... go on without me. I'll see you tomorrow sometime."

"We could stay here with you," Kathrael said, a furrow forming between her eyebrows.

Favian waited for Ithric to dispute that idea. When he didn't, Favian said, "No, don't worry about it. Look, I'm not good company tonight."

Ithric raised a sardonic brow. "Really? You shock me."

Irritation flared, but Favian tamped it down. "I'm just tired. I need some uninterrupted rest, that's all. We've all had a hard time of it lately."

Ithric looked pained. Kathrael still looked worried. "I'll stay here, tonight, in the room I was using before," she said, "in case you change your mind later about the company."

Ithric stood up. "If you want space, I'll give you space, no problem. You know where to find me if you need me." He stalked away a moment later, and the weight on Favian's shoulders pressed down a little bit harder.

"Don't mind him, Favian," Kathrael said when Ithric's footsteps had faded. "I don't think he quite knows what to do with himself when he can't wade in and solve a problem with his bare hands. Do you really want to be alone right now?"

No, Favian thought.

"Yes," he said.

When she nodded and stood up, wrapping her arms around him from behind and pressing a warm kiss to the top of his head, it somehow made everything even worse than before.

It was growing late when Favian finished cleaning up the dishes from the evening meal and slunk back to the room he'd shared with his sister Frella for so long. Though it had been mere weeks since he'd called the place his own, everything had changed. He found himself knocking softly on the doorframe rather than simply barging in.

"Come in!" Frella called cheerfully, not even looking up to see who it was.

"Hey, little sister," he said. "Looks like you're stuck with me tonight after all."

He saw the moment Frella took in his tone and appearance, and did a double take. She frowned, peering at him closely. "Something happened. Did you and Ithric fight?"

"No," he said.

She gave him a faintly mistrustful look, as if not sure she believed him. "Did you and Kathrael fight?"

"No," he repeated. "She's right down the hall, in her old room."

"Oh. Did Ithric and Kathrael fight?"

He couldn't help the snort of laughter that broke free as she methodically went through the list of possible permutations for an argument between the three of them. "No one fought, Frella. I just need some time away. To think."

Frella crossed her skinny arms. It seemed to Favian that she'd had another growth spurt while he'd been away, shooting up like a bean sprout.

"It's never good when you start *thinking*, Favian," she said in a tone of disgust. "But it's still your room. You can stay here if you want."

As it always did, her presence drove away some of the darkness in Favian's spirit. "How generous of you, little sister," he teased. "I feel positively welcome."

"I'm a very generous person, you know," she said primly, her blue eyes sparkling in the candlelight. "It comes from being raised by priests. But if you are going to mope around here tonight, then you can at least tell me more about Teth and Woodhaerst. Do they really have more cows than people there? And does Uncle Vineet really smell like sour milk, the way Papa used to say he did?"

Favian chuckled again. "Not that I noticed, although the *sour* part is accurate enough."

He flopped down on his old bed, happy for the distraction as he recounted a somewhat sanitized version of his travels with Kathrael to an enthralled audience of one, who peppered him with questions and commentary until his thoughts no longer circled back constantly to his troubles.

When Frella finally dozed off, he woke her long enough to get her to wash her face and dress for bed. Hoping that the evening of pleasant conversation would ease his own way into sleep, he followed her example and blew out the candles before sliding into bed... alone.

Sleep took longer than he might have wished, but eventually exhaustion won out and his thoughts slipped into quiescence.

~∞~

In his dream, it was dark. The wind was cold, but not bitter, and carried a promise of rain. His surroundings were unfamiliar. The buildings around him towered over him, larger and grander than anything one could find in Draebard.

He craned around, looking at the huge stone facade of the house he had just left. Flickering torchlight from sconces illuminated the sheer white face of it. Massive double doors swung shut behind him on oiled hinges.

"Stop gawping, Favian," Ithric said from beside him, voice lowered as if he was worried about being overheard. "Act normal, for the gods' sakes, and let's find Kath so we can get out of here."

He felt himself nod agreement. Felt worry tugging at his emotions.

"We need to find the servants' entrance," Ithric whispered, leading the way down wide stone steps that spilled them out into the stinking street below.

*Favian kept his mouth shut. The concept of a building having an entrance just for servants — for **slaves**, he corrected himself — was a foreign one, though it was self-explanatory enough. He hadn't the faintest idea about where to find such a thing, however. Perhaps in the back of the structure?*

Indeed, Ithric led him back to their caravan and untied the horses, then urged Favian into the driver's seat and told him to drive on. They headed out of sight in case anyone from the house was watching their departure, only to circle back on the next road over.

After finding a post in a shadowed alley to tie up the horses, Ithric gestured him deeper into the darkness of the cramped byway between two buildings. "Just hope no one steals 'em," Ithric muttered, ratcheting Favian's worry up another notch. "Should've brought a couple of the boys along to watch it."

As if to punctuate his words, a shout combined with raucous laughter and sounds of breaking glass or pottery came from a nearby road. Favian shivered.

The two of them stole through the darkness. Favian was having trouble keeping his bearings between the gloom and the twisting tangle of roads, but he knew they must have been backtracking toward the sprawling villa they'd just left. Interesting that no effort had been made to make the backs of these great houses attractive. It was all cracking plaster, rotting piles of garbage, and the smell of piss. Favian's boot slipped on something soft that released a new cloud of stench, and he swallowed against his rising gorge.

"This is it, I think," said Ithric, touching his arm. Favian could just about make out the wall to their left, in the glow of the city's torches and bonfires reflected from the gray clouds above them.

A darker rectangle in the amorphous gray plaster signified a recess in the wall, presumably leading down to the musty underground level where the house slaves slept and labored. If Ithric was right about it being the same house, Kathrael should have come out this way. But would she be alone?

"Kath!" Favian hissed into the darkness, as loudly as he dared. "Kath! It's us!"

He held his breath, but could make out nothing other than the distant bustle of the restless city at night. Ithric, however, drew in an audible breath, his superior hearing having evidently picked something up.

His fingers clenched around Favian's forearm, almost hard enough to bruise. "This way," he breathed, and hared off around the corner, dragging Favian with him. Favian kept pace despite the darkness and the churning of his stomach. The two of them slid to a stop halfway down the length of the alley, breathing hard.

"Little Cat," Ithric said, sounding as if the endearment had been torn from him.

Kathrael sat hunched on the filthy ground, back against the rough plaster wall of the villa. She was curled around a small bundle — the unmistakable shape of a swaddled infant — weeping as if she would die...

Anguish stabbed through Favian's heart like a dagger and he jerked upright in the pitch-blackness, disoriented, clutching at his chest as his lungs tried and failed to draw enough breath.

"Favian?" Frella's sleep-roughened voice cut through the darkness, and a moment later a small, warm presence latched onto his arms, steadying him as dizziness threatened to topple him right out of the narrow bed. "Oh, *Favian*. Not again..."

He covered one of Frella's hands with his, needing to make sure she was real, and tried to breathe. His eyes stared blindly into the space in front of him, unblinking as the images from his dream played across his vision.

Instinctively, he wanted to deny what he knew to be a vision. "It's all right," he croaked, sounding anything but all right even to his own ears. "It's just... just a nightmare. That's all. Nothing to worry about."

"Uh-huh," Frella said, still gripping his arm. It took a moment before he realized that she was not the one shaking; he was. "Stay *right* here," she continued. "I'm going to get Kathrael."

"No, wait—" he began, but she was already out the door. He swung his legs over the side of the mattress and hunched over, elbows on knees, scrubbing at his face with trembling hands.

Shit.

In what seemed like no time at all, a flickering circle of candlelight entered the room, Frella's small frame and Kathrael's taller one behind it. The uncertain light stabbed at

Favian's eyes like the noonday sun, and lit the pair's faces oddly, making their eyes appear sunken.

Kathrael lifted the candle close to Favian so she could examine him, and he raised a hand to block the glare, wincing.

"Favian? Are you going to be sick?" she asked matter-of-factly. "Do you want me to get the Wolf Patron?"

"No, and no," Favian said, forcing his voice into some semblance of normalcy. "Frella shouldn't have woken you. It was just a nightmare. Nothing important. Not every bad dream heralds the end of the world, you know."

Rather than leave, Kathrael set the candle down on the table and lowered herself onto the bed next to him. Her movements seemed stiff, as if her muscles were paining her.

"Glad to hear it," she said in a dry tone.

"With you, we can never be sure," Frella added helpfully.

He narrowed his eyes at his sister, but turned his attention back to Kathrael. "Are *you* all right? You're moving wrong."

She made a noise of rueful amusement. "I feel like I've been trampled by angry cattle. It's not a bad thing, though. I... *danced* yesterday, Favian. Alone, in the woods. It was the first time since this happened." She indicated her scars with a careless gesture. "I'm afraid my spirit had more endurance than my body."

Her smile as she looked up and met his eyes was hesitant, and he had an unpleasant moment of double vision, the image of her weeping disconsolately superimposed over the shy look of happiness. He swallowed.

"Your spirit's endurance has never been in question," he managed.

Frella cleared her throat pointedly. "Would you two like me to leave?"

Kathrael laughed aloud, dispelling the ghostly image of abject grief and letting Favian breathe easier. "No, kitten," she said. "I'm not about to chase you from your room. Much easier to drag your brother back to mine, I think."

"Yes, probably," Frella agreed, and Favian had the distinct feeling that he was being ganged up on. "To be honest, I could use the uninterrupted sleep." Her gaze landed on him, and her delicate features twisted into a frown. "You're sure you're all right, though?"

He called up a suitable level of asperity and frowned right back at her. "Yes. *I'm fine*. Stop fussing."

She glared. "Dolt."

"Brat," he shot back, falling easily into the affectionate exchange of insults.

He was forcibly reminded of how much he must have scared her with his abrupt awakening when she darted forward and kissed his cheek. His arm came around her reflexively. "*Hey*. It's fine. Everything's fine. Go back to sleep, Frella. I'll see you in the morning, yeah?"

"Yeah," she said. "Get out, then, both of you, so I can have some peace and quiet."

Kathrael rose stiffly and picked up the candle. "Goodnight, kitten. Don't worry, I'll look after him."

"I know you will," Frella said.

Favian wasn't sure he appreciated the insinuation that he needed *looking after*, but as Kathrael herded him down the hall and into her borrowed room, he couldn't deny the way his chest eased as he remembered the peaceful nights they'd spent here together, taking comfort in each other's arms. The only thing that was missing was Ithric, but Favian knew that if he went to Carivel's hut now, the two of them would just end up fighting.

Meanwhile, Kathrael's occasional bossy streak was coming to the fore. She chivvied him into bed, blew out the candle, and slipped under the blanket with him. When she was pressed up against his side with her arms tight around him — possibly so that he wouldn't be able to leave — she merely said, "Talk, Favian."

He opened his mouth to protest, but she cut him off. "Not about the dream. Not unless you want to, anyway. I mean the other thing."

He could have pled ignorance, but instead his body deflated, the fight going out of him. "I don't want to leave Draebard," he said, feeling abruptly miserable again. "And I don't understand why you and Ithric *do*."

He felt her chest expand and contract in a deep breath. "Me? Because Rhyth is my home, and it's going to burn to the ground if no one does anything to stop it." She swallowed. "Ithric, though? I'm… honestly not sure."

There was a very long, very deep chasm of silence.

"But," Kathrael blurted eventually, "I think maybe you *should* stay here. You have roots here. Family. And, Favian—

to be a eunuch in Rhyth, outside the protection of the Priests' Guild..."

She didn't have to finish. He knew she was thinking of her lost friend, Vesh, stoned to death in front of her eyes while she was powerless to stop it. Even so, the stab of hurt he felt at her words surprised him.

"And to be a shape-shifter in Rhyth?" he asked bitterly.

There was another pause. "If I knew a way to talk him out of it... I would."

"You could stay here," Favian said on a whisper. "If we both stayed, he wouldn't go without us. He might resent it, but he'd stay here."

Kathrael gathered Favian closer against her body. "I *can't*," she said. "I'm so sorry, Favian, but I can't. I can't spend my days chopping vegetables in the temple kitchen and gathering nuts to sell to the cookhouse while my city tears itself apart and crumbles to the ground."

He buried his head in her shoulder.

"I will try to talk Ithric out of coming, though," she said finally. "He should be here, with you."

Favian's muffled bark of laughter was bitter. "Yeah, right. Good luck with that."

"I'm so sorry," she said again.

He squeezed his eyes shut, hard, and took a deep breath, pulling back to put a bit of space between them. "Stop apologizing. You haven't done anything wrong."

"I've done plenty of things wrong," she shot back. "But you and Ithric shouldn't have to suffer for it."

Exhaustion washed over Favian with no warning, inexorable as the tide. "Look. We're not going to fix this tonight. I'm not even sure it's the kind of thing that we *can* fix. Can we... just sleep? I just need to have you here with me tonight."

You and Ithric, he thought with a pang, but did not add.

"Yes," she said simply, and tightened her arms around him once more.

Despite his extreme fatigue, sleep did not come for Favian again before morning.

SEVEN

When Kathrael awoke alone the following morning, her heart sank. How could things have gone from being so wonderful to being so terrible in the space of a single day? And yet, she knew that it wasn't as simple as that. This had been festering under the surface since back in Woodhaerst, when Ithric had first suggested that going back to Rhyth and trying to change things there was something they should actually *do*.

Favian had asked how three people would even begin to accomplish such a thing. At the time, Kathrael's heart had latched onto the words as proof that they would be together, no matter what. Now, in the thin light of a Draebardi dawn, they sounded a lot more like a protest. A suggestion that three people *could never* do such a thing, and shouldn't even try.

The sad part was, Favian was almost certainly right. The sadder part was, she couldn't let that stop her. Not if she wanted to think of herself as a worthy human being, ever again.

But maybe she could at least keep Ithric and Favian safe.

She banished the echo of Favian's bitter *yeah, right* from the night before, and rose to dress. When she arrived at Carivel's hut, though, it was to find the tiny structure empty. She looked around, and saw that the old dagger and sheath was missing from the peg on the wall. He must have left early to go hunting, and there was no telling how long he'd be gone. She sighed in discontent.

With nothing better to do, she grabbed the musty old burlap sack and headed out to gather more nuts.

⋟~ ☖ ~⋞

The next several days were an exercise in frustration. When she finally cornered Ithric and told him that she'd talked Favian out of traveling to Rhyth, and she thought he should stay behind as well, he just looked down at her with a faint frown and said, "Not likely, Little Cat."

After that, all further attempts at talking to either of them — or, gods forbid, getting them to talk *to each other* — had been met with stony silence or one word answers on Ithric's part, and vague, unhelpful replies on Favian's.

In disgust, she eventually left Ithric to work out his frustrations on Draebard's unlucky game animals, and Favian to bury himself in his duties at the temple. Every day, she went out to the woods and forced aching muscles to stretch, then danced until her worries fell away and all that remained was the controlled, furious movement of her body.

After all, it seemed more and more likely that she would end up on her own in Rhyth, whether Ithric returned there to spy for Andoc or not. And, not to put too fine a point on it, she only had one way to support herself if that ended up being the case. Would men pay for a masked woman to entertain and service them? She hoped she didn't have to find out, but if she did, it was best to be prepared so she could be as *diverting* as possible.

After having her little secluded glade completely to herself for a handful of days running, it was something of a shock to find, when she whirled to a stop and dropped to the ground in exhaustion, that she had an audience of two.

Keenan, the artist's wife, stood in the shade of a bent old tree with Carivel, Draebard's Horse Mistress. Both had bows slung over their shoulders, and carried quivers of arrows. Kathrael's heart skipped a beat in surprise, making her briefly dizzy.

"What are you doing here?" she asked sharply — *stupidly*, as if she somehow had ownership of this particular glade.

"Watching a very talented dancer," Carivel said, in that blunt, northern way of hers.

Keenan seemed to shake herself free of something. "Sorry… Kathrael, wasn't it? We didn't mean to intrude, but we didn't want to say anything and interrupt you, either. We kind of got sucked into watching — you have a real gift, there."

Kathrael would have blushed if her face hadn't already been flushed with exertion. Their words put her oddly off balance. She knew she'd been good at dancing, because it had attracted many of her clients in Rhyth. But no one there *complimented* her on her dancing. Compliment a whore on how well she writhed and contorted her body? Ludicrous.

"I'm rusty," she said, since something about the idea of simply saying *thank you* made her quail. "My muscles are weak. I need to get stronger."

Her shawl lay loosely around her shoulders, where it had fallen as she danced. Hating the sudden surge of self-consciousness, she tugged it up to cover her scars and scrambled to her feet on shaking muscles.

"Well, if *that's* rusty..." Carivel said, and shook her head, breaking the awkward moment. "Anyway, sorry we startled you. We just came out to hunt and gossip for a couple of hours, before Ithric strips this entire area clean of game."

"Oh!" Keenan exclaimed. "That reminds me. I should tell you, Kathrael—Ciero is about finished with the piece he's working on for you. If you want to come by the way-house this evening some time after dusk, it should be ready."

Carivel looked curious, but didn't ask—though Kathrael wondered if she would when she and Keenan were alone. Still, she appreciated Keenan's discretion, and Carivel's delicacy in not asking for details in front of her. Kathrael was going to have to try on the mask and see how it made her feel before she could truly decide whether she wanted to wear it in public.

"All right," she said. "I'll stop by after the evening meal."

"One more thing, before we go," Keenan said after a slight hesitation. "Have you ever thought about learning to fight, or to use a weapon? You mentioned wanting to get stronger, and... well... I couldn't help thinking as I was watching you that you'd be a natural, with all that grace."

Her words stopped Kathrael cold.

"Women... don't fight in the south," she said slowly.

Carivel made a noise halfway between disgust and amusement. "Bull," she said. "Someone attacks you, you struggle and fight back—no matter what you've got between your legs."

"It's just a question of how *effectively* you fight back, if and when the situation arises," Keenan put in.

"And I'm guessing that the situation arises fairly frequently, given what I've heard about the state of Rhyth these days," Carivel finished.

Kathrael narrowed her eyes. "If a mob turns on you, knowing how to punch and kick won't save you," she said bitterly.

Carivel sobered. "Maybe not. But there's something to be said for giving a good accounting of yourself before you go down. Make them remember you as they nurse their bruises and broken bones afterward."

"Gods, you two," Keenan said. "Maybe pregnancy is bringing out my long-buried maternal instincts or something, Kathrael, but this kind of talk is just making me want to take you under my wing even more. Seriously, think about it. If you want me to, I'll teach you how to fight."

Keenan's features sharpened as she spoke, focused and intent. Out of nowhere, memory kicked Kathrael in the chest like an angry mule.

"Stop right there!" shouted a female voice with a heavy, unfamiliar accent. Thirteen-year-old Kathrael gaped in amazement as a barbarian woman galloped up from nowhere and reined her horse to a halt. The woman was dressed in leather and fur, with feathers braided in her hair — wild and beautiful. She nocked an arrow into her bow and steadied her mount with her knees as she trained the weapon on Kathrael's tormenter.

Oh, my gods," she breathed, all the blood draining from her face as she looked up at the half-remembered features. "You were there. That day in the field, with the overseer. *You were there, too.*"

Keenan looked taken aback.

"You remember the slave girl we stopped from being whipped, on the way to the summer meeting in Rhyth, all those years ago?" Carivel asked quietly. "I didn't mention it to you before because I wasn't sure she wanted anyone else to know about it."

The Mereni archer's eyes flew back to Kathrael. The bow slipped from her shoulder to fall on the ground, unheeded. Before Kathrael could drag her tattered composure together to speak — and what would she have said, anyway? — Keenan had crossed the glade to kneel next to her and pull Kathrael into an embrace.

Her arms were strong and her grip was sure. Kathrael was suddenly, unavoidably reminded of her older sister's embrace. Unable to stop herself, she sagged into the support.

"Oh, Kathrael," Keenan murmured. "Oh, my gods. You *made it.* You don't know how many nights you've haunted my dreams—you and the others, from that day." She eased back, still supporting Kathrael's shoulders. "Let me teach you to fight, *chachkaa*. Let me hone all that grace and strength into the means to defend yourself," she urged. "Then maybe I can stop feeling like I let you down, that day."

Kathrael stared into that face from the past—still so wild and strong, still with feathers braided in her dark waves of hair.

"Yes," she said. "I'd like that."

⚜

Perhaps sensing that Kathrael needed space to compose herself, Carivel took Keenan away to hunt, as the two had originally planned, leaving her alone in the quiet glade. Kathrael had sat there on the ground for a very long time, looking at nothing, her mind as still as a calm sea with deep currents roiling beneath the surface.

As the light filtering through the leaves angled lower, ghostly voices roused her. Her sister. Vesh. She'd taken a deep breath and risen, muscles protesting the earlier hard work followed by the long stretch of inaction.

Some time later, she walked up to the door of the way-house, flanked on either side by the silent presences of Favian and Ithric. She'd dragged them both along for this appointment and hadn't taken no for an answer. The three of them might be falling apart, but right now they were all still here together in Draebard, and she wanted them with her for this.

Not to mention the fact that it was actually Ithric who had commissioned the mask. Kathrael might have collected a modest pile of copper coins from selling her gathered nuts to the cookhouse, but she suspected it would not be anywhere close to enough for such an extravagant item. Suddenly, Ithric's single-minded focus on catching and selling his hunted game made considerably more sense, and Kathrael had to fight the lump that rose in her throat when she realized he had been doing it all for *her*.

The evening was just on the cusp of full dark, only a faint glow remaining in the west where the bloated orange sun had disappeared some time before. The way-house door opened to her knock, and Kathrael dipped her head to put her face further in shadow as the proprietor looked down at her.

"We're here to see Ciero," she said. "He is expecting us, I believe."

The old man ran his gaze over the three of them and nodded, stepping back to let them in. "Him an' his woman took the rooms at the back of the hall. I'll leave ye to it, then." He scratched his belly absently and wandered off, presumably back to his own rooms.

Kathrael had been doing fairly well on the journey here, but now, as they walked down the hall to the back of the sprawling structure, her heart started to race.

"Nervous?" Ithric asked, the first word he'd spoken since Favian had joined them.

"Yes," she said. "Though it's a stupid thing to be nervous about."

"It's not, you know," Favian said quietly. They had reached the door at the end of the hall, so he stepped forward to knock.

"It's open," a female voice called from within.

Favian pushed the door open on creaking hinges.

"Hello, Keenan," Kathrael said, trying to keep nervousness out of her voice.

The room was well lit, with far more lamps and candles burning than she was used to seeing. Perhaps extra candles and lamp oil were some of the costs associated with living with an artist, she thought. As they entered, Keenan rose from the chair where she had been stringing an ornate, curved bow, and smiled.

"Hello, *chachkaa*," she said warmly. "I was hoping you'd be able to make it tonight. Ciero is nearly beside himself with nervousness about whether you will like what he's created for you." Her attention settled on the others. "Hello, Favian. Hello, Ithric."

Favian smiled, and Ithric said, "Hi, Keenan," but Kathrael's eyes were only for Ciero as he entered from the other room—an object wrapped in soft linen cradled in his good hand.

"Ah! Here we are," Keenan said in a cheerful tone. As a joking aside, she added, "He's been as broody as a hen with one chick over the thing for *days* now."

Ciero rolled his eyes. "*Yes*, dearest. Broody hen, that's me." He turned his attention to Kathrael, and gave Ithric and Favian a friendly nod before continuing. "I suppose I have been a *bit* preoccupied by the piece. I wanted it to be just right, you understand."

His smile was self-deprecating. Keenan rolled her eyes right back at him and prodded, "Well, don't keep them in suspense!"

"Sorry." With a move that was surprisingly smooth and graceful for a man with one hand, Ciero flipped the cloth away with a flick of his wrist. At first, Kathrael's only impression was of bronze and ochre, glinting gold and orange in the light of the many small flames illuminating the room.

All three of them crowded closer, as Ciero set the mask down on the table so they could get a proper look. Kathrael caught a sharp breath, and Ithric whistled low in admiration. None of them could look away.

If the sun goddess Deresta had decided to take the form of her totem, the mythical firebird, she might have worn a mask such as this. The structural part was composed of thin bronze, cunningly crafted in the shape of the left side of Kathrael's face — but smooth and unblemished. Unscarred.

There was no eyehole. None was needed for her blind, milky left eye. Instead, the bronze was formed to suggest a closed eyelid, and lacquered to represent eyelashes outlined with heavy kohl beneath an arched eyebrow. The edge of the mask was adorned with leather decorations in the shape of small sweeps of curling flame, dyed a deep red ochre color that contrasted perfectly with the bronze.

Finally, a plume of perfect feathers burst from behind the leather flames in such a way that they would frame her left temple, cheek, and the left side of her neck. There, a trail of twisted scar tissue ran down to the top of her breast, where the vitriol had dripped. With the mask and a high-necked dress, however, her scars would be completely covered, hidden from even the closest spectator.

"Ciero," said Favian — the first one to regain his voice, "this is stunning. You've outdone yourself."

The artist smiled, but only said, "Let's see how it fits before we drag out the wine to celebrate, shall we?"

"Try it on, Little Cat," Ithric urged. "Let us see."

Kathrael's heart was pounding even harder than before. A moment of panic seized her, and she looked at the hulking, one-armed man who had fashioned this extraordinary piece of art. "Can I... in private—?" she asked, stumbling over the words.

Ciero nodded. "Of course. I took the liberty of borrowing a bronze mirror for you from our host. It's not large, but it should give you an idea of the overall effect. Do you see how to fasten the mask in place?"

He pointed out the beaded black thong that would run across the right side of her forehead, into her hair, and around the back of her head to fasten behind the feathers on the left side of the mask.

"Yes, I can manage it," she said, her voice sounding odd and breathy to her own ears.

Ciero indicated the back room with the stump of his right arm. "Help yourself. Take as long as you need. We'll wait for you out here."

"Thank you," she whispered, and picked up the mask as gently as if it might shatter.

If anything, the room Ciero had been using as a studio was even better lit than the front room. Kathrael swung the door closed, and looked around for the mirror. She could make out the buzz of low conversation coming from the others, but none of the words. She wondered distantly if they were talking about her, or something else. Her good eye alit on the polished oval of the bronze mirror, propped on a table against the wall. It was somewhat larger than the span of her splayed hand, and as smooth as the surface of a still pond.

She faced it, not flinching from the ruin of her face reflecting back at her, though her stomach clenched unpleasantly. Inch by inch, she lifted the mask until the riot of bronze, flame, and feathers blocked her view of the melted flesh. The cool metal settled into place, conforming perfectly to the contours of her skull.

She didn't realize she'd been holding her breath until her lungs started to burn, and she let the air out in a *whoosh*. Suddenly eager to see the effect without her hand in the way to hold it up, she fumbled for the thong and fastened it with a simple knot, arranging her hair around and over it.

When she lowered her hands and straightened, a powerful, fearless woman stared back at her. The closed eyelid of the mask gave the impression of a wink. The expression looked wise and knowing when she schooled her features into something haughty, and cheeky when she smiled. She would have to wear kohl around the other eye to make them match, she thought, admiring the little stylized curl of black at the outer edge of the lacquered eye.

She continued to gaze at the figure in the mirror—all its weaknesses hidden behind the mask's armor. Unconsciously, her spine straightened, her sternum rising and her shoulders rolling back as her lungs expanded, breathing freer than they had in months. She lifted her chin.

It was time to show the others.

⤙ ⚜ ⤚

Favian kept one eye on the door to the other room as he and Ithric chatted with Keenan and Ciero about gossip from Meren, Keenan's pregnancy, and their journey to Draebard.

When the door swung open, all conversation ceased. Kathrael walked into the room, chin held high, her face half tawny, unblemished flesh, half flame and feathers, and all achingly beautiful. In his peripheral vision, Favian saw Ithric's lips part.

"Kath," Favian began, lost for words.

"You look," Ithric said slowly, "exactly the same as you always have. Only, now you're letting other people see it. How does it feel, Little Cat?"

There was a momentary pause, and Kathrael's natural features softened, the expression changing the look of the mask as much as it changed the look of her face.

"Good," she said. "It feels… good."

A huge grin split Ciero's face. "Then the piece is a success."

"I'd say so," Keenan said in wonder, still looking at the transformed woman across the room. "With the feathers, it's not really practical for fighting—but it would almost be worth it anyway for the intimidation factor. What warrior wouldn't hesitate at being attacked by a demi-goddess?"

Favian tore his fascinated gaze away to look at Keenan. "Fighting? What do you mean?" he asked.

Keenan shrugged, still admiring Kathrael. "Oh, we'd talked about me tutoring Kathrael in self-defense. I've been thinking more about that since we spoke, *chachkaa*. Your blind eye will be a detriment to any ranged weapons—bow and arrow, javelin, that sort of thing. You need good depth perception for those. So, I was thinking perhaps quarterstaff and dagger instead."

At the word *dagger*, a faint flush colored Kathrael's right cheek, and Favian assumed she was remembering their first meeting in Favian's sick room. She recovered immediately, though, and nodded. "That makes sense. I'd... like to start as soon as possible. I don't know how much longer I'll be in Draebard."

Just like that, Favian's stomach sank. Before his eyes, Kathrael was... *armoring* herself. Readying for battle. A battle that he wasn't sure he could bring himself to undertake with her. A battle she had already told him she thought he shouldn't join.

A battle that, if he turned his back on it, would ensure that he lost both her and Ithric—either to death, or unimaginable distance. Suddenly, he felt like an old man, stooped under the weight of a burden he could neither carry nor put down.

Female voices washed over him as the two women discussed when they might meet. In a daze, Favian listened as Ithric spoke to Ciero about payment, and Ciero insisted that he would only accept enough to cover the cost of the materials. Finally, the artist asked for the mask back and showed them how the leather and feather decorations could be removed and reattached, leaving only the metal half-mask to make it less obtrusive for everyday use.

Favian found himself offering words of parting without any conscious thought, and then he was being dragged along in the others' wake as they, too, wished the Mereni couple a good evening and departed.

Kathrael was wearing the metal half mask with her shawl draped over her hair, but no longer pulled forward to cover her face. Her bearing was still the same as it had been when she first appeared in the doorway. Upright. Unafraid. Strong.

Stronger than Favian.

"Ithric. *Thank you* for this," she said earnestly. Her gaze moved from Ithric to Favian and back. "Please, both of you. Stay with me tonight. No fighting. No sex. Just... stay with me."

Favian swallowed. "Maybe you should just stay with Ithric tonight." It was incredibly difficult to force the words out.

But she only shook her head, torchlight glinting on metal. "No. Both of you, or neither. I didn't give myself to one of you, and then the other, Favian. I gave myself to the two of you together."

"It's all right," Ithric said in a quiet voice. "Come to Carivel's hut. I'll shift once we're there. We can spend the night that way. No fighting, I promise."

It wasn't necessarily the fighting that Favian wanted to avoid. But, as was becoming ever clearer, he was weak. He nodded silent agreement, keeping his eyes down. A moment later, Kathrael's small hand settled in the crook of his arm.

When they reached the tumbledown little hut, Ithric was good to his word. After lighting the hearth, he stripped out of his clothing and changed, then quietly slunk onto the straw mattress and sprawled along the wall, stretching lean muscles under sleek fur.

"Kathrael—" Favian began, his voice grown suspiciously hoarse.

She cut him off with a soft fingertip on his lips. "I know, Favian," she said, and lowered the finger in favor of urging him toward the bed. "I *know*. Come, now. Just to sleep."

Unable to fight her, Favian bowed his head and stripped off his outer robes before crawling in next to the lion. Kathrael removed her mask and set it carefully on the low table. When she unfastened her outer layers of clothing and stepped out of them, Favian felt the ache in his chest intensify, and hated himself just a little bit more. Was he really ready to abandon this new place with them that he'd only just found, because he was too cowardly to go to Rhyth and fight for the southern slaves' freedom?

But... how could he leave Frella? How could he leave the temple, so soon after achieving the position in the priesthood he'd wanted for so long?

He was already exhausted after several nights of poor sleep. But even after Kathrael fitted herself against his right side, and Ithric's feline form stretched out against his left, sleep did not find him for a long time.

⤛ 🐚 ⤜

Ithric awoke rather unexpectedly in human form after a nebulous, half-remembered dream of fighting a rival male lion that wanted to steal his mates. It was dark outside—closer to morning than evening, he thought, but not yet time for most sane people to rise.

The hearth had burned down to embers, though his eyes adjusted easily after a few moments. He rolled up on an elbow, needing to see his two bedmates properly. Kathrael was wrapped around Favian, one hand tangled in his linen undershirt as if to ensure he could not slip from her grip as she slept.

She had been magnificent last night—a goddess, as Keenan had so aptly put it. Ithric had known that her scars bothered her on a level that they didn't bother him, but seeing the difference so clearly after she donned the mask for the first time was still startling. He was aware that people were mostly stupid and cruel, but he had to wonder about what she had experienced since her injury to have beaten her down so *much*.

His attention turned to Favian, whose brow was furrowed even in sleep.

Favian. How much easier their lives would have been if the two of them had never met. Why could things never be *simple* between them?

Ithric knew the difficulty of what they had asked of Favian. Perhaps, if he were as close to Alyndra as Favian was to Frella, he wouldn't be so quick to wander from the place where he'd been born and raised. But... no. He still would have left. It just wasn't in him to put down those kinds of roots. If anything, he would have made more of an effort to visit occasionally, or send messages.

If Kathrael was fire, and he was wind, then Favian was earth—tied to one place. Grounded. Ithric continued to stare at the handsome features that drew him like a lodestone, and thought of all the things that might happen to an exotic blonde-haired, blue-eyed eunuch in the south. All the things that might be *done* to him.

His breathing grew shallow and his eyes lost focus as he remembered the horrors he'd seen in Rhyth. When they snapped back to the present, it was to find Favian looking up at him.

"Maybe Kathrael's right," Ithric blurted. "Maybe you should stay in Draebard."

Where it's safe, he didn't add.

EIGHT

If anything, Favian's expression looked almost... hurt, as if Ithric had rejected him somehow. Ithric couldn't help the spark of anger that ignited in his chest. Hadn't Favian been acting as though he *wanted* to stay behind?

"Maybe you and Kath should stay in Draebard, too," Favian said, and Ithric's frustration flared higher.

He glanced over to make sure that Kathrael was still asleep, and forced his voice to stay in a low, hissing whisper. "Oh, yes? And are you going to stop her from going back somehow? Good luck with that." He paused, gratified when Favian couldn't come up with an immediate response. "So, given that she is almost certainly going, would you like me to let her go alone? Back to the most dangerous place on Eburos? *Well?*"

"Of course not," Favian said, his features twisting in a combination of pain and anger.

Ithric squeezed his eyes shut, feeling a headache building behind them. "Sorry," he muttered. "No fighting. I know I promised."

"Ithric?" Kathrael's voice was sleep-roughened. "Favian? What's wrong?"

Favian took a deep breath. "Nothing, Kath. Nothing's wrong. It's just... time for me to get up and leave for the temple, that's all."

"You were fighting again," she said, sounding more awake.

"We fight all the time," Favian said. "Don't worry about it."

He rolled up to a sitting position and climbed awkwardly off the end of the palliasse. Ithric watched as he fumbled in the low light for his robes, keeping his lips pressed together lest anything else come out that might lead to more arguing.

"Favian," Kathrael said, filling the heavy silence. "There's still time to figure things out."

"Sure," Favian said, his tone artificially light. "I'll... uh... I'll see you later."

A few moments later, the door opened and closed on creaking hinges. Kathrael made a soft, unhappy noise into the near-darkness.

Ithric breathed in the scent of the three of them, sensing the slow dissipation of Favian's distinctive aura of sandalwood and cedar smoke after his departure.

"I want to talk to Andoc again," he said eventually. "I should tell him about the idea to pose as entertainers. Will you come with me later this morning?"

"Yes, lion-boy," she said, still sounding sad. "I'll come."

At his invitation, they met Andoc informally for lunch in his hut rather than going to the meeting hall. When they arrived, Carivel was there as well. Ithric was relieved to have the discussion without the endless debate that would no doubt have ensued had other members of the council been present. On the downside, though, both Andoc and Carivel knew him well. Better than most other people he could think of, with the possible exception of Senovo. And, well, Kathrael and Favian, of course.

"Senovo apologizes that he couldn't join us as well," Andoc said, as if he'd somehow read Ithric's earlier thought. "He had some duties this morning that he couldn't put off."

Just as well, Ithric thought, feeling Kathrael shift restlessly beside him.

She was wearing her bronze mask without the flames or feathers attached, but apparently even her newfound confidence was not enough to completely overcome her discomfort at being in the presence of Draebard's High Priest.

"That's all right," Ithric said. "You can fill him in on the details later. This is by way of a proposal, really—nothing that directly impacts Draebard's safety."

Carivel had been looking at Kathrael's mask with thinly veiled interest, but she turned her attention to Ithric. "What sort of proposal?"

It was Kathrael who answered, drawing all of their eyes back to her. She sat straight-backed, not flinching from the attention, and Ithric once again congratulated himself privately for the idea of the mask.

"Ithric pointed out that we would need some sort of story to explain why we are traveling together, as well as a way to interact with many different people in all levels of society," she said. "Since we both have some skills as entertainers, he suggested that we travel as a performing troupe. Dancing, music, juggling, fire-eating—that sort of thing."

Ithric took up the thread. "It would give us access to people and places that we might not otherwise have. However, we would need to outfit ourselves with costumes and props. We'd also need a way to move those items from place to place—preferably in a caravan so it could provide shelter for us on the road as well. But, despite all the venison, boar, and shagbark nuts we've sold to Charyal over the past several days, I'm afraid that sort of thing is well beyond our means."

He raised a wry eyebrow, humor creeping into his tone. "And even if we could get it over the mountains somehow, I'm afraid Favian's death trap of a wagon isn't quite up to the job."

He could have kicked himself a moment later when Carivel cocked her head and looked at him.

"Speaking of Favian," she said slowly, "I would have expected him to be here with you."

"He has duties at the temple," Ithric hedged.

Kathrael gave him a look, though, and turned to address Andoc and Carivel. "He is... understandably reluctant to leave his home and his family. Ithric and I have both suggested that it would be much safer for him—as a eunuch outside of the southern Priests' Guild—if he stayed here."

Carivel frowned. Andoc breathed out slowly through his nose.

"I see," said the chief, after a beat of silence.

That silence stretched, and Ithric let it, well accustomed to playing the waiting game. Both Andoc and Carivel obviously had opinions on the matter of Favian, and were just as obviously reluctant to air them.

Kathrael's background made her less willing to stay quiet while the tension grew, and she asked, "Well? What do you think of the idea?"

Andoc blinked and leaned his forearms against the sturdy table around which they were seated. "I think it's an interesting idea, though it will also place you in the public eye — not necessarily a good position for a spy to be in."

"Not necessarily a bad one, either," Ithric retorted. "The person skulking in the shadows is far more suspicious than the one who's busy entertaining you and making your children laugh."

Andoc huffed a breath that might have been amusement. "True enough. Very well, you two. Ithric, I defer to your superior experience in the spying game. I'm willing to finance you for such a setup, though as you mentioned, you won't be able to get a wagon or caravan over the mountains very easily."

"We should wait to buy the costumes and caravan until we are in the south," Kathrael said immediately. "If we were outfitted in the northern style, it really *would* start to attract the wrong kind of attention."

"As you say," said Andoc. "So, then… money. Traveling supplies. Horses."

Carivel had been quiet for some time, but now a shrewd look came over her face. It made the fine hair on the back of Ithric's neck stand up.

"I worry about sending horses along with you for such a long journey, when neither of you are experienced in caring for them," she said. "You should have someone along who can keep them sound and healthy. Someone who would know what to do if one of them were ill or injured."

She was about as subtle as a punch to the nose, and Ithric gave her a flat, unimpressed look.

"I helped Favian care for Ozias and Audris when we were traveling," Kathrael said, but she couldn't keep uncertainty from bleeding through her voice.

"Not good enough," Carivel said, and now even Andoc raised an eyebrow at her. "If you want any of Draebard's horses, you'll need to take someone along who's qualified to look after them."

Andoc lowered his eyebrow. "It looks like the horse mistress has spoken," he said. "Even if I didn't respect her opinion on such matters, I have to live with her, so I guess that's that."

Ithric let his unimpressed look widen to encompass the chief, while next to him, Kathrael gave the pair across from them a look of consternation.

"We're just trying to protect him," Kathrael said softly.

"Yeah, I know you are," Carivel said unhelpfully. "Let's just wait and see what happens, though. A suitable candidate may yet come forward." She leaned forward and served herself food from the bowl in the center of the table, effectively closing the topic. "So, tell me. Are you and Keenan going to start meeting soon?"

Kathrael hesitated for a bare moment before serving herself and responding. "Yes. She suggested quarterstaff and dagger as weapons."

"Quarterstaff, eh? Hmm... I'd actually be interested in sitting in, if you don't mind..."

Ithric dished out some pork and let the sporadic conversation wash over him as he ate, turning over the situation in his mind. Carivel seemed confident that she knew something he didn't, but for the life of him, he couldn't see what it might be.

⚜

Favian returned to his room in the temple after a long day of work and worry. He'd expected to find Frella there, of course, but it was a surprise to find his friend Limdya there as well.

"You've been a ghost pretty much since you got back," Limdya said without preamble. "Something's obviously wrong. Have you and Ithric been fighting again?"

He flushed under her too-knowing gaze. "Why does everyone assume that if I'm not a babbling font of sweetness and light, it means I've been fighting with Ithric?"

Limdya only crossed her arms, not breaking eye contact, and his cheeks grew redder. Not for the first time, he cursed his pale skin.

"Because it's usually true?" Frella offered in a *why are you so stupid* tone.

"Sit. Spill." Limdya gestured imperiously to the second bed.

Favian firmed his jaw and tried to glare at her, holding out for the space of perhaps six heartbeats before collapsing like a wet washrag and flopping onto the old, familiar straw mattress. He slumped forward, rubbing at his face with his hands.

"I don't know what to do," he said, and dug the heels of his palms into his gritty eye sockets.

A weight settled next to him, a soft shoulder brushing his. "Don't know what to do about what?" Limdya asked.

He took a deep breath and let the words free, unaccountably relieved to start talking. "Kathrael and Ithric. They're going south, back to Rhyth. At first I said I'd go with them, but..."

"But?" his friend prompted.

"Draebard is my home," he said in a rush. "How can I just leave it? And now they're both saying that I *shouldn't* go with them. But... I know I probably should?" He dug the heels of his hands in harder, making red starbursts explode across his vision. "Shit. *Shit.* I *hate* this."

"Why are they saying you shouldn't go with them?" Limdya asked, and Favian thought that if she ever got tired of being the first female horse master's apprentice and decided to become the first female priest instead, she would probably be quite good at it.

He let his hands drop. "Because it's dangerous there."

It was Frella who answered, sounding scandalized. "And so you're going to let them go into danger without you?"

"They think it would be *more* dangerous for me than it will be for them. Because I'm a eunuch, and I'd be outside the protection of the temple." He couldn't help the defensive not that crept into his voice, despite the fact that the person he was defending himself against was a *ten-year-old.*

Limdya asked, "Couldn't you... join the temple there?"

His jaw clenched and his face turned to stone in an instant. "*Never.* I will *never* associate with the bastards who kept Senovo as a slave. I'd die a thousand times first."

"*Good,*" Frella said, sounding as angry as he was. "You'd better not. The southern Priests' Guild is *evil.*"

Limdya's voice was soft, barely more than a whisper. "Sorry. I didn't think."

He shook his head and let out a breath, trying to release the sudden surge of cold rage at the same time. "It's all right. No reason you should have. Anyway, there you have it. They think I shouldn't go, and I know I *should* go, but I can't just pull up roots as if it means nothing, and leave everything and everyone behind. You, included."

He looked sideways at Limdya's sympathetic countenance, but it was Frella who spoke.

"You realize," she said in an uncharacteristically quiet voice, "that I would give my right hand for a chance to have an adventure like the one you're about to turn down."

He frowned. "It's not an *adventure*, Frella. It's *dangerous*. If I went, I might not... come back."

"Ithric would keep you safe," she said with complete certainty. "Kathrael, too, I bet."

His headache was pulsing again, and he dug his fingers into his temples. Limdya gently pulled his hand away and held it in hers.

"They'd try, no doubt," he said. "But wouldn't they be more likely to get *themselves* killed if they were stuck with protecting me? It's safer for everyone if I stay behind."

Frella stared at him. "How do you figure *that*?" she demanded. "Draebard isn't *safe*."

There was a beat of silence. "What do you mean? Of course it is," Favian said, looking at her in confusion.

He felt Limdya's hand tighten unconsciously in his. Frella shook her head, sending honey-colored curls bouncing.

"How can you say that? One of my earliest memories is of sitting against Papa's hip, watching a huge funeral pyre that seemed to take up the entire village green," she said. "I didn't understand it then, but I know now that it was because the Alyrions came during the night and killed everyone they could find. Killed *everyone in the temple*."

Limdya shuddered against him. Her mother had been one of the victims of that attack.

"We won the war against the Alyrions," he said, feeling suddenly as if he needed to reassure them both. "The Empire's soldiers aren't going to come back and attack Draebard again."

But... if Kathrael and Ithric were right, the fall of Rhyth could well bring the Empire back to their doorstep. He swallowed. "And... even if they did, that's all the more reason I should be here, Frella—so I can protect you."

Frella's fists clenched. "You're such an *idiot* sometimes, Favian. If soldiers came here and Carivel, Andoc, and Senovo couldn't protect me—if all the warriors and all the priests and acolytes couldn't protect me—you think that *you* could? You'd just die right along with me."

"Frella..." It broke his heart that his baby sister had to worry about such things. He wondered with a twinge of guilt if she often thought about the possibility of being killed, and he had somehow missed it. Her next words were not fearful, though. They were angry.

"No! Don't you *Frella* me! If you don't want to go with the people you obviously love and try to keep them safe, it's because you're a *coward*! I don't need your protection. I have a family, and you're only one part of it, Favian. But you have *mates* now! What kind of person lets his mates go into danger without him?"

She was so upset that she leapt to her feet and hurried from the room, slamming the door after her. She was probably, he thought, heading straight for Senovo's quarters to pour the whole story out to him. Part of him quailed at that idea, but part of him was unaccountably relieved to finally have things out in the open.

"What a mess," he breathed.

Limdya put an arm around his shoulder and squeezed. "Yeah," she agreed. "Pretty much."

Favian was beginning to think he would never have a full night of sleep again. Scenarios wheeled and circled endlessly in his mind like a flock of restless seabirds. Gods help him; Frella had been right about more than he cared to admit. If he really wanted to protect her, and Limdya, and his guardians, and all the other people he cared about in Draebard, then the best thing he could do was try to keep Rhyth from falling into Alyrion hands.

Of course, that didn't address the added danger he would bring down on Kathrael and Ithric by being a eunuch, with his distinctive plait of straw-colored hair proclaiming his status to all and sundry.

He was still torn when, toward morning, the vision of Kathrael weeping hysterically as she held a bundled infant in the cold rain washed across his vision. He'd been deluding himself this entire time, he finally admitted. The strange warren of stone walls and huge, multistory buildings from his dream could only be Rhyth.

Of course he was bloody well going into danger with the two people he loved. What else could he possibly do? Even if it tore part of his heart out to leave behind the only home he'd ever known.

Now, he just had to convince Ithric and Kathrael of his sincerity, as well as his determination. He fell asleep moments later, the bare bones of a plan following him down into dreams.

⤝ ✦ ⤞

The next day, he begged some time away from the temple during the afternoon. Rona's health was slowly improving as her body recovered from the shock of the lost pregnancy, and there were no important ceremonies or meetings scheduled. Senovo let him go with a nod and a look in his eye that was far too knowing for Favian's taste. He'd given up trying to hide things from Senovo years ago, though, so he took a deep breath on his way out of the temple and let it go.

He headed to the horse pens, still mulling over the details of what he had planned. When he got there, he sought out Dalon instead of Carivel.

"Heya, Pipsqueak," said the older man, who still insisted on using the old nickname even though Favian was a couple of inches taller than him now.

"Hey, Dalon," Favian said. "I need to borrow Ozias and Audris, along with a bit of equipment. And I need… someplace to work where we won't draw attention."

Dalon looked at him with narrowed eyes. "Hmm. That sounds awfully mysterious, Favian. Do I even want to know?"

"Probably not," Favian said, and sighed. "You remember what Varin and Tenebral used to dare the other boys to do, with the two horses and the strap attached to the surcingle?"

He looked surprised. "*Seriously*? I think you and Lundis were the only two that ever took them up on it. And as I recall, Lundis fell off and got a royal chewing out from Jorun."

Even years later, mention of the old Horse Master's name brought an ache to Favian's chest, but he only shrugged. "Yeah. Well. If I get a chewing out from Carivel, it won't exactly be the first time, and it probably won't be the last." He paused. "Though if you could avoid bringing it to her attention just yet, I'd consider it a personal favor."

Dalon's lips turned down, and he crossed his arms. With a sigh, he said, "Bring *what* to her attention?" The irony was heavy in his voice.

"Thanks, Dalon," Favian said.

The other man shrugged. "You're a bit off in the head," he replied. "But you always have been, so what's new? Try to be careful, at least. I want you in one piece for long enough that I can find out what in Deresta's name you're actually up to."

"I'll do my best," he said, and headed off to the tack shed to collect a pair of surcingles and two bridles.

The days that followed fell into a sort of pattern. Favian would get up well before dawn and hurry through his duties. Sometimes he'd find an excuse to go out into the village around midday, in hopes of catching Keenan training Kathrael to use a quarterstaff so he could watch from an inconspicuous vantage point. A couple of times, he was surprised to find Carivel there as well, acting as Kath's sparring partner while Ithric lounged against the base of a tree nearby.

It was obvious, even from the little Favian had seen, that Kathrael was a natural. She turned the mock-fight into a graceful dance, whirling and darting to and fro on feet that barely seemed to touch the ground. The stout length of wood she held was slightly longer than she was tall. It flashed in continuous motion, colliding with her opponent's staff over and over in a flurry of blows, the noise echoing through the clearing where they practiced.

After lunch, Favian would once again hurry through the things that needed his attention at the temple, so he could spend two or three hours at the horse pens before darkness fell. He had worried at first that Carivel would find out what he was doing and put a stop to it. Carivel, however, seemed to be going out of her way not to notice what was going on in the flat pastures west of her horse pens every evening. That probably should have worried Favian, but he couldn't really afford the time or emotional effort wondering about her motives. Instead, he simply decided to shrug it off and count his blessings.

He was, however, utterly appalled to find out just how much his body had changed since he was a slender lad scrambling fearlessly onto any horse he could get permission to ride. Whether it was the relatively sedate nature of the temple life, becoming a eunuch, or a combination of both, he discovered the first time he tried to vault onto Ozias' back from the ground that he was no longer the wiry young apprentice he'd once been.

Things that had once seemed physically easy now took an effort of will, and by the third day his muscles burned and ached with unaccustomed use. He thanked the gods for Ozias and Audris—without horses that he trusted, his plan wouldn't just have been crazy, it would have been downright dangerous.

Well, all right.

In all honesty, it was still a *bit* dangerous. But, thankfully, though his strength and flexibility had deteriorated to a shocking degree over the past few years, his balance was as good as ever. And after a solid week of practice with only a single tumble that left a black and blue mark on his hip and a scrape on his shoulder, he was ready.

⤚ ⚜ ⤙

Ithric sat at one of the tables in the courtyard behind Charyal's cookhouse, eating a rather tense and awkward lunch with Kathrael, Andoc, Carivel, and Senovo. He'd been growing increasingly restless over the past few days, frustrated over the situation with Favian; torn between the desire to just *leave*, so they could finally be doing something, and the desire to drag Favian back to Carivel's old hut and hold him prisoner there until they could figure out some kind of solution to a problem that he knew, in his heart, was essentially unsolvable.

Ithric wanted Favian and Kathrael with him. He also wanted Favian and Kathrael safe. Kathrael wanted the southern slaves free, and she was going to Rhyth to try and make it happen with or without them. Ithric had promised to help her. And, in point of fact, so had Favian.

But he still wanted Favian safe even if he and Kathrael wouldn't be. And so his thoughts continued to circle, worrying endlessly at a problem that simply had no good answer. He knew Kathrael was still making an effort to reach out to Favian—to keep the three of them connected somehow. Favian had spent a couple more nights in Carivel's hut, though he was tight-lipped and did not respond to any of Ithric's thinly veiled barbs. Kathrael had even invited Favian to join them for lunch today, though Ithric was not surprised at his non-appearance.

The stilted, sporadic conversation around the table was interrupted by shouts and exclamations coming from the north edge of the village. He and Andoc stiffened in unison—instincts honed by years of conflict. Senovo frowned, and Carivel stood up abruptly, trying to see what was going on.

But the noise was not the sound of fear or anger. It was excitement. A response to some unexpected spectacle—something with which Ithric had become intimately familiar during his time locked in a cage as part of Turvick's traveling show. He, too, rose from the bench he'd been sitting on, his intuition roused and his curiosity burning. He strained to see, and was rewarded a moment later as two very familiar white horses rounded a corner and trotted onto the village green, side-by-side.

"What in the gods' names?" Andoc said faintly.

Across from him, Kathrael sucked in an audible breath, but Ithric couldn't drag his eyes away to look at either of them. Favian stood on the two horse's backs, one foot planted firmly on the muscled haunches of each, knees bent to absorb the shock of their movement. In his right hand, he held the reins of both animals' bridles, as one might do while driving a chariot or wagon. In the left, he gripped a leather strap attached to a ring at the top of the surcingle fastened around the shorter stallion's belly, presumably for balance.

Rather than his novice's robes, he was wearing a loose, flowing linen shirt, half unlaced at the chest, along with a pair of worn but well-cut buckskin breeches. His feet were encased in tall leather boots designed for riding. His blond hair hung loose, free of its customary plait, curling over his shoulders in golden waves.

NINE

Favian's chiseled features were schooled into a look of fierce concentration, his cheeks flushed from the wind as he guided the pair of white horses across the green in perfect tandem. Kohl lined his eyes—a habit employed by some priests for important ceremonies, Ithric knew—Senovo among them. Ithric had never seen Favian wear it before.

Desire slammed into him so hard and unexpectedly that it took his breath away. He tore his eyes from the picture Favian made with considerable difficulty, to gauge the reactions of his companions around the table. Andoc still looked flabbergasted, obviously having had no idea what Favian was up to these past several days. Senovo looked... not *sad*, exactly, but rather, pale and thoughtful. Worried, perhaps, since he would certainly realize what this meant for the young man he considered a virtual son. By contrast, Carivel was standing nearby with her arms crossed, doing a poor job at hiding her look of glee.

And Kathrael... Kathrael's lips were parted, the same expression of rapt attention on her face as Ithric had felt on his own a moment ago. As he watched, her tongue darted out to moisten her lips, and the need to have them both somewhere private *right the fuck now* rose up and nearly swamped him. Ithric's gaze slid inexorably back to Favian as he pulled the horses to a halt in the space in front of their little group. The taller animal tossed his head and pawed at the ground, letting out a great snort. The shorter one champed at the bit, making the buckles on the bridle jingle.

Favian steadied them and looked down, meeting Ithric's eyes directly.

"I figured you should know that I do have a few skills beyond *blessing the onlookers* and *standing around looking pretty*," he said.

Carivel let out a bark of laughter and immediately slapped a hand across her mouth as if she hadn't intended it to be audible.

"*Favian...*" Kathrael breathed, her voice faint.

"Oh my gods," Ithric said, in a voice made rough by desire. "Get down off those horses *right now*."

Favian continued to gaze at him for a long moment, their past and future stretched between them like an invisible cord. Then his eyes moved to Kathrael and softened, before sliding back to Ithric. Without a word, he deliberately stepped onto Ozias' haunches with both feet, crouched, and slid off to the side—staggering a bit when his boots hit the ground.

"Sorry—still haven't perfected the dismount," he muttered, the words cut off when Ithric stalked forward and grabbed him by the shirtfront, crushing their mouths together.

They were far from alone—in addition to Favian's three guardians, a small crowd had gathered, following the sound of the commotion. Ithric could feel Favian wavering back and forth between worry at the idea of so many people seeing them, and his need to let go and sag into Ithric's touch after the long days of tension and uncertainty.

Small hands tugged at them, and suddenly Kathrael was there, clutching at Favian until he drew her into his arms and held her close.

"You didn't have to," she said into his shirt in a shaky voice. "Favian, you didn't have to do this."

Ithric wrapped his arms around both of them as Favian stroked Kathrael's hair.

"I told you," Favian murmured into the mass of dark silken strands. "I don't think *careful* really suits me any more."

Kathrael made a choked noise that wasn't certain if it wanted to be a laugh or a sob, and Ithric felt a suspicious lump rise in his own throat.

"Senovo," he growled, "we're stealing your novice. We'll return him when we're done with him."

There was some muttering from the little crowd of onlookers as the more sanctimonious among them began to whisper, but Senovo merely replied, "In one piece, Ithric, if you wouldn't mind," in a deceptively mild tone.

"But, I need to—" Favian began.

"*Later*," Ithric said. "Whatever it is, you can do it later."

"Tomorrow, maybe," Kathrael murmured against his chest.

"Carivel," Ithric called, "would you take care of the horses, please?"

"Who am I to refuse the request of a shape-shifter?" Carivel still sounded like she was keeping delighted laughter at bay only with considerable effort.

Ithric was dimly aware of her coming forward and taking the horses' reins from Favian, but only because it freed him to drag Favian and Kathrael toward his borrowed hut, and away from the excited—and mildly scandalized—crowd. Their progress would no doubt have been faster if he and Kathrael had been able to restrain themselves from pushing Favian up against random walls and trees along the way so they could kiss him some more.

For his part, Favian seemed to be in mild shock, melting into the press of lips and cupping their faces as if he couldn't quite believe that he was really there with them.

"I'm sorry," he breathed, with a small *oof* as Ithric pushed him backwards against the rough wood of Carivel's crooked door. "I'm sorry I tried to pull away—"

"Shut up," Ithric growled, pressing full length against him even as Kathrael's hand fumbled beside them for the latch.

A moment later, all three half-fell into the tiny hut, staggering in a tangle toward the straw-tick mattress. Kathrael and Ithric were already tearing at Favian's clothing, getting in each other's way. He gasped sharply when they dragged his breeches over his hips, exposing a livid bruise the size of Ithric's spread hand, obviously several days old and already turning from black to yellow and green.

"You're hurt..." Kathrael said, but Favian cupped her face and pulled her in for another kiss.

"I'm really not," he said against her lips. "I'm guessing you've gotten worse than this recently from sparring with Keenan and Carivel. Are you going to let that stop you?"

"Not a chance," she said, breathless, and started shedding her own clothes in record time.

Ithric wasn't about to be left behind in the race to nudity. After toppling Favian onto the bed and practically ripping off his boots, trousers, and smalls, he shed his own clothing and pounced, pinning their prey in place while Kathrael fumbled free of her skirts and chemise. Lastly, she pulled loose the ties holding her mask in place and set it aside carelessly, revealing her scars to them—naked, now, in all ways.

Ithric was a bit surprised when she wrapped her arms around his neck and kissed him, desperation in the press of her lips and the slide of her tongue. "Take him," she said between kisses, "Take him while I have his mouth… while he touches me—"

Favian made a noise in his throat, and her attention turned to him. "Let us, Favian," she begged. "Let us have you, *please*. I thought we were going to lose each other…"

Ithric still had Favian pinned, but he looked up at Kathrael with luminous blue eyes like the sky before a summer storm. "You're not going to lose me. I'm sorry I made you think you would."

Ithric rolled his hips. "Don't be sorry. Just be *here.*'

"I am. I'm here. Take what you need—make me feel you both." He thrust back against Ithric, though his eunuch's prick was soft.

The rumble rolling through Ithric's chest was wholly beyond his control, as was the hard twitch of his cock at Favian's words.

"You. *Stay*," he ordered with a final warning squeeze of Favian's wrists, and practically lunged for the pot of grease on the crooked shelves in the corner of the room. Ithric was not in a mood to be gentle, but he was definitely in a mood to be *thorough*. Very, *very* thorough, indeed.

Unlike their previous explorations together in bed, it didn't look like Kathrael was of a mind to dally either. Ithric's prick stiffened impossibly further as he watched her sprawl out to plunder Favian's mouth and drag his hand across his body to her sex.

Ithric swallowed a moan and set to work with slick fingers, relishing the noises he dragged from Favian—the moans and gasps wrenched from his throat, only to be swallowed by Kathrael's lips. To Ithric's delight, Favian's limp prick twitched as he added a third finger and slid firmly back and forth over the sensitive place inside. Not growing hard, true—but definitely taking an interest, nonetheless.

Kathrael was rocking her hips against Favian's touch, panting through her nose as she continued to more-or-less fuck his mouth with her lips and tongue. Unable to hold back any longer, Ithric pulled his fingers free and slicked himself up so he could lift Favian's hips and kneel at his entrance. He pressed inside with a single inexorable stroke—tight, slick heat clutching him until he thought he would go mad.

Favian writhed under the onslaught, arching and tearing free of Kathrael's lips to suck air into his lungs. He keened as Ithric slid home, the sound muffled when Kathrael grasped his chin and dragged him back into the kiss. His prick twitched a second time against Ithric's belly, apparently in response to their rough handling of him.

Following a hunch, Ithric fisted Favian's prick in the hand that was still slick with grease. He couldn't stroke the soft flesh the way he could an erect cock, but he grasped Favian and milked him base to tip, over and over, not being particularly gentle about it. Favian made a new noise into the kiss, his heels scrambling for purchase in the bedding and finding none.

The sight and feel of it made Ithric's balls tighten.

"You thought if you became a eunuch, you could always be in control," Ithric said in a rough voice, punctuating every few words with a sharp thrust of his hips. "But you aren't. Not with us. We will make it one of our goals in life to have you feel all the messy, frightening, *amazing* things that come with loving someone. You may not feel lust anymore—" He snapped his hips hard enough to make Favian's entire body jerk. "—but I'll wager that between us, we can still make you lose yourself."

He looked at Kathrael, who was rutting against Favian's fingers with slow, undulating movements of her hips as she continued to hold him in place and plunder his mouth. The smell of feminine desire was a thick perfume that settled in his nose and on the back of his tongue as her release grew near.

"Little Cat?" he whispered. "I want you to help me take our prim and proper priest over the edge."

Kathrael hummed into the kiss and let her hand slide down from Favian's jaw, over his throat and along his collarbone. She trailed fingers over his smooth chest and pinched the pebbled brown nipple she found there.

Hard.

At the same time, Ithric grabbed Favian's bruised hip with his free hand, fitting his fingers into the mark he had acquired for *them*, using the grip as leverage to slam himself into Favian over and over, still milking his soft eunuch's prick with firm pulls.

Favian cried out and nearly arched off the bed, his passage clenching so hard around Ithric's cock that his balls drew up and he spilled in great jerking spurts, burying himself as deep as he could and shaking through the powerful climax.

When his vision cleared, it was to find that Kathrael had finally let Favian up for air and was staring at Ithric with her good eye blown wide and dark, mouth open and panting as she hovered on the edge of her own ecstasy. Ithric stretched forward until he could cup her breast in his hand, rubbing the callused pad of his thumb over her taut nipple while Favian resumed stroking her sex.

Her eyelids fluttered half-closed and she came with a choked cry, throwing her head back and trembling for long moments with the strength of her release. The three of them collapsed in slow motion into the questionable embrace of the lumpy straw palliasse. Ithric took care not to jostle Favian in a way that would cause his softening cock to slip free from the warm passage where it was nestled. He was strangely gratified when Favian threw an arm around his shoulders to hold him in place.

There was a long stretch of utterly relaxed silence before Favian finally said, "Well, *fuck*," in a voice scraped completely raw.

"Language." Ithric's contented murmur was muffled by Favian's collarbone, and he could feel the half-hearted huff that came in response. He lifted his hand to sniff curiously at the drops of clear fluid that had dribbled from Favian's prick onto his fingers. Not spend, he decided, but one of the mix of smells that, together, made up the familiar, bittersweet-metallic odor of a man's release.

Kathrael stirred and chuckled through her nose, as if trying to stifle a round of undignified giggling.

Ithric grinned at her. "Have we done something to amuse you, Little Cat?"

She shook her head and lifted a hand as if to wave the subject off, though the movement was lazy and uncoordinated. "No... sorry," she said. "It's only Vesh. He says he wishes he could have met you two while he was still alive and could take *proper advantage*, as he puts it. I think he's jealous."

Ithric laughed, deep and hearty, only to wince in tandem with Favian as the movement caused his spent, oversensitive prick to slip free.

"I've never been propositioned by someone who's dead before," Favian mused, shifting to get more comfortable. "At least, not that I'm aware of."

Ithric yawned. "Tell him he can watch whenever he wants. The more, the merrier, right?"

Kathrael snorted, still obviously amused. "Oh, gods, don't encourage him, you two."

Ithric felt a grin tugging at his lips and didn't try to fight it. "Fair enough," he said, turning his attention back to Favian. The grin turned smug. "So, it looks like you can still come, after all. How was it?"

"Intense," Favian said, after a moment of thought—running his fingers through Ithric's hair in a way that made him want to tumble straight down into sleep. He paused, and then continued. "A bit strange. Different than it used to be." Another beat of silence, as if he was considering. "Good," he concluded. "Though I'm going to be useless for the rest of the day. If a ravenous bear burst through that door right now, I don't think I could be bothered to run away."

Ithric snorted and reached up to flick him on the forehead. "Just as well, since you don't run away from bears. You play dead. I thought everyone knew that."

"Not all of us can count bears among their personal friends," Favian shot back. His chest expanded and contracted under Ithric's cheek. "I suppose we should probably talk now, shouldn't we."

Ithric roused himself enough to roll off of Favian and lie next to him, across from Kathrael.

"Yes," Kathrael agreed. "We should. I don't want any more uncertainty between us. And I'm still frightened of what might happen to you in Rhyth, Favian."

An idea popped into Ithric's head from out of nowhere, brilliant in its simplicity. He smiled at them both. "I've just had a thought," he said. "You two are lucky that I have all my best ideas after sex."

Favian found the strength to lift his head, giving Ithric an incredulous look that spoke volumes even though he didn't say a word.

Ithric blew out a breath in irritation, and relented. "All right. *Fine.* My best ideas *and* my worst ideas. This is definitely one of the good ones, though."

"What are you thinking?" Kathrael asked.

"Simple. Favian, you're going to shave off all of your hair and let it grow back one length. And we're not going to tell anyone you're a eunuch. Problem solved, as long as no one gets a close look at your privates." He grinned. "After all, if Carivel could manage it for three years, I expect you can, too."

Favian blinked, a series of complex emotions sculling across his face like storm clouds. His hand came up to touch his partially shaven skull as if of its own volition. "I'll... have to think about it," he said, sounding uncertain.

Ithric frowned, not seeing the problem. "It's only hair. You'll be every bit as pretty with it short, I feel sure," he finished in a light tone.

It was Kathrael who answered. "*Ithric.* You're asking him to renounce the priesthood — to all appearances, at any rate. He only became a novice priest a few weeks ago, you know."

Ithric opened his mouth to point out that Favian was hardly going to be touring around the south and balancing on the backs of running horses to entertain the crowds while wearing his priest's robes, but he was interrupted by a flurry of knocks at the door.

"Favian?" Frella's muffled voice filtered in from outside, sounding outraged.

Favian jerked upright like a puppet on strings, the threat of being seen by his little sister, naked and debauched, apparently a much more effective stimulant than the threat of rampaging bears breaking into the hut.

"Just a minute, Frella!" he called, before scrambling inelegantly over Ithric and hissing, "*Clothes!*"

Ithric groaned, but rolled out of bed and fumbled for a shirt and trousers. He tossed Kathrael her skirts and chemise while he was at it, and before long they were decent — though he suspected it would still be plenty obvious what they'd been up to, even to a ten-year-old.

Favian pulled the door open to reveal his sister standing there with her arms crossed, tapping her foot. As soon as he revealed himself, she shoved a finger in his chest, glaring.

"You didn't tell me ahead of time what you were going to do," she accused.

Favian looked surprised — maybe even a little hurt. "Frella, we talked about this —" he began.

"No, not the part about you going to Rhyth!" she interrupted, still stabbing him in the chest. "The part with the horses! I wanted to see it, and I *missed it!*"

Her brother seemed to relax, and Ithric couldn't help but wonder about the conversation they'd apparently had regarding Favian leaving.

"It was brilliant, Frella," Kathrael said. "He had them trotting next to each other like a chariot team, and he was standing with one foot on each of their backs, like you or I might stand on the ground. You simply *must* get him to show you."

Favian grasped Frella's pointing hand in one of his and held it gently. "I'm sorry, sis. I was so nervous I could barely think straight, and it didn't occur to me to tell you what I was going to do. I've been practicing every evening, though, so you can come out and see me tomorrow."

In an abrupt change of mood, Frella leaned into him and wrapped her free arm around his waist. Favian immediately returned the hug, holding her close.

"You're certain you're all right with me leaving?" he asked. The hesitation in his voice was slight—but still noticeable to anyone who knew him.

Frella nodded against his chest. "I'll miss you. But at least this way, *one* of us is getting to have an adventure."

"We'll look after him, little Blue Eyes," Kathrael said. "We promise. Just as he'll look after us."

Frella pulled away and wiped at her face with a forearm. "I know. That's what I tried to tell *him*." She looked at Kathrael, a hint of shyness crossing her features. "I like your new mask, by the way. It's really pretty."

Kathrael smiled. "Thank you. I like it, too. It was all Ithric's idea, though. He paid for it and everything. I don't think it even would have occurred to me on my own."

Frella turned shining eyes to him. "Yeah? He's good like that."

To his surprise, Ithric felt a faint flush rising to his cheeks. He cleared his throat. "Why don't you come get me tomorrow after dinner, Frella? I still owe you knife-throwing lessons, and afterwards we can go watch Favian try not to fall off two horses."

Her face lit up. "Deal," she said. She schooled her features into something more severe and turned back to

Favian. "I'm still mad at you, though. Next time, tell me when you're going to do something exciting."

"Noted," Favian said solemnly.

She peered at him for a few moments, as if she suspected him of teasing her somehow, but then her expression softened. "See that you do. Right, I'm supposed to go over to Keesa's house. Her mother is teaching us how to weave. I should leave or I'll be late."

"Does Senovo or someone else at the temple know where you'll be?" Favian asked.

"*Yes*." She glared at her brother, obviously chafing under the restrictions of childhood. Ithric felt for her, though he also knew better than most people that being completely on one's own at a young age was far worse.

"We'll see you tomorrow, kitten," he said. "In fact, if you see Keenan or Carivel, ask them if you can come watch the quarterstaff lessons Keenan is giving. Maybe you could learn that as well as knife-throwing."

Her mercurial mood brightened again. "I will," she said. "See you tomorrow."

When she was gone, the door closed behind her and her footsteps fading, Favian turned to him. "You're going to turn her into a warrior woman. She'll run away to Meren and join Leader Magoldis if we're not careful."

Ithric raised an eyebrow at him. "If she wants to be a warrior, she should be one. Some of our closest friends are warriors, in case it's escaped your attention."

"I know," Favian said, rubbing at his eyes. "She's my *sister*, that's all. I just want her to be safe."

Kathrael approached Favian from behind and wrapped her arms around his chest. "No one is safe, though. Not ever. Not *really*. If you wish for her safety, then surely you would want her to be able to defend herself?"

He seemed to deflate visibly in her arms. "Yes. Of course I do. I just don't want her to ever *have* to defend herself. You know?"

Ithric sighed. "You've known Frella her whole life. So you know exactly how likely it is that she's going to live a quiet existence in the shadows, never looking for trouble."

Favian frowned at him. "Not helping, Ithric."

"It's the truth," he said, unrepentant. "Look—I can practically hear your thoughts running circles like a rat in a cage. We promised we'd return you to Senovo when we were done with you. I think maybe you need to talk to him about a lot of things. Maybe... you should go and do that now."

Favian was still frowning, looking more like Ithric was asking him to go to the executioner's block than to go and pour his heart out to his beloved mentor. "Yeah, I guess," he said.

"You'll come back tonight, though?" Kathrael asked, and Ithric really, really hated that she still had to worry about the answer.

"Of course I will," Favian said, but he still sounded defeated. Unhappy.

For an hour or so, everything had seemed so simple, Ithric thought. It wasn't, though. It wasn't even *close* to simple.

⤞ ⚜ ⤝

Favian stood a short way down the hall from the quiet room in the temple where Rona was still recovering. Both Eiridan and Senovo were inside, speaking softly with her and Nimbral. He took a deep breath and let it out, trying to gird himself for the coming conversation.

It seemed an interminable time before the door opened and the two priests emerged, Eiridan closing it gently behind them. Both men paused when they noticed him, and Favian swallowed.

"High Priest, I really need to talk to you," he said before he could lose his nerve.

Eiridan looked between them and tipped his chin in a small gesture of respect toward Senovo. "Elder Brother, I will leave you two to speak privately. Good afternoon, Favian."

Favian became suddenly, viscerally aware that he had come to the temple still dressed in his loose shirt and breeches, too preoccupied to even think of changing back into his robes before seeking out Senovo. His face heated, and he looked at the floor, overcome by a wave of shame.

"Thank you, Brother Eiridan," he whispered, unable to meet the kind priest's eyes.

Once Eiridan had gone, his worn sandals scraping rhythmically against the flagstones, Favian closed his eyes. He flinched in surprise when, a moment later, a hand closed on his shoulder and squeezed. Senovo's approach had been completely silent.

"Come with me," said his mentor. "My quarters, I think."

Favian balked. "Will the others be there?" The thought of having this conversation with an audience—even one as dear to him as Andoc and Carivel—was unbearable.

"No, Favian," Senovo said. "They both have other tasks to occupy them for some time yet. We will have privacy for you to say whatever you need to say to me."

There was an echo of sadness beneath the words, and it stabbed at Favian's heart. He could only nod, and let Senovo lead him through the familiar corridors that he'd walked so many times over the years. The hand on his shoulder remained, grounding him until they arrived in the large suite of rooms. Inside, Senovo urged him into a comfortable chair.

A cup of wine appeared before him, and Senovo said, "Drink. Then speak."

Favian drank, the strong wine burning on the way down. He set the cup aside deliberately and laced his fingers together, looking at them rather than the man across the table from him.

"You're disappointed in me," Favian said, forcing the words out.

Senovo reached across the table to cover Favian's tightly clasped hands with one of his.

"I am afraid for you, which is a very different thing," he said.

Favian looked up, finally meeting his guardian's striking green-gold eyes. "If... Carivel and Andoc got it into their heads to go off somewhere far away where they would be in constant danger—would you follow them?"

"Of course," Senovo said without hesitation. He quirked an eyebrow. "Though I would hope that such a thing would be a bit more of a mutual decision than the situation you describe."

Favian felt his hands clench tighter, the knuckles straining. "It *was* a mutual decision," he said, aware that they were no longer discussing this as something hypothetical. "But then we got back to Draebard and I realized what going to Rhyth would *actually mean*. Leaving Frella. Leaving... the temple..." His throat closed up and he had to swallow several times.

Senovo was quiet for a moment, and let his hand slide away from Favian's.

"Frella does not wish for you to be tied to her for your entire lives, Favian," he said. "And the temple is not a prison. Nor is it, as you seem to believe, a building. You need not leave it merely by going to a new place."

Favian tried to clear his throat. "I thought, at first, that I could continue to be a priest," he said, his voice rough. "But I refuse to associate myself with the southern Priests' Guild. Not after what they did to you. Not after what they did to Kathrael's friend Vesh. They are *not* the gods' servants, and I will *not* pretend otherwise. It's dangerous to be a eunuch outside of the Priests' Guild in Rhyth, though, and now…"

He trailed off.

"Now?" Senovo prompted.

Favian tried to take a deep breath, but there didn't seem to be enough air in the room. "Ithric wants me to cut off my hair and pass for an uncastrated man, so we'll be safer."

Senovo blinked, looking thoughtful. "That seems like a reasonable plan."

Taken by surprise, Favian could only stare at him. "Are you… saying that as my High Priest, or as my guardian?"

"I am saying it as your Elder Brother who wishes you to remain safe and whole," Senovo replied.

"But, Senovo, he's asking me to *renounce the temple*," Favian said, trying to make Senovo understand.

Senovo shook his head, his brows drawing together. "You just told me that he was asking you to cut your hair and keep quiet about the status of your fertility."

"It's the same difference, surely," Favian argued.

"Little Brother," Senovo said, "a plait of hair does not make someone a priest—as anyone from a temple that has suffered an outbreak of lice will certainly tell you."

Favian opened his mouth to say that it wasn't the same thing, but Senovo raised a hand to cut him off and continued, "nor can someone act as a priest, ever again, *if they are dead*. If a ruse is what is necessary for you to stay alive and relatively safe, then a ruse is what you should employ. There is a time for grand gestures, and a time for doing whatever is necessary to survive. I think that perhaps both of your lovers have some degree of experience with those sorts of choices."

That shut him up rather effectively.

"I thought you'd be upset," he said eventually.

Now it was Senovo's turn to study his hands. "I wish only a long and happy life for you, Favian. But I also know what it is to be bonded to people who place ideals ahead of their own safety, and who fear things other than death." He paused. "In addition, I am acutely aware that if I had fulfilled the destiny which has allegedly been set out before me, you would not be facing this situation now."

The breath caught in Favian's chest, and his eyes flew to his mentor's face. "Oh, gods, Senovo—*no*. Just because Kathrael thinks you're this *Wolf Patron*, doesn't make it true. How is one shape-shifter supposed to stroll in and change an entire society? This is *not* your fault."

Senovo's face was pale. "Perhaps not. Such prophecies are a heavy weight, nonetheless. Particularly when the people we love become embroiled in them against all odds."

Favian frowned as he remembered something else. "Speaking of prophecies—"

Real alarm flashed across Senovo's features.

"No," Favian said quickly, "it's nothing like that. It's... small. A tiny thing, but I don't know what to do about it, or even if I should try to do anything at all."

"Tell me," Senovo said, still looking worried despite Favian's assurances.

Favian shifted in the nest of furs padding the heavy chair where he was seated.

"In my dream, I'm with Ithric, in a place I don't recognize. The buildings are huge. Close together, with narrow, dirty alleys running between them. We've just left one such building, and we're trying to find Kathrael. But we have to be stealthy about it for some reason. We circle around to the next street and retrace our path to the alley behind the house we just left."

"Do you find her?" Senovo asked, his voice tight.

He nodded. "Yes. It's starting to rain when we see her crouched against a wall, holding a swaddled infant to her chest. I can't tell if the baby is dead or alive, but Kathrael is weeping. That's all. That's when I woke up."

Senovo took a slow breath. "You realize that the place you describe is almost certainly Rhyth."

Favian nodded reluctantly. "I'd gathered." His jaw worked for a moment. "I haven't told the others. And I don't know if I should."

"Can you foresee any benefit in doing so?" Senovo asked.

Favian shook his head. "None. I don't see any point within the vision where I could influence events. Whatever happened had already happened before Ithric and I arrived."

"Then telling them or not is a personal choice, Little Brother."

He nodded, knowing it to be true. Knowing, as well, the pain it would cause Kathrael. "Kath has already lost one baby, Senovo. I think it would just be cruel to tell her that she might somehow lose another at some unknown future time."

"You're probably right." Senovo rose from his chair, and Favian followed suit. "I think it's clear, Little Brother," he continued, "that no matter the length of your hair or the style of your clothing, the gods have a use in mind for you. I ask only that you try not to take any unnecessary risks as you join in your loved ones' quest."

"I'll try not to," he promised. "And I'll send messages as I'm able. Ithric will be in regular contact with Andoc, I imagine, so it shouldn't be difficult to add in short personal messages with his reports."

"Then I wish you the best of fortune," Senovo said, and moved slowly around the table. His hands closed on Favian's shoulders, and Favian stepped willingly into the offered embrace. "May the gods smile on your endeavors."

When he had been younger, there had been a number of times in his life when Senovo's arms had felt like the only haven that could keep him from descending into complete madness, shattering like a clay cup dropped on a stone floor. He was a man now, as well as a priest—someone tasked with providing comfort rather than seeking it—but it was still all too easy to let himself sag against that slender, familiar strength, if only for a moment. Senovo's hand came up to rest on the back of his head.

"You are loved, Favian of Draebard," his mentor said softly. "Whatever roads you travel in life, whatever choices you make—know that to be true, always."

Favian's throat closed completely, and he could only nod. When Senovo released him, he ducked his head and hurried from the room, blinking furiously against the burning behind his eyes.

TEN

Kathrael sat propped against a wooden post, polishing the fine dagger Keenan had gifted her after she had shown the Mereni warrior her sad little ceremonial knife. She was here to watch Favian practicing with the two creamy white horses and, as he had put it, *scrape him up off the ground if he went splat.*

After returning to them after his talk with Senovo several nights ago—red-eyed and fragile, with his long blond hair shaven off—Favian had seemed somewhat more at peace. Which was not to say that he shared Ithric's growing excitement at their upcoming departure, or even her own sense of focus and determination. And she understood that. She *respected* it. How much harder was it to commit to something for someone *else's* sake, rather than because you genuinely wanted to do it?

She was truly thankful for Ithric's suggestion about cutting Favian's hair, though. As she watched him trotting around the flat stretch of pasture, guiding the two horses in broad arcs and circles while he balanced atop them, she thought he could still easily pass for an uncastrated man. Honestly, in the south it was likely to be his pale hair and eyes that attracted people's attention, more than anything else about him.

Kathrael held her breath as Favian urged the horses into a rolling canter and pointed them at a fallen log lying at the edge of the area where he was practicing. He'd mentioned that he intended to try jumping them over an obstacle today if they seemed to be doing well. It had sounded dangerous to her, but when it came to horses, Favian was the expert, so she'd only nodded and made a noncommittal noise.

The horses jumped the low barrier slightly out of sync, and Favian lost his footing on Ozias' haunches. Kathrael gasped as he twisted and half-fell onto Audris' back, landing off-center and grabbing for the stallion's thick mane. Ozias spooked sideways at the commotion and ran off, reins dragging, while Audris skittered forward a couple of steps in response to the heavy weight landing on his back. The stallion bounced to an abrupt halt even as Favian dragged himself into a better position, narrowly avoiding a nasty fall.

Kathrael let her breath out and tried to calm her racing heart as Favian gathered up the horse's reins and steadied him.

"Could you grab Ozias for me before he steps on those loose reins?" he called, sounding far less affected by the near miss than Kathrael would have expected.

She swallowed her misgivings and stowed the dagger in its sheath before rising to cross to the loose horse. Ozias snorted loudly as she approached, but allowed her to catch him and lead him back to his brother. The two horses sniffed noses as if to reassure themselves that all was well.

"Are you all right?" Kathrael asked Favian, for much the same reason.

He only smiled. "Oh, yeah. No harm done. In fact, I suspect that would have been a lot more painful if I still had balls."

Kathrael laughed, the tension popping like a bubble. "*Lucky you.* Maybe skip the jumping part from now on?"

Favian shrugged. "Eh, I think I see what went wrong. I'm pretty sure we can get it this time. I'll just work them on the flat for a few minutes first to get everyone calmed down."

She stared up at him. "I feel like I should point out that I didn't *actually* bring a shovel along for scraping-up purposes."

He smiled at her. "Not to worry, Kath. I'll endeavor not to need one today."

With a shake of her head, she helped him reposition the two horses so he could clamber upright on their backs once more. "I'm holding you to that. Next time, Ithric can come and babysit you for this. I'm not sure my nerves can take it."

"I don't think you're allowed to be more worried about it than I am," he called over his shoulder as he trotted off.

"Watch me!" she called back, and returned to her seat by the post.

A short time later, footsteps approached from the direction of the village. Kathrael craned around to see who it was. She scrambled to her feet upon seeing the village chieftain approaching with Ithric at his side. Andoc leaned heavily on his walking stick as they approached.

He waved her to sit down again, but she ignored the gesture. For some reason, she was almost as ill at ease in his presence as she was in the Wolf Patron's, despite the fact that Andoc had been nothing but polite to her since Senovo had extended her the sanctuary of his temple.

While they were still a few steps away, both men's attention moved past her to where Favian was working. Andoc's face drew into an expression of shock. "Good grief," he began, "he's not really going to—"

Kathrael whirled, just in time to see Favian smoothly jump the horses over the thick log, the pair moving as one and barely appearing to jostle him on his precarious perch.

"Apparently he is," Ithric said, sounding suitably impressed.

Kathrael let out a breath. "You both missed the exciting part a few minutes ago," she said dryly.

"I'm not at all certain I want to know," Andoc said. "In fact, I'm pretty sure I *don't.*"

Favian saw them as he wheeled the horses around, and they trotted over. "Ah—my first audience. Just as well I didn't know you were here. I probably would have ended up face first in the dirt. Did you need me for something, Andoc?"

Andoc huffed a breath of laughter through his nose. "Well, first off, I'd tell you to be careful, except even *I* can see what a terrible hypocrite that would make me. I have to say, Favian, the people who come to see you aren't going to know what hit them. That was really quite amazing."

Favian blushed beet red. "Yeah... I'm trying very hard not to think about the part where crowds will be watching," he said, "but thanks."

Andoc smiled at him, a fond expression. Also a proud one, if Kathrael was any judge.

"Actually, I came to talk to you about horses," the chieftain said. "I'm giving you Ozias and Audris, of course, but you'll need at least two more animals for riding and hauling supplies over the mountains."

Favian's jaw fell open, and he dropped down to sit on Ozias' back as if his knees suddenly wouldn't hold him— thankfully a somewhat more controlled move than the one earlier.

"You're… *giving* me…" he began, only to trail off. His hand darted forward to bury itself in the thick mane in front of him.

Andoc had sobered as he spoke earlier, but now one side of his mouth quirked up in a half-smile. "*Favian*. You don't have to look *quite* so shocked, you know. You're my heir. And it's not as if I'm lacking for horses. I am handfasted to Draebard's Horse Mistress, in case it escaped your attention. Every time I turn my back for a few minutes, when I turn around again, we've acquired another horse somehow."

"Andoc," Favian said quietly, "these stallions are worth a small fortune."

"So guard them carefully, in that case," Andoc said. "And tell me which other ones you want."

"Can you spare any black ones that look similar to each other?" Ithric asked. "A matched pair, like these two?"

"Are you thinking of something specific for the show?" Kathrael asked, intrigued.

Ithric smiled. "I am. In fact, I was thinking about the story of Ozias' and Audris' namesakes."

Favian made a noise of interest, but Kathrael frowned in confusion. "I didn't realize they were named after anyone specific. I'd not heard the names before."

"Really?" Favian asked. "They don't tell the story of Ozias and Audris in the south?"

"No," she said, bewildered. "Not that I've ever heard, at least."

"It's true that I never heard them referenced when I was in Rhyth," Ithric mused. "I think it's past time the Rhytheeri were introduced to the legend, in that case."

"I look forward to hearing it," Kathrael said, intrigued.

"It's a good story," said Andoc. "And to answer your question, yes, there are several black horses that look similar to each other in the herd."

Favian was still sitting on Ozias, looking thoughtful. "Geldings would probably be best. These two stallions get along fine, and they're used to working around mares. But having mares around all the time would be difficult to manage—they'd have to be kept separate whenever they came into heat. And adding more stallions to the mix could also complicate things." He tapped his chin with one finger, obviously running through the available animals. "What about Bysh and Fidget? Could we take them?"

Andoc shrugged. "I'm afraid I have no idea which ones those are. It's fine by me, but check with Carivel to be sure."

Ithric gestured to the white horses. "Would those geldings be suitable for this kind of trick-riding, as well?"

Favian threw his leg over Ozias and jumped lightly to the ground. "I don't see why not. They're trained as a chariot team and they've even been battle-tested, so crowds and noise shouldn't bother them too much. If Carivel is all right with us taking them, I'll start working with them right away."

Ozias nudged Favian's hip, and he absently fed both stallions tidbits of apple from one of his pockets. Kathrael crossed to the pale animals and ran her hand over Audris' forehead, scratching under the browband of the bridle—drawn to the beautiful horses as strongly as she had been the first day Favian took her to the pens to see them.

"I'll help you put them away," she said.

Favian nodded. "Thanks. And thank *you*, Andoc. Really. It's incredibly generous of you."

"You're *family*, Favian," the older man said. "But completely aside from that, I learned early on that the expense involved in gathering intelligence about the enemy pales in comparison to the cost of fighting a war. I'm happy to do as much of I can of the former in hopes of avoiding the latter—if it's at all possible."

His eyes moved from one to the other of them, meeting each of their gazes in turn. "And while I hate the thought of any of you being in danger because of it, I deeply appreciate having people I trust doing the job, rather than mercenaries."

Kathrael looked at the Draebardi chieftain—so different in person than the legend of the Great Destroyer that had grown around him in the south. "Rhyth is my home," she told him, "but what is good for Rhyth right now is also good for the north."

"Freedom and self-determination is the birthright of all Eburosi," Andoc agreed. "I cannot go to war against the south, but beyond that, I'll support that ideal in whatever way I can."

She lifted her chin, accepting the statement.

Ithric's eyes crinkled, his satisfaction obvious. "When you two are done with the horses," he said, "I'd like to go talk to Rona and the others. They've all expressed the desire to return to the south, and we need to decide if we're going to travel together."

Favian handed Audris' reins to Kathrael. "We'll meet you at the temple shortly, in that case." He looked again to Andoc. "Thank you again, Andoc. I'll talk to Carivel about the geldings and see what she says."

⤙ ⚜ ⤚

Kathrael had not seen Rona for several days. It had seemed insensitive for her, as a relative stranger, to intrude on the woman's privacy at such a difficult time. And, of course, Kathrael had her own grief to deal with that related to a lost child. The fact that the child's spirit still hovered near her day and night made that loss harder in some ways, and easier in others. Regardless, it was not a subject she looked forward to discussing with Rona or Nimbral while they were still in the depths of mourning, for obvious reasons.

Now, though, it seemed unlikely that she would be called on to do more than offer a brief expression of sympathy, with both Ithric and Favian accompanying her. And the five of them, along with Arnav, really did need to discuss their plans. Kathrael had come up with an idea the previous day, and she wanted to put it forward.

Ithric was waiting for them in the courtyard outside the temple, lounging against the low stone wall that bordered it. He lifted a hand in greeting as they approached.

The three of them were somber as they entered and made their way through the halls to the wing where the three refugees from Turvick's show were staying. Kathrael had spent a few hours with Arnav since they'd arrived back in Draebard, and found him to be entertaining company, if occasionally prone to moments of bitterness or sullen anger, particularly when his past came up in conversation.

Despite having traveled with them from Woodhaerst, though, she had considerably less of a connection with Rona and Nimbral. It was clear, however, that Ithric counted them friends.

The door to Rona's room was open, but Ithric knocked anyway to get the occupants' attention. Rona, Arnav, and Nimbral all looked up. Rona looked terrible, her skin gray, with dark circles under her eyes, but she brightened noticeably upon seeing who was at her door.

"Ithric!" she cried, struggling into a sitting position on the bed.

"Rona," Ithric said, with a depth of feeling that took Kathrael by surprise. "The healer said you were finally able to have visitors. How are you?"

She shrugged a shoulder, and Kathrael could see grief and guilt chase each other across her features. "I'm alive," she said.

Ithric nodded, his brows drawn together in sadness. He crossed the short distance to the bed, and Rona held out an arm to him. Without hesitation, he perched next to her on the mattress and eased her into a hug. She let out a little sob and pressed her face into his shoulder.

"Rona. Nimbral," he said solemnly. "I'm so sorry I couldn't get you to help sooner. I misjudged things with Turvick, and you two paid the price far more than the rest of us."

"It wouldn't have made a difference, Ithric," Nimbral rumbled from his chair next to the bed. "There was nothing to be done."

Ithric let Rona go with a final rub of her back, and rose. "Even so."

"Turvick was an evil bastard," Nimbral said. "You and your friends made him pay for what he did to us. Him and his lapdog, Laronzo. We're free of them now."

He reached out to grasp Ithric's shoulder, and the pair of men shared a brief embrace as well. Though Nimbral was seated and Ithric was standing, the two were nearly of a height.

"Yes," Favian said. "You are free. And it's probably time that we talked about the future. Rona? Are you feeling up to it?"

Rona nodded. "I think so, Brother Favian. Really, though, I just want to be wherever Nimbral is."

Nimbral reached across to cover her hand with his large one. "And I just want to be with you. But winters in the north are hard, and their ways here are strange. I could probably find work keeping the accounts for a trader in one of the large towns down south, but I asked around here and there's not even a call for such things in Draebard."

Arnav shifted in his chair in the corner. "I have no intention of staying here. I want to go home to Rhyth."

Ithric let his gaze move over Favian and Kathrael before returning to his fellow captives. "The three of us will be leaving for Rhyth soon, as well. We haven't talked yet about when, or what route we'll be taking, though."

"With four horses," Favian said, "trying to go by sea would be a nightmare. It would cost a small fortune to transport them by ship, and many horses don't survive that sort of journey in a ship's hold."

"We need to travel overland, in that case," Kathrael said quickly, unwilling to risk Ozias' or Audris' safety.

Ithric nodded. "Right. Well, it looks like we'll be going over the western pass through the mountains, then," he said, and Kathrael couldn't help a shiver at the memory of her earlier travels along the desolate trail through the southern range.

"Rona is too weak for that kind of journey," said Nimbral.

The small woman looked embarrassed. "I'm too weak for *any* kind of journey right now, I'm afraid."

"Nimbral's right, though," Arnav offered. "It might not be good for horses, but traveling by ship is a much easier way for people to get south, Rona. When you've recovered a bit more, it won't be so bad."

Favian thought for a moment. "Draebard has strong ties with the port of Llanmeer ever since the war," he said. "Much more so than with the western ports. There will be several groups traveling back and forth from here to Llanmeer over the course of the autumn. I can arrange for the three of you to travel with one of them if you all agreed that's what you want to do."

Kathrael spoke up, wanting to share her idea. "Llanmeer is in the east, Favian?" she asked, and he nodded. She looked to Ithric. "How far is Darveen from the eastern coast?"

It was Arnav who answered. "The town where Turvick kidnapped the children, you mean? Not far. Maybe two days' walk, or one by wagon. Why?"

Kathrael turned her attention to him. "The twins' parents told me when I left that I would always have friends in Darveen. I'm certain that would extend to all of you, as well. If you went there and explained that you were friends of mine and had also been held by Turvick, you could stay with Shayla and Melko until you found work and got on your feet."

"You don't think they'd mind?" Rona asked timidly.

"They were some of the kindest and most generous people I've ever met," Kathrael said. "Not only that, but the village knows about the twins' gifts, and is obviously very accepting of people who are... unusual. Much more so than Rhyth is, these days."

Ithric looked speculative. "That could work very well. What do you think?"

Nimbral was nodding his head slowly, his expression thoughtful. "I like that idea. Rona?"

"It does sound like a good plan," she agreed. "And it would make me happy to see those poor children again, safe and sound with their family."

Kathrael wasn't quite sure how Arnav was able to convey the impression of stubbornly crossing his arms when he *had* no arms, but he managed it somehow. "I'm still going home to Rhyth," he said. "I'll stop in Darveen first to see the twins and make sure you get settled, though."

Ithric frowned. "Don't take this the wrong way, Arnav, but what are you planning on living on, during the journey? I expect we can rustle up enough money for your passage south from donations to the temple and maybe a bit of additional help from Andoc, but after that, you'll be on your own."

Arnav snorted. "Please, Ithric. I don't need a middle man like Turvick to get money from rubes who think it's entertaining to watch me eat and drink with no hands." His smile turned sly. "Besides, if worse comes to worst, there's usually someone willing to bet on a game of dice."

ELEVEN

The following days were a whirlwind of activity and preparations. It was barely a week later that Kathrael stood with Ithric and Favian on the village green, holding the horses Andoc had gifted them, surrounded by a crowd of well wishers. Ithric was practically vibrating with energy, and Kathrael was torn between excitement and dread at the prospect of seeing Rhyth again, unsure what they would find upon their arrival in the city she had called home for so long.

Favian, by contrast, was pale and somber. He had spent the days since he rode up to them at the cookhouse on Ozias and Audris working from early in the morning until late at night—practicing with the two teams of horses; organizing assistance for Rona, Nimbral, and Arnav to book passage on a ship out of Llanmeer; collaborating with Kathrael and Ithric on ideas for their show and attending to duties in the temple until he was near collapse with exhaustion, before falling into bed with them and sleeping restlessly in their arms for a few hours.

Kathrael was worried about him, but Ithric urged her to let him be. She compromised by watching him like a hawk—searching for any sign that he was about to change his mind, but finding none. Meanwhile, Favian's close-shorn hair began to gradually grow out, covering his skull with a short pelt of gold fuzz that accentuated his fine, chiseled features. He mostly wore trousers and tunics—more practical for working with the horses—but on the day before they were to leave, Kathrael had found a set of dun priest's robes bundled up and stuffed in the bottom of one of their travel packs.

Perhaps it was irrational for her to feel so guilty about the situation. Favian was a grown man, after all, and his decisions were his own. Nonetheless, she still felt awful that they had ripped up his roots when his heart so obviously lay with the priesthood, and with Draebard. Well… not *they*. That wasn't fair. *She* had ripped up his roots. If only she had been content to stay here in Draebard—in this safe, welcoming place with the two men she loved.

If she had not opened her mouth that night in Woodhaerst and talked about her vow to free the southern slaves, she thought Ithric would have been willing to stay with them both, here in Favian's home village. He might have been restless, yes, but he would have stayed.

She knew that guilt would have eaten her from the inside out if she'd abandoned her homeland, though. Was guilt on behalf of thousands of slaves a worse burden than guilt on behalf of a single person? Did it inherently hold more weight? Kathrael wasn't sure, and now it was too late to change her mind, even if she'd wanted to.

They were leaving.

It seemed to her that most of the village had turned out to say goodbye to Favian, and in many cases, to Ithric. She'd been startled to discover that a few were here for her, as well—Keenan and Ciero, Limdya, Brothers Eiridan and Feldes. Indeed, Brother Feldes became a bit misty-eyed while wishing her a safe journey. Eiridan, on the other hand, asked her with considerable enthusiasm to send him any examples of Rhytheeri writing that she might come across.

They were finally getting down to the last few people—those closest to Favian. His guardians. His sister. His fellow acolytes and novices from the temple. Kathrael felt a lump growing in her throat, and faded back to stand a few steps away with Ithric.

Carivel came forward to pull Favian into a hug. "I always knew you were destined for great things, you know," she said. "Be safe. Be together. Take care of those horses, and they'll take care of you."

"I will," Favian said. "Thank you, Carivel. For everything. Look after the others."

Carivel nodded and pulled back, her smile quivering a bit at the edges. Andoc immediately stepped forward to replace her. "I expect regular contact from you, you know. I'd tell you not to do anything foolish, but Senovo would just give me *that look*. You know the one. So instead, I'll tell you not to do anything *unnecessarily* foolish. Fair enough?"

Favian patted Andoc's back and smiled as they separated. "Fair enough. We'll send a message as soon as we get settled and can find a reliable courier. Try not to worry, Andoc. We'll be fine."

Favian turned to High Priest Senovo, and Kathrael could see the new lines that had etched themselves onto the Wolf

Patron's features in the days since Favian made his decision to leave with them. Rather than embrace his protégé, Senovo placed a hand on his head in a traditional blessing.

"May the gods smile on your endeavors, and bless you and yours, Favian," he said. "Child of my spirit, if not my flesh."

Favian's eyes squeezed closed, his handsome features twisting in pain for a moment before he regained control of his expression and it smoothed out. When Senovo let his hand slip away, Favian grasped it and pressed a kiss to his knuckles.

"If we succeed," he said, in a voice hoarse with feeling, "no one else in the south will suffer as you did, ever again… father of my spirit."

Kathrael saw the hitch in Senovo's chest as his breath caught. The bob of his throat as he swallowed.

"Regardless of whether I'm able to return here," Favian continued, "a part of my spirit will reside with you in Draebard's temple, always." His eyes took in the other priests and acolytes gathered around. "You gave me the home I never thought I would have."

Senovo lifted a hand to cup Favian's cheek in his palm for the space of two or three heartbeats. "We will meet again, Favian. Until then, good fortune."

Favian nodded and tried to smile, but failed. Frella had been standing close to Andoc, who had an arm wrapped around her shoulder in support. Now, she ran forward and flung herself into Favian's arms.

"I'll miss you, Favian," she said, "but I'm proud of you, too. As soon as I'm old enough, I'm going to go traveling, and when I do I'll come visit you."

"You're the brave one, Frella," Favian whispered into her hair, holding her tight. "You always have been. Anytime I doubt myself, I'll stop and ask myself what you would do in my place. I love you, little sister. I will always love you."

Frella's breath hitched in a sob, and Kathrael felt tears burn behind her good eye. Ithric left her side to join the siblings, and took them both into his arms. Frella freed one hand so she could hug him in return.

"Keep practicing your knife throwing, Frella, and your quarterstaff," Ithric said. "Someday soon, you're going to have your own adventures. We'll see you before you know it, when you visit us in Rhyth."

"I will, Ithric," Frella said. "I promise. Look after each other, yeah?"

"We promise, kitten," Ithric echoed. "You look after Senovo and the others."

She nodded, and the trio reluctantly parted. To Kathrael's utter surprise, Frella darted over and gave her a hug as well. Kathrael's arms closed around the skinny shoulders reflexively.

"Goodbye, Kathrael," Frella said solemnly. "Now, go and fix things in Rhyth. Save your friends."

Kathrael swallowed hard. "On my life, Little Blue Eyes. Be safe. Be brilliant, just like your brother."

Frella nodded against her shoulder and ducked away, wiping her eyes. Favian wore the expression of one staring into a deep abyss as he slowly turned and mounted Ozias. Ithric took a deep breath and gave the assembled crowd a final look, a sad smile flickering over his features. He mounted Audris, who danced sideways a couple of steps and then settled. The packhorse shook his head as Ithric took up the lead rope connected to his halter. Kathrael clambered up on Bysh, the other black horse, whose rope Favian was holding.

And just like that, they were ready to go.

"Goodbye," Carivel called, and others in the crowd took up the cry. Kathrael settled in the saddle and turned to look back. People were waving, and her eyes fell on Andoc, one arm wrapped around Carivel's shoulders and the other around the Wolf Patron's. Frella huddled in Senovo's embrace, her face hidden in his flowing white robes.

Beside her, Ithric and Favian were waving farewell, and she hesitantly raised a hand to mirror them. Draebard was not her home. But perhaps, in a different life, it might have been.

The three of them were silent for some time as they rode along the southern logging roads that led out of Draebard. At first, they came upon occasional travelers and men working to transport downed logs back to the village — many of whom stopped to wish them well when they recognized Favian.

Kathrael watched him carefully whenever he wasn't looking, not liking either his stony expression or the dazed, lost look in his eyes, but unsure what she would *rather* see there. When the roads grew empty and quiet, Ithric drew them into a desultory conversation about the details of the show and what the bare minimum of requirements for outfitting it would be.

The distraction was more than welcome. Kathrael was relieved when Favian joined in, offering opinions and commentary, though with none of the teasing or quips she might have expected from him under other circumstances.

The riding she had done while they were searching for Ithric, combined with the hours she'd spent dancing, sparring, and strengthening her muscles, seemed to go a long way toward combating the kind of soreness she'd suffered during her first few experiences on horseback. In fact, she thought she might like to try riding on her own before too long, without Favian controlling her horse for her.

"Is horseback getting easier for you, Favian?" she asked. "You're not hovering in the saddle like you were the last time."

"Yeah," he replied. "It seems much better now. Guess I'm pretty well healed. Ithric? Is Audris behaving all right for you?"

"He was a little nervous at first," Ithric said. "Better now. Though the pack horse is eyeing me like he's afraid I'll eat him." At Kathrael's questioning look, he explained, "I tend to make horses nervous. Carivel thinks it's because of the lion."

Kathrael found that intriguing, but didn't comment. "You know, I really like Bysh," she said, scratching the little gelding's shoulder. "I think I want to try riding him on my own tomorrow, Favian, if that's all right."

"He's a sweet-natured little guy," Favian agreed. "I imagine he'll be fine for you. I'll try to keep slack in the rope from now on, so you can get some more practice guiding him."

Despite the easy words, Favian was still giving off that uncomfortable *I'm-all-right-but-not-really* aura, but Kathrael had no idea what to do about it. So she merely nodded and focused on keeping Bysh in place next to Ozias' shoulder. Thanks to the number of people who had wanted to say goodbye, they'd gotten an extremely late start, and it wasn't very long before the autumn afternoon gave way to evening, forcing them to search for a campsite.

With Andoc's generosity and the extra horse to carry things, they were extremely well provisioned. The night was cool, but pleasant. If it hadn't been for her worry over Favian, sitting around the campfire eating hot food and drinking rich wine with the two men she loved would have been utter bliss.

As it was, the silence grew heavy as they finished eating and cleaned up the dishes and cooking pot. Kathrael continued to sneak glances at Favian, whose expression was hollow and distant. They'd erected the tent rather than opting to sleep in the open—though the night was clear, there was enough of a breeze coming out of the north that it would be uncomfortably cold by morning.

As soon as everything was tidied away, ready for the next day's departure, Favian excused himself with a few words and disappeared into the tent. Ithric watched him go from his place lounging against one of the saddles. His chest rose and fell in a sigh, but he only looked across at her and asked, "Did you want to practice our routine tonight?"

They had been working for several days on a particular aspect of the show, but she knew she was far too distracted right now.

"No," she said quietly. "I don't feel right, leaving him alone right now."

Ithric nodded. "Go on, then."

Her mouth twisted in an unhappy expression and she nodded, crouching next to him long enough to place a lingering kiss on his full lips. He brushed his fingertips over her unscarred cheek, making the skin tingle.

"I'll be along later," Ithric said into their shared air. "Maybe he'll be more willing to open up to you if I'm not there."

He wasn't.

When she shed her boots, mask, and leather bodice to crawl into the cramped space with him, Favian was feigning sleep. She bit her lip, torn between calling him out on it and letting him be. She compromised by curling up into the space at his side and resting her head on his shoulder. He said nothing, but after a brief pause, his arm came up to cradle her against him.

She hadn't intended to fall asleep, but she must have done so since she startled into wakefulness some unknown amount of time later. She held her breath for a moment—

disoriented, heart pounding. The previous day filtered into her memory. Leaving Draebard. Camping in the woods. All around her, ghostly voices whispered from the corners of the tent. She pushed them away, trying to focus on whatever had pulled her from sleep.

Favian. Her head was still pillowed on his shoulder, and his chest was moving in tiny, rhythmic jerks. The physical manifestation of tightly controlled tears. An ache of empathy pierced her heart, and she longed for enough light to see him.

There was none within the thick folds of the tent hide, however, so she gathered him to her by feel—a stiff, painfully tense form against her softness.

"Oh, Favian..." she whispered.

"Don't wake Ithric," he breathed, and Kathrael became aware of the third body in the tent.

"Yes, because I can totally sleep through you being in pain," Ithric said, sounding completely awake and lucid. Strong arms wrapped around Favian from the other side, bracketing him between them. "You know, I'm really not thrilled to learn that you apparently think I'm going to... what? Berate you for being sad that you just left your family and the only home you've ever known? Blame you for mourning the loss?"

That was apparently too much for Favian, who curled into Kathrael and wept silently, shuddering between them. Ithric pressed tighter against his back. Kathrael stroked his shorn head and murmured soothing words, trying to tamp down the fresh surge of guilt that flickered at her spirit like greedy flames. Around them, the spirits grew restless. Agitated. Their ghostly voices ran together until she could not distinguish one from another, or make any sense of their words.

She squeezed her eyes shut, though of course it made no difference in the dark. As much as she might dread the idea that her spirits might once again haunt her with their fear and anger as she returned to the southern mountains, it was Favian who needed her right now.

"Ithric," she whispered, as the cries of an unhappy infant pierced the other spirits' confused muttering, "could you... sing for us, please?"

"Always, Little Cat," Ithric said without hesitation, and a moment later his low, pleasant tenor filled the space, cutting through the miasma of grief and fear with a simple song of love lost and found again.

He sang until Favian dropped into an exhausted sleep, his tears drying in the material of Kathrael's chemise, and her restless spirits faded once more into the background.

"I thought you weren't the *care-and-share* type, lion-boy," she managed, though her voice sounded as raspy as if she'd been the one crying.

Ithric reached across Favian to smooth her hair back and hook it behind her ear. "For myself, no. But for you two, Little Cat... I care. More than I can say, in fact."

Favian made a small, bereft noise in his sleep, and something lurched in Kathrael's chest before settling there, deep and heavy.

"I know, Ithric," she said. "*We* know."

Having Favian's grief out in the open seemed to make things easier the next day. He no longer tried to hide behind a facade of normalcy, instead growing quiet at intervals, falling back a few paces and wiping his eyes until the moment passed.

Kathrael devoted herself to controlling Bysh on her own, caught between nervousness and excitement at being free of the lead rope Favian had always held for her before. The little black gelding showed absolutely no sign of wanting to run off or otherwise misbehave, seeming content to wander along the narrow road with his herd mates.

The day passed with nothing out of the ordinary occurring, marred only by a squall of chilly rain around midday. They camped again that night, and this time Kathrael did stay up for a couple of extra hours to practice with Ithric, while Favian watched and offered occasional commentary and suggestions.

The sun was low in the sky the following day when they rounded a bend and the mountains opened out before them, dominating the landscape thanks to a natural break in the forest through which they were traveling. Favian drew his mount to a halt, going very still as he stared at the vista of towering peaks. Kathrael and Ithric followed suit.

"That's really something, isn't it?" Ithric observed. "Kind of puts things in perspective."

Kathrael nodded, staring at the winding, rocky pass where she had very nearly lost her life to cold, hunger and despair. Had it really been only three months ago? It seemed like a lifetime.

"I wasn't sure I'd ever see this place again," Favian said. "And, frankly, it still makes me want to throw up."

Kathrael looked at him, confusion wrinkling her brow.

"I've seen it three times before," he explained in a flat tone. "Once in a dream, once on the way to peace talks in Rhyth… and once in a waking nightmare."

TWELVE

A terrible suspicion came over her at Favian's words. "You saw it in a dream. You mean...?"

He looked at her, and there was an aura about him that she had never seen or felt before. "It was the first prophetic dream I ever had. I was sick with a fever, and I dreamed a mountain on fire, with people screaming. Dying in the flames."

The massacre at the western pass. He had foreseen the insane military gambit that killed hundreds of the Empire's finest soldiers in a fiery maelstrom.

"Favian," Kathrael breathed, unable to come up with anything more.

"And it's just as well that you did," Ithric said into the silence. "Or an army of ruthless killers would have descended on Draebard and razed it to the ground."

"Yes. So instead, we destroyed a mountain, and burned alive every single person and animal unfortunate enough to be trapped on it." Favian's voice was strange. Distant.

Kathrael stared at him, trying to wrap her mind around what she'd just learned. "Favian, if this was a prophecy from the gods, then it was hardly your doing."

He looked at her again, still radiating a disconcerting air of *otherness* that was completely at odds with the affable, occasionally naive persona she had come to know.

"Andoc only had the idea because of my dream, Kathrael. And I lit one of the tinder-fires with my own hands. It was very much *my doing*." His eyes seemed to burn into her, as if sensing her thoughts. "You've come to know me well over the last few months, but you don't know everything about me. I'm really not the person you think I am."

A shiver went through her, but she frowned, dismissing the odd frisson. "Yes you are," she said. "You may not be *only* that person, Favian... but you *are* the kind, giving man I've come to love."

Favian's features softened, but his eyes were still intense as his gaze moved to Ithric.

The shape-shifter merely shrugged. "Don't look at me. I tore a man's stomach open and ripped out his intestines with my teeth when I was thirteen years old. If you didn't have some kind of a dark side lurking in there, I'd feel downright guilty about fucking you on a regular basis."

Kathrael snorted—she couldn't help it. "I'm haunted by the spirits of the dead, and I used to lull myself to sleep at night by fantasizing about stabbing your mentor through the heart. So you won't hear a word from me."

Favian exhaled, some of the tension draining away with the slow breath. "I'm not sure if the slave resistance would do better to welcome us into their fold, or run screaming in the other direction," he said, sounding more like himself.

Kathrael sobered. "If they turn away a shape-shifter and a seer, they're fools."

"They won't turn us away," Ithric said with certainty. "Like I said, I know some of the leaders. They'll be wary until we prove our trustworthiness, but that's only to be expected."

"Come on," Favian said. "Let's get a bit further down the road and find a place to camp. Preferably, someplace away from *that view*."

❧ ✿ ❦

Neither Kathrael nor Favian had good associations with the desolate western pass through the mountains. Though they lacked for nothing in terms of provisions and supplies, it was still a miserable few days as they climbed into the strange, thin atmosphere near the peaks and picked their way down the other side over rocky trails and slippery shale.

Kathrael grew fragile and wan as the ghosts that clung to her clamored for attention. They often seemed more real than the hazardous path under her horse's feet, or the steadfast presence of Ithric and Favian next to her. The only time she could escape them was when she danced or sparred with Ithric. Once the three companions were below the elevation that sapped their strength and made them lightheaded, she threw herself into their nightly practice with an abandon that verged on recklessness.

Ithric, however, was no stranger to recklessness. He matched her energy, catching her from her impossible leaps, spinning her in the firelight to the primal drumbeat Favian set for them using a branch or stone against a hollow log. Afterward, the three of them would collapse into a bedroll together, too exhausted to do more than kiss and hold each other.

You must come back, Kathrael, her dead sister Elarra whispered in the depths of night. *I need you there, little sister. But I don't want you there. Rhyth is a terrible, cursed place, only good for death and pain. Come back to the place where I died. Come and suffer as I did. Come back…*

"I'm coming," she whispered into the darkness. "Rhyth is the curse I deserve, sister. I know that. It's the place that made me."

"Kath?" Favian asked, his voice sleep-roughened.

"My sister needs me, Favian," she said in a quavering voice. "We have to go faster."

A gentle hand tangled in her hair. "Kath. We'll be there soon. But Elarra is dead. You can't help her now."

"I know that," she said. "I *do*. But, somehow… she still needs me in Rhyth."

Favian drew her to lie against him—half on top of him. "Not long now. Tell her we'll be there as soon as we can. We'll be faster if we stay strong and rested, though. So try to sleep."

Kathrael gathered handfuls of Favian's loose shift and clutched them tight, closing her eyes and letting the steady beat of his heart under her ear drown out the whispers around her.

⚜

By mutual agreement, they avoided the area around Penth—the blighted town where Ithric and Kathrael had first met by chance. Instead, they veered further west, toward the coast.

None of them were very familiar with this part of the island, but it was a safe bet that there would be some large villages in the area where they could find the things they needed. Fresh supplies. Costumes. Musical instruments. Heavy cloth to fashion into a hanging curtain large enough to conceal a man standing on two horses. A caravan to transport everything from town to town.

To Kathrael's great relief, the constant haggling with vendors and need for decisions on everything from the color of her skirt to the height of the curtain's rigging seemed to relegate the ghostly voices to the background, where they muttered and worried at the edge of her awareness. It took three long days before everything was settled to Ithric's satisfaction, leaving the trio with a considerably lighter purse, but more possessions than Kathrael had owned collectively over the course of her entire life.

The caravan was freshly painted in bright reds and yellows. In addition to her practical traveling clothes, Kathrael now owned the first bespoke dress she had ever possessed — red, shot through with threads of silver and gold, and a skirt that flared dramatically when she twirled.

With her bronze mask in place to cover her scars, not a single tradesman had flinched from her appearance and tried to send her away. They stared, yes — obviously wondering what lay beneath the smooth metal features — but that was all right. Men had been staring at her since she was barely old enough to bleed with the cycle of the moon.

She met their eyes fearlessly, head held high, knowing that not one in ten of them would have survived what she had survived during her lifetime. Occasionally, she caught Ithric or Favian watching her with pride and approval, and one corner of her mouth would lift for a moment as she realized anew how completely her life had changed over the last few months.

After some discussion, they drove southeast from the port town where they'd purchased the things they needed, wanting to perform for the first time someplace much smaller, where there would be less pressure to be perfect from the beginning.

As they entered a sheltered valley with a sluggish river flowing through it, Kathrael recognized the nameless little settlement where she and Livvy — her sweet, guileless rescuer with the melon cart drawn by a donkey — had stopped on the two-day journey from Rhyth to Penth.

"Here," she said. "We should stop here."

Ithric looked around at the sad little collection of buildings. "Well, if *small* was the goal…"

Favian pointed to the largest building. "Is that a way-house?"

"Yes," Kathrael said, remembering the feel of a rough wooden floor beneath her cheek and the ache of chafed flesh between her legs. "It is. But I'd prefer not to stay there."

"We have a caravan," Ithric pointed out. "And staying in a way-house is an unnecessary expense when we don't have any money coming in yet."

"Fine by me," Favian agreed. "Though I don't think we should try to take *anyone's* money until we know how the performance will go. It could be a complete disaster, and if we don't charge them, maybe we can avoid being pelted with rotten fruit."

"Not to worry, Favian," Kathrael quipped. "They've probably sold all of their rotten fruit to Penth at a steep profit."

Favian laughed and took a deep breath, his nervousness showing through. "So, what do we think? Should we rest for a day first, or jump right in?"

Ithric thought for a moment. "It's harvest time. People will be busy during the daylight hours. If we set up in that flat area beyond the storage building, we could light some bonfires around the edges of the space and do it this evening."

Kathrael's heart beat faster with sudden excitement. "Yes. Let's do that." A thought occurred to her. "Unless fires will make the horses too nervous, Favian?"

Favian shook his head, though he looked a little green suddenly. "It shouldn't. They'd be pretty poor chariot horses if a bonfire fazed them." He swallowed. "So... we're really, actually going to do this, huh?"

Ithric reached across and gave Favian a hearty slap on the back. "We are really, actually going to do this. And it's going to be *brilliant*."

"Yeah," Favian said faintly. "Brilliant."

By mutual agreement, they sent Ithric to put his easy charm to good use by talking to the proprietor of the way-house—finding out who controlled the patch of land they wanted to use and how they might get permission to set up there. He reported back a short time later that it was common ground, and the innkeeper told them to do as they pleased as long as they didn't stay long enough to kill off the grass.

It was just after midday, leaving them the rest of the afternoon to get organized. Favian, who still looked as though he might be ill at any time despite having refused food at lunch, took one of the horses and went to gather wood for the fires. Ithric and Kathrael set about arranging the caravan and the portable rigging for the curtain at one end of the open area.

It was a brisk autumn day, but the combination of exertion and excitement kept Kathrael warm, even as unseen spirits hovered at the edge of her awareness.

Remember when we used to dance at festivals in the great houses, Vesh? she asked silently.

There was a pause. *I remember,* Vesh whispered in her ear, tickling the shell. *They all wanted to have us afterward. We could practically take our pick of them.*

I remember you always went for the handsome ones, Kathrael thought.

And you always went for the rich ones, Vesh replied.

She smiled, though the memory was more bitter than sweet. *I suppose that now, I can take money from the rich ones before I retire to the handsome ones' bed.* Her eyes moved to Ithric.

I suppose you can. Your priest-boy is terrified, though, He doesn't want to do this.

She frowned. *I know. I think it's just nerves. I hope so, at least.*

"Could you tighten that rope and tie it down?" Ithric called from his precarious perch on the caravan's roof, where he was adjusting the curtain's rigging.

Kathrael's attention jerked back to what she was doing. "Got it. Is that better?"

"Yup," Ithric said, and slid off the caravan to land lightly on the ground. "Come on. Let's mark out the best places for the bonfires, so Favian knows where to drop the wood when he gets back."

The setup over the course of the next few hours was perhaps not as smooth as it could have been, but considering it was the first time they'd done it, there were no major disasters. It was suppertime when random people started taking notice as they arrived back at the little settlement from whatever tasks they'd been doing during the day.

"What's all this, then?" called a ruddy-faced man wearing a rough-woven straw hat.

"We're putting on a show this evening to entertain anyone who'd like to come out and watch," Ithric called back, from where he was busy tightening down the leather drum skins on the pair of drums they'd purchased for Favian.

The man frowned. "We're poor folk here, stranger. No money to spend on such things."

"We're not charging," Ithric assured him. "It's free for anyone who wants to show up."

"Not charging, eh?" the man asked skeptically. "How's that work, exactly?"

Ithric laughed. "It's not a good long-term strategy, I'll grant you. The big secret is, this is our first performance. If you don't mind that part, then you and your neighbors can come out and have an evening's diversion. We figure, either we'll be good and you'll be entertained, or we'll fall flat on our faces... and you'll still be entertained." He winked, and the ruddy man laughed.

"Ha! All right then—I like you already, stranger. I'll tell some of the others when I see them. Dunno how much of a crowd we'll be able to drum up for you, but who knows. Not much else to do around here for entertainment, after all." His attention wandered to Kathrael, who was tuning the strings of her *sithaa*. He touched the brim of his hat. "Miss," he said respectfully.

A strange feeling suffused her at the casual courtesy from a complete stranger. She smiled at him and tipped her head in reply. "We look forward to seeing you this evening. The show will start after sunset."

After the man left, Ithric crossed to her and pulled her in for a deep kiss. Taken by surprise, she froze for a moment before melting into the contact, warmth flooding her heart before flowing down to her belly, and lower.

"What was that for?" she asked, a bit breathless.

"That was because I have the sudden, overwhelming urge to drag you and Favian into this caravan and do unspeakable things to you," he said, his voice low. "But, unfortunately, I'm going to have to wait a few hours, and watch you both be amazing first."

Suddenly, Kathrael's sex decided that doing unspeakable things in private with Ithric and Favian sounded like a *wonderful* idea. It ached and throbbed, growing wet and slick as she thought about what they could do together.

Feeling wicked, she stretched up to speak directly into Ithric's ear. "After the performance, I want you to be the one to make me come, while Favian sucks you off... *properly*, this time."

Ithric growled, low in his chest, and fastened lips and teeth to the tender skin at the side of her neck. She gasped, her knees turning to water as he sucked a mark to the surface.

"Be careful what you ask for, Little Cat," he rumbled against the stinging love bite. "Oh… this is going to be *fun*."

She couldn't help the new shiver of arousal that fluttered through her.

"Working hard, I see?" Favian asked, approaching with Fidget, the other black gelding who was now laden with bundles of dry twigs and branches.

"*Always*," Ithric assured him, and drew Favian—still obviously a walking mass of nerves—into a brief, filthy kiss as well. "Just making plans for after the show."

Favian let his forehead rest against Ithric's and just breathed for a moment. "Yes. Right. After the show," he echoed. "Someone remind me again why I'm doing this, please?"

"Because you're brilliant and amazing, and people want to see you balancing on the backs of two horses even if they don't know it yet," Ithric said easily. "And because there are people suffering in Rhyth who need our help, and this is our way to get to them."

"Thanks. I knew there was a reason," Favian said with a sigh. "Will it interrupt the flow of the show too much if I throw up in the middle of it?"

Ithric laughed, and mussed his hair. "Just do it behind the curtain and the rubes won't even notice."

Favian took a deep, centering breath. "I'll keep that in mind."

Kathrael stretched forward and kissed his cheek. "You'll feel better once we actually start," she promised. "Now, do you want some help getting the fires set up? The sun's going down and it's almost time."

If anything, Favian looked even paler than before, but he nodded gamely enough. Kathrael led the way to the first area they'd marked out for a bonfire, eager for the night to begin.

⤙ ♕ ⤚

When the last rays of the bloated orange sun slipped beneath the western horizon, she looked out over the flame-lit expanse of the common pasture. A small crowd had indeed gathered—perhaps a dozen adults and a handful of children. She wondered if the young ones had ever seen anything like this before, and a fresh wash of unexpected warmth flooded her breast at the idea that they might bring a small taste of wonder and joy to these people's lives.

She had retired to the caravan a short time ago to exchange her work clothes for the beautiful red dress and to attach the flames and feathers to her bronze mask. All three of them were ready—or, in Favian's case, as ready as he was likely to be under the circumstances. Both of her men looked handsome enough to eat in the warm, flickering firelight. They wore matching loose white shirts, open at the neck and belted at the waist over dark leather breeches and boots.

Favian had allowed Kathrael to apply kohl around his eyes, since his hands were shaking too badly not to make a mess of it. Something about the unexpected intimacy of the act made her stomach swoop, adding to her anticipation of what was to come *after* the performance, as well as during.

Darkness was falling—it was time.

THIRTEEN

Ithric leapt nimbly onto the wooden platform they had erected in front of the curtain, a lit taper clasped in one hand and a flask of distilled spirits in the other.

"Welcome! Welcome!" he called in a strong, clear voice. "Join us tonight for an evening of song, dance and wonder! Let your cares fall away, and travel with us to a faraway land of wild tales and wilder sights!"

Without giving the audience a chance to respond, he took a mouthful of the spirits and raised the lit taper, blowing a fine mist of the flammable liquid across the open flame. To the onlookers, it appeared that a huge gout of flame shot directly from his lips, and the children cried out in surprise and excitement.

A subtle, insistent drumbeat filled the air — Favian, putting the skills learned by every temple acolyte to a new — and far more secular — use. Kathrael listened for the appropriate cue and swept from her place in the shadows, dancing barefoot into the firelight. There were *oohs* and *ahs* of appreciation as her skirts swirled around her legs, her metal mask shining and the silver and gold threads in her dress catching the flickering light like sparks in the night.

She spun and leapt in time with the beat, peripherally aware of the sound of whistles from the onlookers and hands slapping against thighs in time with the drum as the rhythm intensified. She kept pace, her body set free in the mad whirling, thumping beat of the dance. At the appropriate moment, Ithric blew another plume of flame toward the sky behind her, silhouetting her against a backdrop of fire for the space of a heartbeat.

The sound of the audience clapping hands and slapping thighs, along with Favian's heavy, primal drumbeat, grew louder until Kathrael was convinced that every member of the audience was participating. Ithric extinguished the taper and tossed both it and the flask of spirits aside in favor of picking up her quarterstaff from where they had leaned it unobtrusively against the side of the caravan earlier.

He threw it to her smoothly just as her leaping spin brought her to face him—a move they had practiced endlessly because of her lack of depth perception due to her blind eye. She caught the sturdy wood pole from the air and used it to vault herself higher than her muscles alone could have propelled her in a series of leaps across the open area in front of the curtain, her legs arcing out each time to kick high in the air.

A ragged cheer erupted in the crowd—one with a decidedly male timbre, she thought. Sweat beaded her skin in the cool autumn evening, her heart beating faster with the idea that the men in the audience were watching her, admiring her body and her grace, *and she didn't have to give herself to any of them.*

She twirled the staff in front of her in a fast spin, wrist over wrist, until the ends were a blur. With a graceful sweep, she sank down in a dramatic pose, half-kneeling on the ground as the drums reached a climax. The beat went silent, then started with a new rhythm. Softer. More nuanced.

Ithric would be creeping up behind her, she knew, stalking her vulnerable, recumbent form like the predator he was—his movements silent and achingly graceful. Her skin tingled and tautened with the knowledge, a flutter of arousal growing in her stomach.

Though she had used it as such for many years, never before had she truly *understood* the idea of dance as sexual foreplay. A sensual tease, promising so much more when it was over. She let the feeling wash through her, trembling with it, but still well aware of her role in the game after all the hours they'd spent refining it.

She appeared to be hapless prey, about to be devoured by the man-beast stalking her, until the very last instant when she burst to life, exploding upward and striking out with the staff—the blow pulled at the last moment as Keenan had taught her during sparring. The end of the quarterstaff rested lightly against Ithric's chest, and his exaggerated pose of frozen surprise gave way to a wary standoff, the two mirroring each other as they circled.

Ithric grabbed the end of the staff, using it as a fulcrum for the dance as they grappled for control, first one calling the steps and then the other. The contest ended in a draw as they both dropped the wooden pole in unison, and came together, wary allies.

Kathrael surrendered her body to Ithric's strength more and more, allowing his sure hands to spin and dip her, to launch her into a leap, to slide along her thigh or waist as he supported her in a graceful bascule. They had done this many times over the past weeks, but tonight his touch was like a brand on her skin.

Only in dancing and sex could one completely surrender one's body to another in such a way, she thought... though she had never once in her life stopped guarding herself during sex. Not even with the two of them. Tonight, though, she knew that she would let another of her walls crumble.

When she leapt with complete abandon into arms that were strong and sure, it was with the unshakeable certainty that she would be caught and held safe.

As Ithric lowered her into a sweeping dip and held her there, her unbound hair brushing the ground, the tiny crowd erupted into whoops and shouts. After a moment, he swung her smoothly to her feet, the effortless nature of the move belied by his lean frame. Kathrael stretched up to kiss the corner of his jaw — *not* part of the routine they'd devised — and the skin around his gold-flecked eyes crinkled in the firelight.

"Soon, Little Cat," he whispered in her ear, too low for the crowd to make out.

A new flood of warmth flowed through her body, but she only smiled and swept gracefully back to the shadows, out of view of the crowd.

"Bring her back!" called one of the men in the audience, the shout echoed by laughter and others calling out, "Hear, hear!"

Kathrael picked up her *sithaa* and clasped it to her breast, suddenly feeling lightheaded. The crowd — small though it was — had loved her. They thought her beautiful, not ugly. She had given them happiness, but instead of having to sacrifice her body and soul to do it, she had received this sense of wonder and joy in return.

And they were only getting started.

In front of the curtain, Ithric was launching into a series of jokes and stories that grew increasingly bawdier until the adults were howling in laughter — though his words were always couched in clever metaphors or double entendres that left the children scratching their heads and giggling mostly at the story's seeming randomness and the grownups' amusement.

He was a natural at it, and should she really be surprised? Kathrael wasn't the only one who guarded herself. Much of what Ithric presented to the world was a performance rather than a true reflection of his innermost thoughts and feelings.

She smiled. His lazy, burning gaze that promised all sorts of things for her and Favian after the show finished had certainly been real enough, though. Just as real as her body's response to that look had been. Kathrael dragged her mind back to the present and quietly gave the instrument in her hands a final tuning, plucking at the strings and tightening the top one another fraction. Behind her, Audris blew out softly and shook his head, as if aware that his part in the proceedings was coming soon.

Favian had been pacing nervously back and forth behind the caravan, but at the horse's low snort, he came over to the area behind the curtain to check on all four of the animals tied there. His face was deathly pale, and his lower lip was pink and swollen as if he'd been worrying it with his teeth. Kathrael rose and went to him. She gathered him in a tight hug, trying not to muss the dark wig he was wearing under a broad-brimmed hat.

"It will be all right, Favian," she whispered. "Honestly, it will."

Ithric was still telling his stories, playing the crowd with the same skill she would soon use to play her instrument.

"... and then the donkey said to the blacksmith, 'I dunno, mate, that anvil looks pretty heavy. Are you sure you don't want to grease it up first?'" came his slightly muffled voice from out front, accompanied by peals of uproarious laughter from the villagers.

"That's our cue," she said, her voice quiet enough not to be heard on the other side of the heavy cloth curtain. Favian swallowed audibly and went to untie Fidget and Bysh.

When the crowd's laughter died down to manageable levels, Ithric continued, "But I have an even better story than that one to tell you." He paused for dramatic effect. "Well, that's a lie, actually. It's not a story. It's a song. A very, very old song from far away in the barbarian lands. Do you want to hear it?"

A clamor of affirmatives came in immediate response, and Kathrael slipped through the curtain to her seat beside the platform. She settled the *sithaa* into place between her shoulder and thigh and strummed a series of simple chords. After a few moments, Ithric's clear tenor rang out across the open field.

Ozias and Audris were strong men and true,
The sons of the old village chief.
Dark haired and dark eyed with bold spirits and brave,
They shared a peculiar belief.

The pair claimed to know of the edge of the world,
Where the earth and the sea meets the sky.
They vowed one spring morning that there would they go,
To see what new worlds they could spy.

Favian trotted out from behind the curtain, balanced on the two black horses. The animals had been brushed until they gleamed and had feathers and shiny trinkets braided in their manes. There was a collective gasp of wonder from the assembled onlookers as he guided them around the perimeter of the area they'd marked out with bonfires. The light from the flickering flames seemed to slide over the sleek, dark beasts as they moved in a large oval around the edges of the crowd.

Ithric continued to sing, the words clear and sonorous.

Their father asked, "Go you by land or by sea?"
And promptly "By sea," they replied.
"The world's edge is far beyond land any know,
The ocean is fair deep and wide."

The boat that they borrowed was sleek and full-sailed,
A dragon's head carved on the bow.
It carried provisions for four and ten days,
Their long journey north to allow.

When three and ten days passed they pulled onto shore;
A strange land indeed did they find.
They were met by a fox with a pelt all in white,
Who presented them with a fresh hind.

"You are kind," said Ozias, "to bring us fresh meat,
But what do you wish in return?"
"Go back to your home," said the white fox in truth,
"Leave the edge of the world at your stern."

The two brothers scoffed at the fox's harsh words,
And returned to their boat with the doe.
Again they sailed north toward the edge of the world,
To find what nobody could know.

The villagers watched Favian and the two horses in fascination, several of them swaying in time with the lilting tune of the old ballad.

When the hind's meat was gone they again pulled ashore;
The land was a blanket of snow.
They were met by a hare with a pelt all in white,
And berries so blue they did glow.

"You are kind," Audris told it, "to bring us more food,
What do you desire in return?"
"Go back to your home," said the white hare in truth,
"Leave the edge of the world at your stern."

They laughed at the hare as it scampered away,
Back into their boat they did climb.
And still they sailed north toward the edge of the world,
The answers they sought there to find.

When the berries were eaten they pulled onto shore,
A desolate wasteland of ice.
They were met by a bear with a pelt pale as snow,
Who gave them three fish in a trice.

"You are kind," said the brothers, "to give us this fish,
But what do you wish in return?"
"Go back to your home," said the white bear in truth,
"Leave the edge of the world at your stern."

"We cannot," they told him, "too far have we come,
to return to our home in defeat."
"Fair journey, brave brothers," the bear said in truth,
"Your destiny soon may you greet."

The brothers sailed on for the edge of the world,
And the fate that awaited them there.
At home in their village the years passed in grief,
As the chief dearly mourned the lost pair.

As the stanza finished, Favian and the black horses disappeared from sight behind the curtains. Ithric's voice trailed off and Kathrael let the strings of the *sithaa* fall silent. When the last chord stilled, she raised her voice in a wordless, unearthly ululation that brought shivers to all who heard it, conjuring banshees, demons, and the imagined wail of restless spirits. Several of the children jumped and shrieked in startlement.

She began to play again, as Ithric once again took up the song.

A cry of excitement one morning did rise,
The old man stumbled out of his bed.
In front of him stood the two sons he feared lost.
White hair shining bright on their heads.

Ozias and Audris, shining white in the firelight, galloped from behind the curtain as if wolves were nipping at their heels. Favian crouched low over their hindquarters, balancing against the speed and power of their strides. He had shed his hat and wig, his golden hair pale in the dim light. The crowd cheered in glee as the horses flew over the log they had set up earlier as a jump.

No longer the dark lads he'd sired years before,
Though young men they still remained, true.
The two were as pale as fresh milk in a churn,
The result of the strife they'd gone through.

When asked what had happened, they would not reply;
To ice their lips turned in a flash.
'Til Ozias one evening his silence did break,
Though the words seemed to burn him to ash.

"Hold close to your heart what you have now at hand,
Search not far and wide for what's new.
For you never know what you will stumble upon,

Or what will stumble upon you."

Ithric let the final note linger before trailing off, and Favian pulled the horses to a stop next to the platform, opposite where Kathrael sat with her *sithaa*. He stepped to Ozias' haunches, crouched down, and slid gracefully over the stallion's hindquarters to the ground. Kathrael saw him pull a tidbit of apple from his pocket before he nudged Ozias' left front leg with the toe of his boot. The horse lifted the leg as if to paw, and then followed a gentle tug on the rein to lean down, curling his neck into a tight arch as he bowed to the crowd.

Favian followed suit with a flourish that she and Ithric had needed to teach him, because it didn't come at all naturally. The crowd erupted, startling both Favian and the poor horse so badly they lurched upright—Ozias skittering back a step. The villagers immediately fell silent, and the high-pitched voice of one of the children called out, "Sorry… we didn't mean to scare him!"

Ithric broke into laughter and jumped down from the platform to clap Favian on the shoulder. "That's all right, friends. I believe they'll both recover from the shock without too much trouble."

Kathrael could see Favian's face go bright red with a blush, but he only cleared his throat and said, "It's fine, really. If that's our biggest mishap tonight I think we're doing pretty well."

Several people in the crowd laughed as well.

"I should say you are, strangers," said the ruddy-faced man who had spoken with them that afternoon. "In fact, I feel like we ought to scrape together some coin for you after all, in light of that performance."

Ithric smiled, his hand still clasped loosely on Favian's shoulder. "Ah, that's kind of you. But a free show we promised you, and a free show we will deliver. If you want to help us out, you might mention us favorably to any travelers heading toward Rhyth, so they'll be on the lookout for us."

The innkeeper had come forward to join the ruddy man, his expression troubled. "You'd do well to head for a different destination, young man. Rhyth is not a good place to be these days." His eyes strayed to Kathrael. "Especially not for a lady."

Ithric's smile faded to sobriety, and his voice was deadly serious when he answered. "Again, we thank you for your kindness and your concern. But I can think of few places in more need of what we have to offer than Rhyth. Would you not agree?"

The innkeeper nodded solemnly, as did several of the others. "Perhaps you're right, lad. Just look after yourselves, please. Now, in the mean time, if we can't offer you money, perhaps we can offer you some ale at the inn?"

Ithric's eyes slid left, to meet Kathrael's, and then right, to meet Favian's. There was a sly edge to his expression as he replied, "It's a tempting offer indeed. However, it's growing late and I fear that the only thing that really appeals right now is a bed."

Kathrael couldn't help snorting softly through her nose at his blatant teasing, but that didn't stop her sudden, urgent need to be alone with the two of them.

"Ha! Well, you've definitely earned it," said the ruddy man. "A fair night to you all, and should you ever travel this way again, you're welcome to stop and enjoy our hospitality, such as it is."

"Your kindness has been much appreciated," Kathrael offered, remembering not only this night, but another, months ago, when the way-house had provided nourishing food and the first clean, dry place to sleep that she'd had in ages.

The man touched his hat to her as he had earlier. "As has your entertainment, Miss. Now, though, we'll leave you to your rest."

Rest. Yes. There was a secret edge to her answering smile. *Well… perhaps afterward.*

After the adults had herded the children away to their homes, Favian ran a hand back and forth restlessly through his short hair. "I need to get the horses settled." His voice still had a strained quality to it.

"Of course," Ithric said. "We should get everything packed up and ready to go so we can leave in the morning."

The three of them divided up the tasks—pulling down the curtain and rigging so it could be folded for transport, hauling buckets of water from the well by the inn so the horses could drink, unharnessing the animals and hobbling them to graze in the field overnight, stowing the wooden platform and other sundry props, and, finally, dousing all of the fires thoroughly until the only light came from the small oil lamp hanging next to the door of the caravan.

When the chores were done and he had nothing else to occupy himself, Favian sat down rather abruptly on the stairs leading up to that door and buried his face in his hands.

"Favian?" Kathrael frowned, the small thread of concern within her growing to outright alarm as she settled next to him and felt how badly his body was shaking.

He shook his head without lifting it and raised a hand to wave off her concerns.

Ithric crouched down in front of them at the bottom of the steps. "Reaction hitting you now?" he asked, as if he already knew the answer.

"Merciful Utarr," Favian said in a voice that trembled as much as his body. "I feel like I'm going to faint on the spot. Did we really just do that in front of all those people?"

Kathrael put an arm around his shoulders and leaned into him.

Ithric looked mildly amused, but he did place a hand on Favian's knee and squeeze. "There were fewer than twenty people there, including the children, Favian. And yes, we did."

Letting her hand rub up and down Favian's arm in reassurance, Kathrael tried to understand what he found so difficult. "Favian, didn't you ever have to get up in front of a crowd as a priest, or even an acolyte? You must have done! What's so different about this?"

Favian finally lifted his head. "It's hard to explain. Not that I ever *enjoyed* being in front of a crowd as part of my religious duties, but... well... when I was acting on behalf of the temple, the attention wasn't personal. I was just a novice, or an acolyte, and you could have replaced me with any other novice or acolyte and it wouldn't have made a difference to the people watching. Tonight, they were watching *us*. What if we'd screwed up? Worse than I did at the end, I mean?"

Ithric's response was matter-of-fact. "If Kathrael or I had screwed up, they probably would have laughed, or maybe booed—though, honestly, this was a friendly crowd, so I doubt it. If you'd fallen or something—"

"Don't do that, by the way," Kathrael interrupted, rather vehemently.

"But if you had," Ithric continued, "they'd have been worried that you were hurt. If you were, I imagine they would have run to help. And if you weren't, they'd be relieved for you."

Favian stared at him, perplexed. "You really don't brood about this sort of thing at all, do you?"

Ithric shrugged. "No, not particularly. I mean, we're leaving in the morning. It's unlikely that we're ever going to see these people again. Though—as it stands—if we do, it seems like they'll remember us fondly."

Favian took a deep breath and blew it out through his lips, still tense under Kathrael's touch, though his trembling was subsiding.

"Come on," she told him. "Come inside. Ithric has been teasing me terribly all day. Perhaps if we force him to make good on his promises, it will be a decent distraction from your worries."

FOURTEEN

With a soft snort, Favian pressed more fully against her side. "I'm not sure I can quiet my jitters enough to be much use in bed tonight, you two. But don't let me stop you from enjoying yourselves."

As much as she'd been focused on scratching the itch of arousal that had been building ever since Ithric kissed her that afternoon, she was suddenly filled with the desire to ease Favian's tension.

"You won't," she assured him. "But for now, come into the caravan. I think I know exactly what you need tonight."

The interior of the covered conveyance was a snug fit for the three of them, to put it mildly. It was a large vehicle that required all four horses to pull it, but much of it was devoted to storing supplies for themselves, the horses, and the show. Three bunks were built into one wall, with the bottom one on the floor and the top, only inches below the roof.

They'd quickly discovered, though, that they could pull the stuffed leather sleeping pads from the upper bunks and place them side-by-side on the floor. Doing so took up all the available space, but they compensated by battening some of their supplies into the now-empty berths above them.

Even so, they were practically on top of each other as they closed and latched the entryway behind them, leaving the lamp burning outside to throw some of its illumination through the small window set in the top half of the door.

"Clothes," she ordered, already unlacing the bodice of her dress in the enclosed space.

"Seriously, though, Kath—" Favian began, but she shrugged her arms free of her sleeves and took his shoulders, pressing him back against Ithric's hard body.

"*Favian.* I'm going to massage some of that tension out of your back, that's all," she said. "But I want our clothes off, because first, it'll make it easier, and second, I like looking at you and feeling your skin against mine. We don't expect anything of you tonight beyond lying still while I work on you and maybe groaning every once in a while when I hit a knot. Right, Ithric?"

Ithric shrugged, and wrapped an arm around Favian's chest from behind. "You're in charge tonight, Little Cat. I'm only interested in ravishing people who want to be ravished — you both know that."

Kathrael grinned, and shimmied her dress down over her hips so she could step out of it. "Not to worry, lion-boy. Ravishment is still very much on the agenda. I fully intend to make use of your talents once our reluctant trick-rider isn't on the verge of jumping out of his own skin."

Favian stared at her and craned around to look at Ithric as well. "Were you two *seriously* discussing sex while we were setting up earlier?"

"Yup," Ithric said, his tone unapologetic.

"Favian, I've been thinking about nothing but sex for hours now," Kathrael said. "And before you give me that look again, I'll remind you that *you* were one of the ones who corrupted me. So it's a bit late to start crying about it now." She reached down awkwardly and retrieved the beautiful dress so she could put it away, not wanting it to get crushed on the floor. "At the moment, though, I'm more interested in *helping you relax*. So get those clothes off. Or at the very least, your shirt."

Ithric took the initiative and tugged Favian's loose shirt free of his breeches, skimming his hands up Favian's sides to lift it. All the fight seemed to go out of Favian at once, and he raised his arms cooperatively, letting them fall to his sides when Ithric removed the shirt and tossed it into the corner.

"Boots," Kathrael prompted. "Leave your smallclothes for now. That way you can be sure we won't start molesting you when you're not in the mood. All right?"

Favian toed off his boots meekly enough, but he shook his head at her as he unlaced his breeches and said, "You don't have to coddle me, you know," in a faintly waspish tone.

"Of course we don't have to," she shot back. "But what if we want to?"

He huffed at her, but the furrow that had marred the space between his brows began to smooth out. "Fine," he said. Once he'd kicked his trousers out of the way, he awkwardly scooted around her in the cramped space so he could drop to the sleeping pads lining the floor and stretch out on his stomach. "Just don't do that thing with your elbow, please. I was sore for two days where you dug it into my lower back last time."

"No elbows," she promised, and rummaged around in the chest next to the sleeping area for the stoppered jar of oil Ithric kept there.

For his part, Ithric was taking advantage of the space Favian had vacated to remove his own clothing, not stopping until he was completely naked. The rays of flickering lamplight coming through the window illuminated his chest, flat stomach, and the dark thatch of hair between his legs. He was half hard just from pressing against Favian from behind. Seeing him, Kathrael felt her own arousal settle comfortably over her desire to ease Favian's tension and make him feel good.

Her restless spirits were quiet, perhaps assuaged by the cheerful excitement of the show earlier and the villager's aura of happiness. Whatever the case, the whole night stretched in front of her, and she was free to spend it curled up with the two men she loved — no distractions, no immediate worries.

She unstoppered the little jar of oil and poured a bit into the palm of her hand before carefully resealing it and setting it out of the way. Favian was lying facedown on the leather sleeping pad with approximately the same degree of relaxation usually demonstrated by a fence rail or a drawn bowstring. She shook her head in silent dismay and straddled his hips, settling down to work.

Ithric, meanwhile, used her shoulder for balance as he stepped over and around them so he could flop down to sit next to Favian's head and shoulders, leaning his back against one of the posts supporting the bunks.

Kathrael began stroking her oiled palms up and down Favian's tense back, on either side of his spine. The last time she had done this, he'd still been a virtual stranger to her. She'd been, if not rough, then at least *unforgiving* in her ministrations. This time, she went far more slowly, content to take as long as she needed to release the knots of tension in his muscles without hurting him.

After a few minutes, Ithric reached down and started to run his fingers rhythmically over Favian's scalp, ruffling the hair and scratching lightly with each pass. Gradually, the object of their ministrations began to let himself go, until Kathrael's thumbs pressed into a particular spot about halfway down the length of his spine—at which point he moaned and went utterly limp beneath her.

"Am I going to be like this every time we go out there?" he mumbled into the sleeping pad.

"I certainly hope not," Kathrael said, and continued her journey down the long lines of smooth muscle framing his spine.

Ithric was still stroking through his hair. "I imagine you'll get used to it eventually," he offered.

Favian's answering grunt had a decidedly skeptical edge.

Kathrael, meanwhile, had reached the waist of Favian's smalls. "Do you want me to keep going?"

Favian shrugged his shoulder—a languid movement. "Sure," he said, the words still muffled by the mattress. "As long as you're not expecting me to move at all."

"No," Kathrael said, amusement creeping into her tone. "You're welcome to continue your quest to become one with that sleeping pad. Just let me get turned around."

She maneuvered her body around to straddle him again, this time facing his feet, and continued her hands' journey over his lower back, pressing thumbs into the dimples on either side of the base of his spine—just visible above the waistband of his smalls. His buttocks were firm muscle under the sleek layer of fat the most eunuchs seemed to gain over time. The feel of them was addictive, and she couldn't help the swell of arousal that made her sex ache and throb where it pressed against his spine.

Her voice was low and a bit rough as she said, "I hope you don't mind that I'm getting enjoyment out of this that's not *strictly* platonic in nature."

Ithric laughed.

"Not in the least," Favian said, and indeed, the words were laced with contentment. "Ithric can take care of you when you're finished. That's one of the reasons we keep him around, isn't it? Which reminds me—wake me up before you start, in case I fall asleep between now and then. I want to watch."

The last words emerged as a sleepy murmur, but they still managed to stoke the heat in Kathrael's belly.

Ithric snorted in amusement. "You really have no idea what you're doing to her, do you?" he asked.

"What makes you so sure?" Favian shot back, a decidedly wicked edge entering his tone.

Kathrael pinched him in retaliation, and he yelped. But she immediately returned to kneading her way along his hamstrings. She was pretty sure he actually did fall asleep as she was massaging his calf muscles, but when she moved off of him so she could cradle his left foot and run her thumb firmly over his instep, he came awake with a moan.

"Good?" she asked.

"Strange," he said, though he didn't flinch or make any move to pull away as she kneaded the arch of his foot with confident movements. "Good strange, though. I can feel it in other places in my body."

Ithric raised an eyebrow and caught her gaze. "Makes you wonder if toe-sucking might be something he'd be into."

"What?" Favian sounded taken aback.

Kathrael pondered the idea for a moment. "Hmm. Maybe it would. We should try it sometime when he's more in the mood."

Favian roused himself enough to crane his head around, looking from one of them to the other. "Hang on. You're both serious? That's really a… thing? That people do?"

Kathrael couldn't help laughing, even as she switched to his other foot and began kneading that one until his eyes fluttered closed and he subsided against the thin mattress with a breathy groan.

"Oh, priest-boy," she told him, "you really have *no idea,* do you? Ithric and I could make this massage so completely filthy that it would take you *days* to recover. And someday, we'll do just that." She gave his instep a final rub and lowered his foot gently back to the pad. "Not tonight, though. Right now, I'm tired of waiting, and ready to be selfish for a bit. Lion-boy, as I recall, you made several very specific promises to me earlier."

Ithric quirked a brow at her, all innocence. "Did I? Well, I try to be a man of my word." The innocence was replaced with a devilish gleam. "At least with people I like."

Kathrael moved onto all fours and crawled toward him, even as Favian rolled to the side to give them more room and propped himself up on an elbow to watch. Her target watched her, not moving from his relaxed slouch until she was straddling his lap, stretching up for a kiss.

His hand touched her cheek, stilling her. "May I?" he asked, fingering the edge of her ornate mask. "Beautiful though this is, I prefer to see my scarred lioness without any masks when we're alone."

She smiled, touched, and helped him untangle the thong from her hair so he could ease the mask away and put it carefully to one side. His palm returned to cradle the damaged flesh of her face, and she pressed into it like a cat, relishing the contact.

He used the touch to guide her into the kiss she'd been seeking earlier, and she fell into it with abandon. She had worried, just a bit, that once she was actually here with him, ready to let him touch all the places that he had never touched before, she would somehow slide back into the dark days of the past. But even with his cock twitching against her nest of curls as she straddled him, she knew with utter certainty that she was safe in his arms.

When Ithric said that he only wanted partners who wanted him, it wasn't just empty words. If she wanted to stop at any time tonight, he would do so with easy grace and never say another word about it. He wouldn't take it personally, or use it to punish her or push her away. She was absolutely free to do as much or as little as she liked without fear of repercussions between them. And it was that very fact that made her certain that she *did* want this.

He pulled back enough to speak into their shared air. "Has anyone ever used their mouth on you before, Little Cat? Because that's what I'd like tonight, if you think you'd enjoy it."

She thought of all the countless times she'd made men come with her mouth, and how that service had never, ever been reciprocated. "A few sucked my breasts. And there was one who liked to bite my buttocks before he took me from behind. That's it, though."

"A shocking oversight," Ithric opined. "What a bunch of clueless, selfish pricks."

"What he said," Favian agreed.

She snorted a laugh. "The one with the appetite for female buttocks paid very well, I'll have you know," she said.

"Even so," Ithric said, still sounding offended on her behalf.

"You should let Ithric show you what you've been missing," said Favian. "Amazingly enough, his mouth does, in fact, have some redeeming qualities."

Ithric freed an arm so he could throw a nearby pillow at Favian's head. It boffed him in the face, but he only grabbed it, unperturbed, and stuffed it under his elbow to make himself more comfortable.

"Be nice, you two," Kathrael admonished. "Ithric, it looks like you've been challenged to prove yourself. Best get to it, hadn't you?"

In truth, she was so hot and fluttery at this point that she simply didn't think she could wait. And Ithric's lazy grin really wasn't helping with that.

Before she even realized what was happening, he'd twisted his body, flipping them and depositing her gently on her back beneath him, using the same easy strength he'd used earlier to catch and lift her during the dance. For the first time, she truly felt like prey — though with Ithric poised over her and Favian inches from her side, there was not a hint of fear in her anywhere.

Ithric lowered his lips to hers and continued the kiss they'd interrupted earlier, taking possession of her mouth with his tongue. She melted into the bedding in much the same way as Favian had done earlier. When he'd sensed her complete surrender to the sweet invasion, Ithric pulled back only enough to tip her chin up, baring the vulnerable arch of her exposed throat to his next assault.

His lips pressed along the delicate skin, punctuated here and there with the sharp, bright pinprick of teeth nipping, making her gasp and arch as the sensation jolted through her and settled in her sex. Every nip was followed by an apologetic rasp of his tongue, dragging over the newly awakened flesh and soothing it.

He continued his slow journey downward, spiraling kisses around her right breast, moving ever inward. An inch from her pebbled, aching nipple, he latched onto the tender flesh and sucked, pulling heat to the surface *so close* to where she needed him to be that she cried out with it. Favian's hand stroked through her hair, gentling her until she fell back, panting, giving in once more to Ithric's possession of her body.

He continue to draw blood to the surface of her skin with his lips, in what was sure to leave a livid bruise that would linger for days.

"*Please*," she whimpered, wanting — *needing* — that mouth on her nipple *right now*.

Ithric smiled against her skin and released the suction, moving immediately to where she ached for him. Kathrael didn't recognize the low moan that emerged from her throat as warm, slick lips suckled at her breast like the babe she'd never had, drawing liquid heat from her belly to her heart and flooding her body with tingling warmth.

The exquisite torture continued as he switched breasts, sucking a matching mark to the surface of the left one before having pity on her and teasing the aching point into his mouth, where he worried at it with teeth and lips. A new wave of ecstasy washed over her, leaving her practically incoherent with need.

Awareness returned by reluctant degrees as Ithric abandoned her breasts in favor of kissing his way down her stomach, pausing to dip his tongue in the shallow valley of her navel. She tangled a hand in his wavy mop of hair, urging him lower — unsure what exactly to expect when he reached his final destination. Only knowing that she wanted it.

Ithric gave a low rumble of approval at her neediness and continued down, burying his nose in her dark curls and breathing in, rubbing his cheeks against her, catlike — openly wallowing in her scent.

"Mmm," he said, his voice nearly a purr. "I've been smelling this scent for *hours* now. It's been torture, Little Cat."

Kathrael made a noise that tried to be words — tried to be pleading — but emerged instead as a pitiful little squeak.

To her dismay, he lifted himself away from her, balancing on his arms. "I'm going to lie on my back," he said. "I want you to straddle my face, so you can use me however you wish, until you come all over me at least twice. Maybe more. I want to smell you on me for *days*, even after I wash.

Kathrael was completely beyond speech. She *needed*. If Ithric had asked her to stand on her head so he could pleasure her, she would have been scrambling for a wall to balance against before the last word faded. She allowed him to manhandle her into position the way he wanted her, as he settled onto his back in the spot she'd just vacated.

She was kneeling over him, facing his hard, twitching cock, her sex spread obscenely above his lips and the crooks of her knees curled under his armpits. His hands steadied her hips—long, graceful fingers spanning the soft flesh. His breath puffed against her soaking folds, and she panted as little bursts of air alternately heated and cooled her aching cunt with each slow inhale and exhale from his lips.

"You look wild, Kath," Favian said from beside them, his fingertips running down the outside of her thigh, trailing new fire behind them. "Untamed."

She could only moan, unsure if she was truly allowed to grind herself against Ithric's mouth as she wished to. Fortunately for her sanity, he didn't leave her in suspense any longer, instead using his grip on her hips to pull her down to him properly. The flat of his tongue teased along her folds and pressed inside, igniting her blood until she thought her body must surely go up in flames.

The first touch shattered what was left of her self-control, and she rode his willing mouth, sliding and twisting against the exquisite sensations of his tongue and lips delving into her folds. The two of them settled into a slow rhythm, his tongue pressing ever deeper into her passage and then sliding up her inner lips to circle her aching nub. Ithric's noises of pleasure, muffled by her flesh, drove her to new heights.

She would never have expected a man to get satisfaction from such a thing, but his cock could not lie. It rested hard and heavy on his belly, where it twitched occasionally, leaving little smears of seed behind.

It seemed far, far too soon when Kathrael's release rose up and took her, making her jerk and tremble around him for long moments. He dragged it out until it felt like all the bones in her body had turned into soft willow twigs, threatening to sway and collapse under the strain of staying upright. With difficulty, she moved to climb away from Ithric, not wanting to smother him, but callused hands tightened around her hipbones and held her in place.

"I don't get the impression he's done with you yet," Favian said from beside her, sounding fondly amused.

At the same time, that brilliant, devious tongue delved into her once more, twisting and flexing as stars exploded behind her tightly closed eyelids.

"Men need some time to recover after their release," Favian added helpfully, "But women can come over and over. I've heard of men who accidentally made their bondmates pass out by taking them over the edge too many times in a row."

"*Gods,*" Kathrael croaked, as new pleasure sizzled along oversensitive nerves. Dizziness assailed her, the sensation more potent and addicting than the finest herbs she'd ever smoked at the rich houses in Rhyth. Ithric made a noise of satisfaction as her thighs tightened instinctively around him, and he pressed her mercilessly toward the edge of the cliff once more.

Her good eye flew to Favian, latching onto his presence as a point of solidity amongst her swirling maelstrom of excitement and need. His expression was mischievous, and he placed a finger across his lips in a hushing gesture as he silently eased around on the bed so he could get at Ithric's cock. Without a word or touch of warning, he stretched forward and licked a stripe down its length, from tip to balls.

Ithric groaned and flexed his hips up, chasing the contact, but Favian replaced his mouth with his hand. He fisted Ithric's hard shaft with slow, lazy pulls—enough to tease, but not enough to bring him off. The sight, combined with the way Ithric channeled his growing frustration into his assault on her sensitive cunt, drove Kathrael back to the precipice.

When Ithric fastened his lips around her nub and sucked, she fell over the edge, crying out sharply as she pulsed and twitched, releasing a new flood of wetness over Ithric's face.

Still his hands held her in place, the fingers digging into her flesh deliciously. Favian teased him, and Ithric teased her, until she collapsed forward in slow motion to drape over his body, her face resting inches from Favian's hand fisting up and down Ithric's thick shaft with achingly slow movements.

Favian stretched down until he could kiss her at the same time, the angle awkward, but not awkward enough to stop another languid climax flooding her as two sets of lips slid against her sensitive skin.

As if sensing that he had dragged things out long enough, Favian returned his full attention to Ithric's cock, sliding his mouth over the head and working his way down, licking and sucking as he established a purposeful rhythm.

Kathrael pressed her lips to Ithric's belly and raked her nails gently over the thin skin at the crease of his hip, leaving four light pink lines visible in the flickering lamplight.

Ithric went still, his lips pressed intimately against her. He was completely silent as he came, only the flutter of his stomach muscles under her cheek and Favian's strange noise of combined surprise and satisfaction as come flooded his mouth, attesting to the power of his release.

Favian swallowed a couple of times around Ithric's softening prick and let it slide slowly from his lips. Kathrael was almost completely limp, but she managed to scoot forward a few inches so Ithric could breathe properly, and rested her head in the dip under his hipbone. Oddly fascinated, she trailed a fingertip up the length of his spent cock, and he shivered beneath her.

"I really enjoyed that," Favian said, flopping down so he could rest his head on Ithric's thigh like a pillow. "Thank you both."

"Mmm," Kathrael managed, floating serenely in a warm pool of happiness.

"*Mmm.*" The lower rumble of Ithric's agreement vibrated through her belly where they were pressed together. His hands moved from her hips to clasp possessively across her lower back, holding her in place on top of him. She figured that meant she wasn't crushing him, so she let her mind sink down into the hazy depths of darkness for a while before she was awoken by Favian stirring and stretching beside them.

Several joints in his shoulders and back popped and crackled, releasing the last of the day's tension. This time, she did manage to roll off of Ithric, despite his sleepy protest. Both she and Favian clambered awkwardly around until they were all facing the right direction. Kathrael collapsed straight back down onto the mattress, pleased when Ithric snaked an arm around her shoulders and pulled her close.

Favian, on the other hand, bent down to capture Ithric's lips with his. The kiss was slow, deep, and more than a bit sloppy. A little quiver went through Kathrael as she realized that Favian was methodically exploring the taste of her on Ithric's lips, while Ithric was licking into Favian's mouth, chasing his own essence.

Her lips parted as, once again, she was overcome with the realization of how much she had never truly understood about sex and pleasure, despite having sold her body to men for years. Outside, the light of the lamp flickered and went out, the last of the oil consumed. In the darkness, Kathrael burrowed closer to Ithric and stretched her hand forward until it bumped into Favian's. Their fingers tangled and he gave a little squeeze.

With a sigh of utter contentment, Kathrael let sleep claim her, knowing beyond a doubt that no dreams would trouble her tonight.

FIFTEEN

For nearly two weeks, they traveled from town to town, refining the show and moving ever closer to Rhyth. Even though there were no major mishaps, Favian continued to be a nervous wreck before each performance and a tightly wound ball of tension afterward — at least until they could get him alone and ease the strain from his coiled muscles by fair means or foul.

The three of them started taking donations from the crowd after their third performance, and when they reached the larger towns close to Penth, Ithric began hiring local men to collect an entry fee in exchange for a small percentage of the proceeds. When Favian pointed out that the men were almost certainly pocketing some of the money they collected before turning it over to them, Ithric only shrugged and replied that they were still netting far more this way than they had by asking for voluntary donations.

As they moved slowly southward, the spirit of Kathrael's sister visited her more and more often in the night. *Hurry, please,* she would whisper, over and over. *Hurry!* Each time, Kathrael would try to reassure Elarra's ghost that they were coming, that they would be there soon. Despite how smoothly things seemed to be going for their little troupe, the nightly visitations put Kathrael on edge.

No matter how she tried to phrase the question, she couldn't get Elarra to tell her *why* she needed to hurry to Rhyth. Her sister seemed frightened. Confused. Distracted. All Kathrael could do was try to keep her own focus and not be sucked into Elarra's anguish.

Finally, almost four full weeks after they'd left Draebard, the caravan rounded a bend and the city of Rhyth spread out before them in the distance. Kathrael's heart clenched in a painful twist of tangled emotions — fear and grief and excitement, as well as the sharp ache of homesickness.

"Stop for a moment, please," she said, her voice hoarse.

Favian immediately drew back on the reins, bringing the four horses to a halt. "Kath?" he asked. "Are you all right?"

Kathrael swallowed. "I just need to look at it. Just for a minute."

Ithric, seated on her other side on the driver's bench, slipped an arm around her shoulders. "Been awhile, yeah?"

She shook her head. "That's the thing. It's only been a few months. Not even half a year. But *everything's changed*. What if Rhyth has changed as much as I have?"

Favian transferred the reins to one hand and placed the other on her knee. "Then we'll still have each other, and we'll get to know it together."

"Rhyth has always been all things to all people, Kathrael," Ithric added quietly. "There is a place for us there, as long as we're willing to make it."

She let the words soak in, staring at the distant walls and buildings with her good eye. Rhyth was completely different from anyplace else on the island of Eburos—a churning cauldron of wealth, poverty, art, philosophy, love, hate, cruelty, and corruption. As she watched, an oily plume of smoke curled into the air over the merchants' quarter, far too large and black to be from a hearth or controlled bonfire.

This, at least, had not changed. Rhyth was still tearing itself apart like a wild beast caught in a trap.

⚜

Ithric kept his arm around Kathrael's shoulders as Favian clucked to the horses and started them moving again. His head was full of plans. They would need to find a relatively safe place to stay, which was likely to be an adventure in and of itself. They would also need to scout out locations where they might perform without too much likelihood of a riot randomly breaking out around them. And, perhaps most importantly, he would need to locate his old contacts, assuming they were still alive and in the city.

As foot and horse-drawn traffic increased on the road around them, Favian moved the caravan to one side so people could get around the large vehicle and the four-horse team pulling it. Even this far outside the city, the black and white horses and colorfully painted wagon attracted attention—some of it curious, some of it suspicious. Some of it calculating.

As much as Ithric might fancy himself the powerful shape-shifter protecting his mates, he knew that they would need to gain allies, and quickly, or they would end up as three more unmarked casualties of the war that Rhyth was currently waging against itself. His small arsenal of throwing knives and Kathrael's quarterstaff would not be of any real use in holding off armed gangs identifying with the cult of Deimok.

As they traveled, Ithric had been thinking over what he knew of the city, and he had the vague outline of a plan. The question would be whether he had enough money—and enough bravado—to carry it off.

"We're going to the warehouse district," he said. "It's not far from the waterfront. Since trade through the port has dried up, there are several abandoned buildings there whose owners can no longer afford to keep them up. Many of them are damaged, but I'm confident we can find something that will work as shelter and a home base for us and the horses."

Favian frowned. "It's late in the season, Ithric. Nearly winter. In fact, I'm surprised it's not colder than this already. We'll need some proper shelter, not a drafty storage building with holes in the roof."

Now it was Kathrael's turn to frown. "This weather is seasonable, Favian. I'll admit I got cold sometimes, but I was completely homeless for a good part of the last winter— sleeping on doorsteps with Vesh—and we survived all right. Anything with walls and a roof should be sufficient for us as long as we have fuel for a fire."

"The winters in Rhyth aren't anything like the winters up north," Ithric explained in response to Favian's look of confusion. "Especially right near the ocean like this. We won't freeze. The rain will be the biggest problem—it rarely snows south of the mountains."

Favian's eyebrows rose. "Huh. I hadn't realized," he said, as he guided the horses around a large wagon traveling in the other direction. "That will simplify things, I guess. I'd been wondering how we were expected to put on performances when the weather was too cold for people to come out."

"Wet weather will certainly put a damper on the crowds at times," Ithric said, "but not every day."

Kathrael nodded. "Yes, that's true enough. There are outdoor events all year in Rhyth." She looked up at Ithric.

"That said, if we try to stay in an abandoned area of the city, we'll hardly be alone. It won't take the gangs long to find us and realize we have things of value—money, horses. Even the caravan itself."

Ithric smiled his sharpest smile. "Oh, believe me. I'm counting on it."

Favian shot him a side-eyed glance, and Kathrael frowned at him in consternation.

"There are rules to how the game is played, you know," he continued, "even when things are falling apart. Someone will always step in to fill an empty place in the power structure. And once you know who the new power broker is, you can negotiate with him. You'll just have to trust that I'm not going to lead us straight into danger."

Surprisingly, it was Favian who spoke first. "Ithric, I've left my home and traveled halfway across the island with you, to a place where I have no contacts and no way of surviving on my own. I've placed myself completely in your hands because, while I may not trust you to look after your own skin, I trust you to look after ours as much as is possible under the circumstances."

Kathrael looked down. "I trust you, Ithric. But I've also seen the realities of life in Rhyth."

Their words affected him more than he had expected, and he had to clear his throat. "I know, Little Cat," he said softly. "But the realities you saw were the realities of a prostitute with barely enough money to get by. Sad to say— but in Rhyth, money changes everything."

They were silent as they approached the northern gate. Kathrael was clearly still lost in memories of the last time she had been this way, while Favian was largely absorbed in avoiding any collisions in the busy roadway. It was no great surprise when the guards at the gate waved them to a halt and wandered over to speak with them, eyeing the fancy horses and caravan with speculative gazes.

Ithric sighed. And so it began.

"I've not seen you lot around before," said the taller of the two. "Think I'd remember a wagon and horses like this."

Favian's brows drew together. He was clearly unprepared to be singled out, and he replied. "We've just arrived, after traveling down from—"

"From the towns south and west of Penth," Ithric cut in smoothly. Not that the guards could fail to notice that he and

Favian weren't southerners, but there was no point in offering unnecessary detail.

The guard's eyes narrowed. "And why should we let you in?"

"Why *wouldn't* you let us in?" Favian asked, still clearly taken aback.

The guard laughed. "You could be anybody, now, couldn't you, Blondie?"

Ithric sighed, unwilling to devote time to the exchange when it wasn't necessary. "How much?" he asked.

The guard didn't even pretend not to understand. "Fifty coppers, or two silver pieces if you've got 'em, stranger."

"Thirty coppers," Ithric countered, still making sure to sound bored.

"Forty," insisted the guard.

"Thirty-five," said Ithric.

"Done," the guard replied with a smug grin.

"Just a minute," Ithric muttered, and climbed through the hatch behind the driver's bench to retrieve the money. When he reappeared and tossed the cloth purse to the guard, the man gave it a quick bounce in his hand to assess the weight and immediately made it disappear inside his jerkin.

"On you go, then," he said, slapping the nearest horse on the haunch. "Stop holding everyone up."

Favian very nearly growled in irritation, but he urged the horses on through the city gate and into the maze of streets and byways within.

"I see what you mean," Kathrael observed, nudging her shoulder against his.

"Yup. Welcome back to Rhyth, Little Cat," Ithric said wryly.

Favian let his shoulders relax a bit as the bustle of the roadways around them diminished. The warehouse district was in the eastern part of the city, on the side of the river that was less prone to flooding. The place smelled of dead fish and stale damp, an odor that was different from—but no less overpowering than—the thick miasma of unwashed people, waste, and rotting garbage evident in the more populated areas.

It was really starting to make his head swim. Not to mention his stomach.

As Ithric had promised, the area around them appeared nearly deserted, though Favian thought he felt eyes watching them from the shadows of derelict buildings on several occasions. Many of the structures were massive—larger by far than the temple back in Draebard, and Favian immediately had to quell the pang of homesickness that came hand in hand with that comparison.

It was, quite frankly, an eerie journey. Even the horses seemed unusually skittish. He kept a steady hand on the reins, and split his attention between driving, watching their surroundings, and observing Kath. She seemed oddly quiet after her homecoming, and he hoped she wasn't being troubled by her sister's spirit as she had been so often lately.

"Here, what about that one?" Ithric said, pointing to a building with a portion of one wall missing and a section of the roof fallen into the gap.

It looked... well, it actually looked pretty horrible, to Favian's eyes. But then he took in a broader view of its surroundings, and realized that it was flanked by a large vacant space where it appeared that a similar building had burned to the ground some time ago. The area was grown up in grass and weeds and would, he realized, support four horses for a week or two while they sorted out a source of fodder. The grass sloped down to the edge of the river, which flowed gray and sluggish past a questionable looking dock that must have been fairly impressive at one time.

Kathrael shrugged, breaking free of her reverie. "One place is as good as another."

"There's grass to feed the horses for a while," Favian said, and she nodded.

"Then we should stop here, at least for now. Assuming no one else is here already, of course," she said, and just like that, it was settled.

Favian pulled the team onto the rutted and overgrown track leading from the main road to the abandoned warehouse. When he'd brought them to a halt, Ithric slipped a knife from his boot.

"Stay here," he said. "Kathrael and I will see if it's deserted. If it's not, be ready to move on. Potentially with some haste. It's a good spot, but I'm not willing to fight for it."

Favian narrowed his eyes at the shape-shifter. "I should hope not," he said.

It was an unpleasant feeling to be the one left behind in relative safety as Ithric and Kathrael slipped away, weapons held at the ready. Favian might have been the only one of them to ever fight in a proper battle, but he'd been a boy barely into his teens at the time, and he hadn't even been armed. He'd been driving a chariot.

He hadn't actually fought with another person since he was a very small boy, scuffling with other boys over childish taunts. As seemed to happen often these days, his stomach dipped as yet another aspect of their crazy undertaking suddenly hit him. Would the three of them end up physically fighting other people? Could he be part of a rebellion without lifting a weapon at some point?

If it came down to it, *could* he lift a weapon against someone? He was still a priest... in his heart, anyway.

Senovo had killed, he knew — but only ever as the wolf. Favian didn't honestly think he could do it. He sincerely hoped he wouldn't have to find out. He shook his head to dislodge the unsettling trail of thought and dragged his attention back to the others, where it should have been all along. He would have to get better at keeping his worries from distracting him.

"Hullo!" Ithric called, not making any attempt at stealth. "Anyone around?"

He and Kathrael were at the entrance to the building. The proper entrance, that was to say, since the collapsed wall offered access of a sort as well, strewn with rubble though it was. There was no answer.

"We're coming in," Kathrael said loudly. "We don't mean any harm. We'll leave immediately if you tell us to!"

Still nothing. Ithric glanced back at Favian, and Favian nodded his understanding. The pair disappeared through the huge doorway — built large enough for cargo to travel in and out easily in wagons. Favian clenched his jaw and tried not to worry. Time passed like thick treacle. The horses stamped occasionally, tossing their heads. A chill wind picked up, ruffling the edge of his traveling cloak. No sound came from the damaged building.

Finally, when he was just starting to seriously contemplate going in after them, Kathrael appeared at the doorway and waved him forward. "It's clear!" she called, sounding strangely excited. "You can drive the horses right inside!"

Favian tried to let his growing tension flow out on a sigh. The horses perked up as he steered them down the long drive to the entrance. Fidget balked at entering the huge structure, throwing the team into momentary confusion until Favian slapped him smartly on the haunches with the reins and got him moving forward again.

He could understand the animal's nervousness—it was a strange feeling to drive an entire caravan inside a building and still have room to spare. The place was *huge*. Detritus from its previous existence as a working warehouse littered the floor, but it appeared that everything of real value had been looted long ago. What remained was mostly broken barrels, rotted planks, moldering rags, and other bits of trash no one had cared to bother with.

Ithric nudged one of the barrels with the toe of his boot. "We'll have plenty of fuel to burn until we get money coming in," he observed.

Favian looked up at the distant roof—what was left of it. "Ithric, it would take a bonfire the size of a house to keep this place warm, with the wall and a quarter of the roof gone."

Kathrael's expression was still lit with enthusiasm that seemed all out of proportion to their surroundings. "No, Favian, come and see! There's an enclosed area at the back. I'm sure it's where the owner stayed when doing business. It's perfect!"

Ithric came and held the horses so Favian could climb down from the driver's seat and follow her. Indeed, there was a small door set in the back, leading to a sort of building within a building. The inside was dusty, cobwebbed, and smelled like mildew. But it was, as Kathrael had described, a livable space obviously designed for human comfort. A hearth area was set up in one corner, blocked all around with stone, and a rusted metal hood above it directed smoke out of an opening high in the wall—an innovation Favian remembered from his trip to Rhyth years ago.

"It's very... um..." he began, trying to think of a suitably neutral word to describe the dark, unwelcoming room.

Kathrael stretched up and kissed him on the cheek, surprising him. "I know you're used to nice places, Favian, but I've never had anything remotely like this that didn't belong to someone else." Her brow furrowed. "Well, all right. Obviously this *does* belong to someone else, but it's not someone who's going to be coming here and turning us out tomorrow. We can *stay* here. Fix it up. Make it ours, for the time being. I'm not just bedding down here for a night. I'm not here on someone's *sufferance*."

A wash of fondness swept through him, chasing away his misgivings. "I think I understand, Kath. It's easy to forget that, even though the hut I grew up in was hardly grand, I've been lucky to always have security and a roof over my head. I can't promise not to moan about the dust or the smell or the draft, but this is a good place for us right now, and I'll help you and Ithric make it a home for as long as it makes sense to stay."

Her answering smile was every bit as bright as the light glinting off of her metal half-mask. "I knew you'd understand, Favian," she said, and kissed him again—properly this time.

He smiled into the gentle press of lips and pulled her close, needing to feel her reassuring warmth in his arms in this strange and foreign place. "Come on," he told her when they parted. "Let's go get the horses taken care of."

⊱ ♕ ⊰

Kathrael helped Favian unhitch the horses and lead them down to the water's edge to drink. The river wasn't safe for people to drink from, but it would suffice for the animals. And it was a huge convenience to have it nearby for bathing and washing.

While Favian took the team out to graze for a couple of hours before dark, Kathrael returned to help Ithric set things up inside. It quickly became obvious that they would have to sleep in the caravan tonight unless they wanted to spend the night sneezing from all the dust. Rather than tackle any serious cleaning, they focused on clearing a safe place to pen the horses inside, where they were less likely to attract attention, or be stolen.

They eventually decided on a central space where they could tie some of the old boards to the heavy beams supporting the roof in order to make a small pen. Afterward, they started clearing the area around the pen so Favian could drive the caravan in a broad circle to get it back out of the warehouse the next time they needed to leave.

They were losing the light by the time Favian returned with the animals flanking him. He made an impressed noise as he took in the changes.

"Will this work, do you think?" Kathrael asked.

Favian examined the boards in the failing light, testing the partly rotted wood. "I think I'll tie them to the posts for tonight, until we can reinforce this a bit more. They're still nervous in the strange surroundings. But, yes, I think the general idea is a good one. And there's even room for the caravan to turn around. I was wondering earlier if I'd have to try to back it out the door."

"I'll fill the buckets up for the horses, in that case. We can hang them from the posts where they'll be tied," Ithric said, and disappeared into the deepening gloom.

Kathrael was still caught up in wonder at the idea of this huge space being theirs. Well, *sort of* theirs.

"Do you think we could put a fence around the grassy area outside for them?" she asked, taking Bysh's lead rope and rubbing his soft nose.

Favian smiled at her. "That would take an awful lot of wood or stone. Not to mention time and labor. I'm also not sure I trust our unseen neighbors not to spirit them away when our backs are turned."

Kathrael's spirits dampened minutely. "Oh. Yes, I suppose you're right. We can make this area nicer for them, though. We'll do it first thing tomorrow."

Still smiling, Favian took Bysh from her and tied him to one of the corner posts in the makeshift enclosure. "That sounds good," he said.

Ithric brought back the first two buckets and went to fill the other two. She and Favian worked in comfortable silence, hanging them for the horses to drink during the night.

When all four animals had water and were settled, Ithric turned to them and said, "It would be best for someone to stand guard tonight. No telling who else might come around, or what kinds of animals are in the area. I can do it so you two can get some sleep."

Kathrael frowned. "Nonsense. We'll take it in shifts."

"I'll take the first turn," Favian said. "I couldn't sleep right now anyway. I'll wake one of you when I get tired."

⊱ ⚜ ⊰

The night passed quietly enough, though Elarra once again visited Kathrael as she sat on the steps leading up to the caravan's door, watching over the horses.

Hurry, little sister. We need you! Why do you tarry so? her sister whispered, sounding lost and sad.

"We're here, Elarra," she whispered into the dark. "We're here, in Rhyth. I've come back, just as you asked."

But Elarra only repeated, *hurry,* the word tailing off until silence reigned once more.

As the sun rose, illuminating a cloudy day beyond the open doorway, movement near the collapsed wall caught Kathrael's attention.

"Hello?" she asked, her hand moving instinctively to the staff leaning against her side.

A skinny child of perhaps eight or nine years of age looked back with wide eyes for a moment before darting through the irregular opening and disappearing. Kathrael rose quickly on legs that were stiff after hours spent seated in one position.

"Come back," she called, knowing better than to run after the child. "We don't mean you any harm!"

Ithric was at the caravan's door before the last word had faded to silence, naked from the waist up. Favian's sleepy face appeared at his shoulder a moment later.

"Was someone there?" Ithric demanded. "Did you get a good look at them?"

Kathrael nodded. "A child. Not yet ten, I don't think, though I couldn't see if it was a boy or a girl."

The tension in Ithric's shoulders eased. "It doesn't matter. I expect we'll be getting more visitors at some point today. The kid was most likely a lookout."

"A lookout for whom?" Favian asked, looking more awake now.

"For the people who will be paying us a visit," Ithric said unhelpfully. "The question is, will they be open to reason, or will they be a bunch of religious crazies?" He glanced back at Favian. "No offense."

Favian flicked him on the ear. "None taken." He took in the morning light and sighed. "Let me get dressed. I'll take care of the horses."

Ithric nodded. "If you're taking them out to graze, don't go alone. We should stay together for now."

Favian shrugged and retreated into the caravan. Kathrael swallowed a yawn, knowing that there was much to do today even though they were all tired after standing watch overnight. She stretched stiff muscles and went to check the horses while Favian dressed.

⌁ 🐚 ⌁

The day passed slowly. They worked at a steady pace cleaning the warehouse up and making it habitable. It was late afternoon when Ithric whistled to get their attention, his sharp senses having detected the approach of several men outside. Even though he had warned them to expect it, Kathrael felt her heart speed up. She grabbed the quarterstaff she'd been keeping close by all day, but Ithric shook his head sharply at her.

"Leave it," he said, and headed toward the entryway to meet whoever was coming. "Don't make any aggressive moves. Just let me talk to them."

Favian joined her, and the reassuring squeeze he gave her arm was belied by the tension in his jaw. They followed a few steps behind Ithric, ready to back him up if necessary, weapons or no. Just outside, a group of burly men stood in a rough half circle around the large door, essentially blocking their exit. Kathrael was willing to bet there were more hanging around outside the hole in the wall where the roof had come down, and near the smaller door that led out the back, down toward the old dock.

They were conspicuously armed with the sort of weapons meant to terrify—clubs, spiked maces, wickedly curved, ostentatious daggers. As much as it frightened her, Ithric had probably been right to make her leave her weapon. There were half a dozen of the thugs at the door, in addition to any others that might be skulking around. Kathrael knew Ithric was decent in a fight, but she doubted Favian had ever struck someone in anger in his life, and Kathrael's fighting experience amounted to a couple of weeks of sparring and basic self-defense techniques.

They wouldn't stand a chance.

Ithric walked right up to the men, his hands hanging loosely at his sides. "Hullo," he said. "I figured we might get a visit soon. Which one of you is in charge, if you don't mind my asking?"

He looked from one to another of them, until a huge mountain of a man with a wicked scar over one eye jerked his chin toward the man standing next to him—smaller, but heavily muscled and dressed in slightly better clothing than the others.

"Qaden is," the huge man said.

Ithric and Qaden regarded each other for the span of several heartbeats before Qaden drew a vicious-looking blade from his belt and casually used the point to pry dirt from under a fingernail.

"You're trespassing," he said at length.

Ithric raised an eyebrow. "Well, we're *squatting*, certainly. Trespassing implies that the owner is actively engaged with his property, which is patently not the case for this warehouse." He grinned before continuing—the sharp, vaguely unhinged smile that always set Kathrael's teeth on edge. "I prefer to think of it as offering the owner free repair and cleanup services in his absence. I can guarantee we'll leave the place nicer than we found it."

He was purposely playing the fool. At least, she *hoped* it was on purpose. Whatever the case, Qaden and his lackeys appeared deeply unimpressed.

"I wasn't talking about the owner," Qaden said laconically. "Owner's dead."

"Ah," Ithric said. "So… the owner's son, perhaps?"

Qaden put his knife back in his belt with a measured, deliberate movement. "I'm guessing you're not as stupid as you're pretending to be, northerner," he said, still unperturbed. "You lot want to stay here, you'll pay us for the privilege. Eight silver pieces per week."

"What?" Favian burst out, clearly appalled by the demand. Kathrael grabbed his wrist and gave it a hard squeeze, knowing that their position was precarious.

Qaden gave him a condescending look. "Rhyth's a dangerous place, pretty boy. Without a little something to grease the wheels, who knows what might happen to three people out here all alone, with your fancy horses and painted wagon? I'd hate to hear that something bad happened to your little girlfriend in the middle of the night."

Kathrael could hear Favian's breathing go ragged, and his pulse was pounding under her grip on his forearm. Before he could do or say anything rash, though, Ithric nodded as calmly as if they were discussing the weather.

"I don't think any of us want that," he said. "So I'll tell you what. I have a counter-proposal for you."

SIXTEEN

Several of the thugs unsheathed their weapons—a clear threat.

"You want eight pieces of silver a week from us as protection money?" Ithric continued, ignoring them. "We'll give you twenty-five. But in return, we ask for real protection. No worries about our safety; no concerns about someone making off with the horses when our backs are turned."

Qaden gave a subtle signal, and the men returned their weapons to their belts. "Twenty-five pieces of silver a week, eh?" he asked.

Ithric inclined his head. "That's what I said. We might also have work to offer sometimes, in exchange for either money or food. But the deal rests on your men's ability to keep us safe. If the price suddenly goes up, or your protection isn't adequate, we'll disappear in the night like smoke, and find someone else willing to do business in exchange for the kind of money we're prepared to offer."

Kathrael held her breath as Qaden stared at Ithric for a long moment, before a smile twisted one corner of his broad mouth. "Not sure I've ever had someone offer me triple payment and then threaten me in practically the same breath, boy. You've got guts, I'll give you that."

Ithric inclined his head, but only said, "Do we have a deal, then?"

Qaden lifted a burly shoulder and let it fall. "Sure we do, stranger. Assuming you can come up with that kind of coin. Twenty-five in silver isn't anything to sneeze at."

"I wouldn't have offered it if we didn't have it," Ithric said mildly. "Kath, would you go get these men their money, please?"

Kathrael swallowed and nodded, though it was surprisingly hard to let go of her death grip on Favian's arm and walk back to the caravan. She forced her knees not to wobble as she climbed up the steps and entered, her heart pounding like Favian's drum as she went to the money stash and carefully counted it.

As she had thought, Ithric had offered the men almost everything they had. Only a single silver piece and a handful of coppers were left after she counted out the money. Her hands were shaking as she transferred the twenty-five shiny silver coins into a cloth pouch before making her way back down the steps and across the echoing expanse of the old building.

Ithric smiled at her as he took the pouch, though there was a hint of tightness about it. He handed the money to Qaden without comment, and waited patiently as the other man counted it.

"Well, boy," he said. "Looks like you're good to your word. For now, at least."

"As I'm sure you will be," Ithric replied.

Qaden laughed, a low rumble. "Ain't no one going to mess with you or your friends once they know the lads are looking out for you. You need help, or someone for a job, you just catch whichever one of them is around at the time and ask. As long as the money keeps coming in when it's supposed to, we'll make things nice and cushy for you."

"Excellent. I'm glad we could do business," said Ithric.

The gang leader smiled broadly, though his eyes narrowed at the same time. "We'll see if you're still glad a week from now. Until then, we'll let you get on with your work. Someone will be nearby to make sure you're all safe and snug."

His gaze traveled over all three of them, lingering on Kathrael's mask. She shivered, even though there was no overt threat in his stance that she could detect. Still... she'd known men like this. Running in packs like wild animals, living off the weaker people around them. The idea of relying on them...

She looked at Ithric, trying to take strength from his carefree confidence.

Qaden lifted the cloth pouch in his hand and gave it a final contemplative look before motioning his men to depart with a jerk of his chin. Kathrael waited until they were completely out of sight to let herself sag against Favian's shoulder. His arm came around her immediately, and she could feel a fine tremor running through him in counterpoint to her own shivering muscles.

"Well," Ithric said in a philosophical tone, "I'd say that went quite well."

"You are completely and utterly insane," Favian said matter-of-factly. "I realize that by now, this shouldn't come as a surprise to me, but you are *bent in the head*, Ithric."

"We just gave them almost all of our money," Kathrael pointed out. "There's barely anything left, and we'll need supplies and feed for the horses soon."

Ithric's expression softened, but his voice was wry. "Yes... well. Consider it added motivation to succeed with the show."

Favian made a noise of frustration, and Ithric crossed the couple of steps separating them and took both of them in his arms.

"Look, you two," he said. "It's a different world, here, and honestly, there wasn't much choice. I think we've lucked out—though the next few days will tell for sure. But my sense is that this bunch wants our money bad enough to play nicely with us to get it. And the alternative would be to pay them eight pieces of silver and still be surrounded on all sides by thieves and bullies."

Kathrael leaned into both of them, still trying to calm her racing heart. "We need to start bringing in more money right away."

"Yes," Ithric agreed. "We should find someplace tomorrow and put on a free show, then use word of mouth to draw a larger crowd for a paying one the following day. With luck we can draw some attention—and some coin—sooner rather than later."

"Bigger crowds," Favian echoed in a flat tone. "Wonderful."

⚜

From then on, there was always someone around their borrowed building. It seemed that Qaden was good to his word, as no one bothered them and their belongings remained unmolested. Ithric even went so far as to leave a skin of wine out in the open while they left to scout locations for the show, as a sort of test. It was still there, full and untouched, when they returned.

To Kathrael's surprise, none of their impromptu guards ever made a move toward her or spoke to her with anything other than respect. Again, she was struck by how true Ithric's words of wisdom had been. Money changed *everything*.

Money also became their overwhelming concern over the following days. There were many plazas and market areas where people congregated in the daylight hours to meet and do business. They put on a free show during the afternoon in the largest such place they could find, drawing a few dozen curious onlookers. The little crowd seemed enthusiastic afterward when Ithric urged them to tell everyone they knew that the show would return at the same time the following day.

They set up the next day with the assistance of the huge mountain of a man who had been by Qaden's side when they first met—Ciryl, by name—and the tiny waif of a child who had spied on them. Kathrael still didn't know the child's name or gender. The odd pair collected a copper coin apiece from would-be audience members, though they still let children in for free when accompanied by a parent.

That afternoon was the first time Favian made good on his threat about vomiting behind the curtain. He made the mistake of peeking out before the show started, saw the hundreds of people waiting to see the spectacle, and turned white as a ghost. Moments later, he was spilling the light lunch he'd managed earlier onto the cobbles, and Kathrael's stomach clenched in sympathy.

Ithric sighed and kicked some dirt and straw over the mess before making Favian swill out his mouth with wine, then dragged him into a short, rough kiss. Afterward, Favian still looked dazed, but in a somewhat different way, and the show proceeded with no major mishaps.

Again, Ithric asked the crowd to spread the word. They performed in the same square for two more days, until the crowd grew smaller than the day before. Then they moved on. By the time Qaden showed up to demand the next payment, they had amassed enough to give him his twenty-five silver pieces. After paying the gang, what was left sufficed to buy a wagonload of cut hay for the horses and some simple food for themselves.

As the days passed, Ithric seemed to grow increasingly restless. One evening, he sat poking at his uninspiring bowl of parched grains, a sour look on his face.

"I would kill for some meat to go with this," he said eventually.

Favian looked up from his own bowl. "There are probably fish in the river. If we can figure out something to use for hooks, I'll try setting a few lines and see what happens."

Ithric's expression remained frustrated. "I don't mean *fish*. I mean *meat*. Proper meat."

Favian set his spoon down, his face clearing with understanding. "The lion is getting restless." He didn't bother to phrase it as a question.

Ithric shrugged.

"What do you mean, *restless*?" Kathrael asked.

It was Favian who answered. "Shape-shifters need to shift. Too long spent in one form or the other isn't good for them."

"Oh," she said, taken aback. Back in Woodhaerst after they'd first found him, Ithric had made mention of the lion being restless once or twice. At the time, she had put it down to the thick tension between him and Favian. It hadn't occurred to her that it might be something more.

She frowned. "It's not safe for anyone to see you, but perhaps you could shift here, at night, when it's just us?"

Ithric smiled, but it was tight and didn't reach his eyes. "Favian?"

Favian looked unhappy as he answered. "The sudden appearance of a lion in the same building where we're keeping the horses at night would probably generate a lot more excitement than we're really prepared to deal with. If nothing else, the commotion would attract the attention of whatever gang member was patrolling the area at the time."

"I suppose that's true," Kathrael said.

"If I'd been thinking, I would have tried desensitizing the horses to the lion when we were safely back in Draebard," Favian went on, clearly irritated at himself about the oversight. "It can certainly be done—horses are endlessly adaptable. I just don't know that it can be done *safely* in an enclosed area like this."

Ithric shook his head. "Don't feel bad, Favian. I didn't think about it either. Besides, the lion really wants to get *out*. To run. To hunt. Shifting in here might help for a while, but not forever."

"If it's a problem, though, we can't just ignore it," Kathrael pointed out.

After a moment's thought, Favian said, "It's not ideal, but there's a pretty good wind blowing tonight. If it's still breezy in the morning, I'll take the horses out to graze before first light, as far upwind from here as I can get so they won't smell you. You can shift for an hour or two, Ithric, and if anyone comes around, Kath can distract them and send them on their way."

"That could work," Ithric said. "Though the horses will still be nervous when they get back and smell the scent of lion inside the warehouse."

Favian shrugged. "That's probably not a bad first step to getting them used to you. Smell of a lion, but no actual lion. We'll just have to watch them carefully, but we'll be heading out by mid-morning anyway." He paused. "I'm not sure what to do about meat, though. Until we bring in more money we can keep for ourselves rather than just paying Qaden, I'm afraid barley and ground tubers is about all we can afford."

"Maybe I could take a morning and hunt," Ithric mused. "In human form," he added in response to Favian's sharp look.

"There's no game left around Rhyth," Kathrael said. "There hasn't been for years. Not unless you plan to hunt some poor shepherd's goats, anyway."

Ithric grunted. "Then the best thing to do is focus on making more money. I apologize ahead of time if I snap at anyone." Sly humor touched his features. "Oh, and for what it's worth, I should mention that sex is a fairly useful distraction when things get really bad."

Favian let out a snort. "You think sex is a useful distraction regardless of whether things are good or bad, Ithric."

Kathrael laughed, the tension broken, and Ithric's smile seemed more genuine when he replied, "And? What's your point? I mean... it is, isn't it?"

They finished their uninspiring meal and bedded down for the night in the back room—clean now and with a cheerful fire burning in the hearth. The following morning, Favian took the horses away as he had promised, and after giving him plenty of time to get a good distance upwind, Ithric shifted with a sigh of relief.

Kathrael watched with the same bone-deep sense of awe she always felt upon seeing the strange transformation.

Ithric's animal form had changed noticeably since she'd first stumbled upon the skinny, caged lion with the sparse, ragged mane and coat roughened by hardship. Now, the sleek body—though still scarred from a lifetime of fighting—was filling out with solid muscle. His mane had grown longer and thicker, too.

"You're turning into a proper beauty, Ithric," she told the animal, affection coloring her voice. "It suits you."

The lion stretched luxuriously and yawned, shaking itself from head to tail before padding over to push its blocky head against her hip, rubbing its scent over her. She pushed her fingers into the heavy mane and scratched, grinning as the animal tumbled her to the floor and flopped a heavy front leg across her to keep her there.

His tongue rasped over her shoulder, pulling at the fabric of her work clothes. She pushed his head away with a laugh. "Sorry, but that's one thing that's considerably more pleasant when you're human, Ithric. No offense."

The lion grumbled, making her smile again as she went back to scratching fingernails along his neck and back. After the initial burst of enthusiastic affection, he seemed content to soak up her touch, twisting this way and that under her hands to put her rubbing fingers where he wanted them.

They passed a pleasant stretch of time that way until the sun breached the eastern horizon—their agreed upon signal for Favian to return with the horses. When Ithric shifted back, he was still stretched out under her touch, lying naked on the sleeping mat and looking up at her with dark, dilated eyes.

Her breath caught for a moment at having him sprawled naked and vulnerable beneath her hand, gazing up at her so trustingly. She felt a surge of combined tenderness and lust for the eccentric shape-shifter who had protected her even from himself, never pushing her for what she was not ready to give, never demanding more than she offered.

Her palm slid down his stomach with sudden purpose, and his muscles fluttered under the touch as he schooled himself to stay still. When she cupped his hard length, his hazel eyes slid closed and he arched his head back, baring his neck.

"No," she said softly, "let me watch your eyes. Let me see what you feel."

He obeyed the whispered command, meeting her gaze in the dawn light filtering through the chinks in the shuttered window. It didn't take long for her sure touch to bring him to completion. He was beautiful when he came, his eyes giving her a glimpse behind the walls he usually erected against the world.

Soon, she knew, the last of her own walls would crumble, falling to rubble under the combined onslaught of two men's love. The depravity of her past life would blow away like dust in the wind, leaving her virginal… ready to be claimed for the first time with love rather than cold, rough indifference.

Soon, yes, echoed Vesh's ghostly voice. *I'm happy for you, Kath.*

Ithric made a noise of deep pleasure and rolled over to curl against her hip, catlike. The banked fire in the hearth still gave off enough warmth that there was no real impetus for them to move, so they didn't. Outside, in the main part of the warehouse, the sounds of hooves on packed dirt and nervous snorting heralded Favian's return with the horses.

Another few minutes passed, and Favian entered quietly, having tied the horses up safely in their pen.

"Hmm," he said. "He does appear quite a bit more relaxed now. If I didn't know better, I'd wonder if you hadn't employed multiple methods to that end, Kath."

Kath smiled at him as he flopped down on Ithric's other side. "I might have done. He did look very tempting when he shifted back."

Favian ran a hand down Ithric's spine from neck to tailbone, drawing a fresh sigh of pleasure from him. "He always looks tempting," Favian said. "It's what keeps people from punching him in the face more often than they already do."

"Fuck you, Favian," Ithric said in a voice of utter contentment, the words muffled against Kathrael's skirts. "Oh, and don't let me fall asleep."

Kathrael ran her fingers through his hair. "Why not? You could nap for a bit. There's time."

But Ithric shook his head. "Can't. Need to have a fight with both of you about something first."

"Oh, good," Favian said. "I knew there was a reason I got up early this morning."

Kathrael huffed in amusement as Ithric dragged himself more or less upright and used a corner of the nearest blanket to clean the spend off his stomach.

Favian eyed the soiled blanket and raised an eyebrow. "Is it about who will be doing the washing, by any chance?"

Ithric's return glance was quelling. "I'm going into the city alone tonight, after we pack up the show and you two get back here safely."

"No, you bloody well aren't," said Favian.

"Why?" Kathrael asked, a bit more reasonably. "You know how dangerous it is, Ithric. It's bad enough during the day—let alone after dark, and by yourself."

"Now that we have a place to stay and some money coming in, I need to see if I can track down any of my old contacts," Ithric said. "The best time to do that is at night."

"We'll go together, in that case," Favian insisted.

Ithric's gaze was uncompromising. "And these people will disappear the moment they see someone they don't know. If this is going to happen, it will be with me going *by myself*, Favian."

Kathrael could feel the moment when Favian's frustration and fear boiled over.

"And if you disappear without a trace and don't return?" he demanded. "How are we supposed to find you? What are we supposed to do then?"

"If I disappear and don't return, there most likely won't be anything left for you to find," Ithric said evenly. "So I very much hope that you'll both turn right around and ride for Draebard immediately." His gaze turned to Kathrael, who felt a surge of stubbornness stiffen her features.

"So we should leave, just like that? Without knowing what became of you?" she said sharply.

No! Elarra's otherworldly voice was threaded through with panic. *Don't leave, sister! You mustn't!*

Kathrael gritted her teeth and lifted a hand to her forehead, squeezing her temples. Ithric's eyebrows furrowed as he looked at her in concern.

"I have no intention of letting trouble find me, you two," he said. "I'll remind you both that I skulked around Rhyth for months and survived the experience with no ill effects."

"You don't have to let trouble find you when you're out *actively looking for it*," Favian flared. "And I'll remind *you* that you spent part of those months *locked up in a cage!*"

"I'm not leaving Rhyth," Kathrael said. "I can't."

"Favian," Ithric said, sounding tired. "What we're here to do is dangerous. Ridiculously dangerous. It's also important. And not only will it be impossible for us to stay joined at the hip the entire time, but being together won't necessarily keep us safe."

Favian still wasn't ready to back down. "Oh, I see. So if this was some plan where Kath would be going off on her own at night, you'd be fine with that?"

Suddenly, Kathrael felt as tired as Ithric looked. "Don't use me as a pawn for your argument, Favian."

Ithric regarded Favian seriously. "I don't control what Kathrael does or where she goes. If she went off alone, I'd be worried sick until she returned safely. As you know perfectly well."

Finally, Favian deflated. "I'm sorry, Kath." He met Ithric's eyes. "I hate this, Ithric. But you knew that already. Promise me that you know what you're doing, and that you won't take any stupid risks."

"I know what I'm doing, and I won't take any *unnecessary* risks." Ithric said, before sighing and scrubbing a hand over his face. "Gods I'm tired."

Favian still looked worried, but resignation colored his expression as well. "Then sleep for an hour or two, you clod," he ordered. "It's early yet. We'll still have time to get where we need to go and set things up for this afternoon."

"Yeah. All right," Ithric said, and grabbed a blanket so he could curl up on the mat again, a few inches away from Kathrael this time. She tried not to mourn the loss of contact.

You won't leave? Elarra asked her, sounding young and lost.

I won't leave, sister, she assured. *We won't leave. I just wish you could tell me what it is that troubles you so.*

That evening, after returning from another show — exhausted, but with a heavier purse — Ithric quietly took Ciryl aside to speak with him away from the others.

"I need your word on something," he told the big man, who looked down at him with a curious gaze. "I'm going into the central district alone tonight. In fact, I may have to go there several nights in a row. I could easily be away until dawn. I want you to make sure that nothing happens to the others while I'm gone."

Ciryl shrugged. "Me an' the boys'll keep an eye on things whether you're here or not, Ithric. You lot have got hold of the purse strings, after all. You know that."

Ithric knew his expression had turned dangerous, but he didn't try to cover it. "I don't think I've made myself clear. If anything happens to them in my absence, I will hunt down everyone involved and rip their guts from their bellies one slow, agonizing twist at a time."

Ciryl's eyebrow flickered up, stretching the scar that bisected that eye. "I suppose you can try, boy. But don't get yourself into a state. I wouldn't like ta think of anything bad happening to your friends. They're nice people. Don't get many nice people around these days. You an' me both know that, don't we?"

Ithric nodded, confident now that his point had been made. "That we do, Ciryl. That we do."

⤛ ⚜ ⤜

Kathrael slept poorly that night, and she was aware that Favian did, as well. There was no avoiding the worry they felt for Ithric, even though she knew that he was right. Without allies, they couldn't hope to move forward.

Her restlessness communicated itself to the spirits that hovered nearby, setting her baby to crying. The tiny wraith had mostly been happy and contented in recent days—apparently the spectacle of the daily show delighted her. Kathrael had felt her cheerful burbling and excited, babyish squeals on several occasions as Ithric sang and Favian galloped around the square on horseback. Her daughter's joy warmed Kathrael straight through, but the ghostly infant still needed reassurance when she became upset.

So she hummed the song about Ozias and Audris for a bit, and wasn't surprised when Favian's arms came around her in the dark, pulling her against him and adding his voice to hers. They lay awake together until a soft whistle—like a birdcall—proclaimed Ithric's return. The horses stamped restlessly at the nighttime disturbance, and a few moments later the door to their room at the back creaked open on rusty hinges.

"Everything all right?" Ithric asked.

"Fine," Favian replied. "Did you have any luck?"

Ithric eased himself down to the floor to join them. His clothing reeked of cheap spirits, though his voice was stone cold sober. "Not tonight. Maybe tomorrow. It's a big city, and people with things to hide don't tend to stay in the same place for very long. None of the old haunts had any familiar faces."

"How bad were things on the streets?" Kathrael asked, not sure she wanted the answer. Even during the daylight hours when they were out and about, the three of them had been grateful for Ciryl's armed and intimidating presence on several occasions. Robberies were commonplace within the city walls, as were fights both large and small. Amidst the chaos, city dwellers tried to do business and keep up with the day-to-day tasks of living.

There was a rustle as Ithric removed his jerkin and trousers and tossed them aside. "It's about what you'd expect—though I didn't see much of a city guard presence at all, so that's new. Lots of gangs. Qaden and his lot aren't unusual; they're the rule. Groups controlling various-sized areas and fighting with each other to try and gain more territory so they can extort money from the common folk and merchants."

"And the cult of Deimok?" Favian asked.

Ithric's voice was grim. "They're around. Hard to say if they're getting bigger and bolder—they were pretty fucking bold to start with."

Kathrael shivered.

For the next several nights, Ithric continued to venture out into the city. None of them got much rest, and they were on edge. On the third such day, Favian bobbled during his gallop around the crowd at the climax of the show, and had to drop onto Audris back and finish the circuit astride in order to avoid a fall. There was a collective gasp from the crowd at the near miss, and a smatter of nervous laughter afterward. It was hardly disastrous, but Favian was beside himself after the mistake.

On the fourth night, Kathrael was awakened from a light doze by the sound of someone moving around the warehouse, but there had been no bird-like whistle from Ithric preceding it. Favian sat bolt upright, and hissed, "Kath! Get your quarterstaff. Quickly!"

One of the horses snorted in alarm as Kathrael fumbled for the staff in the near darkness. A moment later, Favian grabbed one of the grass-wrapped wood branches that they had been using as torches and lit it from the burning embers of the hearth fire.

They were sleeping half-dressed these days—too wary to strip down completely at night—and Kathrael was glad of it now. Favian hurried barefoot into the chill expanse of the warehouse, the torch held in front of him like a weapon.

The flickering light illuminated one of the gang members Kath didn't really know at all—a wiry, muscular man with a straggling, unkempt beard and crooked yellow teeth. He was standing perhaps eight strides away, and had obviously been heading for their room at the back.

Kathrael could feel fear rolling off Favian in waves, but he immediately stepped in front of her, blocking the man's progress and setting himself as if for an attack—ready to defend her against an experienced fighter twice his size with bare feet and a smoldering stick of wood. Kathrael was caught between dread at what might happen and awe that anyone would truly try to protect her in such a way.

"What are you doing in here?" Favian snapped, none of his apprehension coming through in his voice.

Kathrael gripped her staff, holding it ready. Perhaps the two of them together could make a fight of it.

The unsavory man eyed them with a jaundiced expression. "Keep your shirt on, Blondie. If I wanted to do something to you, I wouldn't be crashing around out here fit to wake the dead. Me and Shuggan caught a girl sniffing around the place like she was gonna sneak in. Need to know what you want us to do with her."

Most of the tension bled from Favian's frame, even as Kathrael felt herself relax a bit at the man's explanation.

"A girl?" she asked. "Do you think she was here to steal from us?"

The thug lifted a shoulder. "Dunno. Don't really care. Qaden wants us to look after this place, so we do it."

"Bring her in," Favian said.

"Whatever you say, Blondie."

Favian gritted his teeth, the line of his jaw shifting in the guttering flame from the torch. "That nickname was old by the third or fourth time it was used. My name is Favian. Now, please let us talk to the girl and find out what she wants."

The man only smirked at him before calling outside to his partner. "Oy, Shuggan! Bring the girl in here!"

The torch was in danger of burning out, so Favian used it to light a small fire on a patch of bare dirt so they could see. Shuggan dragged their late-night visitor inside, bringing her into the small circle of firelight. She was thin and dirty, with lank, unkempt hair and ragged clothes. Her face was gaunt with starvation. Her eyes—huge and scared—still held a hint of defiance. She gasped in shock when her gaze landed on Kathrael's unmasked face, and went pale.

Kathrael felt an abrupt jolt—aside from the absence of scars on the younger girl's features, she might have been looking into a mirror that showed the past. She had *been* this girl, starving and making the daily decision whether to beg or steal in order to survive.

"So? What d'you want us to do with her?" Shuggan asked, not releasing his bruising grip on the girl's upper arm.

Kathrael heard Favian's sharp release of breath. "Merciful Utarr," he muttered, and then continued in a stronger voice, "I want you to let her arm go while I get some food for her."

The first thug scowled. "You gonna waste food on a thief? You'll have every ne'er-do-well in the district at your doorstep."

"Then it's a good thing we have you to protect us, isn't it?" Favian returned, his tone sharp.

"I'll get something for her," Kathrael said, and tore herself away from the warped reflection of her own past to get the girl some gruel left over from that evening.

When she got back, the men had left, leaving Favian and the girl on opposite sides of the fire. The girl looked like she was torn between staying and fleeing.

"Here," Kathrael said, and set the bowl down a short distance away from her before retreating to Favian's side.

After a long moment spent peering at both of them as if trying to determine their motives, the girl darted forward and retrieved it, shoveling the simple meal into her mouth greedily. When she was done, she clutched the bowl to her thin chest.

"What does he want in return?" she asked, her voice flat. "My mouth, or my quim...?"

Favian made a low noise, too quiet for the girl to have heard, Kathrael suspected. "No." There was a hoarse note to his voice. "Nothing like that. Nothing at all, in fact. We have food, and you need food, so I'm giving it to you as the gods decree. That's all."

She looked at him like he was mad.

"Not long ago, I was where you are now," Kathrael said, drawing the girl's attention again. "And Favian helped me, as well. He just… does that. Now I'm going to try to help you, if you'll let me. Do you know the temple of Naloth, in the central district?"

The girl nodded cautiously.

"I want you to go there, and ask for Novice Hameen. Ask to speak to him privately, using whatever story you think will sway the acolyte at the door in your favor. When you are alone with him, tell him that a friend of Ta'Vesh sent you there for help. Say it back to me."

"A friend of Ta'Vesh sent me," she muttered, looking down at the dirt.

"That's right," Kathrael said. "Don't forget. Novice Hameen. Friend of Ta'Vesh."

The girl nodded, still not meeting their eyes.

"Here," Kathrael said, and handed her the ten copper coins she had pulled from their moneybag when she went to get the food. "But remember—this will only help for a day or two. Novice Hameen can help more."

Without another word, the girl turned and hared off. Kathrael heard one of the men outside shout, "Hey!" as she ran past.

"Let her go," Favian called to them.

A moment later, Shuggan stuck his head in, looking irked. "Not sure why we should bother looking out for you lot if you're just gonna pat the thieves on the head and let 'em go, Blondie."

"Because we're paying you for it," Favian said tiredly.

Shuggan scoffed, but disappeared outside into the darkness. Kathrael came up behind Favian and put her arms around him. "The priesthood is showing around your edges," she told him, pressing her face into the space between his tense shoulder blades.

He placed a hand over hers, but said nothing in reply.

On the sixth night, Ithric returned early.

"We're to meet with a woman named Sephira tomorrow night," he said, sounding utterly exhausted.

"You found one of your contacts?" Favian asked.

Ithric nodded. "I did. He wasn't willing to tell me directly where the leaders of the underground are congregating these days, but he *was* willing to set up a private meeting elsewhere with one of them."

Relief flooded Kathrael at the prospect of finally *doing* something. "That's wonderful, Ithric!" she said.

He shrugged. "At least we can move forward now," he said, echoing her thoughts before adding, "Though of course there's no guarantee that we'll be able to win her trust."

Favian took Ithric's shoulder and guided him to remove his outer clothing and lie down. "There's no guarantee about any of this, but that hasn't stopped us yet. Now get some rest. You look like shit and you're about to fall over from exhaustion."

"Flatterer," Ithric murmured.

"Yes, do please excuse me for wanting you rested enough so that I don't have to worry about you dropping Kathrael on her head during the performance," Favian said wryly.

"Agreed," Kathrael put in, hiding a smile.

She and Favian curled up next to Ithric on the sleeping mats, pleased to finally be getting a decent stretch of sleep together. Despite the anticipation for the coming meeting, they drifted off within moments, and Kathrael woke feeling more rested than she had in some time.

After moving the show to a new venue for the day, they collected their takings, drove the caravan back to the abandoned warehouse, cared for the horses, and paid Ciryl two skins of ale to stay in the old building and guard everything while they were gone. She and Ithric packed as many small weapons as they could conceal, and the three of them headed back into the city to meet the mysterious Sephira.

SEVENTEEN

Favian was glad of their hooded cloaks as they trudged along the same route they'd driven earlier in the caravan, and not just because it was cold outside. Both he and Kath would have attracted far more attention than was wise without them—he for his blond hair and pale eyes, she for her distinctive metal half-mask. Even Ithric's features looked northern enough that he might have stood out to some degree, though—as he had pointed out several times with varying degrees of asperity—he'd already spent quite a bit of time prowling around Rhyth over the past year.

As Favian had lived something of a sheltered life in many ways, he hadn't been sure exactly what to expect of the city after dark. Fires were everywhere, throwing flickering shadows against the buildings. Mostly, the flames were contained in makeshift braziers, surrounded by groups of rough-looking men and undernourished women who stared at the three of them mistrustfully as they walked past in their dark, muffling cloaks.

Elsewhere, the bonfires were just piles of wood and trash thrown in the street and set alight, sending plumes of acrid, stinking gray smoke afloat on the chill breeze. It was hard to separate the sounds of raucous laughter from the shouts of anger and fear. The noises always seemed to come from a block or two away, never within sight, and he realized that Ithric was leading them along the less-used side roads and alleyways to avoid as many people as possible.

Favian stiffened the first time an unmistakable scream rent the air, and he felt Kathrael shiver at his side. He turned in the direction of the sound, and Ithric's hand landed on his shoulder, making him jump.

"No," Ithric said, his voice uncompromising. "You won't be able to stop it, whatever it is. You'll just get us all killed if you try."

He stood frozen, poised with all his senses trained in the direction of the desperate cry. Kathrael's hand closed on his other arm a moment later. "We're trying to help them,

Favian. Just… in a different way." Her voice was unsteady, and it was the obvious regret in it that finally allowed him to unlock his muscles and continue on.

"This place is insane," he said. The words were barely more than a hoarse whisper.

"Yes," Ithric said, his tone heavy with disgust. "It is."

A few minutes later, they passed through a shadowed alley, rank with the smell of garbage and piss. Kathrael cried out in surprise, and when he turned to look, Favian could just make out the silhouette of a thin, ragged figure dragging her back by means of a grip on the flowing cloth of her cloak. The sharp edge of a knife glinted in the reflected light of a fire from the next street over.

"Gimme your money or I'll cut this one's throat," the man snarled at them.

Favian's heart skipped a beat and juddered into life against his ribs, but before he could even draw breath to speak, Kathrael's elbow came up and the knife arced to one side, away from her. There was a confusing whirl of violent movement in the darkness. When it stilled, Ithric was holding the man by the scruff of the neck and had one of his thin arms twisted painfully behind him.

"We've no money," Ithric said, low and dangerous, "and believe me when I tell you that if you end up in possession of one of the daggers we're carrying, it will be blade first."

Feeling ill prepared and useless, Favian stepped half in front of Kath, taking her forearm in his hand and sheltering her behind him — as much of a joke as that might be in reality. She was shaking under his grip.

"Now," Ithric was saying, in counterpoint to the man's ragged breathing, "if I let you go, are you going to run away like a good little mouse, or are you going to give me an excuse to do something that one of the two of us will deeply regret?"

"I'll g-go," the man stammered.

"Probably the wiser choice," Ithric agreed. There was the sound of a boot scuffing packed dirt as he kicked at something on the ground, followed by a metallic clatter against the alley wall some distance away. "You can come back in the morning and get your knife if it's still there. Oh, and if you're so desperate for money, they've been saying in the taverns that a fleet of cargo ships from the continent is due in a few days. They'll need people to unload the cargo.

Not an easy occupation, I grant you—but definitely a safer one than trying to steal from the wrong people."

The man said nothing, the rasp of his panicked breathing still audible as Ithric manhandled him back in the direction they'd come. "Off you go, then," he said, and gave their would-be assailant a shove. "If we see you again tonight, things will go badly for you."

Without another word, the man righted himself and hurried away, limping a bit.

Ithric returned quickly. "Little Cat?"

"All right," Kathrael said, though Favian could still feel a fine tremor of tight muscles under his hand. "When you send a message to Draebard, though—tell Keenan I owe her one."

"What about you, Ithric?" Favian asked.

Ithric craned around, looking at his shoulder. "I think he put a slice through my cloak, but it didn't reach the skin." He let the fabric fall. "Come on. Either we won't see him again, or he's run off to find some friends and come back for us. Whatever the case, we need to move. It's not far to the meeting place, but we don't want to be late."

The idea that there might be an angry gang of criminals coming after them didn't do anything to help slow Favian's pounding pulse, but he merely nodded and slid his hand from Kathrael's arm to her hand, tangling their fingers together. She squeezed back hard, and they both moved after Ithric, who was already leading the way to the mouth of the alley with long strides.

When it opened onto the road, Favian was immediately surrounded by the reality of the noise and disturbance they'd been hearing all night. Men were drinking in large groups, passing around wineskins and guffawing at their companions' bawdy jokes. Others were quarreling, and he saw at least two fistfights surrounded by rings of jeering spectators. Elsewhere, a man leaned against a wall while a girl who was barely more than a child knelt between his legs, sucking his cock. More men stood nearby, laughing and jabbing each other with elbows as they waited their turn.

Favian's stomach clenched as he thought of Kath's past, but she appeared to give the tableau only a cursory glance. The three of them kept to the edges of the street. He had the urge to hunch over and keep his head down as he walked, but Ithric was looking up, head held high as if he knew exactly what his business was and wouldn't welcome any attempts to get in his way. Beside him, Kathrael was doing the same thing, though with a tightly held wariness about her that Ithric lacked.

Knowing that they were both far more familiar with their surroundings than he, Favian did his best to copy them, projecting an air of confidence that he did not remotely feel. A young horse in training would have seen through his act in moments; he could only hope that the gangs of men around them were less perceptive.

A few minutes later, they fetched up in a tavern that had obviously seen better days. The barkeep and customers alike looked up at them with decidedly unwelcoming expressions as they walked in, but Ithric ignored the glares and walked straight up to the till.

"Ruben sent us," he said quietly. "We're supposed to meet with someone downstairs."

The proprietor stared at him for a long moment. "Oh, yes? Tell me, how are Ruben's children doing these days?" he asked in a tone that might have been casual.

The corner of Ithric's mouth twitched down. "Still dead. They died of the paralyzing sickness four months ago, as I'm sure you're well aware."

"Ah, so they did," said the man. "How forgetful of me." He nodded his head toward a rickety door in the back that barely looked big enough for a child. "Go on down and don't make trouble. Got enough problems on my hands already."

Ithric gave a single, tight nod and jerked his chin towards Kath and Favian to follow him. They had to bend nearly double to squeeze through the small, crooked opening. As soon as Favian was inside, hovering at the top of a narrow stone staircase, the door slammed shut and latched behind them, plunging them into complete darkness.

"*Brilliant,*" Favian said, fighting a sudden feeling of vertigo — knowing there was a steep drop in front of him. Kath, whose night vision was poor to begin with due to her blind eye, clutched a handful of his cloak.

"Give it a minute and I'll be able to see," Ithric said from a few steps down. "Someone's got a light burning down here."

"What is this place?" Favian asked, as damp, mildew-scented air tickled his nose.

It was Kathrael who answered. "Catacombs. They run under parts of the city. Several levels deep in places, although they say a lot of them are flooded."

A shiver chased itself up Favian's back. "Sounds lovely," he said. "Don't the southerners burn their dead like civilized people?"

"Well—yes, mostly," Kathrael said, her hand still clutching the fabric of his cloak. "But in the old times they buried them down here instead. I've heard that the Alyrions have been reviving the practice of late."

Favian felt a little nauseous at the idea. "That's horrible." How could the spirits of the dead rise to rejoin the gods if they were trapped underground? And—he swallowed—if those spirits *were* trapped—

He looked at the place where he knew Kathrael would be, if he could only see her. "Kath, will you be all right down here, surrounded by the dead?"

He sensed the shrug, her clothing rustling. "I have no idea. As far as I know, I've only ever heard *my* spirits. Not the spirits of random dead people." She paused. "Elarra is upset, though. Vesh is trying to calm her."

Favian fumbled with the hand that wasn't pressed against the dusty stone wall for balance, until he could twine her fingers in his again.

"I can see enough now to guide us down without breaking our necks," Ithric called from a short distance ahead of them. He returned and took Kath's elbow, leading her down the carved stairs a slow step at a time, with Favian following behind.

When they were almost to the bottom, Favian could begin to make out gray shapes in the darkness, along with the faint glow that Ithric had described, emanating from the tunnel ahead.

"Hello, there!" Ithric called, once they were safely on flat ground. "We're here on Ruben's recommendation! There are three of us—we can see your light and we're coming to you now!" His voice echoed strangely in the tunnels.

Favian held his breath, but there was no answer. His foot kicked against something that rolled to the side with a dull, hollow clatter, and he was suddenly thankful not to be able to see much of anything. They walked cautiously ahead toward the light's glow, trusting Ithric to warn of any unseen dangers in their path.

The flickering lamplight grew brighter, until they rounded a bend in the tunnel and a large, illuminated vault opened up around them. Favian had a brief, horrific impression of walls of human bones before his attention jerked to six large, armed men with swords and shortbows pointed at them.

Ithric froze in place and slowly raised his hands to show his lack of weapons. Favian and Kathrael followed suit.

"We're here to talk, as arranged," Ithric said, speaking carefully and making no sudden moves.

The man on the far right eyed the three of them up and down. "Weapons," he said, sounding unimpressed.

Ithric nodded. "All right," he said. "The woman and I are armed. The other man isn't."

The man snorted. "The fuck he's not."

Favian swallowed to make sure his voice wouldn't waver. "I'm really not. One of you can search me if you'd like."

The leader's attention moved back to the others. "You two. Weapons on the ground and kick them away."

Ithric and Kathrael slowly removed their knives and placed them on the ground before kicking them out of reach. One by one, the leader of the men dragged them off to the side by the arm — not blocking the archers' line of fire. Favian tensed as Kathrael was searched, but — somewhat to his surprise — the man was merely practical about the process, not lascivious.

He left Favian until last, and seemed taken aback that he was, indeed, unarmed.

"They're clear," he called into the darkness beyond the reach of the lamp.

A moment later, a hooded figure emerged into the light — roughly Kathrael's height, but plump rather than slender. A hand lifted the cowl away and let it fall back, revealing the face of a woman between forty and fifty years of age, with dark hair pulled back in a braid and unusual light gray eyes. Favian thought he heard Kathrael draw in a surprised breath beside him, but the woman spoke, dragging his attention back to her.

"What sort of man comes unarmed into the city after dark?" she asked. Her voice was rich and deep for such a small woman.

Ithric took a half step forward. "The sort who would have no idea what to do with a weapon should the need to use it arise."

Favian couldn't work up enough offense to protest, especially since it was true. Instead, he shrugged. "I've always preferred words as weapons," he said.

"Then you are ill-suited to life in Rhyth, I fear," said the woman.

Favian breathed out. "You're not the first to say so—and yet, here I am."

She looked over the three of them with sharp gray eyes, her gaze pausing on Kathrael's mask before moving back to him. "So you are. Why? And how do you know Ruben?"

It was Ithric who answered. "We are here to help change things for the better. Ruben was one of my contacts when I was here a few months ago, spying for a powerful leader in the north. You are Sephira, I take it?"

Favian was surprised. For Ithric to speak in such a forthright manner on *any* subject was unusual—particularly one so sensitive.

"I am." Sephira frowned. "So you ask me to trust an admitted spy? And what of your companions? Are they also spies?"

"I was a slave. I escaped my owner six years ago and was forced into prostitution," Kathrael said, lifting her chin and meeting the woman's eyes with a challenging gaze.

Sephira looked at Favian. "And I am their friend," he said, having nothing else to offer her that he was willing to share.

She raised an eyebrow and looked back at Kath. "Of the three of you, you're the only one I would even consider trusting," she said. Her gaze returned to Favian and Ithric. "You two are outsiders, not children of the south. What business of yours is any of this? What do you think you could possibly offer us?"

There was a beat of silence, broken by the sound of scrabbling among the bones—rats, probably.

Ithric cleared his throat. "Until we learn what you need, that's a difficult question to answer."

"No," Sephira said. "It really isn't. The answer is clear— you and your pale-haired friend cannot help us. Moreover, you seem to know far too much about us for comfort."

Favian tensed, not liking where this was going. Beside him, Kathrael drew breath to speak, but Ithric beat her to it.

"I can't offer specifics of how we may help you in the future," he said, as calmly as if they were discussing a meal or the weather. "But I can show you easily enough why you need us, if you'll allow me a moment's indulgence."

Favian frowned at him, a bad feeling creeping over him. "Ithric..." he warned.

Ithric shot him the tight smile that had disconcerted so many people over the years. He turned away, his hands moving under his cloak. The guards raised their weapons, wary.

Favian grit his teeth. "Ithric, *don't—*"

Clothing fell, and Ithric whipped off the cloak even as his form shifted, twisting and rippling until the lion dropped onto four legs in the space where he'd been. The guards fell back in superstitious fear and awe, even as Sephira murmured, "Gods above..."

As one, Favian and Kathrael stepped between the lion and the guards' weapons, knowing if Ithric had miscalculated, they were all as good as dead. Their eyes met for an instant, a single thought passing between them.

They burn shape-shifters in Rhyth...

Ithric shifted back before the guards had time to decide that the lion was a threat, looking up at Sephira from his position on the ground.

"So," he said, "does that answer your earlier question?"

She was still staring at him with wide eyes. "You're a shifter," she breathed, shock evidently lending her a firm grasp of the obvious.

"I'm a shifter who has just placed my life in your hands," Ithric clarified. "Which seems only fair, since that is essentially what we are asking you to do in return."

Favian was still mired somewhere in the vicinity of *killing Ithric for being such a complete idiot*, but Kathrael seemed to have recovered more quickly.

"Allow us to join your cause," Kathrael said. "While we may not have delivered the Wolf Patron into your hands with an army of beasts marching behind him, ready to lead the slaves into battle, I think you'll agree that we still offer you much of value."

Sephira was quiet for a long moment, looking at Ithric, still crouched naked on the cold stone floor. The silence seemed to echo around the chamber of old skulls and bones, until Favian became uncomfortably aware of the hundreds of empty eye sockets staring down at them from the walls.

"So you have," Sephira said eventually. Her gaze flickered down the length of Ithric's body as he reached for his discarded cloak and straightened, shrugging it around his shoulders. "You are not a member of the priesthood," she observed.

"I would make a very poor priest," Ithric said.

A touch of humor tugged at Sephira's lips before she hid it. "I daresay you're right about that," she agreed.

"Believe me, you've no idea," Favian couldn't help adding.

Sephira nodded to herself, as if coming to a decision. "Very well. One can hardly question the gods' will when they bestow such an unusual gift under such unexpected circumstances. There is to be a meeting two days hence, at moonrise. Come back here and someone will meet you to take you there. Events in the city are presently at a crossroads, and there will be much to discuss."

"Thank you," Kathrael said solemnly. "We'll be there."

Without another word, Sephira made a curt gesture to her guards and turned to leave. One of the men picked up the lamp as they swept out in the opposite direction from the way Favian, Kathrael, and Ithric had come in. As they disappeared around a corner leading into the twisting tunnels beyond, the light was cut off almost completely, plunging the vault into near total darkness.

"Nice," Ithric said, and Favian could hear him patting the ground around him, searching for his clothes and, presumably, their weapons.

"Perhaps we would do well to bring a lamp with us next time," Kathrael observed. There was an undercurrent of tension in her voice that made Favian wish he could see her expression.

"Probably a wise idea," Ithric agreed, the rustle of clothing evident as he dressed himself in the dark. "Do you want me to go up to the tavern and see if the barkeep will lend me a light, so you two can see where you're going?"

All Favian wanted was to get out of this place of moldering death and trapped spirits as quickly as possible. "Just lead us to the base of the stairs. Then you can go up and knock while we wait below. Once the door is open we'll be able to see." He absolutely refused to consider what might happen if the barkeep wouldn't open the door. *Nope. Not going there. Not even thinking about it.*

"Right then. Let me just get my trousers laced up so I don't give the patrons a show," Ithric said. "And if you'd like, you can take this opportunity to yell at me for being reckless, Favian."

"What would be the point?" Favian asked with a sigh, feeling suddenly and unutterably weary. "Apparently, it worked."

Ithric's voice came from much closer this time, and a hand closed on Favian's shoulder. "No point at all. I thought it might make you feel better, that's all."

"Not so you'd notice," Favian told him. "Kath? Ready to go?"

"Yes," came the reply from the darkness next to him. She still didn't sound right, and he frowned.

"Come on then," he told Ithric, wanting to get her back up to the light and untainted air. "Can you see to lead us, Ithric?"

There was a faint pause. "Let's just pretend that I can, and get moving."

Favian swallowed another sigh and followed Ithric's light grip on his shoulder, feeling his way a step at a time along the ancient corridor of stone and human remains.

⚜

Kathrael tried to keep her focus on Ithric's hand in hers and her boots on the uneven stone floor of the catacombs. She'd managed to keep her attention on the land of the living while speaking with Sephira—*just*—but now Elarra's frightened weeping and occasional wails of distress echoed in her ears, threatening to buckle her knees and send her tumbling to the hard ground. When her infant daughter joined in with unhappy cries, she clenched her jaw, biting the inside of her cheek until it bled.

Stay strong, she chanted. *You must stay strong or it will be even worse.*

When they reached the base of the stairs, Ithric let her go to head up to the tavern and knock on the door. Favian's hand fumbled against her back, and his arm closed around her shoulders a moment later, bracing her.

"Something's wrong, I can tell," he said. "What is it?"

"I just need to get out of here, I think," she managed, leaning into him shamelessly. He turned to face her so he could put both arms around her in a proper embrace, and she sagged against his solid body in the dark.

"No argument here," he said, still sounding worried. "Not much longer now."

As if in response to his words, hinges creaked above them and a shaft of uncertain light from the tavern illuminated the uneven stone stairs.

"Come on," he said, urging her to climb up ahead of him.

The dizziness that she had been fighting for several minutes in the blackness persisted even though she could see again. She started cautiously up the steps, crouching with one hand held out in front of her, balancing against the steps further up. Favian kept a hand on her hip as he followed her slow progress, the touch grounding her a little.

Physical grace was beyond her at the moment, and she had to crawl through the low door on her hands and knees— Favian still right behind her. Ithric's sure grip lifted her to her feet and steadied her as she regained her balance.

"We need to find someplace quiet—or at least private— for a few minutes," Favian said as soon as he had joined them.

Ithric looked at Kathrael, and said, "Might be easier said than done," in a voice too low to be overheard by the people around them. "Can you walk?" he asked her.

Since the alternative was staying here, with a room full of drunken men watching them with various degrees of curiosity and suspicion, she nodded. She knew showing weakness was foolhardy in a place like this, but she was immeasurably grateful for Favian's discreet grip on her arm as they walked toward the door leading out into the stinking city beyond.

Two men leaned against the wall next to the entrance, arms crossed, looking at her with hungry eyes that made her stomach churn even more than it already was. As they approached, the taller of the two pushed away from the wall. Her hand fumbled at her belt under the cloak, but she realized with a jolt that Ithric still had all of her weapons— assuming he'd even been able to find them in the dark after Sephira and her guards left.

Beside her, Favian's grip tightened, and ahead of them, Ithric seemed to grow in stature as his spine straightened and his shoulders pulled back. She could feel possessiveness rolling off of him in waves—an aura of danger and unhinged recklessness that caused her breath to catch. She could almost picture his eyes flashing gold as the lion stirred within him.

The tall man hesitated mid-step, and his companion grabbed him by the shoulder of his jerkin and dragged him back, clearing the way through the door. Ithric paused and ushered her and Favian through, his eyes still pinning the two men in place. When they were outside, he let the door swing shut behind them.

"Let's try to find an alley," he said. "We can't afford to linger, though."

Kathrael let herself be led, the shouts and bonfires, laughter and brawling a confusing blur around her. She tried not to stumble over the trash and debris in the street, and before long darkness surrounded her. Gentle hands cupped her jaw—Favian. Strong arms wrapped around her from behind—Ithric.

"Is that better?" Favian asked. "Can you tell us what's happening?"

She swallowed, and took a deep breath. "I think so. It's my sister. She was terrified when we were in the catacombs. Completely distraught, beyond all reason." Around her, the ghostly wails were fading now, subsiding into exhausted sobbing.

Ithric's voice was calm and strong, close to her ear as he continued to embrace her from behind. "Do you know what upset her? Was it Sephira, or her guards? Or being underground?"

She could only shake her head. "I don't know. She won't talk; she just screams and cries. She's still crying. My daughter, too."

Favian's thumb brushed her unmasked cheek tenderly. "All right," he said. "All right. Do you know the prayer for the dead? Does she?"

Kathrael nodded. "Sort of. It's been a long time since I heard it. What are you—?"

"Shh," Favian soothed. "Just listen."

His light voice seemed to gain a lyrical depth, filling the narrow alleyway where they were sheltering as he chanted,

"Gods are calling,
Weary spirits, come to rest.
Join your loved ones,
Rise up, rise up on the smoke.
Day's toil is done.
Time now for love and laughter,
peace is yours forever more."

Kathrael's chest hitched, thinking of those she had lost—those who still clung so tenaciously to her, for reasons she could not comprehend. Favian moved forward until she was resting against his chest, pressed between his body and Ithric's. Surrounded by warmth. He repeated the prayer, and this time Vesh joined the chant, tentative and unsure, but gaining confidence as the familiar words came a third time, and a fourth.

Her own voice was a bare whisper as she echoed the old verse. Her daughter's cries slowly calmed, and Elarra's presence grew less hysterical, grieving quietly in the background until the sense of her slipped away between one breath and the next—like someone falling into exhausted slumber.

Kathrael sagged in relief, her whispered litany stumbling to a halt. Favian finished the prayer and went quiet as well, still holding her.

"Better now?" Ithric asked, and she nodded against Favian's chest.

"They've gone," Kathrael said, wishing she could fall asleep exactly like this, but knowing they still had to make it back to the river somehow.

"Good," he replied. "We need to go, in that case. And you two should be aware that we've gained an audience."

Kathrael stiffened, straightening away from their support with difficulty, even as Favian turned back to the mouth of the alley to look. Three ragged girls crouched at the edge of the light, watching them with wide eyes. She recognized one as the girl who had been sucking off men at the edge of the plaza when they'd arrived earlier. A livid bruise now decorated her cheek.

Their eyes connected, shared understanding passing between them.

EIGHTEEN

"Who did you lose?" the girl asked.

"Everyone," Kath replied, the word emerging hoarsely. "Who did *you* lose?"

"Everyone," the girl echoed.

Favian took a slow breath next to her, and made his way toward the little group. They watched him warily, but did not flee when he lowered himself to one knee in front of them.

"One may lose everything today, only to find something new and beautiful tomorrow," he said. "The past is the past, and the future is yet to be written. That is the gods' gift of hope."

There was a beat of silence.

"Your hair is gold," the oldest girl said, looking at him intently.

Kathrael could hear his huffed breath of almost-amusement. "I'm from far away, that's all. It's not so unusual there."

The girl with the bruise rose to her feet. "You sound like one of the priests, only the priests never talk to us directly. We don't count."

Favian rose as well, followed by the other two girls. "Then you must stand up and be counted. These so-called *priests* are not following the gods' will, for we are all the gods' children—every one of us, from the greatest to the smallest."

"That's what the Sisters always say," said the oldest, still watching Favian with drawn brows, as if trying to get his measure.

"I don't know who the Sisters are," Favian offered, "but it sounds like they speak sense. For now, though, please accept the gods' blessings from my hand, since the people who are charged with sharing them have been remiss."

The third girl— a pale slip of a thing who hadn't spoken, seemed to waver for a moment before darting forward and taking Favian's hand—lifting it to her forehead as she must have seen many times in her young life. Favian brushed a thumb over her skin in the expanding spiral of a blessing mark, his touch gentle and sure.

"The gods' blessings be upon you," he said formally. She looked up at him with wide eyes for a moment, before blinking slowly and darting away into the square.

The bruised girl was next, accepting the simple blessing with an expression of wonder. Favian looked at the older girl, a question in his eyes, but she shook her head.

"I want to stand up," she said. "I want to count. But that is not the way of things."

Kathrael managed to rouse herself enough to speak. "Maybe not now. But change is coming, sister. Be ready for it."

The girl stared at her with a hint of defiance. "Our life is change. We are always ready for it." With that, she turned and slipped away like a ghost, disappearing into the chaos outside.

Silence reigned for the space of several heartbeats before Ithric spoke. "That was probably not the safest thing you could have done," he told Favian, "but I can't bring myself to get onto you about it."

Favian's eyes found his in the shadows. "Pot," he said succinctly. "Kettle."

"Home," Kathrael countered. "Sleep."

"Agreed," the others replied, their voices overlapping. Lifting their hoods to obscure their faces in shadow, they left the shelter of the alley and made their way back through the chaos of Rhyth at night.

The next two days seemed to drag interminably. Despite her exhaustion, Kathrael's sleep was restless and plagued by dreams.

Her love for performing the show did not prevent it from seeming like an obstacle between the present and the time when they would attend the upcoming meeting. Fatigue and worry made the three of them snappish with each other. If it had been possible for them to take a day and rest, it might have helped, but money was not so plentiful that they could afford to lose an afternoon's takings.

Eventually, however, the evening of the meeting did finally come. Once again, they paid Ciryl to stay with the horses and caravan—the man had proved himself trustworthy over the time they'd known him, and it was worth a few coins and some good wine for them not to have to worry about what they would return to find.

"Will you be all right, going back down in the catacombs again?" Favian asked as they made their way into the central district.

Kathrael shrugged. "I'll have to be," she said, though in truth, the prospect had weighed heavily on her mind.

Favian shot her a look from under the hood of his cloak, but he only said, "Maybe you could try reciting the prayer again if the spirits start to get upset. Or some other prayer or verse that's meaningful to you."

"But if you get into real trouble, squeeze one of our hands twice and we'll figure out some way to get you away from there," Ithric added. "I'm not thrilled about it, but we can't exactly back out because the meeting takes place underground."

"We are *not* backing out," Kathrael said emphatically. "I'll manage."

They arrived at the tavern in good time. The owner seemed slightly less hostile toward them on this second visit, and the small lantern they'd brought with them went a long way toward making the trip down the stairs and through the twisting tunnels more bearable.

That said, Elarra once again grew agitated as they approached the place they'd met with Sephira. Kathrael silently chanted Utarr's prayer of solace in an attempt to keep them both calm.

It didn't help when the same six guards as before met them, waiting for them with cloth bags to cover their heads and prevent them from seeing the route to the place where the meeting would occur. Even though it made her heart race to be blindfolded and then marched along the uneven tunnels by a large man she didn't know, Kathrael could understand the reasoning behind the precaution. This way, if Sephira had been unwise in placing her trust in them, they would not be able to guide the group's enemies straight to its leaders.

The guards still seemed wary of Ithric, but he submitted without complaint to the treatment, and allowed the leader of the group to escort him without a word. Every few minutes, Favian would quietly ask Kathrael if she was all right, and she would murmur a short reply.

Oddly, instead of getting worse, Elarra's fear seemed to ease as they trudged along the seemingly endless corridors of bones. Kathrael wondered at it, but was not willing to speak of it in front of the guards. She settled on being grateful and worrying about the implications later.

She heard the meeting long before she saw it—a low buzz of conversation echoing oddly off of the walls of stone and skulls. Finally, after what seemed to have been a very long walk, their escorts brought them to a stop and pulled the hoods off. Kathrael blinked rapidly as her good eye adjusted to the glare of torchlight.

"Go in," the guard leader said gruffly, jerking his chin in the direction of a portal to their left, and a huge cavern beyond.

There were no bones here, just rock and seeping rivulets of water. The floor was packed dirt. Kathrael wondered if it was a natural cave, or if tools had shaped it. Inside, there was a group much larger and more varied than she had expected. She had thought it would be mostly slaves, and while a good proportion appeared to be just that, there were also people dressed as merchants and tradesmen, guardsmen, and a contingent of women draped in long robes the color of red ochre. There were even a handful of men and women wearing fine clothing such as the wealthy might own, and Kathrael wondered at it.

As they entered, many people turned to look at them—some wary, some curious. The lull in conversation spread outward like a wave as more and more people took in Favian's pale hair and Kathrael's bronze mask. Before things could turn hostile, Sephira appeared, slipping through the crowd to join them. She was wearing the same ochre robes as the group of women Kathrael had noticed earlier.

"These three are here at my behest," she said, loudly enough to carry throughout the cavern, now that people had stopped talking. "I have met with them before, and I am convinced they offer things of value to the group."

Kathrael was relieved that Sephira did not immediately blurt out the fact that Ithric was a shape-shifter. While doing so might have lent support to her claim and won over some of the people here, it would also have placed Ithric's continued safety in the hands of more than a hundred people, any one of whom might have ulterior motives.

Sephira turned to them. "You are welcome at our meeting, but do not ask the name of anyone here. Likewise, you are under no obligation to give your own names. This is one of the ways we safeguard ourselves. If captured and interrogated, we can only give up the identity of a few."

Before they could respond, a voice rose from nearby. "Not sure how well that's going to work, Sister," said an older man with gray running through his neatly trimmed beard. "I imagine many people here recognize the masked woman and the man who stands on running horses."

There was a new murmur of conversation as people craned to get a better look at them. Sephira sighed.

"If they didn't before, they probably will now, friend," she said tartly.

Ithric cleared his throat. "It's all right. We're aware that we aren't exactly keeping a low profile. Nonetheless, our current activities do allow us to go places and have contact with people that we might not otherwise be able to."

"There's wisdom in that, stranger," said the man. "Risk, too—but, then, there's risk aplenty for all of us."

"There is risk in merely stepping outside one's door, these days," Kathrael pointed out.

The man snorted. "Aye, so there is, lass. But perhaps we've diverted the meeting long enough. I think things were just about to get down to business."

After a bit more staring and whispering, most people went back to what they'd been discussing before Kathrael, Ithric, and Favian had arrived. As she looked around at the sea of faces, though, Kathrael's eye caught on a slim young man who was still looking straight at her, his eyes burning with some emotion she couldn't name.

He didn't look away when he saw her staring back at him, and Kathrael felt a flush of unease rise. After an uncomfortable beat, she tore her gaze away and purposely looked elsewhere, though the fine hair on her neck still prickled.

At the far end of the cavern, two figures were ascending a set of rough wooden stairs leading to a raised stone ledge. The ledge overlooked the rest of the cavern like a dais. One of the two wore the same red robes as Sephira. Her hair was iron gray, pulled back in a thick plait that trailed almost to her knees. From her place at the back of the cavern, Kathrael had the impression of strong features, wrinkled by time but still showing some of the vitality of a woman in her prime.

The other figure was a man, with thick, well-defined muscles and a back bowed by years of heavy labor. His hair was still dark, except for two silver streaks sweeping back from his temples. Even so far away, his eyes were striking in their intensity.

The conversation tailed off as the two took their places looking over the crowd, and quieted completely when the man raised his hand.

"Greetings, comrades," he called, his voice rolling through the echoing space, deep and commanding. "We meet here tonight to discuss a proposal by the Sisters of Avlan, to organize a secret governing council that would represent the true interests of the people of Rhyth."

Beside Kathrael, Favian jerked in surprise, his attention moving from the man and woman on the raised ledge to the knot of red-robed women standing off to the side, near the front.

"Favian?" Kathrael whispered, but he only shook his head and gestured to indicate that they should be quiet and listen.

"Such a council would be useless," called someone from the crowd. "The king rules Rhyth with an iron fist. He would never tolerate the people forming their own council."

Another voice rose, bitter. "The *gangs* rule Rhyth, you mean. When was the last time you saw guardsmen patrolling in the central district after dark? They're too scared!"

Several of the guardsmen present raised their voices in angry protest, but the woman at the front lifted her voice and spoke over the shouting. "The point of a people's council would not be to seek the approval of the king." Around her, the arguments subsided to muttering. "The point would be to have leadership in place in anticipation of the government's collapse. The city teeters on the brink of a precipice, as you all know. It may well need to fall before it can be rebuilt into something better."

"You are talking of revolution!" said one of the guardsmen. "That's a far different thing than freeing the slaves!"

It was the stoop-shouldered man on the ledge who answered. "Is it? Do you think the king and his nobles will nod quietly and step aside, allowing their slaves to go free?

Will the cult of Deimok get down on bended knee and submit to the gods' will? Perhaps the gangs will join hands with us and sing happy songs when all is said and done."

The crowd exploded, shouting opinions and arguments back and forth.

"We appear to have shown up at just about the right time," Ithric said into their ears, though his voice was tense.

The leaders let the arguments run for a bit before calling for order, which was restored reluctantly. To Kathrael's surprise, Favian stepped forward and called, "Where do the temples stand in all this?"

Behind her, Kathrael heard Sephira make a sound of disgust.

The woman on the plinth answered. "Your words mark you as a stranger to Rhyth as surely as your features do, young one," she said, her tone not entirely unkind. "The priests stand where they always do — safely behind their thick temple walls, with their child-slaves and their hypocrisy. One wonders, sometimes, what the gods must think of it all."

"One does, indeed," Favian said thoughtfully, once the meeting had returned to other matters. He turned to Sephira, who still stood close enough to converse in relative privacy. "The leader mentioned the Sisters of Avlan. You are a member?"

Sephira raised an eyebrow. "None of us hide our affiliation."

"And that doesn't put you at risk?" Favian asked, still looking at her very intently.

She laughed, as if the sound had been surprised from her. "Of course it does. Any of our number who are caught unawares end up dead or thrown in a cell to be tortured and raped. We have lost twenty-eight sisters just since the last solstice."

Around them, the crowd was now discussing the group's recent efforts to free individual slaves from the great houses and smuggle them out of the city. Favian, however, was still focused on his conversation with Sephira.

"You identify with Avlan?" he said. "A minor god largely shunned by the priesthood? And you consider yourselves his... what? His priestesses?"

"Wait — isn't Avlan the trickster god?" Ithric asked.

"Yes," Favian said. "The half-mortal son of Deresta and a warrior who deserted his chieftain during a battle—not generally considered a being worthy of devotion."

Sephira watched the exchange closely. "You are surprisingly knowledgeable for a street performer."

Favian frowned. "I wasn't always a street performer. But, again… why Avlan?"

Sephira gestured around them, taking in not only the cavern and the meeting, but also the city above. "Can you think of any more appropriate patron for Rhyth than the Trickster? A god, I might add, shunned largely because of the sins of his father."

Favian blinked. "No. I suppose I can't."

Sephira's gaze moved to Ithric. "Avlan has another little-known association, as well."

His eyes following hers, Favian said, "He is the god of shape-shifters."

Sephira's eyebrow flickered, and she dipped her chin in acknowledgement. "Just so. Again, your knowledge of our oral history surprises me. It is not the level of education one generally picks up outside of the priesthood." Her gaze settled on Favian, weighing him.

Kathrael saw Favian's throat bob up and down once, and knew before he spoke that he was about to give Sephira even more power over them. She only hoped they would not live to regret it.

"There is a very good explanation for that," Favian said. "I am, in fact, a novice priest from the temple of Senovo, the Wolf Patron of Draebard."

Kathrael caught the flicker of shock in Sephira's expression before the woman covered it. She held her breath.

Sephira seemed to consider her words for a long moment before saying, "You don't look like a priest."

Favian stared at her, not backing down. "Neither do you, Elder Sister."

That startled a short bark of laughter from her. "Ha! Well, yes. Quite. Your point is taken… *Little Brother*."

Kathrael took the opportunity to ask something that had been plaguing her since their first meeting with Sephira two days ago. "Sister," she began, "if I may ask a personal question—I couldn't help noticing that you share an unusual eye color with someone else of my acquaintance. Someone who helped me at a time when no one else would."

Sephira's light gray eyes grew wary, but there was curiosity behind her expression as well. She folded her hands into the loose sleeves of her robes. "Indeed?"

Kathrael nodded, watching her closely. "Yes... a eunuch by the name of Hameen, in the temple of Naloth. He risked his High Priest's displeasure by giving me food, money, and supplies for traveling at a time when I had nothing."

The priestess' expression closed off, but she answered nonetheless. "Hameen? Yes, I am a relation of his, as you have obviously surmised. I lived with his parents for a time, years ago, after my bondmate died."

"I had wondered," Kathrael said. "Does that mean that Novice Hameen is also part of the underground?"

Sephira's face remained stony. "Again, these are not the sorts of questions that are encouraged, for the safety of all involved." She paused for a moment. "However, in this case, I suppose there is no harm in saying that while my nephew seems willing to break small rules now and again to ease his conscience, he shows no inclination to act in a way that will truly make a difference to the world."

"Oh," said Kathrael, finding herself strangely disappointed that she would not run across Hameen at a meeting such as this one. That she would not be able to speak with him, and show him what changes his small act of mercy had wrought in her life.

"Few have the will to stand up openly when doing so may mean death," Sephira observed, still cold. "Fewer still within the Priests' Guild, it seems." Her eyes slipped to Favian for a moment. "Present company excepted, apparently."

Favian looked at her shrewdly. "And that is why the Sisters came together? To stand up for the gods' teachings when the priests will not?"

"Just so, Little Brother. Someone must serve the gods' will. If those who are charged with doing so become fat and corrupt, then others must step forward to do the work they will not."

At her words, Favian nodded. "I honor what you are doing, Elder Sister. I would like to speak with you about it in greater detail, when the time is more suitable—and perhaps meet with some of the others if they are willing."

Sephira tilted her head. "We shall see, Little Brother. For now, though, it appears the meeting is drawing to a close.

The guards who brought you will take you back to the vault underneath the tavern. I will consult with the others about you, and someone will contact you after one of your public performances if we agree to allow you further access."

Ithric had been splitting his attention between the wider goings on of the gathering and their conversation with Sephira. "Thank you, Sephira," he said. "We'll be waiting."

"May the gods keep you safe and whole until then," Sephira said, and tipped her chin to them before leaving their little group to return to the other priestesses.

"Well," Favian said, once they were more or less alone again. "That was certainly interesting."

"In more ways than one," Ithric said. "I think you were both distracted, but after going to the trouble of bringing all of these people here and arguing for well over an hour, it doesn't sound like a single thing was properly decided."

A frown wrinkled Kathrael's brow. "Really? Nothing at all?"

Ithric shrugged. "My impression is that most of the people here are involved in some way with smuggling slaves away from their owners. And… that's about it. It sounds like the leadership, such as it is, wants to organize for bigger things—but if tonight was any indication, they're not having much luck."

She and Favian mulled that over for a moment or two.

"Come on," Favian said eventually. "It's late. Let's go find the guards so they can take us back."

Kathrael nodded, and the three of them started skirting the edge of the crowd toward the familiar, imposing figures of their escorts. Before they'd closed half of the distance, however, the slender man who had been staring so fixedly at Kathrael earlier intercepted them. She felt a small jolt of foreboding as he reached out a hand to stop her progress. Ithric immediately stepped between them—not *threatening*, precisely… but with a definite hint of warning in his stance.

"Can we help you?" he asked, his voice giving nothing away.

Even now, the man seemed to find it difficult to tear his gaze away from Kathrael's face. This close, she could see that he had the gaunt, overworked appearance of a slave. His hair was disheveled and his beard unkempt, though his clothing was carefully mended.

He answered Ithric with hesitant words, while still looking straight at Kathrael. "I need—" He swallowed. "That is, may I... speak with your woman for a moment? Privately?"

Favian was standing shoulder to shoulder with her, and looked at her with a question in his eyes. "Kath?"

She dragged in a deep breath, struggling to tamp down the odd sense of disquiet flooding her chest.

Please, little sister, Elarra whispered from beyond the veil. *Please...*

Kathrael lifted her chin and held the man's eyes. "You may say to me what you need to say." Her good eye flickered to Favian and Ithric. "Give us a moment."

Her companions nodded, obviously wary, and faded back just far enough to allow them some privacy.

"You've been staring at me all night," she said, once they were alone. "Normally, I'd be flattered, but I don't get the impression it was that kind of stare."

He still appeared fascinated by her. "No," he said. "No, it's not anything like that."

With a deep breath, the man opened his mouth and began to talk quietly. As he spoke, Kathrael felt herself growing cold and empty, his words bringing her world crashing to the earth like crumbling brick.

She knew all the blood must have drained from her face by the time he'd finished, leaving her pale and gray. She was barely aware of parting from him... barely aware of Favian taking her elbow or the look of alarm he shared with Ithric.

"Little Cat?" Ithric asked, but she shook her head.

"Not now. Not here," she said, the words coming out strangely flat. "Let's go back to the warehouse. Favian was right—it's late."

If she could have felt anything at that moment, she would have felt gratitude at their ready acceptance of her words. She was vaguely aware of the way they watched over her, at least until the bags were put over their heads again and they were once more led through the winding corridors and tunnels of the catacombs.

When they arrived back where they'd started, there was still a bit of oil in the lantern to guide their steps up the stone staircase to the tavern. Once inside, they found grim faced customers drinking ale behind a barred door.

"Mob out there," warned the taciturn barkeep, the words punctuated by the sound of something heavy hitting the wall outside. "Best hunker down."

Ithric looked at Kathrael, shared a glance with Favian, and turned back to the man. "Is there a back entrance? Besides the one we just came through, I mean."

The barkeep shrugged, as if their apparent suicidal tendencies were no business of his. He led them through a warren of rooms and hallways that grew progressively dingier until they came to another barred door. "Once you go through, you're on your own, strangers. I'll be barring it behind you and going straight back to my customers."

Ithric returned a shrug of his own. "Stay safe, in that case." He listened at the door for a moment, his head cocked, and indicated Favian and Kathrael should follow him.

The alley into which they were disgorged was narrow and dark. The lantern, of course, chose that moment to sputter and die, out of oil at last. Kathrael was staying upright and moving by force of will alone—only distantly aware of the angry rumble of a crowd on the far side of the row of buildings containing the tavern. It was different than the usual raucous noises of the city at night. Larger. More focused.

Still, Kathrael could only turn inward, her mind whirling, a chariot wheel upended uselessly in the air, spinning and spinning but going nowhere. The route Ithric led them along was unfamiliar, skirting the mob and keeping to the shadows.

Twice they were accosted. The first man was so drunk that Ithric shoved him to the side, sending him staggering to where he braced himself against the wall of a nearby building, cursing them with slurred words. The second was frighteningly sober, but slunk away after a brief scuffle that ended with Ithric's dagger pressed under his jaw.

It took far longer to get back to the riverfront than it had taken to get into the central district. By the time the familiar falling-down building came into view in the pale moonlight, Kathrael's head was swimming so badly she couldn't even feel her feet hitting the ground as she walked. Ithric whistled to let Ciryl know it was them. A moment later they were inside, the sound of the horses moving restlessly and Ciryl giving a mighty yawn bringing her marginally back to herself.

"All good?" Ciryl asked, rising from where he'd been seated and stretching his back until it popped.

"That remains to be seen," Favian said, his attention fixed on Kathrael.

"We're fine," said Ithric. "Though I won't be surprised if part of the central city burns tonight. Thanks for watching the place; tell Qaden we'll have the money a day early this week when you see him."

"Sure thing, Ithric," Ciryl said, adding, "Now get some sleep, yeah?" around another yawn.

"Goodnight, Ciryl," Ithric told him as the man wandered out into the darkness with a wave of farewell. When he was gone, Ithric turned back to Favian. "A fire first, I think. Do we have any of the strong wine left?"

Favian had barely looked away from Kathrael since they arrived, but he nodded. "I think so. I'll check the horses and then fetch it."

Kathrael let Ithric lead her back to their room and set her on the low stool they used for a seat. A few minutes later, a fire was burning in the hearth, beating back the damp chill that had set in. Favian arrived and closed the door behind him, dropping a mostly empty wineskin in the corner before crouching down in front of her. Ithric folded himself into a cross-legged position next to Favian.

"Now. Tell us what he said to you," he prompted.

Kathrael swallowed, still feeling disconnected and strange. "It's Elarra," she began.

"What about her?" Favian asked.

Kathrael stared into his blue eyes, trying to gain strength from him.

"My sister—she's—" The horrible truth twisted up in her throat. "She's... *alive*."

NINETEEN

"Alive?" Favian echoed. "Are you sure?"

Ithric reached out a hand and placed it on her knee, anchoring her. "But... that's good news, isn't it? Do you know where she is?"

Kathrael nodded, still unable to feel the emotions that she should be feeling right now. "The man... he kept staring at me during the meeting. He recognized my features, even with the mask." She paused, her good eye losing focus. "Elarra and I always looked very alike, from the time we were young children."

A second hand covered Ithric's where it rested on her knee—Favian. "And this man knows your sister?"

"Yes. He was in service at one of the great houses. The estate of Master Pendreth, heir of the Great Southern Forest." The reality of what she was about to relate rose around her like murky floodwater, threatening to choke her. "When Elarra... came into the city, all those years ago, she wasn't killed. She was recaptured. By one of Pendreth's overseers, who recognized her as being an escaped slave and pretended to pay her for sex so he could get her alone."

Favian drew breath as if to say something, but she shook her head and plowed on, the words coming faster, nearly tumbling over themselves to get out. "The overseer told her afterward it was because of the pale skin around her neck, where the sun couldn't reach. He could tell she had recently worn a collar. He dragged her to Master Pendreth for judgment. Pendreth... took a liking to her looks and spirit. He decided to keep her in his service rather than executing her."

She swallowed convulsively against the bile rising in her throat. "She was in Rhyth the entire time I was here. We were in the same city for *years*, and I never even tried to find her."

The hands on her leg squeezed, drawing her away from a rising spiral of self-loathing at her inexcusable failure.

"You had no way of knowing, Kath," Favian said. "Rhyth is a huge place. You had no way of finding her."

"But now we do," Ithric added. "We'll figure out a way to free her. Is she still in the same house?"

She nodded. "I think so. The man said he was sold a few months ago and had only been able to sneak back and see her twice before he was caught and thrown out. Now the guards won't let him back in. I... think he might have loved her. He seemed to believe that she would have sent word to him somehow if she'd escaped or been sold. But... there's something else."

Something she didn't want to acknowledge, but had to.

"What is it, Little Cat?" Ithric asked.

It almost seemed selfish to dwell on it. Yet she couldn't avoid it. "Elarra isn't dead. Her spirit cannot be speaking to me from beyond the veil." Kathrael's voice had regained the flat, detached cadence from earlier. "I don't have a gift from the gods. The dead do not haunt me. I'm just a madwoman hearing voices that aren't there."

Oh, Kath. Favian silently berated himself for not making the connection sooner. And what could either of them say to that, really? As much as he hated to let the silence hang for even a heartbeat after such a statement, he needed a moment to step back, and look at this new reality from a priest's viewpoint rather than a lover's.

As he suspected, Ithric had the *lover* angle covered already, in any case. "Hey," he said. "You don't know that. Maybe... I don't know, maybe you're hearing her somehow even though she's alive. Like the twins from Darveen. It's not unheard of."

But Kathrael shook her head angrily. "Vesh... *is dead.* My daughter *is dead.* I saw the bodies. It's all been a delusion. *All of it.*"

She grimaced and lifted a hand to her head, making Favian wonder if they were speaking to her, even now — protesting their reality, proclaiming their own existence. He slipped his hand from where it rested atop Ithric's, so that he could grasp her leg directly through the thick material of her skirts.

"Kathrael," he said solemnly, "I realize you may not be able to believe me about this right now, but nothing has changed."

She looked at him with incredulity. "Everything has changed!"

He shook his head. "It hasn't. Your perception of it has changed, which is different. You are exactly the same person you were when we walked into that meeting. Your voices are precisely the same as they were when you woke up this morning."

"How can you say that?" she hissed. "I thought... I thought that there was some kind of *meaning* behind it all. Some *reason*. But the only reason behind it is that my mind is broken! My sanity snapped months ago in a field north of Rhyth, when I first heard Vesh speak to me like a whisper rustling through the grass!"

Her gaze turned inward again, as it tended to when she was listening to things only she could hear, and her fingers tightened in the hair of her temple. Favian could almost imagine Vesh saying something hurt or scathing in her ear. He ached anew for the pain this curse — if it truly was a curse — had brought her.

Ithric rose to his feet in front of her, abandoning his grip on her knee in favor of covering her hands with his, easing the one at her temple away and pulling both to rest against his chest.

"No, Little Cat," he said. "Favian is right, in a way. Look at what you've accomplished, haunted as you have been. Whether your ghosts would exist without you doesn't change or diminish what *you* have done. It won't change or diminish what you will do in the future, either — not unless you allow it to."

That was a bit more blunt than Favian would likely have put it, but at least Ithric's words seemed to be holding Kath's attention. "They're talking to you right now, aren't they," Favian said, not even bothering to make it a question. "They're upset."

She nodded, a reluctant, jerky movement. "Vesh is trying to convince me he's real. Elarra is begging me not to push her away. Our mother is crying. So is my dau —" She cut herself off. "So is... the baby."

Favian's heart ached at the way she was obviously trying to divorce herself from what was, for better or worse, a part of her. "You're forgetting what we already know about your voices," he pointed out gently. "When you are upset... when you try to push them away... everything gets worse."

Her temper flared. "So what would you suggest? Shall I just gibber quietly to myself in a corner, talking to imaginary people and singing them songs? Perhaps I'll have better luck begging in the streets now that I'm obviously deranged in addition to being disfigured!"

"Stop," Ithric said, no-nonsense. "Just... *stop*, Kathrael. You're not going to be begging in the streets. You won't have time, because we'll be too busy performing the show, meeting with the underground, and helping Elarra escape from this *Pendreth* bastard. Besides, the show makes more money than begging by quite a margin."

Kathrael's head bowed, as if she had no more strength to hold it up. Her voice quavered as she said, "I just thought... that maybe you and Favian wouldn't want—"

Now it was Favian's turn to feel anger rise, though he knew it was probably due to lack of sleep more than anything. "Well, stop thinking it," he interrupted, before she could say something that truly would make him angry. "Do you honestly think that of us? Have we given you some reason to believe that we'd—what? Discard you like unwanted garbage because we found out new information about your voices? *Really*, Kath?"

Kathrael *flinched*. Ithric's voice was chiding as he murmured, "Favian. Not helping."

"I'm sorry," Kathrael said, sounding unbearably young. "I—I don't know what to think right now. I'm so tired, but I know I won't be able to sleep, and that makes it all worse. I just want it all to stop, but it's never going to, is it?"

Favian let his breath out slowly, feeling his frustration deflate. "I don't know, Kath. It does seem pretty unlikely after so many months. And I'm sorry I snapped. I'm tired, too. I think we all are."

Ithric lifted Kath's hands to his lips and kissed them. "Even if we can't sleep, we can at least rest. Come on. We'll talk more in the morning about what to do next. All right?"

"Yes, Let's go to bed," Favian agreed. "Things will look better in the morning."

Kathrael was surprised to find that she did eventually fall asleep for a short stretch before dawn, held between Ithric and Favian in their snug little sleeping nest on the floor in front of the hearth. Favian had been wrong, though—things didn't look any better this morning than they had last night. They looked pretty much the same, in fact.

She was still a madwoman. She had still failed Elarra in the worst possible way, leaving her to suffer for years without even bothering to look for her.

Fine, said the hallucination that sounded like Vesh. *You fucked up. Haven't we all. Now go do something to fix it.*

Go away, Kathrael thought, somewhat desperately.

No, said the hallucination. *I'm not going anywhere until you get yourself together.*

"How can I when you won't *leave me alone?*" she snapped, only becoming aware that she'd spoken aloud when Favian and Ithric stirred next to her in the bed. Mortification flooded her at the lapse. Was this to be her life now? Talking to the imaginary voices? Fighting aloud with no one?

"Kath?" Favian asked, and she hated, hated, *hated* the careful worry that she had caused in his voice.

Ithric grunted. "*Ugh.* Is it time to get up already? Shit."

His voice was a bit gravelly. He'd stayed up for hours last night, singing and humming to try to calm her. He would benefit from some honeyed wine before he tried to perform at the show this afternoon. Except that of course they didn't have any honey, because they couldn't afford anything except the basic necessities.

And would they even be able to perform now? Would she be able to—

You're being an idiot, the hallucination of Vesh said, sounding about as edgy as she felt. *Would you please. Just. Stop.*

She very carefully did not respond, instead forcing her attention outward, to the people who were real. "Sorry," she said. "I didn't mean to wake you."

"Don't worry about it," Favian said. "We need to get up anyway. Are you feeling better?"

"No," she said honestly. "But I guess I need to muddle forward regardless."

Well, thank the gods for small mercies, muttered the voice that couldn't really be Vesh.

Ithric cracked a huge yawn and eased his arm out from under her shoulders so he could stretch. "Right," he said. "After giving things quite a bit of thought last night, I have an idea."

Favian rolled up on an elbow. "Is it a good idea or a stupid, dangerous idea?"

"It's a good, only somewhat dangerous idea."

Their half-hearted, early morning sniping was oddly calming. "An idea about getting to Elarra?" she asked.

He nodded. "We need to start performing in the southern district, where the great houses are located. I assume it won't be difficult to find out where old Pendreth's estate is. Then we can put the word around that we're looking to give private performances in hopes of gaining a patron, but only among those with very high status. If we can make contact with someone who works in Pendreth's household and talk up the idea, maybe we can get ourselves an invitation to exactly where we need to be."

Favian looked thoughtful. "It would take some doing. But it seems a lot safer way to get to her than trying to sneak in or break in."

A tiny thread of hope wove its way through the darkness shrouding Kathrael's spirit. "Maybe. But, if..." She swallowed. "If we find her and are able to get her out, what then? It won't be much of a mystery what happened, once she's discovered missing."

Ithric shrugged. "Her disappearance probably wouldn't be noticed right away. We can leave the city if we have to. Maybe take her to Darveen. And that may not even be necessary. You might recall that we have contacts now in the slave underground. And the one thing they actually seem to be competent at doing is helping individual slaves escape Rhyth."

It was all so nebulous; it could barely even be called a plan. And yet, it was better than Kath could have come up with on her own, given the state she was in. Of course, it also meant that she had no choice about going on with the show. She would have to perform and hope that the madness would let her get through her dance routine and music without making the wrong kind of spectacle of herself in front of a crowd.

Don't be ridiculous. The voice that wasn't Vesh sounded tired. Irritated.

Again, she clamped her jaw shut and forced herself not to respond.

Ithric watched Kathrael carefully over the following days, and he knew Favian was doing the same. It was painful to see her losing ground against her own mind. It seemed fairly obvious that she had taken it as a personal challenge not to accept or interact with the voices that haunted her, since she had decided that they weren't real spirits. It was as if she feared that continuing to converse with them would somehow seal her fate as a madwoman.

Though he could hardly say so without coming across as a complete cad, Ithric thought that was a foolish decision on her part. Neither he nor Favian seemed able to convince her that the two of them *genuinely didn't care* if the voices were real, objective presences or the inventions of her own mind.

What did it matter, at the end of the day? He supposed Favian had some views on that, given his lifelong fascination with religion and the spirit world. But as far as Ithric was concerned, as long as Kathrael was able to function and experience a well-lived life with the voices hovering around her, their true nature didn't make a single whiff of difference.

After all, they seemed to steer Kathrael in the direction she needed to go, for the most part. They were even entertaining company, on occasion. And while they sometimes caused her emotional pain, he'd never sensed anything actively malicious about them.

People like him and Kath were doomed to fight painful memories of loss on a daily basis, whether they heard voices in their heads or not. Maybe Favian was, too, with his dead parents and history of dire, prophetic dreams.

At least twice a day, Ithric found himself bemoaning the fact that he couldn't have transformed into a lion for the first time *five fucking minutes* earlier than he had, and thereby saved his parents' lives. He also continued to play his last interaction with Alyndra over and over, looking for some way he could have made things come out the way he'd wanted.

He wasn't oblivious enough to think he was a particularly sane individual, but that certainly hadn't stopped him from living a pretty damned good life so far. Sanity was why they kept Favian around. Well... one of the reasons, anyway.

It pained him to watch Kathrael struggle, but he knew that in the end, it was *her* struggle. Not his. Not Favian's. All they could do was be there to offer help when she reached for it.

And, right now, helping meant getting her sister back.

Which was why he was currently sitting across from Ruben in a seedy inn, pretending to drink the mug of watered down piss that he'd been nursing since soon after they arrived.

"Mob burned down the Painted Lady last week," Ruben was saying, referring to the tavern housing the entrance down into the catacombs. "Same night you and your friends was there, in fact. The barkeep and a bunch of his regulars were trapped inside. Burned to death, every one of 'em. Ain't no one gonna hang for it, neither. It's a travesty, if you ask me."

Ithric remembered the sound of the angry crowd outside the inn, pounding on the walls and battering the barred door. He was surprised that the owner, at least, hadn't followed them out of the back entrance once the fire had started. Perhaps the mob had found it and blocked the way after they'd left.

"The city is trying to chew its own leg off, like an animal stuck in a trap," Ithric said in disgust. "Me and the others want to start moving into the safer parts of town if we can."

Ruben snorted. "The richer parts, you mean."

Ithric allowed himself a smirk. "That, too, yeah. Which reminds me, did you get that message delivered to my friend, like I asked?"

After their admittance to the meeting in the catacombs, Ithric had eked out enough money from their takings to send his first message north, to Andoc. He felt bad about having left it so long before sending word, but in truth such things were expensive. And until then, there hadn't been much to report beyond the fact that they were all alive and in Rhyth. With money so tight, Ithric had thought it best to wait until he had more important information to pass on.

"Aye," Ruben said. "Sent it with a lad I know. He's a sharp one. He'll get it to your friend, right enough."

"Good. I also wondered if we could speak again to one of the group you introduced us to. I have a... business proposition that I think might interest some of them."

"I'll see what I can do," Ruben said with a shrug. "Can't promise nothin', though." He lifted his empty mug in the air and waved it around to attract the attention of the barmaid.

When she arrived, looking harried, Ithric threw down a couple of coins that he couldn't really afford to spend. "His drink's on me," he said, and rose to leave, clapping Ruben's shoulder on his way out.

It was late. Or, perhaps more accurately, it was early. The sun would be up in a handful of hours. Ithric was bone-tired, not to mention restless and worried. The only saving grace was that the city seemed relatively quiet tonight. Perhaps it was the chill wind carrying the threat of cold rain ahead of it, or perhaps the cult of Deimok was holed up somewhere drinking the blood of rats and chickens under the full moon, or whatever they did in private.

Though it would delay his return to his lovers' bed, Ithric found a relatively quiet place down by the river in the warehouse district, still some distance from the building they had taken over. Ignoring the prickle of gooseflesh as the wind bit into him, he stripped efficiently and folded his clothing into a neat pile by a jut of exposed rock. With a sigh of relief, he shifted, allowing the lion to take over for a much needed few minutes.

The beast rumbled in satisfaction and scented the air, taking in the smell of a city in chaos. Beneath it, he sensed the faint musk of a beaver or muskrat, foraging in the underbrush some distance away, near the water. Ithric padded toward the smell on silent paws, the troubles of the day falling away to be replaced by the simple pleasure of the hunt.

⚜

When they moved the show to the richer areas of Rhyth, they discovered that it yielded smaller crowds, but the people who did come paid handsomely. After the first couple of performances, Ithric berated himself for not suggesting this sooner; despite the sparser audience, they were making more money than they had ever made in the central city.

Of course, getting access to the area was more challenging than it had been in the shabby squares and plazas near the marketplace. There were still guardsmen patrolling here, though once they figured out that Ithric and the others had money to pay bribes, things smoothed out considerably.

On the fourth day, they were approached after the performance by a stooped old woman in a rough-woven, hooded cloak. Shuggan was with them today, rather than Ciryl, and he stepped forward belligerently, blocking the woman's path.

"Oy," he snapped. "You've got no business back here, Grandmere. Move along."

Ithric sighed. "*Shuggan*," he said, moving the man aside with a hand on his arm. "Please don't threaten the rubes."

Shuggan backed off, looking sheepish. "Oh. Sorry, Ithric," he mumbled. "Sorry, Ma'am."

"I've been threatened by worse, believe me," said the old woman, a hint of amusement lacing her tone.

Beside Ithric, Favian frowned, and Kathrael drew in a breath. That voice was familiar, not to mention unexpected in their current surroundings. The woman tilted her head just enough to bring her features out of the shadow of the hood for a moment.

It was the leader of the Sisters of Avlan. The woman whose powerful voice had echoed through the cavern at the meeting, calling it to order. Her acting skills were superb—Ithric would never have recognized her had she not spoken.

Thinking quickly, he turned to Shuggan. "Shuggan, would you mind taking down the curtain and packing things up? This is the older sister of an acquaintance of ours. We need to have a word with her about a family matter."

The hired thug lifted a shoulder and let it drop, obviously having no interest in the topic of their conversation. "Yeah, whatever. I want to get back to my woman before it gets too late. Didn't realize we'd be stuck here all afternoon."

"This will just take a few moments," Ithric assured him, and turned back to their unexpected visitor once he'd shambled off to start packing things up.

Favian seemed off balance, but he was still the first to address the priestess. "Elder Sister," he said, quietly enough not to be heard beyond their little group. "This is quite a surprise."

"Please," she said, "call me Zandreen. I wanted to speak with you in person, after Sephira related some things to me. It is true, what she said?"

"Well," Favian hazarded, "that's difficult to say without having been privy to the conversation. But if she told you that I had another vocation before becoming a street performer, and that Ithric is… uniquely gifted… then, yes, it's true."

She nodded. "What is your name, young one? No doubt Sephira warned you against exchanging names, but I have reason to believe that we will have business together in the future."

"I am Favian of Draebard." Favian's eyes sought Kathrael, seeking her permission. When she nodded, he continued, "This is Kathrael of Rhyth."

Zandreen raised an eyebrow. "So you are from Draebard." Her gaze flicked to Ithric, and back. "It seems you are well acquainted with… *uniquely gifted* individuals, Favian."

"I suppose you could say that," Favian allowed.

"How can we help you today, Zandreen?" Ithric asked.

"We had already been discussing you within the group, as it happens," Zandreen said. "But recently a mutual friend sent word that you wished to meet with us again. At about the same time, we heard that you had moved your performances to the southern district, so I decided to come myself. You're all rather talented, I must say. I quite enjoyed the dancing and the horses in particular."

"Thank you," Kathrael said quietly. Ithric didn't like how withdrawn she had seemed so far, so it was a relief that she was finally speaking up.

Zandreen's attention moved to her. "You have been the quiet one, child. Yet I gather you are the one closest to the evils we seek to right."

"Perhaps so," Kathrael murmured.

When it became apparent that she would not continue, Ithric said, "Kathrael's sister is held in thrall at the estate of Master Pendreth." He didn't try to hold back his sneer at the word *master*. "We intend to remedy that situation, sooner rather than later. We'd hoped you might be able to help us if we are able to find and free her."

The old woman was sharp. Her eyes lit with understanding almost immediately. "You intend to walk in his front door rather than sneaking in the back, I gather."

Ithric raised his chin in acknowledgement. "We're told the household guards are on the lookout for intruders these days. This seemed like a better approach."

"It is bold, I'll grant you," Zandreen allowed. "But you'll still need a plan for afterward, if you are successful."

Favian spoke up. "You must have a system in place. This is what you and the others *do*, is it not?"

"Indeed it is," Zandreen said with a dry smile. "It is, in point of fact, *all* we seem to do these days. Send word through Ruben when you know what night you will attempt it. If you are able to smuggle her out, bring her to the abandoned granary at the eastern end of the street running behind the temple of Utarr. Someone will meet you there and help her get out of the city."

"Thank you," Kathrael said, still unnaturally subdued. "But I won't send her away on her own. I'll be going with her, if leaving Rhyth is the only way for her to be safe."

"*We'll* be going with her, I think you mean," Favian said, beating Ithric to it.

Kathrael flushed and nodded, looking down at her feet.

"It is not necessarily the only way," Zandreen replied placidly, "but it is certainly the simplest way, even if she only leaves for a while. Regardless, whoever meets you at the granary will be able to direct you. That said, if you are caught absconding with a slave, there will be no help for you."

"Then we'll take care not to be caught," Ithric said, his smile sharp and grim.

Zandreen regarded him for a long beat. "Avlan runs strong in you, Gifted One. That can often be both a blessing and a curse."

"You've no idea," Favian muttered.

"You think not?" Zandreen asked, sounding amused again. "Remember to whom you are speaking, Favian of Draebard. May the gods smile on your worthy endeavors, and return you to us when they are complete. I sincerely hope we will speak again soon. Things in Rhyth are coming to a head."

"That they are," Ithric agreed readily. "Stay safe and strong, Zandreen. We will send word as we can. And if you are able to put us in touch with someone from Pendreth's household... or just have that person put a word in Pendreth's ear that we would like to perform privately for him, it would be immensely helpful to us."

Zandreen nodded her understanding and headed away, once again an anonymous, stooped old woman, of no interest or threat to anyone. Favian watched her depart, strangely intent.

"They fascinate you, don't they?" Ithric observed. "These Sisters."

It took a moment before Favian shook himself free of his reverie. "I can't deny it. I have so many questions about them. Where did they learn the religious histories in such detail? Why choose the Trickster as their patron god? I really want to talk to them more."

"It sounds like they want to talk to us, as well," Kathrael said. "Hopefully we'll all get the chance." She frowned, then, and Ithric knew she was once again focused inward, on the voices she strove so desperately to ignore.

"Come on," Ithric said. "Shuggan looks restless. Let's get him back to his woman before he decides to stage a one-man mutiny on us. Maybe now we'll get the contacts we need and start to make some faster progress."

⁓ ♕ ⁓

It was another three days before they had their first breakthrough, and if Kathrael hadn't already been mad as a barrel of rats, the waiting would have sent her there regardless. Since they'd started performing in the southern district, Ithric had added a plea for any servants in the great houses to convince their masters to let them put on a private performance for them.

He couched it in joking terms, alluding to the great wealth they hoped to gain by securing a powerful patron, but he also made the idea sound just enticing enough that—hopefully—some ambitious servant would try it in hopes of currying favor. The first nibble on their fishing line, as Favian put it, did not come from Pendreth's estate. That was really no surprise, though it didn't stop the stab of disappointment she felt at yet more waiting.

No, this is no good! insisted the voice that sounded like Elarra, but wasn't. *It has to be Pendreth!*

Hush, Elarra, said the voice that wasn't Vesh. *Kath may not believe in us, but I believe in her.*

Kathrael clenched her fingers to her temples, the horrible, trapped feeling she felt whenever the voices started in on her intensifying until tears burned behind her good eye. She refused to let them fall, though. There was too much to do.

The show required considerable reworking to perform in a potential patron's private courtyard. Favian compensated as best he could for the lack of space and the fact that he could only maintain a serene trot on horseback rather than a headlong gallop. To increase the excitement, he started adding acrobatic maneuvers—pivoting with a brisk leap to stand backwards on the animals, balancing on one foot with the other leg stretched out behind him like a dancer as he steadied himself with a hand on Ozias' neck, kneeling and leaping to his feet without using his hands, scissoring his legs up so that his whole body was briefly parallel to the horses' backs. And one trick that made Kathrael's stomach clench, as he swung off the animals completely, maintaining a hold on Audris' thick mane and using momentum to propel himself back up into a riding position, his feet touching the ground for only a moment.

Their performance for Master Ayala of the Oxbow River seemed to open the floodgates, though, and suddenly they were the new, sought-after status symbol as rich men vied for their presence. Soon, offers of patronage began to filter in— sums of money that Kathrael had never expected to see in her lifetime.

Ithric hemmed and hawed, putting them off; making a show of hoping for a better offer… a more prestigious offer.

The whole thing was surreal. Not that Kathrael's life hadn't already been surreal. In fact, her acquaintance with reality was arguably a passing one, these days. She knew she was scaring Favian and Ithric, but she didn't know a way to stop. All she could do was put one foot in front of the other, do what was necessary to further their goals, and pour her misgivings into the wildness of her dance with Ithric as greedy male eyes watched her from sumptuous, throne-like chairs and calculated how best to make her theirs.

The days ran into one another, a long gray blur punctuated by their public performances in the afternoon and their private ones at night. Favian fretted over the horses' health and soundness. Ithric plotted and schemed, seeking some new angle to draw in the one fish they wanted—the very fish which seemed intent on evading the hook. Kathrael did what was required of her, and tried not to feel.

When a neatly dressed servant appeared after their public show one chilly afternoon and requested their presence at the estate of Master Pendreth, Heir of the Great Southern Forest the following day, it was almost a surprise.

TWENTY

Up until this point, the venues at which they had been performing had been grand, but still nothing that Kathrael hadn't seen before, when she was a prostitute. She and Vesh had provided entertainment at many such places during the lavish parties that rich men used to flaunt their wealth.

Pendreth's city holding was something else, again. She had known, intellectually, that a handful of nobles in Rhyth wielded money and power on a scale that none but the king himself could surpass. Apparently, this area of the southern district was where that money and power laid its head at night.

She had never been around this part of the city before. She would never have been *allowed* near this place in days past, and it was only the scrap of parchment covered in dense, undecipherable writing that got the three of them past the guards now. Kathrael was actually rather surprised that Elarra's friend from the meeting had managed to sneak in here twice before being caught. He must have been very determined indeed, not to mention very stealthy.

The houses here—if they could properly be called *houses*—were as close together as they were elsewhere in the city. However, they were on a scale she had never seen before. Practically palaces in their own right, they towered over everything around them, dwarfing the smaller homes that huddled nearby.

The sun was just setting as she, Ithric, and Favian drove up to the massive white marble facade of the building that the messenger had described to them. Fluted stone columns rose as high as five tall men standing on each other's shoulders, each pillar so thick that if she and Favian had wrapped their arms around it from opposite sides, they could not have touched fingers. Elaborate carvings marched across the portico above their heads—gods and animals and warriors locked in battle. The double doors were easily two stories high.

Favian appeared even more stunned by the place than she was, staring fixedly at it with an expression gone slightly pale. Ithric was the only one of them who seemed unimpressed — or, at least, not overwhelmed — by the structure they were about to enter.

The doors swung open on oiled hinges, eerily silent, and a pair of servants in fine clothing appeared. The one on the left was the same one who had extended the invitation to them yesterday. The one on the right was an older man whose bearing could not have been haughtier had he been the master and not a slave.

"Welcome, honored guests," he said, somehow making the polite term sound as though it referred to dirt on his polished boot. "May I please see your invitation?"

This seemed a bit ridiculous to Kathrael, since the other servant would obviously be able to recognize them. Favian looked perplexed as well, but Ithric merely sighed and climbed down from the caravan, invitation in hand. He strode confidently up the low stone steps separating the door from the road, acting as if he visited such places every day, and handed the slip of parchment to the haughty servant with a charming bow thrown in for good measure.

"Greetings, Honored Sir," he said, and only one who knew him well would be able to detect the faint, mocking tone behind the formal words. "We are but a poor band of traveling entertainers, here to provide an evening's amusement for your Master and his household."

Amusement, yes. Among other things, Kathrael thought grimly.

Hurry, sister — you're so close now! Elarra's imagined voice was desperate and ragged. Kathrael tried to ignore it, and wondered if there was any chance that the delusion would finally fade away once she was reunited with her *real* sister. Could she be so lucky?

"Yes. This all seems in order," said the sneering servant. "You will be performing tonight in the atrium."

Ithric frowned. "I see. Is it large enough to accommodate horses?"

The man appeared affronted by the question. "Of course it is large enough for horses. What a strange question. You may bring the animals and whatever other paraphernalia you need inside via the tradesmen's entrance on the northwest corner of the building. The valet will direct you."

With a dismissive wave, the old man turned on his heel and headed into the house, presumably to announce their arrival. The valet led Ithric back to the caravan and climbed aboard with them to direct them around the side to an entrance large enough for animals and supplies to pass through, out of sight of the main entrance.

Again, Kathrael was struck by the sheer *scale* of the place. It was many times larger than any temple she'd ever been in—almost like a self-contained village of its own with people bustling around, carrying out all kinds of business even at this relatively late hour.

The young valet seemed considerably less frosty than his superior. "Do you need help unhitching the horses and moving things inside?" he asked. "They're beautiful animals, I must say."

"Thank you," Favian said, obviously still a touch wary. "We can handle the horses, but if you don't mind carrying supplies, there's a trunk containing curtains, rigging, and musical instruments stored in the back."

The valet nodded readily and flagged down a slave in plain dress to help carry the heavy case. Favian climbed down and chocked the wheels of the caravan to anchor it. Kathrael helped him swiftly unhitch the horses and tie them to the vehicle so they could go inside to see how the atrium was set up.

The valet led them down a hallway with a ceiling two stories high, and wide enough for a good-sized wagon and team to pass through. He seemed to take pleasure in providing commentary as they walked, gesturing this way and that with his free hand.

"This turning leads to the kitchens, and this one to the lumber storage area. His Excellence keeps an entire crew of builders and carpenters on staff, as he is in the process of improving and adding another story to the south wing."

The fashion these days among the rich in the city was to build *up* rather than *out*, since the houses were already practically on top of each other. Two stories were almost a given, and three story structures were becoming more common. Apparently, Pendreth had an architect who insisted he could design a fourth story for him without compromising the building's integrity. The young servant chatted away about the additional prestige such a thing would bring by towering over its neighbors in the area.

Eventually, they came to the atrium—a truly spectacular space with a stone floor containing blocked-off areas of dirt where exotic plants and flowers grew, even in the early winter chill. It was surrounded by the rest of the massive house on all sides, but open to the sky above. Balconies overhung it on both ends—one positioned right over their heads as they entered the open space. Torches and braziers lit the entire area with a flickering glow.

"His Excellence and his family will be seated over there," said the valet, pointing to the opposite balcony.

Ithric nodded. "That's perfect. Can we get some assistance to hang the curtains from this balcony, so they drape across the entrance right here?"

The servant nodded. "Yes, certainly. I'll get some more help."

The help turned out to be a gaunt young stripling and a middle-aged man with dull eyes and a beaten-down air. Both, of course, were slaves. Kathrael had to grit her teeth to keep from peppering them with questions, knowing that it would be foolish to start asking outright about her sister. And yet, being *so close* but still knowing nothing was sheer torture.

Torture made worse by the litany of *hurry, hurry, please hurry, sister,* whispered in her ear.

When they had everything set up with the help of the two sullen, taciturn slaves, the valet went to announce their readiness to the master. Kathrael knew she needed to focus, but—despite her best efforts—she could feel her breathing growing ragged and her body shaking.

Favian's graceful, long-fingered hand closed around her shoulder. His body pressed against her side, warm and solid. "I'd tell you to breathe slowly and try to relax, but that would make me a laughable hypocrite since I'm a bundle of nerves, too," he said. "So, instead, I'll tell you that you're not alone. And I'll remind you that if you need to throw up, you should do it here, behind the curtain so the rubes don't see. Or so I've been told."

A bubble of hysterical laughter choked its way past her lips. She covered his hand with her own and clutched it convulsively, her lungs settling. The frantic *thud-thud-thud* of her heart eased incrementally. Ithric appeared next to them on silent feet and kissed her temple, then Favian's.

"Our audience is arriving," he murmured, and slipped past them to disappear through the curtains—ready to apply his charm and wit to a new target, one who held a prize far more valuable than money or prestige.

Kathrael had to consciously pry her fingers free of Favian's, and he gave her a quick, fierce hug. "Stay strong, Kath," he whispered. "No matter what. Not much longer now."

With that, he was gone—off to set up his drums. Kathrael pushed her fear and dizziness aside through an act of will, and awaited her cue to come forward and dance for the man who had enslaved her sister.

>--- ♕ ---<

In the end, the performance went better than some they had put on, but worse than others. There were no major gaffs, though the smooth stone floor and the patchwork pattern of garden beds set within it limited what Favian was able to do with the horses. Their hooves slipped on the polished surface, and he was forced to keep them at a walk or very slow trot in order to minimize the risk of a serious accident.

Kathrael shot furtive looks at the opposite balcony as often as she was able. Pendreth was a fat old man with a fringe of gray hair framing a balding head. His bondmate was much younger and very beautiful, though a bit vacuous. She also seemed too young to have been responsible for the impressive array of richly dressed offspring seated around them, so she was probably a second or third wife.

The family and a handful of favored servants had watched politely, applauding at the appropriate points, though the only genuine enthusiasm seemed to come from the very young children. Kathrael knew that their presence here was more about Pendreth's status and appearances than a genuine desire for entertainment. The old bastard was probably so jaded that he'd need three fingers up his arse and someone sucking his cock before he'd even start paying attention, she thought uncharitably.

A surge of bitterness rose in her throat, fueled by sudden, burning anger at this fat lump of a man who thought he could own other people—who thought he could own *Kathrael's sister*.

I hate him, Elarra whispered. *I hate his fat chin and his stinking sweat and the way his breath always smells of garlic and strong spirits. I hate his house and his freezing slave quarters and his pampered dogs that are treated better than the servants. I hate this place...*

I'm sorry I left you here, sister. So terribly, terribly sorry, Kathrael thought before she could catch herself and dismiss the ghostly voice. She shook her head sharply, as if trying to dislodge something, and felt Favian glance her way, worried.

Above them, the vacuous woman whispered something in her husband's ear. He nodded, and waved a careless hand toward the haughty servant who had met them at the door when they first arrived. The servant stepped forward and spoke loudly enough to be heard in the echoing space below.

"His Excellency thanks you for an interesting diversion, and extends his invitation for you to dine with him tonight."

Ithric bowed with a flourish. "We accept His Excellency's generous offer of hospitality with gratitude. If you will allow us a short break to pack everything away and care for the horses, it would be our honor to join him."

A small flush of relief washed through Kathrael. Things were going to plan, so far at least. Their previous performances for some of the lesser nobles had fallen into this same pattern, with their host inviting them for a meal or drink after the show, but there had been no guarantee that Pendreth would follow suit.

The same two taciturn slaves who had assisted them with setting up returned to help them take down the curtains and rigging. The valet tagged along as they hauled everything back outside to the caravan, talking excitedly about their performance. Ithric and Favian responded in friendly tones designed to win the young man's trust.

As they passed the hallway leading to the kitchens, Kathrael swayed and caught herself against the wall. "Oh, dear," she said faintly, lifting a hand to her forehead.

The valet was at her side immediately. "Miss?" he asked, obviously worried. "Are you all right?"

She leaned on him for a moment and then straightened slowly. "Yes, I think so," she said. "I'm very sorry—I felt quite faint there for a moment."

Ithric was watching her in mild concern. "Sometimes the intense exertion of the dance affects her this way. Could we trouble you for a cup of ale or watered wine? That will help restore her."

Kathrael tried to wave the suggestion away. "No, no. I don't want to be a bother—"

"Nonsense," said the valet. "The kitchens are right down here. Come with me and you can sit down for a little bit, while the others load the trunk and get the horses settled. I'll get you something to drink. It's no trouble."

She smiled tremulously. "That's very kind of you. Again, I apologize for making such a scene."

With further assurances that he didn't mind at all, the valet led her to the echoing kitchens while the others went on.

"Goodness," she said, looking around the space with interest. "I've never seen kitchens this large in my life. This place is so huge I'm amazed the servants can get from one end of the house to the other without having to stop halfway for rest and provisions."

The young man laughed. "I can see how you might think so, but really, it's not that bad." He seated her on a padded stool and bustled around, bringing her back a cup of wine. "The stairwell leading down to the common slaves' quarters is right over there—" He gestured to an unobtrusive doorway in the corner of the large room. "—and those of us who serve the master's family personally have quarters in the private wing. It's all laid out very sensibly."

Kathrael knew from the man at the meeting that Elarra had been a common slave in the house, cooking and cleaning. She nodded, feigning polite interest. "I see! Though I still can't imagine living and working in such a grand place." *Because I'd rather die than be a slave again*, she didn't add.

She sipped her drink for a few moments and took a deep breath, setting it down on the rough counter and rising. "That's ever so much better. Thank you again. I imagine the others are almost done by now, and I'd hate to keep His Excellency waiting. Really—you've been very kind."

The valet flushed with pleasure. "It was nothing, Miss," he said, and escorted her back the way they'd come. As they walked, he seemed to be struggling with himself over something. Eventually, he blurted out, "If... uh, if you don't mind me asking, why do you wear that mask? I mean, it's very beautiful and all—I just haven't seen one like it before, only covering half your face. Not that it's any of my business, of course—"

She cut across his stammering, not offended by the guileless question. "My face was injured. People tend to find the scars disconcerting; that's all. It's easier to cover them."

"Oh." The valet was obviously taken aback. "Well, I suppose that would explain it. I would never even have guessed. And I apologize if it's a painful subject. I shouldn't have asked."

"A few months ago it would have been a painful subject," she said truthfully. "It's really not anymore. I don't mind you asking."

It was true, and that was a rather startling revelation in its own right. But now, they had reached the large tradesmen's entrance. Beyond stood the caravan, the horses hitched to it once more in readiness for their departure later.

"Feeling better?" Favian asked. "We're just about done here."

She nodded. "Yes, much. Thank you."

"Let's head back in, then," said Ithric. "When someone offers you free food and drink, it doesn't do to tarry."

They trooped back inside to the atrium. While they'd been putting away their props and supplies, other servants had set up low tables and piles of cushions in the airy space, surrounded by more braziers to provide light and drive back the night's chill. Sumptuous food was arrayed generously on the flat surfaces, along with flagons and carafes of wine, mead, and ale.

Pendreth was installed at the head of the largest table, with an empty pile of cushions at his right that was clearly intended for the three of them. Ithric approached it without hesitation and bowed easily. Kathrael and Favian followed his lead, albeit a bit more stiffly.

"You honor us with your generosity, Your Excellency," Ithric said, employing his charm at full strength. "I dare say we have never eaten so well."

Personally, Kathrael thought she was going to have trouble choking anything down, but that was all right—a bit of queasiness would actually play into their plans quite well. She couldn't help noticing that Favian looked a bit green around the edges, too.

Pendreth waved a pudgy hand in response to Ithric's words, as if dismissing his own largess. "Sit, sit," he said, revealing a faint lisp and a rather effeminate voice with no strength behind it. "Have your woman serve you whatever you'd like."

Ithric smiled, though Kathrael could detect a dangerous glint in his eye, carefully hidden. She knew this role all too well, even if it chafed under the circumstances. Ithric made himself comfortable on the cushions, and Favian mirrored him awkwardly, obviously never having eaten while reclining at a table before.

Kathrael filled a finely crafted metal plate with a selection of meats, cheeses, and fruit for them to share. She curled gracefully into the space between Ithric and Favian. Ithric casually cinched an arm around her—they had decided ahead of time to play up the fact that she was his woman, after Favian insisted that she was less likely to be molested that way.

"He's scarier than I am," he'd said wryly. "Something about the eyes, I think. One good look and you can tell he's mentally unhinged."

The look Ithric had thrown him was less *unhinged* and more *long-suffering*. Nonetheless, Kathrael found herself curled up half in his lap, feeding him and being fed in turn while Favian casually nicked bites from the plate. She could find no resentment within herself, beyond wishing that Favian could curl around her as well.

Pendreth still seemed bored and distracted as they ate, but his bondmate made an effort to engage them, superficial and trite though it was. Kathrael had to hide a sneer. How could anyone—no matter how privileged and sheltered—think that clothing fashions on the continent and the latest hairstyles were an appropriate topic of dinner conversation when riots were breaking out practically every night?

It was a huge relief when the evening finally progressed to the point that she could take action. After a few moments of growing quiet and withdrawn, she stretched so she could whisper into Ithric's ear.

He nodded and cleared his throat. "Forgive me—I'm afraid Kathrael isn't feeling very well. She had a moment of dizziness earlier, after the show, and it seems to have returned."

Pendreth showed the first sign of real emotion they'd seen, alarm crossing his heavy features. "She doesn't have some kind of an illness, does she?" he asked.

Fear of disease was common in the city, where a virulent sickness could burn through the crowded population like wildfire. Kathrael hurried to reassure him.

"Nothing like that, Your Excellence," she said in a meek tone. "I think it's far more likely to have been the fish I ate for lunch. I thought at the time that it smelled a bit off." She looked up at him through her lashes, the picture of helpless pathos. "Perhaps I should return to the caravan, where I can rest while the others enjoy your hospitality."

"That might be best," Ithric said, playing along. "You're sure you'll be all right, though?"

She nodded. "Oh, yes, I'll be fine. I'm certain I'll feel better if I lie down for a few minutes."

Favian, who had been watching the exchange, rose. "I'll go with her, in case she gets dizzy again on the way."

Kathrael took his offered hand and let him lift her to her feet.

"Thank you, Favian," Ithric said. "Hopefully it's just a passing weakness. Rest well, dearest."

"I'll be back once I've got her settled," Favian said.

"*Hmph,*" harrumphed the nobleman, clearly still flustered by the minor drama.

Kathrael let Favian usher her away with a hand on her back before anyone could say or do anything else. They made their way to the now-familiar hall leading to the tradesmen's entrance, moving steadily but not rushing. Favian glanced over his shoulder.

"No one's following," he said quietly, his voice tense.

She gave a short nod.

"I think the valet is still outside watching over the caravan and horses," he continued. "I'll go out and tell him I've come to move them around to the front of the house. That will give me an excuse to linger outside for a bit before coming back in."

They were approaching the turning that led to the kitchens... and, more importantly, to the slave quarters below. Favian stopped Kathrael with a hand on her arm. She was eager to get started, but she looked up at his earnest face and deep blue eyes.

"Stay safe, Kath," he said. "We'll meet you near the servants' entrance at moonrise, as we planned."

"*Us,* you mean," she corrected, thinking of her sister. "You'll meet *us.*"

Favian's smile was brief and tight—not very convincing. "Yes, I hope so. Be careful. Don't take any unnecessary risks."

He kissed her forehead, lingering a moment longer than she expected before pulling away. As if drawn by a lodestone, her attention turned back to the kitchens, and the shadowed doorway beyond. She pivoted and started toward it, Favian's hands falling away as she did so.

It was time.

The kitchens were by no means deserted — not a surprise, given that there was a feast going on in the atrium. Kathrael scanned the pale faces and sunken eyes, looking for Elarra's familiar features. When it became obvious that she wasn't present, Kathrael moved on quickly, striding past in her flowing red dress and feathered mask.

A few watched her with varying degrees of curiosity or indifference, but none made a move to stop or question her as she headed swiftly for the stairs leading down to the lower level.

That didn't mean she was alone, however.

Yes! Elarra whispered. *Yes, that's it! Hurry!*

The slave quarters were damp and poorly lit, smelling of mildew. The place was more of a cavern than a room, obviously hewn long ago from the same rock that served as the building's foundation. Rough wood and cloth partitions served to break up the space into sections, where some slaves were sleeping, and others were talking or playing games of chance using painted bones for dice.

She thought there were perhaps twenty adults in all — more women than men. There were also infants and children, thin and poorly dressed. Those old enough to walk darted to their mothers' sides and clung to them at Kathrael's approach.

Here, her presence spurred fear and distrust in a way that it hadn't upstairs in the kitchens. Her fine clothes marked her as *other*. Someone who didn't belong in this space — a threat. The irony was not lost on her.

Now, though, she was only interested in searching the faces around her — looking for the one as familiar to her as her own. She rushed through the warren of makeshift rooms, heedless of the whispers and restlessness growing in her wake.

Where *was* she? *Where was Elarra?*

"Who are you, lady?" demanded a skinny adolescent girl, bolder than the rest. "What do you want, barging around down here? You're not supposed to be here!"

Kathrael whirled to face her. "I'm looking for Elarra. Where is she? I have to find her!"

The girl eyed her suspiciously. "What d'you want with her?"

Hope beat a painful rhythm in Kathrael's chest. "She's my sister. Do you know where she is?"

The girl continued to peer at her in the inadequate light. "You look like her."

"We're sisters," Kathrael repeated. "Where is she? *Please*—you must tell me!"

The slave shrugged a bony shoulder, a bitter look crossing her face like clouds over the sun. "She's not here. Died about three months ago, didn't she. Fever took 'er."

TWENTY-ONE

The words opened like a dark abyss, swallowing the fragile light of hope that had briefly illuminated Kathrael's spirit. Her stomach heaved, bile burning at the back of her throat. She choked it back down.

"A fever?" she echoed hoarsely.

You're so close now, sister, Elarra whispered. *Don't give up!*

The slave nodded. "'S right. She was so weak after she had the baby, she never really got better. When she caught the summer sickness a few weeks later, she just kind of... faded away." The girl paused, as if remembering. "I miss her sometimes. She was nice."

There was a pause as the girl's words penetrated.

Oh, gods. Elarra had given birth. She'd had a child.

Now you finally understand, her sister said, sounding relieved beyond measure.

"*Elarra,*" Kathrael murmured, utterly bereft.

It's all right, little sister, said the ghost. *Or, at least, it soon will be.*

"Did the baby live?" she asked, barely recognizing her own voice.

"Yeah," said the girl. "He's weak, too, though. The other women who have babies nurse him when they can."

"Show me," Kathrael said, clenching her hands into fists to stop their shaking.

The girl shrugged again. "He's in the back. Follow me."

Kathrael trailed after the girl in a daze. Elarra had been right; it was cold and damp down here. Mold bloomed on the walls. The floor was gritty under her boots. The stench of chamberpots in need of emptying washed over her as they headed toward the back, and then they were entering a small, curtained off area apparently used for storage. The edge of a tattered blanket trailed out of a basket sitting in the corner. Kathrael's good eye flew to it as a thin, unhappy squall emerged from within.

They had thrust her sister's child into a storage room, like a piece of broken furniture or a torn set of curtains. Black rage rose in her chest, but it was as if she was observing it from afar, watching from outside as someone who looked like her turned to the skinny slave girl in cold fury.

A defensive expression slipped across the girl's face, and she rubbed her own arms as if to warm them. "I come back here sometimes and sit with 'im," she said. "'S hard though—the master works us so much." She shot Kathrael an assessing look. "You gonna take him with you?"

Kathrael had never been as sure of anything in her life as she was of her answer. "Yes. I'm taking him away from this place right now."

"Good."

Still feeling distant and untethered, Kathrael tried to focus on practicalities. "Has he been fed recently?"

Another weak, fussy cry emerged. The spirit of Kathrael's own dead daughter answered in kind, and Kathrael's jaw tightened.

"Yeah," the girl told her. "'Bout an hour ago, I think."

Unable to stay back any longer, Kathrael crouched in front of the basket and reached down to draw away the tatty blanket. The baby hidden underneath was pale with cold, and thin from lack of milk. The swaddling smelled as though it had been soiled.

She watched herself cradle the tiny boy in both hands. Watched herself lift and hold him close to her chest, rearranging the blanket snugly around him. Watched herself straighten and turn back to the girl, the small, warm weight tucked close to her bosom.

"You will tell anyone who asks that he died in the night. You will not tell them about me taking him away. Do you understand?"

The girl nodded hesitantly. "All right." She looked at the baby in Kathrael's arms, and a note of wistfulness crept into her voice. "Will he be free now? You won't let him grow up a slave?"

Again, Kathrael watched as if from a slight remove. "I will die before I let him be owned by anyone, ever again."

A look of longing came over the young slave girl's face. "I'm glad," she whispered.

Kathrael spared a moment of sympathy for her, but she had no time for more.

"Tell me how to find the servants' entrance. What is the quickest way to it?" She didn't know how long it was until moonrise, but she knew she needed to move. Time would not be their friend with a hungry infant in their care and no way to get milk.

The girl led her back out into the warren of the slave quarters and pointed to a different staircase. "Turn right at the top, and then left," she said. "It's not far. There's a guard, though."

"It doesn't matter." They had expected such a thing, after all. A final question occurred to Kathrael. "What is his name?" she asked, looking down at the restless babe in her arms.

"He doesn't have one," the girl said quietly. "No one thought he'd live, so no one bothered to give him one."

Her heart lurched.

That's not true, sister, Elarra said, her ghostly voice sounding as serene as Kathrael had ever heard it. *His name is Daeniel.*

"He's called Daeniel," Kathrael repeated aloud. "And he will know all the love the world has to give."

Without another word, she angled the threadbare blanket up to cover Daeniel's face, and left. He snuffled a couple of times and went quiet in her arms. She ascended uneven stone steps without feeling her feet touch a single one, and turned right, then left into the echoing hallway at the top.

A door stood at the end of the corridor, barred with a sturdy plank. A bored looking guard sat on a stool next to it, though he scrambled to his feet in surprise at her approach. His hand went to the hilt of his dagger, but he did not draw it, obviously confused by her fine dress and feathered mask.

"Miss?" he asked. "What are you doing back here? You shouldn't be here. Do you need someone to direct you back to the atrium?"

She looked him directly in the eye, still detached, floating amid a cloud of unnatural calm. When that calm finally crumbled, she knew she would shatter into brittle shards. Not yet, though.

Not *yet.*

"No, guardsman. I do not need an escort," she said. "I only need you to let me through this door, and tell no one about it. There is money in it for you, if you agree."

His brow furrowed, and his gaze flickered down to the bundle in her arms. "What do you have there?"

"I have my dead sister's baby."

The man looked back up at her face, studying her features on the side not covered with the mask. Recognition dawned. "Your sister — she was the one called Elarra, wasn't she? I remember when she fell sick. I helped transport her remains down to the catacombs."

Kathrael shivered, remembering Elarra's dread of being in the underground caverns. The place where her rotting bones now lay.

The guard stepped forward and drew a corner of the blanket back, revealing the listless infant. "The baby is weak," he observed.

"Her baby is starving," Kathrael said. "He is reliant on the other women with nursing children, but he is not their main concern — their own infants are. Eventually, he will die from lack of care, but in the mean time, he drains resources that could be put toward the healthier babies. Let me take him away, and no one needs to know that he did not simply die in the night."

The guard stared at the baby for a few moments longer, then back up at Kathrael. His expression was uncertain. "You said there was money?"

Kathrael reached into the hidden pocket in her skirts and pulled out a purse. "I have thirty silver coins here. It's yours if you allow us to pass and keep your silence about what you saw."

Thirty silver coins constituted practically all of the money that they had saved after performing for the last many days in the rich southern district. It was a marginal bribe for the theft of an adult female slave. For a sickly infant, it was ridiculously high. Kathrael was not inclined to take chances, however.

The guard took the purse and opened it, pouring a few of the shiny coins into his hand and examining them before letting them slide back into the purse. He was silent for a long moment, still appearing torn over what to do. Kathrael watched him, feeling nothing — merely waiting to see what would happen.

He drew his lower lip between his teeth and chewed on it, taking a deep breath and letting it out, as he seemed to come to a decision. He pulled the drawstring of the purse closed and proffered it back to her.

"Take your money back, Miss. And take your sister's boy. The master has no use for a sickly infant with no dam to feed and care for it. You will be doing him a favor by taking the child away. If anyone asks, I will say that I saw nothing this night, but that I heard the boy weakened and died."

A chink appeared in Kathrael's armor, and she swallowed hard. Unable to form words, she only nodded her thanks and moved past him to the door. She lifted the plank that was barring it one-handed and let it clatter to the ground. Outside, the night was cold and the air carried the threat of rain. It could have been past moonrise or not — with the clouds, there was no way to tell.

She was having difficulty breathing now, as if the air was too thick to flow into her body. Her chest began to hitch as she tried to force her lungs to fill. She walked forward, practically unseeing — knowing on some level that she should stay near the door, but not truly in control of her stumbling feet.

The world around her felt dreamlike — the only real thing was the quiet weight of the baby boy in her arms. Or perhaps that wasn't the only real thing. There were voices, too. Vesh, quietly humming a lullaby to himself. Her mother, murmuring words too softly for the sense of them to come through.

Elarra — warmth suffusing her voice even through the cold veil of death.

Thank you, Kathrael — my dearest sister. You came when I needed you, and now I can finally rest. I love you. I love you both more than anything. Don't mourn me. I'm finally free.

The voice faded away to a whisper of memory. Kathrael fetched up against the wall of the massive building next to her and slid down. Filth from the alley seeped into the skirts of her fancy red dress, but she didn't even notice.

She sat that way for what felt like a long time before the first drops of cold rain began to patter against her — softly, to start with, but gaining strength as the gusts of wind intensified. The hitching of her chest grew more violent, and hot tears overflowed her good eye to slide down her unscarred cheek, mixing with the rain.

Favian's relief was palpable when Ithric finally made their excuses and began a final round of gratitude for their host's hospitality. The nobleman had remained taciturn throughout the meal, only deigning to join in the awkward small talk on a handful of occasions.

Now, he looked down his nose at the two of them. "I will consider your petition for patronage, young man," he said, addressing Ithric. "Of course, should I choose to endow you, I would expect your availability for any events at which I needed to provide entertainment."

"Of course," Ithric said smoothly. "We look forward to your decision, though it was an honor to perform for you, regardless."

"I hope your young woman feels better soon," said Pendreth's wife. "Thank you for coming."

They thanked her in return and mustered more genuine smiles in response to the enthusiastic goodbyes from the younger children. The haughty servant came forward to escort them out.

"Oh, sorry—I should have mentioned," Favian said, when he started to lead them in the direction of the tradesmen's entrance. "I moved the caravan out front earlier. I hope that's all right."

The servant scowled, but made no comment, changing direction to take them along the smaller hallway leading toward the front doors. The hall opened out into a massive entryway, manned by two more servants in fine clothing.

"A very good evening to you, sirs," said the old man, his cold tone at odds with the polite words.

At his gesture, the other servants swung the double doors open. Favian and Ithric each gave him a last, abbreviated bow, and exited the massive building. The wind outside was cold, but not bitter, and carried a promise of rain.

A strange, but not completely unexpected wash of surrealism surged through Favian, leaving him dizzy. The buildings around him seemed to loom above his head as if they were leaning over him, ready to topple.

He craned around, reeling a bit, staring dazedly at the huge stone facade of the house they had just left. Flickering torchlight from sconces illuminated its sheer white face. The massive double doors swung shut behind them on oiled hinges.

"Stop gawping, Favian," Ithric said from beside him, voice lowered as if he was worried about being overheard.

"Act normal, for the gods' sakes, and let's find Kath so we can *get out of here.*"

Favian nodded agreement, worry tugging at him as the details of his dream came into sharp focus, syncing with the reality of the waking world around him.

"We need to find the servants' entrance," Ithric whispered, leading the way down wide stone steps that spilled them out into the stinking street below.

Favian kept his mouth shut. The concept of a building having an entrance just for servants — for *slaves*, he corrected himself — had been a foreign one, though he supposed it was self-explanatory enough. He hadn't the faintest idea about where to find such a thing, however. The back of the structure, perhaps.

Ithric led him quickly to their caravan and untied the horses, then urged Favian into the driver's seat and told him to drive. They headed out of sight in case anyone from the house was watching their departure, only to circle back on the next road over.

After finding a post in a shadowed alley where they could tie the horses, Ithric gestured at him to follow deeper into the darkness of the cramped byway between two buildings. "Just hope no one steals 'em," Ithric muttered, glancing back at the animals and ratcheting Favian's worry up another notch. "Should've brought a couple of the boys along with us to watch the caravan."

As if to punctuate his words, shouts combined with raucous laughter and sounds of breaking glass or pottery came from a nearby road. Favian shivered.

The two of them stole through the darkness. Favian was having trouble keeping his bearings between the gloom and the twisting tangle of roads, but he knew they must have been backtracking toward the sprawling villa they'd just left. Interesting that no effort had been made to make the backs of these great houses attractive. They were all cracking plaster, rotting piles of garbage, and the smell of piss. Favian's boot slipped on something soft that released a cloud of stench, and he swallowed against his rising gorge.

"This is it, I think," said Ithric, touching his arm. A soft drizzle had begun to fall, but Favian could just about make out the wall to their left, the glow of the city's torches and bonfires reflecting from the gray clouds above them.

A darker rectangle in the amorphous gray plaster signified a recess in the wall, presumably leading down to the musty underground level where the house slaves slept and labored. If Ithric was right about it being Pendreth's house, Kathrael should have come out this way. But would she be alone?

"Kath!" Favian hissed into the darkness, as loudly as he dared. "*Kath*! It's us!"

He held his breath, but could make out nothing other than the ever-increasing patter of rain and distant bustle of the restless city at night. Ithric, however, drew in an audible breath, his superior hearing having evidently picked something up.

His hand clenched around Favian's forearm, almost hard enough to bruise. "This way," he breathed, and hared off around the corner, dragging Favian with him. Favian kept pace despite the near-darkness and the churning of his stomach. The two of them slid to a stop halfway down the length of the alley, breathing hard as the skies opened, the rain pouring down in earnest.

"Little Cat," Ithric said, sounding as if the endearment had been torn from him.

Kathrael sat hunched on the filthy ground, back against the rough plaster wall of the villa. She was curled around a small bundle—the unmistakable shape of a swaddled infant—weeping as if she would die.

Please, Merciful Utarr — let the baby be alive, Favian prayed, breaking free of his paralysis to rush to the huddled pair.

"We're here, Kathrael," he said aloud, dropping to his knees and sheltering them with his body. She was already soaked, and the infant probably was, too. Stupidly, they'd been in such a hurry that neither he nor Ithric had thought to retrieve cloaks before going to meet her.

"The caravan's not far," Ithric said, "But we need to get there quickly."

Favian stroked Kathrael's wet hair back from her face. She was trying to choke back her heartbroken sobs, but with little success. "Kath," he said softly. "Let me take the baby. Ithric will help you get back to the caravan. Once we're safe and out of the weather, you can tell us what happened."

She didn't answer, but she allowed him to ease the tiny, swaddled form from her arms. To Favian's immense relief, the infant was warm and breathing. It began to cry at the jostling, though the sound was weaker than he would have liked.

Ithric crouched next to them and levered Kath to her feet, bracing her as she stumbled and sagged against him. "Come on, Little Cat. Time to move. Do I need to carry you?"

She shook her head, still weeping, and put one foot in front of the other, leaning heavily on Ithric's sturdy strength. Favian focused on trying to keep as much of the rain as possible off of the baby, and on keeping the others in sight through the darkness and the weather.

Eventually, the pale forms of Ozias and Audris swam into view, still hitched and tied where he had left them. Favian didn't even try to stifle his sigh of relief. He and Ithric bustled Kathrael up the steps and into the shelter of the caravan. Favian handed the child to Ithric once they were both under the shelter of the roof.

"Cloak," he prompted, and took the item when Ithric handed it to him, shrugging it on. He was already wet, but at least the heavy cloth would lend a bit of extra warmth while he drove. "Now, where are we going? The granary?"

"Little Cat," Ithric prompted. "Will anyone be looking for this child? Is anyone coming after us?"

"No," she croaked.

"The warehouse, in that case," Ithric said firmly. "We need a fire, and we need to find someone who knows a nursing mother. Let's just hope that one of Qaden's men has a family, and is well enough disposed toward us to let us near them."

Favian nodded his understanding and closed the door. He untied the horses, giving all four of them a quick once over before climbing up in the driver's seat and heading toward the river.

⤚ ♕ ⤙

Ithric handed the baby back to Kath once they were settled. He pulled off his sodden shirt and tossed it aside as the caravan jounced over the muddy road. The only saving grace of the situation was that the foul weather would clear the roads of traffic and—*hopefully*-dissuade the rioters from leaving the warmth of their hearths to cause trouble in the city.

His night vision was just about good enough to make out the familiar interior of the caravan, and he rummaged for something dry and warm. Gooseflesh prickled his skin, but he'd always run a bit hot, so he ignored it in favor of unswaddling the baby in Kathrael's arms and wrapping it up in a clean, dry blanket.

He didn't think he'd be able to get Kathrael out of the complicated fastenings of her dress until she came back to herself a little more, so he contented himself with holding the baby, tucking them all close together and pulling both his and Kathrael's cloaks around them.

She was cold against him where she huddled into his side, but she began to warm quickly under the muffling folds of the heavy cloth. Her hand crept along his arm until it found the infant, and rested there. They were silent for a while as the vehicle rattled along the nearly deserted streets, rain pattering against the wood of the roof.

"My sister is dead," Kathrael said eventually.

The air escaped Ithric's lungs in a slow sigh. He had suspected that might be the case, but he'd hoped he was wrong.

"I grieve your loss, Kath," he said, wishing that Favian were here instead of sitting up front, driving the horses. He would almost certainly have been better than Ithric at offering comfort. A sudden insight entered his mind. "Is this her child?" he asked.

He felt her nod against his shoulder.

"Girl or boy?"

"A son," she said. Her voice sounded as hoarse as if she'd been screaming. "She says his name is Daeniel."

It was a good name. A strong name. Ithric liked it. A moment later, a new thought occurred. "Her spirit is speaking to you now?"

Of course—if Elarra had died, depending on the timing, it could mean that her spirit had, in fact, been free to haunt her sister. It would mean that Kathrael's voices were not mere inventions of her own mind, after all.

"No," Kathrael replied, her voice quavering on the word. "She's not. She left right after I found Daeniel. She said she was finally free. She could finally rest. Ithric, she's... *gone*. My sister is gone."

The pain in Kathrael's normally lyrical voice tore at Ithric's heart. He gathered her closer, wishing again for Favian's comforting presence as he searched for something to say. The tiny form curled against his chest stretched and let out a little cry, drawing his attention.

"She's not gone, Little Cat," he said. "Not really. Part of her is right here in our arms."

He only hoped they could keep the sickly little boy alive and nurse him back to health. The alternative was too awful to contemplate.

TWENTY-TWO

It took too long for Ithric's liking to make their way back to the abandoned warehouse and get everyone dry and warm. Eventually, though, he had the other two installed in front of a blazing fire with Elarra's baby, wrapped in blankets and sipping hot mead.

Once he was satisfied that they were as comfortable as possible for the time being, he pushed his damp hair back from his face and rose.

"I'll take Audris and go find one of Qaden's men," he said. "Hopefully someone around here has a woman with a nursing baby. It might take me a while, but I'll be back with a wet nurse as soon as I possibly can."

Kathrael had remained quiet and pale, still mourning her loss keenly. Now, though, she looked up. "I still have the money," she said. "The guard wouldn't accept it. He just let us go."

It was a mark of how jaded Ithric had become that the guard's actions surprised him considerably. But the money would make everything in the coming days easier than it would otherwise have been. The thirty silver pieces had been nearly all they'd had, and while he would not have begrudged trading it for Elarra's escape, it would have left them unable to pay Qaden, among other things.

"That's good to hear," he said. "If nothing else, it will make finding a wet nurse much simpler. We already know that Qaden's men are fond of our money."

Favian frowned at him. "Would you rather I go look for a nurse? It's still pouring down out there—difficult conditions for riding."

Ithric crouched down to brush a soft kiss against Favian's lips. "Kath needs you right now. Stay here. I'll be all right."

He kissed Kathrael as well, tasting the salt of the many tears she'd cried that night. Her half-mask had been set aside earlier, its feathers wet and drooping. He cupped her scarred cheek in his palm and she closed her eyes, leaning into the contact.

Seeing her like this, with Daeniel's tiny form held against her breast, roused every protective instinct he possessed. It was good that he had something active to do—he only hoped that he could find someone with milk quickly. With luck, once he did, the generous application of money would be all that was necessary to convince them to venture out on such an unpleasant night.

"I'll be as quick as I can," he promised, and went to saddle the horse.

⤝ ♕ ⤞

Favian sat in front of the fire, holding Kathrael even as she held her sister's son. After cleaning and drying the baby boy earlier in the warm light of the fire, he had examined the child as best as he was able. The baby's lower body had been encrusted by filth from dirty, unchanged swaddling, and Favian had applied some of the balm they used for everything from cuts and scrapes to harness sores on the horses to soothe it.

One of the boy's arms had a livid bruise circling around it above the elbow, and Favian's stomach had churned at the idea that he'd been shaken or dragged by an angry, uncaring adult. As far as he could tell, there were no broken bones, thank the gods, but it was clear that no one had cared for the boy as an infant should be cared for.

He was gaunt, wasting away when he should be fat and happy and growing. Favian longed for Healer Sagdea's presence, and wondered if there was a healer nearby that they could trust.

He had extracted the story of what happened from Kathrael a bit at a time as they sat together. The idea that Elarra might have stayed tethered to the living world for the sole purpose of leading Kathrael to her ailing child was one that he intended to ponder at length when his mind was a bit clearer. He wondered what High Priestess Zandreen might have to say about it.

Ithric had been gone for some time. Kathrael was practically falling asleep on Favian's shoulder, though her sure grip on Daeniel never wavered—a mother's instincts awakening within her as naturally as the birds wake at dawn. They would need to talk, once the baby's immediate needs were taken care of. There were decisions to be made, since with this one tiny addition to their lives, everything had changed.

Outside the snug back room where they were huddled, Ozias whinnied, and an answering nicker returned a moment later. A familiar whistle followed, and Favian relaxed.

"Kath," he murmured, nudging her dozing form with a small movement of his shoulder. "Ithric is back."

They rose and lit torches before emerging into the main part of the warehouse to meet him. It was the middle of the night, and the plain-faced woman riding behind Ithric looked less than pleased about being dragged from her bed to travel in the cold, steady rain. Shuggan was with them, on foot, and helped the woman down from Audris' back.

"Now you can say you've ridden on a fine white horse, Teesa," the rough man said as he shrugged off his rain cloak. "You looked like a real princess, sitting up there."

"Well, I feel like a drowned rat," the woman said in a sour tone. She let Shuggan take her cloak as well, and looked around. "Where's this baby, then?"

Kathrael came forward, Daeniel cradled against her. Shuggan's woman sucked in her breath and took a step back. Favian realized that Kathrael had come out, half asleep, without donning her mask or draping a shawl across her face.

Shuggan frowned, following Teesa's gaze. "So that's why you wear that mask, eh? I'd wondered."

Kathrael flushed, but said nothing.

Shuggan tore his eyes away and spoke to Teesa. "Stop staring, eh? These three are good people, and their money will buy that ox cart we need."

Teesa shook herself free of her startlement and blushed as red as Kathrael, meeting her eyes sheepishly across the expanse separating them. "Sorry, love," she said. "I'm not usually so rude. That your sister's boy? He's quiet."

"He hasn't been getting enough milk," Kathrael said, coming forward until the other woman could get a good look at him.

"Ach! Poor wee thing," Teesa tutted. "He's far too thin. Come on, then. Let's see what we can do about that."

Favian helped Ithric get Audris untacked and settled before they followed the others into the warm back room. It was a bit crowded with five adults and the baby, but Teesa and Shuggan made themselves comfortable without prompting while Favian puttered around getting drinks and hanging their cloaks to dry by the fire.

Teesa unlaced her blouse and bared a pendulous breast, full with milk. Favian held his breath as she accepted Daeniel and arranged the infant against her. He still seemed listless at first, but when she squeezed out a bit of milk and dabbed it on his lips, he made a noise of interest and his mouth moved in a weak suckling motion.

"That's it, precious," Teesa encouraged, stroking his downy black hair for a moment and offering the nipple again. This time, he latched on and began to suck, little wet noises audible in the expectant silence of the room. Favian exhaled in relief. If Daeniel was strong enough to nurse, they had a chance.

Talk was sporadic as the baby drank his fill, though the intimate little gathering was surprisingly comfortable. When the baby's hunger was finally sated, Teesa lifted him to her shoulder and patted his back with the ease of long practice. When she was done, she smiled and handed him back to Kathrael.

"There you go, love," she said. "He'll be all right for a while now. I need to get back to my own brood before the older ones get themselves into all kinds of trouble with no one watching them, but you bring him over as soon as the rain stops in the morning and I'll feed him again. If there's one thing I've never lacked for, it's milk," she added wryly, gesturing at her generous breasts.

"Thank you," Kathrael said quietly. "I don't know what we would have done if you hadn't come."

Teesa's eyes crinkled. "You'd've found somebody else, I expect. Your man here was pretty determined." She tilted her chin towards Ithric. "But rain and lost sleep aside, I'm glad he found me first. We really do need that ox cart."

✂ ⚜ ✂

Over the next few days, Kathrael spent much of her time at the old building Shuggan had taken over for his family. Favian split his days between staying with her and taking care of things at their own place—feeding and watering the horses, making sure they had food prepared and a continuous supply of clean, soft cloths for swaddling.

Ithric, meanwhile, ventured out to the city and earned as much coin as he could on his own with fire eating and storytelling. There was no word from any of the fat nobles they had entertained regarding further offers of patronage. Kathrael could not bring herself to be upset by this, since it saved her having to make the decision as to whether she was willing to accept tainted money from slave owners if doing so would make Daeniel's life easier.

The morning after they'd rescued the child, Favian had tried to talk to her about the future. At the time, she'd pled grief and exhaustion, telling him truthfully that she could not deal with that right away. She was painfully aware that there were urgent decisions to be made, however, whether she wanted to face them or not.

Now, they were not only risking their own lives by courting a slave rebellion in a city on the brink of chaos. They were risking an innocent baby's life as well. Kathrael thought that perhaps the thousands of infants living in bondage should outweigh the risk to a single child, in the gods' eyes. When she held Daeniel in her arms, though, feeling him fill out and grow livelier day by day, she could not make herself believe it.

She had vowed that he would live free, surrounded by love.

She had also vowed that she would give her life, if necessary, to change Rhyth for the better. She wasn't at all sure she could do both, and the uncertainty left her paralyzed.

Favian let her stew for several days before he finally sat her and Ithric down and decreed, in no-nonsense terms, that they would talk things out for better or worse. Ithric shrugged and deferred to her.

"We can go back to Draebard if that's what you want, Little Cat. It's a much safer place to raise a family than Rhyth would be." He frowned, only to consciously smooth his expression an instant later. "Or, alternately, you and Favian can go back, while I stay here and do my best to help the underground."

"No," she and Favian said in unison.

Favian continued, "Together or not at all, Ithric. We've already played that game once, and I don't intend to play it again."

The line of Ithric's shoulders relaxed. "Together, then," he agreed. "But where? Rhyth, or Draebard?"

Kathrael would have expected Favian to jump at the prospect of returning to his home village, where they could be a family. Instead, though, he laced his fingers together in front of him and stared at them as he said, "There's another possibility that we haven't discussed. One that would give Daeniel a loving, secure home while still leaving us free to do what we came here to do."

Kathrael looked up at him in confusion, her expression clearing as he began to speak. Hope and pain mingled in her breast as she contemplated what he was proposing.

Three days later, the caravan pulled into the village of Darveen. No doubt they made quite a spectacle in the quiet little town, with their showy black and white horses, brightly painted vehicle, and a long-suffering milk goat tagging along behind, tied to the back.

Indeed, it didn't take long for a cry of greeting to go up from passersby, people poking their heads out into the crisp winter afternoon to see what the fuss was about. Kathrael was thrown back to the memory of her first visit here. She had arrived, tired and aching, with two rescued children in tow—only to be dragged before the elders, accused of kidnapping and threatened with criminal branding as punishment.

What a difference a few months made. Now, excited youngsters milled about, asking questions and jostling forward to touch the unusually colored horses. Kathrael emerged from the back, wearing her metal half-mask and cradling Daeniel in her arms.

"We're here to see Melko and Shayla," she called to the crowd. "Are they nearby?"

"Melko's at the trading house," a man shouted in reply. "I expect Shayla is at home. Do you know the way?"

"I do," Kathrael assured him, and handed Daeniel over to Ithric, who was still inside the caravan.

She climbed up to sit with Favian in the driver's seat and indicated that he should drive on. The little crowd parted to let them through, excited conversation swelling in their wake.

The house was just as she remembered—good sized and welcoming, neatly kept, though still with a homey, lived-in air. The shutters were closed against the winter chill, but the noise of their arrival alerted the occupants and the door swung open as she and Favian were climbing down.

Rona peeked out, her features lighting with surprise, then joy as she recognized them. "Favian? Kathrael! Whatever are you doing here?" she asked, bustling forward to meet them. "Shayla!" she called back toward the house. "Shayla, come quickly!"

Ithric opened the back door of the caravan and descended as she approached, the baby wrapped in warm blankets and held securely to his strong chest. "Hello, Rona," he said with feeling.

"Ithric!" She hurried forward and he crouched to accept her embrace. Rona gasped when she saw Daeniel. "Oh my goodness! Come inside where it's warm, all of you!"

Shayla emerged. "Kathrael?" A smile lit her face like the sun coming out from the clouds. "Oh, my dear! You've come back! Yes, come inside, all of you. The twins were napping, but I imagine the commotion will have woken them. They'll be thrilled to see you, as am I."

"Do you have anywhere I could pen or tie the horses?" Favian asked.

"Here, I'll come and show you," Rona said quickly, leaving Ithric to direct him behind the house.

Kathrael followed Shayla inside with Ithric, where another joyous reunion took place as the young twins, Dex and Petra, came stumbling into the room, bleary-eyed. They stared for a moment, frozen in place, before practically flinging themselves at Ithric, wrapping around his legs and squeezing tight.

"Told you it was him," Dex muttered to his sister, who nodded and clung tighter.

Kath took Daeniel, freeing Ithric to deal with the pair of limpets attached to his legs. "Look at you two," he said in wonder, crouching down to get to their level. "I can hardly believe it."

They darted in for another hug, and he held them tightly to his chest, eyes closed. Shayla's face shone, and she wrapped an arm around Kathrael's shoulders, squeezing.

"I'm so glad you're here. Both of you," she said, her voice trembling with feeling. "I didn't know if I'd ever get the chance to thank you for everything you've done, Ithric. It's so good to finally meet you."

Ithric looked up at her, his face more open and vulnerable than Kathrael had ever seen it. How seldom in his life, she wondered, had anyone ever thanked him for the things he'd done? He liked to put on a front of being unconcerned—unaffected by such things, but it was clear that his fellow captives from Turvick's show adored him.

It warmed her, to see him among people who valued him as much as she did.

"I'm just glad to see them safe with their family," he said.

In her arms, Daeniel sucked in a deep breath and began to squall, so much stronger than he had been, even a week ago.

"Who's that?" Petra asked, wide-eyed.

"He's hungry," Dex declared.

Ithric laughed. "You don't need second sight to figure that out, squirt. Let me up so I can go tell Favian to milk the goat before he comes in."

With a shy smile for Shayla, he headed back outside, leaving Kathrael alone with the twins and their mother.

"I'll admit to the same burning curiosity," Shayla said, smiling down at the crying infant. "He can't be yours, I don't think. You would have been as big as a house when we met this summer."

"No," Kathrael said, her mixed emotions rising now that they were actually in Darveen. "He is my sister's. She died."

Sympathy clouded Shayla's pleasant features. "Oh, Kathrael. I'm so sorry. He's a beautiful baby, though. What's his name?"

"Daeniel," she said, her voice catching a bit.

"Hello, Daeniel," Shayla crooned. "Not many babies your age have their very own goat. I think your auntie and uncles must love you very much."

Daeniel paused in his fussing to grasp at Shayla's finger, distracted for a moment by the friendly stranger.

Favian, Ithric, and Rona came in a few minutes later. They disappeared into the kitchen to prepare the slurry of wheat and rabbit liver, boiled in goat's milk, that they had been using to feed Daeniel while they traveled. It was a concoction, Favian explained, that they had used for Frella as a baby when no wet nurse was available, on Healer Sagdea's recommendation.

It wasn't ideal, of course, but Kathrael had been reassured by how bright and healthy Frella had turned out.

While Favian was seated in the corner, patiently feeding Daeniel from a special clay jar with a spout that he had purchased in Rhyth, Melko and Nimbral arrived, setting off a new round of excited greetings and introductions.

"What in the name of the gods brings you traveling all the way out here in winter, Ithric?" Nimbral asked, clasping his hand forearm-to-forearm and giving him a hearty pat on the shoulder. "And with an infant, no less?"

"Ah, that's a bit of a long story," Ithric said, "and one that we'd like to talk to you and Rona privately about. Perhaps this evening." He looked around. "Looks like you've done pretty well for yourself, mate. How have you two been?"

Nimbral looked pleased. "Good. Things are good. It's mostly thanks to Melko and Shayla, of course, but I've got a job keeping accounts at the trading house, and I've no complaints about life, these days."

Melko joined them and smiled at the tall, thin man. "Nimbral's too modest. He and Rona have been a huge blessing. They're both hard workers, generous to a fault, and Rona has been a huge help for Shayla with the twins. We're immensely glad to have them here."

Nimbral flushed under the praise, and Ithric grinned. "I'm glad it worked out for all involved. But now, I do believe Shayla wants to feed us."

After a fine meal, Shayla shooed everyone except Melko and the twins out of the kitchen to talk. Kathrael had been both dreading and anticipating this moment, knowing that it was the perfect solution for everyone involved, but selfishly grieving what she would be giving up.

"You said you wanted to talk to us privately, Ithric," Nimbral prompted.

Ithric deferred to her rather than replying, and Kathrael almost wished that he wouldn't. That he would make the decision for her. Take it out of her hands. Favian, seated beside her, rested his palm between her shoulder blades, grounding.

"Daeniel is my sister's child," she began haltingly. "She... died a slave, and we rescued him from the house where she had been held in service."

Rona made a noise of distress, but did not interrupt.

"I vowed to my sister's spirit that I would give her son the best life any child could hope for," she continued. "But I made another vow to Elarra, long ago when we were both children. I vowed that I would help change things in Rhyth. That I would free the slaves, and make it so no human being would ever be treated as property again. I don't... think that I can do both."

"What are you saying, Kathrael?" Rona asked.

Kathrael swallowed hard and took a centering breath. "I would like... for you and Nimbral to raise my sister's son as your own. If you are willing."

A complicated mixture of hope, joy, and empathy flickered across Rona's face. Her eyes flew to the tiny child nestled in Kathrael's arms.

Nimbral cleared his throat. "We owe you three everything, Kathrael. We'd do anything for you, but instead, you just keep offering us more gifts."

Rona found her voice, though it was shaking. "Nothing would give me greater happiness than raising your sister's child. But are you sure you want him to grow up with people like us?" She gestured from her tiny, misshapen frame to Nimbral's unnaturally tall one.

"People like you?" Kathrael echoed. "Kind people who will love him as much as you love each other? Brave people who have seen the worst of life without letting it taint them? Yes, I am sure that I want him to grow up with people *exactly* like you."

"Well said," Favian said quietly, still resting his hand on her back. Steadying her.

"I couldn't agree more," Ithric added. "We have a bit of money to go toward his care. For wet nurses, and whatever else you may need."

Nimbral smiled. "While I look forward to hearing how you've been making your dosh since we parted in Draebard, we're not doing too badly here, ourselves, Ithric. I'll speak to Melko and make sure they don't object to another addition to the household, but I don't believe the added expense will be a strain. Having a head for numbers comes in useful when you're living with a merchant and working in a village that specializes in trading commodities."

Nimbral excused himself shortly thereafter to speak with Melko and Shayla before it got too late, leaving them alone with Rona. The small woman regarded Kathrael for a long moment before speaking.

"This is hard for you. I can tell," she said carefully. "If you want to change your mind, I'll understand."

Daeniel yawned and stretched in her arms. Kathrael felt like her heart was being ripped from her chest, but she said, "I think it's the right thing to do."

Rona still looked pained. "If it helps, you should know that we'll love him as our own. You will be welcome in our house at any time, and he will grow up hearing about the amazing things you've done, and have yet to do."

A lump settled in Kathrael's throat, making it difficult to speak. "I know," she managed. "That's the only reason I'm able to do it."

Rona bit her lip, and nodded. Hesitantly, she got down from her chair and crossed to stand in front of Kathrael, her arms extended. Passing the child over to her was one of the hardest things Kathrael had ever done. She wished desperately that Elarra's spirit was still present, so she might know if she was really doing the right thing.

But Elarra was gone.

It was Vesh's ghostly voice that murmured, *Of course it's the right thing, Kath. You already knew that. But knowing doesn't make it any easier.*

TWENTY-THREE

The remainder of their visit was bittersweet. Kathrael was happy to see the twins thriving, but they also made her ache for the child she had lost and the child she was willingly giving up for a greater purpose.

The adults' mixed feelings also transmitted themselves to the sensitive twins, who frequently grew sad and quiet in Kathrael's presence. Rona's joy, on the other hand, beamed from her like light from the sun—though she tried to hide it as best she could out of respect for Kathrael's sadness over her loss.

The three of them performed a single show in Darveen, mostly because they needed the money for their return to Rhyth. Melko was an excellent promoter, well known in the village as he was. The crowd was a large and enthusiastic one, given the size of the town, and they recouped the cost of the milk goat in a single afternoon, with a bit to spare for provisions of their own.

Kathrael had been worried that her grief would leave her unable to perform, with nerves that rivaled Favian's plaguing her ahead of time. Once she began to dance, however, she found that the movement brought comfort and a sense of release, especially when she was in Ithric's strong hands, giving her body over to him.

Something of her overwhelming emotion must have come through in the movement of her body, because silence reigned for a long moment after the two of them came to rest in each other's arms. It lasted long enough for her to worry that she had made some sort of horrible gaffe, but then a single person began to applaud slowly. More joined in, the noise swelling all out of proportion with the number of people, some of them whistling and shouting approval.

Favian's act on horseback was flawless. By the end, they were swamped with well-wishers expressing approval and thanks for the evening's entertainment. It was all a bit overwhelming to her, under the circumstances, and she longed for the few moments of peace she'd felt earlier as she gave her body over to Ithric's strength and care.

They left the following morning after a tearful goodbye, and repeated invitations to visit soon. As they drove away, heading south, Kathrael had to fight the sudden urge to grab the reins, pull the horses to a stop, and rush back to Shayla and Melko's house to retrieve Daeniel. She dug her fingers hard into the edge of the rough wooden seat and clenched her jaw until the urge passed, replaced by the unnatural detachment and apathy that had plagued her intermittently since the night at Pendreth's villa.

It frightened her in a way, yet it was less painful than feeling. She thought it worried Ithric and Favian, too, but she didn't know what to do about it. Right now, she just wanted to get home. Home might have been a falling-down warehouse with part of the roof gone that didn't even belong to them, but that didn't stop her from needing to be there.

She lay awake in the caravan that night, unable to sleep. The points of warmth where Ithric and Favian touched her were all that kept her from turning to ice; her body had no heat or life of its own. Again, she thought of the dance. The relief that had come from trusting herself to another. When the morning eventually dawned, pale and gray, she finally knew what she needed to do.

She waited until they were back in Rhyth. Until Ithric had delivered Qaden nineteen of the twenty-five silver pieces they owed him, with the promise of the rest in a few days. Until the horses were settled in their pen, eating hay, and Favian had chivvied them into eating a hot meal in front of the roaring hearth fire.

"I... need something from you both," she said when they had set the plates and cups aside, the request coming unnaturally to her.

"Anything, Little Cat," Ithric said without hesitation. "If it's within our power to give, it's yours."

Favian tenderly tucked a strand of her hair behind her scarred ear. "What do you need?"

She swallowed, though it did nothing to steady her voice. "I need you to help me let go. To help me forget, even if it's just for a little while. I need to feel something other than this constant... *ache* of loss."

Favian drew her against his side and tucked her head under his chin. "Tell us exactly what you're asking for, Kath. No misunderstandings, all right?"

"I want you to hold me, Favian. And I want you to take me, Ithric. I want you to drive every thought from my head except the two of *you*." A lump rose in her throat. "I already belong to you. It's time to stop holding back."

Ithric's large, callused palm slid against the side of her face and neck. "You don't belong to us, Kathrael," he said, low and intense. "We belong to each other. Let us show you how much we belong to you, too."

Her chest hitched, tears burning behind her good eye, and she nodded. She let them undress her, a piece at a time, kissing and stroking each newly exposed patch of skin. When she was naked, stripped of her half-mask as well as her clothing, they took turns possessing her mouth, stealing her breath until she was dizzy, her body sinking into the soft sleeping pad beneath them.

They were both still clothed, but it didn't matter. She trusted them with her vulnerability; they had never once abused it, and she knew they never would. Eventually, when her body was warm and pliant, her sex wet and swollen with need, Ithric drew Favian away so she could watch as he removed Favian's clothes with the same slow deliberation that they had removed hers.

When he was done, he guided Favian down to lie with her so he could strip for both of them. Favian urged her to sprawl back, resting between his legs, her head pillowed on his chest.

"Shameless exhibitionist," he accused fondly as Ithric made a show of unlacing his trousers. The tone of his voice was warm honey.

"Ah... you love it," Ithric teased back. "Admit it— you've never been able to keep your eyes off me."

"I never said you were an exhibitionist without an audience," Favian said. "Now hurry up, before we get bored over here."

Ithric smirked and pushed his trousers and smalls down so he could step out of them. Favian wasn't lying—Kathrael never tired of looking at their bodies, and probably never would. Ithric had filled out over the time she'd known him. There still wasn't an ounce of fat on his body, but access to decent food had added bulk to his wiry musculature, broadening his shoulders and thickening his arms and legs.

The patchwork of pink and silver scars painted over his skin told the story of a life lived on the edge. His angular, northern features were strong and distinctive, the neatly trimmed beard he had adopted for the show lending him an air of maturity and rakish charm. His mane of russet-brown hair was still long and unruly, hinting at the wildness inside him.

By contrast, Favian was all smooth lines and soft skin. Days spent working and performing in the sun had lent color to his complexion while simultaneously bleaching his hair to a light spun gold. He had not cut it again since shaving it close in Draebard, and while it was not yet long, it was no longer close-cropped.

Hard, physical work had slowed the changes associated with being a eunuch, but he was still gaining a certain softness around the edges that Ithric lacked. It made him, she reflected, an excellent pillow, among other things, and she burrowed against him a little more. The soft velvet of his limp prick nestled against her back, but the fact that he was unaffected by either of them physically did nothing to make her question his love for them.

Naked now, Ithric prowled forward to join them, dropping to all fours and kissing his way up her body until she was caged beneath his arms and legs, pressed between his hard body and Favian's soft one.

When he reached her lips, his kiss was demanding and deliciously filthy, leaving absolutely nothing to the imagination. She marveled at the way her body responded, still amazed even after all they'd done that she felt no fear or need to protect herself. No need to retreat into her mind, hiding from the reality of what was being done to her.

When Favian's hand trailed down to cup her breast and tease her sensitive nipple to a taut point, she moaned into the kiss and rolled her hips, seeking friction and finding none.

Ithric grinned against her lips, sharp and predatory. He kissed his way back down and dragged her knees apart, delving into her folds with his tongue. He showed no hesitation or mercy, driving her to a crashing climax and lapping up her juices while Favian continued to run graceful fingertips over her breasts, throat, and lips.

She panted and clutched at whatever part of Favian she could reach, little aftershocks racing up and down her body. Despite the powerful release, her sex ached for more... ached to be filled. As if he sensed that she was finally, truly ready for him, Ithric pressed a kiss to her inner thigh and slid sensuously over to recline next to Favian, pressing a wad of blanket behind himself so he could lean back against the wall with his legs stretched out in front of him, his cock curving up toward his stomach.

He extended a hand to her with the same grace and assurance as when they were dancing, and guided her to straddle his lap, facing him. "I'm yours, Little Cat. Take all of me," he said, drinking in her scarred face with the same expression of desire and acceptance that had first cracked her brittle facade of pain and fear back in Woodhaerst.

The tip of his cock brushed her folds, sliding through the wetness there. She *yearned* for him, but the part of her that had been hurt and used so many, many times still felt fear. Then Favian was there, kneeling behind her, pressing against her back and wrapping an arm around her.

"Let go, Kath," he whispered in her ear. "You won't fall. We won't let you."

A sound like a broken sob escaped her throat. Her body sank down, taking Ithric inside. Her walls stretched and fluttered around his hard length, but there was no pain — only pleasure. A deep, overwhelming sense of fulfillment washed over her as she gave herself over to her two lovers, letting the last of her fear dissipate like mist in the morning sun.

She was safe. They would take care of her. She could finally set down her burden, and let other strong arms carry it for a little while. A tear trailed down her cheek, and Ithric wiped it away with the pad of his thumb.

"All right?" he asked.

She nodded, staring at him with a liquid gaze. His thumb trailed down to rub over her lower lip, and he smiled, soft and unguarded.

"Move, then, Little Cat," he said. "Make us both feel it."

Favian's supportive arm around her loosened, his hand coming up to tease her breasts again. She rolled her hips as his lips fastened on the juncture of her neck and shoulder, trailing biting, sucking kisses down the line of muscle. Ithric flexed beneath her in counterpoint to her languid movements, meeting her with every thrust.

Favian's free hand gathered her hair and swept it over her shoulder. Fingertips trailed down the bumps of her spine and back up, repeating the hypnotic caress over and over, dipping lower each time. A deep pool of rippling heat filled her belly, and instinct propelled her to lift herself up and slide back down Ithric's shaft, bracing her hands on his strong shoulders.

The three of them moved together in a new dance, though it was actually as old as time itself. Ithric stretched up to kiss her, never breaking the rhythm, and she could taste herself on his lips. Favian's clever mouth still sucked hot marks to the surface of the skin on the back of her neck. His fingers, which had progressed to stroking along the cleft between her buttocks with every pass, delved the final inch and teased at her puckered rear opening.

Ithric reached between them to rub firm circles around her nub as his length disappeared inside her, over and over. She cried out into the kiss as her senses took flight, her muscles clenching hard around him and intensifying the sensations even more.

Her release dragged him over the edge with her. He moaned and shuddered, his measured movements growing sloppy as he pulsed into her. When it finally ended, he slumped back, spent. She followed, lying limp against his chest, his softening length still buried inside her.

"So beautiful," Favian murmured, still peppering kisses over their skin. "Kath, you are both so beautiful."

She could feel... *everything*. And it should have been frightening. It should have been too much. But it wasn't. Instead, it was a moment of the sharpest clarity.

"I love you both," she said, the words pressed into Ithric's skin. Punctuated by Favian's soft kisses. "Favian... Ithric... I love you so much. *I love you.*"

"We love you, too, Kathrael," Favian said. "Never doubt that. Never question it."

"It's true," Ithric echoed. "Favian, Little Cat—I would be lost without you. You are my world."

Kathrael had once believed that men would say anything in bed—whatever they thought would get them what they wanted. Now, she knew that it could also be a place for the deepest truths to be shared. She squeezed her eyes shut, wanting to freeze the moment somehow. To preserve it, so she could pull it out and experience it again whenever times were hard.

Two pairs of arms wrapped around her and held her close, long into the night.

⚜

They rested for a single, precious day after their return from Darveen, sleeping and eating, fucking and holding each other close. But they could not rest forever. Qaden wanted the rest of his money, and they had to find out if their failure to appear at the granary and subsequent unplanned flight to Darveen had damaged their relationship with the underground.

On the evening after a somewhat lackluster performance of the show, Ithric ventured into the city to see if he could find Ruben and get the latest news. It was only a couple of hours before dawn when he finally returned, obviously exhausted, but nonetheless drawn tight as a bowstring.

Kathrael was instantly wide-awake. "What happened?" she asked. "Tell us."

Ithric tossed away his outer layers and dropped to his knees between them. "There's news. It's big. Really big."

Favian rolled upright and dragged a hand through his hair. "Well? Don't keep us in suspense, Ithric. Spill."

Ithric took a centering breath, and Kathrael felt her tension ratchet up. She had seldom seen him look so shaken.

"An Alyrion arms dealer has arrived in Rhyth. He's brought a shipment of state-of-the-art crossbows with him from the continent. A *large* shipment. The kind of shipment that could arm a rebellion. Someone in the underground got word of it. The warehouse is heavily guarded, of course. But we know where it is. We know where *he* is, and *who* he is."

Favian stared at him with wide eyes.

Kathrael's breath caught. "This could be it. This could be the tipping point."

"The spark that ignites the tinder," Ithric agreed.

"A bloodbath," Favian said hoarsely. "Ithric, it could be a bloodbath."

Kathrael shook her head. "The bloodbath will happen if the slaves try to rise up unarmed. They'll be slaughtered *en masse.*"

"The question is, will the underground be able to take advantage of this?" Ithric said grimly.

Gods. It was true. "They can't even organize a citizen's council," she murmured. "They'll let the opportunity slide by, and the weapons will end up in the hands of the king's guard." She looked at Favian's troubled blue eyes, and Ithric's stony, gold-flecked ones. "We have to act. This is it. This is the moment. We have to do something, before the city becomes a battlefield."

"What are you suggesting, Kathrael?" Ithric asked.

She thought over what she knew of the underground. "We need to speak with Zandreen. Ithric? Can Ruben arrange another meeting?"

"I'll find out," he said. "Favian?"

Favian hesitated before nodding. "Yes. Do it. There are only two possible reasons the Alyrions would be selling weapons to the king of Rhyth. Either the king intends to attack the underground, or he intends to attack the north. Either way, we can't let it happen."

"I'll do it tonight," Ithric assured them.

⚜

The following evening, Zandreen appeared on their doorstep in the warehouse district, once again in the garb of an old beggar woman.

"Tell me what you intend," she said. "Tell me how the three of you think you can turn this to our advantage."

Ithric's eyes flashed gold. Kathrael took a deep breath and explained what they planned to do.

⚜

Three days after that, they were once again in the catacombs—a different area accessed via a pit at the base of an abandoned textile mill that Zandreen had described for them. Even though they had been forced to use this new entrance since the Painted Lady was destroyed, Kathrael had held her breath as they descended, half-hoping for Elarra's familiar presence to return. It had not.

She's gone, Kath, Vesh had whispered. *Her day's toil is done.*

And what of yours, Vesh? she'd asked, unsure whether she wanted the answer.

Her baby daughter snuffled and let out a soft cry.

Not yet, Vesh said. *Not quite yet.*

Once again, they were waiting for Sephira's guards to arrive and guide them through the warren of passages toward the cavern where the group was to meet. This time, however, when the leader came forward with the cloth bags to tie over their heads, Kathrael stepped forward and raised a hand.

"No," she said. "Not this time."

She was wearing her mask with feathers and flames, her hair piled up on her head in a riot of dramatic curls. The gold and silver thread woven into her red dress reflected the torchlight.

Favian stepped forward to stand next to her. He was dressed in priests' robes, the front half of his skull shaved bare. His eyes glittered, hard and blue. A moment later, a huge lion padded out of the shadows, fluid and menacing as it came to stand between them.

The guard captain took an uncertain step back. "What is the meaning of this?" he asked.

"If you want to win this war, take us to the others," Kathrael said. "Bloodshed is coming to Rhyth on a scale you've never imagined. We have one chance to turn the tide our way."

The guard's free hand had gone to his sword hilt, but now it dropped. "You've heard about the weapons," he said.

"We have," Favian confirmed. "And you know what will happen if those weapons end up in the king's hands."

The man's wary stance relaxed. "I do." He regarded them for a long moment, his eyes intent. "Give me your word as a priest that you intend no harm to the movement, or its leaders," he said, addressing Favian.

Favian held his gaze. "You have my word that we intend no harm. We wish only for all Eburosi to live free, with control of their own lives."

After another beat of silence, the guard looked down at the lion, and nodded, as if to himself. "Very well. Come with me."

The route to the cavern seemed shorter this time, or perhaps it was an illusion since they were walking freely rather than being blindfolded and marched along the uneven stone corridors. When they arrived at the gaping entrance to the vast meeting space, the guard leader stopped them with a hand on Favian's shoulder.

"Don't make me regret trusting you," he said.

Favian only nodded, his eyes already moving toward the flickering light inside the cavern. Kathrael felt his body expand as he took a deep, steadying breath. She lifted her chin, armoring herself for what was to come. The lion nudged up between them, its lithe strength and aura of quiet power bolstering her will.

"Come," she said. "It's time."

She strode forward, and Favian paced her. Each of them rested a hand on the lion's mane as it stalked between them on silent paws. She watched as their presence registered with those nearest the door. More and more people turned to see what had caught the others' attention. Jaws dropped, conversations trailing away as they walked without hesitation through the parting crowd to the stone ledge on the far end of the space.

By the time they mounted the rough-hewn steps to join Zandreen on the raised platform above the onlookers, silence reigned in the echoing cavern. Every eye was focused on them, a sea of faces registering a spectrum of surprise, fear, curiosity, and superstitious awe.

The space beside her twisted and warped, as Ithric rose smoothly to his feet amid the collective indrawn breath of the crowd. He stood tall and proud next to Favian, unconcerned by his nakedness.

The High Priestess of Avlan faded back, and Kathrael stepped to the front of the ledge, looking down at the assembled men and women.

"*People of Rhyth*," she said, loud enough to carry around the cavern. "*Civil war is coming to the city, but salvation is still possible if we all work together. It is time to act, lest we be trampled underfoot.*"

The crowd muttered, clearly in shock.

"*A shape-shifter has come to lead Rhyth's slaves to freedom, as was foretold*," she continued. "*But he cannot do it alone. We must unite against the forces that seek our destruction. Join us, and stand against those who would see us dead or enslaved.*" She gazed over the mass of faces gathered below her and straightened her spine, her head held high. "*Now is the time to make your choice. Who's with us?*"

The silence stretched for a beat. Two. A shout rose up from the back of the crowd, echoed by another, and another, until the sound grew into a deep roar of noise, filling the cavern until it shook. Kathrael let the sound wash over her.

She looked at the two men standing shoulder to shoulder with her, a current of understanding passing between them.

The slaves of Rhyth were rising up, and there would be no turning back.

End of Book 2

THE LION MISTRESS:
BOOK 3

ONE

The problem with being the figureheads for a rebellion, Kathrael thought, was that their new roles didn't really do anything to change the reality of what was happening around them. The slave underground was still... *underground.* Still hiding. They still needed to obtain weapons. They still needed a plan. Allies. An agreed-upon military strategy.

In pursuit of the aforementioned *allies*, she, Ithric, and Favian were currently discussing the situation with Qaden — the leader of the gang that controlled the old warehouse district where the three of them had made a home of sorts over these past weeks. And Qaden was looking at Ithric like he'd grown a second head, now that the lion-shifter had given him an abbreviated version of the relevant facts.

"I told you when we first met that I didn't think you were as stupid as you were pretending to be, boy," Qaden said. "I'm rethinking that assessment as we speak."

Ithric only raised an eyebrow, lounging with crossed arms against the corner of a rough wooden table in the old building Qaden used as a base. "Civil war is coming, Qaden. It doesn't take a master strategist to see that. We just thought you might want to be on the winning side when it did."

Qaden barked a laugh. "And yours will be the winning side, will it? How do you figure that, then?"

Favian cleared his throat. "There are a couple of points Ithric hasn't touched on yet."

"Such as? Because they'd have to be pretty fucking good ones to convince me to risk my men on a half-cocked scheme to commit treason against a king who executes people for skimping on their taxes by a handful of coppers. A king, I might add," he continued pointedly, "with an *army* behind him."

Kathrael met Qaden's gaze. She had been terrified of him when he and his followers had first shown up on their doorstep, demanding protection money. Since then, however, he'd proven himself surprisingly honorable for a street thug.

Still, she was painfully aware that they were putting their lives in his hands by talking to him like this.

It was a calculated risk. She didn't *think* he'd turn on them. And with his loyal men and his weapons, he would be a very valuable ally if they could talk him over to their side.

"We're planning to capture a warehouse full of weapons from the continent, in the coming days," she said. "Crossbows. The best the king's money can buy."

The gang leader's heavy eyebrows drew together. "Crossbows? A whole warehouse full? And you plan on... what? Just walking off with them? A stash like that will be heavily guarded, you realize—unless the weapons dealer is a fool."

Ithric shrugged. "Of course it will be. But we know where the warehouse is located. We know where the dealer is staying. One of the slaves on loan to the villa where the king is putting him up is in the underground. He's put a word in the man's ear about a certain troupe of traveling entertainers who have been staging performances at all the most prestigious houses. That's our way in."

"You're actually serious about this," Qaden said, and gave Favian a sharp look. "You said there were *a couple* of points this one hadn't touched on, Blondie. What's the other one?"

Favian took a deep breath and turned his attention to Ithric. "Ithric? Your call."

Kathrael felt her heart beat faster, as it did whenever another person learned Ithric's dangerous secret. If it could even properly be called a secret anymore, now that the entire underground knew about it.

But Ithric didn't move from his relaxed slouch. "I'm a shape-shifter," he said.

Qaden stared at him for the space of several breaths. "Pull the other one," he scoffed. "It's got bells on."

"Oh, *please*. It's not something you'd really lie about in this city, now is it?" Ithric said. "But it's cold tonight, and I don't much feel like stripping down and shifting just so you can gawp at me."

He stared at Qaden, and his hazel eyes flashed green-gold, glowing unnaturally in the low light of the hearth. Kathrael could feel an aura of *otherness* rolling off him in waves.

So could Qaden, obviously.

"Deresta's tits," the man breathed, before seeming to drag his composure back together. Kathrael had never seen him on the back foot before. She got the impression it wasn't a state of affairs he had much experience with, either.

"You... turn into a wolf?" he asked, after another short stretch of silence.

"A lion," Ithric said. "Though all three of us are well acquainted with the Wolf Priest of Draebard, as it happens."

Kath swallowed the surge of bitterness that always rose at the mention of the Wolf Patron who had been prophesied to lead them all to freedom, and hadn't. Though she had come to know Senovo as a person, in addition to knowing him as a legend, it was still a point of contention between her and the others.

They had grown up with Draebard's High Priest as a guardian and, in Favian's case, a father figure. *She* had grown up reviling him. And while she no longer blamed him for every bad thing in her life, she continued to resent his easy dismissal of the prophecy of the Wolf Patron.

Still, even the mention of Senovo was apparently enough to penetrate Qaden's carefully cultivated facade of indifference.

"You three are barking mad," he said. "You'll get yourselves killed, and I'll be out twenty-five pieces of silver a week in protection money. Why the fuck would I want to get involved in your suicidal scheme?"

Ithric didn't even bat an eyelash. "Because you're a natural leader who's shown the ability to maintain order within a large territory, and inspire loyalty in others. What kind of people do you think are going to be running things when the king's government falls to the rebels?"

Favian added, "Without leaders like you to help keep order, there will be chaos. *More* chaos than there is now, I mean."

"You've already shown that you can do a better job protecting people than the ones who are charged with doing so," Kathrael said persuasively, not above stroking Qaden's ego—especially when the words were true. "Think about it. You could be a regional governor. A man of real power and influence, respected by everyone in the city."

"And you can promise me that, can you?" The words were skeptical, but Kathrael heard the waver of uncertainty behind them.

It was Favian who answered. "Qaden. If a shape-shifter who's just brought down the king of Rhyth endorses you before the rebel leaders and the freed slaves, do you *really* think they're going to ignore his suggestion?"

Qaden chewed his lip, thoughts flashing behind his eyes like quicksilver. "*Fuck,*" he muttered under his breath. "I must be bent in the head to even be considering this." Then, louder, "Lemme think about it for a day, you mad bastards."

The villa where Tullus Coruscanus Abito of Alyrios was staying was not really on the same scale as the houses of the nobles she and the others had entertained in recent weeks. After all, that would be unseemly, since the weapons dealer was still a mere *commoner.*

Worse, Kathrael knew, he was a commoner who had dared to accumulate vast amounts of personal wealth. That alone made him suspect in the eyes of Great Houses, but Tullus was content to rely on the fact that the king needed his crossbows badly enough to hold his nose against the stench of low breeding and do business with him.

She, Ithric, and Favian were just finishing up the version of their show adapted for smaller spaces—the villa's courtyard, in this case. Kathrael had watched the dealer as much as she could during the performance, and was confident she had him pegged. She'd run across his type many times before, during her years as a prostitute—a tourist from the continent, no doubt full to bursting with stories of the debauchery which might be found in the rich areas of Rhyth.

For such men, Rhyth offered a taste of forbidden fruit. A sweet nectar unavailable within the strict social order of Alyrios, where the vengeful religion and draconian government threatened ruin to anyone who dared step publicly beyond the bounds of morality.

Though it would offend the king and his fat nobles no end, most Alyrions still considered Rhyth to be part and parcel of the barbarian lands of Eburos. A place where the people threw great festivals in honor of their pagan gods, drinking and dancing and engaging in unashamedly public sex while high on the smoke of potent herbs.

It wasn't a completely fabricated perception, to be fair. In the north, she'd seen just such a festival while staying in

Draebard. The townsfolk cast themselves into their carousing with a refreshing sort of light-hearted innocence, and truly believed it to be a form of worship—a sort of thanksgiving to the Old Gods for their bounty.

At the time, she'd been in no fit mental or physical state to truly take part, but she thought now that it must be a wonderful feeling to surrender oneself to such carefree pleasure and happiness amongst friends and loved ones.

In Rhyth, such events had long since become mere stage shows, as the rich strove to outspend their peers on the biggest, the most depraved, the most flamboyant displays. Any sense of spiritual renewal had been wrung out of the practice, leaving only the spectacle behind.

We made a lot of money at those spectacles, Kath, Vesh's ghost chided. *Working the festivals was a damned sight better than hustling for marks on street corners or in the brothels.*

Her lip twitched upward. *I suppose. I remember you always seemed to enjoy them. Though I didn't like the feeling that we were only there on sufferance, enjoying the largess of the rich for a few hours before being shunted back to the streets and alleys where we belonged.*

And now? Vesh asked. *Do you still resent it?*

Her eyes drifted to Ithric, just finishing up the final verse of the Ballad of Ozias and Audris as she accompanied him on her *sithaa,* and over to Favian, who brought the two white horses on whose backs he was standing to a smooth halt before Tullus and his retinue.

Give me a choice between this fancy villa and our little room back in the abandoned warehouse by the river, she thought, *and I'd be back there before the last echoes faded.*

But that was not to be. Not yet, anyway.

She had a very good idea now of what they might do to tempt Tullus Coruscanus Abito of Alyrios into the net they had woven for him. She'd watched him watching her, as she danced and twirled in her feathered mask and flowing skirts. She knew that look very well, indeed—for all that she'd never expected to encounter it again after a vial of green vitriol ruined the left side of her face.

The question would be whether Ithric and Favian would follow her lead as she tried to lure Tullus into her trap. She thought that Ithric probably understood the use of sexual power as a tool, with no other meaning behind it. She was far less sure of Favian, however.

And, if she were to be brutally honest with herself, she was not entirely sure how far *she* was willing to take the ruse. Once, the answer would have been *as far as necessary, no questions asked.* Now…

Her eyes strayed back to the two men who owned her heart.

Then you'll need to be smarter than that, Vesh chided. *The Alyrion already covets you. Make him jealous. Make him start to lose judgment.*

A new smile pulled at the corner of her lips. *Were you always so devious, Vesh?* she wondered.

Just be glad I'm on your side. The response was dry.

Her smile widened. *Always,* she thought.

Favian and Ithric were bowing, accompanied by the enthusiastic applause of the dealer, his bodyguards, and his little group of hangers-on. Kathrael set her instrument aside, rose gracefully to her feet, and joined them, dropping into a deep curtsey and meeting the weapons dealer's gaze through her eyelashes. His clapping slowed as his attention caught on her, and held.

Yes, she could definitely work with this.

Their purpose tonight was reconnaissance. Somehow, they needed to capture Tullus and transport him in secret to the warehouse holding the crossbows. The question was where and how best to do so. It had quickly become obvious that plucking him directly from his borrowed villa would be a difficult prospect, and one fraught with risk.

In addition to his two hulking bodyguards, the household was populated by a gaggle of servants, some of whom were Rhytheeri slaves on loan from the king, and some of whom were Alyrion and had traveled over with Tullus from the continent. There were also the status seekers, Rhytheeri from lower stations who hoped to curry favor or make connections by cozying up to the powerful visitor.

Even if members of the underground snuck into the residence in the middle of the night with help from their slave contact, there was every likelihood that the resulting commotion would draw attention and end with fighting, or at least end in someone raising the alarm. They needed a different option. A way to get the dealer somewhere relatively isolated, and off his guard.

They had one good chance to accomplish such a thing, and this was it.

"Please," Tullus was saying in his heavy, continental accent, "you must all join me for a drink. I find your talents intriguing, and have many questions for you."

Kathrael stepped in before either of the others could answer. "We would be honored. Favian and Ithric will need to care for the horses first, but that will only take a few minutes. Perhaps I could beg a glass of wine from you while we wait for them? I always feel so parched after I've danced."

She threw Ithric and Favian a swift glance, wishing—not for the first time—that she shared Dex and Petra's gift for silent communication with them. *Trust me*, she tried to convey.

Favian drew breath and opened his mouth as if to say something, a furrow forming between his eyebrows. Ithric's expression remained smooth as glass, even though his gaze on her narrowed. He placed a hand on Favian's arm, cutting off whatever he might have said.

"Yes, of course," he said. "Why don't you keep our host company for a bit, pet? We won't be long."

He shot Tullus one of his sharp, disconcerting smiles and steered Favian away, toward the entrance where they'd parked the caravan. Kathrael let her breath out, confident that Ithric understood the general thrust of her plan. She would be the flighty female lover, susceptible to seduction by a rich, powerful man who might offer her more comforts and shiny baubles than she could get from a pair of street performers.

Not only would Tullus stand to gain the pleasure of a fleeting conquest—for fleeting it would surely be, if she were actually foolish enough to desire such a thing. He would also gain the satisfaction of cuckolding another man, taking his woman from under his very nose. It would make an amusing story for cold nights back in Alyrios, to impress his acquaintances over a bottle of wine. Based on the way he surrounded himself with sycophants, she gathered that such things were important to him.

"Slave," Tullus ordered one of the servants with a snap of his fingers, "fetch this woman and her friends the best wine we have."

Kathrael looked down demurely as Tullus ushered her to the low table that had been set up at the far end of the courtyard. Lit braziers crackled merrily on either side of it, pushing back the winter chill and dark night.

Furs and pillows were strewn around, and she allowed Tullus to guide her down onto a pile of them with a touch to her elbow. He reclined across from her, and studied her for a moment as the servant hurried back with wine.

The Alyrion was not an unattractive man, by any means — fit and of medium height, with patrician features and dark, shoulder-length hair swept back from his face. Kathrael imagined that he was well practiced at beguiling naive young girls and luring them into his bed.

Don't let him... don't let him, daughter! Her mother's spirit, usually a quiet, unhappy presence lurking in the background, had grown deeply upset. *That's what happened to me...*

The ghost of Kathrael's unborn daughter began to whimper, roused by her grandmother's distress.

Hush now, Thea, Vesh warned. *You'll wake the baby. Kath is just pretending. It's only a ploy to steal away his shiny crossbows. Favian and Ithric won't let anything bad happen to her.*

Her mother subsided, only muttering, *Careful, daughter... be careful...*

I will be, Mother. I promise, she thought.

Despite the distractions lurking in her mind, Kathrael made herself focus on the here and now. She smiled shyly and accepted the flagon of wine set before her, taking a sip.

It was quite good.

"So," Tullus began conversationally, "your companions are certainly an exotic pair. Not from Rhytheeri stock, I gather?"

She looked up at him through the eyelashes of her good eye, playing the role of coquette to the hilt. "No, indeed," she said. "They're from up north somewhere. The barbarian lands. But as long as I dance and play the *sithaa* for their show, and warm their beds at night, they are surprisingly good to me. I have a safe place to stay, and enough food to eat. It is more than many in Rhyth can say, these days."

His eyes darkened. *"Warm their beds,"* he echoed, surprise coloring his tone. "What... both of them?"

TWO

Kathrael hoped Favian would be able to keep his reaction under control when he found out what tack she was taking with their intended victim. She blinked up at Tullus. "Well... I am the only woman in the troupe, you understand. And the two of them are very close; they share *everything*. As I said, they are both good to me, in their way. I can't really complain, even though they can be quite... *insatiable*, at times."

Tullus was still taken aback. "Goodness. I'd heard tales about the sorts of things that went on here on Eburos, but I never thought—"

Kathrael blinked innocently. "What? Is it truly so unheard of? I've heard people say that Alyrion men take many wives. Surely that's not so different?"

A faint flush rose to the man's face. "Heavens, no. That's... an old custom. Hundreds of years old. Men used to take many wives so they could have more sons, and strengthen their family's position in the world. But the first Emperor decreed at the beginning of his reign that marriage could only be between a man and a woman. That is what the One God commands."

"Oh... I see," she said. "We have a similar thing here on Eburos—a handfasting. Tell me then, Tullus, are you married?"

His expression soured for a moment before he covered it. "I am. To a woman who has borne me two fine sons, and three daughters."

Kathrael trailed a fingertip around the rim of her flagon. "A good wife, indeed. And yet, I'd think a man would eventually grow weary of seeing the same face, day in and day out for year upon year. Surely, one begins to crave... *variety*. A taste of the exotic."

Tullus looked at her as if trying to see through her mask, both literally and figuratively. "Variety? And tell me, do two men provide variety enough for you?" he asked. The question might have been flippant, but she knew better.

She looked down, toying with her cup of wine. "I told you," she said. "They provide me with food and a safe place to sleep. In today's world, that should be more than enough for a life of contentment. Should it not?" She allowed a hesitant note to enter the final words.

Whatever Tullus might have said was interrupted by Ithric and Favian's return, but the seed had been planted. The weapons dealer blinked and took a breath, visibly donning the persona of the rich host once more.

"Ah, you're back. By all means, join us," he said, with forced joviality. "We were just having the most fascinating conversation about Alyrion and Eburosi marriage customs."

Ithric and Favian took places on either side of Kathrael, dropping down to the cushions and accepting wine from the servant. Ithric slung an arm around her.

"Marriage?" he asked, looking down at Kathrael. "That's like bondmates, right? Surely you're not scheming behind our backs to tie the handfasting knot, pet?"

Kathrael laughed, a light sound. "Oh, come now. How could I ever choose just one of you, my dears?"

She pressed a playful kiss to Ithric's cheek, and leaned the other way to stroke her hand across Favian's temple. Favian—bless him—went very still in surprise for an instant, but Ithric must have told him to play along with her, because he recovered quickly and grasped her hand, pressing a kiss to her knuckles.

Tullus cleared his throat. "Well, I must say you three are quite an intriguing trio. Tell me, wherever did you learn such an unusual assortment of skills?"

Ithric relaxed back, his arm still around Kathrael. She leaned against his side, letting him play with the curls of her hair—subtly reminding Tullus of what Ithric had, and Tullus wanted. Kathrael thanked Ithric silently for being so perceptive, though perhaps it should have come as no surprise to her. He was as much of a natural actor as she was, after all.

Not to mention a storyteller.

"Well," he began, "I can't speak for the others. But I spent part of a winter way up north, when I was much younger. I stayed for a while with a tribe that traveled around during the warmer seasons doing more or less what we do these days—entertaining people in exchange for money."

"Albeit, not very *much* money," Favian put in.

"It gets really cold, that far north," Ithric continued as if Favian hadn't spoken. "They pretty much hibernated during the winter months—which is about as boring as it sounds, I'm sorry to say. I think it was boredom that motivated some of them to teach me a bit about fire-eating and sleight of hand."

He flexed the fingers of the hand that had been playing with Kathrael's hair, and pulled a copper coin from her riot of wavy curls. He flipped it to Tullus, who caught it out of the air with a jerky grab, obviously taken by surprise.

The Alyrion examined the tarnished disc for a moment before his brown eyes returned to them, assessing.

"Keep it," Ithric said, and Kathrael could hear the sharp smile in his voice, even if she couldn't see his face. "A token to remember us by."

Tullus placed the coin on the table in front of him. "So, you learned fire-eating from traveling performers in the far north. Very interesting. But where does a person learn to stand on the backs of horses?"

Favian fiddled with his flagon of wine. "No great secret there, I'm afraid. As a youth, I was apprenticed to the Horse Master of my village. Boys will always dare other boys to do things that are both stupid and dangerous. Standing on the backs of a galloping chariot team was only one such thing."

Tullus huffed a breath of amusement. "Boys will be boys—yes. That much is true the world over. Pray, tell me though. I would not presume to inquire why the lady goes masked. But I will indulge in at least a hint of unseemly curiosity. I could not help noticing that you wear your hair in the rather unconventional style favored by the pagan priests here..."

Favian did not change expression. "Yes. I do."

The silence stretched, Tullus clearly expecting him to expand on that. When he did not, the man eventually laughed. "Well, if you've intended to lend yourselves an air of the mysterious, then I suppose the three of you have succeeded admirably," he said.

"We've told you a bit about ourselves, Tullus," Kathrael offered. "But I would be very interested in hearing more about you. What brings you across the straits in the middle of winter?"

He hesitated. "I am... a trader,' he answered after a moment's pause. "I have business to conduct which cannot wait for spring."

Kathrael pretended disappointment, as if she had hoped for something more exciting. "Oh," she said. "A trader. That must be very interesting." The last word was delivered as if she were trying to put it in a good light, so as not to offend him.

"Interesting... perhaps not," he allowed. "It is, however, quite lucrative. As it happens, I am here to do business with King Flenaar himself."

"The king?" Kathrael echoed, playing at being taken aback, and perhaps skeptical. "Really?"

"Just so," Tullus said. "I am pleased to be his honored guest in the city while we complete our transaction. This is one of his Highness's villas, in fact. And he has extended me other amenities for the course of my stay, as well."

Ithric shifted next to her. "That must be a nice state of affairs to find yourself in," he said, as if grudgingly impressed.

Tullus was clearly pleased to have regained the upper hand in the conversation. "Rhyth isn't quite up to the cultural standards of the Alyrion capital," he said airily. "But, no, I can't complain. For one thing, the royal bath houses here are actually rather impressive."

Kathrael sat up, her sudden interest only half-feigned. "You have access to the royal baths?"

Tullus lounged back against his cushions, clearly aware that he had hooked her. He nodded, humming an affirmative. "His Excellence has given me use of the *caldarium* at the eastern edge of the Old Quarter for the duration of my stay, yes." He inclined his head, as if an idea had just come to him. "You three should join me there tomorrow for a few hours. It's the least I can do to thank you for such a diverting evening."

His eyes played shamelessly over Kathrael, and she made sure to look suitably excited at the prospect. Truth be told, it was no great feat of acting—though she reminded herself firmly that they were working to a plan, and this invitation could be a real benefit to them.

"That's a very generous offer," Ithric was saying. "We'd be delighted to."

Favian made a vague noise of agreement, still obviously uncomfortable with the whole ruse. Hopefully, it would come across as his naturally taciturn demeanor, and nothing more. Certainly, there was no suspicion in Tullus's voice as he said, "It's settled, then. Good! I'm acquainted with so few people here, it's nice to have some stimulating company to pass the time."

An idea sprung to Kathrael's mind, fully formed. "In that case," she offered, "perhaps I could invite a few of my female friends to join us? I'm sure they would jump at the chance to enjoy an afternoon in the royal *caldarium*. And the baths are far more... stimulating... with the right sort of open-minded company, if you take my meaning."

She could see the look of surprise, followed by a split second of indecision, before desire won out. She was offering Tullus that forbidden Rhytheeri fruit, peeled, sliced, and laid out on a silver platter. Of course he was going to reach for it.

"Why not, eh?" he said. "Meet me at the south door when the sun dips behind the tower of the palace. We'll make a private party of it, courtesy of His Majesty's generosity."

The irony was palpable, but Ithric only smiled and said, "We look forward to it. Now, though, we'd best head home before it gets too late. The streets aren't safe late at night."

They took their leave from the weapons dealer and his fawning retinue shortly thereafter. Tullus pressed an ostentatious kiss to the back of Kathrael's hand that was no doubt intended to be seductive. She resisted the urge to wipe her fingers on her skirt until they were safely back at the caravan, where Ciryl was waiting for them, guarding their horses and belongings.

When they were crowded onto the driver's bench of the caravan, Favian took up the reins and guided the team of horses along the narrow streets of the central district; past rows of huge dwellings inhabited by Rhyth's corrupt nobles.

"Right," he said grimly, not looking at her. "Did you, or did you not just arrange an orgy at a royal bath house, Kath?"

Vesh snorted his amusement in the back of her mind.

"Only a little one," she said, already planning how to contact some of the prostitutes they had met who were acquainted with the Sisterhood of Avlan.

"Wait. You *what*, now?" Ciryl asked from his perch on the roof behind them, and Ithric let out a bark of badly stifled laughter.

"No, this is good, though," Ithric said. "There are too many people at the villa. We need to draw Tullus away from his household, and this is one way to do it."

"You're trying to seduce him." Favian did not sound happy about it.

Kathrael frowned, a stab of disquiet going through her. "It's only an act, Favian. He's the enemy. I wouldn't really—"

"Oh, for the gods' sake," Ithric said. "We both know that, Little Cat. I think you may have offended Favian's sensibilities, that's all."

She glanced at Ithric in the reflected glow of the lit braziers illuminating the streets. "But not your sensibilities?"

"If he does much more than kiss your hand, I'll start removing body parts," Ithric said, his tone still conversational. "But what you have planned may well work out in our favor."

"Just make sure not to remove any body parts he'll need to get us access to the warehouse," Favian muttered, still sounding unhappy.

Kathrael turned her attention to him, taking in the way his lips turned down as he skillfully guided the horses. "Are you going to be all right with this?" she asked seriously. "While you were taking care of the horses, I told Tullus I was sleeping with both of you to put him off balance and get him thinking with his prick rather than his head. But it means you'll have to play the part tomorrow, Favian, if we're going to do this."

Favian shot her a dark glance. "You accused me of being a prude shortly after we met. Do you remember? The answer now is the same as it was then. I'm a priest, and I'd be a pretty piss-poor one if I had any kind of a problem with sex, public or otherwise."

She continued to study him. "This isn't sex, Favian," she said. "This is a scheme to kidnap someone."

His jaw worked for a moment before he said, "What do you want me to say? I hate the fact that you're bartering your body and the bodies of whatever girls you get to service this man tomorrow, in exchange for the chance of victory in a civil war? All right—I hate it. But this is what I've agreed to do, and I'll do it."

Kathrael was at a loss for the right way to respond to his tightly controlled anger, and she didn't like the feeling at all. She wanted to wrap her arms around him and press against his side until he wasn't upset any more, but she didn't think he would accept the gesture right now.

Surprisingly, it was Ciryl who broke the tense silence. "Women make their own choices, Favian. Me, I don't like to judge 'em for using whatever power they have over men, when men don't seem to hesitate in using the power they have over women."

Favian was silent for a moment longer before some of the tension bled out of him. "You've been harboring hidden depths, Ciryl. How'd I manage to miss that, then?"

"Other things on your mind, I reckon, Blondie," Ciryl said, unperturbed.

"*Are* you going to be all right with this, Favian?" Ithric asked. "Because if not, it would be better for you to stay away completely. We could tell him you're feeling ill, or—"

"Don't make me laugh," Favian said. "Of course I'm bloody well coming."

"And playing the part of the possessive barbarian lover?" Ithric prodded.

Favian huffed a breath of irritation. "Within the obvious limitations."

It was a valid point, since Favian was a eunuch. "I'll make sure Tullus is too distracted to pay attention to anything below your waist during the short space of time after you take off your robe and before you enter the baths," Kathrael said. "Just stay in the water as much as possible."

"Yeah," Favian said. "Sure. I can hardly wait."

THREE

Even with a four-horse team and a caravan, it was no joke transporting thirteen people at once — six of whom had to stay hidden from view at all times. After leaving Tullus's villa, Kathrael had successfully tracked down one of the three young prostitutes they'd met previously, in the plaza adjacent to where the Painted Lady had stood before it burned down.

The girl contacted her two friends, and the three of them were currently perched on the caravan's roof with Ciryl, who had come along ostensibly to guard the horses while they bathed. That part was true, as far as it went — he *would* be guarding the animals.

He would also keep prying eyes away from the caravan's windows, where they might catch a glimpse of a half dozen of Qaden's men crammed inside, armed to the teeth and waiting to overpower Tullus, along with whoever he might be bringing with him.

After considerable discussion, they had decided to try to nab the arms dealer on the way out of the baths rather than on the way in. There were several potential benefits to waiting. It would be nearer to dark by then, better shielding them from casual onlookers who might raise the alarm. Tullus would be more relaxed at that point — very, *very* relaxed if the three girls accompanying them were worth their salt. With luck, that would put him off his guard.

Also, most importantly, waiting would give Kathrael time to attempt a half-formed plan that might make all of this considerably safer for them if it succeeded. None of them were too thrilled about the idea of dragging an angry, kidnapped man halfway across the city without drawing unwanted attention from either the guardsmen or the gangs.

So, they would take the waters together and play nicely with the man who was planning to sell Rhyth's ruler a warehouse full of the deadliest weapons the continent had to offer. Kathrael would tease him and press him and see if she could mold his actions into the shape she wanted. And, in the course of doing so, the three of them would spend an afternoon in one of the finest bathhouses in the city. She wondered what the king's reaction would be if he knew he was playing unwitting host to a cohort of revolutionaries.

Favian guided the horses to a halt near the south door of the *caldarium*, far enough out of the road that other travelers could get past them, but parked in such a fashion that they could leave quickly when the time came. Ithric was calm and watchful at her right shoulder. At her left, Kathrael felt Favian draw in a deep breath and let it out slowly. He was still tense and unhappy. She studied his set features, sincerely hoping he'd be able to play his role.

⚜

Favian let his breath out through his nose, trying to expel his sense of foreboding at the same time. He secured the reins and slid down from the driver's bench to chock one of the caravan's wheels so it wouldn't roll. He was aware of Ithric and Ciryl helping the three girls down from their perch on the roof above him.

Kathrael appeared at his side a moment later. When he straightened, it was to see three figures on horseback approaching, one of whom was Tullus.

"Two bodyguards," she murmured. "That's manageable, if it comes to it."

He nodded, hiding his misgivings. Manageable it might be, but that didn't stop him from picturing all the ways their plan might go wrong and get people hurt or killed. As it did periodically these days, a wash of panic, of wondering what in the gods' names he was even *doing* here, playing spy and kidnapper and revolutionary, swept over him. And, a moment later, the answer — he was here because the southern slaves were suffering in bondage, and because the two people he loved would not rest until they'd changed things, or died trying.

It was the *died trying* part he couldn't afford to think about too closely.

Tullus and his guards dismounted and tied up their horses before Tullus turned and hailed them. "Well, now! You've arrived with full regalia, I see," he called, gesturing at the caravan and four-horse team.

Kathrael laughed gaily. "My friends were nervous of riding double on horseback, and it would have been a long way for them to walk," she said. "Besides, this way, people will see the caravan and know that we're guests at the king's baths. That sort of gossip brings more spectators to the shows, and that means money for us!"

"Ah, there's that entrepreneurial spirit," Tullus said, coming up to clasp Favian and Ithric hand-to-wrist in greeting.

"Whatever it takes to keep the horses fed, and us well supplied with bread and wine," Ithric said with forced joviality.

Favian merely nodded as he clasped the Alyrion's wrist in a firm grip—well aware that he was incapable of playing this game with the same degree of skill as either Ithric or Kathrael. His job was to be the quiet one. The mysterious one. He would keep his mouth shut unless addressed directly, and act like Kathrael was a possession he feared losing to the wiles of a smooth, rich foreigner—as much as the idea rankled.

Tullus turned his attention to the three giggling girls clustered next to Kathrael. They had cleaned themselves up as well as they could and were wearing borrowed clothing that hovered on the edge of respectability—the best any of them had been able to manage on such short notice.

Not that clothing would be likely to remain an impediment for long, considering the venue.

Kathrael introduced the young women with a smile. "These are my friends—Brenna, Maryn, and Jessamiel. Girls, this is the man I told you about, Tullus Coruscanus Abito of Alyrios. I just know we're all going to get along famously."

Jessamiel took the lead, stepping forward and looking up at Tullus with wide brown eyes as he lifted her hand and brushed his lips to her knuckles.

"Charmed," he said.

"Hello. Is it true that you're a friend of the king's?" she asked, breathless, and Favian wondered idly if acting ability was a prerequisite of surviving as a prostitute.

As if the words had been a signal, the other two came forward to join her, all three practically fawning over Tullus, who clearly relished the attention.

"Ah, now—*friend* is far too strong a word," he said. "His Eminence and I share a particular business interest, you could say, though he has certainly been more than generous to me since I arrived here in Rhyth."

The girls *oohed* and *ahhed* in a way that made Favian feel vaguely nauseated.

"Now, though," Tullus continued, "let's not stand out in the cold discussing tiresome matters of commerce when we could be inside, taking advantage of His Majesty's largesse. Come, let's bathe. I've been assured that we will have the place to ourselves except for the attendants."

Favian glanced quickly at Ithric, who gave an almost imperceptible nod in return. They would have to keep the presence of the attendants in mind—more people who were presumably loyal to the king, and who might raise the alarm if they saw anything amiss.

In the meantime, however, they would bathe, and Kathrael would try to enact her rather unlikely sounding plan of getting Tullus to take them to the warehouse voluntarily. Maryn, Brenna, and Jessamiel would offer sex to a man they didn't care for or even know, in hopes that it would somehow aid in bringing change to Rhyth. Ciryl would guard the caravan, with its cargo of six gang members—who would no doubt be seriously cranky after being stuck inside the cramped space for hours on end. Ithric would play territorial games with their host, and Favian would try not to do anything to fuck it all up.

It was a real pity that they weren't here under less dire circumstances. Favian had only just remembered a snippet of conversation he'd had with Kathrael on the day after they'd found Ithric in Woodhaerst. She had dragged him to the modest bathing room at the back of the temple to wash, and talk. It had been the first time she'd really opened up about her love for the city she called home. She'd waxed lyrical about the bathhouses, built by rich families over sites where the hot springs that dotted the area bubbled to the surface.

And now, here they were. Tullus led them into the grand building through a door set in an arched recess. The architecture was different from anything else Favian had seen in the city. Everything was open and airy, the space delineated by cylindrical columns set at precise intervals, each one appearing identical to all the others. Everything was made of stone, and polished to gleaming.

He couldn't help but catch his breath as they entered the first chamber. Every wall was encrusted in brilliant mosaics, depicting gods and mortals cavorting together in brilliant blue water. The colors were so bright as to seem unreal, drawing and holding the eye with their intensity. His attention caught on a mural of Naloth driving a chariot through frothy ocean waves, drawn by two creamy white animals with the heads and front legs of horses, but the tails of fish.

"Impressive, isn't it? Tullus asked.

Suddenly aware that he was staring like a simpleton, Favian snapped his mouth shut and swallowed. "I hope whoever glued all those tiny little pieces of stone and glass onto the walls was paid well," he managed, striving to sound unaffected.

Tullus laughed long and deep, as if this were the funniest joke he'd ever heard. "I'm afraid I've no idea, my friend. Though the work does display considerably more natural artistic talent than one would expect to find from slaves. So it's possible."

Just like that, Favian was firmly back in the moment. He glanced at Kathrael to see how she'd taken the comment, but she was lounging, apparently unaffected, against Ithric's side. When she saw Favian looking, she smiled and moved to him instead, reaching up on tiptoe to kiss his cheek.

"Come on," she said. "Why are we waiting here? Let's go in and get in the water."

"Why indeed, my dear?" Tullus said indulgently. He led the way to the attendant standing patiently at the door to the next chamber, a girl on each of his arms and the third following a step behind—all three craning around to see everything around them, drinking in the grandeur.

"Good afternoon, honored guests," greeted the young attendant, who was barely more than a boy.

Tullus gave him a pleasant smile. "Good afternoon. My friends and I require robes and towels. After that, we will need only a good supply of wine, some bread and cheese, and privacy."

The lad bowed. "Of course, sir. Shall I send servants to the cabinet room to assist you in undressing?"

Kathrael laughed. "Oh, my. I shouldn't think that would be necessary. I daresay that between us, we can all manage somehow. Don't you think so, Tullus?"

"I've never been the sort to keep a valet," Tullus said, clearly amused. "It's my view that if a person can't dress and undress themselves without help, they don't need a valet; they need a more proficient tailor."

"Hmm. You and I will have to disagree on that point, I'm afraid," Ithric said. "There's a certain piquancy to unlacing a woman's bodice for her and peeling away all the layers, one by one."

Tullus raised an eyebrow.

Let the male territorial games begin, Favian thought.

"I'll admit I've never looked at the matter from that angle," Tullus said. "Perhaps we should proceed to the changing room and examine your idea in more detail. From all sides, if you will."

Favian swallowed a sigh, aware that his feelings of awkwardness were about to increase tenfold. Kathrael had put her finger on the cusp of it with uncanny accuracy yesterday. What they were about to do would not be sex. It would be a performance. And, just as he had never fully come to terms with performing on horseback in front of huge crowds during the show, he suspected he would not be coming to terms with what they were going to do today.

The cabinet room was just that—a space for changing from street clothes into the soft robes that guests apparently wore when moving from room to room through the large complex. Clothes and belongings were stored in one of the many individual cabinets lining the walls, waiting securely for their owners' return. The nine of them trooped inside, and Tullus's two bodyguards arranged themselves next to the door.

The young prostitutes who had accompanied them set to removing each other's dresses, making a show of it. Kathrael caught Favian's eye, and he took advantage of the ready-made distraction to shuck his own clothing and don a robe, trying not to draw attention as he did.

He needn't have worried. Tullus was fully engaged by the emerging female flesh in front of him, and even more distracted when they finished with each other and started on the fastenings of his richly embroidered tunic and tailored breeches.

Aware of the part he was meant to play, Favian stepped behind Kathrael and started to undress her. He was joined a moment later by Ithric, now wearing a robe as well. Favian chewed the inside of his cheek, truly hating the way they were using her—even though the whole thing had been largely her idea.

He especially hated the sense of distance he felt from her as her clothing fell away, revealing the lithe dancer's form beneath. It was a distance he had not felt since very early in their acquaintance—a sense that she was holding her mind separate from whatever was being done to her physically. That she was doing so under his and Ithric's hands made him feel decidedly ill.

Nevertheless, it was working as she had intended. Despite having three girls' attention focused firmly on him, Tullus's gaze wandered back to Kathrael as if drawn by a lodestone, drinking in her body, bare now except for her bronze mask.

Favian saw the flash of Ithric's razor-edged smile as he helped Kathrael into a robe, hiding her once more from the view of his supposed rival. *Their* supposed rival, he corrected. Kath glanced up at Tullus and quickly back down again, as if overcome by a moment of shyness.

Tullus cleared his throat. "Well, now. No servants needed after all, just as you said, my dear. Now, bath or steam room?"

"Bath!" Jessamiel declared. "I don't understand why rich people want to sit around in a hot room getting sweaty and thirsty before bathing."

Her companions chimed in with agreement on the subject, and Tullus huffed in amusement. "Very well, it's decided. The attendants should have had time to ready the room with the warm pool for us. Shall we?"

They passed through the steam room with its heady mix of cedar smoke and burning herbs without stopping. Beyond was the first cold pool. Maryn dipped one foot in and jerked it back out again.

"That's as bad as bathing in the river!" she said, gathering her robe around her as if for warmth.

"I expect it's more appealing after you've roasted in the steam room for a bit," Ithric offered.

"It is indeed," Tullus confirmed, casually reminding them that he was the only one present who was able to regularly take advantage of such places.

Beyond the cold pool lay the centerpiece of the *caldarium*—the warm pool. It was large enough for a person to swim in, surrounded by marble colonnades and open to the gray winter sky above. The water was a soothing green-blue. Tendrils of steam rose from the surface and wafted across the ripples like mist. The smell of sulfur filled the air.

"Now *that's* more like it!" Maryn exclaimed, dropping her robe and rushing for the steps at the edge of the pool like the excited girl she was. She splashed down into the pool, her pert breasts jouncing just above the water level as she turned to them, grinning. "Oh, it's *gorgeous*! Come in with me."

Brenna and Jessamiel needed no further prompting to tumble in after her. The three of them laughed in glee and splashed each other, clearly having the time of their lives. Tullus smiled indulgently and followed at a more sedate pace, setting his robe neatly to the side before stepping down into the pool and retiring to a spot on the submerged bench running around the pool's perimeter, where he could relax and enjoy the sight of the young women at play. His guards took up places against the wall, where they could watch over their employer without being too obtrusive.

Kathrael let her robe slip to the ground and followed Tullus into the pool, with Ithric right behind her. Favian used the distraction and partial barricade of their bodies in front of him to take off his robe and slide down until the water covered his lower body.

The sulfur smell took some real getting used to, but the warm, mineral-rich bathing pool truly was divine. Favian felt his way to the bench around the edge and sank down, little waves lapping at his clavicles. Occasional swirls of cooler air wafted against his exposed skin as the winter chill did battle with the heat and steam rising from the water. Kathrael settled beside him. Ithric dunked himself completely, emerging wet and shining a moment later.

One of the girls giggled and took advantage of his moment of vulnerability to splash him full in the face. Ithric sputtered and laughed, diving into the fray with abandon while Kathrael, Favian, and Tullus shrank back to avoid becoming collateral victims of the impromptu battle.

After the skirmish moved on to the deeper parts of the pool, Tullus returned his attention to Kathrael, who leaned against Favian's shoulder as they lounged on the bench.

"I had thought perhaps you would shed your sense of mystery for something as informal as bathing, my dear," Tullus said. "Yet even here, you wear your mask."

Though Favian had worried about playing his part, it was surprisingly easy to let a growl creep into his voice. "No. No one sees Kathrael unmasked except us."

FOUR

This was a blatant lie, of course. But he could hardly add, "… except people she trusts," when they were trying to earn that very thing from their host.

"My, my," Tullus replied mildly. "Now, I fear I'm even more curious than before."

Favian was rescued from having to answer by Ithric's return. The shape-shifter heaved himself up to sit on the edge of the pool, his legs dangling in the water next to Kathrael, unconcerned as always by his nakedness. "Ah," he said, "you have to understand, though, Tullus. Some sights are simply too beautiful to squander."

He lifted a hand to cup Kathrael's chin and tilt her face up toward his, as one might do with a pampered pet. At that point, Tullus was distracted from any answer he might have made by the three girls descending on him, their play forgotten for now.

"This is wonderful!" Brenna gushed, climbing unashamedly into his lap and kissing him briefly on the lips. "Thank you for letting us come."

Tullus's hands hovered a few inches away from her shoulders for a beat or two, the whole situation of being blatantly propositioned in public obviously far outside of his experience. The other two girls settled onto the bench, flanking him.

"You're allowed to touch her, you know," Jessamiel said with a laugh, sliding a wet fingertip down Tullus's cheek. "You can touch all of us. Girls know what it means when a man invites them to the bathhouse, even one as grand as this one. *Especially* when they arrange to be practically alone with them."

Tullus still had the look of someone who was half-expecting to awake at any moment and find that this had all been a dream. His gaze flickered across to where Kathrael lounged between Favian and Ithric. Favian could see that his eyes had grown wide and dark.

He cleared his throat, though the words still emerged hoarse. "But... we're *not* alone—"

Ithric laughed, and reached out a hand to tangle in Kath's long hair, using it to draw her up to his level. "*Please.* This is Rhyth, Tullus. There are no rules here."

With that, he pulled Kathrael in for a demanding kiss. She made a small noise into his mouth, and Favian heard Tullus let out a harsh breath. He turned back in time to see the man surrender to the allure of the three girls surrounding him, his hands closing on Brenna's naked shoulders as she kissed him again, more deeply this time.

Favian swallowed a sigh, still feeling vaguely repulsed by the whole thing, rather than titillated. Aware that he should probably be *doing* something as opposed to sitting there staring while everyone else kissed and groped each other with ever-increasing levels of shamelessness, he settled for sliding over until he could wrap an arm around Kathrael's waist and press kisses to the swell of her hip. She rewarded the rather sorry effort with fingers twining in his hair, holding him in place.

The young prostitutes were playful, giggling and murmuring filthy suggestions in Tullus's ear as he gradually relaxed into their attentions. Sadly, Favian suspected that this truly was a holiday for them, servicing a man without the ever-present threat of violence, while surrounded by beauty and comfort.

Kathrael still had that aura of disconnectedness that he hated so much, as she moaned and twisted and did all the things that he could tell she wasn't really feeling. Ithric was half-hard; a far cry from his usual response to sex with the two of them, but still enough to make Favian roll his eyes when he was sure Tullus was otherwise engaged. Ithric surfaced from his lip-lock with Kath to shoot him a brief scowl and mouth, "What?"

Favian only shook his head, wishing that they could all be somewhere else. *Anywhere* else, really.

Ithric eased Kathrael away from him. "Let me have your hand on me, pet," he ordered, nonchalant. "Take your time with it, mind you. Favian, do you want her quim?"

As subtle revenge went, it was fairly effective, and Favian covered another sigh. As a eunuch—not to mention someone who had only really been physically aroused by men *before* becoming a eunuch—he was not in any position to have that kind of sex with Kathrael, as Ithric knew full well.

But they would be hidden by the water, and Favian had promised to play his part in the farce. Also, it would mean that Kathrael would not *actually* have to fuck anyone while she was hiding herself away, acting in this role. That, in itself, was reason enough to go along with it.

The words had certainly caught Tullus's notice, even with Brenna draped over him, kissing his neck while the other two stroked their hands over his body, tweaking his nipples and sliding down between his legs.

"Come here, then," Favian told Kath, not worrying that the words sounded gruff. He and Ithric arranged her pliant body so she could straddle Favian's lap on the bench, facing the same direction he was. He looped an arm around her as she made a show of settling down onto him, pretending to take him inside.

Favian belatedly manufactured a low groan, feeling very much the fish out of water. Ironic, he supposed, given their surroundings. From the corner of his eye, he saw Kathrael reach out and take Ithric in hand, teasing him to full hardness with slow strokes.

Across from them, the three girls were daring each other to duck under the water and try to take Tullus's prick in their mouths, only to emerge laughing and sputtering a few seconds later. Tullus still seemed overwhelmed by it all, attention flicking back and forth between his three admirers and Kathrael, pretending to ride Favian as she lazily fisted Ithric.

Under the water, her free hand closed on Favian's forearm and guided it up. He realized she was steering him toward her breasts and took the hint, grasping one small globe in each hand and using his grip to guide her up and down in what seemed like a reasonable rhythm for fucking.

"How does she feel, Favian?" Ithric asked, sprawling back to rest his weight on his hands.

Favian cast around for something suitable to describe being inside a woman. "Tight and, uh, hot," he said. "Hotter than the water, even."

Kathrael hummed and ground down on his lap. He thought she was looking right at Tullus—certainly, Tullus was staring at her with his lips parted, gaze flickering between her face and Favian's hands squeezing her breasts.

A moment later, though, their host was distracted by Jessamiel climbing up on the bench to straddle him. "I want to feel you inside me now, Tullus," she said, before adding playfully, "but don't come! The others want a turn with you, too!"

Tullus finally seemed to have come to terms with the reality of what was going on around him. "How could I possibly refuse such a request?" he said, once again oozing continental charm. Jessamiel lowered herself onto his cock and started moving, while Brenna claimed his mouth for a kiss. Meanwhile, Maryn continued to pluck at his nipples and sucked on his earlobe.

Favian tried to remember to make the occasional noise of pleasure, and waited for the whole thing to be over. Growing up in a culture where public sex was part of both the religion and the social fabric, he'd seen plenty of it over the years. And he honestly enjoyed watching people in love give each other pleasure—especially when the people in question were Ithric and Kathrael.

But watching the girls service Tullus was a flat experience, utterly devoid of the beauty he'd come to associate with good sex. By the time Maryn had taken her turn on Tullus's lap, Favian's eyes were in danger of glazing over. He wondered if the two bodyguards were enjoying the show, or if the fact that they couldn't join in made it as tedious for them as it was for him.

Ithric's voice startled him out of his reverie. "I'm getting close, pet. Faster, now."

Kathrael sped up her strokes, and after a short interval, Ithric groaned and spilled over her hand. Completely shameless, as he had been ever since Favian had known him. As if Ithric's moan of pleasure had been a signal, Tullus grunted and jerked through his own release. Figuring he probably shouldn't be left behind, and also that it would be the best way for this fiasco to be over, Favian thought back to the way coming had felt before he became a eunuch, and faked his way through it as best he was able.

Tullus, he suspected, would not be particularly concerned about whether any of the women had found their pleasure.

That was confirmed soon afterward, when he eased Maryn off of him. "Very... *invigorating*... my dear," he murmured. "Perhaps you would be good enough to fetch me some wine?"

Maryn smiled and kissed him on the cheek as if he hadn't just asked her to play servant girl to him, mere moments after she had fucked him. It was a complete waste of time, of course, but Favian still couldn't help driving the point home by tucking Kath in an affectionate embrace against his side and pressing a tender kiss to her temple. He only wished it didn't feel like kissing an empty vessel—Kath was still gone, hidden away in the depths of her own mind.

Ithric slipped down into the water to wash himself off and settle on her other side, bracketing her between them. *Staking out their territory*, Favian thought with an unhappy twist of the lips.

Maryn brought wine for all of them, herself included, and stretched out on the edge near Tullus. "Tell us more about yourself, won't you?" she prompted. "Did you really come here all the way from Alyrios in the middle of winter?"

Tullus was lounging with his head leaned back, eyes closed, wine cup clasped loosely in his fingers. He hummed an affirmative noise. "I did."

"Weren't you afraid to cross the sea when it's so rough?" Brenna asked, wide-eyed. "I'd be far too frightened to get on a boat in winter."

"Alyrion ships are safe and well-designed vessels," Tullus said, still only half engaged in the conversation after his recent exertions. "It was not a pleasant journey, but it was a necessary one."

Ithric spoke up. "And what commerce are you conducting that could be so important? Grain? Textiles?" The words were laced with subtle challenge, as if Ithric were hoping for something terribly boring and provincial.

It worked—possibly because Tullus' wits were dulled by sex, or possibly because he simply found Ithric's prodding annoying. For perhaps the first time since he'd met the man, Favian could sympathize with him—at least on that subject.

Whatever the case, Tullus peeled open one eye and said, "Weapons."

Beside Favian, Kathrael tensed and drew in an audible breath. "Weapons?" she echoed, her voice barely more than a whisper.

Her breathless tone drew Tullus further out of his post-coital stupor, and he looked at her properly. "Yes, that's right."

"Stop gawping, pet," Ithric said, sounding irritated. He sighed, and addressed Tullus. "She's always had an unhealthy fascination with weapons, for a woman. Not sure why. Don't mind her."

Kath straightened away from them, elbowing Ithric in the ribs as she did so. "Weapons mean power," she said, as if irked. "All women like men with power."

Just like that, their fish was hooked. Tullus drew himself up and raised a haughty eyebrow. "Well, by that assessment, I should say that there is quite a bit of power housed in the warehouse I'm renting near the harbor. It's full of the finest and most modern crossbows money can buy. Thousands of them."

Favian scoffed, playing his part. "Bull. No one has *thousands of crossbows*. They're too new." Indeed, Favian had never even heard of a crossbow until Ithric had explained the technology — which was actually a bit terrifying. The idea of an arrow that could travel farther and faster than one from a longbow, and required almost no training to fire —

"Of course he doesn't have thousands of crossbows," Ithric said. "Can you imagine? No offense, Tullus, but I still think it's grain or, I dunno, beans or something. What's that funny kind of wheat they grow on the continent called, again?"

Kathrael gave him a little shove, and he glared at her. She glared right back. "Stop being so rude! I mean, I know it sounds unlikely, but if Tullus says he has crossbows, then —"

Unaware of the slow pull of the fishing line reeling him in, Tullus straightened away from the edge of the pool and stood. "Well now — there's no call for an argument. I can do more than *say* I have a warehouse full of crossbows. If you've had your fill of the king's waters, then dry yourselves off and I'll give you a brief tour. It's not far from here."

Favian schooled himself not to react as Kathrael's plan fell neatly into place. Ithric, actor that he was, appeared to be taken aback at his bluff being called in such a way. "A... tour?" he said. "Now? Well, I don't know..."

"I want to go," Kathrael said, no-nonsense. "Stay here if you want. I'm sure I could ride double on Tullus's horse."

"No," Favian said quickly. "We'll come. I want to see this for myself."

"It's settled, then," Tullus said. "Girls?"

Jessamiel shrugged. "I don't like weapons. I'd rather not."

"We believe you, though, Tullus," Maryn hastened to add.

"I'd rather go to the Wren and get some ale," Brenna put in.

"Fine. Then I guess the three of us will just follow you with the caravan to see... whatever's in this warehouse." Ithric still sounded sour. "You said it's down by the harbor somewhere, right?"

"We should go right now, in that case! It's getting late in the day." Kathrael climbed out of the pool, giving Tullus another view of her graceful dancer's curves. Tullus drank them in as if he hadn't just fucked three other women.

The Alyrion shrugged, and hauled himself out of the water. "Very well. Far be it for me to keep a lady waiting."

Favian shared a brief flicker of a glance with the others, hardly able to believe that Kathrael's plan had worked so perfectly.

FIVE

Kathrael kept her good eye on their surroundings as they rattled down the cobblestone road behind Tullus and his two guards. The warehouse near the harbor was in far better repair than the tumbledown structure by the river that they were currently calling home.

The sun had made a brief appearance during the short journey, slanting low beneath slate-colored winter clouds as it prepared to disappear behind the jumble of rooftops to the west. Despite her warm clothes, the puffs of wind against her damp hair made her shiver.

Favian and Ithric sat tense and straight-backed on either side of her as the three of them perched on the driver's bench. Ciryl was a reassuring presence behind her, and she knew that six more strong, well-armed men waited inside the caravan, ready to spring out at a moment's notice.

Even so, the prospect of the first real battle in the war they had declared against the king had her breath coming short and her heart pounding in her chest. It was largely up to her to get them as far as they could possibly go before violence erupted. She was frankly a bit shocked that her ploy had worked at all.

With many men, it wouldn't have worked—but she'd had an inkling from the beginning that Tullus desired *acknowledgement* above almost everything else. He wanted people to see that he was better and richer and smarter than they were. She had given him the opportunity to prove it to the skeptical audience provided by Ithric and Favian, and he had jumped at it.

Members of the underground keeping surveillance on the warehouse reported the presence of a dozen hired guards posted around it, day and night. So it was no surprise to find them ranged evenly around the building's perimeter in the late afternoon shadows. They looked bored, but professional. One of the two at the main door stepped forward as they approached. His hand rested on the hilt of his sword, but it fell back to his side as he recognized his employer.

"We weren't expecting you today, sir," he said, eyeing the painted caravan curiously.

Tullus dismounted and handed his horse's reins to one of his bodyguards. "It's a spur of the moment visit," he replied. "We won't be here long. Unlock the door for us."

The guard dipped his head in acknowledgement and headed back to the warehouse entrance. Favian climbed down to secure the caravan, and Kathrael followed him. Ithric remained on the bench, looking at Tullus with a sullen expression.

"That's an awful lot of guards for grain or textiles," Kathrael called up to him, infusing the words with sarcasm. "Wouldn't you say so, Ithric?"

Ithric scowled, and climbed down from his perch. "Merchandise is merchandise. If it's worth enough money, you guard it. Doesn't matter what it is."

"Wise words, my friend," Tullus said, peeling off his winter gloves finger by finger. She got the impression that he was carefully disguising his glee at having driven a wedge between the two of them. "Come inside out of the wind, though, and you'll see for yourself."

Kathrael approached, distancing herself from Favian and Ithric in favor of walking next to Tullus. She plastered an ingratiating smile on her face. "Can our servant come, too? He says his brother showed him a crossbow last spring, and he wants to see if these look the same."

Tullus shrugged. "Why not?"

Ciryl grinned and slid down from the caravan's roof, landing heavily. He was not visibly armed, though Kathrael was confident that every hidden pocket held something that could be used as a weapon.

While they spoke, the guard pulled out a heavy key ring and opened the lock. Tullus's two bodyguards had finished tying up the horses and now waited nearby. Ithric stood with his arms crossed, looking irritable. Favian was blank-faced, but she thought he was a shade paler than usual.

The tall doors creaked open, and Tullus ushered them inside, his bodyguards trailing behind them. The interior of the warehouse was lit by daylight filtering through slatted openings in the wall beneath the overhang of the roof. Even so, it took Kathrael's vision a few moments to adjust.

"Well, whatever you've got stored in these crates," Favian said, "you've certainly got an awful lot of it."

The space was stacked from floor to ceiling with rough wooden boxes, not quite as wide and deep as the span of Kathrael's arms. Her breath caught, and it was not entirely an act. Tullus had a truly staggering number of weapons here.

"All of these hold crossbows?" she asked in an awe-filled whisper.

"They do," Tullus said, moving nearer to her. "Well—some hold bolts for the crossbows, but those don't take up too much space compared to the weapons themselves."

She blinked up at him. "Bolts?" she asked innocently.

He smiled. "Arrows. You can also call them quarrels. Crossbows take a special kind." He glanced around, and his eyes settled on a stack of smaller boxes. "Here."

He gestured her to follow and opened one, revealing hundreds of small arrows about the length of Kathrael's forearm. He handed one to her, and she made a show of examining it as Ithric and Favian looked on sullenly.

"It's so straight and perfectly formed," she said, reaching a finger cautiously toward the razor-sharp tip as if to test it.

Tullus captured her hand. "Careful. I'd hate for blood to be spilled unintentionally."

She covered any reaction she might have had to his words with a smile. "Sorry. It does look very sharp."

He took the bolt back from her and moved to one of the larger crates that had been left by itself on the ground, a few paces away from the large stacks. The lid was open, and he reached in, emerging with one of the crossbows resting in his hands.

"The bolts must be formed to fit the crossbow's channel precisely," he said, aware that he had gained a rapt audience as Ciryl, Favian, and Ithric stepped closer to see. He demonstrated, settling the bolt in place.

Kathrael made sure to pitch her voice low and excited. "It doesn't look at all how I'd pictured," she said. "How does it work? Isn't it awkward drawing the bowstring back with that hook in the way?"

Tullus laughed. "Ah, but that *hook* is the secret of the crossbow. Come here. I'll show you."

Kathrael was aware of Ithric bristling as she stepped close and let Tullus position her to place the crossbow in her hands. No doubt Tullus noticed his reaction as well, and reveled in it.

Her skin crawled as Tullus fitted himself against her back, looping an arm around her to guide her arms and hands into position.

"The hook is actually called a nut, or a pawl," he said. "You use a metal lever to span the bow—to pull back the drawstring, that is to say. The string is held in place by the nut while you insert the bolt into the channel and line up your shot. Then you simply squeeze your hand around the trigger, like this."

His hand closed around hers, wrapped around the stock and the long, thin bar of metal running parallel beneath it.

"That's amazing," Kathrael said, and jammed the end of the stock backwards as hard as she could into Tullus's ribcage. He grunted in surprise, and cried out as she stamped the heel of her boot down on his instep. She shoved her shoulder into his chest, throwing him off balance. He stumbled back, and Favian tripped him with an ankle hooked behind his, sending him to the ground.

Meanwhile, Ithric and Ciryl sprang at the two bodyguards, who had been taken completely by surprise and were fumbling for their swords. Ciryl drew a wooden cosh from the sleeve of his shirt and slammed into the larger guard, tangling his sword arm and bringing the stout length of wood sharply against the side of his head. The man dropped like a stone.

Ithric was wrestling the other one, trying to get behind him and pin his arms.

"Guards!" Tullus cried from his place on the ground, winded, but still loud enough to draw the attention of the paid mercenaries outside.

Ithric let out a shrill whistle, piercing enough that the man he was struggling with winced. Kathrael wished for her quarterstaff, aware that Tullus was probably armed with a dagger at least, and that it would be foolish for either her or Favian to get close enough to him to check.

The man Ithric was fighting landed a wild blow to the lion-shifter's face, snapping his head to the side, but an instant later Ciryl was there, knocking him out with a vicious blow to the back of his neck. He sagged, and Ithric let him drop, shaking off the punch.

Tullus had a knife in his hand now and was trying to scrabble to his feet. Ithric stalked over and kicked it out of his hand, drawing a dagger of his own and yanking the unfortunate weapons dealer upright. He whirled Tullus around and pressed the blade to his throat. A purple bruise was already blossoming over Ithric's cheekbone.

The Alyrion was wide-eyed, nervous sweat beading on his face even in the winter chill. Still, his voice was mostly steady as he rasped, "There are a dozen guards out there. You're committing suicide."

Kathrael narrowed her eyes at him. "Stop and listen, Tullus," she said. Outside, she could make out shouting, and metal clanging against metal as Favian approached to stand next to her. "That's the sound of far *more* than a dozen men who would very much like to take possession of the contents of this warehouse."

The blood drained from Tullus's face. "Damn you! You traitorous *bitch*," he hissed, only to suck in a sharp breath when Ithric yanked his head back by the hair and pressed the knife a little more firmly against his jugular.

"Be polite," he said mildly. "That's no way to talk to the person who got you laid by three women in a single afternoon. Even if she did make you look like a complete fool afterward."

At that moment, one of the warehouse guards staggered through the door, sword drawn, looking around wildly as he took in the scene.

"Tell him to drop his weapon," Ithric ordered, "or I start slicing things that you really don't want sliced."

Tullus opened his mouth, but no sound came out. The hapless guard stared at them, clearly unsure of what he should do. Before he came to a decision, three men burst in behind him. Kathrael vaguely recognized two of them as being members of Qaden's gang, while the other looked like one of Sephira's contingent of guards.

The warehouse guard whirled and raised his sword, only to fall beneath the onslaught of three opponents, blood spurting from a nasty gash in his side. One of Qaden's men yanked the sword free of his loosening grip.

"Oi, Ciryl," he said, and tossed the weapon hilt-first to the big man, who caught it smoothly from the air. "Stop mucking about and get out here, will ya?"

Ciryl glanced at Ithric. "You all right with this one, then? I think the other three are down for good."

"We're fine," Ithric said. "Go ahead and help them clean up outside. The quicker and quieter, the better."

The big man nodded and left with the others, grabbing bows and quarrels from the crates on their way out. Kathrael looked around the dim interior of the warehouse. "Help me find some rope, Favian," she said. "There ought to be some around here somewhere."

Even in the failing light, Favian looked pale as a ghost. But he only nodded and went to help her find something to tie up the injured and unconscious guards.

"What are you going to do to me?" Tullus asked, still displaying admirable poise under the circumstances.

Ithric's voice was level. "If you're a very good boy, we'll tie you up and throw you on the first boat back to the continent. You can go home to your fine lady wife and explain why you lost your entire investment and pissed off the king of Rhyth in the space a single night. I'm sure that for someone of your obvious acumen, it will only be a temporary setback."

Favian cleared his throat. "I think we can safely say that you won't want to be stuck in Rhyth over the coming weeks, anyway. It's not likely to be pretty."

"And whose fault is that?" Tullus spat, some combination of anger or bravery overcoming his good sense despite the blade at his throat.

Kathrael felt an answering anger rise in her chest. Anger at powerful men who saw Rhyth as a dice pit, where they could bet money on the backs of the oppressed and grow rich when the numbers fell right.

"It's the fault of a king who thinks the answer to unrest from his subjects is a warehouse full of deadly weapons," she grated. "And the fault of men like you, who would barter death for gold. How many women and children would the bolts in these boxes have killed, Tullus? How many hearts would they have pierced?"

Tullus looked at her. "They would have brought order. In your hands, they'll bring chaos."

"In our hands, they'll bring freedom," she returned.

He scoffed. "Don't delude yourself. Weapons either bring death, or the threat of it. That's all they do. That's what they're *for*."

"Enough," Ithric said, warning in his tone. "Judging by the lack of noise coming from outside, your say in what happens with these weapons is over."

A familiar whistle like a birdcall came from beyond the doors, which opened a moment later to reveal Ciryl. "We're just finishing up. You can bring that one outside when you're ready. One of your red priestesses is out there waiting, too."

Kathrael joined Favian in quickly tying up the downed guards with loops of rough rope that had been lying in one corner of the storage building. When they were done, Ithric manhandled Tullus outside, the dagger still pressed to his neck in clear threat.

Dusk was giving way to dark, lending an eerie quality to the groans of injured men scattered around the space in front of the large double doors. A few of the rebel fighters had lit torches, casting pools of flickering orange light over the scene of the brief, lopsided battle.

Ithric dragged Tullus over to a tall rebel lad holding one of the crossbows Ciryl had liberated from the crate inside. "Guard this one carefully," he said, and shoved Tullus back-first against the wall of the building.

Tullus caught himself and glared, but held his peace in the face of the primed weapon pointing at his chest.

A flash of red ochre in torchlight caught Kath's gaze. She followed the other two to where the priestess Sephira was speaking quietly with her guard captain. The man tensed at their approach, but relaxed when he recognized them.

"We need to deal with the wounded," Favian said without preamble. He still looked as pale as milk—deeply unhappy and far out of his element. Kathrael felt for him, her old guilt at having dragged him into this rearing its head.

"It will be done," Sephira said, her voice showing no hint that she shared Favian's misgivings.

"How many dead? How many injured?" Ithric asked.

It was the captain who answered. "All of them, on their side. One dead and four hurt on ours, though none of the injuries look too serious."

"Have you decided what we're doing with the warehouse guards?" Ithric asked.

The priestess's smile was grim. "Oh, yes. I have, indeed." She raised her voice to carry to the men currently moving around the area, collecting weapons and anything else of value from the downed guards.

"Dispatch any of these men whose injuries are too serious to heal. Don't let them suffer. Tie up those who are not too badly hurt. We will take them with us. Once we're someplace secure, you can dress them as slaves and take them to the far edge of the city under cover of darkness before releasing them. Let them learn firsthand what sort of treatment Rhyth's less fortunate denizens can expect."

There were a few guffaws of amusement from Qaden's men at the pronouncement, as they returned to securing the injured and removing their valuables.

"I can't help being glad she's on our side," Ithric said quietly.

"Priestess of the trickster god, indeed," Favian murmured in response.

A sudden commotion broke the relative peace of the battle's aftermath. Kathrael whirled back toward the place where they'd left Tullus. Flickering light illuminated him, locked in a fight with the young rebel they'd left guarding him.

"*Shit*," Ithric cursed, and sprang toward the fray.

Before he could reach them, the sharp *twang* of a spanned bowstring releasing preceded a cry of pain. Tullus staggered back, a crossbow bolt protruding obscenely from his chest. He fell, one hand scrabbling clumsily at the length of wood for a horrible moment before his arm flopped to the ground. His body seized and jerked, the movements growing weaker until he lay still.

"Merciful gods," Favian whispered, looking ill.

The young rebel looked down at the crossbow in his hands stupidly, then over at Tullus's body, and back down at the bow. "I didn't mean to shoot him," he said in a shaky voice. "He moved so fast, and we were struggling—it just went off..."

Ciryl had come running at the disturbance, and clapped a hand on the lad's shoulder, making him flinch in surprise. "It's all right, boy. Saves us having to deal with him, at any rate. He was the most dangerous one here. He knew names and faces, and if he'd somehow gotten free and gone to the king, he'd've had clout. Probably better this way."

Favian turned and walked a few paces away, staring into the night.

Ithric ran a hand through his hair, mussing it. Kathrael turned inward, searching herself for regret. For something. Anything. Her mother's spirit was muttering distractedly, a low monotone.

He was a bad man... bad man... they kill us and no one mourns. Don't mourn the bad men...

Disturbed both by Favian's reaction and her own lack of one, she turned her mind to practicalities. "The wagons?" she asked.

Ithric answered after a short pause. "I can hear them coming. They'll be here momentarily."

Sephira rejoined them. "Start moving the crates outside. The faster we can get everything loaded and into the catacombs, the better. None of the guards escaped to raise the alarm, but the torches and vehicles may still draw unwanted attention."

SIX

Carts and wagons descended on the warehouse like flies on a gutted corpse. Rebels and gang members worked side-by-side to load the heavy crates of weaponry onto the vehicles and cover them with blankets or straw. It still took hours to get the place cleaned out.

Kathrael joined several of the other women who had arrived with the wagons, keeping watch for the approach of city guards or rival gangs who might have been alerted to their presence. As the last few boxes disappeared under ragged tarpaulins, however, it was becoming apparent that either no one had seen the attack, or—more likely—no one who *had* seen it cared enough to make a fuss or report it to the guardsmen.

Sephira's captain ordered the injured and dead loaded onto the final handful of rickety carts, and Ithric used the iron keys taken from the leader of the warehouse guards to lock the doors after them. A close inspection of the area would uncover bloodstains and a suspicious number of overlapping wheel tracks, but from a distance, nothing about the now-empty warehouse would appear unusual.

The wagons were heading in several different directions, and would take indirect routes to various entrance points into the catacombs. The sprawling, ancient tunnel system would offer hiding places all around the city for small caches of their haul of crossbows. Even if a few such caches were found by the city guard, most would not be.

It was very late—or perhaps, more accurately—very *early* when Kathrael, Favian, and Ithric finally arrived back at their tumbledown home by the riverbank. Favian had been almost completely silent on the journey back from harbor.

"The horses are exhausted," he said in a monotone, as he climbed down from the driver's bench. "I'm going to take them outside to drink from the river and graze for a few minutes."

"I'll go with you," Kathrael offered, even though she was exhausted as well.

"We'll all go," Ithric said firmly. He grabbed one of the lanterns hanging from the front of the caravan to light the way as Favian shrugged his indifference and set to unharnessing the team.

Kath knew that Favian really wanted some time away from them, to think. For some reason, though, the idea of letting him have that time worried her. She took Bysh's lead rope without a word and followed him out of the building, while Ithric tagged along behind with Audris in tow.

The night was chilly, but the clouds had finally dissipated to reveal a wan sliver of moon and a wash of twinkling stars above them. Except for the rustle of their boots and the horses' hooves through the dry winter grass, the silence was absolute. Favian led the way down the sloping riverbank to the murky water, where the horses drank greedily.

Only when they were settled further upslope, the animals picking at the remains of last year's fodder, did Ithric speak.

"All right. Enough, already. Spit it *out*, Favian," he said.

"Spit what out?" Favian didn't look at him. His voice was still flat.

"You're upset," Kathrael said. "You have been since before the bath house."

"And you're *not* upset," he told her, as if it was an answer. "You haven't been... since before the bath house."

She stared at him in the pale light.

"You're also *not here*," he continued. "Not properly."

Kathrael opened her mouth, only to close it a moment later.

Ithric's expression darkened. "And where exactly do you get off, dictating how Kathrael or anyone else deals with things as unpleasant as what we did today? Are you having second thoughts about what we're doing? Well—" His tone grew sarcastic. "I guess they'd be third or fourth thoughts by now, wouldn't they? It's not as if you've ever been fully behind this, after all."

Favian looked at him without expression, and that was somehow worse than if he'd been angry or started shouting. "I've done everything asked of me since this whole thing started. Though I can't help pointing out that you didn't appear to find what we did today at the bath house *unpleasant*."

Ithric stared back in confusion for a moment before real anger clouded his face. As he stalked forward into Favian's space, the horse he was holding snorted nervously and skittered sideways a few steps to get out of his way. Favian, on the other hand, didn't back down.

"Is *that* what this is about?" Ithric hissed. "You think I *enjoyed* playing the entitled asshole?"

"Everyone in the *caldarium* got a pretty good view of at least one part that you enjoyed," Favian said.

With a jolt, Kathrael realized that she was, in fact, standing there watching the argument unfold as if she were not truly present... just as Favian had accused her of doing.

It's over now, Kath, Vesh whispered in her mind. *Time to come back. Your two squalling tomcats need you before the claws come out any further.*

A small gasp slipped past her lips, and both of the others turned at the nearly inaudible noise. Reaction to the day's events slammed into her, and she shivered, her knees wobbling for an instant before she locked them. "Stop!" she said. "Both of you!"

"Kath?" Favian asked, emotion finally creeping back into his flat voice. He shoved the two lead ropes he was holding into Ithric's unresisting hand and crossed the short distance separating them. His hands hovered over her shoulders uncertainly for an instant before settling. She practically fell into his embrace, trembling like a leaf in the wind.

"Don't fight," she said into his shoulder. "Favian, please. Don't fight right now."

His arms tightened around her. "You're back," he whispered. "Kath..."

She nodded. "I'm sorry. This is how it's always been. But I can't just... start it and stop it, like lighting a fire and then dousing the flames."

Ithric had not moved, but he spoke with feeling. "You don't owe him, or me, or anybody else an apology for doing what you need to, Little Cat. *Does she,* Favian?"

"No." Favian turned her around and tucked her under his arm, leading her toward Ithric. "Come on. Leave Bysh to his grass for a minute—he's not going anywhere. You're all right now, though? You're all right with... both of us?"

She let Bysh's rope slide from her hand and looked up at Favian, confused. "What? What do you mean? Why wouldn't I be all right with both of you?"

There was still a hint of anger lurking behind Ithric's reply. "Favian's upset that I let you... *service me...* in the baths. Or possibly just that I pretended to like it. I'm frankly a bit too pissed off right now to delve into the details."

She glanced back and forth between them, bewildered. "Why would that upset you?" she asked Favian, completely lost.

He stared back at her. "Why wouldn't it upset *you*? We're not supposed to *use* you like that... you shouldn't have to play that role for us, *ever!*"

It took a moment to sort out his objections in her head, and she frowned in consternation. "I wasn't playing that role for you. I was playing that role for Tullus." She shook her head. "No, that's not right either. I was playing that role for the slaves who need Tullus's weapons. And, Favian, it was *my idea in the first place.*"

"*Thank you,*" Ithric said with asperity, as if she'd saved him from having to make the point. He rounded on Favian. "And if you think that just because I eventually managed to get off, it means I was having a good time, then *fuck you,* Favian. We can't all be holier-than-thou, sanctimonious prigs — not if we want this revolution to succeed."

He scrubbed a hand over his face. "Deresta's *tits.* I need to shift or I'm going to go mad. Please take the horses back, both of you. I'll be along in a bit so we can hash this out without completely eviscerating each other, Favian."

She and Favian took the horses' ropes from Ithric without argument, and he stalked off. She gathered up Bysh as well, and they headed back to the old warehouse. When the animals were settled for the night, she turned to Favian and took his shoulders in her hands, looking up at him.

"You're being unfair to him, you know," she said.

"I know," he replied quietly.

"He's being unfair to you, too."

"I know. You're all right, though, really?"

She reached up and pressed a soft kiss to his lips. "I'm all right. Really. I'm not going to suddenly forget that I adore having sex with you both, just because I had to play prostitute for an hour," she joked.

The tension flowed out of his shoulders, and she realized with a jolt that he'd *truly been worried* that she might go back to being the broken girl he'd first met in Draebard.

"Oh, *Favian*," she breathed. "My sweet, foolish priest-boy. For the gods' sakes, come *here*."

She dragged him down again, turning the next kiss deep and filthy. His arms came around her, and after a few moments she gentled her movements, confident that her point had been made. He continued to hold her, lips sliding over hers, making the tension and unpleasantness of the day fall away. There was no sexual ardor in Favian's embrace—there never was—but she sensed a different sort of need in him.

He had hated the violence and bloodshed of the battle at the warehouse, she knew, but it was her withdrawal from them that had truly frightened him. The realization was a sobering one.

Soft footfalls penetrated her awareness a moment before a voice said, "Now I'm not sure whether to be more irritated, or less."

She pulled away from Favian and stepped into Ithric's arms, reaching up to kiss him with Favian's taste still clinging to her lips. "Less, I hope," she said.

"I'm sorry, Ithric," Favian said evenly. "I am, in fact, fully aware that you don't have the slightest desire to use Kathrael—or anyone else—against their will. I'm also aware that I sometimes find it convenient to lash out at you when I'm upset. Habit, probably. Or maybe it's just something about your face. Hard to say."

Ithric nodded, and eased Kathrael away so he could walk up to stand a step away from Favian. "And I'm aware that you're here because of us, not because you ever harbored secret ambitions of starting a revolution in a city you barely know. Also, you'd make a shoddy excuse for a priest if you weren't a *bit* sanctimonious. But you're not really a prig."

Favian nodded back. "So. Are we... all right, Ithric?"

Ithric sighed. "Give me a few hours' sleep. And maybe a day or two to ensure that those weapons are stockpiled where they need to be. There's just... a lot, right now. You know?" His gaze widened to encompass Kathrael. "Sephira took me aside earlier this evening while we were loading the wagons. She suggested that we get out of the city for a bit—

invited us to come out to the Old Stones for the solstice, with some of the Sisterhood. I think we should take her up on it."

Favian's brows drew together. "What are the *Old Stones*?"

"Some kind of ancient religious site,' he said. "I've never been there, but I've heard of it. People in Rhyth mostly steer clear. It's supposedly a locus for the Old Magic. I think most of them are scared of the place. Personally, I think it sounds peaceful. And I'm right at home with the Old Magic, so..." He shrugged.

"I'd like to go," Kathrael said, something in her chest easing at the idea of escaping the chaos for a bit.

"We'll do it, then," Favian said. "Even if it wasn't an excuse to get away from things for a day or two, I'm intrigued."

"Good. Now, please can we get some sleep before the sun comes up and we have to head right back out?" Ithric huffed a breath. "I don't know about you two, but I'm about to fall over."

Favian nodded, and reached out a hand to touch Ithric's jaw, tilting it until the livid bruise on his cheek caught the light of the single burning oil lamp. Ithric allowed the liberty without comment.

"Let me smear some poultice on this first," Favian said. "It's swelling up pretty badly."

Ithric gently moved Favian's hand back down. "If it'll make you feel better, mother hen," he said. "But please don't take all night about it."

In reality, it only took a few minutes, and Kathrael was as relieved as Ithric at finally being able to fall into bed. She had expected to drift off to sleep immediately, but instead she lingered in a drowsy, half-aware state mired somewhere between dreams and waking.

She became aware of odd laughter in the distance, swinging back and forth between gleeful cackling and girlish giggles. Gradually, recognition dawned.

"Mother?" she whispered into the dark.

The laughter grew almost hysterical for a minute, before her mother's spirit choked it back under control.

Oh, my baby girl, she crooned. *My tiny little baby girl! You grew up and look at what you did!* She laughed again, and let out a single high sob. *The slaves are going to fight! The slaves are going to cut down the masters and be free! My lovely little girl. I love you... I love you... I'm so proud of you... my tiny little baby...*

Her mother was weeping now, and Kathrael's breath caught in her chest.

Vesh spoke, his ghostly voice soothing. *Thea,* he said. *It's all right. I think it's finally time, don't you? You can let go now. Your other little girl is waiting for you. Are you ready?*

Kathrael gasped and bolted upright as she realized what was happening. She was only vaguely aware of Favian and Ithric stirring beside her as her sudden movement woke them from a sound sleep. "Mother!" she cried. "*No, wait!*"

Yes, her mother mused in a tiny voice. *I believe I'm ready now. Goodbye, baby girl.*

Kathrael clutched at her chest as the familiar, off-kilter presence disappeared between one breath and the next.

A hand closed on her shoulder in the dark. "Kath?" Favian asked.

"Little Cat?" Ithric's voice, sleep-roughened, came from her other side. "Easy, now. You were having a nightmare."

She was silent for a long moment, her hand pressing against the sharp ache piercing her heart. As children, she and Elarra had fled their overseer without thought—without even turning back to look and see if their mother was following. They'd left the woman who birthed them behind without a word of farewell, and to who-knew-what fate.

For all the abruptness of her spirit's departure, her mother had given Kathrael more consideration than Kathrael and Elarra had given her. She had said goodbye.

"No. I wasn't having a nightmare," Kathrael told Ithric, as her infant daughter's spirit began to squall at the sudden loss of her grandmother's presence. "I was speaking to my mother... for the very last time."

SEVEN

Over the next two days, Favian struggled to stay focused on the here-and-now. It was difficult to remain grounded as the three of them moved back and forth between playing the roles of well-known traveling entertainers performing for crowds; of rebels helping organize and stash stolen weapons where the king's forces would not be able to find them; and of mysterious figureheads for the slave underground.

Possibly, it would have been less difficult if he wasn't also sleep-deprived and dealing with the ongoing tension with Ithric, not to mention Kathrael's reaction to the unexpected departure of her mother's spirit. She wasn't... *grieving*, exactly. Or, rather, she *was*, but not in the same way they'd seen her grieve for her sister, or her unborn daughter.

From what little he'd been able to tease out of her in odd moments, he'd learned that Kathrael's mother had been *broken* for a very long time. Favian had only a vague recollection of the gaunt collection of frightened slaves huddled in the field north of Rhyth. He had been a mere boy at the time, passing through on the way from Draebard to the Rhytheeri king's peace talks.

He remembered Kathrael—a child herself, back then— fearlessly clutching Senovo as the wolf had held the overseer who had been whipping her at bay. He remembered that some of the slaves had run away during the confusion, and some had stayed behind, looking lost and hopeless. Kathrael and her sister had run. Their mother had stayed.

While he would never have a child of his own, Favian could well imagine that Kath's mother would have wanted her daughters to escape. To be free. She would have wanted it even though she could not bring herself to flee along with them. Favian had tried to tell Kathrael that. He wasn't sure if she believed him.

"She told me she loved me," Kathrael had whispered in the dark of night, as they lay on the sleeping pad together with Ithric, exhausted but unable to rest. "She said that she was proud of me."

"Of course she's proud of you," Favian had said. "Kathrael—look what you've accomplished."

"No, you don't understand, though," Kath replied. "That was the first time in my life that she ever said either of those things to me."

Favian ached for her.

It was a relief when, two days after the raid on the warehouse, the crossbows were finally distributed throughout the catacombs to the satisfaction of the underground's leaders, ready for whatever action they might eventually take. Favian had already seen more than enough of the echoing tunnels lined with moldering human bones to last a lifetime. He still found the catacombs deeply disconcerting on both a physical and a spiritual level.

"Hopefully the king's guardsmen will feel the same way about coming down here as you do," Ithric offered dryly when Favian mentioned his disquiet—and that was a fair point. The best possible hiding place was one where no one in their right mind would ever want to go.

Still, he was glad to be done with it. He was even gladder to be heading out of the city's western gate, the day before the solstice. It was mid-afternoon, and they'd squeezed in a performance before packing everything they would need into the caravan and leaving the dangerous, congested, stinking city for a much needed break.

At least, Favian *hoped* they would be leaving the city. He swallowed a sigh when one of the guards at the gate waved them to a stop.

"Oi," said the man. "I know you. You're that crazy foreigner who stands on running horses!"

"Yes. I am," Favian said, not really up to adding more.

"Hey, you're not leaving, are you? My sister's been planning to take the boys out and watch your show one of these days."

Thankfully, Ithric rescued him from having to deal further with the situation.

"Not to worry, friend," Ithric said, amiably enough. "She'll still be able to come. We've been invited to perform for a few days in some of the villages further west along the coast, that's all. It seemed like it would make a nice change of scenery, so off we go. Tell you what—have her tell the man collecting money at the show that she's the sister of the guard at the city gate. I'll see to it that she and her children get in for free."

The man's face broke into a sunny smile. "I'll do that! That's real kind of you."

"Don't mention it," Favian said, trying to summon at least a whiff of friendliness.

The guard thanked them again as he let them pass, and they were *finally* outside the confines of the city wall. The road was still crowded, forcing Favian to stay focused on driving. Gradually, the confusion of close-packed buildings and market stalls gave way to smallholdings, and then to increasingly long stretches of uninterrupted woods or fields.

The weather was not what one would call pleasant— little spatters of cold rain pelted them intermittently and the wind was gusty. Even so, the tightness in Favian's chest and jaw eased as more distance opened up between them and the city they'd left behind.

"I've never really been out this way before," Kathrael observed, huddling between him and Ithric, muffled under her heavy cloak.

"Me, neither," Ithric said. "Not beyond the outskirts of the city, anyway."

Favian glanced at him with a raised eyebrow. "Er... you haven't? So, we're going to find this place... how, exactly?"

"We follow the coast for a couple of leagues," Ithric said, unconcerned. "Apparently it's not the sort of thing you can miss, once you're in the general vicinity."

With a shrug, Favian returned his attention to the road. Honestly, at this point he'd be fine with simply finding a nice spot in a field somewhere and camping there in the caravan, cold weather or no.

Fortunately, that turned out not to be necessary. Whoever had given Ithric the rather vague directions had not been exaggerating. The Old Stones emerged from the mist like hulking shadows in the distance, guarding the plateau above the rocky beach and the turbulent ocean beyond.

The city of Rhyth had been built on a promontory abutting a natural harbor. Its placement assured that it was an important port of trade with the continent, since much of the island's coastline was lined with steep cliffs, too tall and treacherous to breach. Indeed, the three of them were only a short distance outside of the city, and already the road they were following had ascended into broken uplands, high enough above the beach that a man falling over the edge would surely die on the rocks below.

The winter scenery of the area had a sort of desolate beauty to it, gray and brown and misty, with the whistle of wind through rocks and the cries of seabirds echoing against the cliffs. Once they saw the Old Stones, though, it was as though everything else disappeared. None of them could look away.

The stones were huge and rough-hewn, arranged upright in an esoteric pattern that curled out from a center point to describe an unfinished spiral. The uprights forming the outer portion of the spiral were capped with massive lintel stones. Favian could not conceive of how people might have lifted stones so large to set them on top of the others—the task seemed impossible on its face.

The site appeared large even from a distance, but the true scale of the thing became apparent as they drew closer. The biggest uprights were well over twice as tall as a man, and even the shorter ones would have come up to the top of the caravan's roof. Every time Favian thought he could make out the underlying pattern of the mysterious structure, some new aspect would come to light that threw off his mental picture.

He had unconsciously slowed the horses to a walk as they approached. Now, the animals snorted and tossed their heads. Fidget tried to shy to the side, jerking at the harness traces and making the caravan lurch. Favian pulled him back under control, steadying the team with voice and rein.

Across from him, Ithric was leaning forward on the bench, frowning in concentration.

"Can you feel that?" he asked, in a tone of voice Favian couldn't remember ever hearing from him before.

"Feel what?" Kathrael asked, staring ahead as intently as Ithric.

"I don't know," Ithric said, his tone still oddly distant.

Favian could feel *something*—a shiver of awareness across his skin, a sense of ancient eyes watching. "It's the Old Magic," he said. "This place is alive with it."

Kathrael pressed her shoulder a little tighter against his. "It does feel a bit like those stones are... looking at us. How old *is* this place, exactly?"

"Very," Ithric said. "I'm not sure anyone really knows."

Movement of the human variety caught Favian's eye. "I can see red cloaks. The Sisterhood are here to greet us, it looks like."

Indeed, they were met a short distance away from the stones by Sephira and a younger priestess Favian didn't know.

"So. You came, then," Sephira observed. "I wasn't certain you would."

Ithric hopped down to meet her. "It seemed wise, and not just due to the appeal of getting away from the madness of Rhyth for a bit. At some point, someone is going to notice the fact that our caravan was seen at the bath house Tullus used, on the same day he disappeared. We may need to give up the show and move into hiding."

They had discussed the possibility earlier, and Favian couldn't really say he was opposed to *anything* that meant he wouldn't have to perform in front of crowds on a daily basis anymore.

"Yes, that might be prudent," Sephira agreed. "Now, though, you have come here to rest, and to celebrate the solstice tomorrow." She gestured to the woman standing next to her. "This is Ayala, my novice and protégé."

"Greetings, Sister," Favian said, and introduced himself, Kathrael, and Ithric.

Ayala was plump and dark-eyed, with a round face and full lips. She dipped her head, lowering her eyes for a moment before looking back up at them. "Greetings, Brother," she said. "You and your friends are welcome in this dwelling of the Ancestors. May I show you a place where you can park your conveyance and care for the animals?"

"Thank you, Ayala," Kathrael said. "That would be much appreciated."

Ayala gestured for them to follow, and Favian wheeled the horses around in a broad arc. He gave a final glance over his shoulder at the amazing structure that the Ancestors had somehow managed to construct, already mentally listing questions about it that he wanted to ask Zandreen while they were here.

As they followed Ayala across the flat, grassy stretch of plain beyond the stones, a familiar scent of sulfur made him wrinkle his nose. "Smell that?" he asked.

Ithric was walking next to the caravan, stretching his legs after the journey. "Hard to miss, yeah," he said with a hint of humor.

"Hot springs," Kathrael said. "They're not just in the city. There are springs all over the southern coast."

The plateau gave way to a slope that was thankfully not steep enough to cause too much difficulty with the caravan. Favian followed Ayala down the remains of an ancient road that cut across the hillside at an angle. The area at the bottom gave them a new reason to stare. It opened out into another flat spot, but carved into the broken slope was the largest natural cave Favian had ever seen — a cave that was obviously inhabited.

"Elder Sisters!" Ayala called as they approached. "We have visitors!"

A few moments later, Zandreen and another woman emerged from the cave's entrance. "So we do," said the High Priestess in her warm, rich voice. "Thank you, Ayala."

"Greetings, High Priestess," Favian said. He waited for Ithric to take Audris's reins and steady the team so he could climb down and help Kathrael down before continuing. "Thank you for allowing us to come. I can't say that I've ever celebrated the winter solstice in a place quite so appropriate."

The woman standing next to Zandreen let out a cackle of laughter. "Wise words, child. Wiser than you know, I'll wager."

Favian studied her curiously. She was quite old — probably older than Zandreen, though the skin of her face seemed oddly smooth. Her silver hair hung in long, thin, twisted mats rather than in the sleek, single braid of the other priestesses. She was gaunt, and her robes were rough-woven, the cloth a plain, un-dyed brown rather than the red ochre worn by the others. With a sudden flash of insight, Favian realized that she must live here, alone in this massive cave carved into the hill beyond the Old Stones.

"Inga," Zandreen said, "these are the three I told you about. Favian... Kathrael... Ithric... I thought you should all have a chance to speak with Inga sooner rather than later. I'm afraid that was the secret motive behind my invitation to you — though of course I am also pleased to offer you a much needed respite for a couple of days."

"And we are pleased to accept it," Ithric said. "Give us a little time to care for the horses before we start to lose the light, and then we can talk."

After a brief consultation, Ayala waited while they unhitched the animals, and showed them a sheltered spit of land covered in tufts of tough coastal grass. They hobbled the horses and left them grazing near a trickling brook that meandered through the area on its quest to rejoin the nearby ocean. By the time they returned to the cave, the daylight was indeed failing.

"Shortest day of the year," Favian observed wryly.

"We're halfway through the dark," Ayala agreed. "But after tomorrow, winter's back will be broken."

"Have you visited this place before, Ayala?" Kathrael asked. "It's a true wonder."

"I have," Ayala replied. "Twice. I can't claim to be able to feel the Old Magic myself, but there's still something about the place, you know? You can tell that the gods hover nearer, here."

Inside the cave, an orange glow proclaimed the presence of a roaring fire—an attractive prospect after a day spent outside in the damp chill.

"Come in," Zandreen called, upon seeing them hovering in the cave's entryway. She was seated next to the hearth with Inga, Sephira, and Sephira's loyal captain of the guard. Favian presumed that the dour man had a name, though he didn't know what it was. He should probably make an attempt to find out while they were here, for the sake of basic politeness, if nothing else.

Favian found it interesting that the High Priestess seemed comfortable making free with Inga's hospitality like this. The inside of the cave made it clear that Inga did, in fact, live here permanently. It was scattered with simple furnishings, and Favian had a confused impression of a multitude of angular painted markings covering the stone walls before he pulled his attention back to their eccentric host.

"Please, sit," Zandreen continued. "Warm yourselves at the fire. There is stew in the pot, and a skin of last year's mead hanging from the hook."

They murmured thanks and served themselves, settling on the thick furs scattered around the hearth to eat and drink.

Conversation was muted while they ate, but when she had emptied her bowl, Kathrael sat back and regarded the old woman sitting next to Zandreen. "Do you live here year-round, Inga?" she asked.

Inga shrugged. "It is the only place that suits me these days." She regarded Kathrael for a long moment. "A question for a question, child. Why do you hide yourself away like that?"

Kathrael looked confused for an instant before understanding dawned, and she lifted a hand to brush at the bronze half-mask she wore. She gave a faint, bleak laugh. "This? I suppose there's no real reason to wear it here, is there?" She fumbled with the thong, half-hidden in her hair, and lowered the mask to reveal her scars. "I was a prostitute when I was younger. The wife of one of the men I regularly serviced found me with him one night, and threw vitriol at my face."

Inga nodded, not flinching as she took in Kathrael's melted flesh and blind, milky eye. "Interesting that the woman chose to punish you, and not her husband."

"Not really," Kathrael said. "If she'd maimed her husband, he wouldn't have been able to provide for her. Or their children, assuming they had any."

Inga tilted her head in acknowledgement and shrugged.

Ithric shifted, setting his bowl aside. "Zandreen said you wanted to speak with us, Inga? I don't know how much she's told you about what's happening in Rhyth—"

"She has told me enough," Inga interrupted. "But the details don't matter. Soon, it will be in the hands of the gods. Nothing you do before then will matter. But the chief goddesses are coming together. When they join forces, no king or army will be able to stand in the way of your cause."

EIGHT

Favian frowned at her. "You speak of Deresta and Utarr? And you say they are *coming together*? I'm afraid I don't understand what that means, Elder Sister."

"You don't have to understand it, child," Inga said. "You have only to heed it."

He hesitated for a moment, still trying to make sense of the cryptic pronouncement. "Are you a seer, Inga?"

Inga threw back her head and cackled. "Oh, that *is* good! The seer asks if I am a seer. I *see* a great deal, young Favian—more than most. That I most certainly do!"

Favian blinked, a thread of shock weaving through his confusion. "Wait," he said. "I never told Zandreen that I was a seer. How—?" He glanced at Ithric and Kathrael, a question in his eyes. Both of them shook their heads, confirming that they had not told anyone about his prophetic dreams, either.

Zandreen looked at him kindly, her voice calm as she replied, "We are the priestesses of Avlan, Brother Favian. You did not have to tell us."

His frown deepened for a moment before he smoothed it away consciously. Settling back, he took a deep breath and let it out. "I suppose that, as secrets go, it pales beside Ithric's. And you already know his."

Zandreen chuckled. "Quite so."

"For what it's worth," Kathrael put in gamely, "the spirits of the dead speak to me sometimes. Either that, or I'm mad. There's still a degree of uncertainty around that point."

"No, there's not," Favian said with a hint of asperity.

"Interesting," Sephira observed from the far side of the fire. "Three gifted individuals, born far apart, who just *happened* to stumble across each other and cleave together."

"Yep. Pretty much," Ithric said.

"Well," Zandreen said, "Inga has said what she needed to say to you. Now, for the next couple of days, you will merely be three travelers in need of a rest—gifted, or not. Please, feel free to sleep here in the cave, rather than in your caravan. Winter is fighting the turn of the seasons valiantly tonight, and you will be much warmer near the fire."

Gratitude colored Kathrael's voice as she answered. "Thank you. The idea of a few nights of uninterrupted rest..."

A sudden yearning for sleep tugged at Favian's spirit as soon as she spoke. "Blissful," he agreed.

At the talk of sleep, a huge yawn cracked Ithric's face, though he tried to cover it. "I can't argue."

Zandreen smiled. "Get whatever you need from your caravan, in that case. We won't keep you awake any longer after your journey. Help yourself to furs and blankets, and don't worry if the rest of us are gone when you wake. We'll be up early, but you needn't be."

It was barely evening, but they were warm and fed, exhausted from an afternoon of travel on the heels of far too many nights spent hauling boxes of weapons through dark tunnels instead of sleeping. Ithric offered to retrieve what they would need from the caravan. Favian and Kathrael agreed readily, and focused on making up a comfortable place to sleep on the hard-packed dirt floor near the fire.

The others were still drinking mead and talking quietly, but when Ithric returned, the three of them removed their boots and outer clothing before curling up in the pile of furs and blankets. Favian was only vaguely aware of the others' breathing settling into the deep rhythm of sleep before his own eyes fell closed, and he knew no more.

⤙ 🐚 ⤚

It was early when Favian woke, but not ridiculously so. It took a moment to remember where he was, as he surfaced from the confused grogginess that follows a long stretch of deep, dreamless sleep. There was a hint of gray light filtering in through the cave entrance. His eyes adjusted gradually to the low light, and he realized that while Kathrael still slept next to him, Ithric was missing from his spot on her far side.

He sat up, looking around the cavernous space. He and Kathrael appeared to be alone, though someone had left a pot of what smelled like spiced barley gruel simmering near the fire for them. He stayed there for a few moments, wanting to wake up properly before deciding if he should be alarmed by Ithric's absence or not.

But, no. They were alone here except for the Sisterhood. The others had warned them last night that they would be up and moving early. And — remembering Ithric's initial reaction as they approached the stone monument — Favian had a sudden, strong suspicion about where Ithric might be found.

He nudged his sleeping companion's shoulder. "Hey, Kath?"

She groaned and mumbled something.

"It's morning," he said. "Just about, anyway. I need to go see to the horses, and I think Ithric must have gone out to the Old Stones. I want to check on him. Would you rather come along, or sleep?"

She gave the matter some consideration before mumbling, "Sleep. Come wake me if you need me, though."

He kissed her scarred temple and brushed a tangle of dark hair away from her face. "I will."

After rising and dressing to face the morning chill, he emerged to find that the clouds had broken, and the first rays of the winter sun were just breaching the eastern horizon. He stretched, vertebrae popping, and filled a wooden pail with some of the grain they'd brought along as a supplement to the poor winter fodder, before heading out to check on the horses.

He received a rather enthusiastic equine greeting, and lingered as the animals ate, checking that the hobbles weren't rubbing their legs and ensuring that all four horses got their fair share of grain. Afterward, he returned the pail to the caravan and started the uphill trek to the plateau where the Old Stones stood like sentinels.

Favian hadn't been sure if he would find the priestesses at the site as well, but in fact, the stone spiral was devoid of human life when he arrived. It was not, however, devoid of *all* life.

As he had half expected, a large, tawny lion stalked within its confines, sniffing at the stones curiously and rubbing his broad head against them, scent-marking the ancient monoliths.

"I'm not sure that's considered polite in a place like this," Favian said, a bit out of breath as he crossed the last few spans of open ground to the outermost of the stones. "Just, *please* tell me you haven't pissed on anything."

The lion looked up from his task and flicked an ear in Favian's direction, somehow managing to make the simple motion look noticeably derisive. Favian snorted and took the opportunity to really look around the place for the first time. Once one got right up amongst the stones like this, the layout became clearer. Which was not to say that it wasn't still overwhelming. It was.

Up close, the fact that people had somehow moved these massive hunks of stone into place seemed even more mind-boggling. Favian was certain that if he hitched their sturdy four-horse team to a stone this size, they would not have been able to move it a finger's width. And, of course, in addition to the question of *how* the stones had been moved, there was also the question of *why*.

The gods hovered near this place. But had the stone spiral been built because the area was favored by the gods, or did the gods favor it because the Ancestors had placed the stones here?

A whimsical thought came to Favian, and he chuckled. It had suddenly occurred to him that Priest Eiridan would fall in love with this place on sight. Between the mystery of the stones and the esoteric symbols covering the cave walls, they would never be able to pry him away and drag him back to Draebard.

The lion was still watching him. Favian made his way to the center of the open space framed by the stones and sat on one that was conveniently and rather invitingly bench-shaped. He faced east, watching the sun rise. Through accident or design, when it crested the horizon, it was *almost* exactly centered in a small gap between two of the stones that were shaped a bit differently from the rest.

The sound of heavy, animal breathing was all the warning he got before a large, blocky head rubbed against his hip, the rough but friendly caress nearly scooting him right off the bench before he braced himself. Ithric sniffed at him, pink nostrils flaring, and nudged him again. Favian sighed and tangled fingers into the lion's tousled, russet mane, scratching the skin underneath with his fingernails.

"You're a lot easier to get along with like this, you know," he said.

Large golden eyes flecked with green watched him calmly, unblinking.

"I *want* to be here, with you and Kath," he continued. "You know that, right? I want what we're working for to come to pass. But, Ithric, I'm still a priest. Well... sort of, anyway. I can't turn a blind eye to the bad things that happen around us, just because they're a means to an end."

The space next to him twisted, and Ithric crouched at his feet in human form, leaning an arm across Favian's lap to steady himself. "Zandreen is a High Priestess. She's also one of the leaders of the slave underground," he said. "How do you think she justifies it?"

"I've absolutely no idea," Favian replied.

"Maybe you should ask her."

"Yeah… probably," Favian said. "Do you want my cloak? It's cold out here."

Ithric shrugged a naked shoulder. "Nah. My stuff's over there in a bundle, by the base of that crooked stone. But I'd actually like to stay a bit longer. The lion loves it here."

Favian nodded. "I'll stay with you."

Ithric gave a faint shiver as the wind picked up. "Does Kathrael know where we are?"

"Yes. She's still exhausted, though. I left her to sleep some more."

"Good," Ithric said. "She needs it. Of course, you probably do, as well."

"I'm all right."

"Yeah?"

"Yeah."

A pause. "Me, too."

Ithric rested his chin on Favian's knee, and a moment later, the lion was once again staring up at him with luminous eyes.

✎ ⟡ ✎

They stayed at the site until the sun rose above the lintel stone in whose shadow they were sitting. Favian was starting to shiver despite his cloak and the large cat curled up against his leg. At that point, Ithric shifted into human form, dressed quickly, and headed back with him to join Kathrael at the cave, after stopping for another quick check on the horses.

When they arrived, she was up and dressed, speaking quietly with Sephira as they sat at the rough table set next to one of the walls. Sephira's guard captain sat silently in a chair near the entrance, sharpening a dagger. All three looked up at their approach.

"I was just about to come looking for you," Kathrael said. "Is everything all right?"

Ithric crossed to her and leaned down, pressing a kiss to the top of her head. "Better after a few hours spent as the lion. Favian's much easier to deal with when I'm in animal form."

Favian snorted at having his own words thrown back at him, and Kathrael smiled. "Were you both at the stones, then?" she asked.

Ithric nodded. "I like it there." His attention shifted to Sephira. "I was a bit surprised we didn't have additional company, given that it's the solstice. I hope the presence of a lion didn't keep you away—"

Sephira shook her head. "No, not at all. It's the day of the solstice, true. But the solstice itself will not occur until this evening. That is when the season will turn, and when the vigil at the Old Stones will take place. We will spend most of the day at the hot springs. Dharnal and I merely came back to get some food."

The guard captain looked up at his name, and Favian made a point to remember it for future use. Ithric had seized upon a different part of what Sephira had said, however.

"So there *are* hot springs here?" he asked. "We'd assumed, because of the smell, but I wasn't sure if they were the sort that you could actually bathe in, or just a smelly little runnel in the side of the hill."

Sephira chuckled. "No, hardly a runnel. The gods favor this place for more than the stones, as it happens. The water emerges near the top of the hill, and the first pool is hot enough to burn skin. But it overflows into a second pool, further down, that's quite large and safe to enter—though still hot. From there, it flows into a mud pit at the base of the hill. The pools may not be enclosed within the trappings of a fancy city *caldarium*, but it's an extremely pleasant place to spend a day."

Favian was still not accustomed to the bathing culture that seemed to have grown up around the hot springs in the south. "Spend a day... doing what, exactly?" Surely one couldn't bathe for an entire day?

Sephira huffed a breath of laughter. "May the gods preserve us from northerners and eunuchs. It's a day of celebration, Brother Favian. Soak. Relax. Have sex. Whatever would give you pleasure." She cast an assessing eye over them. "Do I have the measure of you three? You are all lovers, are you not?"

Favian couldn't help the heat that rose to his cheeks, but he answered before either of the others could. "We are."

The priestess smiled, one corner of her lip curling up. "Hmm... I thought so."

"I can't imagine the Priests' Guild in Rhyth would be as accepting of such a thing as you seem to be," Kathrael said, looking at her curiously.

Sephira's expression soured. "The Priests' Guild is made up of corrupt old men. They are also hypocrites, given that a large proportion of them are inverts whose families sent them to the temple so they would be castrated and hidden away." She huffed out an irritated breath. "Why in the name of all that's sane should the gods care how — and toward whom — we show love?"

"*Thank you,*" Ithric said with feeling. "I've been saying that for *years*, but would anyone listen to me?"

Favian sighed. "Yes, well. It took awhile, admittedly, but I think you've finally got me convinced."

"And it's not as though Rhyth isn't full of men sleeping with other men, regardless of what the priests say," Kathrael added wryly.

"Or women sleeping with women," Sephira said. "And the gods made every one of them, from the greatest to the smallest, so..."

She trailed off with a shrug.

Ithric nudged Favian toward the pot hanging by the fire. "Come on. Enough philosophy. Food, then bathing. Thankfully, without the kinds of complications we faced at the king's *caldarium*."

Favian frowned at the reminder of that rather awful day, but let himself be herded. The porridge was thick and hearty, with chunks of meat jerky stewed into it. The blend of spices flavoring it was unfamiliar, but pleasant, and he ate with gusto, as did Ithric.

Afterward, Sephira and Dharnal led them around to the far side of the rocky hill, the sulfur smell growing ever stronger as they walked. They followed a dirt trail that had obviously been formed by the passage of many feet over the years. Oddly, except for a few sickly looking, straggling bushes, there was no vegetation on this side of the hill at all. Favian wondered if the mineral-rich, sulfur-smelling water somehow kept the plants from growing.

As Sephira had described, there was a pool of smooth gray mud near the bottom of the trail. The air grew warm and humid around them as they passed it, and Favian unfastened his cloak. He really could have done without the ever-present smell of rotten eggs, but even so, the warm air—cut through by little gusts of cooler breeze every now and then—was pleasant.

As they climbed higher, Favian followed the path of the water with his eyes. It had cut a channel over the eons, down the gentle slope of the hillside, washing away the loose dirt and rock until it exposed the granite beneath. Clouds of steam rose from the rivulet where it bubbled out of the rocks near the top, filling a small depression and overflowing. That must be the dangerously hot part that Sephira had told them about.

They were drawing even with the second pool now, which was far larger than the upper one, as she had said. Piles of clothing and folded blankets lay at the edge near the trail.

"We're back. I brought the others," Sephira called, and movement drew Favian's attention to the figures lounging in the water, partially obscured by wisps of steam.

Ayala was near the middle, the water lapping at her collarbone. Inga reclined in Zandreen's arms near the edge of the pool, her head leaning back against Zandreen's shoulder. Favian could not stop his brief double-take. It was unmistakably a lover's embrace.

The High Priestess craned around to look at them; Inga did not even bother to open her eyes or lift her head.

"Ah. Good," Zandreen said. "I assume Sephira warned you to avoid the upper pool. Other than that, enjoy yourselves. Kathrael—while you're here, child, try putting some of the mud on your scars. It has rather extraordinary healing properties, or so I'm told."

Favian wondered who on earth had first decided to randomly smear mud on themselves and discovered that fact. It seemed… a decidedly odd thing to do, if he was honest. He was curious what Healer Sagdea would have to say about it.

Kathrael only nodded. "I will, thanks." Her expression grew speculative, a smirk playing briefly at one edge of her lips. "In fact…"

She met Ithric's eyes, and some silent communication passed between them that Favian couldn't quite parse. A slow smile spread over Ithric's face, and both of them turned to look at him.

"What?" he asked cautiously.

Behind him, he heard Sephira's faint snort of amusement. She and Dharnal skirted around them on the trail and headed for the area where the clothes and blankets were piled. Ithric's grin sharpened, and suddenly he and Kathrael were at Favian's side, pulling at his clothing—tugging and unlacing.

Favian let himself be undressed, since obviously they *would* have to be naked to bathe. Which… was perfectly fine… only he'd pictured the process being a little more *dignified*, somehow. But now, they were pulling off their own clothes as well as his, and Kathrael was crouching, tugging his boots from his feet. Ithric was dragging Favian's breeches and smallclothes down his legs, nudging him to step out of them… and… yeah. That breeze really *did* carry a chill against bare skin.

A moment later, the others were naked, too, wearing matching expressions of near-glee that Favian *really* didn't like. Then each of them had an arm linked with one of his, and they were tugging him backward down the trail, confused and off balance.

"Wait," he said. "Uh… what are you doing?"

Kathrael threw back her head and *laughed*, clear and light and girlish. Favian had never heard her laugh like that before. It was a beautiful sound. He wanted to hear it more often. But—

"What does it look like we're doing?" Ithric asked in a pleasant, conversational tone. He was still wearing his dangerous, cat-with-the-cream smile.

Favian stumbled clumsily backward along the trail, his mouth open, but no words coming out. He could have set his feet, thrown his weight against them, and stood his ground. Or, well, he could have *tried*, anyway. He knew, though, that he was no match for Ithric when it came to strength, and that was *without* Kathrael also helping to manhandle him in the direction they wanted him to go.

Besides, he wasn't sure he wanted to call a halt to anything that made Kath laugh like that—happy and carefree. And… surely they wouldn't *actually*—

They dragged him down to the edge of the mud pit, their feet sinking in to mid-calf, and tossed him backward into the middle. He flailed and let out a girly yelp—a noise that ranked rather high among the most embarrassing noises he'd ever made in his life—before landing on his ass with a splat and sinking into the mud.

NINE

The slop was more liquid than not, and almost as deep as the length of his arm. He was completely covered except for his head, neck, and part of his chest that hadn't gotten splashed when he landed.

"*Eww*," he said, after reaching for something wittier to say, and finding nothing.

There was a moment of pregnant silence. Kathrael descended into laughter once more, only to let out a short shriek when Ithric picked her up bodily and threw her in after Favian. She was still giggling as she righted herself.

Favian looked back and forth between the two of them. "I *cannot believe* you just did that."

Ithric was still smiling his predator's smile. "No?" he asked, and waded toward Favian with purpose.

Favian tried to backpedal, only to give it up as a bad job when he realized he was making almost no progress. Instead, he set himself for Ithric's pounce and wriggled sideways, trying to get on top. The resulting wrestling match was brief, one-sided, and seemed to involve a lot more groping and rubbing together than was strictly necessary.

It also ended with Favian pinned on his back, splayed open and vulnerable beneath the cage of Ithric's body, while mud oozed into his hair and tickled the shells of his ears. Kathrael slid up next to them and dabbed a muddy fingertip over the tip of his nose. The complete absurdity of the situation overwhelmed him without any warning, and he dissolved into choked laughter, trying to stifle the noise for only a moment before giving up and letting it come.

"You know, I enjoyed doing that far more than the situation probably warranted," Ithric said, once Favian had subsided into quiet snickering.

"What?" Favian managed. "Dragging me down to roll around in the muck with the rest of you?"

"Oooh," Kathrael offered, and drew a muddy line up the bridge of his nose, finishing with a dot between his eyebrows. "*Symbolism.*"

He scrunched up his face and wriggled a bit in Ithric's firm grip.

"Yes," Ithric said, pretending thoughtfulness. "You know, I think that's exactly what it was, Little Cat. Symbolism."

Favian shifted his lower body where Ithric was straddling him. "And that stiff, pointy thing that's poking me in the stomach? That's symbolic as well, I assume?"

Ithric flexed his hips. "What, this? No, that's just my cock."

Favian closed his eyes and tried not to succumb to laughter again. The grip pinning him down eased and lips covered his—too soft and full to be Ithric's. *Kathrael*. He made a small noise into the kiss, the initial shock of what they had done wearing off enough now that he could take things in a little better.

The mud was warm and silky. It was also *everywhere*. It eased the slide of Ithric's prick against his belly as effectively as any oil or grease could have done. He imagined it felt pretty good from Ithric's perspective, too.

Kathrael pulled away, smiling down at him. "That's better," she said. "It's not as if we tipped you into the muck in a dirty animal pen, you know. There was probably a room somewhere in the king's fancy bathhouse with mud exactly like this. People in Rhyth pay good money for this kind of thing!"

He rolled his eyes at her. "I think we've already established that most people in Rhyth are bent in the head," he said dryly. "But... maybe this isn't so bad."

Ithric reached back and ran a hand between Favian's legs, closing his fingers around his soft prick and sliding along the length it, base to tip—slick and filthy and perfect.

"Yeah..." Favian said, his voice growing dreamy. "Definitely not so bad."

Ithric leaned down to kiss him, and then leaned across to kiss Kathrael before getting an arm around Favian's shoulders and helping him lever his upper body out of the mud. "Come on," he said. "Let's find a spot that's a little shallower, and something I can lean back against. We've got most of a day to kill. All the time in the world."

Almost despite himself, Favian felt the warm pool leaching the tension from his body, leaving him loose and relaxed, and suddenly, strangely needy. It seemed as though he was only now feeling all the things that he'd kept himself from feeling since the day at the bathhouse. He let Ithric lead him closer to the edge of the pit, half wading and half crawling, with Kathrael sticking close on his other side.

Ithric made himself comfortable against a flat rock that was propped against the edge of the pool at an angle, reclining against it. When he pulled Favian down to rest against his side, Favian didn't object, even though the well-muscled shoulder his cheek was resting against was covered with mud. Kathrael pressed herself against his back, bracketing him between the two of them.

A wash of lightheadedness passed over him and he shook in their arms for a few moments, his body releasing the last of the emotion that he'd been keeping bottled up. Hands slid over his chest and flank, smooth and frictionless... soothing.

"At least when I hold things inside, I don't do it for days and days like this," Kath murmured in his ear. "We're going to ravish you now. *Slowly*. Let us?"

He nodded, wordless. She kissed him on the temple, one of the few places on his body that was still relatively clean. A thought occurred to him, and he craned around to look at her.

"Hold still a minute," he said softly, and lifted a hand to dab mud carefully over her scars, as Zandreen had suggested. She closed her eyes, not moving a muscle as he worked. When he was done, he turned to Ithric. "You, too."

Ithric let him smear a layer over the ugly bruise from where Tullus's bodyguard had gotten in a lucky punch. When Favian was satisfied, he settled back against Ithric's side.

"Finished now?" Ithric asked, supporting him with one arm and running his free hand over Favian's chest.

"Mm-hmm," Favian said, as slippery fingers tugged at his left nipple, worrying it to a pebbled point.

Kathrael's hands worked down the length of his spine, pressing into the muscles there without resistance or friction. She dug into the flesh below his hipbones, and massaged along the length of his leg until she got to his foot. She pulled it into her lap and pressed slippery thumbs along his instep, sending confusing signals of pleasure buzzing up the length of his body.

Ithric's hand slid down from his chest to his navel, and lower, milking his cock again with slow pulls. Favian moaned a bit as Kathrael's clever fingers massaged his insoles and slid into the spaces between his toes; he couldn't help it. She had once threatened to turn a massage so filthy that he would feel it for *days* afterward. He got the distinct impression that she and Ithric were about to make good on that threat.

His suspicions were confirmed when she abandoned his tingling foot to work her way back up his leg. This time, she did not skirt his most sensitive places as she had always done in the past. Her hand slid up his hamstring and cupped his left buttock, her fingertips sliding into the crease and stroking, firm and slick.

Sparks flickered behind his closed eyelids as he lay trapped between the leisurely slide of Ithric's hand along his prick, and Kathrael's fingertips rubbing over the pucker of his ass. That she would breach him was less a threat and more of a promise, with the mud, slick as the finest oil, easing her way.

His breath stuttered, and she drew things out, teasing until he squirmed between them — not quite far gone enough to thrust himself back onto her finger, but getting there more quickly than he cared to admit. Somehow, all of the control and dispassion that supposedly came along with being a eunuch slipped away from him when he was in their arms, melting into their touch.

His hips flexed as if of their own accord, and the finger that had been teasing open his outer ring slipped past the inner constriction as well, hot and slick. His muscles fluttered around it, clenching and relaxing in time with Ithric's slow pulls on his cock. Kathrael pressed in to the third knuckle and crooked her finger in a beckoning motion, rubbing over the place inside him that made Favian shudder and go boneless.

"Oh gods yes," he breathed, and fumbled a hand around Ithric's hard cock.

"Careful, now," Ithric said, amusement and a hint of strain tangled up in the word. "Don't make me come. When we're done with you, Kath and I are going to take out our mutual frustrations on each other."

"Right, good, you do that," Favian mumbled, floating on the feelings they were producing in his body.

"Though our Little Cat is already touching herself with her free hand while she fucks you," Ithric added, amusement gaining the upper hand for a moment.

"What can I say? I didn't feel like waiting." Favian couldn't see Kathrael from his current position, but her voice was breathless. "Everything's warm and slick, and it feels so good."

She was surprisingly adept at multi-tasking, it had to be said. There was no urgency to their lovemaking, but as time went on, the slender finger penetrating Favian from behind became two, and then three, stretching and filling him, sliding over the center of his pleasure again and again, over and over, never letting up.

It really was like melting, he decided. Like slowly turning to liquid, his body and awareness expanding to fill the space between the two of them. His mind drifted languidly from one sexual fantasy to another, in a way that it never really did anymore during the normal course of things. There was just something about these two. They did this to him. They alone could rouse the sleeping sexuality inside him, and coax it back into the light.

With them, it didn't matter that he'd only ever lusted after men in the time before he became a eunuch. This wasn't lust, for all that it was undeniably carnal. This was the two people he loved, touching him because they wanted him to feel good. This was trust. Trusting his body to others in the sure knowledge that they would not judge him for his reaction or lack of reaction. They would expect no more from him than he was willing and able to give.

He would never, ever be a disappointment to them.

The fingers filling him scissored, stretching him even wider, and the air escaped his lungs all at once in a groan. His hand tightened around Ithric, who hissed and thrust into the muddy circle of his fist.

"I think you're getting close, Favian," Kathrael said, sounding fairly far-gone herself. "Do you want us to make you come?"

Favian considered it for a few moments before letting his head flop back and forth a couple of times. "Mm... no, not today. You'll knock me out completely, and there's something else I still want to do."

"What?" she asked in a breathless tone. "What do you want to do?"

An image that had stuck in his mind earlier returned. "I want to be inside you both while Ithric takes you."

"Gods, *Favian!*" The words were apparently too much for Kath, who gasped and came unexpectedly. Favian could feel the telltale rhythmic jerk of her body through the fingers that were still inside him.

"I think you have one enthusiastic vote in favor, already," Ithric observed, amused. "What are you suggesting, exactly?"

Favian lifted muddy fingers and wriggled them, by way of demonstration. "Just my fingers. That all right with you? Something you'd both enjoy?" he asked.

Ithric shrugged. "Not something I have much experience with, but when has that ever stopped me?"

Favian roused himself enough to lift his head and stare in disbelief, despite the lovely unraveling feeling flowing through him.

The look drew a snort from Ithric. "*What*? I know you have me pegged as a shameless man-whore, but I haven't done *everything*."

Kathrael sniggered. "Not for lack of trying, though?"

Ithric leveled a good-natured glare at her before returning his attention to Favian. "Cock-sucking, I do. Hand-jobs? Oh… *so* many hand-jobs."

He changed his stroke on Favian's cock, twisting his wrist and swiping his thumb over the tip. It twitched, trying to stiffen, and Favian let his eyes fall closed, relishing the feeling of slipping a little closer to the edge of the precipice, even if he didn't really intend to fall over it right now.

"Getting fucked, though?" Ithric continued. "No one's ever offered, to be honest. One girl stuck a finger inside as I was just about to come, but she didn't use oil and I can't say it really added anything to the experience."

Favian chuckled. "So… virgin territory, then? More or less?" he quipped. Kathrael, who had draped herself along his back after coming down from her climax, laughed aloud and carefully slid her fingers out of him.

"Just be gentle with me," Ithric begged in a quavering falsetto, before continuing in a normal voice. "Or, y'know, *don't*. But whatever the case, you'd better let go of my cock now, or I'll be following Kathrael's example. In fact, give me a minute or two to calm down, will you? Get her worked up again instead."

Favian hummed agreement and pushed away from Ithric's side. Figuring he owed at least one of them some sort of revenge for dragging him down here and tossing him in, he took advantage of his size and Kathrael's post-orgasmic haze to press her down in the mud and pin her as Ithric had pinned him earlier. She made quite a show of wriggling and sliding against him, the pupil of her good eye blown wide and dark.

With the echo of sexual pleasure still pulsing along his nerves, it was surprisingly easy to take aggressive possession of her mouth in a way he wouldn't have, normally. She writhed under him, giving as good as she got, her tongue dueling with his. He released one of her wrists in favor of kneading a slippery breast, and she jerked free of the kiss, throwing her head back and gasping.

"*Yeah...* did I say something about calming down?" Ithric asked, sounding decidedly strained now. "You know what? Never mind. Calming down is overrated."

Favian laughed, and rolled off of Kathrael, pressing a final kiss to her lips as he did so. Ithric replaced him, bracing himself above her with one hand and running the other down her body to delve between her legs, stroking and rubbing.

"You're going to be finding mud in odd places for *days*, Little Cat," he observed.

"We all are," Favian said wryly. "I guess it's a good thing that it has *healing properties*, whatever that even means."

"I don't mind. It's worth it," Kathrael gasped. "Now, please will you just *take* me—both of you—before I crawl out of my own skin, thinking about it!"

Ithric rumbled, low in his chest, and spread her legs wide, lifting her hips a bit to line her up. They both groaned as he slid inside. Ithric trembled, obviously resisting the urge to thrust with considerable difficulty.

"*Favian,*" Kathrael begged, breathy and high-pitched. The entreaty tugged at something that lived deep in Favian's chest.

"I'm here," he said, infusing his voice with as much certainty and calm as he could. "Kiss her, Ithric?"

Ithric lowered himself until he and Kath were chest to chest, and kissed her. Favian knelt at their hips and nudged Ithric's knees apart, sliding his hand into the slick space where the two were joined. Ithric's balls twitched and drew up as Favian ghosted his fingers over them. He felt the hard base of Ithric's shaft, disappearing into the soft folds of Kathrael's sex. She wriggled and cried out at his touch, the sound muffled by the kiss.

He followed her contours down, teasing her rear entrance. The mud made everything warm and slippery, and it didn't take much to breach her body's fluttering defenses, sliding in to the first knuckle. He waited until her muscles stopped clenching around him to press in further, somewhat amazed by the way he could feel Ithric's twitching cock through the thin wall of flesh separating them. Kathrael broke the kiss with a moan of pleasure; Ithric cursed, low and filthy.

"Favian," he grated, "if you really want to be inside both of us, you'll probably need to be quick about it."

Favian smiled. Though he was careful not to jostle Kathrael accidentally, he wasted no time in sliding the slick fingers of his other hand between Ithric's well-muscled buttocks, and screwing one inside the tight passage he found there. It was *so* tight, in fact, that it took a bit of stretching and searching around to find what he wanted, hidden away on the front wall.

Ithric shuddered and jerked deeper into Kathrael, who nearly sobbed with pleasure.

"Buggering *fuck*," Ithric choked out. "Do... do that again."

"Language," Favian admonished with the *greatest* of satisfaction... and did it again.

TEN

It was barely any time at all before Kathrael came around his finger — and Ithric's cock — with what was very nearly a full-throated scream. Favian took a moment to hope their hosts lounging in the pool further up the hill would recognize the sound for what it was, and not immediately come running to check on them. He was distracted from that rather disconcerting thought by the feeling of Ithric clamping down on him and following Kathrael over the edge, still cursing creatively as his body jerked.

"Good?" Favian asked innocently, once the spasms had quieted, easing his hands free as he did so.

"*Smug bastard,*" Ithric muttered, sounding completely wrecked.

"Kath?" Favian prompted.

"Unngh..." was all she managed.

Favian prodded Ithric until he rolled off of Kathrael, rather gracelessly, by his standards. While Favian would have preferred to go scrub off the mud at this point — not least because he really wanted to scratch his nose, and couldn't — it was apparent that neither of the other two would be moving much of anywhere quite yet.

So he contented himself with curling up on Kath's other side, cinching an arm around her. He passed the time by drawing spiral patterns in the mud covering her breasts. She hummed in drowsy approval every so often, the sound nearly a purr.

Little Cat, indeed, he thought affectionately.

He was starting to worry that Ithric had actually fallen asleep when the shape-shifter stretched and groaned.

"Reluctant as I am to, y'know, *move,*" Ithric said around a yawn, "I think I'm in danger of drying into a clay statue."

Favian snorted. "Then we'd best go clean up before someone decides to paint glaze on you and fire you in an oven."

Even so, it was a few more minutes before they could truly be bothered to extricate themselves from the wallow and climb back up the trail. When they finally did, Zandreen took one look at them, covered an amused smirk, and raised an imperious finger to point to the far edge of the pool.

"Clean up on the downstream side," she ordered, eyeing them up and down. "You three really don't do anything by halves, do you?"

Ithric grinned at her, shameless as ever. "Anything worth doing is worth doing all the way."

Favian ignored the banter, pushing past him with single-minded focus to pick his way over the rocks that formed the edge of the pool and step into the water. Sephira hadn't been exaggerating—it was *hot*. Shockingly so. Much more so than the warm pool at the king's bath house had been.

But it was also *wet*, and with a bit of scrubbing, it loosened mud from skin, which was mainly what he was after at this point. So, he made his way to a spot that was deep enough to cover his entire body when he ducked down, and set to work. The others followed, the water turning murky around them, and before long they were working on each other—which made it easier to reach the hard-to-get spots.

Favian happened to glance down at his right forearm and stopped, struck.

"Huh," he said.

"What is it?" Kathrael asked.

"My arm," he replied absently. "I've had a rash on it for the last few days. There was some summersweet ivy mixed in with the horses' hay, and I grabbed a sheaf of it without realizing. The little raised blisters are all dried up, and it doesn't itch now."

"The mud healed it?" Kath asked.

"I guess it must have done. Ithric, how's your cheek?"

Ithric shrugged and gingerly wiped at the mud-covered bruise with a wet hand. "I suppose it's a *bit* less tender than before."

Kathrael ducked under the water for a few moments and emerged with her face mostly clean. She wiped the water from her eyes. "Nope," she said dryly, "my scars are still there. Ah, well. My skin does feel very nice, though, so there's that."

"Yes," Ithric said, the corners of his eyes crinkling. "Your skin does feel very nice."

She laughed and splashed him. Favian left them to it and focused on washing the mud out of his hair.

Eventually, they were all clean. They lounged with the others for a while, letting the day slip by without work or care. Favian thought about talking to Zandreen, asking her some of his many questions, but it seemed rather rude to do so when she was curled up with Inga. Who knew how often the pair got a chance to relax and spend time together in such a way?

He spent a pleasant enough stretch of time chatting with Ayala, and tried not to stare upon realizing that Dharnal was apparently Sephira's lover as well as her bodyguard. Later, he acted as a pillow for Kathrael when she dozed off against his shoulder around mid-afternoon.

Eventually, the group straggled back to the cave to eat, and from there, to the stone spiral. Standing among the Ancestors' mysterious construction, they observed the sun setting in perfect alignment with a notch carved into the recumbent slab of rock set west of the bench in the center.

"The solstice is past," Inga intoned. "The days have turned."

Favian joined in the familiar prayers that followed, the words little different from those he had learned as a young acolyte, despite the distance separating Rhyth from the temple in Draebard. Hours later, they returned to the cave by torchlight, ready for sleep.

In fact, Favian was shocked at how tired he was, given that he had basically done nothing that day except rest and play. Once again, he contemplated the luxury of another full, uninterrupted night of slumber. He lay on his back between Ithric and Kathrael, staring up at the darkness in the cave.

A bit more of this, he thought, and he might eventually be ready to face the realities of their return to the city, and what awaited them there.

Later that night, Favian dreamed.

The street was chaotic, full of people running and shouting. The air crackled with potential, like the atmosphere before a thunderstorm. Favian glanced upward from under the hood of his winter cloak. It was cloudy, and the sky was growing darker —

*perhaps a thunderstorm really **was** coming, even though it was the wrong season for it.*

*Because of course, that was **all** they needed right now.*

Sephira was walking next to him. They were near the front of a large group of people. A strange mix of priests, slaves, and common folk, many of the latter carrying weapons, including some very familiar-looking crossbows. As Favian watched, a gang of men wearing the yellow sashes of the cult of Deimok emerged from a side road near him, yelling and swinging swords and clubs. He fell back a few steps in instinctive reaction, his heart pounding as they headed straight for him and Sephira.

An answering cry arose from behind him, a dozen or so of the armed slaves and commoners in the group surging forward to clash with the newcomers. Crossbow bolts flew, and a handful of the attackers fell, screaming.

"Keep the crowd moving! Hold firm, Little Brother!" Sephira called, the words hard to make out over the noise, even though she was only a few steps away.

"Come on!" he cried, pitching his voice loud enough that it wouldn't accidentally quaver. It was hoarse. For some reason, his chest ached as if he were recovering from the coughing sickness, but the words still carried. "Forward, to the palace!"

The cry was taken up by others close to him. The ragged chant of "To the palace! To the palace!" growing in volume as more and more people in the mob around him took it up.

For it truly was a mob now. The crowd had turned into a living thing, a beast that clawed out in self-defense as a disorganized squad of city guardsmen bore down on its flank, trying to cut it in two like a snake. All the while, the main mass continued forward, too large to stop.

A heavy body slammed into Favian and he staggered, clutching the man's shoulders and trying to keep them both from falling. He had a brief impression of wild eyes and yellow teeth bared in a snarl before the man jerked free and staggered off. When Favian looked down, there was a smear of blood on his left hand.

The din of screams and clanging metal was growing loud enough to make his ears ring. He could see Sephira's mouth moving, but he couldn't hear her voice at all anymore as the fighting continued behind them. He tried to focus ahead, in the direction they needed to go, knowing that the most important thing now was to keep moving and not get boxed in.

So far, the way forward was clear. The street they were on entered a large plaza perhaps sixty or seventy paces away, and as they grew closer, Favian could see into the open square. More bodies jostled his from behind, but it was the sight ahead of him that made his breath seize in his throat.

Kathrael walked across the large space, dressed all in red, wearing her mask of flames and feathers, flanked by a lion on one side and a wolf on the other. The three unearthly figures strode along at the head of what could only be called an army. An army of the dispossessed.

The pounding of Favian's heart in his ears grew so loud that the chaos around him faded away. He couldn't breathe, and all he could see was the vision of beauty and powerful magic before him.

His feet stumbled to a halt, and he was still staring a moment later when running figures dressed in guardsmen's armor — armed with swords and longbows — blocked his view of the plaza. He tore his gaze away, dragging in breath to yell something to Sephira. A warning, or —

An arrow slammed into him, sending him crashing to the ground as blinding agony enveloped the left side of his chest. The back of his head hit the flagstones with a sharp crack, his vision swimming crazily.

He could dimly make out people screaming and running, others falling to the ground around him, but the confusion seemed somehow unimportant, as though he were observing it from across a vast distance. His body felt strange. Heavy. Enveloped by an all-consuming numbness.

"Zandreen!" Sephira's voice sounded flat and far away, like someone shouting through a long tunnel. "Zandreen! He's shot — he made me promise not to stop for him if he fell!"

"Then don't stop." Zandreen's voice sounded oddly distant as well. "Sephira, you must take charge of the crowd and join up with the main group in the plaza! Go, now! Keep your word — I will stop for him in your stead."

Favian tried to take a breath deep enough to speak. Without warning, his body jolted back to full awareness. Pain like nothing he had ever experienced in his nineteen years of life sliced through him, and his consciousness wavered.

Awareness washed in and out like the tide, time stuttering forward in fits and starts. Jerking back to cognizance, he was surprised to find that the chaos had lulled, and the street now seemed almost peaceful. He stared at the fallen body of a young woman lying near him, obviously dead. His surroundings seemed dim, as though his vision were going dark for some reason.

Zandreen crouched over him, speaking to him, though he couldn't understand her words over the buzzing in his ears.

With no warning, she grasped the arrow protruding from under his collarbone and yanked it out sharply. The world exploded. Favian tried to scream, but his lungs would not inflate. Blood was filling his mouth. He was choking on it, drowning in it, his struggles to draw breath growing ever weaker as his body succumbed to the lack of air.

The sense of disconnectedness from his physical form returned, as if he were floating up, looking down at himself from above.

No, please... no, please... I'm not ready... no no no, he thought desperately, as the world grew dark around him —

Favian jerked upright like a puppet on strings, choking on nothing and clutching at his chest. His empty lungs heaved, but his throat was closed tight—no air could get past the obstruction. Panic clawed at him, and flashes of light popped in front of his wide-open eyes despite the darkness surrounding him.

"Favian!" Kathrael's voice was sleep muddled and high-pitched with worry. A hand clasped his arm, but he threw it off violently, flailing, hardly aware of where he was—only that he was suffocating, dying—

"What the *hell*—" Ithric's voice came from his other side, and this time the grip on him was too strong to shake off. He struggled, his panic rising to new heights.

"I think it's a dream!" Kathrael again. "I saw something like it in Draebard, but not this bad! *Favian!*"

"*Shit.*" Ithric's voice was a low growl. "Right—I'm sorry about this..."

Pain exploded across Favian's cheek, and the band constricting his throat and chest snapped. He drew in a sobbing gasp, shockingly loud in the darkness. The air entering his lungs felt like hot knives. The strong hands returned to support him by the shoulders, while other fingers fluttered over his cheek and temple, stroking his hair back.

"Careful, Ithric," Kathrael said. "He might throw up on you."

Fortunately, Favian's body seemed too preoccupied with breathing to manage vomiting at the same time, which was really just as well. Awareness of his surroundings returned by degrees, and the first hint of mortification encroached on the blind panic.

"What's wrong with him?" He identified Sephira's voice, coming from farther away. "Is he ill?"

"No." A less familiar voice—*Inga*. "He's not *ill*. He's a *seer*."

"Stay back. Give him some space." Zandreen's rich voice sounded worried.

Sparks flew in the hearth as someone stirred up the banked fire. The orange light illuminated the High Priestess's face, turned toward him and watching intently. Kathrael was a pale and worried figure on his right side, and Ithric, tense and stony-faced on his left.

His cheek throbbed.

"Sorry," Favian croaked, barely recognizing his own voice. "It's… it's nothing—"

"That was not *nothing*," Ithric growled.

Favian eased back, control of his body gradually returning. "No, I mean… just a dream. It was just a dream." He swallowed convulsively, implications swirling in his head, knowing he needed to get away, think it through… figure out what he could tell them. He swallowed hard. "I need—sorry. I need… some fresh air. C-clear my head. It's fine—"

He wasn't making much sense, and he knew it. But the wood Zandreen had dropped in the fire was catching now, throwing flickering light around the cave. He thought he could orient himself well enough to find his boots and cloak, and get away from them all for a few minutes. Long enough to think and regain control of his emotions.

He freed himself from Ithric and Kathrael's hands, relieved when his tenuous balance did not desert him as he rose. His boots were by the bedroll. He grabbed them and stumbled a bit while pulling them on. His cloak was hanging near the fire. He dragged it across his shoulders.

"Favian—" The fear in Kath's voice tore at him, but he couldn't stay here another moment without knowing what words might unintentionally pour from his lips.

"It's fine," he said again, a bit desperately, already heading for the cave entrance.

He was vaguely aware of Ithric behind him, murmuring, "Don't worry. I'll follow and keep an eye on him."

Favian fled, his feet carrying him without thought out of the cave and up the hill toward the stones. The cold night air hit him like a splash of frigid water to the face. He knew Ithric was behind him somewhere, trailing him, but if he kept walking fast enough maybe he'd still have enough time to figure out what to do.

What to say.

In the dream, Kathrael had been walking between a lion and a wolf. And Favian was going to die.

His chest tried to hitch, ridiculously. Could a person grieve for himself? Just as suddenly, a hysterical laugh tried to rise behind his ribcage, which still ached like he'd been kicked by a rowdy colt.

They were going to succeed. Kathrael was going to march on the palace at the head of an army with Ithric. Ithric *and Senovo.* But how could such a thing possibly come to pass?

The Old Stones swam into view in the pale moonlight. He stumbled forward and braced himself against the nearest one with both hands, aware of Ithric's eyes on him, watching from a distance.

He would have to… send Senovo a message. Yes. But would his guardian really come? Favian shook his head, trying to clear it. Senovo had already come. Would already have come. Favian had seen it, and the visions were never wrong.

He would send the message. He would send it tomorrow. And Senovo would come. Favian would get to see him one last time before he —

Oh, gods. He couldn't tell the others about his death. If he told them, they would try to stop it. And they probably wouldn't be able to change it, but if they somehow did, they would also be changing things so that they didn't march on the palace, and he *couldn't* be the reason that they failed in their quest after everything the three of them had been through to get to this point.

Favian was going to die. It was unavoidable. But he wasn't going to *tell* them that he was going to die. He would tell them the rest of it and omit that one tiny little point. And he would pretend that he'd never looked down and seen an arrow sticking out of his chest, so much worse than the one that had lodged above his collarbone as a youth. He would pretend he'd never felt what it was like to drown in his own blood, never watched the world go dark around him as his spirit parted from his body.

His shoulders were shaking, his forehead pressed against the frigid, ancient stone of the monument. Warm hands closed on his arms, and he flinched violently.

"That's enough fresh air, Favian," Ithric said. "We're going back."

"Yes," he replied faintly. "All right. Let's go back now."

Favian straightened, steeling himself to tell the most convincing—the most *important*—lie he had ever told in his life. In Rhyth, he had become a performer. An actor, like the others. He was no longer the naive, open-faced youth he'd once been. He could do this… and none of them would ever know the truth until it was too late.

ELEVEN

Later, he sat next to the fire with a heavy fur draped over his shoulders and a cup of hot tea cradled in hands that barely shook.

"… and then my view of the plaza opened up. I could see Kathrael walking with a lion and a wolf at the head of a huge crowd of people, many of whom were armed with the crossbows we stole. That's when I woke up."

Kathrael frowned at him. "But… that's all good, right? You were upset when you woke up, Favian. You were *frantic*."

Favian shrugged, feeling vaguely proud of his steady voice and calm expression. "Well, I was surprised to see the wolf, that's all. It was something of a shock, to put it mildly."

Ithric let out an audible sigh and tossed the dregs of his tea on the fire, where the liquid sizzled and steamed. He set the cup aside and rested his forearms on his knees, hands hanging loose as he caught Favian's eyes and held them.

"No offense, Favian," he said, "but you're a shit liar and you always have been. Tell us the part of the dream that you're *not* telling us."

Well, damn it anyway.

Favian made himself hold that amber gaze, his own eyes wide and innocent. "I don't know what you mean," he said, brazening it out. "That was everything."

"No, it wasn't," Kathrael said.

"Yes, it was!" he insisted.

Ithric continued to stare at him, not even *blinking*. How did he *do* that, anyway?

"No. It wasn't," said the shape-shifter, in a tone of finality. His eyes narrowed. "But have it your own way for now. We'll drag it out of you eventually."

"There's nothing to drag," Favian protested weakly, aware on some level that he should probably shut up and take the temporary reprieve he'd been offered.

Misdirection. Maybe that was the key.

"Ithric, I need to talk to the contact who sends reports north for you. I want to send a message to Senovo right away," he said.

And that part *was* actually true. Maybe some bizarre circumstance would arise, regardless, and result in Senovo's presence here so that the vision would come true. But that wasn't an experiment Favian felt much like conducting under the circumstances.

"All right," Ithric said, still studying him like some strange and interesting insect.

Kathrael was frowning. "The Wolf Patron will not come back to Rhyth, Favian. He made that clear enough before we left Draebard. Perhaps... your dream was not a prophetic vision after all?"

If only that were true, he thought.

"I should still send the message," he said. "Just in case."

Ithric rocked back to lean on his hands. "I'm overdue to send a report to Andoc, anyway. He should know about the crossbows. No reason you can't add a message for Senovo at the same time. I'll contact the courier as soon as we get back to Rhyth."

"Great," Favian said. "You do that."

In the end, after obsessing over the wording of the message for more than a full day, Favian took a deep breath and held the eyes of the gaunt youth who carried Ithric's reports north to the port of Llanmeer and, from there, inland to Draebard.

"I dreamed the wolf in wintertime," Favian said slowly, "walking through the streets of Rhyth at the head of an army. If you ever loved me, father of my spirit, please, *please* come. Seek out the Sisterhood of Avlan, for that is where you will find me."

He repeated the words four more times, and had the courier repeat them back three times. Even so, he worried afterward about all the ways it could get garbled, and all the things that could happen to the messenger on the long trip between Rhyth and Favian's home in the north.

Meanwhile, Kathrael and Ithric fretted about what he wasn't telling them. And all three of them worried about how they would feed themselves and the horses, now that it was too dangerous for them to perform their show to get money.

Amidst all this worry, Favian lay awake in the back room of their borrowed warehouse, staring into the darkness above him. Because he had just realized something else. Something *important*.

Favian knew exactly when he was going to die. It was preordained. Inescapable. But the flip side of that coin was what had his pulse thundering in his ears as the others slept on beside him, oblivious.

He knew when he was going to die. Which meant that, until Kathrael marched on the palace with Ithric and Senovo beside her, he *wasn't* going to die. He was, for all intents and purposes, untouchable until then.

Between now and whenever Senovo arrived and the slaves rose up, Favian could do *anything he bloody well pleased.*

🙠 ♛ 🙢

Kathrael caught her breath, her heart pounding as Favian finished speaking, explaining what he planned to do.

"That's insane," Ithric said. "You can't possibly be serious. It's suicide."

"It's not suicide," Favian said, "and I'm doing it. I should have done it long ago. This isn't who I am, Ithric. *I'm a priest*. It's time I started acting like it."

"How is this not suicide?" Kathrael demanded. "Favian! You can't just start preaching dissension and rebellion openly in the city!"

The horrible vision of a mob dragging Vesh's broken body through the streets made her sway, and she shot a hand out to steady herself against the wall where she was standing.

To be fair, Vesh said, *I wasn't preaching in the streets when they took me. I was going someplace private to suck a man's cock for money. Bit of a difference there.*

That's not the point, Vesh! she thought. She was still having trouble breathing.

"It's not suicide, because I know that I'll be fine when the slaves rise up," Favian said, interrupting her silent exchange with Vesh. "Until Senovo arrives and you march on the palace, Kathrael, nothing is going to happen to me."

His certainty only frightened her more. "You can't know that, Favian!"

Ithric was watching Favian very closely. "That assertion might be more reassuring if you weren't so obviously lying about what you dreamed."

Favian's brows drew together. "I'm not lying about the dream! Every word I told you about it was the truth."

Of course, Kathrael thought, it was the words he *hadn't* told them about it that were the problem. But before she could tell him so, he continued.

"This isn't a negotiation," he said, "and I'm not asking your permission. The common people need to have some idea of what's happening in their city, and they deserve to hear what the gods *really* teach."

"So you're going to… what?" Ithric asked, combative. "Go stand on a box in a random square in the city and start preaching the Old Religion until the cult of Deimok shows up? And then what will you do? *Run really fast?*"

"No," Favian said, unperturbed. "Hardly. I'm going to go stand in front of one of the temples and start preaching the Old Religion, because the cult of Deimok still isn't quite bold enough to attack the temples directly and draw the ire of the city guard. Then, when the priests come out and try to make me leave, I'm going to point out that I'm *also* a priest, and have every right to speak about the gods in front of the temple."

A tiny bit of Kathrael's panic ebbed. But, still—

"You're *not* going alone," she said. "Take some of Qaden's men to act as protection."

"That's not necessary," Favian said, gentling his voice in response to her obvious fear. "And since we won't be paying Qaden once the last of our money runs out, I'm not sure that our original agreement with him still applies. He may have no interest in offering protection to *any* of us."

Ithric took a slow, deep breath and let it out. "Ask Ciryl. And maybe Shuggan. They might do it anyway. And we'll be there as well, obviously." His eyes flicked to Kathrael, who nodded.

Part of her was queasy at the idea of potentially being a helpless spectator *yet again* as someone she loved was attacked, but a larger part knew she couldn't possibly let Favian go alone.

"Fine," Favian said. "It's settled, then. I need to talk to the Sisters of Avlan. They're already preaching openly among the poor."

And being killed or arrested for it, in many cases, Kathrael thought unhappily.

"I'll try to coordinate something with them," Favian continued. "We need to do a better job of spreading the word about what's coming."

⤛⬥⤜

So it was that Kathrael found herself huddled in a cloak next to Ithric, her breath puffing in white clouds in front of her, as Favian and Ayala spoke to a handful of passersby who had stopped to see what was going on in front of the Temple of Deresta. Ciryl was lounging against a cart nearby, watchful, accompanied by the quiet child who sometimes ran errands or acted as a lookout for Qaden's gang.

After all these weeks, Kathrael still didn't know the youngster's name or gender. Ciryl referred to the child as *Mouse*, with the air of one using a fond nickname, and Mouse seemed content to follow him like a silent shadow, taking in everything with wide brown eyes.

"Do you think it's wise to have a child along, if things start to go bad?" Ithric had asked earlier, frowning.

Ciryl only shrugged. "It'll be safe enough with us right in front of the temple. Worst that'll likely happen is if the priests send someone for the city guard. And if they do, we'll have plenty of time to clear out before they get there. Besides, it'll be good for the li'l runt to hear what Favian has to say. There's too much crap dressing itself up as religion in this city these days.
"

Mouse certainly did seem to be caught up in what Favian was saying as he railed against slavery and the treatment of the poor in Rhyth. They all were, to be fair — though Ciryl, at least, was splitting his attention between the spectacle and their surroundings, she was pleased to note. Around them, more people joined to watch, the crowd growing from a handful to more than a dozen.

Kathrael had never seen Favian in quite this light before. Though he'd been a newly fledged priest at the time of their fateful meeting in the Temple of Draebard months ago, she hadn't ever really seen him in his element like this. His normally diffident demeanor was transformed into a sort of righteous certainty as he outlined the evils perpetrated and enabled by the southern temples.

"The Priests' Guild is corrupt," Ayala said, to the accompaniment of murmurs of agreement from a few of the women in the crowd. "It is soft and rotten at its core."

"How can those who keep slaves and forcibly mutilate young men against their will be trusted to serve the gods and the people of Rhyth?" Favian asked. "One might just as soon ask a fox to care for the hen's nest in her absence."

"That's why the cult of Deimok is growing in the city!" called a man from the back of the gathered spectators.

"Relying on the cult of Deimok for protection is akin to setting fire to the henhouse to root out the fox," Favian said, and several people laughed.

"Nothing is more dangerous than a religion which insists that no other religions can be allowed to exist," Ayala added grimly. "Rhyth welcomed the Alyrions' god into its borders, and we have been repaid with nothing but terror, death, and cruelty. That is not religion. That is invasion."

The little crowd grew restless, people muttering to each other until a commotion at the entrance to the temple drew their attention.

"What is the meaning of this?" demanded a middle-aged eunuch with flabby cheeks and heavy bags under his narrow eyes. He strode out of the temple, flanked by two nervous acolytes, and made a beeline for Ayala. "How dare you profane Deresta's house with your heresy and sedition?"

Favian stepped in front of him, physically blocking his progress toward the Sister of Avlan, and Kathrael's heart fluttered — partly in fear, but partly in… something else.

"Heresy?" Favian asked blandly. The crowd watched with avid eyes, obviously hoping for a new spectacle as the confrontation simmered. "To what heresy do you refer, *Elder Brother*?"

Cool disdain colored the traditional term of respect, and the priest's face grew red. "You have no business here — you and this… *harlot*."

Favian remained unmoved. "What does that even *mean*?" he asked. "I am a priest. Where else would I have business other than at a temple? And what earthly connection does a person's sexual behavior have with their ability to speak about the gods? It's not as though temple acolytes don't have a well deserved reputation for sleeping with pretty much anyone who offers, man or woman. And I don't hear you questioning *their* qualifications to serve the gods."

There was an audible gasp from the onlookers, and the two acolytes flanking the priest abruptly looked as though they wanted to sink into the ground and disappear, their cheeks flaming red. Despite her misgivings about the whole situation, Kathrael found herself mentally cheering Favian on. Beside her, she felt Ithric's chuckle more than she heard it, his chest shaking with silent mirth.

"Oh, gods above," he muttered once he'd regained control, "he's gone all shameless on us. What on earth have we unleashed, Little Cat?"

She could only shake her head helplessly.

Ayala glared at the Rhytheeri priest, stepping up to stand shoulder to shoulder with Favian. "And tell me, *servant of Deresta*, what teachings of the gods prevent a woman from speaking about religion?"

The priest opened his mouth, but Favian cut him off again. "Hmm… now let me think. Oh, dear, *there aren't any*."

"Don't be ridiculous, you insolent boy!" the eunuch snapped. "A woman cannot be a priest! Such a thing is preposterous."

"Why?" Favian asked. "Why is it preposterous? Is the *goddess* Deresta so insulted by her own sex that she would shun a female servant? What about the *goddess* Utarr? In what part of the religious histories does it state that only a man can serve the gods?"

"And only a man whose balls have been cut off or crushed, at that?" Ayala added dryly. "If the gods are so offended by testes, then utilizing female priestesses sounds like a much simpler — not to mention, less painful — solution."

Some of the spectators laughed aloud. Others hooted.

The priest's jaw worked for a moment before sound emerged. "Blasphemy! Eunuchs have always served the temple. It is simply *the way things are done*."

If it weren't for the potentially fatal danger inherent in publicly striking red-hot sparks near the pile of tinder that was Rhyth, Kathrael would have enjoyed watching Favian and Ayala's relentless evisceration of this self-important old hypocrite.

Shut up, Vesh said, his ghostly voice sounding deeply amused. *You're enjoying it regardless, and you know it.*

So are you, she accused.

Too fucking right, I am. This is the most fun I've had in ages, he agreed easily.

TWELVE

The unlucky acolytes accompanying the priest really did look like they were contemplating escape by this point. She wondered if either of them were slaves.

"Oh," Favian said, "well, if it's *the way things are done*, then I suppose we're stuck with it in perpetuity. Just like we still make swords and chariots and everyday tools *exactly* the way our distant ancestors did, even though better ways have been found."

Ayala smirked. The Rhytheeri priest's face turned from red to puce, and he raised a trembling finger to the acolyte on his left.

"Enough of this! Go find guardsmen and bring them here," he ordered.

Someone in the crowd booed, and several others began to heckle the priest.

Favian spoke over the noise. "That won't be necessary. I can see that we've upset you. Perhaps you simply need some time to rally your arguments. We can easily speak another day. Sister?"

Ayala shrugged. "I have no other pressing engagements. I'm pleased to return another time to continue the discussion."

Ciryl pushed away from the cart he was leaning against and called to the crowd. "All right, clear out, you lot. Show's over. Don't want to make a scene and upset the nice man and his acolytes, do we?"

There was more laughter, and the little gathering reluctantly broke up. Kathrael, Ithric, and Ciryl moved forward to form a sort of human barrier behind Favian and Ayala as they left, discouraging anyone from trying to accost them, and the group headed back toward the riverfront. All in all, it was strangely anti-climactic, given the various horrible scenarios Kathrael had constructed in her head.

No need to go borrowing trouble, Kath, Vesh chided.

Ayala took her leave a few streets over, heading for wherever she usually stayed when she was not assisting

Sephira, Kathrael assumed. For her part, Kath was feeling positively shaky and lightheaded by the time they reached the old warehouse and bade Ciryl goodbye.

A banked fire still warmed the sleeping room at the back, and she half-collapsed into a rickety chair in the corner, intent on getting her emotions under control. Vesh had gone quiet since his earlier admonishment. Something about the silence in her mind tugged at her, bringing a frown to her face.

Favian shrugged off his cloak and hung it on a hook before turning to face them. "So, didn't I tell you? That wasn't so bad, now was it?"

Ithric grunted. "Better entertainment than the show we've been putting on for the rubes, yeah. Which isn't to say that things couldn't go straight to shit tomorrow, or the next day, or the next."

"Only they won't," Favian said slowly, as if to an imbecile, "because I've already seen that they won't."

Kathrael finally put her finger on what was wrong with the silence in her mind, and inhaled sharply in surprise. Both of her companions' attention turned to her in an instant.

"Kath?" Favian asked.

"My baby," she said faintly.

"What's the matter?" Ithric asked, frowning. "Is she upset? Do you need me to sing to her?"

"No," Kathrael said, "she's quiet. I... I can barely feel her."

Favian looked understandably confused. "But, that's good, right? Maybe she's just sleeping?"

She shook her head, a deep sense of unease growing in her chest on top of the undercurrent of fear for Favian's safety. "You don't understand. She's never quiet like this when I'm upset. She's always fussing, or crying."

"Hey." Favian crossed the few steps separating them and took her shoulders, leaning down and pulling her forward in the chair so he could hug her. "Maybe she's starting to learn not to be so scared whenever you're worried about something. Surely that's better than her being frightened."

Kathrael gathered the folds of Favian's dun priest's robes in her fingers and gripped them, focusing inward, prodding at the silence like a painful tooth. "I don't know," she said uncertainly, unable to adequately put her misgivings into words.

Ithric's callused hand smoothed her hair back from the side of her face. She hadn't heard him approach.

"Is there anything we can do?" he asked. "Aside from not fighting any more today?"

Kathrael chewed on her lower lip for a few moments.

Vesh?

Yes, Kath? The response came immediately.

Do you know what's wrong with my daughter? she asked.

Nothing's wrong with her, Vesh said, sounding confused. *She's right here.*

Kathrael took a deep breath and tried to let the worry go. "No," she said aloud. "I'm all right. Let's... just... eat something and go do what we need to do today. I'm sure it's nothing."

The following days fell into a sort of uneasy pattern. Favian continued to draw ever-larger crowds in front of Rhyth's temples, sometimes accompanied by Ayala and sometimes alone. Ciryl or Shuggan tagged along most times to keep an eye on things, and Mouse could usually be seen hovering around the edge of the crowd, drinking in Favian's words.

Things occasionally got a bit rowdy with dissent or jeering in the crowd, but, much to Kath's surprise, it was nothing that couldn't be quelled with a few sharp words or, in a couple of cases, by their unofficial bodyguard wading in and *gently suggesting* that the troublemakers either pipe down or remove themselves completely.

The spectators did not appear to be gang or cult members. They were just everyday people, trying to go about their lives in a city teetering on the edge of chaos. Favian's words obviously struck a chord with them, and Kathrael couldn't deny that what he was doing seemed to be having an impact among the common folk.

This became even more obvious when coins and little gifts started appearing at Favian's feet after he finished speaking. It was nothing compared to their takings from the now-defunct traveling show, but it was at least enough to pay for a bit of simple food for them, with some left over to put aside for buying hay for the horses when their current supply ran out.

An unexpected highlight came one drab day while they were gathered outside the temple of Naloth. Ayala was absent, but Kathrael caught her breath when, instead of an irate elder priest, a very familiar portly young novice emerged from inside, taking in the scene with striking light gray eyes.

Well, well, Vesh observed with interest. *Imagine that. Hello there, my old friend.*

It was Hameen, the novice priest who had defied his superiors to give Kathrael aid when she had first decided to travel across the mountains to Draebard. Hameen was also Sephira's nephew, and had been a fellow acolyte of Vesh's before Vesh had fled the temple. Kathrael had appealed to their common friendship with Vesh, and Hameen had acquired food, money, and a pair of ill-fitting sandals for her at a time when she'd had nothing but the clothes on her back.

"Greetings, Brother," Hameen said to Favian, pleasantly enough. "These last days, it seems you've been preaching more than those of us who actually serve here, which is a rather sad state of affairs. I thought perhaps we might speak with each other this morning, and see what can be gleaned from the discourse."

Kathrael held her breath, debating whether to make herself known to her erstwhile savior. In the end, she stayed quiet, her face hidden in the folds of her hooded cloak. As much as she might have wished to show Hameen what his small act of kindness had wrought, her masked features were too well known in Rhyth these days, and if she were recognized, it would only complicate things.

Favian, too, had mostly been keeping his own hood raised as he preached, to cover his distinctive blond hair and throw his blue eyes into shadow. It was unclear how many people had connected him with the man from the traveling show who stood on the backs of running horses — or if anyone at all had done so.

"I'd be honored to speak with you," Favian said amiably. "Talking to myself does grow dreadfully boring after awhile."

"An occupational hazard, I fear," Hameen agreed, and excused himself for a moment to retrieve a couple of stools from inside the broad double doors. "Here. We might as well be comfortable on this rather dreary day."

Favian thanked him, and the two sat a few paces apart, regarding each other curiously. Kathrael wondered if Favian had noticed the light gray eyes Hameen shared with Sephira, and figured out to whom he was speaking.

"So. I'm intrigued by your assertion that eunuchs are not uniquely qualified to serve the gods," Hameen began. "Surely you would agree that a eunuch is the only appropriate choice to oversee a handfasting or a fertility ritual, since they are unaffected by the lures of the flesh."

"Whereas men and women are... what? Incapable of controlling themselves?" Favian returned. "Goodness, it's a wonder that every public handfasting ceremony doesn't devolve into an orgy, if that's the case."

"I would never claim that men and women have no control over their urges," Hameen said. "But you must understand that people demand a degree of dispassion from their priests at such times. A degree of emotional detachment, if you will. A priest must not under any circumstances become entangled with those he serves in such an intimate capacity."

Favian leaned forward, intent, and his voice was very, very serious when he spoke. "Tell me then, Brother. Are you," he asked, "equating sexuality and sexual function with the ability of a eunuch to love?"

The people watching were utterly silent, obviously fascinated by this rare glance inside the priesthood—a shadowy, mysterious world populated by beings who were... *other*. By men who had given up their manhood—or had it stripped from them—to become something neither man nor woman.

Kathrael realized she was actually holding her breath, so focused was she on the interplay between the two priests. She knew, on some deep level, that she was seeing Favian laid bare before her, exposing the heart of his being and refusing to apologize for it.

Hameen had the grace to look thoughtful, at least, but he replied, "A priest should love the gods. And, indeed, he should love the gods' children, to whom he ministers. But that is a different sort of love than a man experiences for a woman. There is no escaping the fact that sexuality and *romantic* love are hopelessly intertwined."

"And yet," Favian said in a quiet tone, "a man may grow old with his bondmate. He may reach the point, as many men do, where he can no longer perform sexually. His partner may reach the point, as many women do, where her desire for sexual contact wanes and even disappears. Are the pair no longer in love?"

"That is..." Hameen faltered for a moment. "That is not precisely the same situation. The hypothetical couple still retains the memory of their romantic union from the past."

Favian's gaze sharpened. "Ah, I see. So, each time they share a loving kiss or a tender embrace, they must bring to mind a memory of carnal union to nurse the dying flame of their romantic love back to life for a few short moments?"

Hameen's pleasant features sank into a thoughtful frown. "Not... necessarily," he allowed. "Though I confess the thrust of your argument escapes me. The point is that men and women—of whatever age—are prone to emotional entanglements, and therefore would make poor candidates for the priesthood."

"Tell me, Brother, have you ever been in love?" Favian asked evenly.

There was a minute pause before Hameen replied, "I have not."

Liar, Vesh murmured softly in Kathrael's ear, making her wonder what had transpired between the pair before Vesh left.

"I have." Favian's voice was quiet, but firm. "Which is how I know that the guarantee of a priest's objectivity and detachment is an illusion, and always has been. Priests... *eunuchs*... may love, and be loved in return. Which makes them no different from anyone else. If they are objective in matters of intimacy, it is because they have been trained to be so. Just as anyone with dedication and a heart inclined toward service to the gods may be trained."

Now, a murmur grew within the onlookers. Hameen was silent for a bit, thinking. "You are a persuasive logician, Brother," he said eventually. "However, one wonders if you are an exception to the rule, rather than an argument against the rule. Perhaps you are merely a very unusual eunuch."

Favian lifted his chin. "Unusual, because I love, and I am loved? If that's what you mean, then I sincerely hope not."

Beside Kathrael, Ithric tangled his fingers with hers. She squeezed back hard, a desperate ache flooding her chest until she thought it might squeeze the air from her lungs.

Weeks passed with nothing more alarming than a handful of shouting matches and a couple of brief scuffles in the crowd of Favian and Ayala's onlookers. Perhaps the combination of daylight, proximity to the temples, and the presence of one or two armed, burly men with no tolerance for rowdy behavior was enough to ensure that the cult of Deimok did not attempt anything untoward.

Meanwhile, the underground resistance was busy training anyone willing to learn how to fire a crossbow. Only two of the dozens of small weapons stashes had been discovered by the king's guardsmen, though a number of rebels had been killed and captured during the confiscation of the second one.

Almost despite herself, Kathrael had started to grow complacent about Favian's preaching. Even Ithric seemed to have come to terms with the fact that the crowds mostly just wanted to hear someone heckling the great and the good of the Priests' Guild—providing them a brief moment of entertainment in a dull and difficult existence.

So, when Ciryl arrived at the warehouse one morning with a message from Qaden that he wanted to talk to Ithric about money—or rather, about the recent *lack* of money—it didn't seem that big a problem for Kathrael and Ithric to go talk to the gang leader while Ciryl, Favian, Ayala, and Mouse went on ahead to amuse the crowds and annoy the priests.

"I'll keep an eye on them, don't worry," Ciryl said with a wink.

"We'll be at the Temple of Utarr today," Favian said, "in case you want to join us later. Remind Qaden that if he ends up as some sort of regional mayor or governor, he'll have all the money he could ever want, all right?"

"We will." Kathrael gave Favian a distracted kiss on the cheek—already worrying about what else they could offer Qaden in return for his continued support—and let him go.

Favian wrapped his cloak a little tighter around his body. The day was a blustery one, but a decent crowd had gathered in front of the Temple of Utarr, regardless. Ayala seemed to be in rare form today. She had grown bolder over the last few weeks. Now, she had the spectators chanting a call for one of the priests inside the temple to come out and debate them— which had so far gone unheeded.

With rare exceptions, only the gray-eyed novice from the Temple of Naloth seemed willing to come forth and cross metaphorical swords with them on any kind of a regular basis. Favian had been very interested to learn that the novice also happened to be Kathrael's one-time benefactor, not to mention Sephira's estranged nephew. It still seemed possible that Hameen might turn out to be an ally, when push came to shove.

Favian often wondered if what they were doing was truly making any sort of difference. But then he would hear two common folk debating some point of religion as they wandered away when the crowd broke up, and comfort himself with the idea that if nothing else, at least they were making people *think*. These days in Rhyth, there didn't seem to be nearly enough of that going around.

From the corner of his eye, Favian saw Ciryl straighten and uncross his arms, looking at something. He followed the big man's gaze to where a young woman was trying to force her way through the press of people, her words swallowed up by the chant.

"Ayala," Favian said.

"I see it," the priestess replied. "She looks frightened—"

As one, they lifted their hands in a quelling gesture.

"Quiet!" Favian called. "Let that woman through!"

The chant trailed off raggedly as the woman reached the front and stumbled to a halt, panting.

"What is it, sister?" Ayala asked, walking forward to take her hands.

The newcomer clutched at her. "Priestess, a mob has taken my mother—they're accusing her of witchcraft!"

A potent swirl of fear and righteous fury rose up from Favian's belly to lodge in his chest, but he didn't allow it to reach his voice. "Cult members? Where are they? Where did they take her?"

"They were followers of Deimok," the woman said. "They're near the riverfront, where the waters bend and widen. Please help me—they're going to burn her!"

Favian felt a moment of dizziness, his vision swimming, before everything crystallized into diamond-sharp clarity. "*No*," he said. He would *not* let this happen.

Ayala looked at him with wide, worried eyes. He turned to the crowd. "The evil that threatens Rhyth grows more brazen with every day that passes. An innocent woman is about to be murdered, not five minutes' walk from here. Come with me and stop it, or every time you see your reflection from now on, you will know you are looking at part of the problem."

Worried muttering spread through the onlookers like a fast-burning flame. Ciryl came up to Favian and bent down to speak to him quietly enough that the crowd couldn't hear.

"This is stupid beyond belief. But you already know that, and you're going to do it anyhow, aren't you, Blondie?"

"You bet I am," Favian said grimly. "Ayala, you probably shouldn't come—"

"I'm coming," Ayala said, though fear still lurked behind her eyes.

He nodded, confident that Ciryl would look after her—already focused once more on getting to the riverfront before it was too late.

"Join us, or don't," he called to the crowd. "Just be certain you can live with whichever choice you make." With that, he grasped the distraught daughter's shoulder, and said, "Lead us there. Quickly, now."

He was vaguely aware of Ciryl bending over to say something to Mouse, who scampered off, hopefully to safety. Several other people hurried away as well—mostly women with small children in tow. He and Ayala were left with a crowd of maybe two dozen people, ranging from those who were obviously angry, to those who were curious, and a few who looked fearful.

Favian had to jog to keep up with the woman, who hurried along the winding roads at a fast pace, despite her obvious exhaustion after her earlier flight to the temple. If ever there was a time to make use of his current invincibility, Favian thought, this was surely it. He had a crowd at his back, a mountain of a fighting man at his side, and he knew with utter certainty that the cult of Deimok couldn't harm him before Kathrael marched on the palace.

He could stop this.

Ayala was huffing and puffing, and he was a bit out of breath himself when they reached the mob gathered on the banks of the river, near one of the old docks. They were, Favian realized, not so terribly far from the warehouse district he and the others called home—just a bit further upstream, where things were in better condition and more of the buildings were still in use.

There was no time to get his breath back. The mob was pressing in tightly toward something—or someone—in the middle, crying, *"Witch! Witch! Witch!"* in a ragged chant.

"Stop!" he yelled, barely recognizing the way his voice boomed, cutting through the noise. Fueled by outrage and the certain knowledge of his own safety, he marched right up to the people in back and started dragging them out of his way, grabbing tunics and cloaks by the handful and heaving. Beside him, he could just about make out Ciryl cursing under his breath, drawing an old shortsword and brandishing it, jamming the pommel into chests and backs when people didn't get out of his way fast enough.

Ahead, a man was standing on a raised platform on the dock, and others were piling bundles of wood and branches around a sturdy pole nearby.

"Mother!" the woman behind him cried.

He glanced back, seeing the accused woman's daughter struggling through a sea of arms grabbing at her, then forward again, where two men held a gray-haired woman.

"Enough!" Favian roared, feeling his forward progress slow as more bodies pressed around them. "In the name of the gods, *let that old woman go!"*

There was the barest of pauses in the confusion, and then an answering roar rose around him.

"Eunuch! Get him!" someone called. Others took up the cry. *"Eunuch! Eunuch! Eunuch!"*

THIRTEEN

The crowd surged around their little group, grabbing and tugging at Favian's cloak and robes. Blood sprayed — a scream piercing the air as Ciryl's blade hacked at one of the cult members trying to overwhelm them. Favian whipped his head around to see several of the people who had followed him engaged in fistfights, while others turned and fled back the way they'd come.

"Get the bitch!" shouted someone in the crowd. "Get the witch's spawn!"

Several men fell on the young woman who had led them here, and she went down under the assault, shrieking.

"*Stop!*" Favian shouted, his stomach dropping as things spiraled out of control. Ayala's hand shot out toward his and he grabbed it, trying to keep them from being separated as Ciryl slashed at anyone who got within range of his blade.

"Get the red woman, too! The harlot!" someone nearby called.

Ayala's eyes were wide and terrified as she clutched at Favian's hand and arm. Ciryl's sword sliced into the neck of a tall, thin man who tried to grab her, and blood splattered against Favian's cheek, hot and sticky.

Three men with daggers leapt at Ciryl, who roared and threw the first one off. One of the others jumped on his back and plunged a short, wicked blade into the junction of the large man's neck and shoulder. He bucked and cried out, his sword slipping from nerveless fingers as his injured arm fell limply to his side.

"*Ciryl!*" Favian cried, fighting against the hands that caught at his clothing and dragged him away from Qaden's loyal lieutenant, pulling Ayala along in his wake.

Two more men joined the fray, their knives lifting and plunging over and over. Ciryl fell beneath the onslaught, hidden from Favian's view by the press of bodies. A cloudy red haze passed in front of Favian's vision. The stench of unwashed bodies surrounded him. Hands dragged Ayala away, breaking their grip on each other.

He couldn't... see clearly... but there didn't seem to be anyone left nearby from the group at the temple. They were alone—

"Bring them to the dock!" called a new voice, sharp and authoritative.

The grip on Favian shifted, dragging him forward rather than pulling him back. The crowd opened up in front of him. He could hear scuffling behind him as Ayala was pulled along, and more from off to the side—maybe Ciryl? A sharp band of worry tightened around Favian's chest.

It wasn't Ciryl. Two men dragged the old woman's daughter to the space at the front of the crowd and threw her down. She landed on her hands and knees with a pained cry. Favian's captors shoved him forward a moment later. He staggered, but kept his feet, catching Ayala when she got the same treatment. The priestess of Avlan was trembling like a leaf, her face pale as a ghost.

Favian looked around wildly, taking in the bloodthirsty crowd. The pile of wood. The gray haired woman struggled weakly against the men holding her—her anguished eyes pinned on her daughter cowering on the ground. She was unable to do more than moan around the dirty rag stuffed in her mouth and tied into place, gagging her.

"Bring more wood," called the commanding voice, and Favian's eyes sought out the source of the order.

A tall, dark-haired man stood off to the side of the empty space in front of the dock. He wore the yellow sash favored by those who openly supported Deimok, and his brown eyes held the light of fanaticism. Those eyes played over Favian, Ayala, and the hapless woman who had led them here, studying them like some kind of noxious insects.

"It appears we have three witches' souls to send to the One God for judgment today, not just one," he continued. "And a heretic, to boot."

Ignoring his hammering heart and shaking knees, Favian gathered Ayala and the daughter behind him, sheltering them with his body. "Nobody is burning anybody today," he said, a surge of hatred burning its way up his throat for this butchery masquerading as faith.

The look the cult leader gave him was almost pitying. "The words of a pagan blasphemer hold no weight here, half-man. Once we've dealt with the witches, we'll see how well your imaginary *gods* come to your aid."

Favian tightened his grip on the women's arms, pressing them closer behind him. "You will not touch them," he vowed. *He knew he would survive. If he made sure that they had to go through him first —*

The leader smirked, exhaling a dismissive sound of amusement. He looked to the crowd, and his voice was almost casual as he said, "Stone them."

Those in the front rows reached down for rocks and bits of rubble, their eyes lighting with excitement. Nausea flooded Favian's gut, but he turned his back on the crowd so he could wrap his body around Ayala and the woman. "It will be all right," he said, hoping that if he somehow willed it hard enough, it would be true. "It'll be all right, I promise."

But the depths of his folly were even now becoming clear. The daughter sobbed, her mother's muffled cries growing more desperate as the old woman struggled against the men holding her. In the expectant silence, Favian could hear Ayala reciting a prayer, over and over, her breath puffing warm and wet against his collarbone as he tried to shelter her.

The first stone struck him in the hip, and he grunted. As if it had been some sort of signal, the crowd roared, and a hail of stones and chunks of bricks rained down on them. Some missed, some glanced off his body, and others landed with bruising force. He staggered, desperate not to accidentally expose the women huddled in his grasp as targets.

A heavy missile slammed against his temple, its rough edge tearing open the skin. The impact seemed to echo through his skull, making his ears ring and leaving him dizzy. He realized in horror that he was no longer sheltering Ayala and the other woman. Rather, they were trying to brace him and keep him on his feet. He was too heavy, though, and his knees had turned to water after the last blow.

He fell to the ground, their terrified cries following him down into darkness.

⚜

When Favian's aching skull dragged him back to consciousness an unknown amount of time later, those shouts of fear had turned into screams of agony. He gasped and rolled his head toward the terrible noise, blinking until the wavering orange light stabbing into his eyes resolved into a raging bonfire burning in the space in front of the dock.

Even from here, he could feel its heat, and he could smell...

He rolled onto his side and vomited as the reality of the fading screams combined with the smell of charred meat penetrated his dulled wits. As he heaved onto the rocky ground, he became aware of his bound wrists and ankles. His head pounded as if someone were driving a spike through his temple.

Oh, gods. Gods have mercy on him. *Ayala...*

"*You bastards!*" he cried hoarsely, riding the crest of his guilt and rage, ignoring the way the words drove fresh pain through his skull. "Fucking *bastards*! You've already lost! *I've seen your downfall!*"

Legs appeared in front of him, blocking the horrible view of the pyre, and a booted foot prodded his shoulder, rolling him onto his back again. His vision was still wavering in and out of focus, but he recognized the cult leader. Revulsion for the man standing over him flooded him, stronger than any hatred he'd ever felt for a human being.

"So, my friends," the man said, playing to the crowd, "what shall we do with the golden-haired heretic who claims to have visions of the future?"

"Drown him in the river!" someone called.

A ragged cheer went up, and the chant grew. "*Drown him! Drown him! Drown the eunuch! Drown him!*"

Favian struggled against his bonds, feeling every bruise from the stones that had struck him earlier. The ropes were heavy and tight, the fibers of hemp scraping at his skin. A grinning man came up and crouched beside him, forcing a rough cloth sack over his head. More rope circled his neck, too tight, tying the bag in place.

"Where are your false gods now, boy—eh?" the man asked, as hands lifted him carelessly into the air. The words were muffled by the heavy cloth.

"May the One God judge you as you deserve, heretic," the leader intoned.

Dizziness threatened to send Favian back into unconsciousness for a moment as many hands carried him with no more care than one would carry a sack of grain. The cloth of the bag pressed against his mouth and nose, smothering and claustrophobic when he tried to inhale.

But he knew everything would be all right in the end, because—

The hands rocked him back and forth a couple of times, and then he was sailing through the air, his heart skipping a beat at the unexpected sensation of weightlessness. The shock of the freezing river water threatened to drive the breath from his lungs as it swallowed him whole—blind, bound, and helpless.

"Look, Qaden," Ithric said, trying to hold onto his patience, "as soon as we can figure out a way to get it out of the city, I'll send someone to sell the caravan in one of the surrounding towns and pay you out of that. But right now, it's too recognizable."

"So sell your fancy horses instead," Qaden said, and it was clear his patience with them was worn equally thin.

Kathrael shot Ithric a wide-eyed look, but Ithric already knew that option was out. Favian would probably burst something at the mere suggestion.

"The horses are just as well-known as the caravan," Ithric replied.

"Maybe the white ones are," Qaden shot back, "but one black horse is the same as any other—"

The gang leader was interrupted by a scuffle of movement at the door. All three of them turned in surprise at the sudden commotion, only to find Mouse clutching the doorframe as if about to collapse. The child's chest heaved like a bellows.

A heavy weight settled in Ithric's chest, pressing outward. Kathrael grabbed his arm, her fingernails digging into the leather of his jerkin.

"C-c-come quickly!" Mouse said, huge eyes moving from one of them to the next with an expression of pleading. "F-Favian and the others went to try and stop the c-c-cult from burning a witch!"

Ithric felt Kathrael shudder next to him, even as his heart hardened to cold steel.

"Where?" His voice cracked like a whip, and Mouse flinched.

"Upriver, by the d-d-docks. F-fifteen minutes fast running."

"What about Ciryl?" he asked.

"He went, too," Mouse said, tears welling.

"*Son of a whore*," Qaden cursed, and shoved his chair back, lunging for his weapons belt.

Ithric was on his feet at the same instant. "Kathrael. You have your quarterstaff?" She nodded, looking like a woman whose worst nightmare was playing out before her eyes. "Knives?" he added.

"Two," she said in a tiny voice.

"I can't ask you to come with me—" Ithric began, but she cut him off.

"I'm coming," she said.

"Qaden," he snapped. "Men. Weapons. I can take you with me on Audris, while Kath takes Mouse and one other man on Bysh. Four more men can run to our place and ride double on the other two horses. The rest will have to follow on foot."

Qaden rounded on him and stuck a finger in his face. "I'm only doing this for Ciryl, you rat bastard. I knew you three were going to be more trouble than you were worth."

Ithric ignored him and started pulling off clothes under his winter cloak. Qaden looked at him like he was mad, but Kathrael asked, "The lion?" in a quavering voice.

"The lion," he confirmed grimly.

Qaden blinked, and went to call the two men patrolling outside. One joined them where the horses were tied to the side of the building, while the other ran off to organize reinforcements. Ithric helped Kathrael mount her sturdy black gelding and lifted Mouse up to sit in front of her. Qaden gave his man a leg up to sit behind her, and she steadied Bysh as he sidestepped and shook his head, protesting the extra weight.

Wrapping the heavy cloak around himself, Ithric mounted Audris and hooked his elbow with Qaden's so the other man could swing up behind him. The gang leader had possessed the presence of mind to grab a crossbow and bolts as well as his sword and dagger. The guard had been carrying a crossbow as well.

"Go!" he shouted, and Kathrael wheeled her mount around, following Mouse's pointing finger as the two horses galloped upstream along the river road, laboring under their heavy burdens.

It wasn't much of an attacking force, but with two crossbows and an enraged lion, Ithric prayed it would still be more than a mob of religious fanatics would be expecting.

It took only a few minutes, riding flat out, until the knot of humanity gathered around one of the docks came into view. The first hint they had of what was happening was the plume of greasy black smoke rising into the gray winter sky. The bottom fell out of Ithric's world. They stopped only long enough for Kathrael to help Mouse slide down. The child immediately darted for the nearest building that could be used as cover.

Ithric's sensitive hearing picked up hoof beats behind them in the distance — their reinforcements. Ahead of them, a ragged cheer went up.

"Drown him! Drown him! Drown the eunuch! Drown him!" The words were barely intelligible, but that was all Ithric needed to hear.

"Hurry!" he barked, and spurred Audris into a flat run with his heels. He could hear Kath following a few lengths behind.

Favian had often boasted of their pair of white stallions being battle tested, and Ithric was about to find out just how true that was. He bore down at full tilt on the oblivious crowd, just as another jubilant cheer rose up.

The cheer turned to screams as the burly stallion plowed into the milling mob from behind, bowling several of them over and trampling them. Ithric gripped hard with his knees as the horse plunged, hooves slipping on the cobbles. He reached back and hooked elbows with Qaden again, helping him slide down to the ground where he immediately shot one man with a crossbow bolt before drawing his steel sword and hacking at anyone close enough to feel the bite of his blade.

Ithric spared a single glance behind him to see the other gang member on the ground and fighting as well, while Kathrael, still mounted, smashed a cult member in the side of the head with a smooth sweep of her quarterstaff. Beyond, their other two horses approached at a fast gallop, carrying more fighters.

"Go!" Kathrael shouted, spinning the staff overhand to take out a man coming up on her right. "Ithric, *go!*"

Ithric growled and whipped off the winter cloak, launching himself from Audris' back and shifting mid-leap. The lion landed in a fury of teeth and razor-sharp claws, ripping and tearing at anything that got in his way. The screams grew louder, panicked, and cult members scrambled over each other in their haste to flee the deadly beast in their midst.

It would have been all too easy to descend into mindless bloodlust, chasing down anything too slow to escape his reach. But even in animal form, the chilling cries of, *"Drown him! Drown the eunuch!"* still echoed in his ears. Ithric cut a bloody path through the fleeing crowd, heading straight for the dock and the river beyond.

A short distance downstream, a shapeless bit of waterlogged cloth bobbed at the surface. The water rippled and splashed as if something was moving violently beneath it. More cloth floated into view — a dun color that was horribly familiar. The ripples grew weaker, and the shapeless lump of cloth sank beneath the murky water, disappearing.

Without slowing, the lion charged down the length of the wooden dock and launched itself into the river's freezing, sluggish depths.

⚜

Favian held his breath against the burning cold of the water. The sudden soaking was every bit as stunning as the blow to his head had been. His heart stuttered at the shock of it, kicking irregularly against his ribs like a fractious horse before settling into a steady pounding that echoed in his ears like thunder.

He *would not* panic. He *wouldn't*, because there had to be a way out of this. The bag tied over his head had pressed against his face as he'd tried to drag in breath earlier, but now it billowed out, holding a bubble of air that tugged gently in the direction where the surface must lie.

He forced cramping muscles into an awkward dolphin kick, fighting the heavy weight of his waterlogged robes. Rolling and wriggling and kicking his bound legs until he thought he must be on his back at the surface — though it was impossible to know for sure with the bag muffling him. Still, he couldn't seem to rise any further, at least.

He let out a burst of air, inflating the wet bag, and tried to drag in breath. The wet cloth immediately collapsed over his face, frigid water crawling up his cheeks and threatening to close over his airways. He flailed and sank, kicked and rose again.

Breathe out.

Breathe in.

Less air, more water. Harder each time to get back to the surface. He couldn't feel his hands or feet, only the deep ache of burning cold. He clenched his jaw to keep his teeth from chattering uncontrollably.

Don't panic. There's a way out.

He kicked, but it felt weak. Uncoordinated. Was he at the surface? His lungs screamed. He let the breath go, but instead of inflating the bag, it bubbled away, his nose and mouth still an inch beneath the surface, the ever-shrinking pocket of air inside the hood just out of reach.

There was nothing to inhale but freezing water.

He flailed, his bound limbs jerking uselessly. Instead of propelling him to the surface, the clumsy movement dragged him down. He could feel the faint tug around his neck as the little bubble of air still trapped in the top of the bag tried to rise, losing ground against the inexorable sinking pull of his heavy robes and wooden limbs.

There's a way out.

There's a way out! There's —

Favian panicked.

FOURTEEN

The lion crashed into the freezing river and surfaced a moment later, powerful limbs cutting through the water in an age-old, instinctive rhythm, pushing him downstream toward the place where the dun cloth had disappeared from view moments before.

Favian's body was still being swept along by the sluggish current as well, the occasional tantalizing glimpse of a robe's hem wafting up close to the surface, always just out of reach.

Even a thick pelt was insufficient protection against the merciless winter river, and already Ithric could feel his muscles weakening. Just when he feared that his strength would not hold out, the claws of one front paw snagged something under the surface. Not even stopping to think, he dove and clamped strong jaws around the nearest fabric he could reach, dragging upward against the pull of the water.

Even the lion's strength was barely sufficient to keep them at the surface; he couldn't untangle the mass of waterlogged cloth twisted around Favian, and trying to shift to human form would just end with both of them drowning. They were some distance downstream from the dock now, and he struck out for the muddy shore as fast as he could swim.

The lion plunged through the thin crust of ice clinging to the river's edge. The muck of the shoreline sucked at his paws as he dragged the limp, heavy form out of the water and onto the half-frozen riverbank beyond. As soon as Favian's upper body was on solid ground, the lion dropped him and gave himself a massive shake, sending water flying as he shifted. Ithric steadied himself in a crouch, the winter wind biting at his naked skin.

He clenched his teeth and lunged for Favian's head, dragging at the wet ropes wrapped around his neck with numb fingers until he could yank the hood free. Water ran out of the rough cloth bag as he threw it aside with a violent movement.

"No, no, no… come on, Favian…" he muttered, taking in Favian's blue-tinged lips. His unnatural stillness. "No, you son of a bitch, you do *not* get to do this to me—"

Favian's body hitched weakly, and a trickle of water ran out of the side of his mouth—then, he was still again.

Ithric grabbed a handful of his wet robes, over his heart. "*I said no,*" he growled. "Fucking bastard. *Try. Harder!*" The words grew into a hoarse shout, and Ithric balled his free hand into a fist, driving it into Favian's stomach.

The reaction was immediate. Favian's body curled around the blow and convulsed, a gout of water spraying from his mouth and nose. The awful gurgling, wet noise as he dragged in a tortured breath of air was perhaps the sweetest sound Ithric had ever heard.

Favian rolled onto his side and vomited more river water, choking and jerking as his body fought to purge itself. Ithric wrapped his body around Favian's, clinging to him as he shivered and convulsed.

"You bastard," he whispered. "You *bastard*. Don't ever do that again. Not ever!"

They were still in serious trouble. Ithric could feel his body temperature dropping dangerously after only a few minutes in human form. Favian's lips were still a frightening blue-gray. Dark purple smudges underlined his eyes.

He didn't know if it would be worse to take off Favian's soaking robes or leave them on. He didn't even know if he *could* take them off with his fingers already turning to blocks of ice. Favian couldn't walk; Ithric couldn't carry him. They were probably less than ten minutes' ride from their old warehouse by horseback, but it might as well have been across the southern sea.

It seemed unlikely that anyone from the cult would come after them, with Qaden's men attacking the mob, but there was no way to rule it out completely. And Kath was in the middle of it. *Gods.* She'd told him to go after Favian, and she'd been right. Favian would be dead if he hadn't. But… he'd left her there—

A shudder wracked his body. It might have been the cold. The two of them were quite possibly fucked, regardless. But if the wrong people found them here, he could protect Favian better as the lion. Favian's choking convulsions had quieted to tremors, his breath rasping in and out weakly.

"I'm shifting back," Ithric told him, unsure if he was aware enough to understand the words. "The lion can survive the cold better, and I'll put out more body heat that way. You *hold on*, Favian, do you hear me?"

There was no reply.

Misgivings flowed through him. Should he shift and run back to the site of the battle? Try to get help and bring it here? How long would it take? Would Favian still be alive when he returned?

He hated this feeling of helplessness. Telling himself that he would wait a few minutes and see if anyone came before leaving Favian to try to get help, he shifted. Immediately, the bone-deep cold eased from life threatening to merely uncomfortable.

The lion nudged Favian and curled around him, flopping a front leg over him and squirming until no space separated them. Within moments, he could feel the faint spark of warmth where they pressed together, even through his wet fur and the wet cloth of Favian's robes.

In the part of himself that remained human, Ithric debated how long to wait. Just when he had half-convinced himself that he would have to try running for help, the lion's sensitive nose picked up the scent of a wounded horse.

The horse knew he was there, as well. He could smell its fright. He lifted his head, ears pricked.

"*Ithric!*" came a sweet, familiar cry, shot through with desperation. "*Ithric! Favian!*"

Ithric shifted back into human form with a gasp. "*Kath!*" he bellowed. "Kath, *over here!*"

He held his breath, and a familiar black horse appeared at the top of the riverbank — Bysh, heavily favoring a hind leg as Kath guided him down the hill in an awkward, hitching gait. Ithric could see a bloody slash across the gelding's haunch, blood trickling sluggishly from the wound. His eyes flew to Kath, raking over her but finding no obvious injuries as she practically hurled herself from Bysh's back.

"Oh, gods — *Ithric!*" She slid to her knees beside Favian, her good eye wide and panicked.

"He's alive," Ithric said grimly. "Help me. We've got to get him someplace warm."

Kathrael stared at Favian, lying still and pale as Ithric shivered naked over him, and tried to latch onto the shape-shifter's words.

He's alive, Kath.

Vesh's voice in her ear was uncharacteristically stern. *Pull yourself together. Think now. You can fall apart later.*

She swallowed against the images of death and loss from the past that wanted to rise up. Pulling off her gloves, she untied her cloak and swept it off, throwing it over Ithric's shoulders. Ithric tried to take it off with hands that were obviously numb beyond usefulness. "He needs it more—"

"And he'll get it," she snapped, dragging at Favian's wet robes and boots. "As soon as I get these off."

The fabric was already stiffening in places as it froze, and she bit the inside of her cheek hard. When he was naked except for his smallclothes, his skin pale and blue-tinged, Kathrael turned back to Ithric. "You'll have to help me get him on Bysh's back. I'm not strong enough."

Ithric nodded, and she helped him wrap Favian in the cloak. Between them, they managed to haul Favian up to sprawl over the little gelding's back. The injured horse sidestepped, still unnerved by the lingering scent of lion, and his haunches dipped alarmingly before he righted himself.

"Did anyone follow you?" Ithric asked. "Is the cult coming after us?"

She shook her head. "They have other things to worry about. No one followed me."

Ithric's tense shoulders sagged a bit before the cold drew another shudder from him. "Good."

"Bysh is too badly hurt to carry both of you," Kathrael fretted.

"Take Favian to Shuggan's place," Ithric said. "Teesa should be there, and she's still reasonably well-disposed toward us. She'll have a fire going to help Favian warm up, and they have oxen. They might know how to treat the horse's wound."

She nodded, and frowned. "What about you?"

Ithric wrapped his arms around himself and rubbed briskly. "I'll give you a head start and then shift. The lion has a fur coat, even if it's a bit damp right now."

It was reasonable, as much as the idea of splitting up pained her. She'd found them mostly by virtue of forcing Bysh in the direction he least wanted to go—the direction of a lion. If Ithric shifted form this close to him, he'd probably panic, and Favian was in no condition to stay astride a panicking horse.

"You're sure you'll be all right?" she asked.

He pulled her in for a quick kiss, his hand like ice against her cheek. "The quicker you go, the sooner I can follow. I'll manage."

She nodded and took up Bysh's reins, urging him back up the riverbank. Without her cloak, she could already feel the wind nipping at her, and she silently cursed the late season cold snap. She could hardly conceive of what it must be like to be naked and wet in the winter chill. She gripped Favian's thigh to steady him and urged Bysh to increase his hitching gait once they reached the river road.

Every now and then, Favian would moan and cough weakly as he was jostled. Kathrael clung to these small signs of life, and forced herself not to think of anything else until she knew Favian and Ithric were safe. Forced herself not to wonder if Shuggan would throw them out of his home the moment he learned what had happened today. If Qaden would hunt them down to take retribution.

In the space of a few hours, the bottom had fallen out of the life they'd carved for themselves in the warehouse district. Kathrael tried not to think about how Favian would react when he found out exactly what his impulsive act had wrought.

If he survived.

Her hand tightened on his thigh through the folds of the cloak.

Kath. Stop. Vesh's voice was kind. His ghostly presence seemed almost to enfold her for a moment before fading once more into the background. *Now is not the time. Shuggan's place is just ahead. Keep putting one foot in front of the other, eh?*

It might have been *just ahead*, but it still seemed to take forever to get the injured horse and his freezing burden to the converted storage building that Shuggan had claimed for his family. Kathrael knew the place well from her days spent there with Daeniel. Teesa, Shuggan's woman, had acted as a wet nurse for Kathrael's sickly infant nephew after she and the others had rescued the babe from the slave quarters of a fat, corrupt noble.

She could only hope that the tentative bond she'd formed with the kindly woman would hold in the face of what had just happened.

"*Teesa!*" she cried at the top of her lungs as soon as she was within shouting distance. "*Teesa! Shuggan! Anyone! I need help!*"

Favian moaned and tried to stir at the sound of her cracking voice, only to fall back weakly against Bysh's neck. Kathrael felt as though she was nearly dragging the poor horse forward by virtue of brute strength at this point, and she choked back a sob.

The sight of a dowdy figure in a plain brown dress sticking her head out of the door almost sent Kath to her knees with relief. "Help me!" she called. "Hurry, *please!*"

Teesa raised a hand to cover her mouth, and immediately bustled outside, meeting Kathrael halfway. Her face was pale. "Gods above! What happened? Quickly, get him to the house—he's half frozen."

"Is Shuggan here?" Kathrael asked, dragging Bysh forward again.

The other woman shook her head. "No, he was called away." Her expression was frightened. "Was it because of—"

Kathrael nodded. "Yes, this is why." They arrived at the front door, which was flapping open. Two of Teesa's brood— a boy and a girl—stuck their heads out curiously, looking at the horse and its burden with wide eyes.

"Out of the way, children!" Teesa snapped. "Go put wood on the fire and stir it up high. Send your older brother to fetch water and warm it. Be quick!"

The youngsters scampered off.

"Help me get him down," Teesa said, taking charge. "We'll have to drag him inside, I think. He's too heavy to carry."

The process of getting Favian off Bysh's back and over the threshold was awkward. Kath's back protested the strain as they used handfuls of the cloak wrapped under his shoulders to pull him a step at a time toward the hearth. When they got him close enough to the fire, she collapsed next to him, drawing him half into her lap. Teesa tugged the cloak around to cover him better before bustling off to get blankets and other supplies.

"The horse..." Kathrael said, knowing that if the choice were between helping Favian and helping Bysh, there *was* no choice—but feeling awful about it nonetheless.

"I saw," Teesa said, arranging what seemed like a small mountain of blankets and furs around and over them. "Poor thing'll have to wait for a few minutes, but once Ange has the water heating, I'll send him out with some poultice. He helps Shuggan with doctoring the oxen when they get hurt. He can tie the animal up in the barn afterward, and at least give it some hay and water."

She nodded, not speaking or lifting her gaze from Favian's still face. Already, Kathrael was starting to sweat under her clothing from the proximity to the blazing fire, but Favian's skin was still clammy and damp where her hands grasped him.

Teesa's oldest boy returned with two buckets and hung them next to the fire. Just then, Bysh squealed outside, uneven hoof beats retreating into the distance. A moment later, there was a knock and Ithric appeared, naked and human.

"I startled the horse, but he didn't go far. Just around the back," Ithric said. "Sorry, Teesa."

Teesa stared at him, shivering on her threshold, and tossed him a blanket. "Are you mad, Ithric?" she asked. "Come to the fire before we have two frozen bodies to deal with, not just one. Ange, go outside and catch the horse. Put him up in the barn and get some poultice for the wound on his haunches. Come back here as soon as you're done."

"Yes, Mum," Ange said and hurried off.

"Thank you," Kathrael said, starting to shake despite the heat, now that both Ithric and Favian were here with her, and alive.

"Yes—thank you, Teesa," Ithric echoed, dropping down to check on Favian, who still had not woken. He looked up, meeting their hostess's eyes. "I have to ask... did Shuggan tell you about me?"

Teesa rubbed her hands in her apron, a nervous gesture. "About you being a shifter, you mean? He did, though I could hardly credit it. Why?"

"I can help Favian better if I shift. The lion is large, and it puts off heat like a banked fire. We have to get him warm, and we have to do it fast."

A tremor ran through Favian's body, breaking his terrifying stillness. Kathrael gathered him a little tighter in her arms.

Teesa stared at Ithric, her expression going hard. "Can you give me your word, both of you, that my children won't be in any danger?"

Kathrael spoke up. "You have my word. I've seen the lion protect and care for human children as if they were his own cubs."

"I won't harm anyone here. I only need to help Favian." He paused. "Though if your oxen are downwind, they may get nervous."

Teesa appeared to waver for a moment, biting her lip. After a pause, she gave a single, tight nod. "All right. But I've got one of Shuggan's swords here, and I'm going to hold onto it until I see what's what for myself. You so much as give any of my brood a look that I don't like, and being cold will be the least of your worries, gifted or not."

"That's fair," Ithric said.

"You wait until Ange gets back from the barn, too. I don't want him in with the oxen or that horse of yours if they get upset."

"Of course," he agreed, and set himself to warming his hands at the fire.

Favian shivered again, and Kathrael stroked his waxy forehead, trying to transfer the warmth from her fingers to his cold skin. When Ange got back, Teesa drew all her children to huddle behind her and dragged Shuggan's sword over to lie across her lap.

"All right, then," she said nervously.

Ithric gave her a brief, grim smile and shifted. The lion shook off the blanket and sniffed at first Favian, then Kathrael. She guided him to settle in a long sprawl against Favian's back, with the fire at Favian's front. Then she tucked the blankets around them.

"Merciful gods," Teesa breathed when they were settled. "I never dreamed that I'd see the like." She seemed to shake herself free of her superstitious awe with difficulty, and cleared her throat. "Check the water, Kathrael. It should be warm enough to dip his hands and feet in to thaw them out. Dry them carefully afterward, but don't scrub."

"I know," Kath murmured. Unfortunately, while she'd escaped any serious episodes herself, frostbite was not an unknown problem among those who lived on the streets. She bundled up her discarded cloak and lowered Favian's head to rest on it, then tested the water and brought one of the buckets over.

Taking care not to spill water on the blankets, she submerged his hands and feet one at a time in the warm water until the skin was no longer blue and translucent, but rather a bright pink. She knew they would have to watch for blisters, but she thought he'd escaped serious injury, at least in that regard. By the time he was dry and the blankets were tucked in again, he was shivering continuously, his teeth chattering.

"That's a good sign," Teesa said. "His body's fighting the cold now. Sorry, I should've asked before—you're not hurt, are you, dear?"

"No," she said. She'd escaped with only a handful of bruises and scrapes. The rage she'd felt as she'd flailed at heads and legs with her quarterstaff was shocking, now that she looked back on it. She must've taken down half a dozen men as they crowded around, seeking to pull her from Bysh's back. One of them had wielded a sword—

She shivered at the memory, and sought out the oldest boy—Ange. "How is the horse?"

The lad looked nervous, as though he hadn't expected to be addressed. "He... uh... he's cut pretty bad, but the bleeding's slowed and I don't think it severed the muscle. I did m'best for him, ma'am."

"Thank you," she murmured. "One of the cult members swung at me with a sword. He was on my blind side. If Bysh hadn't whirled and kicked at him—"

The lion rumbled, low and unhappy, making Teesa and several of the children jump.

"He's a good 'orse," Ange offered.

For some reason, that was the thing that was finally too much for Kath. She looked away, hiding the burn of tears that threatened to overflow from her good eye. The lion stretched out a paw and laid his blocky head on it, his cheek brushing her hip as he looked up at her with glowing eyes.

Shh, now, Vesh soothed, and Kathrael wanted more than anything at that moment to be able to feel his arms around her.

But Vesh was dead. And right now, she needed to focus on ensuring that no one else joined him anytime soon.

Just so, he agreed.

Once again, she was struck unexpectedly by the quiet space where her daughter should have been. With Kathrael this upset, there was only one reason why the infant would not be crying, frightened by her mother's fear and worry. Her baby had finally left her for the spirit world. It was yet another stab of loss, threatening to bleed her heart dry.

Vesh's voice was bewildered. *You keep saying that, Kath. And I keep telling you — she's right here.*

I can't hear her, Vesh, she thought. *I can't feel her. She's gone.*

Vesh had no answer, though his confusion was clear in the silence.

Teesa eventually relaxed enough to herd her children away and start preparing food for the evening meal. Kathrael wondered if she was worried about Shuggan, who still hadn't returned. She must be, surely.

The afternoon dragged on, Favian's violent shivering subsiding into occasional tremors, and eventually stilling as his skin grew warmer under her hands. She thought perhaps he'd finally fallen into a natural sleep, albeit a restless one.

His chest rattled wetly in a way she really didn't like the sound of. Occasionally, his body would twist as if in a nightmare, and the lion rasped a broad tongue over his shoulder until he quieted. Kathrael sat in a daze, waiting for something to happen. For the other shoe to drop.

The shoe came in the form of the front door flying open to reveal Qaden, incandescent with rage. The gang leader was steadying Shuggan with a hand on his arm. Teesa gasped and ran to him, even as Shuggan tried to wave both of them off, looking testy.

"Don't fuss," he groused. "It's only a damned scratch. Teesa, get me a cloth to bandage it and it'll be fine in a few days, for the gods' sakes."

Qaden left his lieutenant to Teesa's clucking and rounded on Kathrael, Ithric, and Favian. She felt the lion stiffen, a warning rumble rolling through his chest, and tangled a hand in his mane to keep him still.

Their erstwhile ally looked like he wanted to eviscerate anyone stupid enough to get near him, and Kathrael's heart pounded against her ribs. He strode over and glared down at Ithric.

"Change back," he growled.

Kath was frozen, terrified that the lion would attack, or Qaden would. But instead, Ithric shifted and rose, squarely blocking Qaden's approach to Kathrael and Favian despite his lack of either clothing or weapons.

Kath clutched Favian's shoulders convulsively. She'd seen Ciryl's crumpled body as she was fighting, lying in a pool of blood by the docks. Even if Qaden didn't intend them bodily harm, he would surely drive them out of his territory now. And they couldn't move Favian like this — they *couldn't*. Outside, with no shelter so soon after nearly freezing to death, he would not survive.

Her breath locked in her throat.

"*You*," Qaden said, pointing a finger at Ithric. "You and I are going to talk."

Ithric watched Qaden warily, but without fear, and Kathrael knew with sudden and complete certainty that, should the circumstances require it, he would change back into animal form in an instant, and kill the other man before letting him put either Favian or Kath in danger.

"All right, Qaden," he said. "Talk."

"This is war now, you mad bastard," Qaden said. "I dunno what it was before, but as of today, it's a fight to the death."

FIFTEEN

Kathrael felt Favian shift in her arms, and realized with a jolt that he was awake.

"Qaden," he said, his voice a bare croak. He descended into coughing, and she tightened her grip on his shoulders to steady him.

Qaden's finger moved to point at Favian. "No. You shut your trap, Blondie." His voice rang out like hammer blows. "I dunno what it was before, but today those cult bastards killed one of *my* men, and I won't rest until I see them wiped from the face of this city."

Teesa was still fussing with the cut on Shuggan's upper arm, but she drew in a sharp breath and turned. "Who?" she asked.

"Ciryl is dead," Qaden said, "stabbed in the back by a piece of trash without enough bravery or honor to face him properly."

Favian made an awful, choked noise and squeezed his eyes shut, his teeth bared in a rictus of guilt and self-loathing as he curled in on himself.

Qaden continued, "I just saw three defenseless women *burned on a pyre while they were still alive.* I will find these rats dressed up like human beings, no matter what hole they've scurried into. I will find them *and I will end them.*"

Kathrael saw Ithric relax his wary stance a fraction, even as the meaning behind Qaden's words penetrated her frazzled wits and took root. Relief flooded her, so profound and unexpected it made her dizzy. In her arms, Favian had covered his face with his hands. His body vibrated like a pane of struck glass in the brief moment before it shattered.

Ithric stepped forward, meeting Qaden's eyes squarely. "There are some people you and I need to talk to, so we can make that happen. I'll set up a meeting as soon as possible."

"You fucking do that," Qaden said. "Because someone needs to pay for this."

Over the following couple of days, Kathrael grew more and more frightened for Favian, and not just because of the ugly, wet cough that wracked him at odd moments.

Ciryl was dead. Ayala was dead, burned at the stake for witchcraft along with the two women Favian had originally been trying to help. Some of Qaden's men had retrieved the bodies — what could be found of them, in the women's case — and brought them back to Qaden's territory for safekeeping until a funeral ceremony could be arranged.

Three of their four horses were gone, abandoned during the fighting at the dock, and probably spirited away by whomever was lucky and enterprising enough to catch them. Kathrael's heart ached at the loss of the beautiful white stallions Favian had cared for so deeply, as well as the black gelding who had once pulled a chariot with her horse, Bysh.

It terrified her that, when he had learned of the loss the evening after Ithric rescued him from the river, Favian's only response had been to retreat even further into himself, his pale blue eyes going even flatter and deader than before. She wanted him to shout, to rail against Ithric and the gang members who had lost the animals during the fighting. She wanted him to *say something*, but instead, he'd only nodded his understanding and returned his gaze to the hot cup of medicinal tea in his hands.

The sword slash in Bysh's haunches — the slash that had been meant for her — was the only thing that seemed able to rouse Favian to action. The following day, while Ithric and Qaden left to set up new meetings with the leaders of the underground, Favian donned borrowed clothing and made Kathrael help him out to the converted building their hosts used as a barn to check on the injury for himself.

"Will he be all right?" she asked, desperate for some small speck of reassurance in the midst of the horror and loss.

Favian smeared fresh poultice over the gash with a shaking hand, steadying himself with an arm thrown across Bysh's back. "I've seen worse wounds heal," he rasped, barely able to make the words heard. "It just depends."

She stroked the horse's forehead and offered him a tidbit of dried mayapple she'd begged from Teesa's pantry. Bysh lipped it from her hand and chewed with his head down, listless.

"He saved both our lives, Favian," she said quietly. "Yours and mine."

Favian was silent for a beat too long before he nodded and said, "Let's go back."

When Ithric returned with Qaden, he was carrying the clothes and boots they'd dragged from Favian's half-drowned body and left by the riverbank. The capricious weather had risen back above freezing, but Favian's things were still damp and covered with mud. Teesa tutted and took them from the shape-shifter, hanging them around the hearth to dry so the mud could be brushed out.

Ithric handed Favian a red bundle of cloth. "From Sephira."

Favian shook out the red ochre robes and looked at them stupidly for a long moment.

"She said if you're facing the same danger as the rest of the servants of Avlan, you might as well dress the part," Ithric continued. "I get the impression you've just been adopted."

Kathrael swallowed hard. "Does she know about what happened to Ayala?"

"She knew something must have happened when Ayala didn't come back yesterday. We told her the details. She's a hard one to read, but I get the impression this sort of thing… isn't that unusual an occurrence." Ithric's voice was grim.

Kathrael remembered something Sephira had said during one of their early meetings. "They've lost dozens of members this year alone, she said."

Favian was still staring at the robes. Without changing expression or saying a word, he stripped out of the borrowed tunic, revealing the bruises peppering his back and ribcage. A moment later, he shrugged into the red robes and fastened them.

Kath felt a moment of dizziness upon seeing the unmistakable marks of the stoning, without the partial cover of a blanket or cloak to hide them. The bruise on his temple was bad enough, but—

He's alive, Vesh soothed. *Try to focus on that.*

Again, the sudden, deep *ache* at not being able to cling to Vesh and bury her face in his shoulder assailed her. Favian had survived *his* stoning, yes… but her closest friend had not.

I'm sorry, Vesh said. *I didn't want to leave you.*

She took a deep breath and let it out. *You didn't leave me, though, Vesh. You're still here.*

As much as I can be, yes. For as long as I'm needed.

Remembering the horrible, empty week after Vesh had died and before she had heard his spirit speak to her for the first time, Kathrael couldn't imagine *not* needing him.

Ithric interrupted the silent exchange, eyeing Favian up and down. "Much as I admire our allies, I do have to wonder what possessed them to choose *red*. I hardly think garnering *more* attention is what you really need right now."

"You're wrong. It's exactly what I need." The croaked words were unexpected, as was the brief flare of fire in Favian's eyes. "As soon as my damned voice works properly, I'm going back out there to preach. *Alone*, this time."

"*No*," Kathrael and Ithric said in unison.

Favian glared at them. "I can't protect other people from the mobs. But they can't do anything to me. *I can't die.* I think we've proved that pretty conclusively."

Kathrael gaped at him. "*That's* what you took away from this? *Favian—*"

Across from her, Ithric had gone stony, one hand clutching convulsively into a fist. Before he could lay into Favian as well, however, Qaden spoke up.

"You can go out in your red robes and preach all day, every day, if it'll bring the rats out of the woodwork so I can stomp on them, Blondie," he said. "But you won't be doing it alone. You'll be doing it with every armed man I can muster at your back. And we'll start with the public funeral you an' the priestesses will be performing in a couple of days, for Ciryl and the women."

Now, Kathrael's eyes flew to the gang leader in disbelief, but Teesa beat her to the punch.

"You're going to have the ceremony in public, Qaden?" she asked. "Wouldn't it be safer to have a quiet one here by the river? There could be trouble."

Shuggan spoke up from his chair near the fire. "Qaden's right, Teesa. This is supposed to be *our city*. Our home. When did things change so much that we can't hold a funeral for good people in public, for fear of what might happen?"

After his brief flash of emotion earlier, Favian's eyes had once more turned flat and dead. His raspy voice was a monotone as he said, "All right. I'll preside. I owe the four of them that much. Sephira can join me, or Zandreen. They're protected, too."

Qaden stared at him. "You know, I expect to hear crazy shit from priests, but that's the second time you've talked about someone being *protected.*"

"Favian has the second sight." Ithric was still glaring holes through Favian, looking like he wanted to grab him and shake him until his teeth rattled. "He had a dream about us marching on the palace, and now he's convinced that he can't be killed before that happens."

"I can't be," Favian agreed. "You can't be, and Kath can't be. Sephira and Zandreen were there, too, so they're safe. I might recognize other people from the vision if I saw them. But I didn't notice you, Qaden—or Shuggan, either. You're not safe."

"Crazy religious nutters," Qaden muttered under his breath. In a louder voice, he said, "I'll take my fucking chances, Blondie. And your woman's right—you don't look all that indestructible right now from where I'm standing."

Favian only shrugged his disinterest and turned his back on them, staring into the dancing flames of the hearth fire.

On the fourth day after the disastrous confrontation at the docks, Kathrael walked with Ithric behind Favian and Sephira in the slanting late-afternoon light, part of an ever-growing procession winding its way from the warehouse district toward the city center. At the front, two dozen heavily armed men surrounded the pallbearers supporting the sheet-wrapped body of Ciryl, along with the scorched bones which were all that was left of Ayala, and the nameless mother and daughter. The remains rested on long wooden stretchers borne on their shoulders.

More armed men flanked the people following, allowing the curious and devout to join the swelling crowd as they wound their way through the twisting city streets, but alert for troublemakers. Anyone wearing the yellow sash favored by militant members of the cult of Deimok was shoved back at weapons-point, under obvious threat of injury or death.

The procession was under the protection of several territorial gangs, and not obviously fronted by slaves or rebels. The addition of curious city folk to the ranks further obscured any connection to the underground. The city guard largely let the gangs go unmolested these days, since they kept order—of a sort—on the streets. So there was no official reaction to the growing column of people marching behind the stretchers.

Kathrael's head was whirling from more than the dense crowd and the sound of voices raised in chanting and prayer. When Sephira had arrived at their home near the river earlier that day, her eyes were sunken with grief over Ayala, and new lines had etched themselves in her face. Nonetheless, she hadn't said a word about the circumstances surrounding her young protégé's death. She also hadn't arrived alone.

Inga had been with her.

The elderly prophetess from the stone circle had left her cave and come into the city to give them a single message.

"The final pieces of the goddesses' plan are falling into place, child," she'd said, staring straight at Kathrael. "The palace will fall at mid-morning, two days hence."

Ithric had frowned. "We can't possibly be ready to move in two days' time, Inga."

Inga's only response was to shrug. "It does not matter if you are ready, Gifted One. The goddesses will come together to depose the king whether you are ready or not."

Kathrael had looked to Favian, hoping for some insight into the cryptic pronouncement, only to find him looking pale and... resigned? It was hard to tell, so distant and untethered had he been since learning of Ciryl and Ayala's deaths.

But how could the palace *possibly* fall two days from now? They had scarcely begun to discuss the actual military strategy needed to move on the king's forces. True, Qaden was fully committed now, and had started talking to other gang leaders about joining the cause. But he was currently obsessed more by the idea of rooting out the cult of Deimok than rooting out the king, it seemed.

She could not foresee any conceivable scenario under which they would be ready to march on the palace by the day after tomorrow.

Those at the front of the funeral procession slowed, dragging Kath's attention back to the present. The sun had disappeared below the buildings, leaving them cloaked in the deepening shadows of evening. They had arrived at the entrance to a large square in one of the poorer districts of the city—their final destination. The raised voices grew somber, joining together in the death chant that every person in the south who had been raised in the Old Religion learned from childhood.

Slave or free, rich or poor—in the end, it didn't matter. Death claimed them all, and those left behind to mourn for them, or at least to pause and mark their passing, chanted,

Rise up! Rise up!
Gods are waiting,
Beloved spirits, time to rest.

Large processions like this one used to be a fairly common occurrence in Rhyth, at least for important or well-known people. Like so many things, they'd grown less common as the threat of violence and conflict with cult members became more pronounced.

She had never been a part of one before, not even as a paid mourner. There was something oddly compelling about it. Perhaps partly because it was comforting to think that all of these people had come to see Ciryl and Ayala off to the spirit world... but there was more to it than that. Being part of the crowd brought a sense of belonging. Of *power*, in a situation where the living were, in the end, utterly powerless.

The procession spread out, taking over the square. Many people were carrying torches, passing them out and helping light them. Others, Kathrael and Ithric included, carried wood for the funeral pyre. Since they were near the front, they were among the first to lay their logs in the center of the square, under the direction of one of the priestesses. By the time it was finished, the pyre would rise chest-high to a tall man and be large enough for the four sheet-wrapped bundles to rest on.

Seeing the pyre take shape only made Kathrael feel more disgust and hatred toward the Cult of Deimok. To corrupt Deresta's purifying funerary flames for the purpose of torturing and murdering the living was surely the pinnacle of blasphemy. Kathrael could not conceive of any person with a soul or a heart standing by—much less cheering—as someone was burned alive in a god's name.

At least the spirits of Ayala and the two women would feel Deresta's sure embrace tonight as they rose on the sacred smoke to ascend to the afterlife. Now that they were dead, it was quite literally the only remaining thing that the living could do for them.

The chanting continued as the pile of logs and branches grew, the space lit now by flickering, ever-shifting torchlight.

Kathrael tried to keep herself grounded by gripping Ithric's hand as she craned to keep Favian's pale form in sight. By the time the pyre was laid, full darkness had descended over the city, the stars twinkling above them in a black sky.

The pallbearers lifted the stretchers into place, arranging their sad burdens in a neat row on top of the pile of wood. Favian walked slowly around the structure, tossing handfuls of the flammable powder the priesthood used in ceremonies over the evenly spaced piles of tinder at the edges of the pyre.

When he was finished, he joined Sephira at the front, their robes the color of blood in the orange firelight. The Priestess of Avlan was carrying a ceremonial bowl cradled in her hands. She raised it above her head, and the crowd's chanting trailed into expectant silence.

"Mighty Deresta, She-Who-Burns," Sephira began, her rich voice rolling through the square. "Goddess of sunlight. Goddess of immolation. Tonight your children stand before you in grief. We commend our dead to your purifying caress, that their ashes might return to feed the earth, and their souls might return to the sky, carried upon your smoke."

"Ever shall it be so," the crowd responded.

Sephira lowered the bowl, balancing it in one hand. She turned to the pyre and dipped the fingers of her other hand into the sacred oil contained within, before flicking a few drops on the first shrouded figure, then the second.

"Mother and daughter, we know not your names," she said. "Your love for each other shone clear and true. You were blameless victims of a creeping evil that cares not for its own cruelty. The city of Rhyth failed you, but the gods take you to their breast, offering peace and comfort forevermore. You are together now, never to be parted again."

She moved to the third shroud, her head bowing for a moment before she squared her shoulders and flicked oil over the burned remains of her protégé.

"Ayala, Sister of Avlan. You died as you lived, serving the gods and protecting the innocent. The spirit world will be the richer for your presence, while the land of the living is all the poorer for your loss. Your sisters mourn you... and none more than I."

Sephira took a deep breath and turned to Favian, passing him the ceremonial bowl of oil with a dip of the head. He took it and shook a few drops of oil onto the largest shroud-wrapped body.

When he spoke, his voice was rough as broken glass, despite the honey and berry-bark tea he'd been swilling in an attempt to soothe his chest and throat. He forced the words out loudly enough to be heard across the plaza, though it must have cost him to do so. Certainly, the result was painful to listen to, for someone used to his normal mellifluous tones.

"Ciryl," he rasped. "Loyal lieutenant, stalwart and trustworthy. You harbored hidden depths, and always acted honorably. I failed you in life, but in death, I humbly commend your spirit to the gods. May peace be yours, forevermore."

Kathrael's throat closed up, and she heard a choked sob from nearby. When she looked, it was to see Mouse sheltered between Shuggan and Teesa. The child's cheeks were wet with tears.

Favian stepped back, and two of the Sisters came forward bearing lit torches. They circled the pyre at a stately pace, touching the flames to the tinder piles Favian had primed with fire-starting powder. Each touch of the torch produced a *whoosh* of climbing flames, and by the time they completed their circuit, the whole thing was ablaze.

The crowd watched in silence as the flames shot into the air, consuming the remains of the departed.

"Mighty Deresta," Sephira intoned, "accept your faithful children into your embrace. Return them to the earth and sky from whence they came."

"Ever shall it be so," the crowd chanted, and Kathrael heard Vesh whisper the ritual response along with her.

She got the sense that he was regarding the flames with fascination, as though he could actually perceive Ciryl, Ayala, and the others rising on the smoke to rejoin the gods—as he had been unable to do. She shivered.

"Go in peace," Sephira told the onlookers in a clear, strong voice. "Celebrate the lives that return to the gods this evening. Blessings be upon you all."

The silence continued for another long moment before murmurs of conversation began to break the stillness. Gradually, the crowd broke into small groups as people wandered off, many discussing the spectacle. Members of Qaden's gang moved to stand guard around the pyre, ensuring that no one would attempt to disturb it. Kathrael saw Qaden himself standing nearby, deep in discussion with a small group of tough looking men—rival gang leaders, perhaps.

Meanwhile, Favian and the priestesses retreated to a quieter area near the edge of the square. She and Ithric followed. Kathrael wanted desperately to drag Favian somewhere private and convince him to stop blaming himself for what had happened on the dock. She knew it was useless, though—he had closed himself off to a frightening degree, and right now she had no idea how to breach the gap.

Indeed, when they reached the group of red-clad figures, the priestesses were exchanging embraces and words of comfort with Sephira, while Favian stood removed, a few paces away. When Kathrael walked up to him and drew him into her arms, it was like holding an empty husk. His arms rose to circle her shoulders, but Favian's spirit was far away, hidden from her.

Ithric didn't even try to elicit an emotional connection, instead focusing on the practical. "If your duties here are complete, we should go home. You're still weak."

Favian's distant eyes wandered back to the funeral fire. "I should stay and watch over the pyre," he rasped.

Ithric put a hand on his cheek and guided his attention back to the two of them. "Qaden's men will watch over the bodies until they burn to ash. You can't do anything more for them now."

If he'd meant to shock Favian into some kind of genuine reaction with the words, he failed. Favian only nodded, his eyes still far away. "All right," he agreed, his voice a whisper.

Ithric moved to join the knot of priestesses surrounding Sephira, and Kathrael followed, hooking an arm with Favian's and bringing him in her wake.

"Sephira," Ithric said. "Sisters. We grieve with you for your loss. Is there anything we can do before we leave and take Favian back to the riverfront?"

"No, Gifted One." Sephira was pale, but her voice was steady and her expression, composed. "Take him back and make him rest. He should not have exerted himself in such a way when he is obviously still recovering from his ordeal."

It was yet another mark of just how far Favian had retreated into himself that he didn't even protest the two of them talking about him as if he wasn't standing right there. Before Kathrael could echo Ithric's expression of sympathy for the loss of Ayala and say their goodbyes, Sephira's eyes moved past them, her expression growing sharp.

Ithric followed her gaze, and Kathrael turned to do the same. A cloaked figure was approaching them, face obscured in the depths of a hood. For a moment, Kathrael thought it was Zandreen, in her guise as an old beggar woman. But the cloak was too new and clean; the figure's bearing, too upright.

And Sephira would surely recognize her High Priestess, cloak or no.

Ithric drew in a sudden, sharp breath, his eyes glowing gold. He strode forward, blocking the figure's progress toward the Sisters with one arm raised, his fingers splayed across the stranger's chest.

"You came," he breathed.

The figure lifted a hand to push back the hood of the cloak, and Kathrael couldn't suppress her gasp of shock. The Wolf Patron's striking green eyes slid over both her and Ithric before settling on Favian, who stood frozen a few steps away.

"Hello, Favian," said Senovo. "It's good to see you. I told you when you left that we would meet again, did I not?"

SIXTEEN

Favian felt a moment of vertigo that had nothing to do with his lingering weakness. Overwhelming emotion at seeing his mentor again threatened to shatter the brittle armor of numbness in which he had clad himself, after waking in Shuggan's home to learn of the fates of Ciryl, Ayala, and the two women he'd tried to protect.

At the same time, he realized that his death had slipped a step closer, dogging him, icy and uncaring in its bleak inevitability.

Senovo was here, in Rhyth. Inga had claimed the palace would fall in two days' time. There was now nothing material remaining to prevent Kathrael marching through the city, flanked by a wolf and a lion.

He became aware that he was still standing there like a ridiculous, open-mouthed statue. The others would expect him to greet Senovo warmly — perhaps to embrace him. But Favian knew that doing so would break him, and that was something he could not afford right now. Indeed, Senovo was already regarding him with concern. Favian didn't dare look at the others, but he was willing to bet they were, as well.

"Elder Brother," he rasped.

When Senovo moved past Ithric to stand in front of him, Favian lifted his right hand. After a hesitation so minute it was barely perceptible, Senovo grasped him forearm to forearm, in lieu of an embrace. Favian thought his mentor looked haggard, as if he hadn't been eating or sleeping well. Now, though, Senovo's expression was one of deep concern.

"How long have you been ill, Favian?" he asked.

"Since the Cult of Deimok stoned him and tried to drown him in the river four days ago," Ithric said bluntly, before adding in a tone of heavy irony, "Welcome back to the friendly city of Rhyth."

An expression of horror slid across Senovo's face. Favian had to look away, once more on the edge of falling to pieces. His gaze landed on Kathrael, who appeared... utterly dumbstruck. It was clear she had truly believed Senovo wouldn't come, and wasn't at all sure how to respond now that he had.

Sephira had joined them now, as well. "He called you *Senovo*?" she echoed. "As in, Senovo of Draebard? Forgive me, but proper introductions are *clearly* in order."

Ithric looked around the plaza, gauging the number of people present and the general atmosphere. "Yes, they are. But not here. Come back with us to the warehouse. Senovo, are you alone?"

Senovo lifted an eyebrow, though his attention was still mostly for Favian. "Yes and no," he said. "If you have someplace private we can retire to discuss things, Ithric, that would certainly be preferable to holding this conversation in a public square."

Ithric nodded. "Sephira? You should join us."

"Too right I should," Sephira said. "Come. It's getting late, and it's obvious there is much we need to talk about."

⚜

Favian remembered very little of the walk back to the abandoned warehouse they called home. Ithric stopped on their way out of the square to speak briefly with Qaden, who shot them a sharp look that Favian didn't even try to decipher.

The evening was cold, but clear. He could recall the trip in flashes—seeing their small group walking through the restless streets of Rhyth as if he were a spectator looking down on himself from above. It was only when the five of them were installed in front of a crackling fire in the snug back room of the old warehouse that his whirling thoughts began to untangle themselves.

After Ithric performed a formal introduction between Sephira and Senovo, Favian sank down on a low stool and looked up at the man who had raised him after his father died.

"You got my message," he croaked, his chest sore and his heart aching.

Senovo crouched down in front of him, searching his face with familiar, piercing green-gold eyes. The silent regard forced Favian to clamp down yet again on the emotions that wanted to shake free from his tight chest.

"I got your message, yes," Senovo confirmed. "We left for Rhyth the following day."

Favian frowned. "*We*? The others are here with you?"

Senovo's lips ticked upward for the space of a heartbeat, but the expression did not touch the worry clouding his eyes. "Where else?"

"How long ago did the three of you arrive?" Ithric asked.

"We've been here for several days," Senovo said. He took a deep breath and let it out, rising from his crouch in front of Favian's stool. "I am posing as a visiting priest from Penth, staying at an inn near the palace. Andoc has taken up the role of a lame beggar in the temple district, in hopes of hearing the gossip. And Carivel..."

He trailed off. Favian felt a flash of foreboding.

"What about Carivel?" he asked.

Senovo's nostrils flared as he drew another centering breath. "Carivel took a job at the royal stables."

Shock pierced his shroud of numbness. "She *what*? That's... that's..."

"Fucking insane?" Ithric offered. "Female body or not, Carivel's hauling around a massive pair of hairy balls forged out of solid iron."

Senovo's eyebrow flickered. "She did point out in rather forceful terms that it was a situation with which she had extensive previous experience."

Apparently, Kathrael had regained the capacity for speech. "But... if they find out she's a woman—"

"Then the results will be unfortunate," Senovo said. "Just as the results will be unfortunate should anyone discover that Andoc is the man who burned the southern mountains and organized the defense at Llanmeer six years ago. I... could not stop them from accompanying me. I did try."

"There's danger aplenty for anyone in Rhyth who dares to stand up and be heard," Ithric pointed out. "Not just them."

With no warning, and for the first time in several weeks, Favian was hit with a wave of homesickness so intense it made him catch his breath. "How is Frella?" he asked hoarsely. "Who's looking after her, if you're all here?"

Favian got a glimpse, then, of the misgivings Senovo must have been fighting since getting Favian's cryptic message.

"She is under the care of the others in the temple," he said, none of the turmoil coming through in his voice. "I left Brothers Eiridan and Feldes in control of things, in case I do not return. I also charged them with Frella's care. Andoc gave Varanis and Jacun joint chieftainship over the village, and Carivel handed over the title of Horse Master to Dalon. Draebard is in excellent hands."

Movement caught Favian's eye as Kathrael sank down to sit on the edge of the palliasse the three of them slept on, as if her knees had suddenly gone weak. "You… gave up your titles and positions to come here?" she asked, the words sounding faint.

Senovo regarded her steadily. "We arranged matters so that those who rely on us would not be left adrift, should something unforeseen happen."

Something unforeseen. Right. Favian had to swallow a bark of choked laughter, though in reality, it wasn't remotely funny.

"However," Senovo continued, "Should I return intact, I have no doubt that Feldes and Eiridan would step aside and allow me to return to my position as High Priest. Dalon would do the same for Carivel, as would Jacun, for Andoc."

Ithric raised his eyebrows. "And Varanis?"

The briefest flash of dry humor lit Senovo's eyes before disappearing behind the wall of worry. "That is another matter entirely. Let us hope that the three of us have the opportunity to return to Draebard and address it." His attention returned to Favian. "Now, though, I wish to hear more about your dream, Little Brother. And then, I will hear the details of this attack."

Senovo's burning green-gold gaze moved to Favian's temple, where he knew the sickly green and yellow bruise left behind when one of the stones had knocked him out was still visible. Favian nodded, steeling himself, and recounted the same sanitized version of the dream he'd given to Ithric and Kathrael.

"I was an idiot, though," he said, the words slipping out unguarded. "I thought just because I'm untouchable—just because the other people present in the dream are untouchable until the vision comes to pass—it meant that no one around me would get hurt. But then—"

He cut himself off, clamping his jaw shut to prevent anything else from escaping. Senovo frowned, his eyes growing dark.

"But... then?" he prompted.

Favian only shook his head, his gaze slipping down to rest on the packed dirt of the floor as fresh horror and guilt flooded him.

"But then," Sephira supplied, "your protégé and my protégé were preaching in front of the Temple of Utarr when a woman ran up and told them that her mother was about to be burned as a witch by the Cult of Deimok. They... tried to stop it. They failed. Ayala, along with a man who was acting as their bodyguard, paid for that attempt with their lives. Favian nearly did, but his lovers managed to rescue him from the river before he drowned, gods be praised."

Favian squeezed his eyes shut, the heavy silence that followed broken by the memory of Ayala's screams as she was burned alive. Because of him. Because of *his* hubris. His stupidity.

He realized he was shaking.

"This is my fault." The words, barely more than a whisper, came from Senovo.

Hearing his thoughts echoed in such an unexpected way shocked Favian into opening his eyes and looking up at his mentor. There was *anger* in the shape-shifter's eyes. He couldn't tell if it was directed inward or outward, but it hardly seemed to matter since he'd never *seen* Senovo angry in all the years he'd known him—

"No." It was Kathrael, who had remained uncharacteristically silent through most of the conversation. "It was the fault of the mob, and those who led it. It's the fault of a corrupt king and spoiled, decadent nobles who care nothing for the common people beyond how much money they can be bought and sold for, and how much labor can be extracted from them."

The others were silent, all eyes in the room now focused on her. She, in turn, was focused on Senovo.

"The question is, now that you're here, Wolf Patron—what are you going to do about it?"

The two regarded each other for a long moment, something unspoken passing between them.

"I will act. Tomorrow, I will face my final reckoning with the southern Priests' Guild," Senovo said. "But be aware, Kathrael of Rhyth, if the temples fall, the city will descend into chaos in short order."

"We have stores of weapons hidden throughout the catacombs, and an organized network of sympathizers," she shot back. "We have the beginnings of a citizens' council, and several thousand slaves who would like very much to have a say in their own futures. *Chaos* is what we have *now*. What you describe is *opportunity*."

"It is change — nothing more and nothing less. But, by its nature, change is unpredictable." Senovo took a steadying breath. "I must return to Andoc soon, or risk worrying him more than he is already worried. Favian and Kathrael — meet me at the Temple of Utarr tomorrow at midday. Ithric, you should speak with Andoc to discuss strategy, rather than coming with us. It is best that you and I are not together any more than necessary, for now."

Ithric nodded, grim. "You don't want to risk both of us being killed, in case Favian's dream was wrong."

"It's not wrong," Favian murmured.

But, oh, how he wished parts of it were.

"Such things are capricious," Senovo pointed out gently. "If the worst happens, there should still be one shape-shifter available to lead the slaves to freedom."

Something occurred to Favian, and he frowned. "Wait. How do you plan on keeping Andoc from accompanying you tomorrow? And Carivel, for that matter?"

Senovo flickered a finely arched brow. "Simple enough. I will tell them only that I have located you, and plan to bring you back with me to see them. Which is the truth, even if we will be taking a somewhat... circuitous route to get back, with a handful of stops along the way."

Ithric let out an indelicate snort. "You realize that Andoc's going to *completely lose his shit* when I show up and he realizes what's happening."

"No doubt." Senovo's tone was dry.

"There is a reason that the Trickster is considered the patron god of shape-shifters," Sephira observed. She tilted her head, giving Senovo an assessing look for a moment before continuing, "The Sisters of Avlan will stand with you tomorrow, Senovo of Draebard."

"Thank you," Senovo replied.

"You should go to the Temple of Naloth first, though," Kathrael said. "Not the Temple of Utarr. There may be at least one priest there who will be ready to listen to what you have to say."

She exchanged a look with Sephira, and Favian knew they were thinking of Hameen, the priestess's gray-eyed nephew. Senovo also took note of the silent communication, and after a moment, he nodded agreement.

"Very well, the Temple of Naloth, then," he agreed. He eyed Favian critically for a moment. "I should go. Favian, you need to rest. You've been overexerting yourself."

Favian truly *looked* at Senovo, then, and saw the brittleness he was hiding. He nodded, agreeing easily. Though he hated himself just a little more for it, rather than disappointment, Favian mostly just felt relief that he would not have to face Andoc or Carivel tonight.

Senovo was circumspect, and not generally given to outright confrontation. He was also distracted by the fact that, come tomorrow, he would be facing unavoidable reminders of the worst day of his life. Andoc and Carivel, on the other hand, would take one look at Favian and roll straight over his carefully erected defenses.

Hopefully, tomorrow they would both be thoroughly distracted by the day's events, when and if he saw them. Senovo was going to need their support, whereas Favian mostly just needed them *not to focus on him*, and on the things he wasn't telling anyone. Things about the dream. About his utter culpability and crippling guilt over the deaths of good people.

The good news was, he only had to hold onto his composure for a couple more days. After that, it wouldn't matter any more.

⚜

The following day, Kathrael walked next to Favian, approaching the Temple of Naloth as the sun climbed toward its zenith in a hazy, winter-gray sky. Her worry for him persisted, even though his cough had seemed somewhat improved that morning. She had awoken several times the previous night from confused dreams that left her heart beating fast and her skin clammy. Each time, it was to find Favian awake, too... staring blankly at the rafters above them.

The fact that he had not seemed to notice either her awakening or her turmoil was so far out of character that it made her heart pound even harder.

Talk to him, Kath, Vesh had urged silently. *Please.*

But... what could she say, that she hadn't already tried to say to him a dozen times in the past few days? *Ciryl and Ayala's deaths weren't your fault, Favian? Please stop lying to us about the dream, Favian?* In the end, she kept her silence.

Ahead, the temple came into view as they rounded a corner. In a way, the Temple of Naloth was where her journey had begun. When she tried to think back, many things about her former life were hazy, but she still vividly remembered her conversation with Novice Hameen. They had reminisced about Vesh that day, and debated the truth behind the prophecy of the Wolf Patron.

Now, the Wolf Patron himself approached the temple from the opposite direction, wearing the same concealing cloak he'd worn last night at the funeral ceremony. He was flanked by a group of figures in red.

Kathrael could not deny the spark of vindication she felt at the prospect of calling Hameen out and saying, *look, he's real, he's here, and now you have to choose a side.* Mostly, though, she still felt a profound sense of shock and disbelief at Senovo's presence.

So much of her life had formed around the belief that Senovo of Draebard was a traitor to the prophecy that defined him—a callous demigod with no care or sense of responsibility toward the slaves he was supposed to save. Yet... he was here. Favian had called for him, and he'd left everything behind to answer that summons.

She'd had a sense, last night, of how much it must have cost him to do so. For the first time, she wondered what personal demons had driven him to reject his title of Wolf Patron and distance himself from the prophecy so thoroughly. No doubt Favian knew the answer... not that he was likely to tell her when she could barely pry two words out of him at a time.

The two of them met Senovo and the group of Sisters a few paces away from the doors. A single nervous-looking acolyte stood next to the temple's entrance, his gaze roving over the Sisters' red robes, Kathrael's feathered mask, and the pale-faced, blond northern priest who had been systematically heckling and terrorizing his superiors over the past few weeks.

In short, Kathrael thought, he looked everywhere except where he *should* be looking.

She turned to the Wolf Patron. His features were shadowed under the cloak's hood, but she could still make out the deep currents roiling beneath his impassive facade, barely held under control.

"Are you ready?" she asked, since Favian was still mired in his self-imposed silence.

"It is time," Senovo said.

Kathrael nodded, and turned her attention to the bewildered acolyte. "Fetch Novice Hameen," she ordered. "Tell him that the friend of Ta'Vesh has returned, and that the day of reckoning is at hand."

The acolyte swallowed and hurried away, wide-eyed.

You are surprisingly good at this, Vesh whispered in her ear.

I've been waiting my entire life for this day, she replied, feeling something in her chest loosen and slip free.

Silence reigned, and a sharp twist of movement caught the corner of her good eye. Senovo's cloak slid to the ground, and a huge, rangy wolf stepped away from the pool of heavy fabric. Several of the Sisters caught their breath. The animal padded over to stand between her and Favian, its gold-green eyes fixed on the open doorway before them.

Favian's fingers clutched convulsively for a moment in the thick ruff of fur framing the wolf's shoulders, and when she looked up at his face, she caught the tail end of a spasm of... grief? Regret? It was gone an instant later, and she couldn't be sure.

Hurried footsteps approached them from inside the building. Novice Hameen emerged, blinking, into the light, his striking, pale gray eyes landing briefly on Sephira before taking in Kathrael's presence, and the presence of the menacing four-legged predator next to her.

He gaped at them, looking from the wolf, to her, to Sephira, to Favian, with whom he had engaged in several philosophical discussions over the past few weeks.

"The Wolf Patron has returned to Rhyth, Novice Hameen," Kathrael said. "It's time to choose a side."

SEVENTEEN

To Hameen's credit, he didn't sputter or try to deny Kathrael's proclamation. Instead, he swallowed hard, collecting himself. Again, he glanced at Favian, and at his aunt with her eerily similar light gray eyes.

"I am on the side of the gods, and the people of Rhyth," he said carefully. He returned his attention to Kathrael. "I hope that my actions toward you in the past have shown that to be true, friend of Ta'Vesh."

Kathrael nodded, satisfied. "They have... friend of Ta'Vesh. Now, take us to the High Priest."

"Tell me what you intend, first," Hameen insisted. His eyes slid to the wolf, and Kathrael thought he must be remembering the story of Senovo's escape from the temple, and the torn bodies of the priests the animal had left behind.

It was Favian who answered, his voice stronger than it had been the day before, but still raw from the river water he'd inhaled during his near-drowning.

"We intend to end the practice of slavery, and turn out those who have behaved cruelly while hiding behind the cloak of false piety," he said. "There will be no bloodshed unless it's instigated by someone within your temple."

Hameen hesitated for a bare instant.

Sephira regarded her nephew steadily. "This is happening now, kin of my kin. It would pain me to find you on the wrong side of the battle."

Some of the tension in Hameen's shoulders eased. He drew his spine straight, lifted his chin, and nodded. "Kin of my kin, I regret that I have given you cause to question where my ultimate loyalty lay. Come. The High Priest is in the altar room. No doubt young Terrek is running through the corridors as we speak, alerting the others to the Wolf Patron's return. I expect you'll have half of the temple assembled to watch... and the other half fleeing out the back rather than face you."

Without thought, Kathrael placed a hand on the wolf's shoulder, her fingers brushing Favian's. The animal was trembling nearly imperceptibly. Its demeanor did not project fear, however—rather some other strong emotion she couldn't identify.

"Lead on, then, Brother Hameen," she said.

The priest turned and swept into the temple. She and Favian followed, with the wolf prowling between them and the Sisters of Avlan at their backs. Kathrael vaguely remembered the building's layout from her visit the previous summer. Rather than leading them into one of the side corridors, though, Hameen continued along the main hallway, their way lit by oil lamps in recessed sconces.

Ahead, the building opened out into a massive two-story space dominated by a slab of stone in the center. The acolyte—Terrek—must have run straight to the High Priest and told him what was happening, because the old eunuch stood facing the doorway with his back against the altar, his face nearly as pale as his white robes.

"Novice Hameen!" he barked. "What is the meaning of this?"

His voice was strong, but everything else about him screamed of weakness. His shoulders sloped, his small, deep-set eyes were glittering with fear, and his receding chin was framed by heavy jowls that jiggled as he spoke.

Hameen's eyes dropped to the floor, no doubt the result of a lifetime of subservience toward the man cowering in front of the altar, but his voice was clear and level. "The Wolf Patron has returned, High Priest."

The High Priest's fingers clenched around the edge of the altar behind him. "*Wolf Patron?*" he snarled derisively, his angry voice still at odds with the waves of fear rolling off of him. "Lies and fairy stories! How dare you allow this... *animal* into Naloth's most sacred space—"

The wolf stalked forward, Favian and Kath's hands sliding from his back as he left them. She heard a gasp from the far side of the room, and saw a collection of younger priests and acolytes huddling at a second entryway, watching with wide eyes.

The wolf paused a few steps away from the High Priest. Reality twisted, and Senovo rose gracefully to two legs in his human form. The last hint of color drained from the High Priest's face, and his fingers dug harder into the stone behind him. Senovo circled to the side of the altar, his eyes glowing in the low light, the pair's gazes locked on each other.

"The *animals* were here already, O High Priest of *nothing*," Senovo said in a low, dangerous voice, "and any sanctity that lingered in this place of lies disappeared long ago."

A shiver skittered up Kathrael's spine at Senovo's deceptively silky tone, and she didn't think Favian was even breathing as he watched the confrontation.

The High Priest locked his knees enough to slide around and put the stone slab between them, his palms braced against it as if he needed the altar's support merely to stay upright. Beyond the tense tableau, a few of the acolytes trickled into the altar room from the hallway beyond. They were gaunt. Hollow-eyed. Kathrael recognized the look of slavery. She spared a thought for her closest friend, who had once been one of these boys, and felt his spirit stir in her mind.

My brothers, Vesh agreed. Wonder suffused his words. *Can this really be the day they walk free?*

Senovo and the High Priest continued to circle each other, step by deliberate step. The Wolf Patron was hugging the edge of the room, his attention split between the elderly priest and the beaten metal idols adorning the walls. Many of them appeared to be made of solid gold and silver, and Kath couldn't help wondering how many starving people could be fed and clothed with the wealth displayed so carelessly around them.

The High Priest moved only enough to keep the altar between himself and Senovo as they circled the echoing space. Nearly a dozen acolytes and novices now stood huddled inside the room, watching.

"*Lupiandas*," one of them asked as Senovo approached the tightly huddled group, "have you truly come back for us, after so many years?"

Kathrael caught her breath, and Favian's fingers tangled with hers. The words were nearly identical to those she'd spoken six years ago, when Senovo and his fellow Draebardi clansmen had saved her from an overseer's whip and aided her escape from her masters.

"I have," Senovo said, though it sounded as though the words had been punched from him.

"Silence, boy!" the High Priest shouted, some combination of stupidity and desperation not to lose his grasp on power lending him a foolish flash of bravery. "Remember your place!"

Senovo growled and tore one of the heavy idols from the wall, sending it crashing to the flagstone floor to the sounds of a collective gasp from the onlookers.

"Remember yours!" he thundered. "Are you not the gods' servant? What gives you the right to own another human being?"

"It is the gods' will—"

Another idol crashed to the ground. "*It is not the gods' will!*" Senovo stalked toward the altar, his eyes flaring gold. "The gods command us to offer comfort to the grieving, and rest for the weary! They command us to feed the hungry and protect the innocent! They do not command us to *enslave and mutilate innocent children against their will!*"

Favian's hand clutched hers convulsively, and she could hear his ragged breathing as Senovo's words echoed through the chamber of stone and wood. The High Priest appeared frozen in place as the shape-shifter stormed toward him. Kathrael gasped and started to cry out in warning as the old man drew a tiny ceremonial dagger from the loose sleeve of his robe, but Senovo was already moving—hitting it out of his hand with a violent swipe of one arm. His normally placid features were set in hard lines of righteous anger, terrifying to behold.

The High Priest backed up a step, casting around as if looking for allies, and finding none. Kathrael wondered if the rest of the senior priests had truly fled, or were merely in hiding elsewhere in the temple. Seeming to realize that he was on his own, the old eunuch scrambled backward, trying to get to the door without turning his back on Senovo as the shape-shifter continued his inexorable approach.

Favian's fingers slid free from hers, and he moved silently forward to stop the old priest's retreat with a firm hand in the center of his back. Hameen and the Priestesses of Avlan closed in from one side, and the hollow-eyed acolytes and novices closed in from the other, hemming him in. The Rhytheeri priest stood rooted in place, trembling from head to foot, as Senovo came to a stop one short step away, his eyes still blazing with inner light.

It was Sephira who spoke, however.

"Leave the temple and do not return, old man. Your reign is over," she said. She raised her voice, addressing the acolytes and novices. "The rest of you—join us, or don't. The old order is falling. The new order offers you freedom and self-determination... but you will have to fight for it first."

The slaves and former slaves looked at each other, communicating silently, it seemed. After a few moments, the boy who had addressed Senovo earlier said, "We choose to join you, Elder Sister. We will stand with the Wolf Patron."

Senovo's gaze did not waver from the High Priest's. "Are there others remaining in the temple who are loyal to this man?" he asked.

"Most of the senior priests ran away when Terrek started yelling that you were here, *lupiandas*," said the boy. "There may still be one or two hiding in the back. There are other acolytes and novices back there who were too scared to come out, as well."

Senovo nodded. "Take us to them. The senior priests must leave, but we will offer the others the same choice we offered you, to join us, or vacate the temple peacefully."

The youngster swallowed. "All right. But the priests who ran away may already have gone running to the city guard for help."

Sephira scoffed. "The city guard will shortly find that they have other things to worry about. That's assuming they're even willing to brave the gangs' presence to come here in the first place."

High Priestess Zandreen, Kathrael knew, was busy behind the scenes, organizing the underground for... whatever Inga seemed to think was going to happen tomorrow. Kathrael was still skeptical that such a large, disorganized group would be able to move that quickly, but Sephira seemed confident that the king's guard would be too preoccupied to descend on them in force. Besides, they were already committed to their course of action at the temples, and there was, at this point, no real direction to go other than forward.

Senovo stared down the former High Priest of the Temple of Naloth. "Leave," he commanded. "There is no longer a place for you here."

The man seemed frozen in place for a beat, but the priestesses opened a path for him toward the main hallway and the doors beyond. He backed away, his eyes roving over them wildly. Before he reached the entrance to the altar room, he lifted a shaking finger to point at them, or perhaps at Senovo.

"You are all traitors to the natural order of things. This outrage will not stand," he said, trying to claw back a modicum of dignity, and failing.

"Yes," Senovo said. "It will."

When he was gone, Senovo closed his eyes for a moment, and when he opened them again, they were no longer glowing. One of the Sisters had retrieved his robes after the wolf shed them, and proffered them hesitantly. He waved her off.

"Come. Let us find anyone who may be hiding, and then we will move on to the temple of Deresta."

"Senovo?" Favian asked in a tentative tone, and Kathrael could hear his worry for his beloved mentor behind the single word.

But Senovo only stilled for a beat, then shook his head and shifted, dropping to all fours and sniffing the air. The new additions to their group took a few nervous steps back, but when the animal made no threatening move, the boy who seemed to be their unofficial leader gestured to the entrance at the far end of the room and led the way to search for stragglers.

⚜

When they emerged from the temple an hour or so later, it was to find a crowd gathered outside, drawn by the commotion of fleeing priests. Kathrael knew Favian had done a shockingly good job over the past few weeks at drawing spectators to his and Ayala's heckling of the Priests' Guild — especially here at the temple of Naloth, where his debates with Hameen provided surprisingly intellectual entertainment for those who cared to stop and watch.

Some of those same people were here now, and the buzz of conversation swelled as people pointed at Favian surrounded by the red-robed priestesses. The murmurs turned to shouts and cries of surprise as the first people noticed the wolf walking with them — shock traveling through the crowd like a wave.

Favian gestured sharply to Hameen to follow him, and the two stepped forward before the surprise could transform into panic.

"Peace!" he called, as loudly as he could with his raspy voice. "Many of you know me, and you have seen me speak with Novice Hameen on the subject of religion. Today, we are no longer opponents. We stand united."

His eyes flicked to their new ally, who cleared his throat and took a deep, centering breath before speaking.

"My brother speaks the truth. The Wolf Patron has returned to Rhyth. The city stands poised on the precipice of change. The downtrodden are rising up from under the boot-heel of the rich and powerful, and we must all prepare. I entreat you to join us, and stand against the forces of hate, terror, and cruelty."

Kathrael felt a small frisson race up her arms as someone in the crowd raised a fist and cheered, joined by others until *dozens* of onlookers were yelling and whistling their support. She thought she saw Sephira's chin rise and a small smile of pride hook one corner of her full lips.

Favian raised a hand, and after a few moments, the noise died down enough that his hoarse voice could be heard over it.

"Come with us! Lend your support to the Wolf Patron as we march on the other temples and cast out the corruption at their hearts! *Who's with us?*"

The cheer rose again, and Kath could see the crowd swelling as more passersby were drawn by the sounds of excitement. Her heart started pounding against the cage of her ribs as she was overwhelmed by the feeling of being at the birth of something that would grow and grow until it was unstoppable.

Sephira stepped up to Favian's side. "Come, citizens!" she called. "On to the temple of Deresta!"

The five of them—Sephira, Favian, Hameen, Kathrael, and the wolf—started toward the next temple at the head of a column of priests, acolytes, priestesses, and common folk, which continued to grow as they walked. Much like the funeral procession the day before, it seemed that the citizens of Rhyth had merely been waiting for someone to offer direction, and were eager to finally take some kind of action—*any* kind of action—to wrest back control of their lives, and their city. By the time they reached the temple of Deresta, the group had grown from dozens to a couple of hundred, at least.

It quickly became apparent that some of the fugitives from Naloth's temple had run straight to the other temples to warn the occupants about what was coming for them, because they arrived to find the doors of the building flung open. Two acolytes and a novice awaited them. When they saw the wolf, their eyes went wide and they dropped to the ground, abasing themselves.

Favian and Sephira moved forward almost as one, and knelt to urge them to their feet with gentle words. The novice was weeping openly.

"Is it true? Is it really true?" he asked over and over.

Hameen came up and grasped the young priest's upper arms, his own voice sounding a bit unsteady as he answered, "If we are dreaming, Brother Vellen, then it's the same dream."

Vellen choked on a surge of strong emotion and nodded, clasping Hameen's arms tightly in return.

Hameen patted him and let him take his own weight. "Have the ones with cause to fear fled before us already?" he asked.

Vellen nodded and swallowed hard. "I think so, yes. At first, they didn't believe it, but little Terrek came sprinting through here, crying that he's seen the wolf with his own eyes as he was hiding outside the altar room, and he'd come to rip out the High Priest's throat. He was so pale that you couldn't help but believe him."

Sephira spoke up, her tone wry. "Never fear. The former High Priest's throat remains quite intact. One assumes it has been tempered to the consistency of solid iron over the years, with all the lies and vitriol that have passed through it on the way to his lips."

Vellen looked at Sephira's red-cloaked figure with a combination of wariness and confusion.

Hameen cleared his throat. "Brother Vellen, this is my father's sister, Priestess Sephira of the Sisters of Avlan. The Sisters are our allies in the coming fight, and they have, I fear, been stauncher supporters of the Old Gods than we have been."

Vellen blinked, and after a bare moment of hesitation, dipped his chin in a gesture of respect. "Elder Sister," he said haltingly. His wide eyes traveled back to the wolf, which still stood unmoving by Kathrael's side. "How... may I serve?"

"Show us where those who did not flee may be hiding, and then join us with your fellows who are true to the gods' will and the people of Rhyth," Sephira said.

They repeated the process of clearing the temple and gathering up the acolytes and novices who either had been slaves or had shown themselves to be allies of the slaves. Meanwhile, Hameen, Vellen, and several of the Sisters of Avlan remained outside with the crowd, leading them in prayer before lifting their voices in song.

The simple melody continued as the procession pressed on toward the Temple of Utarr. The sound of singing and chanting drew even more people as they walked. Kathrael's sense of watching something grow from a tiny seed into something vast and powerful intensified as they arrived at the last of the temples dedicated to the Old Gods.

The temple of Utarr relied less on stone and more on wood, as befitted the goddess of bounty and growing things. This, Favian had informed her, was the place where Senovo had been held in service until the pain of his castration had shocked him into his first transformation. The wolf had killed four priests outright, and mortally wounded a fifth before escaping into the wildlands beyond the city.

Somewhat to Kathrael's surprise, the wolf halted a short distance away from the structure and shifted. Senovo straightened in human form, and this time he accepted the white robe and sandals that one of the priestesses had been carrying for him.

With a shock, Kath realized that he intended to confront his former owners in human form — assuming they had not already fled. He turned to her and Favian, his expression set in stony lines that did not suit his kind face.

"Stay here," he told them, his voice as hard as his features.

Next to her, Favian scowled. "Not bloody likely," he said.

Senovo lifted an eyebrow in surprise, as though he had not expected open defiance from such a quarter. "I have no wish for an audience, Favian," he said, modulating his voice somewhat.

Kathrael could sense the stubborn set of Favian's jaw; she didn't even need to look.

"Too bad," he ground out. "At some point, I'm going to have to face Andoc and Carivel. It'll be bad enough when they learn I was in on your plan to ditch them today. If you think I'm telling them that I let you return to this house of poison alone, you're not nearly as smart as I'd come to think."

"I can't disagree," Kathrael put in. Deciding that action was the quickest way to break the unexpected stalemate, she gathered in Favian and the Sisters with a look. "Come on, then."

They started toward the stone steps leading up to the door, forcing Senovo to either join them or be left standing outside the entrance. He gave them a shuttered look, and she thought perhaps he was coming to some kind of realization about the changes the last few months had wrought in the boy he'd raised and come to think of as a son. His chest rose and fell, his expression going blank in the instant before he turned and resumed his place at the front of the small group.

The temple doors were shut, and no acolytes were present to admit them. Senovo's hands closed around the handles, white-knuckled, and the doors swung open easily under his touch. No surprise, since temple doors were not made to be locked or barred shut. Supposedly, the temple was open to all. The architecture reflected that, even if the reality was not necessarily so straightforward.

It was dark and quiet inside as the doors swung shut behind them, muffling the sound of singing and chanting coming from outside. Kathrael moved forward, cautious, waiting for her good eye to adjust to the change in light. A few moments later, she could make out lamplight coming from ahead.

The altar room contained a granite slab similar to all the other altars Kathrael had seen, but where stone and metal dominated the central spaces in the other temples, Utarr's altar room was dominated by wood and woven wicker. Evergreen boughs formed into the shapes of animals and geometric patterns hung from the walls, and live plants in clay urns reached toward small openings in the ceiling, which let in narrow shafts of natural light. The sound of trickling water reached her ears.

Utarr's temple was always my favorite, Vesh observed philosophically. *Too bad it's run by arseholes, just like all the others.*

A man in High Priest's robes stood in the center of the altar room, his hands folded into his wide sleeves. Senovo stopped a few steps inside the door. Kathrael, Favian, and the others filed into the room behind him, spreading out to form a line flanking him.

The High Priest of the Temple of Utarr was a eunuch who appeared to be in his late forties. His hair was still dark, except for twin streaks of gray that swept back from his temples to the tight plait of hair at the back of his skull. His bearing was upright, lacking the weak, flabby appearance that afflicted so many of the older priests.

No fear was visible in his expression, though there was something haunted hiding behind his dark eyes. Senovo regarded him, and Kathrael could see tension in the line of his shoulders.

"Shen," the wolf-shifter greeted, breaking the silence.

The High Priest of Utarr lifted his chin. "Senovo. So you truly have returned. The priests from the other temples urged me to flee, but I had to stay and see for myself if it was really you."

"And now that you have seen?" Senovo asked.

Shen drew himself straighter. "Now that I have seen, I will tell you to abandon this ill-considered quest before blood flows through the streets of Rhyth like floodwater — and pray to the gods that it is not already too late."

"It was *too late* long before now. That Rhyth will crack down the middle is unavoidable. Now, we must concern ourselves with what will be rebuilt from the rubble. The mob chanting outside of your door will not rest until corruption has been rooted from the temples."

Shen remained carved from stone, immovable. "A mob does not dictate to the Priests' Guild, Senovo."

"I would not like to see you put that belief to the test." Senovo's chest rose and fell on a deep breath. "Particularly since there is another way. When I was held in service here, we were not friends, but you were never cruel. Join us. Lend your support to our cause and march with us on the Temple of Deimok. Your enemies are not the common people outside. The true enemies are those who would murder innocents in the name of religion, and those who would treat human beings as chattel."

A look of hard anger crossed Shen's face. "Those who would murder? And what of the murderer standing before me now? What of the escaped slave masquerading as a barbarian High Priest? There is a reason the slave-born are not allowed to rise above the rank of novice, and I am looking upon it *right now*." He paused, breathing hard. "You could have had your freedom, Senovo. You could have had a place here. Who knows? As a shape-shifter, perhaps you could even have risen above your station, given time."

Next to Kathrael, Favian was practically trembling with the urge to speak out. She clamped a hand on his forearm to forestall him, knowing that this was for Senovo to answer, and no one else.

"Risen above my station and given tacit approval to the same sort of inhumane treatment I received as a slave, you mean?" Senovo replied. "Once upon a time, you disapproved of such treatment—even if you did so silently. Now you are a High Priest... or rather, you were, until today. Is that what you have done, Shen? Handed over your morals, in exchange for power and wealth?"

Shen's face closed off. "You know nothing of my morals, or this temple."

Kathrael glanced to the side and saw a muscle at the corner of Senovo's jaw tighten.

"If you still sanction the buying and selling of children... if you still oversee the mutilation of the unwilling... then I know everything I need to know. So I ask you again, what is your choice? Will you join the cause of freedom and dignity, or will you leave this place, never to return?"

Shen scoffed, a choked noise. His voice was harsh when he replied. "*Dignity*? Shall I walk out that door and join hands with red-robed heretics who make a mockery of our religion?" His hands were by his sides now, his fists clenched as his passion flared. "You claim to stand against the foreign god Deimok, but who do you think has stood against the cult before now? The Priests' Guild utilizes slaves because otherwise, it would whither and *die*! Without slaves, the number of acolytes would be far too low to maintain the ranks! And as those ranks shriveled, we would be overrun by the foreign religion."

Senovo looked at him with something like pity. "You are wrong."

"I am *not* wrong! Unless you'd prefer to leave our faith in the hands of unbonded whores who have stolen some bastardized version of the religious histories from the gods only know what source."

Sarcasm grew heavy in Shen's voice, and Kathrael could swear she heard Favian let out an *actual growl* beside her.

Shen wasn't finished, though. "You asked me to choose between fleeing like a whipped dog, and joining a misguided cause that will bring ruin on the city. I choose neither. This is *my* temple, and you are the ones who will leave."

"Saying a thing does not make it so," Senovo replied. "And you are playing a dangerous game by defying the will of the people, now that the sleeping beast has awakened."

Shen's lip curled into a snarl. "Am I indeed? What danger is there for me here in Utarr's sanctuary, *Gifted One*? Will you transform into a beast and rend me limb from limb, like you did my predecessor?"

Senovo went very still. "No. I will not."

"Then what possible motivation could I have to flee into the arms of a mob?"

There was a moment of tense silence. Kathrael realized that they had reached the limits of what the Wolf Patron was willing to do to this man he had once known.

"Favian," she said, "take the others and clear the rest of the temple. First, though, is that fire-starting powder?" She indicated a pedestal next to the altar, which held a stone bowl of brown powder.

Good gods, Kath, Vesh whispered with a hint of awe. *Have you been hiding a ruthless streak from me all this time?*

Had she been? She wasn't sure.

Ruthless? Maybe, she allowed. *Practical? Definitely.*

Favian's gaze locked with hers, and understanding dawned in his face, followed by shock, and then a predatory gleam that would have looked more at home behind Ithric's gold-flecked eyes. He brushed past Shen without giving the man a second glance and lifted a pinch of the powder, sniffing it.

"It is." He picked up the bowl and brought it back, handing it to her before turning to the Sisters. "Come on. Let's see if anyone in the back cares to join us."

"Check all the rooms carefully," she admonished.

He nodded and kissed her forehead. "We will. Don't worry."

Shen watched the exchange with growing alarm, and Kathrael casually drew a dagger from one of the hidden sheaths in her skirt—not threatening, but letting Shen know that she was not suddenly vulnerable now that she and Senovo were alone with him.

Cornered animals could be dangerous, after all.

Shen's dark eyes flickered between them with growing alarm as Kath moved to stand shoulder to shoulder with the Wolf Patron. His worried gaze settled on the stone bowl in her hand, and she knew he was thinking of all the wood and greenery surrounding them.

"Will you sanction this new outrage as well, traitor?" he asked Senovo.

Senovo tilted his head. "It is not mine to sanction. I am not the driving force behind this uprising. I am merely its messenger."

Something kindled in Kathrael's chest at his words. Some new piece of understanding in the complicated puzzle that was her history with the Wolf Patron. She glanced at him quickly, but his attention was still fixed on his old acquaintance.

The wary standoff lasted until the others returned to the altar room with a gaggle of youngsters and three novices in tow. All of them wore dazed, wide-eyed expressions. Several clasped drawstring bags, presumably filled with their meager belongings.

"This is everyone," Favian assured her.

She nodded. "Take them outside, please," she told the Sisters. When the sound of the large doors opening and closing reached them a few moments later, Kathrael turned her attention back to Shen. "You asked earlier what possible motivation you could have for leaving. But as you see now, that is a very simple question to answer."

She moved along the wall until she came to the first piece of the woven evergreen wall art—a downward facing triangle symbolizing female power. Being careful not to spill any of the fine powder on herself, she tossed the contents of the bowl onto the interwoven branches of fine green needles. The dust coated the lower half of the wall hanging in light gray, and some of the powder drifted down to settle on the planks of the hardwood floor beneath.

From the corner of her good eye, she saw Shen make an aborted move toward her, only to find his way blocked by a solid blond-haired figure and a slender, dark-haired one.

"What kind of priests are you," Shen hissed, *"to stand by while a temple is willfully destroyed?"*

Favian's reply was as bland as his ravaged voice would allow. "A wise man once taught me that a temple is not — as I had previously believed it to be — necessarily a *building*."

"Leave this place, Shen," Senovo said, sounding suddenly weary. "Or don't. Just realize that the events in which we are embroiled are not some sort of random happenstance with no foundation beneath them. They were inevitable — a sure and inescapable reaction to what has come before."

"The only inescapable thing is the bloodshed and death that will soon descend on Rhyth," Shen snapped. "I will content myself with the knowledge that you will be at the center of it, and pray that the gods' judgment will come surely and swiftly."

"No doubt it will be so," Senovo said. "Though I have tried to avoid my destiny, the gods' hands have been behind this from the very start."

Kathrael moved to a stone plinth a little further along the wall. An oil lamp burned cheerfully on its flat surface, held safely away from the wooden walls and floor. She wrapped her sleeve around the hand that wasn't holding her dagger and picked it up, the heat from it seeping through to warm her palm even through the fabric.

Standing well clear, she tossed the lamp onto the floor at the edge of the gray stain left by the fire-starting powder. The oil from the reservoir splattered, forming a messy puddle, and the flame from the wick danced across its surface, orange and blue. When the expanding edge of the spill reached the powder, there was a loud *whoosh*. Fire exploded up the wall. The woven evergreen branches sputtered and crackled, sending new gouts of flame toward the rafters.

"Come," she said, watching the flames spread with startling speed. "The people outside are waiting for us."

EIGHTEEN

Favian kept a hand on Senovo's elbow as they exited the Temple of Utarr, smoke and heat at their backs. He wasn't so far gone in his own troubles that he didn't worry about his mentor's possible reaction to watching this place—where he'd been hurt and degraded so badly as a youngster—go up in flames.

The three of them passed through the doors and into the chilly late winter light, where the crowd was still singing. Senovo seemed steady enough, but he did turn and stare for a long time as smoke began to rise from the roof.

Favian wondered if Shen had exercised the better part of valor and escaped out the back. He hoped so. Whatever the former High Priest stood to lose in the coming struggle, it wasn't worth dying for.

Senovo took a deep, centering breath, though the air around them was already growing heavy with wood smoke. To Favian's mild surprise, he turned to the crowd with purpose, slipping free of Favian's light hold on his arm.

They were still standing at the top of the stone steps leading up to the temple entrance. They would need to move away from the burning building soon, but for now, it was still safe. Senovo raised a hand, and the chanting faded away.

"People of Rhyth." His smooth voice rolled over the assembled crowd, which had grown shockingly large while they were inside. "The old order is falling. What will follow is up to us. Come with me to the Temple of Deimok. Let us show the cult what peaceful revolution looks like. Let us show them that love and courage are more powerful than fear and violence."

A cheer rose, the noise gradually giving way to a new chant. *"Wolf Patron! Wolf Patron! Wolf Patron!"*

Senovo started down the steps, Favian and Kathrael falling in behind him. The crowd parted for them, hands reaching out to touch them as they walked past. It was surreal. Favian glanced at Kath's face. She didn't meet his gaze, but her expression clearly asked, *am I dreaming?*

Clad only in robes and sandals, Senovo should have been freezing in the winter chill, but he didn't appear to feel it and showed no sign of changing back into animal form. Favian, on the other hand, felt chilled to the bone as they moved slowly through the assembly chanting for Senovo, and led the crowd away from the flaming building behind them.

Leading them toward the Temple of Deimok, and whatever awaited them there.

It wasn't far to walk. Only a few streets away from the other temples, in fact—and a few streets more from there to the palace itself. Favian pushed the thought away. What was coming for him would come regardless. If he spent the hours remaining to him focused on how little time he had left, it would be a waste. He would not be able to do the things that had to be done.

Deimok's temple was very different than the temples dedicated to the Old Gods. It gleamed white, the walls constructed of polished marble imported from the continent—no doubt paid for by a mere fraction of the untold riches belonging to the Emperor of Alyrios. The way the building seemed to clash with its surroundings, drawing attention by virtue of its gaudy splendor, offended him.

To be honest, Favian had half-expected them to run straight into a mob of cult members intent on a battle, even though he knew intellectually that Kathrael and Senovo were both perfectly safe until tomorrow. The idea that they might be harmed at some point after the events in his vision was another thing that Favian was pushing firmly down and away, into the dark space behind his ribcage.

If that happened, he would be powerless to do anything about it, or even to know about it unless he somehow met them in the afterlife. Much better to simply work on the assumption that they would be safe, and their quest, successful.

Indeed, his worries about leading the crowd behind them straight into a clash with cult members turned out to be unfounded. The open space around the temple was strangely deserted. Or perhaps not so strangely. As he watched, figures armed with crossbows appeared around the edges of the plaza. Their attention was not on the approaching crowd, though. Rather, they were guarding the entrances to the square and watching the doors of the temple for anyone who might emerge.

The rebels were here, and they were armed—poised to protect the common people who had joined the march on the temples.

Something brushed his hand, and a moment later, Kathrael's fingers tangled with his, squeezing *hard*. He squeezed back.

As was the case in many of Rhyth's plazas, there was a raised platform in the center of the open space that might be used for anything from official announcements to executions. Two figures mounted it—one wearing red robes, and one wearing laborer's clothing. Favian recognized Zandreen and the middle-aged man who had frequently presided over the meetings in the catacombs. Zandreen caught Senovo's eye and gestured him to approach.

"Come," he said, his voice pitched for Favian and Kathrael's ears alone.

The three of them climbed the steps leading up to the platform and turned, looking over the sea of faces spread out before them. With a jolt, Favian realized that they were starting to lose the light. The afternoon seemed to have passed as a blur.

"People of Rhyth," Zandreen called, her strong voice cutting through the noise of people talking and muttering. "Tonight, we gather in joy and celebration of change. For too long, fear has ruled our city. No more! This evening, we gather secure in the knowledge of strength in numbers. Tonight, we rejoice! The Wolf Patron has returned to us! By following him, you are unlocking your shackles and emerging into the light of freedom."

Kathrael was still clutching Favian's hand like a lifeline. He could feel her trembling with emotion, so close to fulfilling the vow she had made half a lifetime ago.

Below them, the crowd was roaring approval. Favian saw that several of the armed men had approached the platform while he was distracted, and were keeping the mass of people from getting too close. He recognized some of the guards as members of Qaden's gang.

Zandreen faded back a few steps to join the rebel leader, brushing a hand over Kath's arm as she did so. Kath's fingers tightened in Favian's convulsively, before she took a deep breath and very deliberately released her grip on him. She stepped up to the edge of the platform.

"In the morning," she called in a clear voice, "we will march on the palace and make our demands known to the king, under the combined banner of Deresta and Utarr. The goddesses have made it known that, come tomorrow, Rhyth will no longer suffer under the grip of corruption and the yoke of slavery. They have sent not one, but two shape-shifters to lead us, and our victory is guaranteed."

Favian felt a lump rise in his throat and try to choke him. His own prophetic vision had shown no such thing. It had shown that they would march on the palace, nothing more. He could only hope that Inga's odd insistence about the support of the goddesses and the king's ultimate fall was accurate.

But—once again, fretting about it was a waste of his emotional resources, which were frighteningly limited at the moment. Either way, he would not be here to see the outcome.

Excited muttering spread through the crowd on the heels of Kathrael's words. After a moment, she continued. "Tonight, we show the Cult of Deimok our numbers, and our determination. Tomorrow, we show the Alyrion puppet king our might."

Again, cheering and applause erupted around the plaza. The priests and priestesses who were scattered throughout the large assemblage guided the crowd back into song, a multitude of voices melding into one, as more and more people joined in.

Favian spared a long look at the shining Temple of Deimok, which dominated the far end of the square. The doors remained firmly closed, the flicker of torchlight shining through the high, narrow windows the only indication of the presence of life within. He guessed that those trapped inside were probably priests, not cult members.

He suspected they were terrified at being surrounded by the devotees of the religion they had tried to crush—and not without cause.

Around the square, people were lighting braziers and bonfires to hold back the chill of evening. Here and there, he could see others moving through the crowd with baskets of flatbread and skins of wine acquired from the-gods-only-knew-where. Movement next to him caught the corner of his eye, and he turned to see Zandreen gesturing them to get down from the platform.

The line of armed men were still acting as a barrier between them and the crowd, dissuading the curious and the excited from getting too close. The grizzle-haired rebel leader ushered them toward a corner of the square that was quieter, sheltered under an overhang. He and Zandreen exchanged a few words with Kath and Senovo before turning and disappearing into the crowd. Favian still didn't know the leader's name, and it niggled at him—a small worry to help keep the larger worries at bay, he supposed.

He was just steeling himself to enquire about Senovo's wellbeing without inadvertently giving away his own state of mind when a disturbance off to their right had the informal line of bodyguards stiffening and raising their weapons in warning. With a jolt, Favian recognized Ithric walking next to a tall man dressed in rags, who moved with a very familiar limp.

"Let them through!" he and Kath called at nearly the same instant.

The guards looked back, confused, but made way for the newcomers nonetheless. A moment later, Ithric had one arm around Favian and the other around Kath, pulling them both into a rough embrace.

"You made it," he said, sounding a bit awestruck. "You *did* it. I... wasn't quite sure what to expect when you got here. But I have to say, I didn't expect *this*."

Favian didn't have a ready reply, since he was every bit as gobsmacked by the size of the crowd as Ithric. Mostly, he just focused on the feel of Kath and Ithric's arms around him, and tried not to collapse against them and cling like a desperate child.

Kathrael made a choked sound halfway between a laugh and a sob. "What can I say? Apparently, the gods really are on our side."

A few steps away, Ithric's raggedly dressed companion pulled back his hood as he descended on Senovo. Andoc's hair and beard were unkempt; his expression a bit wild. He clasped Senovo's shoulder hard with one hand, their eyes locking.

"Tell me you're all right," he said in a tight voice. "We saw the smoke earlier. Was that—?"

"A final piece of the past, crumbling to ash." Senovo's reply was hoarse, but steady. "We are all unharmed."

Favian knew that wasn't the real question Andoc had been asking, but after continuing his intense scrutiny of Senovo's face for another few heartbeats, the Draebardi chief relaxed and loosened his tight grip on his bondmate's shoulder. Senovo's eyes flicked to Favian as he and Kathrael straightened away from Ithric's embrace. Andoc's eyes followed the tiny movement.

"Favian," he said. "Merciful gods. I don't know whether to hug you or shake you until your teeth rattle for enabling this madness."

He belied the words by crossing and immediately pulling Favian into a crushing, one-armed embrace, his walking stick clasped in his other hand for balance. Favian swallowed another rush of dangerous emotion and squeezed him back. "Andoc. It's good to see you. Where's Carivel?"

Andoc released him with a huff. "Still at the stables. I sent Ithric's little friend Mouse off with a message letting her know what you idiots had done, but that you were back and all appeared to be in one piece."

Thoughts of Mouse inevitably brought with them thoughts of Ciryl and Ayala. Favian managed a nod.

Andoc turned to Kathrael. "Well. It looks like you're about to fulfill that vow of yours after all," he said. "I've been talking to Ithric—"

"He talked to me once he got done shouting at me, anyway," Ithric interrupted.

"—and he introduced me to your High Priestess, along with some of the other leaders here," Andoc finished. "Zandreen made it clear that we'll be moving on the palace tomorrow morning. I have to say, I was skeptical about the tactical wisdom of that decision until you arrived with what looks to be half of the city in tow."

Senovo came closer, the five of them forming a rough half-circle.

Ithric caught their eyes one at a time, intent. "This isn't the only gathering tonight. Groups of slaves and sympathizers are massing elsewhere in the city, as well—armed with crossbows and ready to move. This is going to happen. I don't think we could stop it now if we tried, to be honest."

"No," Favian agreed quietly, thinking of the dream. "You couldn't."

Ithric nodded. "Anyway, first thing in the morning we'll need to head out and gather the various groups together to march on the palace."

"Actually," Favian said around the heavy ache in his chest, "you, Kathrael, and Senovo will need to head out. I'll be staying here with Sephira and Zandreen to help lead this group."

Kath frowned. "Favian, *no*. I don't like the idea of us splitting up like that. The Sisters and the freed acolytes from the temples can take care of this group. You should come with us."

He forced a smile, knowing that it probably looked off. "Sorry, but I can't. Like I told you—I've seen it already. I'm with this group. Don't worry, Kath. It will be fine."

The ache in his chest grew sharper.

"What would happen if you just ignored what you saw in the dream and left with us anyway?" Ithric asked, sounding both unhappy and genuinely curious.

Favian shrugged, trying to project nonchalance. "No idea. I suppose something unforeseen would happen that forced me to stay behind. The way I see it, since we're trying to achieve what I saw in the vision anyway, it seems foolish to risk going against it."

Kathrael exhaled through her nose, clearly still worried. "I suppose," she allowed. "Just promise to be careful, Favian, *please*."

"I will if you will," Favian shot back, assuaging his guilt over the lie with the sure and certain knowledge that the odds of Kathrael and Ithric being *careful* tomorrow were basically nonexistent.

"Fair enough," Ithric said, the cagey look in his eyes pretty well confirming Favian's suspicions.

Ithric would do his best to protect Kathrael and Senovo, Favian was sure, and they would do their best to protect Ithric. At the end of the day, however, they were still marching at the front of a largely untrained army of common people heading into battle with both the king's guard and a bunch of angry religious fanatics.

Andoc had been watching the exchange. "Come on," he said into the lull. "Let's find someplace where we can be a bit more comfortable overnight. This looks to be turning into an all-night gathering, but we should still try to get some rest if we can."

"Agreed," Ithric said, and the others nodded.

This corner of the plaza was bounded by two-story buildings with a shared portico running along their fronts. They weren't shops — indeed, Favian couldn't have said what purpose they served during the daylight hours. Now, though, they appeared dark and empty.

The one nearest them had an open entryway with no door. Andoc and Ithric led the way inside. A central corridor led deeper into the building, with locked doors spaced at intervals on either side. Light from the bonfires in the plaza barely sufficed to illuminate their way, and Kathrael kept a hand on Favian's arm, letting him guide her.

The hallway wasn't long. It opened into an atrium — a much smaller and less ornate version of those favored by the rich families of Rhyth within their extravagant homes. As his eyes adjusted, Favian could make out a couple of stone benches and some potted plants in the reflected starlight coming from the opening in the roof above. The plants appeared rather droopy and pitiful after the cold snap a few days ago. Favian could sympathize with them.

"This will work, I think," Andoc said, hobbling over to a brazier already laid with logs and rummaging through his tattered beggar's clothing. Favian saw a spark fly as he struck a flint, and then a second. On his fourth attempt, the kindling at the base of the brazier caught, and he nursed the fire to life.

The walls of the building muffled the singing and chanting coming from outside, turning it into low background noise, rather than something over which it was difficult to speak. When the fire was burning cheerfully, they all stood around it for a few moments, warming themselves.

"Won't Carivel have trouble finding us in here, though?" Favian asked.

Andoc shook his head. "She won't be here tonight." He didn't look happy about it. "She sent a message with Mouse earlier. Apparently she has plans for tomorrow morning and doesn't want to raise any suspicions before then."

"What kind of plans?" Kathrael asked.

"She didn't specify," Andoc replied.

Favian almost asked, *will she be safe*, before thinking better of it. She would be no more or less safe than any of the rest of them in this ridiculously dangerous situation. No doubt Andoc and Senovo were already painfully aware of that fact. There was no point in drawing more attention to it.

Andoc's eyes moved to him. "I'm afraid this isn't exactly the reunion I'd envisioned, Favian. But I'm still very glad to see you—more or less—in one piece. Frella asked me to tell you that she loves you, and she's considering becoming a priestess now, after hearing Ithric's report about the Sisters of Avlan."

A combined surge of fondness and homesickness threatened to further chip away at Favian's thin armor of numbness. He huffed out a breath as he pictured his baby sister, with her honey-colored curls and sky blue eyes.

Gods. He was never going to see Frella again, was he?

"I'm not sure even the devotees of the Trickster god are quite up to dealing with Frella as an acolyte," he managed.

In a week or two, when they returned home, one of their three guardians would have to break the news to her that her brother had been killed. Favian was the last blood relation she had left in Draebard. And if anything happened to Andoc, Carivel, and Senovo tomorrow…

He shoved the thought aside with considerable difficulty.

Andoc smiled, unaware of his inner turmoil. "Oh, I don't know. She might fit right in." He cleared his throat. "Also, Limdya asked me to tell you that she misses you, and that she and Dalon are planning on tying the knot after the spring equinox."

"Good for them," Ithric opined. "I don't think anyone saw that particular match coming, but somehow, it works."

Kathrael arched a brow at the Draebardi chieftain. "So, I have to ask. Have you really been posing as a beggar in the temple district these last few days?"

Andoc shrugged.

The look she was giving him was hard to decipher. "How has the trade been?" she asked.

He snorted. "Well, I probably wouldn't starve, but let's just say it's a good thing we brought enough coin with us from Draebard to pay for our stay here and our passage back. Carivel's doing a bit better on the *earning a livelihood* front, I think. Though even in the royal stables, an apprentice's pay isn't exactly what you'd call generous."

Ithric's tone was wry. "No real reason to be generous, when you can simply bring in slave labor if the freefolk you're employing try to complain about the pay."

"After tomorrow, that will no longer be an issue," Kathrael said, her voice growing hard.

Andoc met her gaze with a tilt of his chin. "I must say, what you three have accomplished here is truly stunning, Kathrael."

Ithric snorted and waved a hand. "Eh. The groundwork was already laid. It only needed a shape-shifter, a religious rabble-rouser with no sense of self-preservation, and a beautiful, mysterious masked woman to set a spark to the tinder."

Senovo had been noticeably silent as they spoke. At the mention of shape-shifters, Andoc turned to study him.

"Perhaps we should try to get some rest now," he suggested. "Tomorrow will be a very long day, regardless of how much the gods favor us."

Ithric stirred. "Let me go out and see if I can find some bread and wine for us first. I doubt these three have had anything since this morning."

"I'll go with you," Kathrael put in. "I can help carry everything back."

Favian stifled a sigh. It was painfully obvious that they were throwing him to the proverbial wolf, in hopes that Andoc or Senovo could get him to talk about the things he was refusing to talk about with *them*.

Traitors.

NINETEEN

Favian hated the fact that circumstances had made this reunion with the people who were like family to him stilted and awkward—nothing at all like what he would have pictured, before the disaster at the docks. Before his vision. Under no circumstances could Favian afford for the others to find out the secret he was keeping, however. To deflect his guardians' attention, he took a breath and went on the offensive.

"How are you doing, Senovo?" he asked, once the others had left—trying to minimize the painful rasp of his voice as the words emerged. "You've been very quiet."

As he'd hoped, Andoc's attention remained largely focused on the white-robed figure standing next to him. Senovo, on the other hand, shot Favian a look that said he knew exactly what his apprentice was trying to do.

"I might ask the same of you, Little Brother," he replied, sounding tired.

There was an uncomfortable beat of silence. Andoc huffed and limped over to drop down on one of the benches, leaning his walking stick against the edge as he narrowed his eyes at them. "Senovo, I blame you for the way he turned out. Your hard-headedness has clearly rubbed off on him over the years."

Senovo continued to warm his hands by the brazier. "He was already hard-headed. Just ask Carivel."

Favian felt his cheeks color, and tried to glare at them.

"And meanwhile," Andoc continued, "neither of you have answered the question."

"I'm fine," Favian muttered. "Just tense. Like you said, tomorrow's going to be a long day."

"You nearly died, Favian," Andoc said.

Favian made a noise that tried to be a snort of dismissal, but came out sounding ugly and bitter. "I can't die." *Until tomorrow*, he failed to add. "The vision hasn't come to pass yet. I was perfectly safe the whole time."

He didn't like the way Andoc was watching him with perceptive brown eyes.

"Other people died," his guardian said.

Favian jerked around, turning his back on both of them and taking a couple of steps away. He was breathing heavily, his congested lungs aching with each painful inhalation.

"What do you want me to say?" he ground out, unable to keep the words from escaping. "That I got good people—*friends*—killed because I did something stupid, and that I had to listen to the screams of innocent people being burned alive? That I feel like shit and the guilt is eating me alive? *Is that what you want to hear? Well, fine, I said it.*"

Panic started to crawl up his throat as he heard the words pouring from his mouth. He clamped his jaw shut to stop the flood. His hands were shaking. He clenched them into fists, hiding them from view in the wide sleeves of his ochre robes.

Long fingers closed on his shoulder, and he jumped nervously at the touch.

"Favian," Senovo said.

Oddly, that much-loved voice, laced with sadness and regret, was enough to help him regain control.

"Look," he whispered. "Don't... make me have this conversation right now. Please? Not when I need to be focused on what we're doing in the morning."

The hand on his shoulder slid away.

"We *will* talk about this... after we both fulfill our duties to the people of Rhyth." Senovo's tone brooked no argument.

Favian nodded, still facing away, relief and pain flooding him in equal measure. "Yeah. Sure. Tomorrow. We'll talk tomorrow."

Andoc sighed. "Stubborn bastards, the pair of you. Favian, sit down before you fall down, and for the gods' sakes, eat something when the others bring it back. Senovo, since you obviously don't want to talk either, just... tell me what you need right now."

Favian took a moment to make sure that his eyes were dry and his expression more or less under control. A ripple of movement caught the corner of his eye. When he turned back to the others, the wolf was slinking toward Andoc, Senovo's white High Priest's robes dragging behind, half caught over his haunches.

"That's better than nothing, I suppose," Andoc said tiredly. He freed the mass of heavy cloth from the animal's hindquarters and lowered himself to sit with his back propped against the edge of the bench closest to the brazier, using Senovo's wadded-up robes as a cushion.

The wolf crowded close and half-climbed into Andoc's lap, laying his pointed muzzle on the Draebardi chieftain's thigh. His green-gold eyes closed in contentment as Andoc's fingers stroked through the heavy fur framing his neck and shoulders. A small whine emerged from his throat, the tension draining from his rangy body.

The animal looked up a few minutes later, ears pricking in the direction they'd come from earlier. Soon, Favian heard footsteps returning down the corridor leading to the atrium.

"Nothing but cold tea to drink, I'm afraid," Ithric announced. "And I hope no one was too desperate for a hearty meal, because all you're getting is a fifth of this piece of flatbread Kathrael got from one of the Sisters."

Kath paused, looking at the wolf curled in Andoc's lap, then shook herself free of her momentary reverie and sat on the other bench to break the bread into equal pieces.

"That's all right," Favian said, flopping down against the end of the second bench in a pose that mirrored Andoc's, and dragging his cloak around him more snugly against the chill. "I'm not really all that hungry."

Andoc gave him a flat look. Favian sighed at the silent admonition and accepted the chunk of coarse bread Kathrael handed him without a fight, mostly just to keep the peace.

"Did he talk to you?" Ithric asked Andoc, flicking his chin in Favian's direction.

The older man lifted an eyebrow. "He agreed to speak with Senovo once things die down a bit tomorrow."

Favian felt irritation creep up on him, despite the fact that he'd gotten a reprieve, of sorts. "I am sitting *right here*, you know."

Ithric shrugged, unconcerned, and handed the skin of tea to Andoc. He took a drink and lowered it from his mouth. The wolf craned up to sniff at the contents, only to curl his upper lip in distaste and return his head to its comfortable spot on Andoc's leg. Ithric took the skin back, and Kathrael got up to share out the rest of the bread.

The wolf took his share delicately from her fingers, and again, Favian saw Kath look at him with that expression which said she was having trouble reconciling his presence here with the bitterness she'd harbored toward him for so long.

Ithric lowered himself to sit on the bench with his leg brushing Favian's shoulder, and gave him a nudge with one knee. The skin of tea appeared in Favian's field of vision. He grabbed it and drank, grimacing a bit.

"Wow. That's utterly foul," he observed.

"Yup," Ithric agreed.

Kathrael scoffed and returned to sit on the ground on his other side. "It's not *that* bad. Don't you drink sweetleaf tea in the north?"

Favian took another cautious sip. *Nope. Still terrible.*

"No," he said. "We don't. Though I suppose we might if it were actually, you know, *sweet*. This tastes like someone steeped damp kindling in dirty river water."

Ithric snorted. "For what it's worth, it probably *was* steeped in dirty river water."

Favian shrugged and dribbled a bit of the tea onto his brick-like slab of bread, in hopes of softening it up enough so he wouldn't accidentally break a tooth. He handed the tea to Kathrael when he was done, shaking his head at her as she downed it with every appearance of neutrality.

They ate in near silence. Despite Kathrael's shoulder pressed to his on one side, and Ithric's leg brushing him on the other, Favian felt a sense of distance—of *aloneness*— growing in the pit of his stomach. This was to be his last night of life. He was surrounded by the people he loved. Yet, he could not reach out to them. He could not tell them any of the things that he should be telling them.

He could barely bring himself to speak at all, for fear of letting slip some hint of what he knew was to come. So instead, he choked down the stale bread a bite at a time until it was gone. He drank the disgusting tea. He looked at the wolf, curled against Andoc, affectionate and unselfconscious. Then, he took a deep breath, and shivered a bit. He didn't even have to manufacture it.

"Ithric," he said quietly, "would you mind shifting before we try to sleep? It'll be warmer that way, and Kath and I can use your cloak to sleep on."

Kathrael looked at him, and Favian thought for a moment she might question him again. But she only turned her attention to Ithric and said, "It's not a bad idea. The wolf and the lion will wake if anyone comes back here. No need for a watch that way. And it's true, you do put off heat like a hearth fire when you're in animal form."

Ithric lifted his shoulders and let them fall, his mouth still full of the dry, unappealing bread. He swallowed it with a bit of difficulty, and coughed. "Sure. I can do that."

Favian carefully did *not* slump in relief. He was reasonably certain both Andoc and Kathrael would respect his desire to wait until tomorrow to talk to them. But, Ithric? Not so much.

The others were finishing up their meager meal and scoping out the best sleeping positions. After looking around, Andoc huffed out a breath and stayed where he was, propped up against the bench. Favian suspected he would regret it tomorrow morning when he tried to get up, but, to be honest, the ground or the benches weren't really much better when it came to comfort.

Ithric stripped off his cloak and undressed quickly, handing Kathrael the clothing so she and Favian could use it to cushion themselves a bit. He shifted without ceremony. The wolf opened one eye, a brief rumble of noise rolling up from his chest at the disturbance before he settled again.

The lion curled his lip and yawned wide, showing teeth. He padded over and flopped down near the lit brazier. A moment later, his broad, pink tongue rasped over one front paw as he idly groomed himself.

Kathrael bumped her shoulder against Favian's. "Come on. I'm exhausted, even though I'm probably also too jittery to fall asleep."

I know the feeling, Favian thought. Aloud, he said, "We can at least lie down and rest, even if we can't sleep."

While she removed her mask and pulled her hair back into a simple braid, he gathered up Ithric's clothing. The cloak, he folded in half and laid on the cold stone floor by the lion. He handed Kath the jerkin and undershirt to use as a pillow, while he rolled up Ithric's breeches for the same purpose. The lion stopped grooming as they lay down next to him. Kathrael nudged Favian to lie between them, and he did not protest.

He *couldn't* protest, because the ache of inevitability had risen in his chest again, and words were impossible. It was just about all he could do to help Kathrael arrange the remaining two cloaks over them like blankets. When they were settled, he lay there wondering how much physical contact he could initiate without it coming across as suspicious. A moment later, Kathrael spared him the decision by rolling half on top of him and wrapping an arm and a leg around him.

"You're more comfortable than the floor," she muttered, and snuggled into him.

His arm closed around her shoulder—though he was very careful not to cling. Instead, he focused on keeping his breathing as slow and even as he could. The lion stretched, pressing its long body against his other side from shoulder to knee. Favian tangled his free hand in Ithric's mane, telling himself it was just to keep his fingers warm.

"Goodnight, you three," Andoc said.

"Goodnight, Andoc," Favian whispered.

Despite her earlier words, Kathrael did, in fact, fall asleep after a few minutes. A short time later, Favian heard soft snores coming from Andoc's direction. He thought the wolf and the lion were dozing as well, though the faintest disturbance would no doubt have them both awake in an instant, alert to any approaching threat.

Favian... did not sleep. To slumber his last hours away when he could be awake and feeling Kathrael's breath fluttering against the side of his neck... feeling Ithric's sleek ribcage rise and fall under his hand?

He couldn't do it. He *wouldn't* do it. They might have been lying on a stone floor in a freezing atrium with a restless mob singing and chanting outside, but right now, this was exactly where Favian wanted to be. Here, with the others sleeping peacefully so he could drink in their presences curled up next to him. So he could savor the feeling of them in his arms.

Just for a little while longer. Then, in the morning, he would let them go. The two of them had always been destined for greater things, long before he'd dreamed of them leading an army. Whereas he—

Well. He had only been along for the ride.

Favian wished now that he'd taken more time to speak with other, more experienced priests about the spirit world and the afterlife. He was terrified that, when he died, his spirit would attach itself to Kath instead of passing through the veil, tormenting her with his presence instead of letting her grieve him normally and move on. Terrified, because a part of him *wanted* to stay close to her—close to *them*—even if doing so would cause her pain.

Would he have a choice? If so, would he have the strength to make the *right* choice?

He thought of his mother. Of his father. Perhaps he could see his parents again in the spirit world. Then he thought of Ciryl. Ayala. The nameless mother and daughter who had burned to death because Favian had been foolish and arrogant. They would be waiting there for him, too.

His breath hitched. The people whose deaths he had caused deserved a chance to hold him to account before the gods. Favian deserved *every single thing* that was coming to him tomorrow. He could only hope that someone would bother to pick up his body and give him a proper funeral, at least, rather than tossing him into the catacombs with the rest of Rhyth's moldering bones—including those of Elarra, Kathrael's sister.

These thoughts plagued him throughout the long, cold, lonely night. Several times, Kathrael woke from restless dreams, and each time, Favian pretended to be sleeping until she dozed off again. Towards morning, his exhaustion finally pulled him into a light sleep despite his attempts to stay awake.

By the time the sky above the atrium finally lightened from black, to navy, to pale blue, the fire in the brazier had burned down to nothing. Favian's head ached from worry and lack of sleep; his toes were numb inside his boots.

Kathrael stretched against him. He closed his eyes, savoring the feeling of her sleepy body moving against his for the final time. She sat up, freeing his arm, and he shook the blood flow back into it. When he could feel his fingers again, he rubbed at his dry, gritty eyes. Beside him, reality twisted. Ithric rolled over, muffling a very human yawn against Favian's shoulder. Favian gave into the impulse to run a hand over the sleek, hard-muscled body that had driven him to distraction for *years* before Kath finally came along and banged their thick heads together.

In the end, Favian had gotten what he'd always longed for—love, and a family of his own. Indeed, he'd gotten love twice over. And while he might selfishly wish that he'd been able to hold onto it for a lifetime rather than a scant few months, he still knew that it was far more than many people got.

"Good morning. You look like shit," Ithric observed, gathering his clothes from where they'd been used as bedding and pulling them on. "Didn't you sleep at all?"

"A bit," Favian said. "Nerves, I guess. I think Kath got a bit more."

"More than I thought I would, certainly," she said, dragging fingers through her hair to unravel the braid she'd put it in the previous evening. She blew out a sharp breath. "So. Today's the day, I guess."

A smile tugged at one corner of Ithric's mouth, as though he were genuinely excited at the prospect. "Are you ready, Little Cat?"

"As I'll ever be," she replied.

Favian's attention wandered over to the far bench. True to form, Andoc was still asleep, though at some point he'd slid down to lie prone with his head pillowed on his arm. Favian frowned. Senovo was gone, though the absence of his robes and sandals proclaimed that he'd left in human form, rather than as the wolf.

He'd probably gone to speak with someone outside, or perhaps to find food for them.

Favian shook his head, dismissing his irrational flash of worry. Senovo was perfectly safe until mid-morning. Nothing would happen to him before he and Ithric left with Kathrael to gather the people from elsewhere in the city. Favian rose and crossed to wake Andoc, nudging his foot with the toe of a boot.

Nothing.

He kicked a little harder, and his guardian snorted awake, looking around groggily.

"Oh. Right," he said, after a moment of confused silence. "It's morning, then? Where's Senovo?"

"Outside somewhere," Favian said. "Maybe looking for breakfast." Some time during the night, the singing and chanting had died away. Favian hadn't noticed when it happened. "It's quiet out there."

"So it is." Andoc stretched, wincing a bit, and accepted Favian's offer of a hand up. Several of his joints cracked and popped in protest. "Argh… son of a *bitch*. This… is going to be a long day," he said with a grunt.

"Maybe we can find you a horse," Ithric offered, eyeing him.

Andoc waved him off. "Don't worry about me, Ithric. I'll manage. Come on. Let's go see if we can find Senovo. He wouldn't have gone far without letting one of us know first. Everybody ready to move?"

"Just a minute," Kathrael said. They waited while she finished tying on her mask with the flames and feathers attached. She quickly arranged her long, wavy black hair around the thong holding it in place and straightened, looking exactly as she had in Favian's vision with her red dress and dark cloak.

Not yet, he told himself. *Don't get ahead of yourself. It's still early, There's still a bit of time left.*

He followed the others out to find the crowd wandering around, the people looking groggy and restless. A southerly breeze blew through the plaza, bringing with it warmer air from across the sea. The atmosphere seemed heavy with anticipation.

Favian craned around, trying to catch a glimpse of white robes through the mass of people. Andoc gave a sharp whistle, and jerked his head toward the portico running along the buildings on the eastern edge of the square. Favian followed the movement and saw a knot of red robes, along with the white one he'd been looking for.

The four of them made their way across the distance separating them, Andoc leaning heavily on his walking stick. Favian frowned. Despite his earlier attempt at waving off the suggestion, they really should try to find Andoc a horse. Favian presumed he would go with Senovo's group, since he hadn't seen the Draebardi chieftain with the group from the plaza in his vision. They would be covering a great deal of ground, and it would be nearly impossible for a lame man to keep up on foot.

Senovo looked up as they approached. His face was drawn, dark smudges under his eyes. He looked about the way Favian felt, not to put too fine a point on it.

"Good morning," he greeted them, none of his obvious turmoil coming through in his voice. "I came out to get news. There have been messengers from other parts of the city arriving over the course of the last hour. We will need to leave soon."

Favian's breath caught. Of course, if they were to gather the other groups and make it back to the palace by mid-morning, they would have to leave early.

"What about the city guard?" Andoc asked, all business now as he slipped effortlessly into the role of military strategist.

Sephira answered. "Oddly disorganized — so far, at least. The last messenger made mention of some kind of disturbance near the guards' garrison. They didn't get close enough to find out details."

Andoc nodded. "Probably wise. Not to mention fortuitous. We'll take that piece of good fortune and be glad of it."

"Any news about the Cult of Deimok?" Ithric asked.

"They can't have failed to notice that we have their temple surrounded," Kathrael observed. "We haven't exactly been stealthy about it."

"I have no doubt that they're planning a response," Sephira said. "Though it remains to be seen how bold they'll be when faced with these kinds of numbers."

Favian swallowed. "Both the Cult and the guardsmen will try to attack," he said, having seen it already. "Our side is better armed, though."

Andoc's chest rose and fell. "It's only to be expected, of course. And as Sephira says, we also have numbers on our side."

Most of those people were not fighters, Favian knew. And many of them would be caught in the crossfire, regardless. His stomach churned, and he was suddenly glad that no one had tried to press food on him this morning.

A disturbance from across the square caught their attention. Whatever it was, the bulk of the platform in the middle of the plaza blocked it from view. But they could hear raised voices and see people moving out of the way, like the sea parting.

"*Make way!*" called a very familiar contralto with a pronounced eastern accent. "*Let me through! I have urgent news for the Wolf Patron of Draebard!*"

TWENTY

Favian's mouth dropped open as Carivel appeared, riding a stocky cream-colored stallion with a second, nearly identical stallion at her side. She was leading a string of nervous horses, which also included a thick-barreled black gelding with a long mane and tail. His heart stuttered, kicked hard against the side of his chest, and belted into double-time. Beside him, Kathrael gave a short cry of excitement.

"The horses!" She grasped his arm almost hard enough to bruise, and he covered her hand with one of his, barely able to believe his eyes.

Carivel was peering around, obviously looking for them. Andoc let out another shrill whistle, and her eyes landed on them an instant later. She urged the group of animals forward, pushing through the crowd until she reached the relative quiet of the portico. Her smile was grim, and when her eyes landed on him, Favian realized that his mouth was *still* open. He snapped it shut.

"Hello, Favian. Lose something, did you?" she asked sweetly.

He pulled his feet free from where they had seemingly been rooted to the cobblestones, half-stumbling forward to place a disbelieving hand on Ozias' shoulder. The stallion shook his head and nudged Favian playfully, while Audris snorted and pawed with a front foot, pinning his ears as one of the unfamiliar horses moved too close.

"Carivel," Favian whispered, choking on the ridiculous sting of tears. He looked up at her, his fingers tangling in the stallion's creamy mane. "Where—? How—?"

He was vaguely aware that Kathrael and Ithric had come up to join him, several of the horses snorting nervously at the lion-shifter's approach. Affectionate warmth crept in behind Carivel's tense expression, and she stepped gracefully down from Ozias' back.

"Here," she said, handing a tangle of reins and ropes to Ithric and Kathrael. "Hold onto this lot for a moment. Mind your feet, though—they're a bit on edge."

When her hands were free, she turned and wrapped her arms around Favian, hugging him fiercely. He clung and buried his head against her neck, fighting to rein in the hitch of his breathing. How utterly typical—weeks of grief, weeks of holding in a terrible secret, and it was a damned *horse* that finally threatened to unman him completely.

"Missed you, Favian," Carivel whispered, strong arms still wrapped around him.

He screwed his eyes shut for a moment, and took a deep, rasping breath, making himself ease back until he could look at her. "Carivel... I thought these horses were gone forever. How on earth did you find them?"

She snorted. "Well, they're a bit hard to miss, really. I saw all three of them munching hay in the royal stables on my second day on the job. Apparently, someone found them and saw an easy way to make some coin by selling them into the king's herd." Her face grew sober and worried. "I'd yell at you for being careless with them, but Senovo already told us what happened to you that day."

"Yeah... definitely don't yell at him," Ithric said. "He couldn't have done anything about the horses; he was a bit busy drowning in the river at the time. You can yell at me if you'd like. It was completely my fault. And, unlike me, Kathrael was able to hold onto her horse during the fight, though he was slashed pretty badly by a blade."

"Bysh saved my life, and Favian's, too, even though he was hurt in the battle," Kathrael said quietly.

"You three made it out alive, and that's all that matters," Carivel told them in a firm tone. She gave Ithric a brief hug, and Kathrael, as well—much to Kathrael's apparent surprise. Then she moved to where Andoc and Senovo stood watching the little reunion, pulling each of them down for a kiss. "Is he all right?" she asked Andoc, jerking her head toward Senovo.

"Yes," Senovo said tiredly.

"No," said Andoc.

Senovo cast a brief, long-suffering glance at Favian, who returned it with an unexpected flash of fellow-feeling over the way people continually discussed them as if they weren't present.

"Yeah, I didn't think so," Carivel said. She glared at Senovo, wrinkling her nose. "When I got that message from Andoc yesterday saying you'd ditched him and gone to the temples, I nearly burst something important. I'd ask what the *fuck* you thought you were doing... only, I already know the answer."

Andoc nodded. "There's no way out except forward, now," he said. "Do I want to know where you got the rest of these horses? The ones I don't recognize, I mean?"

Carivel grinned, sharp and dangerous. "Oh, these? Funny story, that. *Somehow*, all of the other horses in the royal stables appear to have gotten loose this morning. Someone must have been *terribly* careless."

A bubble of laughter tried to escape Favian's throat, his emotions jerking back and forth violently enough to give him whiplash.

Ithric *did* laugh. "Oh, gods. And by any chance, does that include the horses that belong to the king's guardsmen?"

Carivel blinked, still smiling. "It might have done."

Andoc snorted. "You're a menace, *caradi*. It's one of the many things I love about you."

"Just be glad I'm *your* menace," she shot back.

"We are," Senovo said. "Passionately so."

"Anyway," Carivel continued, "these are the ones I was able to catch, afterward. The stables were pretty much in chaos, so I thought I'd bring them here instead of taking them back."

Her innocent tone wouldn't have fooled anyone.

"And they just *happen* to be saddled and bridled because—?" A smile was tugging at one corner of Andoc's lips.

"Because they wouldn't be much use to the rebels bareback and bridleless," she said, all business now.

Andoc turned to the priestesses, who had been watching the whole exchange with keen interest. "Sephira, can you find ten people trained to fight from horseback? It's not a huge number, but it will at least increase our speed and mobility against potential attacks."

Sephira nodded curtly and turned to one of the acolytes. "Go find Dharnal and tell him we have horses for ten men. He'll know who to send."

The girl nodded and hurried away.

Carivel pointed a finger at Andoc's chest. "*You*. You're riding Ozias. No way are you doing this on foot with your bad leg. I'll take Audris." She turned back to them. "Kathrael? Do you want Fidget?"

Kath shook her head, stroking a hand over Ozias' forehead. "No, I'll walk up front with Ithric and Senovo."

"And you two will be doing this in animal form?" Carivel asked, looking between the shape-shifters.

"Yes," Ithric said. "I don't know about you, Senovo, but I've no desire to stop halfway to the palace and strip off my clothes in front of the crowd. It doesn't seem very dignified, somehow."

Carivel nodded. "All right, then. If you're up in front, we'll have to keep the horses back a bit in the procession. The smell of wolf and lion might panic them. We can probably get closer on Audris and Ozias if we need to, since they're more familiar with you."

"They were getting better about being around the lion," Ithric admitted, "but I may have traumatized Audris by shifting as I was leaping off him when we went to rescue Favian."

Carivel waved the words off. "It'll be fine," she said. "I'll be riding him, and if I need to get him close to you for some reason, rest assured that I will."

Armed men started to come up to them, and Carivel handed out the mounts as they arrived, firing off brief questions about their experience and skill level. Since Kathrael wasn't riding, she handed Fidget's lead rope to the last one, and told him to find one more rider among his comrades.

When he nodded and headed back into the crowd with both his own horse and the black gelding in tow, Kathrael took a deep breath. "We should go, if there's nothing else left to do here. Favian, are you sure you won't come with us?"

Favian smiled, hoping it didn't look as much like a death rictus as it felt. "No, Kath. You know why I have to stay here."

This was it. This was goodbye.

Kathrael sighed unhappily. "I know why you *say* you have to stay here." She wrapped her arms around him, and he tried not to shatter into a thousand sharp-edged pieces. "Please," she whispered. "Don't do anything foolish. I couldn't bear it."

He eased away so he could cradle her face in his hands, one palm cupping warm flesh, the other, smooth metal.

"Kath," he said solemnly, "You're about to confront a king and tell him to stop treating his people like dirt. If there was ever a case of the pot calling the kettle black, this is it."

Her good eye welled up, and Favian leaned down to kiss her before he had to watch the first tear fall. She melted against him, fitting into the space in his arms in a way he'd never really expected to experience with anyone. For all that their first meeting had taken place with her dagger pressed against his neck, Favian thanked the gods that she had stumbled into his life, desperate and starving and holding one of the missing puzzle pieces of his soul.

"I love you, Kath," he murmured against her lips. "This is it. This is your time. You wrested this day out of *nothing*, and molded it into being with the force of your will. I am in awe of you."

Her hands gripped the material of his robes, and she rested her forehead against his for a long moment. Her voice wavered a bit when she said, "I'm in awe of *you*. You took me into your heart at a time when my spirit was teetering on the brink of ruin. I love you, Favian. Please be careful. I'll see you in a few hours, and together, we'll finally make things right."

"I want that more than anything," Favian said truthfully. "Now, go and be brilliant."

He kissed her again, and pulled away before his resolve could weaken. She took a deep breath and looked up at him, a single tear track streaking down her bare cheek. Her good eye held fear, but also a steely determination to force the world into the shape she wanted. Favian could hardly breathe in that moment, for how much he loved her.

A strong hand closed on his shoulder, and he turned to meet gold-flecked hazel eyes under a mane of russet hair.

"You'll talk to us properly, tonight," Ithric told him. It was not a request.

Favian nodded. "Tonight," he agreed.

"Good," Ithric said. "I'm not going to say goodbye. No point in tempting fate."

Favian wanted to weep, but he managed to keep his voice light as he said, "Tempting fate? Pfft. Remember who you're talking to."

Ithric's full lips hooked into a smile. "Fair point. C'mere..."

Favian let himself be pulled into a kiss, no longer giving a whit about who in the crowd might see, or what they might think about it. Ithric had always been the spark to his tinder, and now, he let himself burn without a second thought, bright and hot in the moments before he would be extinguished forever.

Lucky, he thought. *You were lucky to have this.*

When they parted, Ithric angled Favian's head down and pressed a second kiss to his forehead. Favian clasped his shoulders, leaning against that steady strength for a bare moment before he straightened away.

"Look after Kath and Senovo," he said. "I know better than to ask you to look after your own flea-bitten hide."

"I will if you will," Ithric said, repeating the same words Favian had said yesterday.

Favian shrugged. "See you soon," he said, hating the hoarse quality of his voice.

Ithric gave him a tiny smile and nodded, wrapping a hand around the nape of Favian's neck and squeezing. "So you've told us," he said. "We'll try to make a suitably impressive looking sight. See you soon, Favian."

His fingers trailed away, leaving Favian's skin feeling cold where they had rested. He turned to his three guardians. Andoc stepped forward and pulled him into a one-armed embrace.

"Make sure to watch your flank when you leave the plaza," he counseled. "Try to stay toward the middle of the group if you can. That's a selfish thing for me to ask, I know, but there it is."

Favian nodded, knowing that he wouldn't be doing any such thing. "Watch over the others for me. And... thank you."

Andoc pulled away and frowned down at him. "For what?"

"For coming when I asked."

Carivel scoffed. "Please, Favian. What else were we going to do? Don't be daft! Being daft is Ithric's job."

He turned and hugged her, thinking of the years he'd known her, and all the things they'd been through since the Alyrions had attacked Draebard, so long ago.

"I know," he said into her spiky, close-cropped hair. "But thanks for coming, all the same."

With a feeling akin to dread, he let Carivel go and turned his eyes toward his mentor.

"I'm sorry." The words were pulled from Favian's lips without his permission, but he didn't think he'd ever meant anything more sincerely in his life. No doubt Senovo would think he was referring to his summons... and Favian truly was sorry for that. But he was also sorry for what was to come in a few hours. Not only had Favian forced Senovo to come here and face his painful past; now he was going to make him grieve the loss of someone he considered a son as well.

Senovo still looked like he was hanging onto composure by a thread, but his embrace was sure and solid. "Don't be sorry," he murmured. "We are all the gods' servants, and this is a wrong that should have been put right long ago. May the gods smile on your endeavors while we are parted, Little Brother, and return you safe and well at the end of them."

Favian should have said something in return. Something wise and learned. Something comforting and priest-like. But his words were gone. He feared that the next time he opened his mouth, all of his secrets would pour out like wine from a cracked cup. So he kept silent, and squeezed Senovo's slender frame long and hard.

He nearly had to pry his fingers free, and after he had, he ducked his head to avoid seeing the eyes of the people he'd just bid farewell for the last time.

There was a long moment of silence before Andoc said, "Come on. We should go."

Favian watched in a daze as Carivel and Andoc mounted the white stallions he thought he'd never see again. He watched as Senovo and Ithric shifted form. He watched as Kathrael straightened her spine and lifted her chin, becoming once more the mysterious masked woman who drew shape-shifters to her side and changed the course of kingdoms. He watched as they turned for a final farewell, wishing him luck and entreating him to be careful one final time.

He watched... as they left, accompanied by the cheers and excited murmurs of the assembled crowd.

Only when they had disappeared into the press of people, hidden from view, did he finally whisper, "*Goodbye.*"

He didn't know how long he stood there, glassy-eyed and feeling nothing but an all-consuming ache of emptiness. When a hand closed on his arm, he didn't flinch. He didn't react at all, in fact. It was only when the hand turned him around and he found himself looking down into Sephira's sharp features that he blinked back into some kind of awareness.

"The secret you've been hiding from them," she said. "Tell me now, Little Brother."

Favian sucked in a breath far more painful than the one he'd taken not so very long ago on a frozen riverbank after nearly drowning... and told her everything.

Sephira was silent as he spoke, her expression giving nothing away. When his words finally trailed away, she continued to regard him for several long moments.

"I understand," she said finally, and Favian sagged a bit in a strange kind of relief.

He'd thought that she might. The Sisterhood had lost dozens of its members. They understood the inevitability of more deaths, as long as they continued to speak openly against powerful groups who saw them as a threat. They understood, in a way that Kathrael and Ithric, Senovo and Carivel and Andoc would not be able to.

The people who loved him labored under the belief that, because they cared for him, Favian was somehow more important—more *worthy* of continued life—than Ayala or any of the other nameless priestesses who had fallen in the name of spreading the gods' true message. Sephira, by contrast, understood that he was not.

He met her eyes with naked gratitude for her practicality. "Please, Elder Sister—I have a single request, You must give me your word that you will not stop for me when I fall, or tell the others what has befallen me at a time when it might distract them from what they are doing and put them in added danger. *Promise me.*"

Sephira continued to study his face for the space of several heartbeats, a small furrow marking her forehead. "I give you my word, Favian," she told him, and Favian let out the breath he'd been holding without realizing it.

"Thank you," he breathed.

She nodded, but only said, "Come. You and I will be assisting High Priestess Zandreen. Together, we will lead this group. We should join her at the speaker's platform. The crowd is already growing restless, and it will be some time yet before we are to leave and rejoin your friends. The people here need direction until then."

Anything, Favian thought. *Anything, as long as it means I don't have to think.*

"I'm right behind you," he said.

>∽∿ ♛ ∿∽<

Sephira had taken him to the platform, urged him to mount the steps, clasped a hand on his shoulder, and told him to preach.

And he did. He preached with more conviction than he had ever felt before in his life, heedless of his still-sore throat and congested lungs. He preached for Senovo. For Ayala. For Kathrael, and for her friend Vesh. For every beggar and slave and prostitute who had ever been forsaken by the Southern Priests' Guild.

He preached even though his hands were shaking with fear at what would soon come. He preached even though he wanted to collapse with grief over the loss of his own life, and the loss of the love he had found such a very short time ago. He preached until High Priestess Zandreen placed a gnarled hand on his arm and gave it a gentle squeeze. His words stumbled to a halt and he looked at her, his throat closing when he heard the distant sounds of people — *thousands* of people — approaching the temple district.

"Your friends are returning," she said. "We must lead the crowd out of the plaza and join them now, for the final march on the palace."

Favian blinked and looked around the square as if emerging from a trance. The sky was growing faintly hazy, no longer as clear and blue as it had been earlier in the morning. At the far end of the plaza, the doors of the Temple of Deimok remained tightly closed, its denizens sheltering inside, hiding from the mob on their doorstep. Favian was painfully aware, however, that both the Cult of Deimok and the palace guardsmen would even now be rallying as the true size and nature of the threat against them became clear.

He swallowed hard and coughed to clear his throat, his pulse thundering in his chest as panic tried to rise and drag him down with tearing claws.

> *Utarr give me solace in my time of need.*
> *Mighty Deresta, give me strength.*
> *Naloth, help me walk the path of justice.*
> *Utarr, give me solace in my time of need.*
> *Mighty Deresta, give me strength.*
> *Naloth, help me...*

He breathed against the rush of animal fear, and fought his way through it.

He opened his eyes and looked out, addressing the crowd once more. "The Masked Woman approaches, leading the people with her companions, the Wolf and the Lion!" he called. "Follow us and join them—throw off your chains. Help us bring freedom to the citizens of Rhyth *on this very day!*"

Someone in the crowd started chanting, "*Rhyth! Rhyth! Rhyth!*" Favian couldn't be sure if it was a member of the underground who was planting the seed, or if it arose spontaneously. Whatever the case, others took up the cry, pumping their fists in the air. The chant grew in volume until the whole square echoed with it.

Figures armed with crossbows had moved in to encircle the platform as people grew more excited. Sephira led the way down the steps and into the crowd, where their unofficial guards cleared a path for them and kept the commoners and slaves from mobbing them. The shift of movement gradually goaded the entire massive crowd in a single direction, out of the square and onto the road leading to a main thoroughfare that would take them to the palace.

As Favian had suspected, those outside the plaza had finally realized what was happening, and the street was chaotic, full of figures running and shouting. He felt queasy as the reality around him started to slide into synchronicity with his memory of the vision. Panic tried to rise again, and he shoved it down ruthlessly.

The air around the crowd crackled with energy, like the atmosphere before a thunderstorm. Favian glanced upward from under the hood of his cloak. It was cloudier now than it had been a few minutes ago, and the sky was growing darker. Perhaps a thunderstorm really *was* coming, even though it was the wrong season for it.

Because of course, torrential rainfall was *all* they needed today.

Sephira was still walking next to him, and Zandreen was somewhere behind, directing and encouraging the main mass of the crowd. He and Sephira were near the head of the group, comprised of a strange mix of acolytes, priests and priestesses, slaves, and common folk. He noticed that many from the latter two groups now carried weapons of various kinds, including some of the stolen crossbows.

Favian alternated between waves of panic that threatened to make him turn tail and flee back the way he'd come, and a dazed sort of mental detachment that he vaguely recognized as the onset of shock. As he watched, a gang of men wearing the yellow sashes of the cult of Deimok emerged from a side road near him, yelling and swinging swords and clubs. He fell back a few steps in instinctive reaction, his heart pounding as they headed straight toward him and Sephira.

An answering cry arose from behind him, a dozen or so of the armed slaves and commoners from the crowd surging forward to clash with the newcomers. Crossbow bolts flew, and a handful of the attackers fell, screaming.

"Keep the crowd moving! Hold firm, Little Brother!" Sephira called, her words hard to make out over the noise, even though she was only a few steps away.

"Come on!" Favian shouted over his shoulder, pitching his voice loud enough so that it wouldn't accidentally quaver. He was growing increasingly hoarse after preaching for such a long time this morning. His chest ached terribly, but the words still carried. "Forward, to the palace!"

The cry was taken up by others close to him. The ragged chant of "To the palace! *To the palace!*" growing in volume as more and more people in the mob took it up.

For it truly was a mob now. The crowd had turned into a living thing, a beast that clawed out in self-defense when a disorganized squad of city guardsmen bore down on its flank, trying to cut it in two like a snake. All the while, the main mass continued forward, too large to stop.

A heavy body slammed into Favian and he staggered, clutching the man's shoulders and trying to keep them both from falling. He had a brief impression of wild eyes and yellow teeth bared in a snarl before the man jerked free and staggered off. When Favian looked down, there was a smear of blood on his left hand. He didn't think it was his.

The din of screams and clanging metal was growing loud enough to make his ears ring. He could see Sephira's mouth moving, but he couldn't hear her voice at all anymore as the fighting continued behind them. He tried to focus ahead, in the direction they needed to go, knowing that the most important thing now was to keep moving and not get boxed in.

So far, the way forward remained clear. The street they were on entered another large plaza perhaps sixty or seventy paces away, and as they grew closer, Favian could see into the open square. More bodies jostled his from behind, but it was the sight ahead of him that made his breath catch in his throat.

Kathrael walked across the large space, dressed all in red with her mask of flames and feathers, flanked by the lion on one side and the wolf on the other. As Favian had foreseen, the three unearthly figures strode along at the head of an army of the dispossessed.

The pounding of Favian's heart in his ears grew so loud that the chaos around him faded away. He couldn't breathe, and all he could see was the vision of beauty and powerful magic before him.

The last view of his loved ones that he would ever get.

His feet stumbled to a halt, and he was still staring a moment later when running figures dressed in guardsmen's armor — armed with swords and longbows — blocked his view of the plaza. He tore his gaze away, dragging in breath to yell something to Sephira. A warning, or —

The arrow slammed into him, sending him crashing to the ground as blinding agony enveloped the left side of his chest. The back of his head hit the flagstones with a sharp crack, his vision swimming crazily.

He could dimly make out people screaming and running, others falling to the ground around him, but the confusion seemed somehow unimportant, as though he were observing it from across a vast distance. His body felt strange. Heavy. Enveloped by an all-consuming numbness.

"Zandreen!" Sephira's voice sounded flat and far away, like someone shouting through a long tunnel. "*Zandreen!* Favian's shot — he made me promise not to stop for him if he fell!"

"Then don't stop." Zandreen's voice sounded oddly distant as well. "Sephira, you must take charge of the crowd and join up with the main group in the plaza! Go, now! Keep your word — I will stop for him in your stead."

Favian tried to take a breath deep enough to speak. Without warning, his body jolted back to full awareness. Pain like nothing he had ever experienced in his nineteen years of life sliced through him, and his consciousness wavered.

His awareness washed in and out like the tide, time stuttering forward in fits and starts. He was surprised to jerk back to cognizance and find that the chaos had lulled, and the street now seemed almost peaceful. He stared at the fallen body of a young woman lying near him, obviously dead, her brown eyes wide and staring at the heavens. His surroundings seemed dim, as though his vision were going dark. Zandreen crouched over him, speaking to him, though he couldn't understand her words over the buzzing in his ears.

With no warning, she grasped the arrow protruding from under his collarbone and yanked it out sharply. The world exploded. Favian tried to scream, but his lungs would not inflate. Blood filled his mouth. He was choking on it, drowning in it, his struggles to draw breath growing ever weaker as his body succumbed to the lack of air.

The sense of disconnectedness from his physical form returned, as if he were floating up, looking down at himself from above.

No, please... no, please... I'm not ready... no no no, he thought in desperation as the world grew dark around him—

TWENTY-ONE

Kathrael's heart thrummed in a heady combination of excitement and fear as she walked across the open square, the two shape-shifters flanking her and an army of slaves and commoners at her back. As they approached the place where she expected to meet up with Favian and the group that had camped overnight in front of the Temple of Deimok, she could just make out the sounds of people shouting and weapons clashing over the noise of the crowd coming from behind her.

Over the last couple of hours, she, Ithric, Senovo, and those who'd accompanied them had covered a loop that wound through the very poorest parts of the city, gathering followers as they went. The throng of people now at their backs far outstripped the group that had gathered in the plaza—easily numbering in the thousands. Slaves and gang members armed with crossbows were a steadfast presence among them, but—as with the throng that had followed Favian and Senovo yesterday—the ranks had swelled with commoners who had no previous connection with the underground slave rebellion.

She had seen beggars, prostitutes, laborers, merchants, and curious youths drop whatever they were doing to follow the crowd, their mouths agape at the sight of the wolf and the lion walking next to her. It was only as they'd made their way back to the central district with its temples, palaces, and government buildings that they'd begun to encounter any noticeable opposition—well-dressed people shouting from side streets and covered walkways, hurling abuse, sometimes throwing stones.

Kathrael and her silent, four-legged protectors were very much at the front of the procession, but as resistance started to materialize around them, armed figures had come forward to array themselves on either side of the trio, guarding their flanks and discouraging those who might be tempted to try to stop their progress.

On five separate occasions as they traveled through the city, Kathrael had seen city guardsmen—alone or in pairs—hurrying ahead of them. Thanks to Carivel, only one of those guards had been on horseback. It was obvious the king's soldiers were still in considerable disarray, scrambling to organize against what was coming their way.

Judging by the noises coming from the temple district, either they had finally managed to mount some kind of organized attack, or the Cult of Deimok had.

Kathrael's heart was in her throat as she, Senovo, and Ithric finally reached the end of the open concourse they were traversing, giving them a view down the street that those from the temple would use to join them. She craned to look for blond hair and red robes, but all she could see was confusion.

There was definitely fighting going on—an ugly tangle of figures wearing yellow sashes and figures in everyday clothing. Crossbow bolts flew, many of them converging on a position out of her line of sight. The higher arc of longbow bolts returned a moment later. The yellow sashes meant cult members, but the longbowmen were king's guard; they had to be.

People in the crowd fell under the onslaught, making her pulse race faster with fear for Favian. She still couldn't see him, though she did catch an occasional flash of ochre amongst the confusion in the distance. It was apparent that the guardsmen were attempting to keep the two groups from merging.

She turned to call to those behind her. "If you have weapons, make for the group from the temple and help clear the way for them!" She had scarcely finished speaking when the first arrow arced toward their group from the guardsmen's position, clattering harmlessly to the ground a few paces in front of her.

Several dozen armed men split away from them and headed toward the group from the temple, closing in on the guardsmen's position from one side even as fighters in the group from the temple continued to attack from the other direction. More arrows flew toward Kathrael's group as the king's soldiers faced the new threat. This time, she heard someone behind her scream as the hail of projectiles fell back to earth. She didn't dare stop and turn back to see what had happened.

Something glanced stingingly against her hip, startling a grunt from her. It was a rock, probably hurled from the hand of a cult member. Next to her, the lion growled a warning, but men from the mob were already surging forward, overpowering the would-be marksman. Kathrael was more startled than hurt; the blow had seemed to come from nowhere. She tangled the fingers of her right hand in Ithric's mane, steadying herself as they continued moving forward, eager to join up with Favian and his group.

By the time they reached the edge of the square, the coordinated pincer attack from the two groups appeared to have crushed the contingent of guardsmen, or at least sent them into retreat. No more arrows flew, and the two masses of people met at the intersection of the temple road and the plaza, milling together in a confused press of bodies. The armed men who had been guarding them as they walked managed to maintain a small bubble of space around Kathrael, the lion, and the wolf. Kath cast around with increasing desperation, trying to peer over the bodies of the people blocking her view. Looking for Favian.

Where was he?

Her grip on Ithric's mane tightened. On her other side, the wolf sniffed the air nervously, perhaps searching for a clue to Favian's whereabouts as well. Despite Andoc's parting advice to him, she knew he would have been near the front of the crowd. Why wasn't he here?

Kath. Vesh's voice was sharp. *Stay focused. This could turn into a full-out battle at any moment.*

She ignored the rebuke. *Favian should be here by now, Vesh! Why can't I see him yet?*

This place is in chaos, Vesh said. *All sorts of unforeseen things could have happened. Just because he's not right up front —*

At that moment, Kathrael saw Sephira's red-cloaked form pushing through a gap in the swarm of bodies.

"Sephira!" she cried. "Sephira, over here!"

The wolf snarled as a knot of strangers pressed too close. They stumbled back in surprise, making an opening big enough for the priestess to squeeze through. She had a scrape on one cheek, but still managed to appear enviably cool and composed.

"Kathrael," Sephira called, raising her voice to be heard over the din. "We need to get the people moving forward before we end up pinned down in this plaza."

"Where is Favian?" Kathrael asked, hearing the naked fear in her own voice.

Sephira didn't even blink. "He was detained near the temple. Zandreen is with him, but we need to go on without them."

"*Detained*?" Kathrael echoed, her instincts clamoring with a deep sense of *wrongness*. "What do you mean, *detained*?"

Sephira's fingers closed on Kathrael's upper arm and pointed her in the direction of the palace. "Walk now, Talk later. There's no time."

Kathrael balked, torn between the scope of the monumental task before her and the nearly irresistible desire to run back toward the Temple of Deimok and find Favian. The lion looked up at her with gold-flecked eyes, watchful, while the wolf paced restlessly, three steps in one direction and three steps in the other, still scenting the air.

She... didn't know what to do. Even now, the mob she had helped create was pressing at their backs. She was supposed to be leading it. Without direction, it could turn into a mindless beast. She wanted to ask Ithric what she should do, but she knew it wasn't practical to ask him to shift now. And what could he tell her anyway, that she didn't already know?

Favian should be here.

Favian *wasn't* here.

If they went to look for him, they would be risking the future of the very rebellion they'd helped foment. This was their moment. This was the tipping point. They would either lead these people to the palace, or they would strand them here, leaderless, until enemies surrounded them on all sides and rained death down on them.

Sephira's grip on her arm tightened. "Don't be a fool, Kathrael," the priestess said. "Don't make this mistake after all we've sacrificed to get here."

"I—" Kathrael stumbled forward, her legs following Sephira's urging before her mind gave them permission to do so.

But Sephira was already lifting her powerful voice, rousing the crowd behind them. "To the palace! To the palace! *To the palace!*"

And others were joining in, taking up the simple chant, raising their fists in time with the words.

The priestess of Avlan kept Kathrael moving forward with an uncompromising grip, ensuring that they — and the shape-shifters — remained at the front of the mob, rather than being swallowed up by it and losing the air of command they now held.

"But, *Favian...*" Kath whispered, the sound swallowed up by the wall of human noise behind them.

The lion and the wolf heard, however. Ithric growled, his glowing eyes fixing on Sephira until she loosened her hold on Kath's arm.

What am I doing? How can I leave him without knowing if he's safe, Vesh? she pleaded within the privacy of her thoughts.

There was a pause long enough to make tears spring to her good eye.

Do you trust me, Kath? Vesh asked in lieu of an answer, his pleasant voice weighted with something she couldn't define.

She wasn't sure what he was asking, exactly, but... *I trust you with my life,* she told him with complete certainty.

And what about... with his *life?* The words still sounded strangely heavy within her mind.

She blinked. *I don't understand —*

Go, Kath. Your destiny lies less than half a league from here, at the palace, and the lives of thousands hang in the balance. Trust me to look after Favian, while you and the lion-boy look after the revolution.

It took her a moment to make sense of Vesh's words. When she did, pure panic flooded her breast. "*What?* No!" she cried aloud. "Vesh, you can't leave me —"

She staggered to a halt again. The wolf and the lion looked up at her in confusion.

It's time. I'm sorry. Vesh's voice was gentle, but firm.

Kathrael clutched a hand to her throat as a feeling of choking terror threatened to suffocate her.

But Vesh wasn't finished. *I love you, you know. I always have, Kath. I'm so sorry I never told you when we were both alive. When we might have done something about it. I'm so sorry you had to watch me die.*

A sob wrenched free of her throat.

Goodbye, Kathrael — my fierce and beautiful warrior. My inspiration.

With a feeling like the fluttering wings of a bird taking flight from her cupped hands, Vesh was gone. Gone, as if he'd never been. She was alone inside her head for the first time since she'd fled Rhyth and awoken in a summer field, surrounded by rustling grass and the sound of Vesh's laughter.

The wolf tilted his head up to the hazy sky and let loose a spine tingling howl. Kathrael shuddered.

The weight of impossible responsibility settled over her shoulders, threatening to crush her. How could she lead an army when her world had just been turned upside down—the bedrock beneath her shattered? She couldn't even draw breath to speak past the choking lump in her throat. She was a scarred and worthless prostitute standing all alone in the middle of a civil war. *What in the gods' names had she been thinking?*

Sephira was holding her by the upper arms again. Her mouth was moving. She gave Kathrael a sharp shake, and suddenly the panicked rush of blood in her ears faded, letting the words come through.

"—and you are bloody well *not* falling apart on us now!"

Kathrael's mouth opened, but she still couldn't make her voice work. The crowd was milling all around them. The chant of *"To the palace!"* was still going strong further back, but confusion reigned here, near the front. The space to her right twisted, and Ithric took her by the shoulders, glaring at Sephira until she backed off.

"Kathrael," he said, low and intense, turning her in his arms until he could look down at her face with eyes that seemed strangely hypnotic. "Talk to me. Quickly, now. Why did you call out for Vesh?"

Excited shouts erupted around them from people who had seen his transformation. The wolf snarled and snapped as some of them tried to press in, holding them at bay with the help of the armed gang members around them—many of whom looked as gobsmacked by Ithric's change of form as the rest of the crowd.

Kathrael swallowed hard. "Ithric, he's *gone*. He... said he was going to look after Favian. Something horrible has happened—I know it has! Favian would be here with us otherwise!"

Ithric held her shoulders tightly, grounding her. "This probably has to do with whatever he's been hiding from us," he said, grim. "But, Kath, the truth is, we may *all* end up dead before the day is out. We've known that from the beginning. You *cannot* falter now. If Vesh went to help Favian somehow, then... well... *let him.* Let him do it. If we're still alive when the sun sets, we'll find Favian—find *them*—and move on from there."

A clatter of hooves broke through the intense moment. Two figures on creamy white horses pushed through the press of bodies, weapons held at the ready as they scanned the crowd until they found Sephira, Ithric, Kathrael, and the wolf.

"You are not alone," Ithric told Kathrael, wrenching her attention back to him—each word delivered like a blow. "Now, let's *do* this, so we can come back here afterward and kick Favian's ass for being such a secretive bastard."

He pressed a brief, fierce kiss to her lips and shifted back into animal form. A sharp curse erupted from a few paces away, and Kathrael looked up, dazed, just in time to see Audris skittering sideways under Carivel at the sudden appearance of the lion.

The Draebardi Horse Mistress wrestled the stallion back under control and urged him forward. She and Andoc converged on them a moment later.

"We heard the wolf howl," she called over the noise of the restless crowd.

Kathrael swallowed, trying to regain her equilibrium despite the empty place in her mind where her spirits were meant to be. "Something's happened to Favian," she replied. "He's not with the group from the temple!"

"Shit," Carivel hissed. Andoc's jaw tightened as he rode up next to them and halted Ozias.

Sephira gave the lion a wary look and joined them. "Please," she said. "I tried to tell you earlier. There's no cause for worry. I spoke to Favian shortly before I left with the crowd. Someone was injured; several people, actually. He and Zandreen stayed behind. Zandreen used to be a healer before she dedicated herself to Avlan, so she stayed to help. Favian specifically asked me to tell you not to worry, and to focus on what you came here to do. We *must* get the crowd moving now."

Andoc and Carivel shared a glance. "That does sound like something he'd do," Andoc said. "And you're absolutely right about this crowd."

Kathrael should have been reassured by the words, she knew. She *tried* to be reassured, but a niggling sense of something *not being right* remained. Also… there was Vesh. Or rather, there *wasn't* Vesh, because Vesh was gone. But the others were correct about the need to keep moving, and she knew it.

Even if the idea of leaving without Favian ate at her like vitriol consuming flesh.

"Yes," she said reluctantly. "Forgive me. I'm all right, now. Let's get going again, before the guardsmen regroup and bring reinforcements."

⤞ ⚜ ⤝

In reality, the king's guard turned out to be less of an issue than the Cult of Deimok as they pressed on toward the palace. The cult was not as organized as a military force might be, but pockets of supporters randomly came at them with whatever weapons they could scrounge, fueled by what seemed like almost maniacal outrage at the demonstration around their god's temple the previous night.

So many figures adorned with yellow fell to crossbow bolts—and to the swords and clubs of Qaden's gang members—that Kathrael started to wonder how many supporters the foreign god actually *had* in Rhyth.

After the confusion earlier when Favian had failed to appear, Andoc and Carivel had braved their mounts' nervousness around the shape-shifters to stay near the front of the procession with Sephira and Kathrael—for which she was grateful. Despite the barely controlled chaos of the march on the palace, it was still a shock when three cult members managed to break through the line of protection around Kathrael and her companions, rushing at them with raised daggers.

"*Witchspawn!*" a wild-eyed man screamed as he barreled toward Kathrael. "Evil temptress!"

Her heart stuttered and kicked against her ribs. She scrabbled for a dagger from one of the hidden sheaths in her skirt and swept her free arm in an arc, trying to block his knife hand and force it to the side as he crashed into her. The man was almost twice her size and she stumbled back, barely managing to step sideways and shove her weight against his shoulder as Keenan had shown her during their sparring sessions.

He lost his balance, but was able to grab her cloak and drag her with him, his knife arm lifting for a second attempt at stabbing her even as they fell to the ground. Before the wild blow could land, a heavy shape slammed into him, and Kath had a confused impression of tawny hide and red, red blood as the lion ripped into him.

She rolled away, dazed, and looked around wildly. Crossbows were useless when firing them might as easily hit allies as enemies, but Andoc bore down on one of the other cult members with Ozias, the heavy wood of his walking stick connecting with the man's head hard enough to split his skull. He dropped without a sound.

Meanwhile, the third man was struggling with Sephira. The wolf's jaws closed on his arm, dragging him off-balance, and Sephira plunged the ceremonial dagger she was holding into his chest. He grunted and collapsed, scrabbling at the jeweled hilt with his right hand, with Senovo's teeth still buried in his other arm. When he went still, the wolf shook his body viciously, as if searching for signs of life. There were none.

Sephira leaned down to jerk the knife free and wiped it on the man's yellow sash, leaving a smear of red behind as she straightened.

"Come on," she said, and offered Kathrael a hand up. "We can't stop."

Around them, the fighting continued as the mob pressed forward, overpowering the enraged cult members by sheer force of numbers. Kathrael saw Carivel fire a crossbow bolt from horseback, her teeth gritted in a grimace as she steadied Audris beneath her and reloaded the weapon. She glimpsed two large men fighting at the edges of the group, a jolt of surprise gripping her as she recognized one of them as Qaden. She hadn't even realized the gang leader was here near the front with them.

Something whistled past her ear, barely missing her. She wasn't even sure what it was. A rock? An arrow? She kept her dagger in her hand in case anyone else made it past the ring of people fighting around them. The press of thousands of people behind her was like a solid thing, pushing her forward despite the small bubble of clear space that the presence of the imposing shape-shifters afforded her.

Time stretched, and she could not have said how much of it passed before the attacking cult members gave way and the street opened up in front of them once more.

"To the palace! To the palace! To the palace!" The cry rose up behind her again, growing in strength, and she wasn't sure who had started it this time. She scanned her surroundings without stopping, making sure that Ithric and Senovo, Andoc and Carivel, Qaden and Sephira were all still with them and unhurt.

Carivel was wrapping a strip of cloth around her upper arm, tying it off with her teeth. Andoc leaned over to ask her something, and she shook her head, grim-faced but steady. The others seemed to be all right, and Kath tried to control her ragged breathing.

Clouds had continued to roll in as they made their way through the central part of the city, lending an odd, vaguely ominous quality to the winter light. It was too warm for snow today, but heavy rain would be even worse for them. She prayed that the support they supposedly enjoyed from the gods would extend to dry conditions for the next couple of hours.

Before she really expected it, the palace grounds came into view as they rounded a bend in the thoroughfare. They were here. Gods above... they had almost made it to their goal.

A moment later, she saw the burnished chest plates of the king's guard, and it became apparent why they hadn't run into any more of the ruler's forces after defeating the small band that had tried to keep the two groups of rebels from joining up near the temple district. It was because the guardsmen had decided to make their stand here, at the palace itself.

Clearly, Andoc had seen them, too. "We need everyone armed with crossbows up here at the front," he said, and she was forcibly reminded that this man with the twisted leg and the tattered beggar's clothing was, in fact, one of the most feared military minds on Eburos. "Kathrael, Sephira, get Ithric and Senovo toward the middle of the group, where it's safer. Teeth and claws and daggers won't be much use for the next little while, and we need you four to stay in one piece if it's at all possible." He flicked his eyes to Carivel. *"Caradi,* maybe you should go with them."

Carivel raised both eyebrows at her bondmate. "Yeah. Not happening. In case you've forgotten, firing arrows from horseback is kind of what I *do*. Now shut up, and let's get these archers organized."

Andoc nodded, looking unhappy. "Ah, well. It was worth a try," he muttered, forcing a brief, cocky smile that was only partially convincing.

Dharnal came cantering up on Fidget, the little black gelding tossing his head nervously as he smelled the lion and the wolf. "How many troops defending the palace?" he asked breathlessly.

"Looks like a couple hundred, maybe," Andoc replied, and the two fell into a brief consultation that Kathrael couldn't hear over the crowd noise. A few moments later, Dharnal gave Sephira a speaking look, then whirled and trotted off again.

"Come," Sephira said in her ear. "Let those who are qualified to do so put the weapons you gained for us to good use."

She led the way deeper into the crowd, toward the center where the elderly and infirm had congregated, along with the women and children. Kathrael blinked. Children. There were *children* here, for the gods' sakes.

She kept a hand tangled in Ithric's mane as they walked. Her other snuck down to rest on the wolf's wiry shoulders, almost without her being aware of it. A boy of perhaps ten, too thin and with huge, brown eyes, stepped up to the wolf without a hint of fear.

"Are you really the Wolf Patron?" he asked, awe behind the words.

Senovo, for obvious reasons, did not answer with anything more than a whine and a short, unhappy yip.

"He really is," Kathrael said, her voice hoarse.

The boy's bright eyes lifted to her. "And this is the Lion Prince?"

"Is that what the people are calling him now?" she asked, feeling a bit dazed.

He nodded solemnly, just as a worried looking woman shoved through the people nearby and called, "Mearka! Stay *with* me, child!"

The woman came to an abrupt stop, her face going pale as she took in the two massive predators.

"It's all right," Kathrael said quickly. "Mearka, go back to your mother, and stay near the center of the crowd. May the blessings of the gods be upon you."

Mearka's mother dipped her head in a nervous gesture of respect and hauled Mearka back by the shoulder. "Th-thank you, Blessed One," she stammered, and quickly disappeared into the press of people.

Kathrael glanced at Sephira, who had watched the exchange silently.

"That was well handled," she said. "Though you're as pale as milk, Kathrael. You must steel yourself for what is yet to come."

Kathrael tried to take a deep breath, but it felt like a tight band was strapped around her chest. "My mind is whirling," she said truthfully, having no one else to whom she could spill her thoughts. "Sephira, I'm an escaped slave. A prostitute with a ruined face. What am I even *doing* here?"

Sephira's lips twitched, though if the expression was trying to be a smile, it fell short. "You are making a difference," she said. "Your companions may be the figureheads, but you are the people's voice, Kathrael. I knew it as soon as I heard you speak at the meeting in the catacombs."

At the time, it had seemed so natural to step forward to the edge of the stone dais and address the crowd of would-be revolutionaries. Now, though, with Favian missing and Vesh gone, she felt wholly inadequate to the task.

The lion pressed against her, a low rumble rolling through his massive chest. On her other side, the wolf was watchful. Wary. Yesterday, she had seen Senovo topple a powerful religious guild nearly single-handedly, despite the fact that by doing so, it was clear that he was also reliving a private nightmare from his past.

She squeezed her eyes shut, her chin dropping to her chest as she breathed and breathed. She owed it to the Wolf Patron to be as strong as he had been, after the long and bitter years she'd spent hating him. She owed it to Favian, whether he was safe as Sephira claimed, or in terrible danger as Kathrael's instincts insisted. She owed it to Vesh, and to her sister. To her mother... to her unborn child... to all the slaves who had labored and died under Rhyth's yoke over the years.

She lifted her head, opening her eyes. She would play the role that fate had assigned her. It might mean her life. It might mean the lives of the people she loved. She might shatter into a thousand razor-edged shards the moment it was done, but until then, she would be the Masked Woman—the companion of shape-shifters and the mouthpiece of the gods.

A roar went up from the front. The battle had begun.

TWENTY-TWO

The wait as the battle raged between the palace guard and the rebels was its own kind of torture. Sephira grabbed a passing red-robed acolyte whom Kathrael did not recognize, and set her to spreading a message among the Sisters and refugees from the Priests' Guild who were scattered throughout the throng.

After she had hurried off, the priestess turned to the common folk around them. "Lift your voices, O people of Rhyth! Let the gods hear our prayers!"

Her voice rose in a melodious prayer to Deresta, the fiery goddess of war, and slowly, the people clustered nearby added their voices to hers.

Give us victory!
Give us justice!
We offer our lives and our blood in your service!
O Mighty Deresta,
We are on the side of right!

Around them, the chant floated up from other pockets of people, no doubt incited by the Sisters and priests who had received Sephira's message. It helped calm the restless and fearful crowd, but inside, Kathrael was still sick with the need to know *what was happening*.

It was clear that the guardsmen didn't have weapons with enough range to reach the center of the crowd, but that also meant that here, they had no sense at all of what was going on. Even Ithric seemed restless now, and the wolf was nearly vibrating with the need to move.

The need to find out whether his mates are safe, Kathrael thought. She felt an unexpected stab of guilt at having dragged Senovo into her battle, and his two lovers with him. She understood what he must be feeling right now — the same sort of piercing need to know Favian's fate had lodged in her own heart like a barb, and it was slowly bleeding her dry.

The feeble shadows cast when the sun peeked through the uneven blanket of clouds proclaimed that more than an hour had passed when Sephira's acolyte finally shoved her way through the crowd again, breathless and disheveled.

"Elder Sister!" she cried, straining to be heard over the crowd's chant, "Dharnal says come to the front! They're falling back! They're retreating!"

Kathrael sucked in a breath, her heart beating like the galloping hooves of a horse.

Sephira caught the acolyte's shoulders, steadying her. "The king's guard is retreating?" she clarified, and the girl nodded eagerly.

"Yes! You must all come quickly!"

Sephira gathered Kathrael and the animals in with a glance, and the four of them followed the girl, the crowd parting before the imposing forms of the lion and the wolf. As they walked, the girl continued to speak, pitching her voice to carry over the noise around them.

"It was the crossbows! One of the boys in front said that they could fire crossbow bolts farther than the guards could fire with their longbows. They could barely reach us with their arrows, and every time they tried to advance and get in range, we just picked them off before they could get any closer!"

Sephira nodded. "Calm yourself, Evie," she said, not unkindly. "The victory is a gift from Deresta, but it is not appropriate to glory in death. Not even in the death of an enemy."

The girl lowered her eyes, chastened. "I ask forgiveness, Priestess." She swallowed and continued in a more somber tone. "Anyway, when the guardsmen saw they couldn't possibly win, the ones who were left retreated inside the palace."

Kathrael met Sephira's eyes. "Heading for the high ground of the parapets, to gain cover and extend their range," she speculated.

Sephira nodded. "No doubt. Nevertheless, a victory is a victory. Every step forward is another step toward winning the war."

It took some time to make their way through the mass of people. When they were close to the front, the wolf lifted his head, scenting the air, and then darted forward, slipping through the final few rows of bystanders like smoke. Kathrael hurried after him, relying on Ithric's presence to open the way. She looked around until she found the two white horses at the edge of the crowd.

Carivel was already stepping down from Audris, holding his reins in one hand as she met the wolf, grabbing him in a one-armed hug as he jumped up and rested his front paws on her shoulders. Andoc stayed mounted—probably because of the difficulty involved in mounting and dismounting with his withered leg—but he urged Ozias closer to the pair and leaned down, reaching a hand out to stroke the animal as Senovo licked frantically at Carivel's jaw. The Draebardi chief's lips moved, but Kathrael could not make out the words over the noise around them.

She motioned Ithric to stay back, not wanting to spook the horses, and went with Sephira to join them. People were cheering all around them, lifting their crossbows over their heads in celebration, but she could also see men lying on the ground, being tended by others. Some of them lay very still.

"How many dead and injured?" she asked, when she was close enough to be heard over the din. The wolf dropped back on all fours, pressing against Carivel's leg, while Andoc straightened in the saddle and regarded her.

"We haven't done a count yet," he said. "Far fewer than I would have expected after facing two hundred trained soldiers with a band of untrained civilians, though. These crossbows are a marvel."

"These crossbows are bloody *terrifying*, you mean," Carivel put in. "Good thing they were mostly in our hands, and not the soldiers'."

"They almost weren't," Kathrael said grimly, trying not to imagine how this day would have gone if the weapons had ended up in the king's armory as they were supposed to.

Dharnal rode up and joined them. "We need to press the advantage while it's still fresh. There's no doubt the ones who retreated are headed up to the parapets to try and pick us off as we approach the palace gates. I don't know that there's any way to avoid heavy losses when they do. The only option I can see is to try and overwhelm them with our numbers."

Andoc nodded and scrubbed a hand down his face. "Those numbers are largely made up of unarmed common folk, Dharnal. Crossbows or no, we'd be leading them into a bloodbath."

Kathrael straightened her spine, aware that she was about to offer up both Ithric's and Senovo's life, as well as her own. "Can you safely estimate their range with longbows from the parapets?" she asked, looking from Andoc to Dharnal.

Andoc frowned. "Not with any real accuracy. Why?"

"But you could keep the front edge of the crowd back far enough so they would be safe, yet still within the palace grounds?" she pressed.

"Yes, we could," he said, glancing at Dharnal, who shrugged and nodded agreement. "But that doesn't solve our tactical problem of how to take the palace."

Kathrael turned to Sephira. "Inga said the goddesses would come together and support us if we acted today. Do you truly believe that?"

Sephira gazed at her for a long moment before a faint smile graced her lips. "I do. I have enough faith in Inga's prediction that I will not only support what you are about to propose, Kathrael; I will offer myself up with you."

Dharnal's face darkened. "Sephira, what—?" he began, but she cut him off with a shake of her head. He subsided, his eyes stormy.

Kathrael took a deep breath. She looked down at Ithric, and the lion met her gaze unflinchingly. Her eyes moved to Senovo. The wolf lifted his head and separated himself from Carivel, returning to stand at Kathrael's left side.

"Keep the crowd back," she said, her voice calm and certain. "We will approach the palace alone and speak with the king."

"The *fuck* you will. That's suicide," Carivel said. Her hands clenched into fists at her side.

Kath met her gaze squarely. "I have it on very good authority that the gods are on our side. I would rather rely on their support and risk the lives of only a few, than risk leading these people to their deaths."

Carivel's eyes flew to Andoc, who returned her look.

"No," Carivel said. "We can't let them do this, Andoc."

Andoc stared at the wolf's gold-green eyes. Senovo met his gaze unflinchingly as he stood unmoving at Kathrael's side.

Carivel followed his gaze. "Senovo, *no*."

Sephira spoke into the tense standoff. "We risk death either way, Wolf's Mate. Whether we approach alone or with a mob at our backs, we are equally likely to fall under a hail of arrows. We will *not* fall, however. The goddesses will protect us."

Carivel's mouth opened, but no words came out. She stared at Andoc again, pleading. The Draebardi chief's face was pale as he spoke. "She has a point, *caradi*. This looks very much like suicide for whoever's in front, and that was always going to be us."

Kathrael could see Carivel's chest rising and falling with her rapid breathing. It took a moment for the sense of Andoc's words to penetrate, and her brows drew together in consternation.

"Wait, you two don't need to risk yourselves—" Kath said, only to be cut off by a ripple of movement on her left.

Senovo straightened, his eyes flashing. "No. You and Carivel must stay back with the others." His velvet voice snapped with command.

Andoc made a noise of disbelief and stepped down awkwardly from Ozias' back, steadying himself against the stallion's shoulder until he could grab his walking stick for balance.

"And you're going to stop us from coming... how, exactly?" he asked, his tone surprisingly gentle. He handed the horse's reins off to a man standing nearby, and Carivel followed suit. They approached Senovo to stand in front of him, shoulder to shoulder, and Kathrael moved back a few steps to get out of their way, taking the lion with her.

She thought of how she and Ithric had insisted on accompanying Favian on his crazy quest to preach in the streets... and of what had happened when they had stupidly allowed him to go alone. Guilt still flooded her at the memory of that awful mistake. At that moment, she knew Andoc and Carivel would be coming with them—even if Senovo was not yet convinced.

"I already allowed you to face battle with the king's guard while I huddled in safety with unarmed women and children," Senovo said. "I will *not* allow you to take this risk as well."

Carivel scowled at him. "And this risk is different from all the other risks the three of us taken, because...?"

"Because it is mine to take... *not yours*." The words seemed to be wrenched from Senovo's chest. They were barely audible over the noise of the celebrating crowd.

It was Andoc who answered, closing his large hands around Senovo's naked shoulders. "Senovo, you are the most powerful High Priest Eburos has seen in a generation. If you truly believe you will be walking to your death, then as far as I'm concerned, *none* of you are going. But if you believe, as Sephira does, that the gods intend this somehow... that it is preordained... then you will not be going *alone*."

Senovo was silent for a long, tense moment.

"I believe..." he began, "that the prophecy of the Wolf Patron is a destiny I cannot escape. I have certainly spent a lifetime trying to do so, yet... here we all stand." A shiver wracked him—the winter chill penetrating his bare skin. Andoc and Carivel moved closer, their hands pressing against him. "I do not know yet whether that prophecy is a curse, or a blessing in disguise."

"It doesn't matter," Carivel said. "Because it's not as though we'd let you face either of those things on your own, now, is it?"

Senovo looked around at the armed slaves... at the fallen fighters. "I do not wish you to risk yourselves for me yet again."

"And we don't wish for you to risk yourself again, either," Carivel replied without hesitation. "But... if this is truly the fulfillment of a prophecy, I can't believe that the gods would punish a lifetime of sacrifice and selflessness by cursing you to death in the very place you are trying to save."

Kathrael's throat grew tight. "Let them come with us, Wolf Patron, please. You know as well as I do that they are meant to be at your side, always." She thought of Favian, her chest aching with the need to have him here with her.

Senovo looked down as another shiver wracked him. "Gods forgive me," he said, lifting a hand to scrub over his face. "I'm too weak to tell you *no* again."

Andoc kissed him. "There's nothing to forgive, *amadi*— no matter what happens here today."

He eased away, letting Carivel take his place. "We love you, Senovo," she said, and pressed her lips to his. "Whatever happens, we'll face it together."

The lion rubbed his blocky head against Kathrael's hip in a reassuring caress, and she clutched at his mane convulsively. Favian was gone, but Ithric was still here. They would do this together and trust in the gods. There was no other choice for them now.

"Sephira," Dharnal began again.

Sephira placed a hand over her lover's heart, palm flat. "Dharnal," she told him, "You are in charge of these people. Do as you think best if anything should happen to us."

He covered her hand with his, and his voice was tight when he answered. "I thought you said the gods would keep you safe."

She shrugged. "I did." A wan smile tugged at her lips. "But I also serve the one known as the Trickster. In such a position, it's as well not to be *too* certain of anything."

Both Vesh and Favian would almost certainly have had a sarcastic quip to share in response to that particular little gem of wisdom. Kathrael wished desperately that they were here to do so. But they weren't.

"We should go," she said. "Dharnal, make sure to keep the crowd well out of range of the guardsmen's bows."

Senovo closed his eyes, took a deep breath, and shifted back into the form of the wolf. Kathrael looked at Andoc.

"Do you need help re-mounting?" she asked.

He shook his head. "No. There's no reason to risk the horses. I'll manage on foot. If this goes to shit, those stallions will be of more use to Dharnal's men if he decides to fight it out."

She and Carivel both nodded their agreement.

"Sephira," Kathrael said, "can we quiet the crowd?"

Sephira beckoned to Evie and spoke with her. The acolyte bowed quickly and darted back into the crowd. "That will take some doing," she said. "Let's get them moving while the message spreads."

The entrance to the palace complex was perhaps a hundred paces away. The courtyard beyond was massive. Kathrael was tense, half-expecting another attack despite the fact that the guardsmen seemed to have retreated for a final stand inside the ramparts. Nothing impeded their approach, however. They poured into the grounds, the crowd spreading out as it passed through the entrance.

Kathrael had never been this close to the king's seat of power before. Several of the others had, she knew. She remembered Favian telling her that he, Senovo, Andoc, and Carivel had been on the way to a meeting here at the palace when they'd stumbled across Kathrael and her fellow slaves in a field north of the city, and turned her life upside down.

The palace dwarfed the finest of the rich houses where she and the others had entertained fat noblemen over the past couple of months. Even at a distance, the structure dominated the central district. And it had clearly been built with defense in mind. She could already make out figures arrayed along the top of the mighty walls, sheltering behind stone parapets, no doubt with bows at the ready.

Kathrael's education in military matters consisted largely of the dreary pillow talk of soldiers who had paid to bed her over the years, along with a smattering of strategy she'd picked up while listening to the members of the rebellion who had fighting experience.

But even she could see that they were in a terribly vulnerable position here. The entrance to the courtyard seemed huge and imposing as you walked through it, but it was the only way in and out unless a person somehow scaled the courtyard walls. If the mob panicked and tried to flee the palace grounds, it would create a nearly insurmountable bottleneck. People would be trampled, and any troops waiting outside would be able to pick them off at leisure, a few at a time.

Meanwhile, the soldiers on the ramparts could attack anyone who tried to enter the palace itself, the added height of their positions compensating for the shorter range of their longbows compared to the rebels' crossbows.

"If the gods *aren't* planning on acting on our behalf," Carivel muttered, "we are *seriously* screwed."

The clouds had once again obscured the sun as they entered the king's domain, darkening the sky even more ominously than before. The air hung heavy despite the winter chill. By all appearances, practically every single thing was arrayed against them — even the weather.

A tiny voice in the back of Kath's mind was chanting, *this is madness, this is madness, what were you thinking?* For once, it didn't belong to someone else; it simply sounded like *her* voice. Somehow, that made it easier to shove it to the side and ignore it.

"This is close enough for the crowd," Andoc said, and turned to limp backwards, raising the hand that wasn't holding his walking stick and shouting, *"Halt! No farther!"* in a booming, battlefield voice.

Fighters at the front took up the cry. The chanting was already fading away as the priests and priestesses spread calls for silence through the crowd. It was replaced by muttering, some excited, some fearful, some confused. Kathrael wondered how many of the bystanders who had been swept up in the mob truly had any idea of what they were getting into.

She could tell there was some confusion and jostling as the forward progress of the massive throng was blocked by those at the front. Before long, the crowd settled, restless but quiescent for now. She briefly considered speaking to the people, but she wasn't sure what she would say. In the end, she decided to simply head for the palace. Those near the front would be able to hear her call out to the king, and no doubt an account of her words would travel through the crowd quickly.

She took a deep breath and lifted her chin, aware on some level of the picture she made—red dress the color of blood, shot through with silver and gold thread. Bronze mask, resplendent with flames and feathers like some mythical phoenix. Flanked by wild beasts who strode calmly at her side as though under her control. Behind her followed a priestess in ochre robes, a slender figure encompassing both male and female within a single body, and a lame beggar who was, in reality, one of the most powerful men on Eburos.

All of them, walking with unhesitating steps toward what should, by rights, be certain death. The rational part of Kathrael's mind was still gibbering in the background, proclaiming the insanity of what she was doing. The larger part, however, descended into a strange, unnatural sort of calm, like sliding into the warm waters of the spring-fed pool hidden below the plain of the Old Stones.

Her life had been one long series of events pushing her inexorably toward this moment. Whether she survived it or not, right now Kathrael was exactly where she was meant to be.

Four people and two beasts walked without hesitation toward the palace, and into the sights of a hundred archers, any one of whom could have rained death on them. When they were close enough to be heard within the walls, Kathrael stopped, and the others stopped with her.

The calm was all encompassing, now, no trace of her fear remaining. When she spoke, it was with the voice of the Masked Woman. The voice of every person who had ever been trampled underfoot and left to rot in the streets of Rhyth.

"*Flenaar of Rhyth,*" she called. "*Your people call you to account. Face them, or prove yourself the coward I know you to be!*"

She could see some of the soldiers huddled on the ramparts above exchanging looks. There was silence for a long time, broken only by the occasional rustle and clink of armor. She let it stretch—let it pull Rhyth's puppet ruler toward her like the marionette he was.

When he appeared on a balcony above them, flanked by two grim-faced guards, she was not surprised, though she sensed that the others were.

The king had donned golden armor, a ridiculous conceit in any kind of real battle. Though it might, she supposed, deflect an arrow. Not that even a good marksman could make such a shot from the crowd's position out of longbow range. For now, the ruler's soft gold battle garb would remain safely unscathed.

"You risk death with this show of disrespect," Rhyth's ruler said from his perch high above them. His long, black hair fluttered in a breath of wind; the sky was dark and threatening above him.

Though Flenaar was a slender man, lacking in both muscle and physical stature, his speaking voice commanded attention. Kathrael lifted her chin, meeting his eyes fearlessly.

"And you have courted ruin by grinding your subjects into the dirt," she said. "You are sworn to protect them, yet they starve and labor in bondage! *No longer*, O King of Nothing. Today, you will surrender to the very people you hold in such disdain."

Flenaar laughed, as if it was expected... as if he was giving a performance for his watching troops. "You amuse me, little jester, with your shiny mask and your performing beasts. I should probably have had you killed as soon as you approached, but listening to you babble entertains me on this dreary winter's day."

More likely, he was feeling out the situation, aware that if the mob stormed the palace, they might overwhelm his remaining guards with sheer force of numbers.

Kathrael remained silent, uninterested in his taunts. In her strange, detached state, she clearly felt her power over this situation. By placing her life and the lives of her companions in the hands of the gods, she was freed from any constraint to respond in the way Flenaar was trying to goad her into responding. As far as she was concerned, he no longer held any sway over the direction of the day's events.

All he could do was kill her. He could not control her. She would never again be a slave to anyone—not even the king of Rhyth.

As she had known he would, Flenaar spoke again, unable to let her silence stretch. "I won't be the one to surrender, jester," he said. "Messengers have already been dispatched for reinforcements. Additional troops will arrive here shortly, and if this rabble has not dispersed, they will pin your mob of traitors in this courtyard and massacre them to the last man, woman, and child."

Sephira stepped forward to stand next to the wolf. "They will not," she said with supreme confidence. "The goddesses stand behind us on this extraordinary day, puppet king. Your troops are as children before them, waving their fists and throwing pebbles."

Flenaar scoffed. "How dare you. Do I take threats from a superstitious harlot? With a word, I could see you burned at the stake, and the hides of your pet beasts hung from the city gates. Blasphemy is dealt with harshly in Rhyth. Your kind is a stain of rot within this city."

From the corner of her eye, Kathrael saw Sephira's mouth stretch into a feral grin, a gleam of something that almost appeared to be glee in her eyes. She bowed low, theatrically, sarcasm dripping from every pore.

"Do *please* forgive me, your most esteemed majesty." Her voice oozed with fake sweetness. "I misspoke earlier. The goddesses do not stand behind us on this extraordinary day." She straightened, her strange gray eyes almost seeming to glow from within in the dim light. She looked up. "The goddesses... stand *above us.*"

"*What in the gods' names?*" The whispered comment came from Andoc, and Kathrael had never heard his voice sound like that before.

She followed Sephira's gaze up toward the dark sky. She gazed at the parting clouds in confusion. The sky had cleared as they stood speaking with the king of Rhyth. But where the sun should be, there was only a bare crescent of light. As she watched, open-mouthed, it was swallowed completely, leaving only an eerie, pale ring hanging high in the east. It had become nighttime in the middle of the day, stars peeking out in the indigo wash of sky, with only a hole where the sun should be. A hole where the moon should be.

Gasps and cries erupted in front of her, within the palace walls. She could hear frightened screams from the crowd behind them. Kathrael struggled to make sense of the impossibility hanging over their heads—a night sky with no sun and no moon, the faintest hint of sunset surrounding them in all directions on the horizon.

Something clicked into place in her memory, and she snapped her jaw shut sharply.

The chief goddesses are coming together. When they join forces, no king or army will be able to stand in the way of your cause.

Inga's cryptic words had been a prophecy after all. Deresta—goddess of the sun. Utarr—goddess of the moon. The goddesses had merged, the sun and the moon cancelling each other out. Kathrael's breath hitched.

She swallowed, refusing to think about what it would mean for the world if the sun and moon were gone forever. She had to *act*. She couldn't afford to *react*. It was the reactions of the men above her on the ramparts that they needed now. *That* was the edge the goddesses had given them.

"Guardsmen!" she cried. "Deliver Flenaar to the common people, or risk the goddess's wrath!"

The wolf howled, the noise cutting through the sounds of human panic. An instant later, the deafening roar of a lion joined the mournful noise.

The faintest hint of light was returning now, but Kathrael did not dare look at the hole in the sky to see what was happening. She peered through the gloom, straining to see the reactions of the king's bodyguards. The king himself was frozen in place with shock. The bodyguard on his left was focused on the sky, his sword hanging limp in his hand. The one on his right was crouched in place, visibly shaking— nearly prostrating himself before the goddess's might.

He looked at the mob milling around in the courtyard. At the wolf and lion. His eyes caught and held Kathrael's gaze, and she stared back, impassive, sensing the world twist and warp around her, sliding into the shape that she needed it to be.

The feeling that suffused her as the bodyguard tightened his grip on his sword hilt, turned to King Flenaar of Rhyth, and plunged his blade into the gap at the edge of his golden chestplate was not relief.

It was inevitability.

Flenaar clutched at the wound as his traitorous guard pulled the sword free, blood gushing from between his fingers. He convulsed, toppling to the ground out of Kathrael's line of sight, but she knew he was dead.

The guard looked frantically toward the sky, as if seeking validation for his actions. And, indeed, the darkness was already starting to lift, becoming once again that strange, murky half-light which Kathrael had taken earlier for an approaching storm.

She could sense his relief from the sag of his shoulders. His fellow guard was staring at him in consternation, clearly unsure how to respond.

"Lay down your weapons," the assassin cried, placing his sword on the balcony floor next to its victim. "See if that makes the sun come back! *Lay down your weapons!*"

A handful of the guardsmen on the parapets laid down their longbows, and the sun brightened incrementally above them.

"Yes! That's it! It's working!" someone called, and more of the terrified guards disarmed themselves, paying more attention to the sky than to the throng in the courtyard.

That throng was moving. Kathrael turned at the sound of people and horses approaching, to see Dharnal leading the rebels forward to the palace gates. The crowd parted around Kathrael and her companions like water.

"Open the gates!" It was the powerful voice of Dharnal, mounted on Audris now, and standing at the head of the rebel force. "Surrender and you will not be harmed. Resist, and you will die before the goddess's might!"

Kathrael waited, still with unnatural calm. Minutes passed, and the massive gates creaked open. The armed fighters entered the seat of Rhytheeri power, and Kathrael followed them, still surrounded by her five companions, animal and human.

She heard shouts from deeper in the palace as the rebels met and overpowered small pockets of resistance. Those guards who foolishly decided to fight back were, however, vastly outnumbered by those who did not. The kneeling figures of soldiers, servants, and nobles waited meekly along the walls by the dozens, humbling themselves before the new citizen-rulers of Rhyth.

They reached a stairway and went up, rising through the halls of power. Kathrael followed the sturdy form of Dharnal, who led them unerringly through the huge building. She realized with a flash of insight that Sephira's lover was not merely a defected city guardsman. He was a defected *palace* guardsman.

And he knew exactly where he was going.

He gestured Kathrael, Ithric, and Senovo toward the open balcony where Flenaar had fallen less than an hour before. Someone had removed his body, but blood still pooled, congealing on the cool stone floor. Kathrael looked at Sephira questioningly when the woman hung back at the entrance, and the priestess of Avlan smiled.

"I told you before, Kathrael," she said. "I may be the voice of the Trickster god, but you are the voice of the people. Speak to them."

Senovo shifted into human form next to her, and Ithric followed suit a moment later. Both men accepted cloaks and shrugged them on. Senovo looked dazed; Ithric looked smug. He cupped her bare cheek in his palm, a secret smile tugging at his full lips.

You did it, his expression seemed to say.

We did it, she tried to reply. *Gods above. We did it.*

Andoc and Carivel each grasped one of Senovo's shoulders, and the High Priest sagged for a moment before drawing himself straight again. He clasped Carivel's hand, drawing it to his lips and closing his eyes as he pressed a kiss to her knuckles. When she slid her fingers free, he repeated the gesture with Andoc's hand, and drew in a deep breath before returning to Kathrael's side.

The three of them walked onto the balcony, the others hanging back beyond the doorway. Kathrael strode to the railing, Ithric and Senovo silent shadows at her side. She looked down over the sea of faces milling below in the winter sunshine, and breathed in.

"*The ruler of Rhyth is dead, and so are his laws,*" she began, her voice rolling over the courtyard. "*From this day forward, no person in the southern lands may own another. Slavery no longer exists on the island of Eburos. King Flenaar is no more. Long live the Rhytheeri people!*"

The roar of approval that rose from the multitude in the courtyard shook the very stones of the palace with its power.

TWENTY-THREE

The mortal world was a strange and confusing place without the tether of Kathrael's brilliant spirit, which had always shone like a beacon in Vesh's ghostly awareness. Whether he was alive or dead, he was drawn to her like a moth to flame, reveling in the conflagration without thought for the consequences. She had always been the righteous anger to his apathy, the unconquerable antidote to his feelings of defeat.

Now, he was trapped in a strange contradiction. The spirit world called to him, promising the final peace of a proper death after the unnatural stretch of half-life he'd experienced — attached to the living world, but no longer truly living. He could not follow the pull of eternal rest, though. His purpose here was not yet completed.

Until today, he could not have even conveyed what, exactly, that purpose was supposed to be. Now, it was the only thing that mattered.

Favian — Kathrael's charming, awkward, kind-hearted priest-boy — had a very unusual mind, as it turned out. It was loosely entwined with the spirit world. Not entwined with the *dead*, as such, but rather with the timelessness of the land beyond the living. His sleeping awareness occasionally latched onto events in the past and future, slipping through cracks in the veil between worlds and dragging back slivers of other times.

Favian's spirit was also inexorably entwined with Kathrael's. As was the lion-boy's spirit. As was Vesh's. Now, Vesh had to somehow find Favian amongst this endless sea of the living.

Vesh knew, with a sort of distant awareness, that time was passing in the mortal world as he searched, looking among the multitude of brilliant spirits for that one unique signature with its fleeting sense of shared familiarity.

Was such a thing even possible? Or was Vesh delusional now, as well as dead? It seemed increasingly likely that he was — but, delusional or not, Vesh knew that he would wander lost and untethered through this ocean of living souls for all eternity, before he would willingly disappoint Kathrael. He couldn't let her down. Not now, when she needed him most.

In another corner of Vesh's fractured awareness, he was aware of the strangeness of the world's natural rhythms on this unusual day. While he had not studied it very much when he'd been a youth at the temple, Vesh found himself intrigued by the movements of the celestial bodies now that he had the perspective of, well... *being dead.*

His visit to the Old Stones had given him an unprecedented appreciation for Inga's combination of mysticism, observation, and painstakingly accurate recording of astronomical data. Trying to understand her scribblings had started as a way for Vesh to distract himself from the bittersweet experience of watching Kath have joyful and uninhibited sex with two men she loved—neither of whom were *him.*

It wasn't accurate to say that he was jealous. Jealousy would imply that he didn't want her to be having joyful and uninhibited sex with the people she loved. It was more that it made him sad. He hadn't really grieved his own death, because doing so felt both strange and selfish. But... seeing her like that made him grieve the loss of all his future possibilities, if nothing else.

So, Vesh spent much of the time they'd been at the Old Stones soaking up Inga's written records and uncovering the patterns she'd observed in the sky. Day after day, night after night, the old woman compared the position of the sun, moon, and stars to the unchanging positions of the Old Stones. And now, this very morning, the sun and the moon— which had been crossing ever nearer to each other—would finally meet.

Based on her written notes, it had not been clear to Inga exactly what would happen when that occurred. But it was starting even now, and it appeared that the moon was going to briefly block out the sun's light. Indeed, the sky was already growing unnaturally dark in the world of the living.

Well, that was inaccurate. It was *perfectly* natural. But it was still strange.

A ripple, barely perceptible, interrupted his musing. It disturbed the fabric of living spirits around him, and Vesh paused. Seeking. Reaching. Following, until—

There!

A flash of second-hand familiarity, which had only been distinguishable from the chaotic background of souls because it was...

Oh. It was *leaving.*

Well, shit. Evidently, the priest-boy was trying to die. Just like that, Vesh's course of action became painfully, blatantly clear. He hurtled toward the fragile flicker, aware that he was skimming the plane between one side of the veil and the other as he did so.

He could sense the landscape of fallen bodies — dead and injured — littering the street leading from Rhyth's temple district to the main thoroughfare. He could also sense the spirit world; the realm that had both drawn and repelled him since he'd ripped his spirit free from Kathrael's.

Favian was floating between the two, drifting inexorably from the living world toward the spirit world.

Vesh slammed into him with every bit of momentum he possessed, and the pair tumbled back into Favian's body, mutually stunned. Vesh wrestled with blind panic and confusion not his own, as it quickly became clear why Favian's spirit had wrenched itself free of his physical form. His physical form was — to put it mildly — a bit of a wreck at the moment.

If Vesh hadn't spent the last several months learning how to separate himself from Kath's feelings, sensations, and emotions, both he and Favian would have been lost in that moment. As it was, Vesh forcibly pulled back from the pain, the fear, and the horrific sensation of drowning in one's own blood, so he could take stock.

Blood was pumping freely from a wound under Favian's left collarbone. Far, far too much blood. Blood also filled his mouth, choking him as he tried to breath. Beneath the stabbing agony of the open wound and the throbbing pain where his skull had impacted the cobblestones, Vesh could barely make out the ache of Favian's third injury.

Steeling himself, he slammed into Favian's consciousness once more, melding them together so closely that his words would reverberate through the priest-boy's panic, impossible to ignore. He'd really never had much experience playing the bully during his short lifetime, but for Kath's lover, he'd give it his best.

You've bitten your tongue, you arse, he snapped. *Spit out the blood. Now!*

The last word was sharp as a whip-crack and Favian convulsed, responding to the tone of command out of instinct. He curled half onto his side, a gout of blood spraying from his mouth as he spat. Vesh was peripherally aware of hands grasping at Favian's body as he jerked and shuddered on the cold ground. The young priest was not alone on the street-turned-battlefield, but Vesh couldn't spare much attention quite yet for the details of what was going on around them.

Now, BREATHE, godsdamn you! Vesh didn't really have to fake angry yelling at this point; experiencing the feeling of suffocation — even secondhand — was threatening to pull him right back into full-blown, animal panic.

The terrible gurgle of air sucked past a throat still full of blood was not one Vesh ever wanted to hear again… though he suspected he was, in fact, going to be hearing it quite a bit for the next little while. He winced at the burning agony they both experienced as Favian's chest rose, jarring the bleeding wound.

… can't…

The thought was barely more than a whimper — the first sign of real awareness Favian had shown since Vesh forced him back into his body. Another flush of unaccustomed anger shot through Vesh at the thought that he might fail to keep Favian alive, even after succeeding in the nearly insurmountable task of finding him.

Too bad, priest-boy, he barked, channeling his childhood overseer's sharp indifference and lack of compassion. *I'm not letting either of us leave, and I have no fucking clue what will happen to us if we stay in your body when it dies. So you might want to… oh, I don't know? Keep. Fucking. Breathing.*

Favian spat more blood, and dragged in another wet gulp of air, the pain no better this time than it had been with the first. Vesh tried not to hate himself for the torture he was inflicting on this innocent soul who had never asked to be party to violence and civil war.

That's it, he encouraged. *Now, keep doing that for a minute while I try to figure out what's going on around us. Open your eyes.*

Favian reluctantly blinked his eyes open, and Vesh could feel tears of pain spilling over and tracking down his cheeks. The world was a dark blur.

... blind...

Oh. Yes. He'd almost forgotten about that. *You're not blind,* he reassured. *The goddesses are coming together, as Inga foretold. The moon is blocking out the sun.*

He didn't really get the impression that Favian understood what he was saying, which, under the circumstances, was probably fair enough. The important part was that Favian blinked a couple of times, and the blurriness cleared enough that Vesh could make out their surroundings a bit better.

High Priestess Zandreen crouched next to them, one hand steadying Favian on his side so he could breathe without choking. She was looking at something—*someone*—out of his field of vision.

"Is it ready?" she called. "It has to be red hot. Get the blade right down into the flames!"

A sinking feeling overtook Vesh as he thought about just how much blood Favian was losing. His suspicion was confirmed when a lad in ragged slave clothing hurried up and carefully handed Zandreen a dagger, the blade glowing dull orange in the dim light. Just exactly the sort of thing one might use to cauterize a deep wound that wouldn't stop bleeding.

Well, *son of a bitch.* Before he could think too much about it, Vesh turned inward, wrapping himself around Favian and holding tight—partly so his spirit wouldn't accidentally be jarred loose from Favian's when the pain hit, and partly because no one should have to face something like this alone.

Sorry, priest-boy, he whispered. *This part is truly going to be unpleasant.*

... what? Favian sounded dazed. Lost.

Hold on, Vesh said. *We'll do it together. I won't leave; I promise.*

Zandreen's mouth pressed into a thin line, and she lowered the glowing knife to Favian's clavicle. Favian screamed, the smell of cooking meat filling the air, and the dim illumination from the false night sky gave way to endless, velvety black.

TWENTY-FOUR

For a long time, the only thing Favian knew was darkness, shot through with strange dreams and interspersed with brief periods of awareness during which blinding pain tore through his chest, chasing him straight back down into the abyss.

The dreams were particularly vexing, because they consisted almost entirely of someone yelling abuse at him whenever he forgot to breathe... or whenever he chose not to breathe, because breathing was too difficult and too painful and he was *completely exhausted.* Some of it was surprisingly creative abuse. Some of it might even have been amusing if Favian weren't so busy trying to die.

But it was also *loud.* And occasionally very personal. Unpleasantly so. He wasn't actually all that thrilled to have someone shouting in his ear at length about all the horrible things Ithric and Kathrael would do to him if he didn't *stop being a bloody useless waste of space and take another damned breath.* It just seemed... *rude,* somehow, to drag his relationship with his lovers into things.

What had Favian ever done to deserve a heckler during his attempts at dealing with an arrow through the chest?

It was under your collarbone, said the heckler. *More of a shoulder wound, really.*

Favian scowled in his sleep. *Under the collarbone counts as part of the chest,* he argued mulishly. *I already got one in the shoulder, a long time ago, and it was nothing like this, all right?*

Whatever helps you sleep at night, priest-boy, the heckler said, as if humoring him. *Now take another godsdamned breath, will you?*

Go fuck yourself, Favian thought, and breathed.

Language, the heckler chided, sparking something in Favian's mind.

How could his mysterious gadfly possibly know about Ithric's favorite taunt?

⤙ 𝗪 ⤚

The first time he regained enough awareness to take in the world beyond the bounds of his battered body, it was to find himself lying on the most comfortable bed he'd ever been in. He blinked until an opulent room came into focus, lit by gentle early morning light streaming through a window.

There was warmth on either side of him—soft and delicate on his left; sleek, hard-muscled, and smelling of animal on his right. Kathrael. Ithric. They were here. They were alive. They were together.

Breathe, the gadfly reminded, in a tone of warning.

Favian breathed, tears springing to his eyes as the pain made his vision waver. With an immense effort, he let his head roll first to one side, then the other, trying to see. More tears threatened as he saw three other figures dozing on a long, padded settle against the far wall. Andoc sat with his head tipped back and resting against the wall, mouth open in sleep. Carivel was curled with her head resting in his lap, and Senovo was propped against his shoulder on the other side.

Favian's small movement was enough to rouse the lion to wakefulness. He felt the odd ripple in reality that he'd thought he would never feel again, as Ithric sat up in human form, looking down at him. He looked like shit, pale and drawn, with dark smudges under his eyes.

"Favian?" he asked, seemingly frozen in place.

Favian didn't even try to speak. There was no point; he was too weak. Instead, he blinked up at Ithric, feeling another tear slide down his face. Kathrael flailed awake on his other side, her voice raspy and breathless.

"Ithric? What is it? What's wrong? Is he—"

"He's awake," Ithric said quickly.

It was harder to move his head this time, as if exhaustion were already pulling at him. Still, Favian managed it, meeting Kathrael's eye. She sobbed, slapping a hand over her mouth as though trying to keep the sound inside.

Rustling from across the room heralded the others rousing from sleep. Senovo appeared in his line of sight, his face the same shade of pale as Ithric's, and with the same dark circles under his red-rimmed eyes. Why did everyone look so terrible?

"I will find Zandreen, and the physician," Senovo said. "Try to get broth into him."

Hands eased under his head and back, lifting his upper body. Stabbing agony shot through him at the movement, turning the world dark again. When his vision returned, he was resting against Ithric, who was supporting Favian cradled against his chest. Cool fingers stroked over his temple in a soothing rhythm, and his eyes traced the arm they were attached to until he was once more blinking up at Kath's scarred and worried visage.

"That's it," she whispered. "Come back to us, Favian."

His lips parted, but speech was still impossible, and probably would be for some time. Interestingly, there was now no sign of his personal gadfly.

The bed dipped, and Carivel handed a cup of something across to Kathrael. Andoc approached to stand behind Kath's shoulder, leaning heavily on his walking stick. His face was etched with lines of worry.

Favian knew there were things he should be remembering. Big things. But Kathrael was lifting the cup to his lips, her other hand moving from his temple to the back of his head, supporting him. She held the metal cup perfectly steady, meting out a tiny sip of the contents—broth of some kind, rich and perfectly seasoned.

He knew before he even attempted it that swallowing was going to be a new kind of torture, but his body craved the nourishing liquid with the intensity of a starving man. Still, he squeezed his eyes shut, trying to brace himself.

It was not as bad as being lifted into Ithric's arms had been, but it was still enough to make him wish for the relief of unconsciousness again. He managed perhaps half a dozen sips before angling his head away, unable to continue. Kath eased his head down to rest on Ithric's shoulder and set the cup aside.

"It's a start," Carivel said. "We can try again in a bit."

Favian was already starting to drift when Senovo returned with other people in tow. He heard them discussing him and knew he should pay attention to what they were saying; knew he should have reacted more when a cool hand peeled up one of his eyelids and an unfamiliar face peered into his. But it was far easier to lie back against Ithric's chest, soaking up his comforting heat, and let the darkness steal away his pain once more.

When he dreamed this time, he found himself standing among the Old Stones, looking through the gap in three large blocks arranged in the shape of a doorway, two massive uprights and a heavy lintel balanced on top. A figure stood on the other side of the aperture, mirroring Favian. He was slender—clad in clothing that was simple, but flattering. Waves of raven-black hair fell to his shoulders, brushing high cheekbones and framing a sharp chin. His eyes were brown and somber, and his nose was a bit crooked, lending a faint sense of asymmetry to his features that drew Favian's gaze.

And... Favian could see right through him, to the scenery behind his body.

"You're Vesh," Favian said, not phrasing it as a question.

The figure smiled. "So I am."

Favian's eyes narrowed at the familiar voice. "You've been hurling abuse at me for days now. I think it's been days?"

"Hmm... so I have," Vesh agreed. "And yes, I believe it's been a couple of days, at least. It's a bit hard to tell."

"I'm not sure whether to thank you or punch you," Favian said. "By rights, I think it's pretty clear that I should be dead."

"Maybe," replied Vesh. "I don't honestly recommend it, though."

Favian raised an eyebrow. "But you *do* recommend living with a horrific wound that makes every breath agony?"

Vesh didn't even hesitate. "If it means more time with the people you love, then you bet I do, priest-boy."

There really wasn't any arguing with that.

"I... was worried that my spirit might latch onto Kathrael when I died," Favian confessed. "I was *terrified*, in fact. I didn't want to do that to her... even though a tiny part of me selfishly kind of *did*."

Silence reigned for the space of several breaths.

"I have to leave soon," Vesh said eventually. "I'm losing my grip on the living world. Growing weaker, the longer I stay with you."

Favian nodded. "Because you don't have Kath as a tether?"

Vesh shrugged. "Something like that. Before I go, I need your word that you won't stop fighting. That you won't lie down and slip away."

Favian's tone turned dry. "Without your gentle and tactful reminders, you mean?"

"Your word, Favian. It's important."

He took a deep breath, blessedly unhindered in the dream state. Weeks of debilitating pain and weakness stretched out in front of him. Months, perhaps... and all with no guarantee that he wouldn't be permanently crippled by his injury.

He thought of Ithric's pale face, Kathrael's stifled sob. The new lines etched into his guardians' faces.

"You have my word," he said. "You can go back to Kathrael now, Vesh. I promise I won't roll over and die as soon as your back is turned."

Pain flashed across Vesh's face, but it was gone so quickly he wasn't sure he'd really seen it.

"All right, then," Vesh muttered. "All right. It's time." He looked around the stone spiral, his dark brows drawing together. "Huh. I wonder if maybe—" He cut himself off, shaking his head. "Well. Anyway. Take care of yourself, priest-boy. And for the gods' sakes, keep—"

"Breathing?" Favian finished, mock-sweetly. His voice turned wry. "Yes, I think I got that part, thanks."

Vesh snorted. "Mission accomplished, in that case. Now, go wake up again so they can pour some more broth down your ungrateful gullet. And tell Kath that I said you're *fucking* hard work when you're being stubborn."

"Tell her yourself," Favian shot back.

Vesh's smile was tight and did not reach his eyes. "Yeah. Sure."

Favian blinked, and when he opened his eyes, he was alone.

⁓⚜⁓

The next time he regained awareness of his surroundings, he was still in the amazing bed. This time, his upper body was propped against the headboard, supported by a small mountain of cloud-soft pillows. Ithric was dozing next to him, his head even with Favian's hip and one hand curled over his thigh. Voices could be heard in heated discussion elsewhere in the room.

Favian swallowed painfully against the dryness in his throat and flinched, trying not to cough—certain that doing so would send him straight back into unconsciousness. The tiny movement was enough to rouse Ithric, who blinked, rolled into a sitting position, and stared into Favian's eyes for a moment as if to determine his level of awareness.

"Broth," Ithric said, and craned around to retrieve a cup from the table by the bed.

The other voices cut off, and several people appeared at the bedside as Ithric supported him and urged him to swallow the cup's contents. Favian tried not to feel like some sort of strange exhibit, being gawked at by a crowd as he carefully swallowed small sips of liquid.

The broth was as rich and delicious as he remembered, warmed to the perfect temperature. His stomach rumbled, impatient with his efforts not to jar his wound while drinking. If he'd been unconscious, how had they kept the cup warm? Was someone swapping it out whenever it started to get cold?

He realized that there were almost certainly more important things that should be vying for his attention. When the cup was empty and Ithric eased his head back to rest on the mound of pillows, Favian looked from face to face, trying to reassemble the broken shards of the past few days into something that made sense.

In addition to Andoc and Kathrael, Zandreen was here, examining him in a way that reminded him of nothing so much as Sagdea looking over one of her patients.

"You look a bit more alert this time, Little Brother," she said kindly. "Blink your eyes for me if you can understand what I'm saying, please."

Favian blinked. Kathrael, Andoc, and Ithric seemed to relax minutely when he did.

"Very good," Zandreen approved. "Don't try to speak or move. For now, you can blink once to convey *yes*, and twice for *no*. All right?"

He thought about it, his mind still feeling like it was wading through treacle, and blinked once.

The High Priestess nodded, her attention moving to Ithric for a moment. "If he can stay awake for a few minutes, we'll try a bit of watered wine with the broth."

"I'll get it," Ithric said, rising from the bed—careful not to jostle it, for which Favian was immensely grateful.

Favian looked at the other person, who was standing a couple of steps from the group with his arms crossed. A chunk of memory slotted into place. *Qaden.*

The gang leader raised an eyebrow. The eye beneath it had been blackened, and there was a cut on his forehead. "Well," he said. "I guess we've finally found one way to shut him up."

Kathrael glared at him.

Zandreen removed the cool hand she'd placed on Favian's forehead—presumably to check his temperature—and snorted. "I might mention that *tact* is an important quality for anyone interested in a future in politics to cultivate," she said. "Favian, do you remember much of what's been happening? It's not unusual for there to be some mental confusion after such a serious injury."

He thought about it for a few moments. He remembered being shot. He remembered Vesh insulting him and yelling at him a lot. He remembered being worried for the people he loved, and vastly relieved to find them present the first time he'd woken up in this... wherever it was.

He tried to cast his mind farther. Wider. Tried to take clues from his surroundings. The room dripped wealth and comfort. He'd never been anyplace like it before...

Oh.

Wait.

Yes, he had.

He'd been someplace exactly like this, years ago. The palace in Rhyth. They had been marching on the palace in Rhyth. In the space between one heartbeat and the next, everything came cascading back. Tullus. The bathhouse. The Old Stones. Senovo casting the priests out of the temple.

The *dream.*

But... he wasn't dead.

He wasn't dead.

He'd beaten the dream. But... the rebellion. Did that mean—

Without thinking, Favian dragged in a sharp breath and tried to sit bolt upright—only to slump back as the resulting wall of pain sent him unconscious again.

⚜

More voices.

"This would be a lot easier with the support of the former members of the Priests' Guild. Even just a few of them." That was Qaden.

"No." Senovo and Sephira that time, speaking as one.

"Look, we understand what you're saying." That was Andoc. "But it needs to be a clean break. If you let the same blight creep back into Rhyth's government, everything will just start rotting from the inside out again, same as last time. You don't need the priests. The wealth you've confiscated from the nobles will pay the salaries for a lot of rebels to become soldiers and guardsmen who can enforce the new laws."

"I suppose," Qaden said grudgingly. "So far, roughly half of the slave-owners are choosing to compensate their freed slaves with a fair wage for their continued employment. Among the ones that haven't, I expect we'll have to extract the lump sum remuneration payment by force."

Kathrael's voice came from close beside Favian, and he blinked his eyes open. "Some of the gold from the nobles and the temples should go to support slaves whose former owners are disputing payment. Otherwise we'll have more people starving in the streets than we've got already."

She was seated on the edge of the bed, her fingers twined with his. Her attention was so focused on the conversation that she hadn't noticed him waking up. He drank in her face with the same thirst he drank in the others' words—shoring himself up. Making this real.

He was alive.

They had *won*.

"That gold also has to pay for running a city with no system of taxation in place, you realize," Qaden said. "Oh, and by the way—Blondie's awake again."

Kathrael's gaze flew to his, and Favian squeezed her fingers. The movement was shockingly weak, but she squeezed back.

"Favian," she said, the word rich with feeling. She leaned forward and carefully pressed a kiss to the corner of his lips. When she pulled back, she added, "Sorry. I thought I'd better lead with that, this time, since you keep fainting before I can get it in."

He couldn't help it; he smiled, despite the pain in his chest. A weight settled on the bed on his other side, and he reluctantly dragged his eyes away from Kath. Senovo perched next to him, holding a familiar-looking cup. His mentor still looked like he was one stiff breeze away from falling over in sheer exhaustion.

"Drink this, Little Brother. You must keep your strength up. I'm afraid Ithric is currently with High Priestess Zandreen," he added, as if apologizing for his role as Purveyor of Broth in Ithric's place. "They are meeting with the group organizing the citizens' council."

Favian gave a tiny nod of understanding, pleased when doing so did not aggravate his wound to any great degree. He submitted meekly to both the broth and the small cup of weak wine that followed, thinking that perhaps swallowing was growing a bit easier than it had been.

Andoc came around to the bedside when Favian was finished. He rested a hand on Senovo's shoulder, studying Favian over his bondmate's head. "We're in the palace," he said. "I don't think anyone's actually gotten a chance to tell you that. Except for you scaring us half to death, everything's all right."

Qaden snorted from across the room, where he was leaning hipshot against a heavy wooden table. "Matter of opinion, that."

"It could be worse," Sephira said. "Believe me."

Andoc ignored them both. "Carivel got a pretty good slash across the upper arm, but it's not festering and it should be fine. She's at the stables, trying to sort out deliveries of feed for the horses they managed to retrieve after she set them all loose. You remember that part?"

Favian nodded again, hoping to hear about the part he *didn't* remember.

"Favian... the goddesses came," Kathrael said, sounding as though she were worried she might wake to discover this had all been a dream. "Just as Inga said they would. They came together and turned day into night, at exactly the moment when we needed them most. One of the king's own bodyguards killed him to try and avert their wrath. The guards started laying down their weapons, hoping to bring the sun back. We hardly met any resistance when we took the palace. And yet, by midday, you would never have known that anything strange had happened in the sky — it was just a normal day."

He squeezed her hand again, wishing he were stronger so he could talk to her properly.

"Oh, and you're lying on King Flenaar's bed, just so you know," Andoc said, and Favian's eyes flew to him.

His guardian looked decidedly amused.

"It's all right, though," Kathrael put in. "It's not like he has much use for it now."

Favian looked from Andoc to her, and back again, before finally settling on Senovo's face in hopes of finding a bit of sanity and normalcy there. His mentor only turned and set the empty cup aside with a deliberate movement.

"Zandreen had you brought here on a litter as soon as it was marginally safe to do so," he said, his tone careful. "She stopped for you when you fell, and cauterized the wound before you could bleed to death."

Sephira moved to stand at the foot of the bed. "The High Priestess was a healer before she devoted herself to Avlan."

He blinked in surprise.

"She and the king's physician have been looking after you these past days," Kathrael said quietly.

"Yes," said Senovo. "And they prescribe rest."

"Well," Sephira said, amusement coloring her words, "the royal physician prescribed rest... *and leeches*. But Zandreen overrode him. Whatever blood you've got left in your veins at this point, you probably need more than they do, according to her."

Favian made a mental note to thank Zandreen when he was able to speak again.

"We will talk more the next time you wake, Little Brother," Senovo said. "For now, rest assured that we are all safe and whole. You needn't worry about anything except your recovery."

"And someone will always be with you," Kath said, leaning forward to kiss him again—the merest butterfly brush of lips.

Reassured, he let his eyes slide closed. When the world faded away this time, it was with a feeling of natural sleep, rather than unconsciousness.

Over the next couple of weeks, Favian gathered snippets of information from the conversations and meetings going on around him. With little else to do in his debilitated state, he spent much of his waking time slotting them together like pieces of a child's wooden puzzle, until he had a reasonable understanding of what had transpired during and after the coup.

The nascent citizen's council was taking over the day-to-day running of the city, though there were constant challenges as all the various groups with a stake in the power struggle vied for position. Qaden had stepped into the fray with admirable skill, and was very obviously taking his newly elevated position with the degree of seriousness it deserved.

Two days after they marched to the palace, a mob stormed the Temple of Deimok, looting it and killing several of the priests. Something twisted in Favian's stomach upon learning of the news, his smoldering hatred for the ones who had burned Ayala alive and killed Ciryl warring with his revulsion over the idea of anyone killing priests in a temple.

He had only been a boy when Alyrion soldiers had attacked the temple in Draebard and massacred almost everyone inside. Was this really so different?

Whether it was or it wasn't, the appearance of shape-shifters and the very public display of the goddess's power had resulted in a backlash against the Cult of Deimok. Rather than causing terror for others, the foreign god's supporters now lived in fear for their own safety. The citizens' council was in an ongoing and somewhat acrimonious debate over the merits of declaring the religion illegal.

Meanwhile, the slaves had all been freed by decree, but it fell on the armed forces of the rebellion to travel around Rhyth and the surrounding areas, making sure that it actually happened. Many of the noble families known to have supported the dead king were stripped of their wealth and exiled in the first few days after the coup.

Others who had expressed willingness to support the new fledgling government had been offered the chance to cooperate with the new laws by compensating their former slaves with money, goods, or property.

The Temple of Utarr was almost completely destroyed by the fire Kath had set. The Sisters of Avlan had taken over the other two temples, and were working with the acolytes and novices who had followed Senovo to open them to the public once again. Slowly, the people of Rhyth were returning to the day-to-day rhythms of life—cautiously emerging from their shells after the last few years of tyranny and fear.

As the days passed inside the opulent bedroom that had once belonged to a king, Favian grew stronger by increments.

He was able to stay awake longer, and perform simple tasks like scooting to the edge of the bed to use the chamberpot. Both Zandreen and the royal physician—whom Ithric had apparently put in fear of his own life should Favian not recover—watched over him like hawks.

And, as Kathrael had promised, the people he loved made certain that he was never alone.

It was, by his reckoning, some three weeks after he'd been shot that Favian woke from a sound and undisturbed night's sleep, to find that the simple act of breathing no longer stabbed at his chest like the point of a knife. Cautiously, he swallowed, moistening his throat, and gave a little cough to clear it.

He rolled up to a sitting position, bracing himself with his good arm. It was already light outside, and the rumpled bedclothes on his left proclaimed that Ithric had already been called away for something or the other. Kath slept on his right, as it was apparently her turn to stay with him while the Ithric dealt with whatever crises chose to raise their heads that day.

Risking a deeper breath and finding that it still did not pain him, Favian licked his cracked lips and looked down at the sleeping woman next to him.

"Kathrael?" he rasped.

The sound of her name jerked Kathrael from a restless sleep. It had been a barely audible croak, but—

"*Favian!*"

He was sitting up, gazing down at her with a tiny, crooked smile in the mid-morning light. "Is... there... wine?" he asked hoarsely.

"Of course!" she said, her heart beating with excitement at seeing him looking so much improved this morning, after the long weeks of nursing him through his terrifying injury.

She pushed her hair back from her face and looked around to see where Ithric had left the cup and flagon. Rising quickly, she poured him some and brought it back to the bed. Favian cautiously arranged himself against the headboard and took it from her. She hovered, ready to help him if necessary, but he lifted the cup to his lips with a steady hand and drank without mishap.

"Oh, that's better," he said, sounding more like himself.

"Very much better," she agreed. "I've missed your voice."

She took the cup away and set it aside, then returned and gathered his right hand in both of hers, raising it to her lips. The events of these past weeks should perhaps have been cause for celebration, but Kath could not begin to dwell on their success while she was alone inside her own skull, fearing every day that Favian might weaken and take a turn for the worse as his body fought to heal.

"Tell me how you feel," she said, refusing to acknowledge the burn of relieved tears threatening behind her good eye.

Favian shrugged his uninjured shoulder. "Weak. Can't move... arm much." He let out a little huff of breath. "Could be worse. Should be dead."

Kathrael's throat tried to close up. "Don't say that," she whispered.

He twisted his hand in hers so that their fingers tangled together, and squeezed. "Saw... in the dream. Saw myself dying. Couldn't..." He swallowed. "Couldn't tell you."

She thought back to that day, to her utter certainty—despite Sephira's reassurance—that something was terribly, irretrievably wrong. She thought of Vesh's parting words, as his spirit had fluttered free of hers and disappeared. She wanted to be angry with both of them. She wanted to rage at them for leaving her.

But Vesh couldn't hear her anymore, no matter how she raged at him. And Favian hadn't left—he was right here in front of her.

"Vesh's spirit... came to me," Favian said. "Saved me. Forced me to fight and... live."

Kathrael's breath exploded out in surprise, as if she'd been kicked.

"Could you tell him... thanks, for me?" he asked. "I might've been... a bit rude when... he left."

The sob that choked free of her chest took her by surprise, though it probably shouldn't have. Her free hand flew up to cover her mouth, but not before the ugly noise of grief escaped to find freedom in the still air between them. She hadn't grieved... there hadn't been *time* to grieve...

She hadn't *wanted* to grieve, for fear that doing so would somehow draw even more bad things into her life. She couldn't grieve while Favian was hanging onto life by a thread. But now, Favian was getting better.

And Vesh had saved him.

Favian was frowning at her. "Kath?" he asked. His hand slipped free of her fingers to cradle her cheek... which was wet.

"Vesh is gone," she choked out, more tears sliding down to pool against his thumb. "All of my spirits are gone, Favian. I'm alone."

He was silent for a long time, stroking her cheek as she wept silent tears.

"Perhaps they finally... completed the tasks... that held them here," he said eventually.

She thought about it, though it did nothing to quell her grief. "Maybe. But, Favian, what possible *task* could a baby have? My daughter is gone, too. Why would a baby want to leave her mother?"

To her consternation, Favian only smiled a secret little smile.

"Oh, Kath." His hand trailed from her face down to her neck, between the valley of her breasts and lower, to rest on her stomach. "Did you bleed... with the moon this month?" he asked.

Kathrael thought back, and felt her lips part as blank shock slammed into her, driving grief from her heart and making it pound like a drum.

"What about... last month?" Favian said.

Her eyes grew wide. She snapped her mouth shut. "B-but... that's impossible," she said. "I can't have children. The miscarriage. It damaged me inside."

He was still smiling. "Maybe it didn't, though. You were starving. And without enough of... the right kind of food—"

"Nothing in the body works the way it's supposed to," she finished in a whisper. Her hand came up to rest over Favian's on her belly. A feeling too big and overwhelming to have a name crept over her, growing and growing until it overflowed into a shout.

"Ithric!" she cried, her fingers clutching Favian's. "*Ithric!*"

Pounding feet sounded in the corridor outside a moment later, and Ithric burst into the room, a bit wild-eyed. "What happened? Is it Favian?"

His eyes fell on Favian an instant later, and the tension in his shoulders eased a bit at seeing him sitting up and lucid.

"I'm fine," Favian said, letting his hand drop as Kath scrambled to her feet. "Much better... today."

A slow grin spread across Ithric's face. "Well, thank the gods for that," he said, and rested a knee on the edge of the bed so he could reach down and kiss Favian in relief. He straightened a few moments later and turned to give Kath a searching look.

"Don't scare me like that again, Little Cat—*please*," he said, his brows drawing together. "I think we're all on edge right now."

"She's had a... bit of a shock, that's all," said Favian.

Ithric looked back at her, worry clouding his expression again. She reached down to take his strong, callused hand in hers, and lifted it to rest over her womb. "I've just found out where my daughter's spirit went," she said. "Not so far away after all."

Ithric stared at her face, then down at his hand, and back up at her face again. He opened his mouth as if to say something, but nothing came out. Instead, he dropped to his knees beside her, gazing up at her as though she'd grown wings.

"I think we... broke him," Favian observed from the bed.

A fresh flood of joyful tears welled up and spilled over, even as laughter bubbled up from her chest.

TWENTY-FIVE

Summer was giving way to the first hints of autumn on the southern coast of Eburos. Kathrael paced back and forth inside Inga's cave, sweat beading her brow and a hand pressed to the aching small of her back. She breathed deeply, trying to calm her nervousness as another contraction made her tense and grit her teeth.

Despite her fears, her twenty-year-old body had managed to succeed where her thirteen-year-old self had failed. Her belly was large and round, and she had felt the quickening of the healthy new life inside her over the past several weeks.

Still, though, she could remember with awful clarity the pain of the miscarriage; the way her womb had rejected its contents in a gush of blood and tissue, taking part of her heart with it. It was hard not to picture all the things that might go wrong.

Much as she loved him, Favian wasn't really helping with that right now. He, too, was pacing, his arms crossed tight across his chest and unease rolling off of him in waves. He hadn't spoken about it much, but Kathrael knew his mother had died giving birth to his sister Frella, and that he had been old enough at the time to remember the screams and understand what was happening. It was clear that he was more focused, at present, on what he might lose than on what they all might gain.

"Favian." Zandreen's voice was calm, but no-nonsense. "You have two choices. You may calm yourself, and concentrate on helping Kathrael bring this child into the world, or you may go outside and gather more wood for the fire."

Favian came to an abrupt halt, his face coloring in embarrassment at being called out. His eyes flicked from Zandreen to Kath, and back again. "Sorry, Elder Sister. I didn't mean to—" He cut himself off, and cleared his throat. "Do you, er, need more firewood?"

"No," Zandreen said. "I do not."

His flush deepened, but he nodded and took a deep, cleansing breath before finding a spot on the wall to lean against that wasn't covered in Inga's cryptic scrawlings.

"Do you need anything, Little Cat?" Ithric asked from his own spot, sitting cross-legged on the bedroll they'd been using.

Inga snorted, not looking up from the section of hide she was marking with the day's astronomical observations. "I imagine she needs that baby out of her belly."

Kath picked at the sleeve of the loose robe she was wearing, feeling both jittery and enervated. "I think I want to lie down for a bit," she decided.

Both Ithric and Favian were by her side in the space of two heartbeats. She let them take her arms and guide her to lie down on the pile of furs and blankets Ithric had just vacated.

"Do whatever you think will make you most comfortable, Kathrael," Zandreen advised. "Your body knows what it needs. There's no hurry."

She nodded, shifting around to try and find a position she could tolerate. With a sigh, she thought back with longing to this morning, which she'd spent soaking in the pool fed by hot springs near the cave. The buoyancy of the mineral-rich water had eased her discomfort and relaxed her muscles when the contractions first began, but Zandreen had made her come out when they started growing closer together.

Now, she ended up on her side with her head resting on the right side of Favian's chest, the crook of his hip going some way toward supporting her pendulous belly. When Ithric slotted himself against her back, cradling her between them, she relaxed a bit, even though the body heat surrounding her made her uncomfortably warm.

She blew out a breath, trying to rest a little while she had the chance. "It's been hours, though, Zandreen," she said, "and I'm not any closer to giving birth than I was this morning."

Zandreen crouched next to them, knees creaking, and reached out a hand to tuck a lock of Kathrael's hair behind her ear. "You're doing fine, child," said the old High Priestess. "It just takes time. It will be easier with your future babies, but you can do this, I promise you."

"All right," Kathrael whispered. Her emotions had been as unpredictable as a wild horse these last weeks, and something about the reassuring, almost maternal words had her sniffling back tears, ridiculous though that was.

"Don't cry, Kath," Favian said, a hint of desperation hiding behind the words. "Please. If Zandreen says it will be fine, then I'm sure it will."

Ithric scoffed lightly from his place behind her, giving her a little squeeze with the arm he had wrapped around her. "Take a breath, Favian, will you? And cry all you want, Little Cat. Scream and growl and curse us until you're blue in the face if you need to."

"I'll keep that in mind," she promised. "I just wish this *waiting* could be over!"

"It will be over soon enough, child," Zandreen said, rising. "I believe Inga and I will go outside and leave you three alone for a bit. We'll let your guardians know that all is well." She paused, considering. "Ithric, Favian, you might recall what I spoke with you about last week. If Kathrael is not in too much discomfort, that might be worth a try."

Favian blushed again, and Kathrael was momentarily confused until she remembered the conversation in question. "What gets the baby in, can often help get the baby out," Zandreen had said, after Kathrael bemoaned the seemingly interminable wait for her pregnancy to be over. Ithric's eyes had immediately lit up, while Favian's had gone rather comically wide.

"Seriously?" he'd asked, sounding skeptical.

Zandreen actually laughed at him, though there was no malice in it. "This is what comes of having male priests, I suppose. *Yes*, Favian. A man's release softens and ripens the neck of a pregnant woman's womb—that's how his essence is able to get inside and start a baby in the first place. And touching or suckling the breasts seems to make her body more eager to birth the babe that will suckle there."

At the time, Favian had looked like he thought she was having him on. Now, though, her blushing priest-boy was all business.

"We'll do anything that you think might help, High Priestess," he said. "And, if you wouldn't mind, please tell Carivel that the horses will need water soon."

Kathrael suspected that Carivel was perfectly well aware of the horses' requirements, but Zandreen only smiled and nodded.

"Of course," she said. "Inga, come away with me for a bit. Kathrael, we will be nearby at all times. Call out if you need me, or send one of your mates to get me."

Another contraction rocked her, stealing her words, so she merely nodded.

"We will," Ithric answered for her. "Thank you again, Zandreen."

Silence reigned inside the cave once the two women left, while Kath tried to breathe around the contraction without tensing up too much. When it finally passed, Ithric asked, "Better now?"

"Mmm," she said—tired already, though the real work hadn't even started yet.

"I think those last two were closer together than the others," Favian offered.

She grunted. "Maybe so."

Ithric's hand stroked over her flank. "Do you want us to see if we can make you come?" he asked. "I gather that's what Zandreen was not-so-subtly hinting at."

"But only if you want to try it, Kath," Favian added. "I think Ithric believes he's found a soul mate in Zandreen. Both of them are convinced that sex fixes everything."

Kathrael couldn't help it; she laughed, as Favian had no doubt intended.

"Hey!" Ithric defended. "I never said it fixed everything. I just said it *helped* with *most* things. Coming makes you feel relaxed and happy afterward, at least for awhile, doesn't it? Seems like that might be useful right about now, that's all. And Zandreen's a healer. She ought to know."

"See what I mean?" Favian asked. "Soul mates."

Kathrael snorted and buried her face in Favian's loose shirt, trying to listen to her body. The idea of basking in the loose-limbed glow of sexual release for a few minutes was undeniably appealing, but, honestly, she didn't think she'd be able to get there in her current state.

"I don't think I can right now," she decided, "though it's not for lack of wanting to. Maybe... just focus on my breasts for a bit and see what happens? That really did seem to help start the little contractions last week."

"Easy enough," Favian said. "Ithric can often be found focusing on your breasts."

"Too bloody right," Ithric agreed readily. His hand slid her robe open. "I mean… just look at them."

"It's a fair point," Favian said. "I thought they were beautiful the first time you dropped your robe for me, back in the bathing room at the temple in Draebard. Now, though, they're truly magnificent."

He eased her onto her back, supported by pillows, so that his right hand was free. Over the past several months, Favian's terrible injury had healed as well as any of them could have hoped. He had the use of his left arm… but not *full* use. He couldn't raise it above the level of his shoulder, and he no longer had any feeling in his thumb or his first two fingers. While he could grasp and manipulate things in a basic manner, it made him clumsy with that hand.

They all knew that it could have been far, far worse.

Kathrael gazed up at them both, a much-needed sense of peacefulness stealing over her. Their presence was a balm to her turmoil. Their gentle teasing, a reminder of the bond between the three of them. She still longed for Vesh's presence, it was true. She wanted him to be here to see her baby finally come into this world — into this *better* world that all of them had helped shape.

But Vesh was gone. Favian and Ithric were here. They loved her, and she loved them. And now, two sets of lips were pressing kisses to her temples… her cheeks… nuzzling at her hair, and nibbling at her earlobes. Favian's clever fingers stroked slow circles around her left areola, while Ithric continued a gradual descent toward her right breast with his lips, taking his time about it.

Her nipples tightened in anticipation, a bit of yellow colostrum leaking out. Favian swiped a finger through it, sending a little jolt of pleasure running through her as his touch tweaked the pebbled point. She watched as he lifted the finger to his mouth and licked it off.

"I still can't quite wrap my head around that," he said, a bit of awe creeping into his tone.

Ithric made a low rumble, and wrapped his lips around her other nipple, licking up the little dribble of liquid he found there. She sighed, letting her eyes slide closed. Favian's fingers returned, closing around the taut bud on his side, squeezing and massaging, giving it a slow pull upward until it slid free, making her breast bounce a bit. Meanwhile, Ithric moved from licking to sucking, drawing another little pulse of liquid from her body.

The sensation was not sexual in the same way it probably would have been a few months ago. It was still deeply, intimately sensual. And it still pulled at a place deep inside her belly. Now, though, her feelings were not those of lust, but rather, a sort of all-pervading, protective surge that wanted to hold and nurture and provide.

It was powerful, that unnamed emotion.

She floated on it as her two lovers continued to tease and caress her flesh, with no sense of urgency or thought to the passage of time. She let the feeling grow inside her, buoying her up, making her feel oddly strong.

Some unknown amount of time later, Ithric's hand came to rest over her distended belly, fingers splayed, his heat penetrating her bare skin. She gasped as a powerful contraction, completely unlike those that had come before, rippled through her body.

Ithric straightened, looking down at her with hazel eyes. "I felt that!" he said.

Favian was watching her, too. "I *saw* that," he added.

The strong ripple of muscle left her breathless. "Get Zandreen," she managed.

The two exchanged a look, and Favian sprang to his feet and hared out of the cave.

Ithric's nostrils flared. "Your water just broke."

She became aware of the warm wetness coating the inside of her thighs in the same instant he spoke, and felt a moment's irrational panic. "It's… just water, though, right? No blood?"

He grasped her hand in his strong one. "I don't smell blood," he said, and eased her robe away from her legs with his free hand. "No, it's clear."

Zandreen bustled back in, and smiled when she saw the wet bedding. "Well, I've said it before, but I'll say it again," she observed. "You three never do anything by halves."

Kathrael laughed, then groaned as a new contraction hit her.

"Good, that was much stronger. Do you feel the need to push?" Zandreen asked.

She nodded, a bit frantically.

"Let's get her up," Zandreen told Ithric and Favian. "Did you decide which one of you is going to support her?"

Favian gestured to Ithric before taking her arm and helping her stagger ungracefully upright. "He is. He's stronger than I am."

Ithric supported her on the other side, and gave Zandreen a tight, worried smile. "And I figure Kath can hold onto Favian's left hand. That way, if she breaks his fingers by squeezing too hard, he won't even feel it."

"Nice," Favian said, as they guided her to the rough wooden chair that had been set out in a clear space lit by sunlight from the cave's entrance.

Ithric sat down, and Favian helped her remove the robe, the bottom of which had become soiled when her water broke. Kathrael squatted down between Ithric's open legs, facing away from him as Zandreen had showed her. He supported her with strong arms looped under hers, his fingers clasped together beneath her breasts and above the bulge in her stomach.

"I've got you, Little Cat," he murmured in her ear. "Lean on me as much as you need to."

Favian went to retrieve the clean, soft blanket that Zandreen would use to catch the baby when it was born. Then he knelt at her side and carefully wrapped her hand in both of his. "All right. Squeeze away. If anything's truly in danger of breaking, I'll make some sort of terribly undignified squealing noise."

She opened her mouth to make some quip—something to try to reassure them—but another labor pang chose that minute to hit, taking her breath away.

Zandreen sat down in front of her and put a gnarled hand on her knee. "Push, child—bear down for me. Don't be afraid. Your body is ready now."

At odd moments, Kathrael had been worried that she would not know what to do when Zandreen told her to push. Push against what? And how? But she needn't have been concerned. As Zandreen had said earlier, her body knew what it needed. She bore down, straining, new beads of sweat breaking out across her forehead as she labored.

The contraction passed, and she sagged in Ithric's hold. As he had promised, his arms didn't waver under her weight. She could feel the corded muscle in them as he held her up.

"Breathe, Kathrael," Zandreen said. "Rest for a few moments."

Kath panted, trying to prepare herself for the next one. When it came, she wasn't remotely ready, but she tried to push when Zandreen told her to. Each time, it hurt a little more, and each time, she felt weaker, exhaustion pulling at her. First she groaned, then the groans became cries, and the cries, screams.

She was only vaguely aware of the paleness of Favian's face, the tension of Ithric's muscles. On some level she knew that it tore at them to see her in pain like this, but she could not spare breath to try reassuring them. And while she didn't curse them, she suspected that her grip on Favian's hands might well leave bruises, if not actual broken bones.

She wanted to rest. She wanted to *sleep*. She wanted the pain to stop, but there was no real respite from the sharp contractions — only a few moments to suck in ugly gulps of air after each one and try to stop the spinning dizziness threatening her.

"You're close now, Kathrael," Zandreen said. "One big push, on the next contraction."

She closed her eyes and tried to shake her head, knowing how much it would hurt to strain her abused and exhausted muscles further than she already had.

Favian freed one of his hands from her clammy, sweat-slicked grip and cupped her cheek, drawing her to look at him. His face was bloodless with worry for her, but his jaw was firm with resolve.

"Kath. We are *going* to have this baby. It's not up for debate." His blue-eyed gaze burned into hers, unwavering.

"You're the strongest person I know," Ithric whispered into the shell of her ear, making her shiver. "Can you imagine how amazing our baby is going to be, with the three of us as parents?"

It was true. If she could just be strong for a little while longer, she would finally — *finally* — get to hold her daughter in her arms. She hadn't told the others, but she was sure it would be a girl. She *had* to see her baby — the tiny spirit she had nurtured for so long.

A new contraction rippled through her abused body and she bore down, a full-throated shriek escaping her lips. She could feel something stretching, maybe tearing, but —

Zandreen's face went very still for a bare instant, but then she blinked and gave Kath a reassuring smile. "I can see the head. Hard part's done now, Kathrael. Just one more push, and we're there."

Kathrael couldn't hold back a little gulping sob of exhaustion, but she pushed on the next contraction and felt something slide free, into Zandreen's waiting hands.

Kathrael's vision was wavering in and out, and she knew that her body blocked Ithric's view. But Favian said, "What—?" only to be interrupted by Zandreen's calm voice.

"You did it, child. Another push to get the afterbirth out, and you're done."

Kathrael was getting deeply sick of the phrase *one more push*, and she wanted desperately to see her baby. It actually took *two* more contractions before the bloody red mass of her placenta slid out, plopping into the wooden bowl Zandreen placed between her legs to catch it.

The priestess had the baby swaddled in the soft blanket and was using it to rub briskly at the tiny form. Listening intently for a cry, Kathrael fell forward to rest on her knees, still leaning on Ithric's strength as she tried to get her breath back.

"Zandreen," Favian said, and the unaccustomed hardness in his tone made Kathrael's heart skip a beat before it galloped back into life. "Let us see the baby."

No, Kathrael thought blankly. *No. Nothing can be wrong this time. Please, no.*

Zandreen unwrapped the tiny bundle with careful hands, and Kath felt Ithric's sharp indrawn breath against her back. She blinked rapidly, trying to clear the sweat from her good eye. When the small form came into focus, Kathrael found herself looking at a perfect, newborn lion cub.

She opened her mouth, but before she could decide what words should come out, Zandreen grasped the tiny animal by its hind legs with one hand, and delivered a brisk swat to its haunches with the other. Before their eyes, the lion cub's body shifted into that of a human baby, and a weak, squalling cry split the air, getting stronger as the tiny lungs grew accustomed to drawing breath.

"And... it's a girl," Zandreen declared, a twinkle of amusement glinting in her dark eyes.

The moment of utter, shocked silence was broken when Favian collapsed forward, slinging one arm around Kath and the other around Ithric's waist as he dissolved into slightly hysterical laughter.

When he managed to choke it back under control, he settled back on his heels and dragged a shaking hand over his face. "All right," he said, "I'm calling this, right now. Ithric — it's going to be your job to keep her out of trouble as she grows up."

Zandreen only smiled, and handed the still-squalling baby to Kathrael. The small weight settled into her arms, warm and red and squirming and *beautiful*. She looked at their daughter, joy and awe fighting for dominance inside her heart as she contemplated the amazing new life her body had made. She thought the emotions must surely be erupting from her face like beams of light as she looked up at Favian, grinning.

"Ithric's job… to keep our shape-shifting daughter *out* of trouble?" she asked, almost giddy with happiness. "Favian, did you really think those words through before saying them?"

Favian reached out a finger to touch their baby's perfect little form. "I didn't have to think them through," he said, growing serious. "The male lion always protects his pride. Especially the cubs."

Ithric extricated himself from behind Kathrael and dropped to kneel by her other side, staring at his child.

"With my life, Little Cat," he vowed. "With everything I have, and more."

"Have you decided what to call her?" Favian asked.

"Lyndarra," Kath said without hesitation, looking up at Ithric. "After our lost sisters."

"That's beautiful," Favian murmured, drawing her attention.

"Beautiful," Ithric echoed, the word barely a whisper. Kath looked back to him in time to see a tear spill down his cheek. She smiled as Favian reached across to brush it away.

✨ ⚜ ✨

After Zandreen had tied off the baby's umbilical cord and cut it… after Favian and Ithric had helped her to Inga's bed, where the priestess had examined her for excessive bleeding… after everything was once more calm and quiet, Kathrael sat propped with Lyndarra in her arms, the infant suckling contentedly at her breast.

By rights, her daughter would surely have a better chance at a fortunate life than most, having already been blessed by both a High Priestess and a shape-shifting High Priest. Lyndarra was surrounded by loved ones on her first day in the world, with Ithric propped up on an elbow next to Kathrael in the bed, watching her nurse, and Favian sitting cross-legged at its foot, watching all three of them with a brilliant smile.

Zandreen had allowed Andoc, Senovo, and Carivel back in once mother and child were settled and cleaned up a bit. The Draebardi chieftain sat in a chair near the bed, and Carivel lounged next to him, an elbow propped on his shoulder. The Horse Mistress was examining Lyndarra like she was some sort of perplexing puzzle. Kathrael wondered idly why she had never borne children of her own with Andoc. Perhaps, she thought, it had something to do with Carivel's strange mixture of male and female. Or perhaps the eccentric trio was content with Frella and Favian—the children they'd adopted.

Indeed, the Wolf Patron stood now at the end of the bed, his hands resting on Favian's shoulders—looking like any proud grandparent, welcoming a new generation into the family. Kathrael thought back to their tangled and troubled history, trying to remember how it had felt to want Senovo dead.

It was as though that had happened in some other lifetime, and someone had merely told her the story. Kathrael looked up, meeting his green-gold wolf's eyes.

"Our debt to each other is paid in full, Wolf Patron," she said, feeling peace wash through her as she let that part of her past float free forever.

Senovo raised a finely arched brow. "You owed me no debt." His voice was mild. Self-deprecating. She thought that perhaps he was not quite as ready as she to leave his past behind.

"I did," she insisted. "You freed me from slavery. Then, you gave me shelter when I would happily have seen you dead by my own hand." She looked down at the bundle in her arms. "In return, I give you and your bondmates a grandchild—and, perhaps, a new future for shape-shifters on the island of Eburos."

He lowered his eyebrow slowly, regarding her. "Then any debt is repaid a hundred times over, Kathrael," he said, in a tone that made her think the two of them truly *had* made their peace.

"Will you stay in Rhyth?" Carivel asked, directing the question to all three of them.

Favian answered, warming Kathrael's heart with his lack of hesitation. "Yes. We're needed here. Will you return to Draebard?"

Andoc laughed. "Yes, of course—though we may or may not be needed there."

The three had spent the bulk of the last six months in Rhyth, only leaving for a few weeks in early summer to return to Draebard and check on Frella. At first, they had stayed on to lend their expertise—and Senovo's reputation as the Wolf Patron—to the emerging government of the liberated city. The transition from a tyrannical king and lawless gangs to citizen rule had been a rocky one, to put it mildly, but as time passed, the newly minted council of elected representatives—which now included Qaden—had grown stronger, weathering a series of challenges from within and without.

After returning from their visit home, Favian's guardians had stayed to help with the baby's birth. "It's what families do," Andoc said simply. Favian had been disappointed when they had not brought Frella with them on the return journey—but he agreed that despite improvements, Rhyth was still a dangerous place. Kathrael could only imagine how much more disappointed Frella must have been at yet again being excluded from what she saw as a grand adventure.

It was something of a running joke that the three would return to find themselves with no gainful employment, forced to go from chieftain, High Priest, and Horse Mistress to penniless beggars, relying on charity from the temple.

Favian laughed. "Oh, please. Jacun worships the ground you walk on, Andoc. He'll be stumbling over himself to hand back the chieftaincy the moment you ride into town."

Andoc only smirked. "Jacun? Probably. Varanis?" He made a waggling, *not-so-much* gesture with one hand. "That said, I think Senovo's status in the temple is safe enough."

"If Brother Eiridan balks at relinquishing his position of leadership," Senovo said, "I suppose I can always send him here to consult with Inga about astronomy."

Favian snorted. "Ooh, *devious*. It would be love at first sight, without a doubt. You'd never see him again."

"Mind your tongue, boy!" Inga called from her writing table. Favian winked at Kathrael, and she stifled a laugh.

"Well," Carivel put in, "I have no doubt I'll need a pile of rocks and a long lever to remove Dalon when we get back, but it takes that much to get him to do just about *anything*. So I'm used to it."

"Get Limdya to help you," Ithric suggested with a smirk.

"Good plan," Carivel approved. "And if worse comes to worst," she added sweetly, "we'll just let Senovo support us in the lifestyle to which we've become accustomed."

"Well, whatever the case," Favian said, "Frella still needs you."

Andoc smiled. "For a few more years, perhaps."

Favian pinned him with a look. "Uh... for a few more years, *definitely*, I think you mean."

Senovo gave Favian's shoulders a final squeeze and moved to stand next to his bondmates. "I fear your sister will only stay in the nest so long before she insists on stretching her wings, Favian."

From what Kathrael had seen of Frella, that was almost certainly true. Just as soon as her guardians allowed it, she suspected Frella would be off in search of the adventure she so clearly craved. Kathrael just hoped that she would eventually find whatever it was she was truly looking for.

"In all seriousness," Andoc said, "when we get home, I'll be offering Jacun and Varanis the position of joint trade envoys to Rhyth. And who knows, if they've developed a taste for the chieftaincy in my absence, maybe I'll take the position myself—bad leg or no."

Ithric made a considering noise. "Honestly, travel between the north and the south by ship isn't so terrible—"

Carivel scoffed. "So you say. Give me a good horse any day of the week."

Ithric mock-glared at her. "The *point* being, that you are all welcome any time, whether you're acting as trade envoys or not. With the Sisters of Avlan building a temple on the plain of the Old Stones, there will even be a safe place to stay away from the city itself, if you want to bring Frella along."

"We'll visit," Andoc promised. "Though I should point out that the sentiment goes both ways. You're free to come visit Draebard just as soon as Lyndarra is old enough to travel, you know."

Kathrael blinked. Northerners always used that word so easily.

But... it was true. And maybe someday, southerners would be able to use it in such a careless manner, as well.

Kathrael smiled up at Favian and Ithric, then down at her baby. "*Free.* Yes. I suppose we are."

⚜

Not long after, the little gathering broke up, with Kathrael pleading exhaustion and Zandreen shooing the others away.

"Don't worry," Carivel said cheerfully. "We'll camp out on the plain so we don't bother you with our comings and goings. Get some rest, you three—you've earned it."

"In other words," Favian said once they'd gone, "the three of them intend to shag like rabbits as soon as the sun goes down."

Kathrael laughed softly, only to wince a bit as her abused muscles protested. "Good gods," she moaned. "It's only late afternoon and I can barely keep my eyes open."

"Sleep while you can," Zandreen advised. "You're exhausted, and having a new baby is not generally compatible with long stretches of uninterrupted rest. Inga and I will be out for most of the evening, observing signs of the upcoming equinox. We'll be at the stones, should you need anything."

"Thank you, Zandreen," Kathrael said, meaning it with every fiber of her being. "And you too, Inga. Thank you for giving us this refuge for Lyndarra's birth."

Inga waved the words off, but Zandreen smiled kindly at her. "Nonsense. You are all the children of Avlan, and Avlan looks after his own."

Not long afterward, Kathrael lay nestled between her two lovers in the soft bedding after nursing Lyndarra again. She was pleasantly drowsy, and knew she would be able to sleep with no problems despite the nagging pain in her belly and loins. She was safe, fed, and sheltered, with the people she cared about most nearby.

Only one thing marred her perfect contentment. Although it had been months, an empty space still lingered in her thoughts—the space where Vesh should have been. Even with Ithric's and Favian's loving arms holding her, and her daughter sleeping peacefully in a wicker basket beside the straw mattress, the dull ache of Vesh's absence followed her down into exhausted slumber.

TWENTY-SIX

Kathrael dreamed she was walking among the Old Stones with Favian and Ithric, Lyndarra cradled in her arms. Ithric's eyes still seemed drawn to their daughter as if by some unseen force, and the smile lines at the corners of his mouth were in real danger of becoming etched there permanently.

"She likes it here," he said.

"She does," Favian agreed, pausing to rest a hand on the sun-warmed bulk of the closest stone. "Maybe she can feel the Old Magic in the air."

"Hmm. That wouldn't be surprising," a new voice observed from behind them. "It is a rather magical place."

Kathrael stumbled to an abrupt halt and whirled toward the sound with a gasp. The voice's owner was unseen, hidden from view at the center of the stone spiral. The others stopped as well, and Ithric took an instinctive step forward, placing himself half in front of Kathrael and her baby to shelter them.

"Who's there?" he called. "Show yourself."

A slender, dark-haired figure emerged from the shadow of the twin stones in the center of the monument. Kathrael's heart thudded against her chest as she recognized merry brown eyes and a crooked nose set in a beloved, much-missed face.

"Hello, Kath," Vesh said, his voice warm and familiar.

Kathrael stared at her closest friend with her mouth open and her breath locked in her throat. Her chest hitched, and the air escaped in the shape of a word that was part sob. "*Vesh?*" She swallowed hard. "Oh my gods... *Vesh!*"

Vesh smiled, and Kathrael's feet carried her forward before she even realized she was moving, closing the distance between them. She stopped a mere step away to drink in the features she'd never thought she would see again. Cradling Lyndarra in one arm, she reached out a trembling hand toward Vesh's face, only to hesitate as realization dawned.

"This is a dream, isn't it?" she said, her joy giving way to sadness. "You're not real."

Warm fingers clasped her hand and pressed it to a living cheek. Kathrael felt the muscles under her palm move as Vesh smiled.

"Hey! None of that, now," he protested. "I'm as real as you are."

It couldn't be true, but Kathrael decided then and there that she didn't care. She freed her hand and flung her arm around his neck, careful not to crush her daughter between them as she buried her face against his chest and breathed in his old, familiar scent.

"It's good to see you," he murmured into her hair. He eased her back a bit, and his eyes dipped to the bundle in Kath's arms. "Now, let me see your daughter. I've missed her over these past months, you know."

Tears welled in Kathrael's good eye as she angled herself to give Vesh a better view. Lyndarra's tiny face scrunched up in a yawn, her arms waving as she stretched and settled again, making little smacking motions with her lips.

"I've missed *you*," Kath whispered, as Ithric and Favian came up to flank her. "Oh, *gods*, how I've missed you. Vesh… *how can you be here?*"

Vesh shrugged, and gave her a final squeeze before letting her shoulders go.

"How does anyone do anything? I wanted to see you again, so I came." He reached down to trace Lyndarra's wispy curl of brown hair with a gentle fingertip. When he looked up, his twinkling gaze widened to encompass all of them for a moment, before it settled on Ithric. "She has your coloring, lion-boy."

"But hopefully not his penchant for attracting trouble," Favian said.

"Says the man who's been shot with arrows *twice in the same shoulder*," Ithric retorted. He stepped closer to Vesh, looking down at him from his slight advantage of height with intense eyes. "Well. This is certainly unexpected. Kath is right, you know… this pretty well has to be a dream I'm having."

"If you say so," Vesh agreed with a shrug.

"Still," Ithric continued, "I'm not likely to get a better chance than this, so—"

He reached out and cupped Vesh's face, lowering his head to press a chaste kiss to his lips. Vesh's eyes fluttered closed, only to open with a look of pleased curiosity when the shape-shifter pulled back a few moments later.

"What was that for?" he asked. "Not that I'm complaining."

"It was a *thank you*, for saving the lives of not one, but both of the people I love," Ithric replied in a solemn tone. "Thank you, Vesh."

Vesh smiled. "You're very welcome, Ithric." His gaze turned to Favian. "And *you*, priest-boy. Your dreams are certainly very interesting."

Favian regarded him with fascination. "*Ah*. So this *is* a dream, then. I thought it must be. It feels very strange, though."

"Just so," Vesh said with a nod. "It took me a while, true—but once I knew the feel of your mind, I was certain I'd be able to use you to find my way back through the veil."

Ithric frowned. "The veil?"

"Of death," Vesh clarified. "Favian's a Seer. His dreams pierce the boundary between the living world and the spirit world. I'm using him as a conduit to visit the four of you." The corners of his eyes crinkled at Favian. "Sorry for the presumption. But I didn't think you'd mind."

Favian snorted and waved him off. "My mind hasn't been completely my own since I was thirteen. What's one more otherworldly visitation between friends?" He gestured to the low stone seat at one edge of the central space. "Here, come on. Let's sit. The baby needs to nurse, and while Kath feeds her, you can answer some of my questions about the afterlife." He lifted a pointed eyebrow. "It's the least you can do. After all, first you called me names and yelled at me for almost three days straight... and now you're apparently using my dreams like a cheap hired wagon to haul your lazy ass back and forth to the land of the living."

Vesh laughed aloud—a carefree sound Kath had missed deeply.

Favian was right—Lyndarra had indeed awoken and started to fuss as they spoke. Kathrael settled herself against Ithric's side on the stone bench. One-handed, she unlaced her blouse and bodice enough to free a breast, still drinking in the sight of her lost friend. She had to keep reminding herself that this wasn't real.

But was there really any harm in pretending it was, just for a little while?

Vesh gave her a look that was almost painfully fond. "No, Kath. There's no harm in it."

She bit her lip and nodded, still hesitant—fresh tears trying to rise as Lyndarra latched onto her nipple and began to suckle. Favian sank down to sit on the ground next to her, his shoulder pressed companionably against her leg. He looked up at Vesh after the familiar figured settled on the other end of the bench.

"So," Favian began, "I gather this means you were able to cross over to the spirit world successfully, even after being tied to Kath for so long?"

Vesh nodded. "I was. Once I completed what I was here to do, the path to the other side became clear. I was able to travel along it, just as Elarra and Thea had done earlier." He met Kathrael's gaze, his eyes growing somber. "Kath, I realize that our presence caused you pain, especially in the early days. I'm sorry for that. I wish it had been otherwise."

She had to swallow hard twice before she could speak. "Don't be sorry, Vesh. Elarra saved Daeniel. You saved Favian. That was worth any pain I might have felt. And it wasn't all bad. You were always there for me when I needed you most—just like when you were alive."

He nodded. "I did my best, anyway. It was so *strange*. It took a long time before I could separate myself from your thoughts and moods. But I'm glad I could be there for you. You and Lyndarra." His eyes drifted back to the infant suckling at her breast, his expression hopelessly affectionate.

"What can you tell us about the spirit world, now that you've been there?" Favian asked. "Is it really the place of peace and respite that we're told it is?"

Vesh looked thoughtful. "It certainly can be. It's whatever you make of it, I suppose. It's… a place of perfect knowledge."

Kath's brows drew together. "Perfect knowledge?"

"Yes." He nodded, still thoughtful. "In the spirit world, you gain an immediate and complete understanding of the effects of the actions you took during your lifetime. All the pain you've caused to other living things; all the good you've done. You experience all of it, directly."

There was a moment of silence.

"That's… actually a bit terrifying," Ithric said, and Kath wondered if he was thinking about all the people he'd fought. All the animals he'd hunted as the lion.

Favian, on the other hand, was obviously fascinated by Vesh's words—as was she.

"It can be something of a shock," Vesh agreed. "More so for some than others, I'm sure. But, as I said, it's what you make of it. When those you have harmed enter the spirit world, you can seek to atone for the pain you caused them. And you can try to help others who are struggling to do the same. For those who desire it, comfort and support are always available."

"Ask and gain the help you need?" Favian said softly, paraphrasing a line from the prayer of Utarr.

Vesh's lips quirked briefly. "Indeed. It's only a place of torment for those who are unwilling to seek that sort of help."

"What of my mother, Vesh?" Kathrael asked, needing to know. "What of my sister?"

"They are at peace," Vesh assured her. "Secure in the knowledge that the things they could not achieve during their lifetimes have nevertheless come to pass, thanks to you."

A tear spilled over, trailing down her unscarred cheek. "You've seen them?" she pressed. "Talked to them?"

"Yes, of course. Many times," Vesh replied. "You can visit anyone you wish in the spirit world, at any time—as long as they agree to meet with you. Well… you can visit anyone who's dead, I should say." He arched an eyebrow, his expression growing mischievous. "Visiting the living takes a bit more maneuvering, as it turns out."

Lyndarra finished nursing and started to fuss. Favian reached up and took her from Kathrael's arms, settling her on his shoulder and patting her back. Kath covered her breast and re-laced her bodice with slow movements, her gaze never leaving Vesh's face.

"There's so much I want to tell you," she said. "So much I want to tell *them*."

"Let's start with what you'd like to tell your mother and sister. I don't mind carrying messages," Vesh replied with a smile.

She thought for a moment. "I want to tell them… that I love them. That I miss them, but that things are also… *good*. Better than they've ever been in my life, really."

"I'll pass it on," Vesh promised. "Now… what would you like to tell *me*?"

Her throat closed up for a moment, and she had to clear it before she could speak. "Before you left to help Favian, you… said something to me."

I love you, you know. I always have, Kath. I'm so sorry I never told you when we were both alive.

"I did," he agreed. "I told you I loved you."

Her breath hitched. "I never knew," she said in a tiny voice. "I always believed…"

"That I preferred men, and thought of you only as a friend?" Vesh finished for her. "I think you saw what you wanted to see in those days, Kath. Not all of my clients were men." He smiled, a bit wry. "My clever tongue was always in demand, you know."

"But you never *said*," she accused.

Vesh rose from the bench and reached out a hand to her. She took it, and he pulled her up to join him. He looked past her, and she followed his gaze in confusion, only to see Favian and Ithric watching him with matching expressions of understanding. Favian smiled softly at her, his elegant, long-fingered hand still splayed over Lyndarra's back as she nuzzled and cooed against his shoulder.

Kathrael looked at Vesh… at his full lips and fine cheekbones. At his deep brown eyes, radiating the soul-deep kindness that had always surrounded him like an aura.

He cradled her cheek with one hand and looked down at her. "I never said anything because you weren't in a place to be able to hear what I wanted to tell you. What would you have done if I'd professed my love? You didn't believe in love. You thought it was a lie men told women to entrap them. You would have seen it as a betrayal, and pulled away from me."

He caressed the delicate skin under her right eye.

"I couldn't bear to take that chance," he finished.

Tears overflowed, and ran down to pool against the pad of his thumb as she realized that he was right.

"Oh, gods, Vesh," she whispered. "I'm so sorry."

Ithric rose and moved to stand behind her, looping an arm around her waist in comfort. Vesh smiled up at him, over her shoulder, and looked back to her.

"Don't be sorry, Kath," he said. "It took me awhile, but now that I know how to reach your dreams, we have all the time in the world. I finally have time… to do this."

He leaned down, narrowing the distance between them. Kathrael closed her eyes against the sharp ache in her chest and tilted her face up, meeting him in a tender kiss. Ithric's palm was warm and grounding on her belly. Her hands came up to frame Vesh's face, holding him as the sweet slide of his lips against hers spoke of the feelings she had never even suspected he held for her.

How blind she'd been, even before a vial of vitriol had stolen the sight from one of her eyes.

When they parted, he brushed the backs of his knuckles tenderly over her temple. Again, his eyes moved first to Ithric, and then down to Favian, gratitude shining in the rich brown depths.

"Thank you," he said. "Jealousy always seemed a ridiculous things for a dead man to feel. But… watching the three of you… sometimes it was difficult *not* to feel it."

Favian rose to join them, Lyndarra cradled securely in the crook of his good arm. "Jealousy is not a part of what the three of us have," he said. "It's not who we are. Kath loves you and she always has, even if she wasn't able to show you how much when you were alive. Isn't that right, Kath?"

Kathrael nodded, her chest jerking silently as she tried to hold back fresh tears.

"It's true," she croaked. "Vesh… *gods*… please don't make me say goodbye. Not now. Not again. I don't know if I have the strength."

"It doesn't have to be goodbye, though, does it?" Favian asked, his shoulder nudging against hers. "I sleep pretty much every night, after all—despite Lyndarra's best efforts to prevent it."

"No," Vesh said. "It doesn't have to be goodbye. Say the word, Kath, and I'll visit you in dreams every single night. I know it's not the life we might have had if things were different." His gaze moved to take in all four of them. "In many ways, though, it's *better* than that life could ever have been."

Favian smiled and handed Lyndarra off to Ithric. "I suppose it *is* a pretty damned good life, isn't it?" The smile widened to a full-blown grin as he reached out and drew Vesh into a one-armed embrace. "Come here, you."

Vesh laughed and squeezed him back. "Yes, I'd say you've done all right for yourself, priest-boy... all things considered."

The corners of Favian's eyes crinkled. "I guess I have. Though I should warn you, given the way Ithric is eyeing you like a succulent piece of roast, you may have more on your hands than just Kath."

Vesh smirked. "I'm sure the lion-boy and I can come to some accommodation. Don't you think so, Kath? We could gang up on him — just like the old days."

Ithric matched him, leer for leer. "You could try, certainly." He looked down and gave Kathrael a mock-frown. "Kath, why didn't you tell me he was this much fun? We could have figured out some way to include him in the sex, back when he was haunting you."

Kathrael covered her mouth with her hand, caught between laughter and tears, a fragile bubble of hope and happiness swelling in her chest. She knew that the hope was foolish; she *knew* this was all in her mind —

"Kath, *hey*. Don't cry. It's all right. Do you still trust me?" Vesh asked, growing serious once more.

The baby gave a little squall in Ithric's arms, probably needing to be changed.

Kath closed her eyes and looked inside herself, reaching for the delicate thread of faith she found there. She nodded. "Yes. I do. I trust you, Vesh."

"Then there's no need to say goodbye. You have my word that I'll visit you tomorrow night in your dreams... and all the nights to come. Look at me, please —"

Kath took a deep breath and looked up at the person who had saved her, over and over in so many ways, large and small. She knew that having hope would make things all the more painful when she woke up... but for now, she took a deep breath... and believed.

"Until tomorrow night, then," she said, and kissed his cheek. "I love you, Vesh."

Vesh's eyes lit with happiness. "Until tomorrow night, Kath. Now, though, your baby girl needs you."

Lyndarra's fussy cries were growing louder, and when Kathrael turned to check on her, the stone circle wavered in her vision, fading like gray mist in the morning light.

Kathrael rolled over on the lumpy straw mattress, reaching instinctively toward the basket next to the bed, where Lyndarra lay crying. The movement roused Favian and Ithric, whose arms were tangled around her. She blinked awake in the gray glow of predawn, the interior of Inga's cave gradually coming into focus.

Ithric shuffled out of her way so she could get to the baby, whose hungry wails were growing louder. Kath was still more than half asleep, her thoughts a jumble as she set Lyndarra to her breast to nurse.

Something about the action resonated within her confused, early-morning awareness. The events of the dream slipped into place, and she inhaled sharply.

The dream.

It had all been a dream. A sharp ache of old pain took up residence behind her ribs.

She chastised herself for her foolishness. *Of course* it had been a dream. Vesh was gone. He had passed over to the spirit world. Even his ghostly voice was lost to her now. Fresh grief over his death stabbed at her like a knife.

Beside her, Ithric yawned widely and scrubbed a hand over his face. "Huh," he mused, rubbing his fingers briskly back and forth through his mane of russet hair, mussing it.

Favian was sitting up, still looking groggy. His face folded into a thoughtful frown. He glanced over at Ithric with bleary eyes. "What is it, Ithric?" he asked, his tone distracted.

Ithric shook head as if to clear it. "Oh… nothing, really. I just had the strangest dream, that's all. We were walking in the stone circle, and Vesh was there. I kissed him, to thank him for saving both of you."

Kathrael's eyes flew to his. Her mouth opened, but no words came out.

Favian was staring at him as well. Unlike Kath, after a moment he seemed to recover the power of speech — at least, to a degree. "Wait. You… dreamed that, too?"

"Oh my gods," Kathrael managed faintly, her eyes darting from Ithric to Favian and back again. The hope that had unfurled fragile shoots inside her heart during the dream burst fully into bloom, chasing the cold ache of loss from her chest. "Oh, my *gods*. You… mean…"

They'd all had the same dream.

Favian looked back and forth between them, his blue eyes sparkling in the predawn light. He stared at them for a long moment that seemed pregnant with untold possibilities, before dissolving into peals of helpless laughter.

End of Book 3

PRIDE OF DREAMS

ONE

In Kathrael's dream, it was nighttime. She was standing in the grand main entrance of the king's *caldarium* — although, to be accurate, it was no longer the *king's*. It was the people's *caldarium*.

The king, after all, was dead.

Now, the opulent bathhouse was available for the public's use in return for a nominal fee that was easily within the reach of most of Rhyth's citizens. It was also open one day a week for everyone, whether they could afford to pay a copper to get in or not. Unsurprisingly, it had quickly become a popular attraction.

Which made it all the odder, seeing it empty and echoing like this. Especially since the whole place appeared to be lit by a multitude of candles at a time of night when the doors should have been locked and barred. The sheer improbability of anyone squandering so many candles on a deserted building — not to mention the time needed to set them up and light them — let Kathrael know that this was, in fact, a dream.

And that was enough to make her smile. The smile widened when she heard the low sound of splashing from further inside the structure. So. Not a *completely* empty building, then.

No real surprise there.

Part of her wanted to hurry along toward the source of the noise, but a larger part held her in place for a few moments, taking in the stunning beauty of the stone and glass mosaic walls lit by the flickering light from hundreds of candles. The effect was truly magical, and whoever had crafted it inside the dream — Vesh, at a guess — had obviously meant for it to be savored. Otherwise, a handful of torches would have sufficed to light the way... or else it would simply have been daylight outside, rather than night.

The warm light deepened the brilliant colors of the mosaic artwork around her, glinting off the glass facets and making them look like thousands of tiny fireflies. Once, during a party, Kathrael had seen a large piece of exotic stone displayed in one of the noble houses. On the outside, it had been brown and dull, utterly unremarkable—but the stone had been cracked in two, and the inside displayed a riot of crystals—deep purple and azure.

That was what the room around her reminded her of—it was like being inside a huge version of such a stone.

The atmosphere was calm and quiet, as though the very fabric of the dream itself was wrapping her up in peaceful happiness. And why not? She knew full well who awaited her deeper inside the building.

As though prompted by her thoughts, the distant sound of male laughter reached her ears—low pitched and filthy. That was Ithric, without a doubt. No one else she'd ever met could make a simple laugh sound so unashamedly sexual. Kathrael's belly tightened in response.

She caught her breath at the sensation. It was the first time in the weeks since giving birth to Lyndarra that she had experienced such arousal. After the delivery, Zandreen had assured her that a lack of sexual desire was perfectly normal as her womb and passage healed from the trauma of the baby passing through. And, of course, in the waking world, she, Favian, and Ithric were constantly exhausted from the demands of caring for a new infant, combined with their ongoing duties to the new government of Rhyth.

In the bedroom, Kathrael had been content to remain an appreciative spectator, of late—watching Ithric and Favian trade lazy caresses whenever they were not too tired.

And here in the dream world, she and Vesh were still locked in a sort of odd, in-between phase after his revelation that he had long cared for her as more than a friend. Each night when he visited, they shared a kiss that was barely on the wrong side of chaste, and then he whisked them off to show them whatever wonder he'd come up with for the night.

Sometimes it was extravagant food. Sometimes it was an amazing natural view. Once, they had all lain together on a warm, grassy plain, looking up at the brilliant wash of twinkling stars on a moonless night. Until tonight, Lyndarra had always been with them in the dreams—Vesh doted on her, and the baby clearly adored him after the months they had spent together as spirits trapped with Kath in the physical world.

Tonight, though, her babe was not nestled in her arms. Kathrael felt no concern—in the waking world, her daughter was sleeping in her basket, an arm's length away. If she cried, Kathrael would awaken within moments to care for her needs, secure in the knowledge that Vesh would still be waiting for her when she next slept and dreamed.

Nonetheless, her daughter's absence from the dream world, paired with the choice of venue, spoke volumes. Kathrael was surprised to feel an unaccustomed flutter of nervousness. That she loved Vesh with her whole heart was not in question. But since his reappearance in her dreams, her body had not been inclined toward sex with him or anyone else. Now that her feelings of sensuality seemed to be emerging from their brief hibernation, would she feel the same flame of arousal toward him that she felt with Ithric and Favian?

It wasn't even that she didn't think of Vesh in a sexual way. In fact, in some respects it was almost the opposite problem. They had both been prostitutes, after all, peddling meaningless sex for money, often separately—but sometimes together. Kathrael had seen Vesh in just about every conceivable carnal situation, just as he had seen her.

And... she had always felt gratitude when they were together, because she knew she had someone with her who would watch over her—someone she could trust. But she had never felt lust. Not for him. Not for *anyone*.

Was Vesh worried that she would not want him in that way? Did he want *her* in that way? She realized with a small jolt of surprise that he'd never actually specified. He loved her. He was *in love* with her. But he was also a eunuch. Perhaps he didn't desire her physically. She had learned early on from Favian that the two things did not necessarily go hand in hand.

Favian always made things exceptionally easy, with his absolute openness on the subject of love and desire. He had done so since the very beginning of their unlikely relationship. But she wasn't naive enough not to realize that the possibilities were rife for conflict when one person desired another person who did not desire them.

Her nervousness ratcheted up a notch. Whatever else did or did not happen tonight, it was clear that she and Vesh needed to talk.

The low laughter came again, uncurling some of the anxiety from her gut and replacing it with a different sort of tension. Suddenly, the desire to know what, exactly, Ithric was doing—and to whom—overrode any lingering desire to gawp at the sparkling, candlelit walls surrounding her. *Or to obsess over all the complications that might arise between her and Vesh now that the two of them had a second chance at happiness with each other.*

Her feet carried her forward into the first chamber after the main entrance. This was the cabinet room, where people changed out of their clothes and stored them in secure boxes for their return. A diaphanous robe of some light, shimmering material hung prominently by the door. She ran a fingertip down the silky cloth, and changed into it. It was cool and felt slippery against her skin, brushing against her nipples in a tantalizing tease as she walked.

She moved on, bare feet padding against the warmth of the tile floors as she passed the steam room. A quick glance confirmed it was empty, though a damp towel lay draped haphazardly across the table used for rubdowns. A bowl of scented oil sat nearby.

The cold pool was next—also empty. Her foot nudged at a discarded pile of fabric puddled near the steps that led down into the water, and she saw that it was a man's robe, larger and of heavier material than her own. A smile tugged at one corner of her lips.

Her heart beat faster in anticipation as she moved on to the warm pool. She couldn't help marveling at the swell of happiness she felt over the prospect of seeing her three beautiful men together, after even the shortest of separations.

Vesh had promised her the rest of their lives—one night at a time. Over the weeks since that declaration, she had come to understand what it meant for them. Even if—gods forbid—one or more of them should die, Vesh had ensured that they could never truly be separated again. In dreams, they could see each other every night. Touch each other. Love each other.

The doorway ahead of her opened out into the massive central atrium, which held the warm pool. Again, hundreds upon hundreds of candles illuminated the space, open to the night sky above. They flickered against the white marble columns surrounding the shimmering green pool like sentries standing guard, and illuminated the three figures tangled together on the submerged bench at the far end.

As if in a trance, Kathrael walked forward and stepped down the set of shallow stone stairs that led into the pool. The gossamer fabric of her robe floated up around her legs as the water rose up to her waist, then her ribcage, then her breasts and collarbones as she waded toward the far end.

Ithric's back was turned toward her, his attention focused on the pair seated on the bench. Favian—gentle, unassuming *Favian*—held Vesh in place in front of him, facing outward and straddling his lap. The young priest had one arm slung around Vesh's bare chest, and his other hand wrapped in Vesh's black, shoulder-length hair. Using his grip on it to hold Vesh still. To hold him in place, neck arched, for Ithric to kiss, deep and filthy.

She must have made some sort of noise of reaction, because three sets of eyes fixed on her—one, hazel and wicked, glinting above a cat-with-the-cream smile; one, blue and heavy-lidded; and one, dark brown and open, utterly vulnerable. Desire for all three of them slammed into her hard enough to take her breath away as she drank in the scene.

"About time you got here, Little Cat," Ithric said, humor lacing his tone. "Favian and I got tired of watching you and the ghost-boy dance around each other, so we decided to warm him up for you. You can thank us later."

Kathrael snapped her jaw shut, aware that she'd been staring at the three of them like a starving woman. "Vesh?" she asked, the word emerging low and hoarse.

"Your concubines are both terrible brutes, Kath," he managed, playing at being unaffected. Favian used his grip on Vesh's dark locks to arch his head back further and roll it to the side, baring his neck for Ithric's sharp, reproving nip. Vesh gasped, and his voice grew breathy as he added, "I approve, by the way."

"Mmm… we thought you probably did," Ithric told him, still amused. He dipped into Vesh's mouth for another brief, demanding kiss, and pulled back to throw a wicked glance at Kathrael. "So—interesting fact," he said, his arm disappearing under the water, into the space between Vesh's legs. "Apparently when you die, if your balls are gone, they grow back. Who knew?"

His arm muscles flexed rhythmically a few times, and Vesh's eyes fluttered shut.

"It's a dream, lion-boy," Vesh murmured. "You can be anything you want. Change anything you—*uhh*—want." He arched a bit against Favian's hold, wriggling in his lap. Favian let out a sharp breath as Vesh continued, "Being a eunuch was my reality, but it wasn't my choice. It was never really… how I saw myself."

The ache of love Kathrael felt for her closest friend merged with the ache of desire she felt at watching the other two hold him in place and ravish him. The liquid warmth of the water swirling against her skin matched the liquid warmth swirling within her belly. She drew in a quick breath and ducked beneath the surface to swim the last few spans separating them, her hand held out in front of her to feel her way, the dark depths she was traversing untouched by the light from the flickering candles above.

Her fingers brushed against legs twined together. She followed them up, smoothly breaking the surface in front of Vesh and Favian, with Ithric at her shoulder. Kathrael reared up, bracing a knee on the bench so she could kiss Vesh while Favian held him still and Ithric continued to pump the hard flesh between his legs with lazy strokes.

His lips parted beneath hers, letting her take control—a tiny, surprised puff of air escaping through his nose as she did. It was incredibly tempting to move Ithric's hand away and straddle both him and Favian, so she could lower herself onto Vesh's shaft and feel his restored flesh sliding inside her, joining them together in a way they had never experienced before.

Reluctantly, she pulled back, giving his lower lip a nip as she did.

"Let him go," she said.

Favian and Ithric's hands fell away, and Vesh made a sound halfway between delicious relief and delicious regret. He slid off Favian's lap, dunking himself and emerging to scrub at his face with shaking hands.

"Sorry—I meant to ask earlier," he began, a hoarse note still coloring the words. "Favian, if you want to, you can be whole again, as well. Just say the word."

Kathrael looked at Favian with interest, but he only smiled. "Maybe we'll do that sometime, but not tonight. This *is* actually how I see myself, most of the time." He lifted an eyebrow, considering. "But, that said, I wouldn't mind it if I didn't have to deal with the bad shoulder tonight. Is that something you can—"

Vesh brushed a hand over the twisted knot of scar tissue left by the arrow, to reveal smooth, pale skin in its place. "Better?" he asked.

Favian lifted his arm, rolling the shoulder and wriggling his fingers. A smile crinkled the corners of his blue eyes. "Hmm. Thanks. That's rather impressive, really."

"It is at that," Ithric agreed, and gave Vesh a considering look. "You could have gotten out of Favian's grip at any time, couldn't you? Just… disappeared and reappeared someplace else, or made yourself much stronger than us, or something."

Vesh shrugged. "Probably. But where would be the fun in that? I haven't had decent sex in ages."

Kathrael laughed, lightness flooding her chest.

Vesh turned to her. "Hold still for a moment, Kath." His palm caressed her scarred temple and cheek. Her eyes slipped closed as his thumb brushed the lid of her blind eye—a gossamer touch.

When she opened them a moment later, she could see the three men around her with a new depth. Her hand flew to her face, encountering smooth, supple skin, and her lips parted in surprise. The look of agonized love on Vesh's features as he looked down at her made her breath stutter and catch.

"Gods," he said, barely more than a whisper, "I've longed to be able to do that since the night it first happened."

She half-fell forward into his arms and clung, feeling Ithric and Favian enclose them in an embrace from either side a moment later.

"It's all right, Vesh," she said wetly. "Please don't look at me like that. The scars don't bother me anymore, truly. I hardly even think about them."

"I know," Vesh said against her hair. "I know you don't, Kath. But every time I see them, it's a reminder that I failed you. That I couldn't protect you."

Her throat threatened to close up for a moment, and she swallowed hard. "I couldn't protect you, either," she managed.

Favian made a soft noise, and spoke. "No. Look… both of you. Vesh, you saved Kath's life by nursing her back to health after the attack. And, Kath—you protected Vesh's spirit when he was trapped in the living world. You tethered and sheltered him when he was at his most vulnerable."

Ithric's strong arms tightened around them. "He's right, you know. And now we're together—all of us. All of the actions the four of us have taken—in life and in death—have led us here, to this night. To this moment. I, for one, wouldn't change a thing."

Kathrael gulped again, trying to compose herself—knowing Ithric and Favian were right. She took a few moments to just *breathe*, resting in three pairs of loving arms. When she was confident her voice wouldn't waver, she pulled back a bit and made herself smile up at Vesh.

"Maybe I should get you to smooth out my stretch marks while you're at it," she joked weakly.

"*No*," Ithric and Favian said in unison.

Ithric's hand slid around to rest over her belly, still flabby and lax after her pregnancy. "No one touches the stretch marks," he said with finality.

A little flutter of feeling made her heart beat faster, and Vesh smiled at her, the tension breaking.

"I believe you've just been outvoted, Kath," he said. His hand trailed down to tangle with Ithric's over her stomach. "Three to one, in fact."

Her smile grew a bit watery, but she straightened her spine and lifted her chin. "Well," she said, "Given what we're trying to do in Rhyth these days, I suppose it would send the wrong message if I ignored the will of the majority."

"Damn right it would," Favian said, pressing a kiss to her temple. "Now, would you two please get on with the shagging? I'm slowly going mad over here."

She peered at him curiously. There was a definite hint of strain behind his voice now, though there hadn't been earlier when he was comforting her. And his eyes still had that heavy-lidded look that she'd noticed when she first saw him holding Vesh still for Ithric.

"Why are you going mad, exactly?" she asked suspiciously, looking between the three of them.

"Because Vesh is evil," Favian said. "Which, of course, I already knew after being stuck with him for days on end when I was injured."

Ithric laughed. "What's the matter, Favian? Something distracting you?"

Favian gave him a flat, unimpressed stare.

Kath returned her attention to Vesh, waiting for an explanation. Vesh smirked, his earlier melancholy falling away to reveal a hint of the playfulness she'd missed so much.

"I… might've used the secret weapon on him," he said, all innocence. "Purely in self-defense, mind you—given what he and the lion-boy were obviously planning for me."

Her eyes widened, and a shocked laugh burst from her. She slapped a hand across her mouth to stop it, not wanting to offend Favian.

"You didn't," she said through her fingers, still trying to hold back giggles.

"Oh, believe me—he did," Favian said dryly. "And I'll probably enjoy it quite a bit, once I'm no longer trying to hold a reasonable conversation at the same time."

"Well, *I'm* certainly enjoying it," Ithric offered, giving Favian an exaggerated leer.

"You don't say," Favian replied, still dry as dust.

The *secret weapon* had been one of Vesh's most prized possessions before he sold it to pay for food for them, shortly before his death. More than one male client had become a devoted regular thanks to the carved and polished wooden plug with the wicked curve at the top, which nestled against the place inside a man's passage that gave incomparable pleasure to many.

Once inserted, the flat base and tapered area just above held it in place. Every time the ring of muscle guarding the wearer's entrance clenched or fluttered, the curved tip rubbed over his center of pleasure—relentless and inescapable until it was removed. Vesh had bragged of bringing men to release three, and even four times in quick succession with the thing.

At the time, Kathrael had not understood the appeal, her own experience with that sort of penetration having been universally painful and unpleasant. Since being with Favian and Ithric, though, she'd come to more fully appreciate its power for many men. And, indeed, she had enjoyed the feeling of Favian's gentle fingers exploring her on several occasions in recent months—even if it had not been nearly such an intense experience for her as it would be for a male.

"Someone should have said something earlier," Kathrael told them, still trying to keep a straight face. "If I'd known, I'd have tried harder to avoid distractions."

She stretched up to kiss Favian, feeling arousal start to uncoil in her belly once more. Unable to help herself, she ran her fingers down his back under the water, brushing over the dimples at the base of his spine and following the valley between his buttocks. Sure enough, her fingertips brushed over the hard, flat base that spread his cheeks. She pressed the heel of her hand against it, moving in small circles. Favian twitched and made a noise into the kiss, pulling away to rest his forehead against hers as he breathed quickly through his nose.

Ithric's body pressed against her from behind. "Make that two votes for commencing the shagging," he said. "Oh, and by the way..." His lips brushed the shell of her ear, his voice lowering to a whisper that tickled the sensitive skin. "Vesh has one in, too."

TWO

It was Kath's turn to make a low noise in the back of her throat. Ithric nipped her earlobe and pulled away, continuing in a conversational tone.

"Favian insisted it was only fair. We figured that since it had been a while for him, we'd take the edge off while we were getting him ready for you. I didn't even have to touch his cock. Just played with his balls and kissed him. All it took was him wriggling around on Favian's lap, straining against his grip and moving that thing around inside him. He came like a geyser, and when I didn't stop playing with him afterward, he got hard again in minutes."

Kathrael licked her lips, feeling her face flush as she pictured it. Just like that, any question that might have lingered about her desire for Vesh dissipated like mist in the sunlight.

When she turned to him, Vesh looked part sheepish, part amused—but his pupils were blown wide and dark. He gave a little shrug, unrepentant. "I did mention that I haven't had decent sex for ages. And it certainly didn't help that Ithric kept whispering all sorts of things about what the three of us would do to you when you got here."

There was nothing to prevent her stepping into Vesh's arms again, so she did. Her breasts pressed against the planes of his chest. "And what are you going to do?" she asked, breathless.

His arms closed around her shoulders, holding her close, and open longing colored his voice when he said, "Everything."

Suddenly needing to feel him and map the changes in him that existed here in the dream world, Kath wormed a hand into the scant space between them and cupped him, exploring the hard length—long and slender, with a slight curve—along with the soft wrinkled weight of his sac, which twitched in her hand, trying to draw up toward his body. He shivered.

"Let me see you, please," she begged. "I want to see."

Vesh pressed a fierce kiss to her lips. He twisted to look over his shoulder as if searching for something, drawing her gaze to a huge, stuffed leather sleeping pad lying on the tile floor next to the pool. Kathrael wasn't sure if she had somehow failed to notice it before, or if it had only just appeared. Either way, Ithric was already levering himself out of the pool on corded arms, twisting to perch on the edge so he could offer the rest of them a hand up.

Kathrael's gaze moved inevitably to the place at the juncture of Ithric's thighs, where a padded leather strap was buckled tightly around the base of his cock and balls. His prick was stiff and engorged—a dusky red.

She lifted an eyebrow, her sex clenching deliciously. "Well, now. More surprises?"

Ithric's grin was brief, sharp, and dangerous. "I'm told I won't be able to come until it's off, and I can't go soft until it's off, either. Also, it's making me so sensitive that even the feel of water moving against me in the pool was almost too much. Your Vesh is a devious man, and apparently one who enjoys playing with fire."

"It keeps death interesting," Vesh said lightly, failing to stifle a groan as he climbed onto the edge of the pool—no doubt feeling the toy inside him shifting as he did.

Favian was next, not faring much better. "I'm about to crawl out of my skin," he muttered. "Good gods, this thing is *maddening*."

Vesh lowered himself rather gingerly onto the soft leather pad, meeting Kath's eye with a wink so quick she hardly caught it. "You can always take it out, priest-boy," he observed.

Favian grumbled something that sounded like, "… and I thought *Ithric* was impossible," with a flush rising in his cheeks. He made no move to remove the wooden plug.

Kathrael let the waterlogged robe slip free from her arms and float away before accepting Ithric's hand up, his strength lifting her effortlessly to sit on the edge of the pool next to him. She kissed him, licking at the seam of his lips as she ran a fingertip lightly along the bottom of his engorged shaft, from the leather strap to the tip. His teeth closed around her lower lip in retaliation, tugging back until it slipped free, tingling from the rough treatment.

"So… go on, then," he said, tweaking one of her pebbled nipples. "Vesh is waiting. What do you want to do to him first?"

Her mouth watered. She didn't even have to think about it. "I want to suck him."

Aside from a bit of kissing and nibbling around Ithric's shaft while she was teaching Favian how to pleasure him orally, Kathrael had only sucked off one man since her face was injured. It had been a painful and unpleasant task; the contracted flesh of her scars stretching until she had feared it might split and bleed. But here in the dream—thanks to Vesh—her skin was smooth and unblemished. She intended to take full advantage of that fact tonight.

Ithric grinned. "Oh, yes—good plan." He lifted an eyebrow. "Tell me, Little Cat—do you think you can take on both of us at once? One in front and one behind?"

Her sex pulsed, but she mustered a haughty look. "I told you early on in our acquaintance, Ithric. There's very little you could come up with that I haven't seen—and probably *done*—dozens of times before. *Bring it on.*"

He waggled his eyebrows. "Well, now. You asked for it."

She smirked at him and rose smoothly, the light swat he landed on her buttock as she turned going straight to her cunt, which pulsed with anticipation. Vesh was sprawled on his back on the pad, leaning up on his elbows to watch her approach. Favian knelt even with his shoulders, sitting on his heels and staying very still—trying, she thought, to keep the toy inside him from moving. She gave him a knowing glance, and received a humorously long-suffering one in return.

After that, her attention was purely for Vesh. He was beautiful to her, as he always had been. Somewhere between Ithric's lean, hard-muscled frame and Favian's sleek, well-fed one, Vesh was slender and pleasingly proportioned. Scarce food and a hard life had kept him from growing plump or flabby as many eunuchs did. And he had always taken care with his appearance—a necessity, in their line of work.

She dropped onto all fours near the edge of the leather pad and prowled forward into the space between his spread legs, holding his burning gaze unblinkingly as she kissed her way along his calf… the inside of his knee… the line of his inner thigh.

Though he was still almost completely hairless, his sac hung heavy beneath the proud jut of his cock. She brushed her lips against each of the round stones inside, watching his eyelids droop to half-mast. He lifted one hand to hook her hair over her ear, trailing fingertips through the dark strands.

"I love you, Kathrael," he murmured. "You know... I never truly thought this day would come."

Rather than reply in words, she kissed her way up the length of his shaft and circled the head with her tongue. His breath caught. From behind her, callused hands closed around her and lifted her hips higher. She let Ithric position her the way he wanted on her knees, her tongue teasing the tip of Vesh's prick the whole time.

"So beautiful," Vesh whispered, as Ithric pressed into her smoothly from behind, driving her onto Vesh's cock. She moaned at the dual sensation of being penetrated; filled to bursting at both ends with hard, slick heat. Ithric pulled back until his tip barely parted her folds, and pushed back in slowly, over and over. Kathrael let the movement drive Vesh's prick deeper into her mouth with each thrust, surrendering to the primal rhythm.

Barely had she relaxed into the slow, deep, mind-melting fuck when a hand gathered her hair away from her neck and soft lips pressed against the top of her spine, trailing hot kisses down the bump of each vertebra, one by one, before starting back up. She hummed around Vesh, the vibrations making him shudder. One of Favian's arms wrapped around her until he could reach her breast, pinching the nipple and rolling it as he continued to kiss her back and neck.

Already, she felt out of control, dizzy with arousal and shivery at the feeling of lips... hands... cocks. Ithric held her hips firmly, dictating the pace, which was maddeningly slow. Favian teased and tortured her nipples, making them ache in the most exquisite way. Her very lack of power over the situation inflamed her, and the more she surrendered to the three men possessing her, the higher her excitement rose.

With almost no warning, her pleasure crested, dragging a muffled sob from her as her body clamped around Ithric's flesh. He cursed, low and dirty, and she distantly remembered that he couldn't come with his cock bound. The reminder of his predicament dragged a final hard shudder from her.

Vesh hissed and eased her off of his prick with a careful hand in her thick hair. She made a noise of dismay, still riding the tail of her release, but he hushed her.

"*Shh*. You and I aren't done yet, Kath," he said, low and throaty. "*Not even close.*"

Ithric pulled out, and she whimpered, feeling horribly empty.

"It's just for a minute, I promise," Vesh soothed. "I really need to be inside of you now, that's all. Favian, help her up so she can ride me, will you? Ithric, come kneel next to my shoulder where she and Favian can both reach you."

"Bossy," Favian observed, clearly amused. "Not that I'm the *least* bit surprised."

Ithric huffed out a breath, though the strain in his voice was very apparent. "Quit your bellyaching, Favian. We are *obviously* basking in the presence of a true professional."

"Seven years of fucking people for money ought to be good for something that's of actual value," Vesh said. "Come here, Kath—it's all right. We've got you."

Arms helped her scoot up, her rubbery limbs gradually coming back under her control as the aftershocks of her climax faded. She fell on Vesh, kissing him as he gathered her in his arms and held her tight. His erection rubbed along her soaked folds, and it was pure instinct to shift until he pressed at her entrance. She canted her hips, changing the angle, and he slid inside her. They both groaned.

He was longer than Ithric but not so thick, and he filled her in a different way. She reared up, looking down at him with something like awe, meeting eyes that blazed up at her with love.

"Gods... it's been so long," he said softly, "and it's *you...*"

"It's us," she agreed, a smile sliding over her face like the sun coming out.

She moved, feeling him rise to meet her with every slow twist of her hips. The other two were leaning together, watching. Favian had an arm slung over Ithric's shoulders, kneading and tugging Ithric's balls with his other hand. Ithric grabbed Favian's chin and drew him in for a biting kiss, the sight further intensifying Kathrael's lust.

Vesh rolled up on an elbow, hooking his free arm around her lower back and holding her to him as he took her right nipple into his mouth and sucked. The sensation burned a direct line to the hard nub of her pleasure, which rubbed against his pelvis every time they moved against each other.

The position also brought her lips within reach of Ithric's cock, which bobbed and twitched within its bondage as Favian teased him. She grabbed Ithric's hip with one hand, pulling him a fraction closer so she could lower her head and swallow him whole. He was large and thick, and he tasted of her slickness. Little beads of salty seed escaped from his tip, and she could feel the fine tremor of tightly held muscles under her hand as he fought to keep control.

She ground against Vesh, the two of them rocking together almost frantically now, making no effort to rein themselves in. Favian had let go of Ithric when Kathrael started to suck him, but now his cheek brushed hers, nuzzling. She pulled back enough to kiss him around Ithric's cock, their tongues tangling as they dueled over who would have him.

Ithric made a low noise like a growl, tangling one hand in her dark waves of hair, and the other in Favian's heavy golden plait. He used his grip on them to guide his length first into her mouth and then Favian's, sliding past their lips and disappearing inside.

That was apparently too much for Vesh, who came hard, spilling into her, crying out as his body clamped around the wooden toy inside him — each spasm reflected in a new jerk of his cock. Ithric pressed his length deep into her mouth as Vesh twitched and pulsed in her clenching passage, pushing Kathrael over the edge as well. A wash of brilliant, blinding white clouded her vision, her surroundings going hazy as new pleasure flooded her limbs, making her body go heavy on top of Vesh's.

When she blinked back to full awareness, it was to find Ithric toppling Favian onto his back next to them and pinning him there with a forearm against his chest. His other hand scrabbled to unbuckle the strap confining his genitals, and he groaned in relief.

"Bear down for me," he ordered Favian, whose eyes were wide and dark with unaccustomed arousal. "I want this thing out of you *now*."

A moment later, he was tossing the curved plug to one side, and reaching for a pot of grease conveniently set next to the leather pad. He greased himself up, and slid slick fingers inside Favian to make sure he was ready, then knelt at his entrance and pushed inside with one unforgiving thrust.

Favian's hands scrabbled for purchase on the smooth leather, his mouth falling open in a soundless exclamation as his head fell back, baring his throat. Impossibly, Kathrael felt a new flutter of arousal, and Vesh made a soft rumbling noise of appreciation.

"Good gods," he whispered in her ear, "I do love watching those two."

"You're not the only one," she murmured in agreement.

"Poor Favian... he's strung tight as a bowstring." Vesh observed idly. "Should we help the lion-boy make him come, do you think?"

"It does seem like the charitable thing to do," she agreed, fresh warmth flooding her as she fell into the old, familiar banter with him.

She stretched luxuriously, her skin sliding against Vesh's, his softening prick slipping free from her body. She took only a moment to mourn the loss—they could do this whenever they liked, as many times as they liked, from now on. She pressed a kiss to his full lips and slid off him, brushing past Ithric's back to get to Favian's other side.

Ithric was balanced on his knees, Favian's legs locked in the crooks of his arms to hold his hips up as he fucked into him hard and fast. After so long enduring the teasing brushes of the toy against his center, Favian writhed and panted with each unforgiving thrust against the sensitive place inside him.

Vesh mirrored Kathrael on Favian's other side. He was clearly unfazed by the fact that Favian was still completely flaccid—being well acquainted of the realities of being a eunuch. Kathrael handed him the grease, and set it out of the way after he scooped up a bit.

She took possession of Favian's mouth and nipples, letting Vesh milk his soft prick with slick, filthy strokes. They pinned him in place, ignoring his increasingly desperate grunts and writhing, never letting up as Ithric fucked him into the mattress. After several minutes, Favian went absolutely rigid, not even breathing, every muscle locked.

His body started to tremble, the shaking growing more violent until he finally convulsed, the breath escaping his lungs in a hoarse shout. Above him, Ithric's spine arched like a bow, his thrusts growing sloppy as his voice joined Favian's in a sharp cry of release.

The two collapsed together, breathing hard. Vesh flopped onto his back next to them and let out a sigh of contentment, clasping his hands behind his head.

"No offense, priest-boy, but you could really use a good, hard buggering more often," he said. "Ithric, if you ever want a hand with that, just let me know. I'll get Kath a harness and the three of us can take turns with him."

"*Ungh*," Favian managed, not moving.

Ithric buried his face in Favian's neck and snorted out a huff of exhausted laughter. "*You* are an absolute menace, ghost-boy," he said. "I knew there was a reason I liked you."

They lay sprawled together until the stickiness and drying sweat inherent in uninhibited group sex started to become too distracting, at which point they slid back into the steaming pool of mineral-rich water. Kath took a deep breath that felt like it chased the last modicum of tension from her body, and slipped beneath the surface.

The silence and absolute serenity under the water quieted some small, hidden part of her soul. That restless fragment had lived inside her, unnoticed and unremarked, since her girlhood as a slave. For perhaps the first time in her life, Kathrael felt whole. Complete. She knew that—dead or alive—she would never, ever be alone again.

She had everything she could possibly want out of life.

The faint sound of a waking infant tickled the edge of her awareness. Her precious, perfect little daughter awaited her in the waking world, as did two of the three men she loved. There, she had a family, a purpose, and a future. Here, she had a haven and a respite, along with more love than she could ever hope to repay during the course of a lifetime.

As the dream world faded slowly around her, Kathrael of Rhyth let out a slow breath of contentment. She was finally… *finally*… at peace.

finis

The Eburosi Chronicles continue with The Dragon Mistress, Frella's story.

For more books by this author, visit www.rasteffan.com.